OUTST[ANDING PRAISE] FOR THE NOVELS OF LISA JACKSON

PARANOID

"Jackson gradually builds up the layers of this tangled psychological thriller, leading to a stunning finale. Jackson knows how to keep readers guessing and glued to the page."

—*Publishers Weekly*

LIAR, LIAR

"Bestselling Jackson jam-packs the plot of her latest nail-biting novel with plenty of unexpected twists and turns, making *Liar, Liar* a terrific choice for readers who enjoy their literary adrenaline fixes on the darker side of the suspense spectrum."

—*Booklist*

"Twisty . . . suspenseful. The many threads of this action-packed mystery are tied together by the mesmerizing, larger-than-life character of Didi Storm, who haunts the book to its final pages."

—*Publishers Weekly* (starred review)

YOU WILL PAY

"This suspenseful thriller is packed with jaw-dropping twists."

—*In Touch Weekly*

NEVER DIE ALONE

"Jackson definitely knows how to keep readers riveted."

—*Mystery Scene*

CLOSE TO HOME

"Jackson definitely knows how to jangle readers' nerves . . . *Close to Home* is perfect for readers of Joy Fielding or fans of Mary Higgins Clark."

—*Booklist*

TELL ME

"Absolutely tension filled . . . Jackson is on top of her game."

—*Suspense Magazine*

Books by Lisa Jackson

Stand-Alones

SEE HOW SHE DIES
FINAL SCREAM
RUNNING SCARED
WHISPERS
TWICE KISSED
UNSPOKEN
DEEP FREEZE
FATAL BURN
MOST LIKELY TO DIE
WICKED GAME
WICKED LIES
SOMETHING WICKED
WICKED WAYS
SINISTER
WITHOUT MERCY
YOU DON'T WANT TO KNOW
CLOSE TO HOME
AFTER SHE'S GONE
REVENGE
YOU WILL PAY
OMINOUS
RUTHLESS
ONE LAST BREATH
LIAR, LIAR
BACKLASH
PARANOID
ENVIOUS
LAST GIRL STANDING

Anthony Paterno/ Cahill Family Novels

IF SHE ONLY KNEW
ALMOST DEAD
YOU BETRAYED ME

Rick Bentz/ Reuben Montoya Novels

HOT BLOODED
COLD BLOODED
SHIVER
ABSOLUTE FEAR
LOST SOULS
MALICE
DEVIOUS
NEVER DIE ALONE

Pierce Reed/ Nikki Gillette Novels

THE NIGHT BEFORE
THE MORNING AFTER
TELL ME

Selena Alvarez/ Regan Pescoli Novels

LEFT TO DIE
CHOSEN TO DIE
BORN TO DIE
AFRAID TO DIE
READY TO DIE
DESERVES TO DIE
EXPECTING TO DIE
WILLING TO DIE

Published by Kensington Publishing Corporation

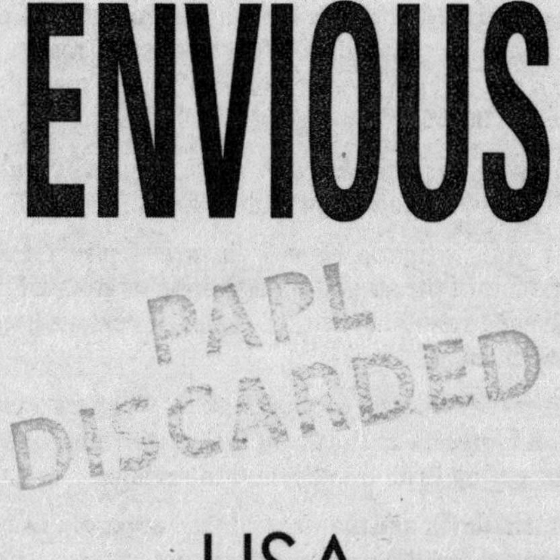

ENVIOUS

LISA
JACKSON

ZEBRA BOOKS
KENSINGTON PUBLISHING CORP.
www.kensingtonbooks.com

ZEBRA BOOKS are published by

Kensington Publishing Corp.
119 West 40th Street
New York, NY 10018

All three titles comprising *Envious* were originally published by Silhouette Books by arrangement with Harlequin Books S.A.

First Zebra Books Mass-Market Paperback Printing: April 2020
ISBN-13: 978-1-4201-4986-9
ISBN-10: 1-4201-4986-5

ISBN-13: 978-1-4201-4987-6 (eBook)
ISBN-10: 1-4201-4987-3 (eBook)

10 9 8 7 6 5 4 3 2 1

Printed in the United States of America

CONTENTS

A FAMILY KIND OF GUY

The books in the FOREVER FAMILY miniseries are dedicated to my family, those who are living and those who have passed on. I was lucky enough to have lived an enchanted childhood thanks to my parents, grandparents, aunts, uncles, cousins, and sister. My adulthood has been blessed with two incredible sons, a fabulous niece, three great nephews, and a host of new members. Thank you all!

Prologue

Bittersweet, Oregon
Ten years past

She was the most beautiful woman he'd ever set eyes upon and she was mad. Mad as hell. At him. He had the sting of her slap to remind him. "Just listen—"

"You listen, Mason, okay? I love you and I don't want to. That's the bottom line."

Blue eyes snapped furiously above cheeks that were flushed in anger. One fist clutched the reins of her intended mount's bridle, the other hand looked as if it itched to slap him again.

"You don't."

Thin lips compressed and she hooked a thumb at her chest. "Don't tell me what to feel, okay? Or what to say or do. Got it?"

"Yes, princess."

She stiffened. "And don't ever, *ever*, call me that again." She stepped forward a bit, dragging the pinto's head with her. "And get this straight, okay? You can't tell me what to do, Lafferty," she said in a voice that reminded him he was but a hired hand and she was, in fact, "the princess"—the daughter of his millionaire boss. "Don't even try." She placed one small, booted foot in the stirrup and hoisted herself into the saddle, then yanked on the reins. "A-di-os." The horse whirled before Mason had time to take hold of the reins.

"Bliss, come on. Don't be a fool."

"Too late for that, don't you think?" she asked with more than a trace of irony. The anger drained from her face and was replaced by sadness. "Way, way too late."

The sky was dark, threatening, the air hot and cloying as a storm brewed over the hills. Clouds moved in the barest of breezes, and Mason wished that he could shake some sense into her.

"Wait a minute, Bliss." Again he reached for the bridle, but she was quick. Too quick. She slapped Lucifer on his rump.

"Just stay away from me!" Leaning forward, she pressed her knees into the pinto's sides. "Hi-ya!"

"No—"

Ears flattened to his head, the colt bolted forward at a dead gallop. His hooves flung mud and dirt. Aptly named Lucifer, the demon tore across the paddock and through the open gate to the grassy fields beyond.

Mason's back teeth ground together. He was torn. Bliss Cawthorne was a stubborn, prideful creature who deserved to get caught in a downpour, but then again, the storm might be worse than just a summer shower.

I love you. Words he'd longed to hear but which scared the stuffing out of him. There was no future for them; there never would be.

You can't tell me what to do, Lafferty; don't even try! Just stay away from me!

As if he could. Hadn't he spent the past weeks trying to do just that?

Thunder rumbled over the surrounding hills and he

silently cursed himself up one side and down the other. He shouldn't have let her go. Should have physically restrained her, but short of hog-tying her, there'd been no way to keep her at the house.

You could have told her you loved her, too, and right this minute you might finally be in bed with her, feeling her hands on your body, kissing those pouting lips and making love to her.

Hell. He didn't love her and wouldn't lie, so he'd been between the proverbial rock and a hard place.

Eyes narrowing against the first spattering of rain, he rubbed his jaw where she'd slapped him as he'd argued with her. The skin stretched over his cheek still stung, but he'd been turned on by the fury in her eyes. "Dammit all." He kicked at a rock and sent it careening into the fence post, but his gaze was fixed on Bliss again, now far in the distance astride Lucifer.

Just the sway of her rump as the horse loped gave him an arousal that ached against his fly. What the devil was wrong with him? The boss's daughter was off-limits. *Way* off-limits. No one who worked on the ranch knew it better than he, yet he'd found excuse after flimsy excuse to be next to her, or close enough that he could watch her.

The smell of her skin aroused him, the way she angled her chin and wrinkled her nose caught him off guard and was sexy as all get-out. But why?

Sure, she was pretty with her pale blond hair and cornflower-blue eyes. Her cheekbones were high, her jawline strong, her eyebrows arched, but, come on, Lafferty, there were lots of pretty women in the world. Yet, this woman—no, make that *girl*, she wasn't quite eighteen yet—was different and appealed to him on another level, a level that scared the living tar right out of him.

She was like no other.

For a fleeting second, he thought of Terri Fremont, the girl he'd dated before Bliss had come to visit her father this summer. At twenty-one, Terri still looked like a pixie. Petite with freckles, short brown hair and huge brown eyes, she'd chased Mason down mercilessly and vowed to love him despite the fact that he had, at the time, been dating several women.

A little prick of guilt jabbed at his brain because he knew in the deepest parts of his soul that he'd never cared for Terri the way she'd cared for him. He'd tried to explain it to her, over and over again, but she had refused to listen, assuring him instead that he would "learn to love her" as much as she loved him.

She was wrong and he'd been forced to break it off with her. They had no future. He had dreams and they didn't include a wife. He glanced at Bliss's form again, just as horse and rider disappeared into the dark shadow of pine trees that skirted the base of the hills. Maybe a woman like Bliss would eventually change his mind. But not now.

The rain began in earnest. Thick, fat drops shimmered from the dark, foreboding sky. In the next field, the horses, sensing the change in the atmosphere, lifted their heads, noses to the wind, nostrils quivering in anticipation. This storm would be a bad one. And Bliss Cawthorne, headstrong fool, was out in the middle of it.

He had no choice but to follow her and haul her back to the ranch.

Just stay away from me.

"No way, lady," he growled, as if she could hear him. He squared his hat on his head and whistled sharply to Black Jack, a rawboned ebony gelding blessed with the speed of Pegasus and the temperament of an angel.

"You and me, partner," he said as he hitched Black Jack to the fence, ran to the stables for a bridle and threw it over the gelding's head. He buckled the leather straps with deft fingers and climbed onto the beast without a saddle. "Let's go," he said, digging in his heels as Black Jack took off.

Lightning sizzled above the hills.

Great. "Come on."

The horse's strides lengthened and they were through the open gate, flying over the bent grass and wildflowers mashed by the rain. Thunder rumbled ominously through the dark heavens.

He should never have let her go and he silently swore at himself as the wind pressed hard against his face and the downpour flattened his hair. There were too many things he shouldn't have done to count them all.

He'd had no right to touch her. No reason other than lust to kiss her. No sane excuse for taking off her clothes and . . . "Oh, hell." This wasn't the time to think about how yielding she'd been, or how, out of some vague sense of duty he hadn't, when offered the chance, made love to her.

"Come on, you miserable piece of horseflesh!" His knees prodded his mount as rain drenched his shoulders. Maybe he should have made love to her and been done with it, but he'd realized, almost too late, that Bliss Cawthorne wasn't the kind of woman to love and leave. Nope, she was the type of female who crawled into a man's blood and settled there—the kind of woman who spelled trouble with a capital *T*.

He gave Black Jack his head and the game horse flattened his ears, stretched out his neck and sprinted through the fields, his legs eating the sodden ground in quick, even strides. Wind tore at Mason's face and hands and he smiled grimly to himself. Bliss Cawthorne, princess and only daughter of John, was in for one hell of a surprise when he caught up to her.

"Son of a bitch," he muttered, swiping at the water on his face. He glanced at the spot in the trees where she'd vanished, then cursed himself for being a fool. Bliss wasn't his kind of woman; but then no one was. He'd make sure of it.

Bliss ignored the rain. She dug her knees into Lucifer's sides and urged him ever upward along the old cattle trail. The colt, incited by the storm, streaked forward, his hooves digging into the soft mud, his sides heaving with the effort. Bliss felt free and unfettered, as if she didn't have a care in the world. Her hair, bound in a ponytail, streamed out behind her.

The rain fell more steadily, in thick, heavy drops, sheeting in the distance. Still she didn't stop. If she got a little wet, so what? Her anger was slowly dissipating, but the thought of Mason with his arrogant high-handedness telling her what to do after . . . after . . . Oh, Lord, she'd nearly made love to him just last night; practically begged him to take away her virginity when he, poised above her, muscles straining, sweat dampening his brow, had rolled away.

"Bastard," she muttered. "Come on, come on," she urged. The pinto, wide-eyed, with nostrils quivering at the smell of the storm, began to lather. Grasshoppers scattered. A startled pheasant flew away in a rush of glistening feathers. Bliss yanked out the rubber band restraining her hair as she leaned over Lucifer's shoulder, encouraging him to speed even faster along the path—upward, through thickets of spruce and oak toward the cliffs that guarded the river. "Run, you devil."

The horse responded, his legs a flash, the wind causing tears to run from her eyes and fly off her cheeks with the rain. Trees were a blur.

The crest was close, just through this last copse of trees. As the saplings gave way, she pulled back on the reins and looked over the valley, this southern part of Oregon her father often called his home. Lucifer, tossing his head, slowed to a mincing walk.

"Thata boy." She was winded and breathless, her heart drumming, exhilaration replacing anger. Who cared about Mason Lafferty, anyway? If she had any brains at all she would forget him.

Telling herself that she'd get over the creep, she urged Lucifer to the crest near the edge of the ridge. From that vantage point she could see for miles, over the tops of the surrounding hills, past wineries and ranches and toward the town of Bittersweet.

Lucifer was spooked and blowing hard; the storm was getting to him. She'd only stay for a few minutes, then double back. By then she wouldn't have to face Mason again. At that thought her heart wrenched and she silently called herself a dozen kinds of fool.

She'd get over him. She had to. When she got back to Seattle—

A sizzling streak of lightning forked from the sky, singeing the air.

Lucifer reared.

"Whoa—" Bliss slipped in the saddle.

Thunder cracked, reverberating through the hills.

"It's okay—"

With a panicked shriek, Lucifer stumbled.

Bliss, already unbalanced, tumbled forward. "Hey, wait—" The reins slipped from her fingers. "Damn."

Crack! Thunder crashed, snapping through the forest and reverberating against the outcropping of stone.

Lucifer shied.

The saddle seemed to shift.

She started to fall, grabbed for the pommel and missed. The rain-washed world spun crazily. She scrabbled for the reins. "Whoa—oh, God."

With a wild, terrified whinny, the horse stumbled again.

Bliss pitched forward. Wet strands of his mane slid through her fingers.

"Stop! Please—Lucifer!" The ground rushed up at her.

Thud! Pain shot through her shoulder, jarring her bones. Her head smacked against the ground. Lights exploded behind her eyes. Her boot, still caught in the stirrup, twisted, wrenching her leg.

A shaft of lightning struck, sizzling and sparking. Crack! An old oak tree split down the middle. Fire and sparks spit upward to the heavens.

Half the tree fell. The ground shook. Bliss screamed as she tried to free herself from the horse and saddle. Lucifer, spooked, bolted.

"No—no—oh, God!" she cried. Frantically she struggled to wiggle out of the boot or yank it from the stirrup as the frightened horse dragged her along the trail near the edge of the ravine.

Hot, blinding pain seared up her leg as she tried to grab at something, anything that she could find with fingers that were bleeding and torn. Still the horse ran forward, bolting at a fever pitch along the jagged edge of canyon that dropped hundreds of feet to the riverbed below.

"Stop! Lucifer, for God's sake . . ."

A blast—a loud, eerie whistle—pierced the sodden air just as some of the rocks beneath them gave way. Through horrified eyes she saw the river, winding silvery and snake-like what seemed a million miles below.

For a second, day turned to night. Another piercing blare of the whistle. Lucifer shuddered to a stop. Bliss's head slid over the edge of the canyon. Hair fell in front of her eyes. She was going to die.

She blinked, rolled over and clutched the rimrocks. Through a heavy curtain of raw pain she saw the vision of a rain-soaked cowboy atop a black stallion. Mason's face, white with fear, came into view.

"For the love of God!" He jumped down from Black Jack and rushed forward as one of Lucifer's hooves slipped over the edge.

"No!" Mason caught hold of her booted ankle. Her thigh wrenched and popped, burning with new, searing pain. Blackness threatened her vision.

Lucifer found his footing and reared, trying to shake himself free of the dead weight still attached to his saddle.

"Hang on!" Mason ordered. His grip was slick. Her weight pulled her ever downward as her fingers found no purchase on the rough stone.

"Mason!"

"I've got you."

Steel-shod hooves glimmered as lightning flashed.

One hoof struck Mason in the temple. Crunch. He toppled, his fingers refusing to give up their grip.

The second hoof hit him in the side and Bliss began to slide over the edge even farther. Something deep inside her tore. His fingers relaxed, and the boot was slipping from her foot. She knew in that instant that she was about to die.

"I love you," she tried to say, but the words caught in her throat. She heard noises. Voices. Panicked voices. Her father? Mason? She couldn't tell as she reached upward, hoping to find his hand but grabbing only air as she began to slide downward.

Chapter One

Now

Bliss snapped off the radio as she wove her convertible through the slick streets of downtown Seattle. Traffic was snarled, horns blared and she couldn't stand to listen to Waylon Jennings talk about cowboys—a breed of man she knew more than a little about.

Hadn't her father started out as a range rider? Not to mention Mason. Not for the first time she wondered what had happened to him. He'd married, of course, and had a child—her heart bled at the thought. In her schoolgirl fantasies she'd imagined she'd be the mother of Mason's child; and in that dreamworld, her mother was still alive—an adoring grandmother—and her father and Mason had reconciled because of the baby.

But of course that would never happen. Her mother had already died and now her father was battling for his own life. As for Mason . . . well, he'd just turned out to be her first love. Nothing more.

Stepping on the gas as the light turned green, she shoved all thoughts of Mason from her mind. Her Mustang convertible surged forward toward the freeway entrance. She didn't have the time or patience to reminisce about a love affair gone sour.

Her windshield wipers slapped rain off the glass as she maneuvered through the traffic. In the distance lightning flashed, and again she thought of that long-ago storm and how its fury had changed the course of her life forever.

She'd never seen Mason after that day.

"Don't think about it," she warned herself as she headed toward the hospital where her father had been a patient for nearly a week, ever since he'd returned to Seattle to sign papers on some property he'd sold. "It's over. It's been over for a long, long time."

Within minutes she'd exited the freeway and was winding through the wet side streets surrounding the hospital. She nabbed a parking spot not too far from the main entrance of Seattle General and braced herself. Her father, irascible and determined, would demand to be released. And would probably insist upon returning to his ranch in Oregon, though he still owned property here. She, as strong-willed as he, would insist that he abide by his doctor's orders.

"Give me strength," she muttered under her breath as she locked her car and sidestepped puddles as the wind tugged at the hem of her raincoat and rain pelted her hair.

Inside the hospital, she ignored the sense of doom that threatened to settle in her heart. Barely three months before, in this very facility, Margaret Cawthorne had lost her battle with cancer. Bliss had been at her side.

But it wouldn't happen again! Not this time. Her father was too strong to let some little heart attack get him. She punched the elevator call button and shook the rain from her hair.

On the third floor, she headed straight for her father's room and found him lying under a thin blanket, his face pensive, turned toward the window. His television was on, the volume low, tuned in to some golf tournament in progress. Flowers, cards, boxes of candy and balloons were crammed onto every inch of counter space.

John Cawthorne looked thinner and more frail than she'd ever seen him. Hooked up to a heart monitor and an IV he was nothing like the man she'd grown up with, the tough-talking, badgering cowboy-turned-real-estate-mogul. At the sound of her footsteps, he glanced her way and a half grin teased the corners of a mouth surrounded by silver beard stubble.

"I wondered if you were gonna stop by," he said, pressing a button on a panel of the bed in order to raise his head. The electric motor hummed and he winced a little as his stitches pulled.

"I wouldn't miss a chance to see you cooped up, now, would I?" she teased.

His blue eyes twinkled. "I hate it."

"I know."

"I'm not kiddin'."

"I know," she repeated, walking to the windows and adjusting the blinds. "Don't tell me—you want out of the prison and expect me to help you escape."

He chuckled, then stopped abruptly, as if the pain was too much. "Look, I'm about to go stir-crazy around here, but the doc, he thinks I need to stay another couple of days."

"I'm on his side. Don't even argue with me about it." She leaned over and kissed his forehead. "So tell me—and I want the truth—how're you feeling?"

"Like I was dragged through a knothole one way, then pushed back through the other."

"I thought so. You're better off here, Dad."

"But I've got things I gotta do."

"Oh, quit whining," she said with a grin. "Whatever it is, believe me, it'll keep."

As quick as a cat pouncing, he grabbed hold of her

hand and wouldn't let go. "No, honey, this time, I'm afraid it won't."

"Oh, Dad—"

His lips compressed thoughtfully for a second. "There's something I've got to tell you, Bliss. Something I should've told you about a long time ago."

For the first time since entering the gleaming room, Bliss felt a premonition of despair. An unidentifiable urgency etched the contours of her father's face and his gaze was steady and hard as it held hers. "Oh, God," she whispered, suddenly weak in the knees. Tears, unbidden, formed in her eyes. "The doctor found something else—"

"No, no," he was quick to assure her. "I'm gonna be all right, just gotta take care of myself."

"Then what?" Her shoulders sagged in relief.

He hesitated, muttered an oath under his breath, then said, "I'm gonna get married again."

"What?" She stiffened. Surely she hadn't heard correctly. "Married? You're joking." He had to be.

"Never been more serious in my life." His expression told her that he wasn't pulling her leg.

She steadied herself on the rail of his bed, clutching hard enough that her knuckles showed white.

"Now, wait a minute—"

"I've waited too long as it is."

She was missing something here. Something important. "But Mom—"

"Is gone."

"Oh, Lord." She swallowed back the urge to argue with him and told herself she'd better hear him out. Maybe he was hallucinating from the drugs, maybe he'd grown attached to one of the nurses attending him and had developed a silly, dependent crush on her, or maybe—could it be?—he had a lover. No way.

"Sit down." He waved her into a chair.

Gratefully, she sank into a chair wedged between the bed and the window. "I think you'd better start at the beginning," she suggested, though she knew she wasn't going to like what she was about to hear. "Who—who is this . . . this woman?"

"Someone I love very much." His smile was weak, but the set of his jaw was as hard as granite, and while the sportscaster on the television spoke in hushed tones as a golfer approached his tee shot, Bliss felt a welling desperation.

"I—I don't understand."

"I know. Trouble is, neither do I, and I've had a lot of time to think about it." His lips, dry and chapped, curled in over his teeth in a second's indecision, and with his free hand he tugged on the crisp white sheet covering his body.

"Is she someone you just met?"

"No." The words seemed to ricochet off the stark hospital walls and echo dully in Bliss's heart. "I've known Brynnie for years."

"Brynnie?" The name was familiar, but Bliss couldn't place it. "But Mom just passed away—"

"That's the hard part." His gaze found hers and she saw the secret lingering in the blue depths—the truth that he'd been in love with another woman for years.

Bliss's heart twisted painfully. "No." Though she had known her parents' marriage had been far from perfect, Bliss had told herself they had loved each other in their own special—if unconventional—way. After all, they had celebrated their thirtieth wedding anniversary just this past year. There hadn't been tension or arguments in the house; just a general sense of apathy and drifting apart as they'd aged. "Who is she?" Bliss asked, cringing inside and feeling suddenly cold as death. "Who is this Brynnie?"

A twinkle lighted her father's faded blue eyes and his

lips turned up in a semblance of a smile. Even the skin on his face, paler than his usual tan, seemed to grow a little rosy. Bliss thought she might be sick. He looked like a love-struck teenager. Shifting in the bed, he pulled on the IV again and winced when the tape tugged on the back of his hand. "Brynnie Perez . . . Well, her name's changed a few times over the years. She's been married more than once, but . . ." He stared at his daughter and reached forward, taking her hand in his again. The cool plastic tubing of his IV brushed her arm. He hesitated, as if unsure of his next words.

"What, Dad?"

His gaze slid away for a second and he squared his shoulders. "This isn't easy for me to admit, Blissie, but I've loved Brynnie most of my life—well since I met her twenty-six—no, twenty-seven years ago."

"You what?" Bliss whispered, feeling as if a thunderbolt had shot through her. "Most of your life?" *And all of mine!*

"Adult life."

"But—" All the underpinnings of Bliss's life were suddenly shifting, causing her to lose her sense of balance, her security, her knowledge of who she was. "Wait a minute. I don't believe—"

"It's true, Bliss."

"No—" Had John Cawthorne been living a lie for years? Bliss's stomach tightened into a hard knot. It was one thing to think that this infatuation had been recent, but to admit to years—*years*—of loving someone other than his wife. This was too much to take. *Way* too much.

Her father's bony fingers tightened over hers. "I've loved her forever. Still do."

"But Mom . . ."

A sadness stole over his thin features—the same sadness she'd witnessed a dozen times before but had never understood. "Your mom and I, we cared about each other, but it was a different feeling . . . hard to explain. She was a good woman, that's for sure. A real good woman."

"Of course, she was." Bliss felt a jab of indignity for the proud woman who had borne her father's name for most of her life. "Mom . . . Mom was the greatest." Tears threatened her eyes and she had to swallow hard.

"No doubt about it."

"But you loved someone else." Despair flooded her insides and she stared at the fragrant white blooms of a gardenia someone had sent him. "Oh, Dad, how could you?"

"I just fell in love, honey. I know, I know, I shouldn't have, but . . . well, there it is. Your mother, she knew about Brynnie, but we thought it would be best for you if we stuck it out together and gave you some kind of normal family—"

"Normal family? You call this normal? Living a lie?" The room seemed to spin for an instant and there was a loud rush in her ears, like the sound of the ocean pounding the shore.

"People do it all the time."

"Do they?" She pulled her hand out from his grip. Repulsed and stunned, she shrank into a corner of the chair. She loved and hated him in one second, even though she herself knew about love gone wrong. Isn't that what had happened with Mason? Hadn't he been involved with two women? Oh, Lord, she felt like she might throw up. She stared at her father and tried to understand. "So why tell me now?"

"I said I was gonna get married. Soon."

Her laugh was brittle and forced. "Don't tell me you expect me to come to the wedding?" When he didn't answer she rolled her eyes and felt the hot moisture that had collected beneath her eyelids. "Oh, Dad . . . please don't even ask. I . . . I can't believe this is happening."

He glanced away, ran his tongue around his teeth and

seemed to weigh his next words carefully. "Listen, honey, there's more."

"More?" she whispered, feeling a sense of doom sneak through her insides. What "more" could there possibly be? She didn't want to hazard a guess.

He sniffed, ran a hand under his nose and sighed. "It's not just me and Brynnie."

Bliss bit her lip.

He hesitated, searching for the right words. "There's a girl—well, a woman now—"

"I—I don't know if I want to hear this," Bliss interrupted, rubbing her hands together to ease the intense cold that had permeated her bones.

"You have to, honey. Because, you see, you have a half-sister."

"Wh-what?" The white tiles of the hospital floor seemed to buckle beneath her chair.

"Well, more than one, actually."

"More than one?" *This was too absurd to be true.* And yet she knew as she looked at him that he wasn't lying. "Wait a minute, Dad. Something's wrong, here. Very wrong." She tried not to glare at her father who was still recuperating, but, damn it, she could barely make sense of his words. "You're trying to tell me that I have a sister—no, make that two?"

When he nodded she said, "But how?" Her mind was spinning in furious, complicated and very ugly circles. Everything she'd believed in, all that she'd trusted in her life, had been a lie—a dirty, dark and shameful lie. "Why?" she asked, trying to sound rational when her entire world was turned upside down. "This . . . this Brynnie is their mother?"

"She's Katie's mother," John said slowly and scratched the side of his cheek. "My other daughter—"

"Does she have a name, too?" Bliss couldn't hide the sarcasm in her words.

"Tiffany. She's older than you by a few years. The result of an affair I had before I met your mom."

"Oh, Dad," Bliss whispered, the tears she'd been fighting beginning to slide from the corners of her eyes. How could she have been so wrong about this man she'd loved all her life? The man who'd taught her how to ride bareback and lasso a wayward calf and swim in a river where the current was strong and swift? "You—you didn't marry her?"

"I was ridin' rodeo at the time. It wouldn't have worked. Matter of fact, she wasn't interested. I offered, she said 'No, thanks,' told me that she was givin' the baby up for adoption. Seems as if she lied about that, though. I found out a few years back."

"Oh, Lord."

"As I said, I didn't know it, but she kept the girl. Tiffany's almost thirty-two now, and . . . well, it's time she and I met. Especially now that she's moved back to Bittersweet. Living in the same town, it doesn't make much sense not to acknowledge that we're father and daughter."

"Are you sure? Maybe she's not interested in meeting you." Bliss, who had always prided herself on her strength, felt suddenly weary. She was usually a woman who moved easily in business circles, handled herself well at sophisticated and elegant social events, could adjust her style so that she felt as at home in a Seattle high-rise overlooking Puget Sound as she was in a low-slung ranch house that hadn't seen fresh paint in twenty years. But this—this complete alteration of what she'd grown up believing to be right and true—was more than she could deal with. Nothing in her life had been this mortifying, except maybe her faith in Mason Lafferty all those years ago.

"It's not so bad," her father insisted. But then he had no

choice but to believe his own words, did he? If what he was saying was the God's honest truth, then he had to trust that the situation would someway, somehow, work out. His graying brows drew together as if he were confused by the puzzle that was his life.

"Not so bad?" she repeated. "Well, it's damned unbelievable." Bliss, raised as an only child had not one, but two half-sisters—grown women she'd never heard of before, never had known existed.

Clearing his throat and squaring his shoulders beneath the thin cotton of his hospital gown, her father mustered up as much bravado as he could. "So now I'm gonna change things. Brynnie and I are gonna get married as soon as the docs tell me I can move back to Bittersweet." He fingered the edge of his sheet. "I'd like you to come with me, Blissie. Meet Brynnie and your sisters."

"Meet them?" Boy, her father had really lost it. "Dad, it's not just that simple. I mean . . . do *they* want to meet *me*?"

"Brynnie does."

"And the others?"

"Don't know."

Could she do it? Go back to Bittersweet, a town that held all kinds of bad memories? She felt a familiar ache in her heart—one she'd tried to bury for ten years—and that old, dark pain seared through her. She rubbed her thigh where she still sometimes felt a jab of pain from the accident so many years before. She could only hope that Mason was roasting in his own private hell. "I don't think so, Dad," she heard herself saying. "My life's here, in Seattle."

"What have you got other than an apartment and a job?"

"Oscar." She hitched her chin up an inch.

"That mutt of a dog can move with you. You can sublet your apartment and work from Oregon, what with fax machines and computer links and all. I know you spent one summer working out of a cabin in the San Juan Islands and another in Victoria. So don't give me any guff about having to be near the office. I'll have the phone company put in more telephone lines to the house for your modem and whatever else you need. The way I understand it"—he eyed her as if expecting her to mount a protest—"or at least what you've always led me to believe, is that you're pretty much independent anyway."

That much was true. She worked with two other architects restoring old buildings in Seattle, but she was between projects right now and had planned to take a vacation to Mexico or the Caribbean or somewhere in the sun. So why not Bittersweet? A dozen reasons why. Mason Lafferty was at the top of the list. If he still lived there. She hadn't heard from him in a decade and had never asked her father about him, though she had, over the years, gleaned a little about his life from people who had run across him. Not that it mattered. He'd betrayed her. Pure and simple.

Like your father betrayed your mother.

Well, she, for one, wasn't about to dwell on the mistakes of her past. Not now. Not ever.

As for the half-sisters she'd never known existed, what would be the point of meeting them now? True, she'd been raised as an only child and had always wished for siblings—brothers or sisters—but now that she was faced with her father's infidelity, she wasn't sure she could accept her sisters. Oh, what was she thinking? Sisters? *Half*-sisters? Two of them? What would she say to them? What *could* she say?

"This is way too sudden for me, Dad."

"And I'm runnin' out of time." He scowled and clicked off the television. "Who knows when the Grim Reaper's gonna knock on my door?"

"Don't talk like that!"

"I've already had one heart attack. I think it's time to live my life the way I want to." He rubbed his jaw, scratching the silver bristles covering his chin. "Besides, you'll like Brynnie, if you only give her a chance."

Bliss wasn't so sure. Brynnie, was, after all, her father's mistress and even though Bliss had known that her parents had drifted apart over the years, she couldn't just accept this other woman as part of her family. Bile climbed steadily up her throat, but she forced it back down.

"Your mother and I . . . Well, we were never right for each other. We were from different worlds. I was at home in the saddle with a plug of tobacco, and she wanted to see the damned ballet."

"I remember." Margaret Cawthorne was from old San Francisco money. John had been a cowboy with a keen mind who had bought land during the recession and made a fortune. He'd split his time between Seattle where he owned property and Bittersweet, Oregon, where his ranch was located.

A cloud passed behind his eyes, as if he still felt some kind of regret.

"But you stayed married."

"Believed in the institution. And there was you to consider."

"You made a mockery of the institution, Dad. And of me." Bliss stood, folded her arms over her chest, leaned against the cool wall and stared out the window to the parking lot three stories below. Rain drizzled from oppressive gray clouds, streaking down the panes. She could scarcely breathe. Her parents hadn't loved each other? Her father had been and still was involved with another woman? How could she not have known or guessed? She swallowed against a suddenly thick throat. Everything she believed in seemed to be falling apart, and more rapidly by the moment.

"I always thought opposites attracted," Bliss said lamely. Heat stole up the back of her neck when she thought of her one experience with a man as opposite from her once-prim city-girl ways as could be. Mason Lafferty, the randy tough-as-rawhide ranch hand who had worked for her father the summer she was almost eighteen, had managed to steal her naive heart before her father had stepped in.

"I suppose there's some truth to the saying, but not as opposite as we were. In the beginning, I guess we didn't realize how different we were and then . . . well, I found Brynnie. . . ." He had the good grace to look sheepish and Bliss felt the bleak ache in her heart thud painfully. He'd cheated on her mother with this woman he intended to marry. He'd fathered a child with her. "Brynnie's had her share of troubles, you know. Been married a few times and has some older boys that give her headaches you wouldn't believe."

From the half-open door Bliss heard the reassuring beep of heart monitors and the quiet conversation of the nurses busying around their station from which the corridors fanned toward the private rooms on the outside walls of the building. A medications cart rattled by and the elevator call button chimed. Sighing, Bliss looked down at her father, her only living parent.

"Come down to the wedding, Bliss," John said, his leathery skin stretched tight over his cheekbones. "It's important to me. Damn it, honey, I know it will be hard for you, but you're tough, like your ma. The way I see it, I've lost too much time already and I think we should start over. Be a family."

"You and Brynnie and her children and me," she clarified.

"And Tiffany."

"Right." She shook her head and blinked back her tears. "Dad, do you know how absurd this all sounds? It's not that

I don't want to, but I need some time to catch up. I walked into this room an hour ago and didn't know anything. Now, you expect me to accept everything you're telling me and be a part of a family I knew nothing about. I don't know if I can."

"Try. For me."

She wanted to agree to anything, to promise this man who had nearly met his Maker that she'd try her best to make him happy, but she didn't want to lie. "I'll give it a shot," she said, wondering why she would even think of returning to Bittersweet, the place where, as far as she knew, not only her half-sisters lived, but where she'd lost her heart years ago to a cowboy who had used her and thrown her away.

As if reading her thoughts, her father fingered the edge of his sheet and announced, "Lafferty's back in Bittersweet." His mouth tightened at the corners and Bliss's heart lost a beat. "Lookin' for property, the way I hear it"

"Is he?"

"His ex-wife and kid are there, too."

Wonderful, she thought grimly. "Doesn't matter."

His eyes narrowed a fraction. "Just thought you'd want to know."

"Why?"

"Well, you and he—"

"That was a long time ago, remember? He got married."

"And divorced."

She'd expected as much. Mason wasn't the kind of man who could commit to one woman for very long. She'd found that out. The hard way. "I couldn't care less," she lied, and cringed inside.

"Good. You'll have enough to deal with."

"If I come."

"I'm countin' on it, Blissie," her father said with an

encouraging smile. "It's time for me to start over and I can't do it without you."

A huge lump filled her throat. *Half-sisters.*

She'd have to meet them sometime, she decided without much enthusiasm, but that didn't mean that she had to like them.

Chapter Two

"Bliss Cawthorne's coming back to town."

Mason froze, his pen in his hand as he sat at his desk. "What?"

"You heard me." Jarrod Smith snagged his hat from the hall tree as he walked to the door of Mason's office. "Just thought you'd like to know."

"You're full of good news, aren't you?" Mason said, leaning back in his desk chair until the old springs creaked in protest. His stupid pulse had jumped at the mention of Bliss's name, but he calmed himself. So she was returning to Bittersweet. So what? He didn't doubt that she cursed the day she'd ever set eyes on him. He didn't blame her.

She was, as she always had been, forbidden.

Jarrod grinned like a Cheshire cat. "Supposedly it'll be a short visit, just coming back for her old man's wedding."

"To your mother." Mason had already heard the news that had swept like wildfire through dry grass along the streets of Bittersweet. In the taverns, churches and coffee shops, the topic of John Cawthorne's marriage had been hashed and rehashed. Not that Mason cared so much about what Cawthorne did these days, except when it came to the ranch, the damned ranch. Behind the old man's back he'd made a deal with Brynnie to buy out part of it. His conscience twinged a bit; he had a ten-year-old deal with the old man, too. One he no longer intended to honor.

"Yep." Jarrod squared his hat on his head and paused at the door. "This *is* a small town."

"Too small." Nervously, Mason clicked the pen.

"But you couldn't stay away."

Mason grimaced and glanced at the picture propped on the edge of his desk. In the snapshot a pixie of a girl with dark hair and amber eyes smiled up at him. Freckles dusted her nose, teeth too large for her mouth were a little crooked in a smile as big as the world. Dee Dee. Well, really, Deanna Renée, but he'd always called her by her nickname. "I've got my reasons for coming back," he admitted.

"Don't we all?"

"I suppose," Mason allowed. He and Jarrod had been friends for years, ever since high school. Jarrod had been everything from a log-truck driver, to a detective with a police department in Arizona somewhere, but he'd been back in Bittersweet for a couple of years running his own private-investigation business. Mason had hired him to track down his younger sister, Patty. So far, no luck; just a few leads that always seemed to peter out.

Jarrod's smile was slow as it stretched across his jaw. "So what're you gonna do about Bliss?"

Bliss Cawthorne. "Not much." His stomach clenched as he remembered her eyes, as blue as a mountain lake, and lips that could curve into a smile that was innocent and sexy as hell all at once. She'd nearly died. Because of him. Because he'd been weak.

Jarrod pretended interest in his knuckles. "You and she had a thing once."

If you only knew. "A long time ago." *But it feels like yesterday.*

"Old feelings die hard."

"Do they?"

"She's not married. Never been." Jarrod twisted the knob and shouldered open the door. "It's almost as if she's been waiting for you."

Mason nearly laughed as he folded his arms over his chest "My guess is that she'd just as soon spit on me as talk to me."

"Still blaming yourself for that accident?"

Mason shrugged, as if he didn't give a damn, but the muscles in his shoulders tightened like cords of a thick rope that had been wet and left to shrink in the sun.

"Hell, Lafferty, it wasn't your fault."

Mason didn't answer.

Jarrod shook his head. "I probably shouldn't have said anything, but you were bound to find out sooner or later. I was just letting you know that she'll be back. She's still a good-lookin' woman—or so her old man brags—and still gonna inherit a pile of money, so if you're not interested, I'm sure a lot of other men around these parts would be."

Jealousy, his old enemy, seeped into Mason's blood. "Including you?"

"Maybe," Jarrod admitted with that lazy smile still fastened on his face. "You know it's nice to keep it in the family, and now she'll be my what? Stepsister?"

"If the wedding of the century ever comes off." He knew that Smith was needling him, and yet he couldn't take anything, when it came to Bliss, lightly. Even after ten years.

"See ya around."

"Right."

Jarrod left the door open when he left. Mason watched as his friend, wearing jeans, cowboy boots with worn heels, and a faded denim jacket, sauntered out of the exterior office, stopping long enough to say a few words to Mason's secretary, Edie, to make her blush.

Jarrod Smith had a knack for breaking women's hearts. Though he owed the man his life, Mason didn't like the idea of Jarrod being anywhere near Bliss Cawthorne. She deserved better than to be another of Smith's conquests.

Oh, right, because you were so good to her.

Frowning, he picked up his coffee cup and scowled as the weak, cold brew hit the back of his throat.

Bliss Cawthorne.

The princess.

The one woman he could never quite wedge from his mind, even though he'd married another.

In his mind's eye, he saw her again at the edge of the cliff, slipping from his grasp. He heard the sound of his own terrified scream, felt that same horrifying certainty that she would be dead in an instant.

But her old man had shown up just in time.

Thank God.

John Cawthorne had arrived on horseback, his foreman with him.

"What's going on here?" Cawthorne had shouted, then reached around Mason and grabbed hold of Bliss's leg just as his own grip had given way.

"Hang on, Blissie— For the love of God, man, pull! Pull!"

Mason's ebbing strength had revitalized. Though pain jolted through his arm, he caught hold of her free leg and yanked. The two men dragged her back to the ledge where she'd lain, eyes closed, blood streaming from the cuts on her head.

"Ride like hell to the truck, call the police and get a helicopter for her," John had commanded the foreman. Rain dripped from the brim of his hat, mud oozed around his boots. His face was etched in fear and his eyes, two smoldering blue coals, burned through Mason with a hatred so intense it nearly smelled. "You miserable son of a bitch, you nearly killed her." He bent down on one knee and touched his daughter tenderly on the cheek. "Hang on, honey. Just hang the hell on."

The minutes stretched on.

Mason was in and out of consciousness and barely heard the helicopter or the shouts from the pilots. Nor did he feel the whoosh of air as the rotor blades turned above him and bent the wet grass skirting the ledge.

All he knew was that when he awoke, battered and broken, the helicopter had taken Bliss away and left him alone with John Cawthorne and the older man's festering hatred. A half-smoked cigarette bobbed from the corner of Cawthorne's mouth.

"Now, you lowlife son of a bitch, you listen to me," Cawthorne commanded in a voice barely above a whisper. His face was flushed with rage, his hands clenched into hard, gnarled fists. "You stay away from my daughter."

Mason didn't answer. He couldn't. Pain screamed up his left arm where the horse had kicked him and his chest felt so heavy he could scarcely breathe. Rain, in cold, pounding sheets, poured from the sky, peppering his face and mud-caked body as he lay, face up, at the edge of the ravine.

"Bliss is half-dead, Lafferty, all because of you. You nearly cost me my best stallion as well as my daughter's life. If I had the balls I'd leave you here for the buzzards." The cords of his neck, above his grimy slicker, were taut as bowstrings. "It would serve you right." He wiped his face with a muddy hand, leaving streaks of brown on his unshaven jaw as he glared up at the heavens. "But you're lucky. Instead of letting you die like you deserve, I'll cut you a deal. Twenty-five thousand dollars over and above your medical bills if you walk away."

Mason blinked, tried to speak, but couldn't say a word.

His arm wouldn't move and his breath came in short, shallow gasps that burned like hell and seemed to rip the tissue of his lungs.

"You leave Bittersweet, never contact Bliss again and marry Terri Fremont."

What? His head was heavy, his mind unclear from the raging pain, but he didn't understand. "No way. I can't—" he forced out in a bare whisper.

"You know Terri's pregnant with your kid."

No! Impossible. He hadn't been with Terri since Bliss had entered his life two months ago, but as he blinked upward at the dark, swollen clouds and into the fury of John Cawthorne's face, he felt a sickening sensation of calamity barreling, like the engine of a freight train, straight for him.

"It's what you've always wanted, Lafferty—money the easy way. Well, now you've got it. Just leave Bliss alone."

Bile crawled up Mason's throat and he turned his head in time to retch onto the sodden grass of Cawthorne's land.

"The way I see it, you haven't got much choice."

Mason couldn't argue.

"Have we got a deal?" He spat his cigarette onto the ground where it sizzled before dying.

No! Mason's nostrils flared and he tried to force himself to his feet, got as far as his knees and fell back down, his head smacking into the mud, his arm and chest searing with agony.

"Moron." Cawthorne's voice had lost some of its edge. "Come on, son. Think of your future. You've got a kid on the way. It's time to grow up. Face responsibility. And then there's that little matter of your sister."

Patty. Two years younger and beautiful, but oh, so messed up.

"She could use the money, even if you and Terri aren't interested, but you'd better talk to the Fremont girl first. My guess is that she's like most women and she'll want all the money for herself and your kid."

No! No! No! A burning ache blasted through his brain and his eyelids begged to droop.

"Now," Cawthorne continued a little more gently, "have we got a deal?"

No way! Mason's head reeled. He spat. Blood and mud flew from his cracked lips.

Cawthorne leaned down, the scent of smoke and tobacco wafting from him. "I'm giving you the chance of a lifetime, boy. All you have to do is say yes."

Mason closed his eyes. Blackness threatened the edges of his vision, but still he saw Bliss's gorgeous face. Cawthorne was right; he'd nearly killed her. If the old man hadn't shown up when he did, if he'd lost his grip only seconds earlier, if he hadn't followed her to the cliff . . . He swallowed and realized with an impending sense of doom that he had no choice.

"Well?"

Bliss, oh, God, I'm sorry. I'm so damned sorry. He felt more broken and battered than his injuries and realized that it was his soul that had been destroyed.

Through cracked lips, he agreed. "Yeah, Cawthorne," he finally mouthed, his insides rebelling at the very thought of giving her up. He skewered the older man with a glare of pure hatred. "We've . . . we've got a deal."

Now, ten years later, at that particular thought his stomach turned sour and he tossed the dregs of his drink into a straggly-looking fern positioned near the window.

So Bliss was finally returning to Bittersweet. With that little bit of knowledge, he knew that his painful bargain with Cawthorne was over. Though he should leave her alone, pretend that what had happened between them was forgotten, he couldn't.

He'd returned to Bittersweet with a single purpose: to gain custody of his daughter and provide a stable life for her. He shouldn't let anything or anyone deter him. Especially not Bliss Cawthorne. But there was that little matter of Cawthorne's ranch. Mason had always loved the place despite a few bad memories. Now, as luck would have it, he had a chance of owning it, maybe settling down with his kid and hopefully finding the peace that had eluded him for most of his life.

Except that he was going to see Bliss again, and that particular meeting promised to be about as peaceful as fireworks on the Fourth of July.

"I should have my head examined," Bliss muttered.

Oscar, her mutt of indiscernible lineage, thumped his tail on the passenger seat of her convertible as they raced down the freeway five miles over the speed limit. The radio blasted an old Rolling Stones tune as the road curved through the mountains of southern Oregon.

Oscar, tongue lolling, black lips in a smile that exposed his fangs, rested his head on the edge of the rolled-down side window. His gold coat ruffled in the wind and sparkled in the sun under a cloudless sky.

Bliss tapped out the beat of "Get Off My Cloud" on the steering wheel and wished she'd never agreed to this lunacy. What was she going to do in the town where she'd been so hurt, meeting half-sisters and a bevy of steprelatives she hadn't known existed, and watching as her father, foolish old man that he'd become overnight, walk down the aisle with his mistress.

"Unreal," she muttered as Mick Jagger's voice faded and the radio crackled with static.

Oscar didn't seem to care. He was up for the adventure. His brown eyes sparkled with an excitement Bliss didn't share, and with a red handkerchief tied jauntily around his neck, he looked ready for ranch life.

Bliss's hands tightened on the steering wheel. She'd changed her mind about driving to Oregon six times during as many days. Her father had recuperated and left Seattle two weeks earlier, then just this past week had called to tell her he was being married at the end of June. He wanted her to come spend some time with him, meet her new family, and be a part of the festivities.

Great.

And what about Mason? her wayward mind taunted. *What if you run into him?*

"The least of my worries," she lied as she stepped on the gas to pass a log truck. She planned to avoid Mason Lafferty as if he were the plague. Her hands on the wheel began to sweat, and she bit down on her lip. She was over him. Had been for a long time. So what if he'd been her first love? It had been ten years ago—a decade—since she'd last seen him or felt his fingers moving anxiously against the small of her back.

At the old, erotic memory, goose bumps broke out on her skin and she closed her mind to any further wayward thoughts. Mason had never loved her, never cared. He'd left without a second glance. Hadn't even had the decency to stop by the hospital where she'd fought for her life after the accident. Hadn't so much as sent a card. In fact, he'd cared so much for her that he'd married another woman. He was the last man on earth she wanted.

An old Bruce Springsteen song, one she'd heard that painful summer, pounded through the speakers.

She snapped off the radio in disgust.

She wouldn't think of Mason. At least, not right now. Besides, she had other worries. What about the two women who were supposed to be her half-sisters, for crying out loud? A nest of butterflies erupted in her stomach when she thought about the women she'd never known. Did she really want to know them? "Give me strength," she muttered under her breath.

She exited the freeway, her stomach tightening in painful knots. Memories, vivid and painful, slipped through her mind. The hills of pine and madrona looked the same as they had ten years ago. The landmarks—an old trading post and an abandoned schoolhouse—hadn't changed much. Barbed-wire fences surrounded fields lush with the spring rains, where cattle grazed lazily.

After a final rise in the road, the town of Bittersweet came into view. She passed by the old water tower that stood near the railroad station. Nearby, a white church spire, complete with bell and copper roof, rose above leafy shade trees surrounding the town square. Fences ranging from white picket and ranch rail to chain link cordoned off small yards within which bikes, swings, and sagging wading pools were strewn. The homes were eclectic—cottages and two-story clapboard houses intermingled with ranch-style tract homes and tiny bungalows.

In the central business district she drove past the old pharmacy where she'd ordered cherry colas one summer. She slowed to a stop at the single blinking red light in the center of town and noticed that the old mom-and-pop grocery store, once owned by an elderly couple whose names she couldn't remember, had changed hands. It was now a Mini-Mart. Time had marched on.

And so had she.

She hadn't belonged here ten years ago. She didn't belong here now.

Thoughts a-tangle, she drove on into the country again and slowed automatically at the gravel lane that cut through fields of knee-high grass. The gate was open, as if she were expected, and the curved wooden sign bridging the end of the lane read Cawthorne Acres. Her father's pride and joy.

John Cawthorne called this spot "heaven on earth." She wasn't so sure. She wasn't seduced by the scents of honeysuckle and cut hay, nor did her heart warm at the sight of the horses milling and grazing, their tails swishing against flies. Nope. She was much happier as a city girl. Margaret Cawthorne's daughter.

She slowed at the barn and parked near the open door. Oscar jumped out his side of the car. She reached into the back seat for one of her bags.

"Look, I thought I made it clear that I wasn't interested!" John Cawthorne's angry voice rang from the barn.

Bliss's shoulders sagged. The last thing her father should be doing after his surgery was getting himself all riled up. She dropped the bag, opened the car door, climbed out and shoved the door shut with her hip. "Dad?" she called as she walked into the barn. Dust motes swirled upward in air thick with the odors of dusty grain and dry hay.

"Bliss—?"

Her eyes adjusted to the dim light and she saw her father leaning heavily on his pitchfork. His jaw was set, his face rigid and he was glaring at a man whose broad-shouldered back was turned to her and whose worn, faded jeans had seen far better days.

"I think you probably remember Lafferty."

Bliss's stupid heart skipped a beat and her throat went dry. "Lafferty?" she said automatically, then wished she could drop through the hay-strewn floor. What was he doing here?

In the shadowy light, he glanced over his shoulder. Gold eyes clashed hard and fast with hers.

She froze.

Gone was any trace of the boyish charm she remembered. This man had long ago shrugged off any suggestion of adolescence and was now all angles and planes, big bones, hard muscle and gristle. A few lines fanned from his eyes and bracketed his mouth. His hair, though still blond, had darkened and was longer than the style worn by most of the businessmen in Seattle.

"Well, what do you know?" he taunted, turning on a worn boot-heel and giving her an even better view of him. The skin of his face and forearms where his shirtsleeves were pushed up was tanned from hours in the sun and the thrust of his jaw was harsher, more defined and decidedly more male than she remembered. A day's worth of whiskers gilded a chin that looked as if it had been chiseled from granite. "It's been a long time."

Not long enough! Not nearly long enough. "A good ten years."

"Good?"

"The best," she lied. She wouldn't give him the satisfaction of knowing that he'd hurt her.

"I knew you'd come," her father said and propped the pitchfork against the wall. He crossed the short distance between them and gave her a bear hug with arms that weren't as strong as they once had been.

"Did I have a choice?"

"Always."

She laughed as he released her. "No one has much of a choice when you set your mind, Dad. Mom used to say that stubborn was your middle na—" She bit her tongue and reminded herself that her mother, proud and ever-faithful, was gone. And her father was hell-bent to marry someone else.

"That she did," John agreed. "That she did."

The moment was suddenly awkward and Bliss, as much to change the subject as anything else, said, "I hope I didn't hear you shouting a couple of minutes ago."

"Me?" Her father's eyes twinkled. "Never."

She turned to Mason. "He's not supposed to get overly excited."

"I'll keep that in mind." Shoving callused hands into the back pockets of his jeans, Mason smiled, a sizzling slash of white that was neither friendly nor warm, just downright hit-you-in-the-gut sexy. Well practiced. A grin guaranteed to turn a young girl's heart to mush.

But she wasn't a young innocent anymore and all of Mason's wiles to which she'd been so vulnerable long ago, couldn't touch her. Not now. Not ever again. Her fingers curled into fists and her fingernails dug deep into her palms.

"Good."

His gaze raked up and down her wrinkled blouse and the tangle of her hair, only to pause at her eyes. "How've you been?"

As if he cared.

"Fine . . . I mean, great. Just great. Really."

"You look it."

She felt a blush climb up the back of her neck. "It must be because of all the clean living I do, I guess."

Mason laughed. "Right."

Her father snorted.

"You don't believe me?"

"I *know* you."

"Did know me. A long time ago. I—I've grown up."

"I noticed."

Bliss wasn't fooled by Mason's well-honed charm. Not a bit. How many nights had she cried bitter tears over this two-timing thoughtless bastard? In an instant, she wanted to strangle him and wasn't about to listen to any of his cheap compliments. She'd made that mistake before. Years ago he'd cut her loose and broken her heart; she'd never trust him again. Folding her arms under her breasts, she asked, "So what're you doing here?"

His smile only broadened as if he were amused by her discomfiture. *Amused!*

"Tryin' to buy the ranch out from under me, that's what he's doin'," her father said, his blue gaze blistering. "I told him I'm not selling."

"Why would you?"

"Because it's too much for him." Mason was matter-of-fact.

"Who're you to determine that? Just 'cause I had a little heart attack don't mean I've got one foot in the grave." Her father was as irascible as ever. Good. That meant he was getting better.

"Just think about it, okay?" Mason suggested. "And while you're at it, you might want to talk to Brynnie."

"Why?" her father demanded, suspicion flashing in his eyes.

"She's going to be your wife, isn't she?"

"Of course."

"Then you probably should ask her what she wants."

"I always do."

One of Mason's brows rose skeptically. "I'll bring you the offer. You can read it over."

John looked about to argue, but clamped his mouth shut.

With a nod to Bliss, Mason strode across the wedge of sunlight that had pierced the gloomy interior of the barn, shouldered open the door until it bounced against the wall and disappeared. A few seconds later a truck's engine roared to life and gravel sprayed from beneath heavy tires.

"No-account bastard," her father said as he reached into his back pocket and pulled out a plug of chewing tobacco. He started to bite into the black wad, then hesitated as if he'd caught the censure in his daughter's eyes. "It's just a little chew, Blissie, and since I can't smoke . . . Oh, hell." He shoved the dark plug back into his pocket. "What's Lafferty want this place for? He owns property all over the West."

John hung his pitchfork on a peg near the door and walked outside where the breath of a breeze cooled the air. Leaves, lush and green on the apple tree near the front porch, turned softly in the wind.

"I was hoping you were down here taking it easy," she said.

"I am."

"I don't think working in the barn and arguing at the top of your lungs is what the doctors had in mind."

"What do they know?"

"Come on, Dad," she cajoled as they reached her car.

"Don't you start in on me, too. I've spent the last few weeks cooped up in bed, so I thought I'd come into the barn and clean up a bit. Nothin' more. Then Lafferty showed up." He glowered at the driveway. "I've thought about sellin' out, but it galls me to think that a no-account like Lafferty wants to buy."

"What do you care?" she asked and her father's eyes flashed. "Weren't you the guy who always said, 'Money is money, as long as it's green'?"

"I know, I know," he agreed as Oscar explored the shrubbery around the house. "It's just that I care about this place, even if Brynnie doesn't."

"Why doesn't she like it?"

He shrugged. "Too many bad memories here for her, I guess." He settled a hip against her fender as sunlight bounced off the convertible's glossy finish.

"Because you were married to Mom?" Bliss asked, her heart wrenching.

"Even though your mother never lived here, it bothered Brynnie."

"Because you were married."

"I suppose."

Oh, God, this was going to be hard. A stepmother. One who had been involved with her father for a long, long time. Maybe this was a mistake. Maybe she shouldn't have come back.

"I'll look over the damned offer," he admitted, "but I'm not gonna accept it."

Oscar romped over, wagged his tail. As Bliss reached down to scratch him behind his ears, she glanced at the wake of dust that was settling on the long gravel drive.

"I know it was tough for you to come here," he volunteered, swiping at a yellow jacket that buzzed around his head.

"I'm worried about you," she admitted.

"Yeah, but it's more than that. You're curious as hell about Brynnie and the girls."

Lifting a shoulder, Bliss hoisted a bag from the back seat and hauled it toward the house. Her father carried a smaller case and followed her. "A little."

"A lot, I'll wager. Don't blame you." He eyed her as he held open the front door and the scents she remembered—of floor wax, smoke and cooking oil—greeted her. She fingered the old globe, sending countries that no longer existed spinning.

She walked along the short hallway and pushed open the door. Her room was as it had been for as long as she could remember. Double bed, old dresser with a curved mirror, tiny closet. Rag rugs were scattered over an old, dull fir floor.

He dropped her small case on the foot of the bed.

"I'm drivin' over to Brynnie's for dinner later. You want to tag along?"

"No." She was surprised how quickly the word was out of her mouth, and hated the disappointment she saw in her father's eyes. However, the truth of the matter was that she still needed time to settle in and grow more comfortable with this new life that was being thrown at her. Seeing Mason again didn't help. Not at all. "Not—not tonight. Just give me a little time to catch up, okay?"

He started to argue, thought better of it and shrugged. “Whatever you say, kid. I just think it’s time to make peace. I’ve made my share of mistakes in the past and now I’d like for you and your sisters to be part of a family.” He scratched at the stubble silvering his jaw. “But I’ll try not to push you too fast.”

“Thanks, Dad,” she whispered, her throat clogging at his kindness. Crusty as he was, he had his good points. Somehow she’d have to get over her feeling that he’d betrayed her mother. She only wished she knew how.

She walked to the window and forced it open. Returning to Bittersweet might have been a mistake. A big one. Not only would she have to deal with this new patchwork of a family, but also, she was bound to run into Mason again.

So? He was just a man. What they had shared was over a long, long time ago. Or was it?

Chapter Three

His first mistake had been returning to Bittersweet.

His second was seeing Bliss again.

"You're an idiot, Lafferty," he told himself as he parked on the edge of Isaac Wells's property just as night was threatening to fall. The woman had the uncanny ability to get under his skin. Just like before.

"Hell," he ground out, chiding himself for believing that he could see her and not care. He'd been thinking about her ever since leaving the Cawthorne spread—a place he intended to have as his own, if only to prove a point.

But he couldn't think of Bliss right now. He had too much on his mind. First he had to fight with Terri over custody of Dee Dee and secondly he had to find his sister. Patty had been in Bittersweet recently. Jarrod Smith had determined that much, and she'd come here to this scrappy piece of land owned by their uncle, a man who had turned his back on them years ago.

Isaac Wells.

A number-one bastard.

Who had now disappeared. Vanished, without a trace.

Mason climbed out of the pickup. In one lithe movement, he vaulted the fence and walked up the short, rutted lane to the dilapidated cabin that Isaac had called home.

An old wooden rocker with battle-scarred arms and a worn corduroy pad on the seat, pushed by the wind, rocked gently on the front porch. The old man had spent hours on the stoop where he'd whittled, read the stars, strung beans from his garden, and spat streams of tobacco juice into an old coffee can he'd used as a spittoon. He'd made few friends in his lifetime, but had unearthed more than his share of enemies.

So what had happened to him? Had someone killed him and taken his body? But why? Or had he been kidnapped? Or had he just taken a notion and up and left? Mason rubbed the back of his neck in frustration and wondered if Patty had been involved. "Hell's bells," he muttered as he scanned the countryside. Berry vines and thistle were taking over the fields, and the barn, which had never been painted, was beginning to fall apart. The roof sagged and some of the bleached board-and-batten siding was rotting away.

What the hell had happened here?

Foul play?

Or had an addled, lonely old man left in desperation?

No one seemed to know and everyone within fifty miles was frightened. Mysteries like this didn't happen in these sparsely populated hills. The town of Bittersweet and the surrounding rural landscape were far from the rat race and crime of the city; that was part of the charm of this section of Oregon. But Isaac's disappearance had changed all that. Dead bolts that had nearly rusted in the open position were being thrown, security companies contacted for new installments, and, worst of all, shotguns cleaned and kept loaded near bedsteads in the event that an intruder dared break in.

The townspeople and farmers were nervous.

The sheriff's department wanted answers.

And there was nothing. Not a clue.

Except for Patty.

Shadows lengthened across the dry acres that made up

Isaac Wells's spread. Mason kicked at a dirt clod, then scoured the darkening sky, as if in reading the stars that were beginning to wink in the purple distance, he could find clues to the old man's disappearance. Of course there were none. Nor were there any celestial explanations for why Mason seemed destined to deal with Bliss Cawthorne again. He couldn't stop himself, of course, and truth to tell, he was inwardly grateful that she hadn't married another man and had a couple of kids.

Like you did.

He'd been foolish enough to think that by seeing her again he'd realize that what he'd felt for her all those years ago—some kind of schoolboy infatuation wrapped up in guilt—would have diminished; that he'd see her and laugh at himself for the fantasies that had haunted him over the years.

"Moron," he growled as memories of his youth, of that time in his life when he was searching, hoping to find something, anything to cling to, flitted through his mind. Boy, had he made a mess of it. He stretched out his left hand, felt the old scar tissue in his arm tighten and was reminded of the horrid, black afternoon when she'd almost died. Because of him. Though John Cawthorne didn't know the whole story and probably never would, the God's honest truth was that Mason had nearly killed her.

He shoved a wayward hank of hair from his eyes and silently leveled an oath at himself. He'd been the worst kind of fool.

She'd turned into the beauty her youth had promised. Her hair was still a streaked golden blond, her eyes crystal blue, her lips as lush as he remembered. Her body was thin in the right places, and full where it should be. Yep, she'd matured into what he suspected was one hell of a woman, and the defiant tilt of her chin as she'd challenged him today in the barn had only added to her allure.

He looked around the outside of the small house, noticed the faded real-estate sign planted firmly in the grass and frowned. Who would want this scrap of worthless land?

"Damn it all to hell," he muttered as he headed back to his rig. He had enough problems in his life. Running his businesses, trying to convince Terri that Dee Dee was better off with him, and hoping to find his flake of a sister were more than enough. Now, like it or not, he would have to deal with Bliss.

Life had just gotten a lot more complicated.

"You know, Dad, I'm still having trouble with all this." Bliss slid a pancake onto the stack that was heaped on the plate before her father. She'd slept fitfully last night, her dreams punctuated with visions of her father strapped to an IV, of meeting women she didn't know and introducing herself as their sister and, of course, of Mason. Good Lord, why couldn't she get him out of her mind? It had been ten years since she'd been involved with him. A decade. It was long past time to forget him.

"What kind of trouble?" Her father slathered the top pancake with margarine, then reached for the honey spindle. Drizzling thick honey over his plate, he looked up at his daughter as if he expected her to accept the turn of events that had knocked her for such an emotional loop.

"You know with what. Brynnie. My half-sisters. The whole ball of wax, for crying out loud. It's . . . Well, come on, Dad, it's just . . . well, *bizarre*, for lack of a better word." She shook her head, then winced as she poured them each a cup of coffee. After setting the glass pot back in the coffeemaker, she settled into the empty chair across from him.

"Not bizarre, honey. It's right."

"Right?"

"For the first time in a lot of years, I . . . I feel free 'cause

I'm not livin'a lie." Blue eyes met hers from across the table. "Your mother was a fine woman—I won't take that away from her—but we weren't happy together. Hadn't been for a long time."

"I know." A dull pain settled in her heart. She'd felt the tension between her parents, known that theirs wasn't a marriage made in heaven, but still, they had been married and Bliss, though she hated to admit it, still believed in "till death us do part."

"She's gone, honey," her father said. "I would never have divorced her, you know."

"Only cheated on her."

He looked down and sliced his hotcakes with the side of his fork. "Guess I can't expect you to understand."

"I'm trying, Dad," she said, unable to hide the emotion in her words. "Believe me, I'm trying." Resting her elbows on the table, she cradled her cup in two hands. Through the paned windows she could see the barn and pastures. White-faced Hereford cattle mingled with Black Angus as they grazed on grass sparkling with morning dew.

The silence stretched between them, with only the ticking of the clock, the low of cattle, the rumble of a tractor's engine in the distance and an excited yip from Oscar as he explored his new surroundings, breaking the uneasy quietude.

John washed down a bite of pancake with a swallow of coffee. "Since I had the heart attack and looked the Grim Reaper square in his black eyes, I've decided to do exactly what I want with the few years I have left."

"And that includes marrying this . . . this Brynnie woman."

"Believe it or not, Bliss, she's got a heart of gold."

"And a string of ex-husbands long enough to—"

"She made some bad choices, I know. So did I. And if it's

any comfort to you, I never ran around with another woman while I was married to your mother."

"Just Brynnie." Bliss couldn't hide the bitterness in her voice.

"Yes."

"Isn't she enough?"

He shoved his half-eaten breakfast aside and skewered his daughter with a look of sheer determination. "I know you don't approve. Can't blame you. But no one was hurt."

"What about Mom?"

"Your mother and I . . . We had an arrangement."

"An *arrangement*?" Bliss sputtered, choking on a mouthful of coffee. "It's called marriage, Dad, and one of the vows a person takes when they get married is fidelity. To be faithful. It doesn't seem a lot to ask." She couldn't help the rising tone of her voice as if she were on the earth solely to defend Margaret Cawthorne's honor. Everything she believed in was being tested and though she was trying, really trying to understand, she was having difficulty. *Rise above it; it's not a big deal, Mom's gone*, her mind argued with the loyalty that burned bright in her heart and the belief that love lasted a lifetime.

Her father reached across the scarred maple table and took her hand in his rough, callused fingers. "I'm sorry, Bliss, really. I never wanted to hurt anyone. Not you. Not Margaret. Not Brynnie. Seems it's all I do." He frowned, patted the back of her hand and picked up his fork again. "But now it's time to heal, to make some peace, to recognize the family that I have." His lips pinched together. "I wanted you to be a part of it, to meet your sisters, to find out about them. This is a chance for all of us to finally be a family."

"Of sorts."

"Yes. Of sorts."

Dear God, why did she feel like a heel? Someone had to

make him face the truth. Now was one of the times she wished she really did have a sister or brother with whom she could share the burden of her father's problems. But she did have sisters, didn't she? Two half-sisters. Certainly they would add up to a whole one— Oh, for the love of Pete, this was making her crazy.

The sound of a truck's engine rumbled through the air, and from the porch Oscar gave an excited "woof." Bliss recognized the pickup from the day before and her heart did a little lurch when she spied Mason behind the wheel.

"Now what?" her father grumbled, looking over his shoulder and squinting against the sun rising over the hills.

"Trouble," Bliss predicted.

"Young upstart pup, Lafferty. Always pushing." He eyed Bliss speculatively. "You'd think with all he owns, he'd give up on this place." His jaw hardened slightly and his eyes thinned in anger. "Then again, maybe it's not the place that's got him so interested. Maybe it's you."

"I don't think so." Bliss remembered how easily Mason had left her ten years before, but couldn't drag her gaze away from Mason as he stepped out of the truck. Tall, lanky, hard-edged, with a walk that bordered on a swagger, he approached the front door. Tinted sunglasses shaded his eyes and a scowl etched deep grooves over eyebrows slammed together.

"I'll get rid of him," she said, wiping her hands on a dish towel and telling herself that she had the guts to face him.

"No way. He's as sticky as hot tar."

Bliss scraped her chair back and hurried to the front hallway just as he knocked. Yanking open the door, she faced him across the threshold and ignored the stupid, wild knocking of her heart.

A slow-growing smile wiped the grim expression from his face. "Mornin', Bliss."

"Hi." Dear Lord, was that her pulse jumping in her neck,

visible in the V neckline of her T-shirt? Great! What a fool she was. A naive, stupid fool. She and Mason had been in love once, or maybe it was even puppy love, but what they had shared, that hot flirtation, was long dead. Yet she couldn't help the fluttering of her pulse or the urge to swallow against a suddenly dry throat. "Do you make it your primary objective in life these days to harass people?"

"Only a few special ones," he teased and she fought the urge to smile.

"Like Dad."

"Or you." He pocketed the sunglasses and stared at Bliss with eyes that were as seductive as cool water in a blistering desert at high noon.

"Wonderful." She managed a bit of sarcasm.

"Look, I just want to talk to your father."

"You talked to him yesterday."

"I know, but I'd like to finish the conversation."

"It's finished, Lafferty. Take a hint."

"I forgot to give him the offer." He glanced over her shoulder. "Is John around?"

"You bet I'm around," John answered, walking in his stocking feet along the dusty patina of the hardwood floor. "What is it you're lookin' for—as if I didn't know?" He glanced at his daughter and scowled. "I already told you. I ain't sellin'. No matter what the price."

Bliss lifted a lofty brow, encouraging Mason, if he had the guts, to draw her father into a battle he would surely lose.

Mason leaned a shoulder against the doorjamb.

"Since you and Brynnie are going to tie the knot, I thought you might want to retire, see a little of the world with your new bride, take it easy."

"You mean the old stud should be put out to pasture?" With a hoarse laugh and a scrape of his fingers against his empty shirt pocket where he searched by habit for a nonexistent pack of cigarettes, Bliss's father shook his head.

"One measly little heart attack isn't gonna scare me away from doin' what I want." He rapped his knuckles against his chest. "The old ticker's just fine and I'm gonna run this ranch like I always have." Again his fingers scrabbled into his pocket and he frowned when he realized that his cigarettes were gone, as his doctor had insisted he give up smoking after the heart attack. Bliss suspected that he still sneaked a puff now and again along with his chew, but she'd never caught him with a cigarette. Not that she could stop him from smoking. No one had ever been able to tell John Cawthorne how to live his life.

Mason reached into his back pocket and drew out a long envelope that he slapped into John's hand. "I think you'd better talk to Brynnie about this. In the meantime, here's a formal offer—for the acres in your name."

"In my name?" John questioned.

"Fair price. Good terms. Think about it." Mason slipped his sunglasses onto the bridge of his nose.

"Don't need to," her father insisted, but he didn't toss the envelope back at Mason as Bliss had expected. Instead, his bony fingers clamped over the manila packet.

Mason's gaze centered on Bliss. "I'll see you later," he said through lips that barely moved as he glared through his sunglasses, and Bliss had trouble drawing a breath.

John wagged the envelope at Mason. "Just remember that a few years back we had a deal."

"A deal?" Bliss repeated.

"That's right. Signed, sealed and delivered." Her father's smile was shrewd and self-serving and Bliss felt a sliver of dread enter her heart.

"I haven't forgotten." Mason's shoulders tightened. The skin over his face seemed to grow taut and his gaze, behind his tinted lenses held hers briefly before he turned and strode back to his truck.

Oscar bounded along behind him and Mason paused long enough to scratch the dog between his shoulders before climbing into the cab of his Ford.

"Pushy S.O.B.," John grumbled as the pickup tore down the lane. He was already opening the envelope, anxious to explore its contents, which surprised Bliss. For someone who was so vocally against selling the ranch—especially to Mason—John Cawthorne was certainly interested in the bottom line. But then, he always had been. That was how he'd made his money.

Scanning the pages, he walked into the living room, picked up his reading glasses from the fireplace mantel, plopped them on the end of his nose and then settled into his favorite battered recliner.

"You know why he's back in town, I suppose?"

"Other than to try and talk you into selling?" she bantered back.

"Seems he's decided to settle down here, be closer to his kid." He glanced up, looking over the tops of his lenses. "Can't fault him for that, I suppose."

"No."

"But rumor has it he's trying to get back with his ex-wife. You remember her? Terri?"

How could she ever forget? "Of course, I remember."

"Good." He looked back to the pages again.

Why it should bother her that Mason was seeing Terri, she didn't understand, but the old wounds in her heart seemed to reopen all over again. Straightening a hurricane lantern sitting on the mantel, she said, "Okay, so what was this business about a deal between you two? As far as I knew, you didn't want anything to do with him."

"Still don't." Her father hesitated a fraction. "I had to do something to get him out of town. So I paid his medical bills and gave him the old heave-ho."

"Then he left to marry Terri Fremont," she said, feeling an odd sensation that something else in the past wasn't what she'd thought it was. But that wasn't much of a surprise, was it? Hadn't her entire life been a lie?

"I just gave him some extra incentive." He cleared his throat. "It wasn't too hard to figure out what was going on between the two of you and it worried me because I knew about the Fremont girl. So . . . I upped the ante a little, offered him a deal and he rose to the bait like a brook trout to a salmon fly."

"No—"

His lips pursed in frustration. "It was for your own good, Bliss. That's why I did it. Remember, he already had a baby on the way."

Bliss rested her hands on the back of the couch. "You shouldn't have gotten involved."

"He needed surgery on that arm of his and his kid needed a father."

"You're a fine one to talk," she sputtered. Then, seeing the pain in his eyes, she wished she could have taken the words back.

"Is that what you think?"

"Yes," she admitted, not wanting to hurt him, but knowing that the lies would stop with her. "You fathered *two* children with women you didn't marry."

"And I didn't want to see anyone, even a snake like Lafferty, make the same mistakes I did."

"But—"

"No buts, Blissie," he said, signifying that the conversation, as far as he was concerned, was over. He tilted his head to ensure that his bifocals were in the right position for reading. "Now, what have we got here?"

Bliss couldn't believe her ears. It was as if her father would use any means possible to get his way. She'd always known he was stubborn and determined, but this side of him was new to her and she wasn't sure she liked it very much.

"You know, for a man who swears up and down that he's not interested in selling this place, it's odd that you can't put down that offer." Bliss swatted at a cobweb that floated between the old blinds on the window and the ceiling.

"Just thought I'd see what Lafferty thinks the place is worth." With practiced eyes he skimmed the printed text and his eyebrows jammed together in concentration. "There's somethin' wrong here. The figures don't add up and . . . What in thunder? Is he out of his mind? This"—he snapped the crisp pages—"this is only for the north half of the property. I thought he wanted the whole place."

"Didn't you say that part of the ranch was in Brynnie's name?"

Every muscle in John's body tensed. His gaze shot up to hers. "What do you mean?"

"Well, if he wanted the whole ranch, he'd have to deal with her for her part."

"For the love of—" John scowled, rubbing the edge of the documents against the stubble of his chin and as he squinted, Bliss could almost see the wheels turning in his mind. "Brynnie's not like your mother, Bliss," he said, though his voice lacked conviction. "She wouldn't expect me to give up what I love."

"I'm not suggesting anything of the sort. And Mom would never—"

"Unless she got herself conned into it." Her father snapped the leg support of the recliner into place and climbed to his feet. Wadding the offer in his fist, he headed for the den. "I think I'd better call my lawyer."

"Why?"

"Just to make sure Lafferty doesn't try to pull a fast one."

* * *

"Damn it all to hell," Mason grumbled, stomping on the brakes as his pickup slid to a stop beside the carriage house of an old Victorian home in the center of town. Four stories counting the basement, painted gray and trimmed in white gingerbread with black shutters, the mansion had been divided into separate apartments sometime between the 1920s and now. There were two other units in the old carriage house as well, and for the next few months Mason would call the upper story of that smaller building home.

Climbing out of the cab, he spied Tiffany Santini, the widow who owned the place, clipping a few rosebuds from the garden. Tall, with dark hair and eyes, she was pleasant and pretty, the kind of woman who took to mothering like a duck to water. Mason didn't know much about her, but he liked the way she dealt with her kids—a teenage boy and a girl of three or four.

He waved and she smiled, hoisting a gloved hand as her little girl chased a black cat through the rhododendrons flanking the back porch.

Mason had decided to rent while he was negotiating for a ranch of his own and had chosen this complex over more modern units because he felt more at home in this charming older place, which had a backyard with a play structure that Dee Dee could use whenever she came over.

He walked up the outside stairs, unlocked the door and stepped into his living room. It was sparsely furnished with only the bare essentials. The hardwood floors were begging for throw rugs and the stark walls could have used more than a splash or two of color. But all that would come later—once he'd moved into a permanent place.

At Cawthorne Acres.

For the first time he wondered if his insisting on buying old John out was wise. True, Brynnie had come to him and he'd jumped at the chance to own a spread he'd fallen in love with as a kid, but now, with the old man's heart condition and Bliss thrown into the picture, he wasn't so sure that he'd made the right decision.

What was the old saying? Buy in Haste, Regret at Leisure. That was it. He hoped it didn't apply in his case.

In the kitchen he tossed his keys on the counter and reached for a glass. Pouring himself a stiff shot of bourbon, he tried to erase Bliss and the complications of dealing with her and her father from his mind. But it didn't work. Ever since seeing her yesterday afternoon and again this morning, he'd thought of her—even made an excuse to give Cawthorne his offer in person so that he could see her again.

Bliss Cawthorne, all grown up. He remembered her as she had been ten years earlier with honey-blond hair and eyes as blue as cornflowers. She'd been a smart mouth at the time, a big-city girl who was pretty and damned well knew it. A dusting of freckles had bridged her nose and she'd been tanned all over from hours of swimming in the river.

Mason had been working for old man Cawthorne, and although all the other hired hands had warned him that the boss's daughter was off-limits, he hadn't been able to keep himself away. Which was where all the trouble had begun and ended.

He tossed back a long swallow of his drink and felt the alcohol burn a welcome path down his throat. Why did he torture himself with thoughts of her? Why couldn't he think of her as nothing more than a love affair gone sour?

Because you're a fool, Lafferty. You always have been, where that woman is concerned.

He finished his drink in another gulp and wiped his mouth with the back of his hand. Ten years. It had been ten years since he'd seen her. A decade of telling himself she meant nothing to him, but then, with one sidelong glance from her innocently seductive eyes, he'd come undone and last night, with the hot breath of a wind blowing the curtains in his room, he hadn't slept, but had envisioned Bliss's face as he'd stared through the window at the moon. Now he remembered in vivid detail her expression when she'd answered the door. For a second he'd seen the glimmer of happiness in her eyes but it had been quickly hidden by a facade of anger.

Why the hell did it matter what she thought? She was just one woman, and John Cawthorne's daughter to boot.

"Idiot," he growled, contemplating another drink before screwing the cap on the bourbon bottle. He jammed the bottle back into the cupboard and slammed the door. Bliss. Gorgeous, sophisticated and intriguing Bliss Cawthorne. Why hadn't she married, had a dozen kids and gotten fat? Why did she still attract him after all these years, all these blasted long, lonely years? "Grow up, Lafferty," he chided. He'd learned long ago not to entrust his heart to a woman. Any woman. Especially Bliss Cawthorne.

Besides, the old man was right. Inadvertently, Mason had nearly killed her years before. And there was more to it than that. He and Cawthorne had made a deal. A pact practically signed in Bliss's blood.

So cancel it, an inner voice suggested and he felt a grim smile tug at the corners of his mouth. He'd always believed in honoring his bargains, but Cawthorne had never played fair. So, technically, the deal was null and void.

Bliss, if she'd have him, was his for the taking.

He had only to figure out if he wanted her and for how long.

Chapter Four

"See that sorrel mare?" John Cawthorne leaned against the top rail of the fence and pointed a gnarled finger at a small herd of horses in the north pasture. The animals grazed lazily, twitching their tails at flies while their ears flicked with each shift of the wind.

"She's gorgeous." Bliss watched as the red mare's nose lifted and her nostrils flared slightly, as if she'd somehow divined that she was the center of attention.

"I want you to have her."

"What?"

"That's right. She's yours."

"But I live in Seattle, Dad. In a condominium that's hardly big enough for Oscar and me." Bliss hazarded a smile. "Trust me, the horse won't fit"

He chuckled. "I know, I know, but I reckon, now that your mom's gone, you'll be spending more time down here with your old man."

"And my stepmother." The words still stuck in Bliss's throat though she was trying, damn it, to accept this new and, she still thought, ludicrous situation.

"And hopefully, your sisters."

"If—and it's a pretty big if, Dad—I'm interested and they're willing to meet me halfway. What're the chances?"

"I don't know," he admitted, clearing his throat. "I just think it's all worth it. I'd hate for you—or them, for that matter—to miss out on getting to know each other."

"We might fight like cats and dogs."

"You might. Then again . . ."

She plucked a piece of clover from a clump near the fence post and twirled the purple bloom in her fingers. "Okay, okay, point well taken. Tell me about them."

"Well . . ." He stared off across the fields to a distance only he could see. "You know that Tiffany's older than you. She's a widow now. Works part-time as a secretary at an insurance agency in town. She's got a son Stephen—my oldest grandkid, mind you—almost fourteen and hell on wheels, the way everyone in town says. Then there's that cute button of a daughter of hers who's around three. My only granddaughter, so far."

He looked away quickly, as if bothered by the conversation, and Bliss fought back a feeling of having the rug pulled out from under her. She'd always thought that she would be the one to give her parents grandchildren—when the time came. As the years passed and her friends married and started families of their own, she'd heard her own biological clock ticking away.

"After her husband died, Tiffany moved down here to be close to her grandmother—you've heard of Octavia—Octavia Nesbitt?"

Bliss nodded. Who hadn't heard of Bittersweet's most prominent and flamboyant citizen? Octavia had inherited the Reed estate years before, as she'd been nursemaid and caretaker of Bittersweet's oldest and most wealthy citizen. When Cranston Reed had died, he'd left his fortune to the widow Nesbitt.

"Well, when Tiffany's husband, Philip, died a few months back, she packed her kids into a U-Haul truck and drove south from Portland. She moved into an old house her husband had bought about a year back—it's been cut up into apartments that she rents out for a little extra money."

Bliss folded her arms over the top rail of the fence and watched spindly-legged colts frolicking beside their docile mothers. "So how is Tiffany with you?"

His eyebrows lifted and he bent down to pluck a long blade of dry grass from the ground. "Not great. In fact, she won't talk to me."

No big surprise there. "Do you blame her?"

He rubbed his chin. "Guess not. She didn't know much about me or that I was even alive for a long, long time."

"What?" Bliss couldn't believe her ears, then mentally kicked herself for being so naive. Hadn't she been hoodwinked all her life? Why not Tiffany, as well?

"Her mother, Rose, finally told her the truth, I guess, but I didn't try to get in touch with her until a couple of months ago, after your mother passed on."

"Oh."

"Anyway, I tried to call her, you know, to break the ice, but she hung up before I could say anything other than my name." He placed the piece of grass between his teeth. "Guess she's a little ticked. As I said, Tiffany's mother told her that her father was dead, had died before they could get married—and then she did a quick reversal." He hesitated, his thinning hair ruffling in the breeze. "Since I never showed any interest until recently . . . well, it's been hard for her."

"Beyond hard," Bliss agreed, feeling a tiny pang of pity for the older half-sister she'd never met. "If I were her, I don't know if I'd ever forgive you."

He sighed. "You're having trouble now because I'm marrying Brynnie."

That much was true, but Bliss didn't want to think about it. Not now. She hardly dared ask her next question, but decided there was no time like the present. "So what about Brynnie's daughter. Katie? What does she think?"

"That's another story," he admitted. "Katie, too, just found out. Her mother told her a couple of weeks back that she wasn't Hal Kinkaid's daughter."

Bliss froze. "Wait a minute. Are you telling me that Brynnie passed Katie off as—"

John lifted a hand. "She had no choice. I went along with it."

"But—"

"It was probably a mistake."

"One of many," Bliss whispered, wondering how deep were the lies that her father had perpetuated over the years. Her head spun with all this new information about a family she hadn't suspected existed.

"I know." He seemed suddenly tired and older than his years. "I've done a lot of damage. To you. To your mother. To the other women in my life. But I'm going to change all that by marrying Brynnie and claiming Tiffany and Katie as my daughters. If they accept me, I'll be a happy man. If they don't, well, I guess I'll just have to understand."

As if he could. No one had ever called John Cawthorne understanding. "I wish I could tell you that everything will turn out fine, Dad, but I'm not sure that's possible."

"It's all right." Her father managed a watery smile. "I've given you a lot to think about. Maybe too much. But I've decided to finally live up to my responsibilities as well as make the most of the few years I've got left." A hawk circled lazily overhead, its shadow passing over the ground as John brushed an ant from the fence post. "Somehow I'm gonna make peace with my daughters and grandchildren."

"Are there more than Tiffany's two kids?" Bliss asked.

He glanced up sharply. "Katie's got a ten-year-old. Josh."

"So she's married?"

"No." He shook his head. "The guy left her pregnant and she wanted the baby, so she kept him."

"Does this never end?" she wondered aloud. Both her half-sisters had children and she, who had always thought herself the mothering kind, had none, nor a husband or any prospects of one. Her mind wandered to Mason and she scoffed at herself. If Mason were the last man on earth, she wouldn't want him to father her child. She knew his true colors. He'd shown them once before and they were ugly and oh, so painful. Even now, ten years later, she still experienced a little burn in her heart when she thought of him and how deeply he had deceived her. *Bastard*, she thought unkindly, then told herself it didn't matter. Mason Lafferty was nothing to her.

"Tell me about Brynnie's other children," Bliss said, forcing her thoughts from Mason. She rubbed her hand across the top rail and a sliver pricked her finger.

"Three boys. Jarrod, the oldest, and the twins, Trevor and Nathan. Brynnie had her hands full with those three and little Katie, let me tell you." He grinned slightly as he stared at the mare, and not for the first time in her life Bliss wondered if John Cawthorne missed having sons, a boy to carry on his name. He nodded toward the mare. "You'll like riding Fire Cracker."

"Fire Cracker?" She plucked at the sliver with the fingernails of her other hand and heard a train rattling on far-off tracks.

Her father laughed. "Fire Cracker looks docile enough now, I suppose, but she's got a little bit of the devil in her." He slid his daughter a kind glance. "Like someone else I know."

Bliss rolled her eyes. "That was high school, Dad. I'm pure as the driven snow these days."

"Not if you're any daughter of mine," he said and slapped

the top of the fence. "I'd better go see about the tractor. Seems to have a problem with the clutch."

"Just take it easy, okay?"

He waved off her concerns as she watched him walk back to the equipment garage, a tall shed of sorts where tractors, plows, harrows, bailers and God only knew what else were stored. As he disappeared into the interior, Bliss bit her lip. John Cawthorne was and always would be her father. A man she'd been able to depend upon. A man she loved.

A man who had lied over and over again. A man who, until recently, had led a secret life. A man she'd trusted.

She wondered if she ever would again.

Even though she was disgusted that he'd been such a liar as well as a cheat, she'd somehow ended up with a couple of sisters. How many times had she, as an adolescent, wished and prayed for a close sibling, someone to share dreams and worries with, a friend to shop and gossip with, another teenager who was as confused as she when she tried to understand the incomprehensible world of adults? Now, as a woman, wouldn't she love a new companion, another person who understood her hopes, dreams, ambitions, and concerns? Someone closer than a friend, a woman bound to her by blood?

Two, she reminded herself. Two women bound to her by blood.

But would either Tiffany or Katie want anything to do with her? Did she really want them to? She frowned as she finally managed to work the sliver free from her fingertip.

There was only one way to find out. Bliss would have to take the initiative and meet both her half-sisters, whether they wanted anything to do with her or not.

Mason drummed his fingers on his desk in his den, which was really the second bedroom of his apartment.

Tonight the room with its glowing computer monitor seemed empty. Hollow. Like his own damned soul.

It had been his night to see Dee Dee, but Terri had come up with another excuse to keep him from his daughter. Only half a mile away and it might as well be half a continent.

Just like Bliss—so near but so damned far. Completely out of reach.

"Where she should be," he reminded himself as he refocused on the illuminated screen, but try as he might, he couldn't concentrate on the spreadsheet for his ranch in Montana. Tonight he didn't give a damn. The numbers didn't mean anything to him now. Nothing did. Not when his daughter was being kept from him.

Or when Bliss Cawthorne was less than twenty minutes away.

"Stop it," he growled at himself and blinked to clear his head.

Restless by nature, he could never sit for long and had always worked off his excess energy in physical labor. But this evening had been different.

After his telephone conversation with Terri, he'd kicked off his boots and jeans, donned sweats and running shoes and jogged six miles across hilly terrain. He'd returned sweating and overheated, his blood pounding, and had taken a cold shower, letting the needles of water spray against his skin as he'd rested his head against the tiles and willed his thoughts away from Bliss.

So what if she was close by? So what if she was still as intriguing as ever? So what if he still wanted her so badly he felt himself stiffen at the thought of her? She was still John Cawthorne's daughter and still off-limits. Way off-limits. He had enough problems in his life without the complication of a woman—especially that one.

Now, as he sat in his boxer shorts, a half-drunk bottle of beer in one hand, he stared at the ledgers on the computer screen and wondered how his life had careened so far out of control.

Oh, come on, Lafferty; it's your fault. You're the one who sent her out riding in that storm ten years ago, you're the one who took her old man's money and you're the one who got Terri pregnant. If your life's on an unwanted path, you've got no one to blame but yourself.

He took a draft from his long-necked bottle. Ever since seeing Bliss again, he'd been distracted. Half-a-dozen times he'd reached for the phone to dial her number, only to stop before he picked up the receiver. Why call her? What could he say? The old torment gnawed at his soul. *"You nearly killed her."*

He snapped off the toggle switch, felt a sense of satisfaction as the screen faded, and took another long swallow. He remembered the first time he'd seen her as if it had been yesterday.

She'd been the boss's daughter, a pretty girl of nearly eighteen, who had come to spend a few weeks on her old man's ranch. He'd been twenty-four at the time, old enough to know better, young enough not to give a damn.

At first he'd wanted nothing to do with Cawthorne's daughter, or so he'd tried to convince himself. She'd been trilingual, for Pete's sake, danced ballet, rode polo ponies, played tennis, sailed, and was rumored to have a portfolio of investments that would have made a stockbroker's mouth water. In short, she hadn't been his kind of woman. No way. No how.

But she'd been fascinating. No doubt about it. And it hadn't just been her beauty. No, there was something more, something deeper that he'd sensed in her; and whatever that female essence had been, it had scared him. It had scared the hell out of him.

With eyes as blue as a mountain lake, cheekbones that a model would have killed for, pouty lips and an easy smile, she had caused most of the men who had worked for her father to think about risking their employment for a few hours alone with her. Including Mason.

Now he damned himself for being two times a fool, but the truth of the matter was that Bliss Cawthorne, curse her sexy smile and twinkling eyes, had gotten to him all over again.

It had taken less than ten minutes.

So what're you gonna do about it, Lafferty? his mind taunted as he peeled the label from his beer bottle.

There was only one safe answer—the same as it had always been. Stay away from the woman.

Trouble was, Mason wasn't known to take the safe path.

"So this is Bliss!" Brynnie Anderson-Smith-McBaine-Kinkaid-Perez breezed into the Cawthorne house in a cloud of sweet perfume laced with cigarette smoke. Her hair was a deep red beginning to streak with gray, her face tanned, her lips colored peach, her eyelids shaded in a soft pewter color. She wore jeans a size too tight and a white T-shirt that showed off her enviable chest. "Well, John, you're right again. She's beautiful." Brynnie winked at Bliss and extended a beringed work-roughened hand. "I've heard a lot about you. All good, mind you, all good."

"Same here," Bliss said, though what she'd found out about this woman had been recent and she wasn't holding her breath that the story her father gave her was the entire truth. Besides, not only had Brynnie wed more than her share of husbands, but she'd been a married man's lover. That thought was sour, no matter how hard Bliss tried to swallow it.

John captured Brynnie in a bear hug, and with his arm still slung over her shoulders, led them all through the kitchen and onto the back porch. A sweating pitcher of iced tea and several glasses were waiting on the picnic table.

"Looks like you were expecting me," Brynnie said.

"All Bliss's doin'."

"Thoughtful."

"Thanks." Bliss didn't know what to say. This was, after all, the woman with whom her father had been involved in an affair, the woman who had knowingly cheated on Margaret Cawthorne, the woman who had gotten pregnant with John's child while he was married.

Forcing a smile she didn't feel, Bliss told herself that discretion, if she could find it, was the better part of valor. Her mother was dead, had known of the affair and dealt with it in her own way. Somehow Bliss should do the same. But as she poured the tea into glasses, watching the slices of lemon dance, she felt a stinging loss, a pain deep in her heart, and she nearly slopped tea onto the table.

They sat in deck chairs in the shade of a larch tree. A breeze moved across the rolling acres, stirring the leaves and bending the grass of a field of hay not yet mown. The sound of sprinklers jetting water to irrigate the surrounding pastures vied with the distant hum of traffic far off on the highway.

"I know this is hard for you," Brynnie ventured as she set her glass on the table. Her fingernails were long, squared off and matched the peach gloss of her lips.

"Very."

"It's hard on everyone," John said thoughtfully, a hint of regret in his voice.

"Well, here goes." Brynnie looked Bliss straight in the eye. "Look, honey, I'm not proud of everything I've done in my life. Lord knows, I've made more than my share of mistakes and I'll probably make a few more before they bury me.

"Gettin' involved with your dad was inevitable, believe me,

but our timing was always wrong. Well, maybe there never could have been a good time. But you have to believe me when I tell you that I never meant to hurt your ma."

Bliss didn't say anything. Her throat was too tight and her eyes stung with unshed tears.

"From all I've heard, she was a good woman. Deserved better." Brynnie's brown eyes shadowed with a pain she'd borne for years, but still, Bliss wasn't completely moved.

"She deserved the best," Bliss said. She slashed a glance at her father and noticed the hardening of his jaw, the determined set of his chin. Her mother had always said he was a stubborn man.

"I'm making no excuses, Bliss. Never claimed to be a knight in shining armor. Sure, I've made my share of mistakes just like Brynnie said. But then what man, or woman for that matter, hasn't?"

Bliss cast a mental glance at her own fractured love-life. Her first and, really, only love had been Mason Lafferty, and surely that relationship had been doomed from the start. With trembling hands, she lifted her glass and took a sip of tea. The cool liquid slid down her throat as she pushed Mason from her mind and concentrated on her father who had taken out his pocketknife and was avoiding her gaze as he cleaned his fingernails with a sharp blade.

"Unfortunate as it is, Blissie, your ma's gone now and Brynnie's divorced. Seems as if we're finally gettin' a break and this time we're gonna grab it. It's about time."

"Amen," Brynnie said and reached over to pat John's hand. Her rings sparkled in the sunlight and Bliss couldn't help but wonder how many of the jeweled bands had been given to her on her various wedding days by her ex-husbands and which, if any, had been gifts from her secret lover.

Brynnie's smile seemed genuine and for the first time Bliss caught a glimmer of what her father saw in a woman who was so unlike her socially upstanding and rigid mother.

Brynnie seemed like someone who could roll with the punches and always land on her feet. Nonjudgmental. No false sense of pride. No matter what challenges life tossed this woman's way, Bliss guessed that Brynnie handled them and managed to end up grinning.

"I, uh, I hope you're happy," Bliss said, more for the sake of conversation than from conviction. In truth, hadn't everyone suffered enough? Reluctantly she conceded her father his point. It was time to make a stand, to recognize his other daughters, to find a place for all his family. She just wasn't sure that she could be a part of it.

"We will be happy, won't we, darlin'?" Her father nodded and his mouth turned up at the corners.

"Absolutely. That's all there is to life, isn't it? Being happy." Brynnie appeared to relax a little, although she avoided looking directly into John's eyes.

"As long as you don't hurt anyone in the process," Bliss interjected.

"Never intend to." John was adamant.

"Never," Brynnie agreed, clearing her throat.

Bliss couldn't remember when she'd been more uncomfortable. She took another long swallow of the tea and watched several honey bees flit from one opening rose blossom to the next. In the lacy branches above them a squirrel scolded noisily, and off in the distance a horse's whinny sounded over the rumble of a tractor chugging through the fields.

"You know, there's someone who's pretty darned anxious to meet you." Brynnie reached into a worn suede bag and pulled out a pack of cigarettes. "Do you mind?" she asked, and Bliss shook her head. "Good. I know it's a nasty habit and I should quit, but . . . Oh, well, what can I say? I just love to smoke." She shook out a long white filter tip, lit up and waved out her match. "My daughter, Katie, is dying to talk to you."

"Is she?" Bliss's stomach knotted. This was what she wanted, wasn't it? To see her half-sister, even if it meant coming face-to-face with the fact that her father had been unfaithful to her mother. She found a little bit of pride deep in her own innards and managed to force some starch into her backbone. "I'd like to meet her, too."

The minute the words were out, Bliss regretted them. This was all happening way too fast. She sensed that she'd just hopped aboard an emotional freight train that was suddenly careening out of control.

"Good." Brynnie's grin was infectious. "I'll let her know and we'll set something up. If you're lucky you'll get to know her son Josh, as well." Brynnie's eyes sparkled. "My first and only grandchild so far, though I'm counting on a dozen more." She sighed and tapped ash onto the lawn. "I'm afraid that Josh, devil that he is, has got Grandma's heart twisted around his little finger."

"Several times," John said with a chuckle as the telephone rang.

"I'll get it," Bliss said, starting to stand, but her father, already on his feet, waved her back to her chair.

"Stay put. I'm expecting a call."

As she watched Bliss's father close the screen door behind him, Brynnie drummed her fingers nervously on the armrest of her plastic deck chair. "I worry about him, you know," she admitted, then dragged hard on her cigarette. "He makes light of that heart attack, but you can't convince me it was nothing. If it wasn't, he wouldn't have had to suffer through that god-awful surgery." She eyed the glowing end of her cigarette, then frowned regretfully. "I'll have to give these up," she decided, her brow furrowing. "I hate to, but I can't have them around the house tempting him." She slid Bliss a conspiring glance. "I guess I'll have to sneak one now and again. Just because I'm gonna get married, I can't give up all my vices." She bit anxiously on the corner of her lip. "This place . . . all the worries and work here, it's too much for him, don't you think?"

"I guess so. But he loves it."

"Lord, don't I know? But his health is the main thing, my big worry. He can't expect to put in fifteen- or even ten-hour days around here."

"No . . ." Bliss agreed, wondering where the conversation was leading.

"He's just got to sell." She took another nervous puff.

Bliss laughed. "I thought you knew him better than that."

"He just needs to be convinced." Brynnie licked her lips. "I guess that's my job. Uh-oh, now who's riling him up?" she asked as John's voice filtered through the screen door.

"Dammit!" The receiver crashed into its cradle and the door was flung open so hard it banged against the house. "What the hell's going on?" John demanded.

"Now, honey," Brynnie said as she squashed her cigarette in the grass with the sole of her sandal.

"I can't believe you went behind my back," he charged.

"Oh, Lordy."

"So it's true!"

"John, just listen," Brynnie placated.

"To what?" Bliss was missing something—something important.

"I got off the phone with my attorney and he's been checking some things out with the county—the deeds and titles and records." Her father's expression was thunderous and he looked more like the hard-driven man she'd known as a girl. "It seems that my fiancée here has been doing some business that I didn't know anything about."

"I can explain," Brynnie said.

"You *sold* my ranch to Lafferty."

"My half," she said, standing and lifting a reddish eyebrow that dared him to argue the point "And I'd do it again. Like that!" She snapped her fingers.

"Wait a minute," Bliss interjected. "I don't understand."

"It's simple. I deeded over part of the ranch to Brynnie for her and Katie—security if anything happened to me—and now I find out that she sold her parcel to Lafferty."

Bliss didn't move.

"John, now, don't get upset," Brynnie suggested.

"I'm already upset. Way past it, in fact. I think it's time you told me what the hell's goin' on." His face was a mask of raw anger, his lips tight over his teeth.

"I—I had to do something. While you were in Seattle, in a hospital bed because of your heart, I had a lot of time to think," Brynnie began, her fingers nervously scratching her throat. "Oh, Lord, I need another cigarette."

"Just finish." John scowled darkly, as if he were already reading his fiancée's mind.

"All right, I will. The truth of the matter is that I've spent too many years waiting for you as it is and I don't want to lose you. That heart attack scared me and I thought, well, I knew that you'd come back here and work yourself to death, so I . . . I knew that Mason was moving back here to be closer to his daughter. He'd always been interested in the place, so I called him up and sold my part of the ranch to him."

"Just like that," he challenged.

"Just like that." Brynnie didn't back down.

"I expected as much from him, but not from you, Brynnie. Never you. He hornswoggled you, didn't he?"

Brynnie swallowed back the tears in her throat. "No, John," she said. "This was all my idea."

John lowered himself onto a bench pushed up against the house. "But you know how much this place means to me."

"I'm hoping I mean more," Brynnie said, her chin trembling as she dabbed at her eyes with her fingertips.

John shook his head and Bliss decided they needed to be alone to sort this all out. "I need to drive into town," she said, "for some supplies. I'm setting up an office in the den and this looks like a good time. You two need to talk. Alone."

"No, please," Brynnie said. "Don't run off, we'll work this out—"

Bliss smiled and lied through her teeth. "I'm sure. Listen, it was great to finally meet you, but, really, I've got to go. Bye, Dad" With a wave, she hurried into the house and grabbed her purse.

She was going to drive into town, all right, but her trip had nothing to do with supplies. Nope. She was going to track Mason Lafferty down and get the straight story.

If the man was capable of anything other than lies.

Chapter Five

Bliss jammed on the parking brake in the shade of an ancient oak tree and as the engine of her Mustang cooled, she tapped her fingers on the steering wheel. Some of her anger should have dissipated during the drive into town, but it hadn't and even though she took the time to call the phone company and locate Mason's apartment, here in this huge Victorian manor, she was still ready to read him the riot act.

Who was he to think that he could deal with Brynnie behind her father's back? Why in the world was he so interested in the ranch? For once John Cawthorne was right There were dozens of other ranches Mason could purchase; all he had to do was talk to a real-estate agent or two.

"Bastard," she muttered as she climbed out of the car and slammed the door shut. She strode up the front walk, past a rose garden and a sign that advertised an apartment for rent. On the front porch, she punched the bell and heard the peal of melodic chimes.

Footsteps scurried inside the house and within seconds a little girl of about three yanked open the door. "Mommy," she called over her shoulder just as a woman with her black hair clipped into a makeshift French braid appeared. She was wiping her hands on a towel and smiled when she saw Bliss.

"Just a second." With a disapproving look at the little curly-haired imp, she said, "Christina, you know better than to open the door without me."

"But—"

"We'll talk about it later." She picked up the pouting child, balanced her on a hip and turned all of her attention back to Bliss. "What can I do for you?"

"I'm Bliss Cawthorne . . . a friend of Mason Lafferty's." That was stretching the truth just a little, but it didn't matter, did it? From the look on this woman's face, though, she might have said she'd just flown in from Jupiter.

"His . . . friend," the woman, obviously stunned, repeated. Maybe she had a thing for Mason, or was already involved with him. So who cared? Right now, all Bliss wanted to do was take Mason to task.

"I have his address, but not which apartment is his."

"Cawthorne?"

"John Cawthorne's my father," Bliss answered automatically, and wondered at the tension tightening the corners of the woman's mouth.

"He rents a unit in the back," the woman said, still eyeing Bliss with a sense of horror—or was it just curiosity?—for she managed a thin, though certainly not warm, smile again. "Upper level of the carriage house."

"Dee Dee's daddy?" the cherub with the dark curls asked.

"Mmm."

Dee Dee's daddy. The thought of Mason fathering a child did strange things to her. "Thanks," she managed to say, though she barely noticed what happened to mother and daughter as she walked around the corner of the house and along a tree-lined drive.

Would she ever have a child of her own? A baby? "Stop it," she muttered, ignoring that empty barb that pricked her soul as she thought about her childless state. She wasn't a hundred years old, for crying out loud. There was still time—plenty of it. She just had to find the right man. *Oh, right. Like that's going to happen anytime soon.*

Rounding the corner of the main house, she spied a second tall building with paned windows, black shutters, and the same gray siding as the main house. A private staircase led to the second story, and despite the perspiration on her palms, she marched up each step. She rapped on the door and was rewarded with Mason, all six feet of him looming directly in front of her.

"Well, Ms. Cawthorne," he drawled, his gold eyes silently appraising. "What brings you here?"

"We need to talk."

"Do we?" His smile slid from one side of his square jaw to the other.

"About Dad."

He leaned a shoulder on the doorjamb. "Come on, Bliss. I bet if you think real hard you can come up with a better topic than that."

"Do you?"

With that same amused, cocky smile, he stepped out of the doorway. "Come on in." As she passed he added, "How about something to drink? Soda? Coffee? Something stronger?"

"I don't think a drink is the answer," she said as she tossed her purse into one of the few chairs in a room with glossy wood floors, windows opened slightly to let in the hot summer breeze, and walls paneled in yellowed knotty pine.

He left the door ajar, allowing a bit of cross ventilation as Bliss realized they were alone for the first time in a decade. Goose bumps rose on the back of her neck and the fragrances of honeysuckle and rose swept through the narrow room.

"Let me guess. You're here because I bought part of the ranch from Brynnie," he said, as if he'd been expecting her.

"Right out from under Dad's nose."

"She approached me."

"And you just couldn't say no, could you?" Bliss said, folding her arms over her chest.

"I didn't want to." The smile fell from his face and she noticed the fan of crow's feet at the corners of his eyes. "I've always liked the place. Dreamed of owning it years ago."

"And now there's a chance to get back at Dad."

"That wasn't the intention."

"Sure."

He crossed the room and stood directly in front of her. She'd forgotten how intimidating he was, hadn't remembered that the scent of him sent unwanted tingles through her blood. The temperature in the carriage house seemed to shoot upward ten degrees, and she found drawing a breath much harder than it had been. "Why, exactly, did you come over here?" he asked.

No reason to avoid the truth. "I think you manipulated this—this ridiculous situation. Somehow you convinced Brynnie that she needed to sell."

"I said, she came to me."

"You're lying."

"Ask her."

"Why would she sneak around behind Dad's back and—Oh!"

Quick as a rattler he struck, grabbing hold of her arm and yanking her toward him. "It was her idea."

"I don't believe—"

"Because you don't want to. Brynnie's a grown woman. She knew I was looking for a place and offered hers. We struck a deal." His face was so close to hers Bliss could see the striations of brown in his gold eyes, and watched as sweat dotted his forehead, darkening his hair. His nostrils flared and his lips barely moved. "I'm not going to deceive you, Bliss. There's no love lost between me and your old man. Never has been. But I didn't have to coerce Brynnie into selling out. She was more than willing."

"Was she?"

"Absolutely."

"You are a bastard, Lafferty."

His smile was cold and cruel, and his hand, rough with calluses, clamped in a vise-like grip over her wrist. But the scent of him, all male and musk and leather, filled the mere inches that separated his face from hers. "I wouldn't be throwing that particular word too loosely around here, if I were you," he warned. "It might hit a little close to home."

Frustration pounded in her pulse. Blast the man, he was right. Her father had sired two children out of wedlock. Two that she knew about. "Let go of me."

"If I only could," he said. Then, as if her words had finally registered, he dropped her arm and backed off a step. "Hell." With both hands, he plowed stiff fingers through his hair.

Idiot, she silently berated herself. How did it come to this—that she was alone with the one man she wanted to avoid, the one man who could make her see red with only a calculated lift of his eyebrow, the solitary man who had touched her unguarded soul?

"Look, I didn't come back to Bittersweet to stir up trouble," he said.

"Too late," she retorted but decided, though her heart was thudding with dread, that there was no time like the present to sort out a few things with this man who seemed to be, ever since she'd glided into this part of Oregon, forever underfoot. "Just because you dumped me ten years ago and—"

"I didn't dump you."

"Ha." She shook her head and started gathering her

purse. Coming here had been a mistake, and really, what had she expected—some kind of rationale for his need to buy the ranch? Or was it something more?

"I didn't mean to hurt you."

"But you married another woman," she said, the words, having been pent up for ten years, tumbling out of her mouth. "What do you call that?"

"A mistake."

The word echoed over and over again in her heart. But it was too late to hear it, far too late for apologies or explanations. "Listen, I shouldn't have asked."

"But you did."

"Never mind, I really don't need to know," she said, starting for the door.

"I should have called you. Shouldn't have been bullied into . . . Oh, hell what does it matter?"

She swallowed hard and turned to face him again. Maybe this was the time to sort things out. "When . . . when I got out of the hospital ten years ago, you were already gone," she said and saw a shadow of pain pass behind his eyes. "Dad said you'd had some surgery yourself, then eloped to Reno."

A muscle worked in his jaw. "That's not exactly what happened."

"No?" She stood straight and met his gaze with her own. "The way I see it, you were two-timing me."

"Never."

Oh, God, how she wanted to believe him, to trust the honesty reflected in his eyes; to think, even for a minute, that he'd cared about her. But she couldn't. He'd been a liar then, and was a liar now. She was shaking inside and realized that the conversation was getting too personal. *Way* too personal, and Mason, blast his sorry good-looking hide, didn't seem afraid to open doors that had been locked for a decade. "I think you should back off with Dad."

"I thought we were talking about us."

"There is no 'us,' Mason. You took care of that. Remember?" She caught the door handle with one finger.

"It might be a good idea for me to explain."

"And I think it might be a good idea for you to go straight to hell, but I told you that already, didn't I? Ten years ago. If not, then consider the request retroactive."

"Damn it, Bliss, don't you think I've been there?"

She arched a cool brow. "I don't really care."

"Liar!" This time he reached forward so quickly she gasped. Strong fingers surrounded her arm.

"Obviously we need to talk a little more," he said, pressing his face so close to hers she noticed the furious dilation of his pupils, felt the warmth of his breath on her already hot skin. Determination glinted in his eyes.

"I don't think so."

"There are things you don't know."

She tried to hold on to her rapidly disintegrating composure and yank her arm away, but his steely grip only tightened. Her heart began to thump so wildly she could scarcely breathe. "I'm sure there are, but I'm not interested in ancient history, Mason."

"Then let's talk about now."

"What about now?"

His gaze lowered to her lips and her breath stilled. A dozen memories, erotic and forbidden, waltzed slowly and provocatively through her mind. Her pulse ran rampant. Swallowing against a suddenly tight throat, she said, "Let me go."

"I made that mistake once before."

She yanked hard on her arm, but his hand only gripped

tighter, his eyes glinting with sheer male persistence. "As I said, I think we should talk about us."

Her laugh was brittle. "Us. Now? You and me? You can't be serious."

"I've never been more serious about anything in my life," he said, though there were doubts in his eyes, as if he, too, remembered the pain and the lies. He pulled her closer to him and she knew in an instant that he was going to kiss her.

"This—this is a mistake."

"A big one," he agreed, his breath whispering across her face before his lips found hers in a kiss that questioned and demanded, that was fragile, yet firm. A kiss that stole the very breath from her lungs and caused her heart to trip-hammer madly.

Every instinct told her to stop this madness, to pull away; but another part of her, that silly, romantic, feminine part of her, wanted more. Her lips parted and his tongue slid quickly between her teeth, touching and tasting, dancing with her own.

Strong arms surrounded her and his hands splayed possessively over her back. She thought she heard a disturbance somewhere behind her, but discarded the sound as part of the rush of blood through her brain. Mason didn't stop kissing her and Bliss's heart, damn it, thundered in her chest.

Stop this lunacy now, rational thought insisted.

Don't ever let him go, her heart replied.

She heard a soft, wanting sound and realized it had come from her own throat. It had been so long, so damned long . . . and she wanted, needed, so much more.

"It's always been this way with you," he said as if disappointed, and she realized that their kiss had been a test, to see if he, like her, would respond.

"And it can't be." Though her breathing was as ragged as his, she was angry with herself for falling into his trap, for letting her body dictate to her mind. She couldn't, *wouldn't* let this happen again. "It . . . just can't."

Slowly he let go of her. Shoving his hands into the front pockets of his jeans, he cleared his throat. "I didn't mean to—"

"Of course, you did," she retorted. "You just didn't expect to be affected."

"So now you're a shrink?"

"Well?"

A muscle worked his jaw. "I was curious."

"So was I." She took a step even closer to him and tossed her hair over her shoulder. "But anyone can get caught up in lust. We did before, remember?" The words as they passed her lips, stung. She'd always thought she loved him, but she had to stop this destructive urge right now, because she wasn't about to take a chance on letting this man hurt her again. "And just for future reference, cowboy," she continued, "that kind of Neanderthal tactic might work on some of the women around here, but with me—"

"I'm sorry."

She couldn't believe her ears. Never had this man apologized to her. "What?"

"I came on too strong. You made me see red and then all of a sudden . . ." He leaned against the wall, sighed loudly, then before her eyes drew himself upright. "It won't happen again."

"You bet it won't!" she said, not sure if she was relieved or disappointed. Her pulse was still beating erratically and the taste of him lingered on her lips. "And as for my dad, just leave him alone, okay?"

His eyes narrowed. "Don't know that I can."

"Why not? What makes you want his place so badly?"

Mason shrugged as he held open the door and she passed through. "It's the right time."

"The right time for whom?"

"Brynnie, to begin with and, yes, me. I need a place down here. Cawthorne Acres has everything I want."

"Except a For Sale sign on the front door." She reached into her purse for her keys and as she extracted the ring, cut herself on a pair of nail scissors tucked into an inner pocket. "Ouch. Oh, damn." A drop of blood oozed from the tip of her forefinger and before she could do anything, Mason took her hand in his and eyed the wound.

"Let's see."

"It's nothing."

"Maybe."

"I said, it's . . ." Her voice faded as he slowly placed her finger to his lips. "Oh, no, don't—"

But his lips were warm, and the flow of blood was quickly stanched, the inside of his mouth so slick and seductive, Bliss could scarcely breathe. Why, oh, why did this one man still get to her? What was it about him she found so damned irresistible?

"I'm okay," she said, retrieving her hand.

"I know." He rocked back on the heels of his boots and had the decency to look uncomfortable. "I, uh, don't know what came over me."

He actually looked perplexed for an instant.

"Listen, Bliss," he said, clearing his throat and walking to the fireplace where he leaned against the mantel, as if he, too, finally realized the need for distance between them. "You'd be doing your father and Brynnie both a big favor by suggesting he sell the rest of his property."

"I think that's his decision. And now I have some advice for you. Just leave Dad and Brynnie alone. They have enough problems without having to deal with you."

"And what about you, Bliss?" he asked.

"What about me?"

"Should I leave you alone, too?"

"Absolutely." She tried not to notice the way his jeans settled low over his hips and the play of muscles in his forearms as he moved. Dark gold chest hair sprang from the V of his neckline, and she remembered exploring the springing curls that covered his nipples with young, interested fingers.

"I think you're afraid of me."

She laughed, and shook her head as she headed for the door again. "Don't flatter yourself, Lafferty. You don't scare me."

"Maybe I ought to."

"Maybe," she admitted. "But you don't." The lie hovered between them in the air for a few seconds until she turned and shoved open the door only to find a young girl, somewhere between eight and nine, hovering on the landing. "Oh."

"Dad?" the child asked, looking over Bliss's shoulder.

"Dee Dee." Bliss heard the smile in his voice and realized that she was staring at his daughter. With a fringe of brown hair and freckles bridging a tiny nose, Dee Dee looked from Bliss to Mason and back again.

"Bliss Cawthorne, this is my daughter, Deanna."

"Glad to meet you," Bliss said automatically, though she felt a stab of deep regret for the child she'd never had, had never had the chance to conceive with Mason.

"Yeah." Dee Dee chewed on her lower lip for a second. "Mom just dropped me off."

"And didn't stick around. Figures," Mason said, eyeing the street as if looking for Terri's car. "Are you hungry?"

"Starved. Can we go to McDonald's?" Dee Dee asked, her eyes suddenly bright with anticipation.

"Sure. You game?" he asked Bliss and she saw the girl's shoulders droop a bit.

"No . . . uh, no thanks," she said, not wanting to intrude on father and daughter. "Another time." She hurried down the stairs and offered a pathetic excuse of a wave. It wasn't

Dee Dee's fault that she'd been conceived when Mason was dating Bliss, and yet Bliss didn't want to be reminded of the man's faithlessness.

She skirted the main house and made it to her car without looking over her shoulder. As she slid behind the wheel, she told herself it didn't matter that Mason had cheated on her, that he'd gotten another woman pregnant while he'd been seeing her, that he'd never loved her. He had an ex-wife and a daughter, and Bliss had her own life to lead—without him.

That night Bliss threw off the covers and glared at the digital readout on the clock near the bed. Two forty-five. Great. She'd been in bed since eleven and hadn't slept a wink. Ever since returning to Bittersweet, she couldn't wrench Mason out of her mind. Seeing him with his daughter hadn't helped. She'd been reminded of just how he'd betrayed her, how much she wanted a child of her own.

Outside, rain fell steadily from the sky; fat, heavy drops pummeling the roof, splashing in the gutters and dripping from the leaves and branches of the old oak tree that stood near her window.

Why hadn't he told her about Terri Fremont years ago when Bliss was falling in love with him? What was the reason he left Bittersweet without even stopping to say goodbye to her? Why was he back now and why was it so important that he buy her father's place? And why, oh, please, God, why, was she still thinking about him, wondering at her response to his kiss while hating herself for caring?

"Stop it!" she muttered, punching her pillow in frustration. She reminded herself for the millionth time that Mason Lafferty was nothing to her. *Nothing!*

So why was she thinking of him? Why? Why? Why? "Because you're an idiot," she told herself.

Knowing that sleep was impossible, she slid her arms through the sleeves of her robe and stepped into her slippers. Oscar, who had been curled up beside her, was already on his feet, stretching and yawning. He followed her into the kitchen and waited at the pantry door until she reached inside and tossed him a biscuit. While he crunched on his snack, she heated cocoa in the microwave.

Mason was a problem, but not one she could solve tonight. She needed to forget him and return to Seattle as she'd planned. Her father was recuperating at a rapid pace, and if he and Brynnie could quit fighting long enough to walk down the aisle and say their vows, then Bliss would leave Oregon and get back to her old life.

Her old, peaceful, and somewhat-boring life.

Sliding into a chair, Bliss cradled the warm cup in her hands and let the chocolate-scented steam fill her nostrils and whisper over her cheeks. She'd told herself again and again that she was over—make that *long* over—Mason, but tonight, while the sky was thick with clouds and the outside air dense with rain, she wasn't so sure of her feelings.

Seeing Mason, touching Mason and kissing Mason had brought back memories, painful and tarnished. She'd spent ten years repressing her thoughts about him, trying not to compare him to other men she'd dated, hoping against hope that someday she'd never think of him at all, believing that he was just a summer fling—a schoolgirl crush. Nothing more.

Now, she was ready to second-guess herself. "Fool," she exclaimed, and when Oscar gave out a disgruntled "Woof," she laughed without any sense of satisfaction. "That's right, dog, your mistress is a first-class, A-one moron, I'm afraid."

Old feelings—excitement, anger, hurt and even a trace of first love—resurfaced. She remembered the tumbling, breathless feeling of hearing his voice or kissing him, or swimming nude in the nearby river with him. "Oh, Bliss," she whispered, stirring the hot chocolate and creating a small whirlpool in her cup, "I thought you were smarter than this."

The memory of the first time she'd seen him, tall and lean, covered in dust as he'd offered to lift her suitcases and trunk from the back of her father's truck, haunted her. And tonight, alone in the kitchen of the ranch house, with only the rain and Oscar to keep her company, that memory stretched out vividly before her. It had been ten years ago, but tonight, it seemed as real as if that summer had happened yesterday. . . .

Chapter Six

Bliss sipped her cocoa and remembered that sultry afternoon when she had come to her father's ranch that summer. The housekeeper had called to John Cawthorne as he'd climbed out of his truck.

"Phone call for you, in the den," she'd said, standing in the doorway of the house and pushing aside clumps of dry dirt left from boots with her broom.

John, swearing under his breath, had dashed toward the front door and had left Bliss standing alone by the truck in the blistering sunlight. As she stood in the dusty gravel parking area near the garage, harsh, unforgiving rays pounded down on her crown and shoulders. She felt totally alone, a city girl plucked out of her nest and tossed here with a father who usually ignored her. As she reached into the bed of the truck for one of her bags, she silently wished, as she had since she could remember, that she had a sister or brother with whom she could share her misery.

"You must be John's daughter," a rawboned, slightly intimidating, cowboy drawled. He was tanned from long hours of hard work under the glare of the sun and his eyes, staring at her from the shade beneath the brim of his Stetson, were a light golden brown. Intense and unblinking, they stared at her in an uncompromising appraisal that caused her breath to catch and warned her that she should run now while she had the chance.

"That's right." Why did her tongue want to trip all over itself?

His grin was a slash of white against bronzed skin. "He's proud of you, let me tell you."

"Is he?" She smiled back, then blushed. This guy was way too old for her and she wasn't one to flirt, but there was something about him that made her want to linger. "Bliss Cawthorne," she said boldly, extending her hand and remembering the manners her mother had drummed into her head from the time she was a toddler.

"Lafferty. Mason Lafferty." He dropped the trunk and covered her soft small outstretched palm with his bigger, callused hand. His fingers were rough, covered with dust and warmer than the breeze that swept through the grassy acres. He tipped his hat and didn't apologize for the dirt that he left smudged on her skin.

"You work for Dad." There was something about him that nudged her curiosity; something that set him apart from the rest of the men who called John Cawthorne their boss.

"Most of the time." He hitched the trunk onto his back and started for the porch.

"And the rest?"

He glanced over his shoulder and winked at her so slowly she felt her knees turn to jelly. "Raisin' hell, if you believe the stories in town."

"Should I?" Lugging her suitcase, she struggled to keep up with his long, easy stride.

His gold eyes glinted. "Every word. Hey, don't carry that—I'll get it." He cocked his head toward the bag she carried.

"I can handle it."

"Can you?"

She knew she was being baited and she flushed. After all,

this guy wasn't a boy; he was a man and he scared her more than a little. "I can handle a lot of things," she said, tossing her head. Margaret Cawthorne might have taught her daughter to be a lady, but she'd also instilled a fervor in Bliss to carry her own weight and be independent enough not to have to rely on any man, especially not a cowboy.

John walked out onto the porch. "Damned mechanics," he grumbled, then noticed Mason. "Take the trunk and the rest of her things into her bedroom—down the hall, second door on the right. Next to the bath."

"I can show him. I know where it is," Bliss said, feeling the fiery rays of the sun beating against the back of her neck. Heat shimmered in waves across the pastures, and dust, kicked up from the movement of cattle and horses in nearby fields, floated in the air. She was beginning to sweat and her blouse was sticking to her back and her heart was pounding so loudly she was sure everyone within ten feet of her could hear it.

"Good."

"When you're finished with the luggage, Lafferty, run down to the machine shed. The combine's acting up again, according to Corky, and the shop in town is overloaded. No one can look at the machine for three weeks at the earliest. Holy hell, how can you run a ranch like this?" Scowling and grumbling to himself, her father strode across the parking lot toward the machine shed.

Mason's jaw hardened. He held the screen door open for Bliss. "Your old man is gonna give himself a stroke if he doesn't calm down a little."

"It's just his way," she said, but felt an unspoken tension in the cowboy walking beside her. His muscles were suddenly strung tight, his knuckles showing white around the handle of the trunk.

Hurrying through the cool interior of the house, she bumped shoulders with him a couple of times and nearly tripped over her feet at the contact. Being alone with him was nerve-racking. She reminded herself that he was just one of her father's hands—a worker on the ranch. Right? So why did she feel instantly that there was something about him, something primitive and sexual, which bothered her and caused her already-flushed skin to break into beads of anxious perspiration? "You can put the trunk in the corner," she said, opening the door of her room and indicating a spot near the small closet.

"Whatever you say, princess."

She bristled at the name. "I'm not a princess."

His lips twitched. "Hmm. Coulda fooled me." He dropped the trunk on its end and hesitated long enough to make her uncomfortable. There was something in his eyes, something wickedly intriguing that warned her he was the kind of man to avoid; the kind of man a woman in her right mind wouldn't trust. "Anything else?"

"No, uh, I think I can handle the rest."

"You sure?" His voice was low and a little raspy, as if he'd breathed too much dust or smoked too many cigarettes.

She wasn't sure of anything. "Yeah. Don't worry about it."

With a wink that bordered on something far more sexual than she'd ever experienced, he left the room as quickly as he'd come in. She set her suitcase on the bed and opened the window. Suddenly the tiny bedroom seemed airless and hot. In the old mirror over the bureau she caught her reflection and nearly died. Her cheeks were a bright shade of pink, her blond hair wild, her eyes wide with an anticipation she'd never seen before.

The breeze that moved the curtains and filled the room didn't help much. Nothing did, she came to find out. Whenever she was around Mason, she couldn't seem to catch her breath or even untangle her thoughts.

* * *

In the days that followed, that summer ten years ago, she saw Mason enough, though most often from a distance. He roped steers, he branded stock, he castrated calves, he shoed horses and strung fence wire. The muscles of his back and shoulders, tanned from long hours laboring in the sun, moved fluidly as he worked, straining, then relaxing and drawing her eyes to the faded jeans that rode low on his hips. Dusty and torn, they offered a glimpse of a strip of whiter skin whenever he stretched, and that tantalizing slash of white, coupled with the curling golden hair on his chest, caused a warmth to invade the deepest, most private part of her, and she had to force her gaze away.

"You're being silly," she told herself on Tuesday evening when she was walking toward the stables and spied Mason leaning against a car—a yellow sedan—she didn't recognize. The driver was a pert woman with short dark hair, an upturned nose and doelike brown eyes that gazed upward through the open window to Mason's face. The car idled, exhaust seeping from the tailpipe, the thrum of the engine competing with the sounds of warblers and sparrows singing in the trees and fields.

Mason, wearing sunglasses and an irritated expression, shook his head, and though Bliss's ears strained to hear the conversation she only caught snippets.

". . . waited all night," the woman said.

"No one asked you to."

". . . we had an understanding."

"Did we? Wasn't my idea."

"Mason, please—" The woman cast a sidelong glance at Bliss who increased her pace as she walked to the stables. The sun was hovering low in the western sky and the air was breathless and still.

Bored with listening to her tapes and reading old magazines, Bliss had decided to go for a ride. Her father had already pointed out the docile horses he wanted her to saddle, but Bliss had other ideas.

"Lousy son of a bitch!" The woman's voice blasted through the hot air.

Bliss turned toward the car.

The driver gunned the engine. Gravel sprayed. Mason leaped away from the fender as the car took off at breakneck speed down the lane.

Swearing under his breath, Mason swung his fist in the air in frustration. "Damn, fool—" He caught his tongue and threw his hat on the ground. Then, turning on a worn heel, he caught Bliss's eye. Rather than be the target of his wrath, she ducked around the corner of the stables and snagged a lead rope coiled around a peg near one of the doors. The last person she wanted to catch in a bad mood was Mason Lafferty. No way. No how. The man was enough trouble when things were going right.

Squinting against a lowering sun, she eyed the horses grazing quietly in the shade of a stand of oak. She wasn't interested in the docile palomino mare or lazy roan gelding her father had pointed out to her, and smiled when she spied the animal who had unintentionally captured her heart—a feisty pinto three-year-old. His eyes were an unusual pale blue—the only blue-eyed horse she'd ever seen—and he was a show-off in front of the mares, always hoisting his tail high, tossing his head and snorting as he galloped from one end of the field to the other.

"Okay, Lucifer, I think it's time you and I got to know each other," she said as he snorted and pawed the dry earth. "Come on," she cooed, uncoiling the vinyl rope. "That's a boy."

Lucifer rolled his eyes suspiciously. He was wearing a leather halter. All she had to do was get close enough to snap the tether to the ring under his chin.

"It's all right," she assured him. She was only three feet away. One more step and—

He bolted. With a high-pitched squeal and a toss of his brown-and-white head, he galloped from one end of the pasture to the other, kicking up a cloud of dust in his wake. His odd eyes sparkled in the sunlight, as if he knew he was taunting her.

"Don't make me chase you," she warned.

"Why not? He loves a good fight. Especially with a female."

She stiffened at the sound of Mason's voice. Glancing over her shoulder, she ignored the sudden jump in her pulse and shot him a glance guaranteed to be as cold as ice. "Seems like you should know," she said.

"Can't argue with that," he admitted, though his jaw was hard as granite.

When he didn't stroll off, she asked, "Was there something you wanted?"

He was leaning against the gate, his arms crossed, elbows resting on the worn top board, eyes still shaded by aviator glasses. His hat was resting on a post and his hair, sun-streaked and ragged, brushed his eyebrows and the tops of his ears. "Just watching you."

She lied and told herself that the absolute last person on earth she wanted observing her was this sarcastic cowboy.

"Don't you have *something* more important to do? You know, like work? Isn't there a cow to be branded, a horse to be shod or something?"

"Not just now. Besides, I wouldn't want the boss's daughter to get herself into some kind of trouble."

She made a disgusted noise in the back of her throat. "Don't worry about it."

He didn't bother to respond. Nor did he move. Bliss gritted her back teeth together and inched her chin upward in pride. She'd die before she'd let him witness her humiliation from this headstrong piece of horseflesh.

"Want me to help?"

"No!" Damn the man, he was enjoying this and making her so nervous she was beginning to sweat. "Give me strength," she muttered under her breath as she approached Lucifer again. In a louder voice she said gently, "Come on boy. That's a good—"

In another whirlwind of dust the colt again thundered away, bucking and showing off as if he and Mason were privately conspiring against her.

"Son of a—" she bit back a curse and stomped a foot, sending up her own pitiful puff of dirt and Mason, damn his soul, laughed outright. "I suppose you could do better," she challenged, then cringed as the words escaped her lips.

"Yep." In one lithe movement he vaulted the fence and gave a sharp, terse whistle.

Lucifer stopped short.

Another commanding blast from Mason's lips and the colt, ears flicking nervously, reluctantly turned. He hesitated, his nostrils flared, and Mason whistled a third time.

To Bliss's complete mortification, the colt trotted docilely to Mason, pressed his nose against the man's chest and was rewarded with a piece of apple.

"Isn't that cheating?" she asked as Mason grabbed Lucifer's halter and with his free hand, slowly motioned for Bliss to approach with the lead rope.

"Everything's fair in love and war and taming horses." He glanced at her from behind his tinted glasses. He was so close she could smell his aftershave as well as the dust and odors of horse and leather that seemed to cling to him. His jaw was gilded with a day's growth of beard and his sleeves were shoved above his elbows to show off tanned forearms where veins and hard muscles stretched beneath his skin.

Swallowing against a suddenly arid throat, she turned her eyes back to the horse.

"You have heard the expression before, right?"

"It was a little different." She snapped the lead onto the metal ring on the colt's halter.

Mason lifted one dark eyebrow. "Well, around here we make expressions fit the situation."

"So I see."

"Be careful with Lucifer."

"I can handle him."

"I hate to give you advice, but if you call what you just did 'handling him,' you're in for a couple more lessons from this guy."

"Am I?" She tossed her hair over one shoulder.

Mason patted the pinto on the shoulder. "You want me to saddle and bridle him for you?"

Her smile was cool, though her hands were sweating on the tether and her heart was beginning to pound erratically. "I'll be fine," she said, clucking to the colt and heading to the stables where she'd already picked out a saddle, blanket and bridle. She didn't need any more help from the sexiest ranch hand on the place. All she wanted to do was ride to the river that cut through the north end of her father's property where she planned to take a long, leisurely swim. Nothing more . . .

But, of course, looking back on it now, she'd gotten way more than she'd bargained for. That night was the night she began to fall in love, the night when all the trouble really started.

"Oh, who cares?" she asked herself as she took a long sip from her cup. Life sometimes seemed to move in strange, fateful circles. Who would have thought that she would be here, at her father's ranch, drinking tepid cocoa at three in the morning? Back in Bittersweet. Involved with—no, not involved with—dealing with Mason again. "Fool," she muttered to herself as she tossed the remains of her drink into the sink and Oscar, panting, tagged along behind her to the bedroom.

She'd made a mistake with Mason in the past, but she wasn't going to repeat it. "Once burned, twice shy, you know," she told her mutt as Oscar slipped through the open door to her room and hopped eagerly onto her bed. "Okay, okay. Since you were already here earlier, tonight you can sleep with me, but that's it."

She slid beneath the sheet and sighed. The rainstorm had moved on, but she was still here, in bed with only a dog for comfort, and the nagging feeling that all the promises she'd made to herself wouldn't help where Lafferty was concerned. He was just one of those kinds of men that slipped under a woman's skin and wouldn't go away.

"Great," she thought aloud as she tugged at the covers. Well, she wasn't an ordinary woman. She was strong. Independent. Margaret Cawthorne's daughter. And she'd be damned if she'd let any range-rough cowboy change the course of her life or mess with her head. Mason Lafferty, damn him, could go straight to hell, for all she cared.

Mason towel-dried his hair roughly while barely glancing at his reflection in the foggy mirror. He hadn't seen Bliss in nearly a week and like it or not, he was going quietly out of his mind. He threw on slacks, shirt, socks and shoes, then walked through his apartment and thought it seemed emptier than before. His heels rang against the hardwood floor, echoing loudly enough to make the rooms seem hollow.

He snagged his jacket from a peg near the back door

and slid his arms through the sleeves. He'd thought of Bliss off and on over the years, but had made a point to keep any lingering and provocative memories of her where they belonged—strictly in the past. Then again, he hadn't expected her to show up in Bittersweet, nor had he thought her old man would remarry so quickly on the heels of his first wife's death. Life, it turned out, was oftentimes stranger than fiction, and a hell of a lot more complicated.

Frowning, he thought of his own situation. How, as a small boy, he'd watched his father drive away in a beat-up old Dodge truck, the exhaust a blue haze in the coming darkness as the pickup rumbled away. He'd clung to his mother's hand, swallowing back the tears that burned in his throat, blinking against the rain that poured from the sky. He'd been five at the time, his sister, Patty, barely two. She'd sucked her thumb as she'd sat balanced on their mother's slim hip.

"It'll be all right," Helen Lafferty had said, her chin held high, her nose and eyes red from endless nights of crying. Mason had heard the fights, listened to his mother beg his dad to stay—to keep the family together, to stay with them. She'd forgive him the drinking. Forget the other women. Ignore his gambling.

But he'd left just the same.

"You go on to bed, Mason," she'd said, swiping at her tears. "I'll rock Patty to sleep out here on the porch."

Only years later did Mason realize that Albert Lafferty couldn't handle responsibility, a family, or just plain settling down. He'd never seen his father again and hadn't missed him.

"Yeah, right," he told himself now. His mother had never remarried and when she'd discovered she had breast cancer the year that Mason turned eighteen, she'd taken matters into her own work-roughened hands. Without insurance or a nest egg, she couldn't afford the operation that probably wouldn't have saved her life anyway. So, stoically, with no word to her children, Helen Lafferty had opened a bottle of sleeping pills, swallowed every one, and never woken up. She'd left Mason and Patty a simple note asking them to forgive her and begging Mason to look after his younger sister.

Well, he'd made one hell of a mess of that. Patty, he suspected, was in more trouble now than she'd ever been, and trouble, it seemed, was her middle name. As for Mason himself, his life had never been more complicated. He was considering suing Terri for custody of Dee Dee, Patty and old Isaac Wells were missing, he'd bought half the ranch and had old John mad as a hornet at him and, to top matters off, now Bliss Cawthorne, "the princess," had strolled right back into the middle of his life.

His back teeth gnashed together as he locked the door of his apartment behind him.

He wouldn't have believed that seeing her again would bring back a rush of memories he'd hoped to have forgotten. It seemed unfair to be haunted by the past, but then, he'd learned a long time ago that life was neither fair nor easy. Growing up in poverty, he'd developed a keen understanding of the fact that in order to even out the stakes in this life, a man had to have money and lots of it. His old man, when he'd been around, had taught him well. A few years later John Cawthorne had only reinforced that theory.

"Jerk," Mason growled and wondered where was the sense of satisfaction he'd been hoping to feel, why had the warm knowledge that he was finally getting even escaped him. Somehow, he suspected, this all had something to do with Bliss and how he felt about her, how he'd felt about her in the past and what the future might hold for them.

Snorting in disgust at the turn of his thoughts, he headed down the stairs and to a space near the street where he'd parked his rig. Traffic was sparse on the quiet streets of town.

He should forget Bliss. She'd stumbled into his life at a

time when the last thing he'd needed was involvement with the boss's daughter, but she'd been the most incredible woman he'd laid eyes upon in a long time and fighting his attraction to her had failed miserably.

Then he'd nearly killed her. He should never have let her take off on that horse in the middle of a storm. He should have risked her wrath and refused to let her saddle Lucifer. It would have been better to risk the old man's anger and lose his job than to have Bliss's life endangered.

But then he'd never been smart when it came to John Cawthorne's daughter. He hadn't been then; wouldn't be now.

Ten years after the accident, he was still drumming up excuses to see her, to be alone with her. Even as he climbed into his truck and silently swore that he'd keep his hands off her, he already knew that he was only kidding himself. Before the day was out, he'd find a reason to see her again.

"Hell, Lafferty," he told the eyes glaring back at him in his rearview mirror. "You've got it and you've got it bad." He threw his pickup into reverse, backed out, then nosed the truck onto the dusty pothole-strewn avenue. "Real bad."

Chapter Seven

Crossing the fingers of one hand, Bliss silently prayed and pushed a button on her new fax machine. "Let this work," she muttered as the machine hummed obediently. She'd tried to transmit the bid she'd been working on for two days to her office in Seattle with no success. This time she was in luck. "Thank you, God of All Things Electronic," she said as she filed her original away and heard the phone ring down the hall.

"For you!" her father yelled.

"Got it," she sang back, conscious of the irritation in John Cawthorne's tone. He and Brynnie were speaking again, but the situation was still tense and the wedding plans, though progressing, were in a constant state of flux. "Hello," she called into the extension.

"Bliss, hi, this is Katie Kinkaid. I, uh, thought you might want to meet for coffee or lunch or . . . well, whatever."

No time like the present, her mind prodded her, although, deep down, she wanted to avoid this meeting like the plague. "Sure, I can meet you, or you might want to come out here. Delores made a killer batch of pecan rolls and I brought some French-roast coffee from an espresso shop in Seattle."

"You're on," Katie said with a lot more enthusiasm than Bliss felt. "I'll be there in half an hour."

"Great." Bliss hung up and told herself it was time to get to know her half-sister, whether she wanted to or not. She straightened the den and told her father goodbye as he and Brynnie were off to talk to the preacher, who, Bliss hoped, was a decent premarriage counselor.

By the time Katie wheeled into the drive, Bliss had heated the gooey rolls, made a fresh pot of coffee and was halfway through the newspaper.

Katie rapped hard on the screen door, then let herself in, meeting Bliss in the hallway to the kitchen. She had curly auburn hair, pink cheeks and green eyes. "Hi." She seemed a little nervous but managed a cute grin. Extending her hand, she took Bliss's fingers in a crushing handshake. "I know this is hard for you. Jeez, it's hard for me and I really don't know what to say to you, but I think—I mean, the best thing is for us to get to know each other."

"I suppose," Bliss acquiesced, ambivalent. What do you say to someone who is the product of your father's infidelity? How do you accept them or they accept you?

"The truth of the matter is," the redhead said with refreshing honesty as she sailed down the hallway as if she'd done it a hundred times before, "I've been torn. From the minute I heard about you and realized that you were my sister, I wanted to meet you, but was afraid and embarrassed and, oh, it's just so damned complicated."

"Isn't it?" *Give the woman a chance, Bliss. She's obviously struggling with this as much as you are.*

In the kitchen Katie paused and eyed the rolls that Bliss had put on the table. "Mmm, smells great."

"Good. Sit, sit." Bliss waved her into a chair and poured them each a cup of coffee. She handed Katie a mug and watched as the younger woman spooned two teaspoons of sugar into her brew. "When Mom told me that John was my father I thought we should get together to shake our heads at our parents' stupidity if nothing else." She rolled her large eyes. "And I thought *kids* were hard to understand. You know, sometimes adults are ten times worse."

"You're probably right," Bliss agreed as she sat across the table, her back to the window. Outside the glass a robin was busy pulling up worms from the morning-damp lawn. Bliss didn't have to like the woman, just hear her out. Unfortunately, Katie seemed to be one of those bubbly, wear-your-heart-on-your-sleeve types that she found endearing.

"I have to admit, though," Katie said, sipping her coffee as Bliss cut the rolls apart and placed one of the sugary confections on a small plate, "after living with three brothers it was a relief to know that I had a sister—well, really, two sisters!"

Katie, all five feet two inches of her, cut into her pastry. She was small and wiry, with quick movements and the exuberance of a brushfire at the height of summer. No moss grew under this little woman's feet. "And what's your name?" she asked as Oscar, slowly wagging his tail, galloped into the room, only to slide to a stop at the table.

"Oscar. I've had him a couple of years."

"Well, you're just adorable," Katie said to the dog who wiggled at her feet. "Do you hear me? A-dor-a-ble." Without checking with Bliss, she tossed the mutt a bite of pecan roll, which he tossed and gulped in one swift motion. She wiped her hands and asked suddenly, "Do you have any kids?"

Bliss ignored the jab in her heart and shook her head. "No. At least not yet. Never been married."

"Neither have I, but I've got a boy—Josh. He's hell on wheels and the most wonderful thing that ever happened to me. I always say kids are the biggest blessing and curse of your life. You love them so much you worry about them day and night." She bit her lower lip and stared out the window, but Bliss guessed she wasn't seeing the horses grazing in the field grass or one of the ranch hands shoring up the ramp to the back of the barn. No, Katie was in her own private world—a world that seemed to revolve around her son.

Bliss felt the same tug on her heartstrings that had become a regular feeling whenever she thought of her own childless state. Ever since coming to Bittersweet she had been conscious of her biological clock. This wasn't a new experience. For the past few years as her friends and coworkers had become mothers, she'd felt her maternal instincts awakening, and she'd only wished she could have given her mother a grandchild while she was alive.

"Lately, Josh—he's ten going on sixteen—has been getting into a powder keg of trouble. I'm telling you, when school's not in session, look out!" Katie flung her arms wide, as if they'd been blown apart, before she finally turned away from the window and met Bliss's uneasy stare.

"Oh, I guess I came on like gangbusters, didn't I?" With a smile, she added, "I'm glad to finally meet you, Bliss, even though this is kind of weird for both of us. You know, I didn't know John was my real dad until just after his heart attack. For all those years I thought Hal Kinkaid was my biological father." She shook her head as if at her own folly and chewed on a bite of pecan roll. "He and I were never close. *Never.* But still, finding out that he wasn't the guy whose genes are running around in my body was a shock."

"I imagine it was," Bliss replied, though, in truth, she couldn't imagine anything of the sort. The whole conversation was surreal in a way. What could she say to this forthright woman who seemed to have no qualms about talking about any subject under the sun, including her own conception, illegitimate though it was?

Katie propped one foot on the brace of one of the empty chairs scattered around the table. "It's really an odd sensation, you know," she admitted, "growing up believing one thing and learning that you were lied to and that everything you believed in is bogus."

Bliss only nodded. Her entire life, it seemed, had been a lie.

"Hal Kinkaid—the guy I thought was my dad—was a real jerk. I mean, a first-class bastard. Why Mom connected with him, I'll never know. He drank too much, always ran around on my mom, left her with a pile of bills. Strange as it sounds, I was relieved that he wasn't related to me."

"Yeah, but what about Dad?"

Katie shook her head and rubbed her arms as if she was suddenly chilled. "That's a tough one. Especially for you and your mom." She propped her chin on one hand and didn't argue when Bliss refilled both cups. She added sugar, and this time, a little bit of cream, watching in idle fascination as clouds rose in the dark brew.

"Thanks," the redhead said, taking a sip. "To think that John Cawthorne had two families. I can't say I have too much respect for him—well, or for Mom, either—but there it is. Now your mother's gone and they're finally getting married. What can I say?"

"It's . . . hard."

"Bingo. On one hand I think they should slow down, let the rest of us catch our breath and deal with all this, and on the other I understand their need to be together. Who knows how much time they have?" Katie shrugged and blew across the top of her cup. "I just hope the rest of us—you, me, Tiffany and my brothers—can handle this.

Well, and of course, I hope John can make Mom happy. She deserves it."

Bliss didn't comment, and Katie raised her hands as if to ward off physical blows. "I know, I know, you probably hate her for what she did."

"*Hate's* too strong a word," Bliss admitted.

"But you have to resent her."

That much was true. Wiping away a drip of coffee from her cup, Bliss said, "Let's just say I loved my mom a lot. She might not have been perfectly suited for my dad, but she deserved him to be true to her. It's him I'm having the problem with."

"Me, too," Katie admitted before taking a long swallow from her cup. "I just hope we can all work this out and be friends." She grinned. "I know, that's beyond optimistic, but it doesn't make sense for anyone to hold any grudges. What would that accomplish?"

"Nothing, I suppose," Bliss reluctantly agreed.

"Yeah, so go and tell your heart, right?" Katie laughed without much mirth. "This is one dandy mess."

"Touché."

"You know, this is probably hard for you to believe, but my mom wouldn't hurt a flea. Lord knows, she tried to break it off with your dad several times—or at least that's what she said—but they just couldn't stay apart. Every time she married another guy in an attempt to get over your father, she swore she'd have nothing to do with John Cawthorne, but then the marriage would begin to fail, probably because her heart wasn't in it in the first place, and John would come back to Bittersweet and it would begin all over again. I was too young and out of it to notice."

"I don't want to hear this," Bliss said, her heart squeezing for her mother and the family they'd been.

Katie pursed her lips. "Sorry. Tacky of me. My brothers

say that I don't know when to keep my mouth shut, and I guess they're right."

"No, I wanted to know, but it's . . . I don't know."

"Painful. I get it. You feel like your dad betrayed your mother and therefore he betrayed you. I understand. I didn't mean to open up any old wounds."

"No, no, it's all right." The last thing Bliss wanted was to alienate Katie, her half-sister, a woman as unlike her as day was to night. But she found Katie Kinkaid refreshing and outspoken, relaxed and honest. No false pretenses. No worries about decorum or what the neighbors might think or say. In short, Bliss found herself warming to Katie whether she wanted to or not.

Katie sliced Bliss a curious look. "I don't mean to pry, but since we're getting to know each other, I wanted to ask a couple of things."

Bliss's back stiffened. "Such as?"

"You visited here when you were growing up, didn't you?"

"The summers— Well, some of them." Unease knotted Bliss's already tight stomach.

"Then you know Mason Lafferty."

It was a statement, and it hung in the air. Bliss had taken a bite of her roll, and it suddenly felt like a lump of wet cement wedged against the top of her mouth.

"He, uh, worked for Dad a long time ago."

"Until he was fired," Katie said, then drained her cup again. "You know, my brother Jarrod was his best friend at the time and thought John—er, Dad—oh, whatever he is—gave Mason a bum rap. There was something about a riding accident and you, right?"

Memories, as dark and dismal as that fateful day ten years past, scraped at Bliss's soul. She cradled her cup in her palms, as if expecting to gain some warmth from its heat. "I ended up in the hospital."

"Because of Mason?"

"No, in spite of him," Bliss admitted, thinking back to that storm-ravaged day and her wild ride to the north edge of the property.

Katie cleared her throat and Bliss came crashing back to the present. Her half-sister was still staring at her, waiting for an explanation. "I took the horse out even though Mason warned me not to, that a storm was brewing."

Katie picked at a raisin left on her plate. "Mason took the fall for you—well, so to speak."

"I told Dad the truth, but he never believed me, thought I was covering up for Lafferty's—what did he call it? Oh, uh, his 'bad attitude, insubordination, pathetic sense of judgment and lack of respect.' That was it."

Katie let out a long, low whistle. "That's not the Mason Lafferty I knew."

"Me, neither," Bliss admitted, but her heart ached just the same, because Mason had used her and lied to her, left her for another woman—a woman pregnant with his baby.

"Ever since his divorce from Terri, he's become one of the most eligible bachelors in the county," Katie said, one eyebrow lifting.

"Is that right?" Bliss wasn't interested, or so she told herself. She drained her coffee cup.

"Well, that's just the recent consensus because he hasn't lived here in years. Just returned a few months ago so that he could be closer to his kid. In fact—"

"I know. He's trying to buy this place but Dad won't sell."

"Yeah, but my mom already owns part of the ranch and she's gone and signed on the dotted line."

"I know. She and Dad are fighting about it."

"Great," Katie said. frowning as she shoved aside her plate. There was a strange, uncomfortable silence for a few minutes and Bliss, to keep the conversation from becoming even more strained, cleared the table.

"Oh, damn." Katie glanced at the clock on the stove. "I've got to call and see if Josh is up. He's got a job doing yard work for Mrs. Kramer next door, so I don't want him to forget and take off on his bike or skateboard. Mind if I use the phone?"

"Not at all."

Katie scooted back her chair and plucked the receiver off the wall. Deftly she punched in the numbers and waited. "Darn it, either he's asleep or already took off— Josh, this is Mom, if you're there, pick up. Josh? Honey, if you're— Oh, about time. I was afraid you'd already taken off." She paused for a minute and then said, "No, don't go back to bed. You've got the job at Mrs. Kramer's, remember?" Another hesitation. "No, there's no way out of it. It'll only be for a couple of hours and I'll be home soon. You don't have to be over there until eleven—"

She stopped in mid-sentence and leaned against the wall. Absently twirling the phone cord in her fingers, she listened to all of her son's excuses.

"Okay, okay, just get ready. After you finish this afternoon you can go swimming and later I'll barbecue for dinner. . . . I don't know—how about hot dogs or hamburgers? Good." She waited and rolled her eyes. "See ya." She hung up and shook her head. "I'd better go before he takes off and ditches out of this job. A workaholic he's not, but I guess he's pretty young." She was already heading for the hallway. "It was nice to get to know you a little better. Maybe . . . well, if we can convince her, we can visit Tiffany some day. You know about her, right?"

"My father's firstborn," Bliss said stiffly. "Yes. I've heard of her." But only recently.

"She moved back to Bittersweet a little while ago, just

about the time school was out, and I saw her once to tell her about John and Mom getting married. She wasn't very anxious to talk to me—in fact, I'm not sure she can handle all this—" Katie gestured vaguely toward the interior of the house and waved her fingers. "Well, maybe none of us can, but I'm sure she just didn't know what to say to me, and she was having trouble with her boy and his uncle. The guy—J.D. Santini—seems to be butting into the kid's life. The whole Santini clan are kind of pushy, I think. Her father-in-law is the patriarch and head of Santini Wines, a big deal up in Portland. Her husband Philip worked for him and I think J.D. does, too, though he is, well, as I understand it, the black sheep of the family.

"Anyway, Tiffany's got her share of problems and I haven't worked up the nerve to call her again."

"You?" Bliss questioned. "Afraid? I don't believe it."

"'Intimidated' would be more like it," Katie admitted. "Tiffany's gone through some rocky times and I think she blames your—I mean, our—father."

"Maybe she's got valid reasons," Bliss suggested as she swiped bread crumbs from the counter and tossed them into the sink.

"Probably. But she's still our sister. I think we should give her another chance." She hesitated. "You gave me one."

Bliss lifted a shoulder. What could she say? It was impossible not to like Katie Kinkaid. "I'll try."

"Good." With a wave Katie was off, scurrying down the hallway like a whirlwind. Bliss followed her to the front door and closed it after Katie's tired old convertible rumbled down the drive.

Left feeling breathless, Bliss walked back to the den. Each and every day, her life became more complicated than she'd ever expected. Her father's impending marriage, her half-sisters and Mason were more than she could expect to handle. Not at all certain she wanted to get to know either of her sisters any better, Bliss wondered if they'd ever come to terms with each other. Katie was a steamroller who seemed determined to take control of everyone's life she crossed, and Tiffany sounded cold and aloof.

"Don't judge," she warned herself, but she was still wary. She had to be careful. Years before, she'd cast caution to the wind when it came to relationships and it had cost her; it had cost her dearly. She'd lost her heart and nearly her life. She wouldn't make that mistake again. Not ever. Or so she tried to convince herself.

Chapter Eight

"So, is there a man in your life?"

Brynnie's question startled Bliss. She nearly dropped the pot of coffee she'd been pouring for her soon-to-be stepmother. Though she and John were still at odds about selling the ranch, they had buried the hatchet in shallow, soft soil. Everyone was treading lightly and Bliss wondered if the wedding would come off as planned.

"A man in my life? No, not really," she said, setting the glass pot back in the coffeemaker and handing Brynnie a steaming cup.

"A pretty girl like you? I don't believe it." Brynnie took a sip. "Mmm, that's good." She set her cup on the marred kitchen table and eyed her future stepdaughter. "You're an architect, isn't that what John told me?"

"When I'm working. Business has been a little slow lately."

"Good. You can spend more time here with your dad." She added cream to her cup. "I would think, in a job like yours, that you'd work with lots of men."

Bliss swallowed a smile. "Too many."

"Uh-uh-uh. That's not the right attitude. By the time I was your age I was through with my second husband and on to my third." She laughed—a deep, throaty chuckle, made raspy by too many cigarettes.

"I guess I haven't met the right man yet."

"Of course, you have. You just don't know it." Brynnie blew across her cup and sighed. "You know, he might be right under your nose."

"Is that a fact?" The conversation made Bliss a little uncomfortable, but she couldn't help being intrigued by this woman who was so different from her mother. While Margaret Cawthorne had always been perfectly dressed, not a hair out of place, her smile somewhat immobile, her fingernails polished, her jewelry refined and understated, Brynnie wore tight jeans, T-shirts that had seen better days and costume jewelry that was outrageous and fun, rather than elegant.

Brynnie eyed Bliss over the rim of her cup. "I heard you saw Mason Lafferty the other day."

Bliss nearly choked on a swallow of coffee. This was a small town.

"I thought you two had some kind of, well"—she waved her pudgy fingers in the air and frowned—"chemistry, for lack of a better word."

Heat stole up Bliss's neck. That "chemistry" was none of Brynnie's business, and yet she'd probably already heard the story of her involvement with Mason from Bliss's father. "There was—once. It was a long time ago. It's over."

"Hmm." Brynnie chewed on her lower lip thoughtfully. "Some loves die hard. Never go away. Oh, they can be put on hold or people can pretend they don't exist, but it's all a big lie and one day you look in the mirror and face the fact that the love of your life might slip away if you don't do something."

"Are you talking about you and Dad?" Bliss asked woodenly. This woman might soon become her stepmother, but, as far as Bliss was concerned, she had no right to hand out advice, especially on the subject of love.

"Right now, I'm talking about you." Brynnie drained her cup as John's boots pounded up the back steps to the porch. "You and Mason Lafferty. You can lie to yourself, if you want to, but it won't do any good. Besides, he's a good man and single."

Bliss bit her tongue to keep from saying something harsh about Brynnie being involved with her father while he was married.

"That marriage didn't seem to take. Over real quick. He and Terri split up years ago." She pointed an accusatory red-polished fingernail in Bliss's direction. "If you ask me, now that he's back in town, Mason Lafferty is the best catch in Bittersweet. Well, next to your father and my own boys, of course."

"Of course," Bliss said dryly as Brynnie shoved back her chair and the legs scraped against yellowed linoleum.

"My boys, now, they're good men, but land's sake, I pity the women they end up with." She shook her head. "I swear the twins were enough to nearly send me over the edge when they were in high school. But that's neither here nor now."

"Stay away from Lafferty, Blissie," John ordered as the screen door creaked open and he walked into the kitchen in his stocking feet. Pausing at the counter, he poured himself a cup of coffee.

"I'm not involved with Mason," she replied.

"I'm not blind, y' know. I see how you look at him."

"Give me a break," Bliss said, though she felt a blush steal up the back of her neck. Was it possible that she was so transparent?

"I shouldn't have to remind you that it was his fault you nearly—"

"No, Dad, you're wrong," she said vehemently. "Mason *saved* my life. I think we've had this conversation before." Bliss stood and tossed the dregs of her barely touched coffee down the drain. Though she was furious with Mason for sneaking around behind her father's back to buy his ranch, she wasn't going to let John accuse him falsely. She slid her empty cup into the dishwasher. "Don't worry about me. I can take care of myself."

"Don't give me all that feminist mumbo jumbo. Women need men to take care of them. Good men," John said, then, the minute the words were uttered, he looked as if he wished he could swallow them back again.

Bliss blanched. She thought of her mother and the years of betrayal she'd borne; of Brynnie, in love with one man while marrying others; of herself, never quite over a silly schoolgirl crush on Mason Lafferty. "I . . . I don't believe that," Bliss said.

"Neither do I." Brynnie's eyes had filled with tears and her chin wobbled. "John—"

"Ah, blast it all, anyway." He rubbed a hand over his head, making his silvering hair stand on end. "What I meant was, Bliss, you could do better."

Just like your mother could have. The unspoken words hung in the air like forgotten cobwebs, visible one minute, hidden the next in the shifting light of mixed emotions.

"Well, uh . . ." Brynnie cleared her throat and dug into her purse for her cigarettes. "I heard you met Tiffany the other day."

"Tiffany?" Bliss repeated, still stung by her father's statement.

"Yes. When you visited Mason."

"You saw Mason and Tiffany?" John's mouth pulled downward.

"I don't think—" Bliss cut herself short as she remembered visiting Mason at his apartment. "Does Tiffany own an old Victorian in the middle of town?"

"Didn't you know?" Brynnie found her pack of cigarettes and shook out a filter tip.

"No, I . . ." So that explained the other woman's cool, stunned reaction to her.

"I ran into Octavia—that's her grandmother—down at the beauty parlor and she mentioned you'd been over."

"Is that right?" John said.

"I didn't realize she was Tiffany. I mean, I introduced myself and she didn't give me her name, just looked shocked and pointed out Mason's apartment."

"So you went visiting him?" He sighed wearily. "You're a smart girl, Bliss. I hoped you'd learned your lessons with that one."

"I have. But—"

Resigned, he waved off her excuses. "It's your life. Just use your head."

"Always do, Dad."

"Oh, honey, I wish I could believe that."

"Trust me."

"She's a grown woman," Brynnie reminded him. "And I'm not so sure either you or I are the right ones to be handing out advice." She struck a match and drew long on her cigarette.

John's jaw hardened. "I just don't want her to make the same mistakes I did."

"Or Margaret did," Brynnie said, shooting a geyser of smoke from the corner of her mouth.

"I won't." Rather than continue the no-win argument, Bliss headed for the den. She heard Brynnie defending Mason and her father going through the roof. The happiness he was certain he would find with his bride-to-be seemed to fade with each passing day, and Bliss doubted he'd find the peace he was so determined to have.

"You should never have sold out to him," her father was saying as Bliss walked the length of the house.

"It was my right."

"Like hell. I've half a mind to call the son of a bitch myself."

"Now, John, don't get all worked up. . . ."

Bliss closed the door to the den behind her and leaned against the cool panels. What a mess. It seemed that John and Brynnie were forever at each other's throats. A match made in heaven, it wasn't.

But her part in it would soon be over; then they could fight it out like cats and dogs if they wanted to. Bliss only had to put up with a few more weeks of living with all this tension. Then, the Good Lord willing and true love, if that's what you'd call it, winning out, her father would be married. Bliss would return to Seattle.

For a reason she couldn't name, the thought of heading back to her apartment overlooking Puget Sound settled like lead in her heart.

Because of Mason. Because you can't forget him and because you haven't had it out with him. Face it, Bliss, what you really want while you're down here, is to find out why he abandoned you; why he ran away and why, when you cared for him so deeply, he didn't return your love.

"All I'm saying, Lafferty, is that you had no right!"

Mason held the telephone receiver away from his ear as John Cawthorne, swearing and yelling, told him seven ways to go to hell for buying out Brynnie's portion of the land. Though it had been days since the old man had found out, he was still furious and had, apparently, had another fight with his bride-to-be over the situation.

"I don't like anyone sneaking around my back, dealing

with a woman, playing on her emotions. You're a snake, Lafferty, and I'll see your sorry backside in court, let me tell you."

"Fine."

"If you think I'm going to sell my part of the ranch, you'd better think again! And stay away from my daughter. You're not going to use Bliss to get to me!"

A quiet anger stole through Mason's blood. "I wouldn't."

"Sure. Like you wouldn't use Brynnie! Hell, Lafferty, you'd sell your own mother if you thought it would bring you a little profit in the future!"

Mason's jaw tightened and his knuckles showed white on the receiver at the mention of his mother's name.

"You're not going to pull a fast one on me, y'know," Cawthorne was yammering.

"Just think about the deal, Cawthorne," he said, managing to keep his voice calm though images of his mother, sad and old beyond her years, cut through his mind like razors. "That's all that matters."

"Like hell." Cawthorne slammed down the receiver.

"Great. Just great." Mason hung up and stood, stretching the tension out of the tight muscles of his back. Why the old man could get to him was a mystery.

Years ago, with Cawthorne standing in the rain, looming over him, offering him a deal for getting out of Bliss's life, Mason had been blinded by pain and had silently sworn he'd get even one day. Now the day was at hand, but the sweet taste of revenge eluded him.

He glanced at his watch. Not quite five, and he'd had a hell of a day even without John Cawthorne's verbal attack. Five cattle—three cows and two calves—had died of black leg on his ranch in Montana. The rest of the herd was quarantined, but there would still be losses—too many of them.

A foreman at the same ranch had fallen from the

haymow, cracked three ribs and broken his ankle, and some neighboring rancher was screaming bloody murder about water rights. The neighbor had hired himself a local lawyer who had taken the case with a vengeance and was now threatening a lawsuit.

Then there was the matter of Patty. What had happened to her? It was strange that she'd quit calling him about the same time Isaac Wells had disappeared.

But John Cawthorne's phone call was the one that bothered him the most. Because of Bliss. Mason couldn't shake her out of his mind no matter how hard he tried. He'd always prided himself on being able to put each portion of his life into perspective, to give appropriate attention to the most pressing problems while letting others simmer until he was ready to deal with them, but Bliss dominated any other thoughts. Where she was concerned, he was beyond a fool.

"Get a grip," he growled as he squared a hat upon his head. He grabbed his jacket from a hook on the brass hall tree and decided to call it a day. It was after six and he needed a drink. A stiff one. Maybe even a double.

He yanked open the door and there she was. Bliss Cawthorne in the flesh. Her cheeks were flushed, her eyes troubled.

"I tried to stop her," Edie, his receptionist-secretary, apologized helplessly, as if there was no way she could deter the intruder. Edie's earphones were still in place, the cord to her transcriber dangling from the headset.

"It'll just take a minute," Bliss said.

Mason doubted it. A minute? No way. An hour? He didn't think so. Whatever was weighing heavily enough on Bliss's mind to prod her down here looking for him, it would take a long time to hash out. "It's all right, Edie."

"But—" the secretary stammered, her feathers obviously ruffled.

"I'll handle it," Mason assured her as she glanced at her

watch. "You can go on home. Just lock the door and have the answering service pick up."

"Are you sure? It's just that I have to pick up Toby."

"I know." He held the door to his office open and Bliss, looking suddenly as if she regretted whatever impulse it was that had driven her here, stepped inside. A cloud of her perfume trailed after her, but Mason refused to be affected by anything remotely feminine, even a scent that reminded him of long-ago years.

He closed the door softly and she nearly jumped.

"What's going on, Bliss?" he asked.

"I—I came down here because of Dad."

"You're sure about that?" He couldn't hide the skepticism in his words.

"Of course." She cleared her throat and her spine visibly stiffened as she impaled him with those incredible blue eyes. "I want you to back off, Mason."

"Back off?"

"Yeah, with Dad and his ranch. Surely there's another parcel you could buy." She tossed her hair over her shoulders. "Dad doesn't need this now—all this pressure. He's already had one heart attack and he doesn't need another. He and Brynnie are at each other's throats because of this mess. Because of you."

He propped himself on the corner of his desk and folded his arms over his chest. There was more to this than money and land; he could see it in her eyes and the set of her chin.

"I told you before, Brynnie wanted to sell," he reminded her.

"That was Dad's land."

"Which he had already deeded over to her."

Bliss took a step forward, placing herself directly in front of him and nailed him with a look that caused an uneven thumping in his chest. "You know, Mason, for years I've stuck up for you whenever Dad tried to pin that horseback riding accident on you."

"Did you convince him?" he asked dryly.

"Never. But he knew what I thought."

He lowered his gaze to the semicircle of bone at the base of her throat where there was a pulse throbbing erratically. "And what was that, Bliss?" Mason asked boldly, painfully aware that her body was placed squarely between his legs, should he close them. His throat was so dry he had trouble concentrating. "What did you think?"

She paused and her gaze shifted. "I was the one who rode out in the storm. You saved me."

"Did I?" He wasn't convinced. Too many years of carrying a load of guilt around.

She didn't answer and through the frosted, pebbled glass of his door, he noticed the lights dim in the outer office. Edie had left. He was alone with Bliss. His palms began to sweat. His thighs, straddling the corner of the desk, began to ache.

"Just stay away from Dad and Brynnie, okay? Don't cause trouble between them."

"You want them to be together?" he asked. "Given all the circumstances, I would have thought—"

"I want my father to be happy," she interrupted. "That's all. He's . . . he's already had one heart attack."

"Which is the reason why Brynnie sold." He rubbed his knees with his hands and felt a tightening in his groin, the start of arousal. He should just cut the lights and escort Bliss and her air of self-righteousness out the door. But he didn't. He couldn't. Being alone with her—so close that he could smell her skin, see the faint freckles bridging her nose, witness the sweep of her honey-brown lashes against her cheeks—was his undoing.

Her eyes narrowed a fraction. "They've been fighting about it, you know."

"No one twisted Brynnie's arm."

Her eyes locked with his, and he felt a catch in his throat "What is it with you, Lafferty? What is it you have against my father?"

He should have been prepared for the question and been able to deal with the silent accusations in her gaze, but he wasn't. Damn it, whenever he was near her, rational thought slipped away and he saw her as he remembered her best, naked as the day she was born, swimming in the rippling current of the river, her hair dark and damp, her skin flushed from the icy water, and her nipples, round pink buttons visible beneath the shimmering surface.

"What is it you have against me?"

"What?"

"You're not here because of 'dear old Dad,'" he said, seeing a spark of passion and the hint of pain in her eyes. "You're here because you wanted to see me again."

"Don't flatter yourself, Lafferty."

"Admit it, Bliss."

"I came because of the ranch—"

"Bull. You just don't know what to do with me."

"What?"

"Strangle me or kiss me."

"That's ridiculous!"

"Is it?" he asked, his heart thumping, his body hard with arousal. The scent of her perfume was tantalizing, the smell of her hair damned near drove him out of his mind. "You've never married."

She froze and the color in her face drained quickly. "Does it matter?" she demanded, then shook her head. "Listen, don't answer that. It's not important—"

"It is to me."

His words echoed through her soul, and she reminded herself to tread carefully, that this was a man to be wary of, a man she couldn't trust, a man who had stolen her heart years ago, only to ruthlessly toss it away.

She stepped away from him and rubbed her arms at the sudden chill in her bones, and he, as if understanding the need for distance between them, stood and walked around the edge of the desk to the window. Still, he was waiting for an answer. So why lie about being single? "Okay. Just for the record, Lafferty, I never found the right guy, okay? I've dated, sometimes seriously, been asked a couple of times, but never felt that I wanted to throw away my independence on some guy who . . . whom—"

"You didn't love."

Oh, God, it was as if he could read her mind, so she turned her back to him, tried to think. "Yes . . . I suppose that's it." He always had a disconcerting way of slicing right to the point. She heard him shift and leave his place at the window. His footsteps thudded dully on the carpet. She felt his hands upon her shoulders, his breath warm against the nape of her neck, and she stiffened. Her idiotic pulse had the nerve to skyrocket. Worse yet, his hands, work-roughened but gentle, felt so natural as they gently rotated her to face him.

"So why didn't you fall in love, Bliss?" he asked in a whisper that wafted through her hair and reverberated through her mind. Oh, Lord, he was too close and oh, so male. . . . She noticed the shadow of his beard, dark gold and rough against his square, uncompromising jaw.

"What?"

"I asked, why didn't you fall in love?"

I did. A long time ago. With you. And you hurt me. Oh, God, Mason, you hurt me so badly. She swallowed hard and licked lips that had become dry in a second. "I, uh, I guess I'm picky." Dear God, was that her voice that sounded so breathless—so filled with a desperate yearning she didn't want to name? "What—what about you?"

"I fell in love with the wrong woman."

Terri Fremont. His ex-wife. Of course. "I see."

"Do you?"

He was too close, *way* too close. She needed to escape, but her feet wouldn't move.

"Terri and I are divorced." His lips turned downward and a private pain pierced his eyes. "We have been for a long time. Ours wasn't exactly a marriage to write home about."

Her heart squeezed even though she'd told herself over and over again that she didn't care about Mason Lafferty, that he could rot in hell, that he was a selfish bastard. "I suppose not."

His mouth twisted and his hands, still upon her shoulders, didn't move. "You know, I never meant to hurt you—"

Oh, no, he was going to apologize! Again! This man who could barely admit to making a mistake. Bliss couldn't take it, didn't want to hear anything he had to say about what had happened between them. "Don't, Mason," she begged, staring into eyes as gold as an October sunset. "Just don't, okay?"

"I thought I should explain what happened."

"I know what happened, and guess what? It doesn't matter anymore," she said, her tongue tripping over the untruth. "I said what I wanted to say."

"Liar."

"Pardon me?" she asked, inwardly telling herself it was time to leave, to get away from him.

"I think you have a lot more to say. More questions that beg to be answered." He stepped even closer, touched the side of her face with one callused finger. Just being alone with him and breathing the same air he did caused her chest to constrict and her heart to pound in a silly, useless cadence.

"Bliss—" His hands captured her shoulders. His expression, harsh only minutes before, seemed suddenly haunted and weary. "Just . . . just believe that I never meant to hurt you."

She swallowed against a sudden lump in her throat as she witnessed a ghost of pain cross his eyes.

"I am sorry," he whispered.

"I know." Oh, Lord, now tears were burning against her eyelids but she forced them back. She'd wasted too many tears on this man years ago. "Believe me, Mason," she said, lying through her teeth again as anger overcame sadness, "it doesn't matter. It wasn't that big a deal. If you think I spent years or even months pining for you, you're dead wrong. I went home to Seattle, pulled myself up by my bootstraps and was dating Todd Wheeler not long after you finished saying 'I do.' So don't flatter yourself into thinking I cared a whit about whom you married or even when."

She tried to pull herself from his grasp, but his fingers clamped possessively over her arms. His amber gaze—hot, wanting and intense—pinned hers. No, she thought desperately. *No! No! No!* This was wrong. So very wrong, and yet, despite the denials screaming through her brain, she couldn't breathe, couldn't think, could only stare at his lips—blade-thin and hard. It took little effort to imagine what they would feel like against hers, how his mouth would open and his tongue would slide so easily past her own lips and teeth, searching, seeking, touching . . .

"If I could do things over—"

"What?" she asked, tearing her gaze from that sexy slash that was his mouth. "What are you saying, Mason? That you'd change the past? How? Sneak around so that I wouldn't find out about Terri? Keep me from riding out to the ridge in the storm?" *Make love to me like I begged you to?* Oh, God. "What?"

"No, I—"

"I don't want to hear it!" Now she sounded like a spoiled teenager, but she didn't care. She had to find a way to break away from him, away from the sweet seduction of his touch. This was all happening way too fast and much too late. "Look, Mason, as I've said, it just doesn't matter anymore."

"Like hell." Their gazes clashed—innocent blue and rugged gold. Like metal striking metal.

"No— Oh, Mason—"

He dragged her against him and as she gasped, his lips crashed down on hers. Urgent. Wanting.

She voiced a soft moan of protest that went unheeded.

His mouth was hard and warm and molded so effortlessly against hers. He smelled of leather and aftershave, musky and male. A part of her let go—after ten long, heart-wrenching years.

His lips were as sensual and insistent as they had been years before, and she was just as lost to him now. In the warm interior of his office, a decade had melted away.

Don't do this, Bliss. Don't let him use you again!

But she couldn't stop herself.

His mouth moved over hers with a wild abandon that touched the deepest part of her. Within a heartbeat her traitorous body began to respond, and desire, hot and long-slumbering, awoke with a vengeance. She could hardly breathe, her knees threatened to buckle and her mouth opened willingly under the sweet, gentle pressure of his tongue.

Somewhere in the back of her mind she knew she was making a horrid, life-altering mistake, but she didn't care. For the moment, she only wanted to close her eyes and drown in the seductive whirlpool of his taste, his smell, his touch.

With a moan, she started to wind her arms around his neck. Then, as his fingers toyed with the hem of her T-shirt, she realized that she was falling into the same precarious trap that had snared her ten years earlier.

He used you before.

He'll use you again.

He never loved you and never will.

"I—I can't," she managed. "W-we shouldn't . . . Oh, Lord, this—this isn't a good idea," she whispered, lifting her head and feeling dizzy. Her eyelids were at half-mast, her blood flowing like lava.

"I know." He kissed her—a soft, teasing brush of his lips over hers.

She melted deep inside. "I don't think—"

Another feather-light kiss to the corner of her mouth. "Don't think."

Sweet heaven, how she wanted him. Her legs turned wobbly. "Listen, Mason, please, l can't do this." Forcing the unwanted words over her tongue, she pushed him away with all her strength. She was breathing hard, her chest rising and falling with each breath, her anger pulsing in her ears. "What we had was over a long time ago. I thought you understood that a few minutes ago, but if you missed the message let me give it to you loud and clear, okay?" Somehow she found the strength to say what her heart so vehemently denied. "I don't believe in reliving the past."

"How about changing the future?"

Her heart stopped for a crazy minute and in her mind's silly eye, she saw herself walking down an aisle in a white dress, swearing to love him for the rest of her life, becoming his wife and bearing his children. Mason's babies. A part of her heart shredded when she remembered he already had a child, one that had nothing to do with her. Tears touched the back of her eyelids and she said dully, "We have no future." And that was the simple truth. They both knew it. "Look, don't . . . don't you have an oil well to drill, or some tractors to sell, or some livestock to brand?"

A slow, sexy smile spread across his face. "I was just about to call it a day." Reaching behind her head, he snapped off the lights. "Maybe you and I should have dinner or drinks," he suggested, and a part of her longed to be with him, to forgive him, to be confident enough to make love to him without the need to think of becoming his wife.

"I—I don't think that would be such a good idea."

"Scared?" he taunted, and a spark of amusement flared in his eyes.

"No way."

"Then, why not go out with me?"

Because I can't take a chance. I don't want to get hurt, and I can't trust myself when I'm around you! "I . . . I have plans." Even to her own ears, her excuse sounded feeble. "With Dad."

He hesitated, his silence accusing her of the lie. His jaw slid to one side. "Then I'll take a rain check."

"Fine. Right."

"I'm serious, Bliss. Any time you want to see me, drop by." Amber eyes held hers for a second. "You know where I live."

"Yes. At Tiffany's."

He nodded and touched her lightly on the arm. "Any time." A tremor stole through her at the thought of being alone with him at his place. He opened the door and she walked through with as much dignity as she could muster, but all the way down the stairs to the first floor, she felt her lips tingle where Mason had kissed her and her cheeks, where the stubble of his beard had rubbed against her skin, were slightly tender. Oh, Lord, what was she getting herself into? She shoved open the front door and heard Mason's keys jangling in the lock but she didn't wait for him to follow her.

Quickly, she hurried outside to the sidewalk. The flow of traffic was lazy in the late afternoon and in the town square across the street, women pushed baby buggies or watched their children play on equipment in the park. She thought she spied Tiffany Santini pushing her daughter on a swing, and again her heart twisted at the thought of children.

Tiffany threw her head back and laughed as the imp in the swing said something she found hilarious. Tiffany's black hair gleamed in the sunlight, and mother and daughter seemed carefree and incredibly happy.

Someday, she silently told herself. *Oh, sure, and when is that going to happen? Remember, Bliss, you've got a long way to go. You're twenty-seven years old and still a virgin.*

Chapter Nine

"So tell me, Lafferty, what is it you're afraid of?" Jarrod asked. He peeled the label from his bottle of beer while some old country ballad wafted through the smoky interior of the bar. From the back room, billiard balls clicked while conversation at the few odd tables scattered around the room was punctuated by laughter. A television mounted high over the bar was tuned in to a baseball game, which the bartender watched as he polished the battered old mahogany with a white towel.

"'Afraid of'?" Mason took a swallow from his long-necked bottle and let the beer cool his throat. He didn't like lying; wasn't much good at it, but knew that once in a while it was necessary. This was one of those times. "Nothing."

"Bull." Jarrod eyed him with the calm of a cougar advancing upon a lamb. He leaned forward. "You're scared that Patty's involved up to her eyeballs in old man Wells's disappearance."

"I don't know how." That much was the truth, though he couldn't help suspecting that Patty, with her penchant for trouble, knew something about their uncle's vanishing act. What, he couldn't imagine, but then Patty always kept him guessing. He never knew what to expect from his mule-headed sister.

"Yeah, and I'm the Pope."

"Why would I pay you a lot of money if I already knew the answer?"

"*That's* what I'd like to know." He hoisted his empty bottle and signaled to a bored-looking waitress. "Hey, Tammy, how about another one?" He motioned to Mason. "For him, too."

She nodded a head of overbleached and kinky-permed hair, and Jarrod swung his gaze to his friend again. "I get the feeling that you've led me on a wild-goose chase, Lafferty, and I don't like being played for a fool. You know that."

"Look, I don't know where Patty is and I sure as hell can't begin to figure out what happened to old Isaac. As much of a pain in the butt as he was, most of the people in this county think it's a blessing that he's gone, but I'm not one of them."

Jarrod snorted as Mason drained his beer. "Right."

The waitress, slim in her blue jeans and white T-shirt, deposited two more bottles on the table. "Anything else?"

"Not just yet," Jarrod said, flashing her a smile that was known to break women's hearts.

She, today, wasn't in the mood. "Just let me know," she said sourly and took the empties.

"You got it." Jarrod rolled the new bottle between his palms.

Jarrod had phoned Mason, invited him for a drink, and Mason had agreed. He needed something—*anything*—to get his mind off Bliss. But he wasn't too keen on being grilled by his old friend.

Jarrod checked his watch. "Look, I've got to go, but there's one more thing."

"Shoot."

"It's about Mom."

"Brynnie?"

With a sharp nod, Jarrod settled back in the booth. “She’s in a pile of trouble because of her deal with you about her acres of the ranch. Old man Cawthorne is fit to be tied and he wants blood. Yours and Mom’s.”

“So I heard.”

“Yeah. He feels that she betrayed him.”

“What do you want me to do about it?”

Jarrod rubbed his jaw. “I don’t know. Maybe sell the ranch back to her.” At the tightening of Mason’s jaw, Jarrod sighed and shook his head. “Hey, you know there’s no love lost between the man and me. I’d just as soon spit on Cawthorne as talk to him, but he’s gonna be my stepfather—like it or not. And for some unfathomable reason, he makes Mom happy. Or he did, until she up and sold out to you. Now he’s hot under the collar, furious with her, and she’s got her back up. They’re barely talking and they’re supposed to be tying the knot.”

“Sounds like a marriage made in heaven,” Mason observed.

“There is no such thing,” Jarrod replied, finishing his drink and reaching into the back pocket of his jeans for his wallet. “You, of all people, should know that. This one’s on me, Lafferty.” He tossed a few bills onto the table.

“I’ll buy next time.”

“Nope.” Jarrod climbed to his feet. “Just be straight with me.”

“Always am,” Mason said, inwardly cringing at the lie.

“Good.” They walked outside where a summer breeze was chasing down the dusty streets and a million stars were visible over the faint glow of the sparse streetlights. “So, are you going to give me a hint about where that sister of yours could be?”

“If I knew that, I wouldn’t have to hire you.”

One side of Jarrod’s mouth lifted. “But you’re holding

back. I can feel it. Don't you know that confession's good for the soul?"

"Got nothing to confess."

"That'll be the day." Jarrod opened the door of his pickup and paused. "By the way, I heard through the grapevine that you've been seeing Bliss again."

The muscles in Mason's shoulders bunched. "That grapevine's all twisted the wrong way. She won't have anything to do with me."

Jarrod pulled on his chin and hesitated for a second before dispensing his advice. "Just tread softly. Old man Cawthorne's already on the warpath."

A smile tugged at the corners of Mason's mouth. "So I'm supposed to back off?"

"Just be careful." Jarrod slid into the seat and jammed his keys into the ignition. "And be smart. Bliss is a classy lady."

"I noticed."

"She deserves the best."

"Don't we all?"

Jarrod started the engine and his mouth tightened. "Don't use her, okay? I know you have a thing—some kind of personal vendetta—against her old man, but don't use her to get back at him."

"Don't worry about it." The last thing in the world he wanted to do was hurt Bliss, but he damned sure wanted to make love to her. And that was a problem—a problem that had been with him since the first time he'd seen her so many years ago, a problem he couldn't begin to solve.

But then again, he was a firm believer in the old "Nothing ventured, nothing gained" theory. Now was as good a time as any to test it.

On Bliss.

* * *

Astride Fire Cracker, Bliss craned her neck and peered over the edge of the ridge. Full from the spring runoff, the river far below slashed wildly over stones and fallen trees, carving a rushing swath through the stony canyon as it had on the day she'd nearly lost her life at this very spot.

Her heart began to pound and her hands sweated on the reins as the memories of that fateful afternoon ricocheted through her mind. She remembered Mason's warnings as clearly as if he'd just uttered them. . . .

"Don't be a fool."

Too late, she thought. She'd always been a fool for Mason Lafferty. They'd been so young, so innocent, and so afraid of falling in love.

It seemed as if everything and nothing had changed. Slowly she dismounted.

The wind stirred, rustling through the trees and causing wildflowers to bend in its wake. Bliss sighed for all the could-have-beens until she noticed the shadow creeping slowly beside her. Squinting against the sun she saw Mason, tall astride his horse, rangy and rugged as the mountains that towered around them.

Her heart squeezed as it always did when she was alone with him, and a tiny voice inside reminded her that he was the one—he had forever been the one—who was wedged deep in her heart, be he bad, good or indifferent. "Mason," she said, surprised that her voice had lost some of its timbre.

"Thought I might find you here." He swung down from his gelding and let the horse roam free.

"Did you? Why?"

"Because, like it or not, Bliss, I know you."

Her throat turned to dust but she wouldn't be so easily seduced. "No, Lafferty, you don't know a damned thing about me. Not anymore."

Slowly he sauntered toward her. "When you weren't at the house and Delores said you'd taken off riding, I thought

I'd be able to catch up with you. So I, well, 'borrowed,' I guess you'd say, one of the horses in the stables and rode out here. After all, this is the scene of the crime, so to speak."

"'Crime'? You mean accident." Oh, God, his eyes were such an incredible hue of gold.

He lifted a shoulder. "Whatever." The corners of his mouth twisted. "I—" His gaze centered on hers and she knew in an instant that he was searching for her soul. "I thought there were some things you and I should get straight."

"Like what?" she asked warily and wished her pulse would slow a little. So he'd followed her out here, so they were alone together in the dying sunlight, so her throat was as dry as a desert wind, so what?

"I wanted to say that I didn't mean to hurt you."

Somewhere nearby a crow cawed loudly.

She stiffened. "You didn't."

"Of course, I did." He closed the short distance between them.

Trying to back away, she nearly stumbled but his hands, rough and large, caught her and held her upright. His fingertips were warm through the light cotton of her blouse and she felt them press intimately against her ribs, as if there were no barrier, no flimsy piece of cloth separating his skin from hers.

"Terri didn't mean anything to me, Bliss," he said, a muscle jumping in his jaw.

"Then why did you sleep with her?"

"It was before I met you. Before I understood."

"Understood what?"

He hesitated for a second. "What caring about a person is all about."

Oh, God, she wanted to believe him. But there was too much time, too many lies. "Mason, you don't have to explain."

"Like hell." Shifting clouds covered the sun in a soft, thin veil.

"It doesn't matter. Not anymore."

"It matters to me." A lick of lightning flared in his eyes and in that split second she knew he was going to kiss her. Not just once, but many times, with a pulsing passion that was certain to be her downfall.

She tried to pull away, but his hands held her fast and when his lips claimed hers the whimper of protest forming in her throat turned into a soft moan of pure female wanting. Dear God, she'd waited so long for this. Much too long. Kissing him seemed so natural, so right, and yet . . . His tongue slid easily between her teeth and beyond, searching and teasing, tasting and flicking against its mate.

Bliss was lost. All thoughts of denial swiftly fled. As the horses, bridles jangling, grazed on the summer grass and a hawk circled lazily in the cloudless sky, Mason kissed her eyes, her cheeks, her throat. Her skin quivered with each brush of his lips and she couldn't protest as his weight pulled them both to the soft carpet of grass covering the ground.

"I told myself to forget you," he whispered.

"I know. I did, too."

"But I couldn't."

She didn't argue, didn't bring up the fact that he'd married another woman. Right now, alone on this grassy ridge, with an outcropping of stone near the edge and the forest so close, she closed her eyes and gave in to the sensations that she'd denied for oh-so-many years.

Her heart thundered; her skin was on fire. Strong arms held her fast, firm lips loved her as if she were the only woman on earth.

As the wind picked up, he lowered himself over her and the intimacy of his weight pressed against hers felt so right. Kissing each patch of her exposed skin, he drew her closer.

With deft fingers, he unbuttoned her blouse and the warm air of summer touched her skin.

Slowly he kissed the dusky hollow between her breasts before he brushed his lips across a lace-encased nipple. "Bliss," he whispered as she arched her back. "Sweet, sweet Bliss."

A yearning, feminine and wanton, swirled deep inside her and seeped into her blood. He lifted one breast from the lacy bounds of her bra, and her nipple puckered in expectation.

"Mason—" she cried as his mouth found her nipple and gently suckled. "Oh . . ." She should stop this madness, stanch the heat flowing wildly through her blood, halt the driving need that was causing her to want him so badly.

"That's it, darlin'," he murmured as his hands moved to the waistband of her jeans. "Let go."

"I—I can't."

"Sure, you can." His mouth was wet velvet, smooth and slick, his tongue wantonly teasing her as he slid her jeans over her hips.

Somewhere in the back of her mind she knew she should stop him, that letting him touch her was downright dangerous, but as he trailed his tongue along her bare skin she melted inside and passion ruled over reason. His lips were hot, his breath a warm summer breeze that rolled over her, and she trembled deep inside.

This was wrong. So how could it feel so right? Through her panties his lips and tongue touched her, parting her legs, creating a hot pool of lust that ached for all of him. "Mason, please . . ." she rasped as he teased at the elastic of her underwear with his teeth.

He slipped his hands beneath the silk. "Trust me," he said, and her heart nearly broke. Hadn't she trusted him with her love—with her very life—ten years ago?

Slowly he touched her. With infinite care he explored

and caressed while his lips pressed anxious kisses to her abdomen. She closed her eyes and the world seemed to swirl on a new and separate axis. He rimmed her navel with his tongue and she felt perspiration soak through her skin. She knew nothing more than the feel and smell of him. Closing her eyes, she gave in to the storm of desire sweeping through her, moved under the gentle tutelage of his fingers, cried out as the world spun out of control and the universe, stars and rainbows, collided behind her eyes.

"That's my girl," he whispered, as she quivered and his arms surrounded her. He kissed her gently on the stomach, then held her close.

Her mind reeling, she looked up into his gold eyes. "But"—she cleared her throat—"what about . . . what about . . . you?"

With a cynical smile, he drew her even closer, his nose pressed to the crook of her neck. "Another time, darlin'," he promised, then kissed the side of her throat. "Another time."

Despite the open windows, the air inside the house was airless and hot. Most of the tension was due to the fact that Brynnie had come over to make amends with her intended, but some of the frustration Bliss was feeling was because she hadn't seen Mason in several days. She didn't understand what had happened to them up on the ridge—why he hadn't made love to her—and she hadn't been able to think of much else.

"A curse, that's what it is," she told Oscar, and the dog, seated on a chair, his chin between his paws, wagged his tail. "Men. Who needs them?"

As for her father, John Cawthorne wasn't ready to reconcile with Brynnie. He obviously felt betrayed and bamboozled and kept reminding the woman he supposedly loved that she was some kind of traitor.

"Oh, I give." Bliss threw down her pencil and walked from the den toward the kitchen. As she passed the dining-room windows, she heard the sound of tires crunching against the gravel in the driveway.

For a split second she thought Mason might have come by the house and her heart did a stupid little leap, but she glanced out the window and spied Katie, all business, striding to the front door. Disappointment settled upon her, though she couldn't explain why. Just because she hadn't seen Mason in a few days was no reason to get a case of the blues. Oh, she was being such a ninny. What did she care about him? Who cared if she spent her nights sleeplessly remembering how he kissed her and caused her insides to tremble?

The bell rang just as Bliss yanked open the door. Oscar let out a few excited barks and scrambled to the doorway, jumping wildly on Katie as she breezed into the house. "Hi," Katie said a trifle breathlessly. "Is Mom here?"

"In the kitchen."

"Good." Katie hurried down the hallway to find her mother stirring a bowl of strawberries, sugar and pectin together as she made freezer jam. John was sitting at the table reading the paper.

"Katie!" Her mother looked up and beamed. "What brings you out here?"

"I, uh, thought it might be a good time for Bliss to meet Tiffany." She glanced at Bliss. "I know it's kind of sudden, but I'm not working today and Josh is over at Laddy's, so I thought if you have the time . . ."

Bliss cleared her throat and noticed that her father, looking over the tops of his reading glasses, was staring at her. There was something akin to hope in his eyes. "Are you sure she wants to meet me?"

"I don't know," Katie replied honestly.

"Why wouldn't she?" John demanded.

"Oh, Dad, come on. If you can't figure it out, I'm not going to spell it for you."

"You're a wonderful person and—"

"And I'm your daughter. Your *legitimate* daughter—the one you claimed."

"We're all adults, now," he said stubbornly. "And she's got a couple of kids. I'm their grandfather."

Grandfather. Bliss held back the argument that was brewing in her mind. Her father was a grandfather—three times over—and though she had trouble with the concept, he didn't. A little spurt of jealousy flowed through her veins. For most of her life she'd thought she would be the only bearer of Cawthorne grandkids. If she could. That was still a question. It was funny, in a bitter way, how life had turned out, and again she felt an empty space, a small hole in her life—one that only a child could fill.

"That's why I think we should talk to Tiffany. See her face-to-face," Katie said.

"Maybe you should slow down a mite." Brynnie patted Katie's hand and Bliss felt a lump forming in her throat. Though she and her mother hadn't been the touch-and-hug kind of mother and daughter, they'd been close, and seeing this display of affection between Brynnie and Katie brought to the surface a part of her she'd tried to suppress—the part of her that missed Margaret Cawthorne so badly that sometimes she still fought tears. "Tiffany might need a little more time, you know, to get used to things."

"It's been over thirty years," John interjected.

"But not for her." Brynnie took a chair at the table so she could face Bliss's father. "You know she might not come to the wedding. You'll have to accept that."

"Don't know if I can." Taking off his reading glasses, he rubbed one hand over his face and Bliss was struck by how he'd aged in the past few years.

"Look, let's not get all tied in knots about it," Katie said. "Just tell me how the wedding plans are coming along."

"Humph!" John pushed his chair back.

"They're fine." Brynnie shot him a look that dared him to argue, but for once, John Cawthorne held his tongue.

In the ensuing silence, Bliss glanced at the calendar. Only a few weeks until her father said "I do" for the second time in his life. Somehow, Bliss had come to terms with her father and his new bride. She had to find a way to lock away her past with him, to concentrate on the future so that she could honestly wish him happiness and maybe some kind of peace that had eluded him for most of his life.

"The invitations went out last week," Brynnie was saying. "The flowers are ordered, the cake is gonna be beautiful and if I can only get those miserable caterers to come up with a decent meal for a price that wouldn't make a millionaire's eyes pop out of his head, we'll be set."

Katie glanced at her watch, then at Bliss. "Why don't you take a ride into town with me and we'll grab a soda or something?"

Bliss hesitated, but just for a second.

"Okay," she said, involuntarily squaring her shoulders as if readying herself for battle. "Let's go."

Katie didn't need any further encouragement. Within minutes they were out the door and on the road in Katie's old rattletrap of a convertible. Despite her seat belt, Bliss clung to the door handle. The car was an older model with a big engine and it practically flew past the dry fields and rounded hills. Telephone poles whipped by and Bliss's hair tangled in the wind. The radio was on and the pounding beat of an old song by The Who rocked through the speakers.

"I hear that you and Mason Lafferty are an item," Katie said as she took a corner so fast the tires squealed.

"An item? Where'd you hear that?" Bliss was trying to

hold her hair into a ponytail with one hand while clutching the door with the other. The last topic of conversation she wanted to deal with was Mason.

"Mom. She seems to have an ear to the ground."

Or a nose for gossip, Bliss thought. "There's nothing going on between Mason and me."

"Why not?" Katie cast her half-sister a grin. "You have to admit he's hot."

"Oh, for the love of . . . Hot?"

"That's the term the kids use. Josh is always telling me who's hot and who's not in the fourth grade."

"This isn't elementary school." And yet her heart pounded like that of a schoolgirl whenever she heard his name.

"I know, but, as I told you before, Mason's one of the most eligible bachelors in these parts."

"I'm not in the market," Bliss said, as if to convince herself. "Why don't you date him?"

"Naw. Known him all my life. He hung out with my older brother, Jarrod, so even though he's sexy as all get-out, I'm immune." She eased up on the gas as she approached town. A wooden sign welcoming visitors to Bittersweet needed a new coat of paint and the railroad tracks that had run parallel to the road curved toward the spindly-looking trestle bridge that spanned the river. Flat, single-story strip malls had sprouted on the outskirts of town, while in the older section, near the town square and Mason's office, shops with false western-style fronts rose two or three stories.

"Do you know his wife?" Bliss asked as Katie nosed her car into a parking spot.

"Terri? Sure." She turned off the engine and tossed the oversize key ring into her purse. With a shrug, she added, "She's okay, I guess. After the divorce, she moved to—Colorado, I think. Either Boulder or Aspen or . . . Well, it doesn't matter. A few years ago she moved back here with Dee Dee, her and Mason's daughter."

Bliss remembered the girl with the soulful eyes.

They walked across the hot sidewalk where tiny particles of glass reflected in the sunlight. Katie opened the door of a coffee shop with her hip and waved to a waitress in a checked blouse and brown pants.

She seemed to know everyone in the place, from an old man with one leg and a charming smile, to a five-year-old blond girl who burst out of the rest room and careened into Katie's waiting arms. "Cindy Mae West, what're you doing here?" Katie asked with a wide grin as she scooped up the urchin.

"Havin' ice cream with my dad."

"You'd better go eat it before it melts." Katie hugged the child and set her on the black-and-white tiled floor. Like a shot, the kid bolted to a booth in the corner where her father was smoking a cigarette and a caramel sundae was dripping over the side of its dish.

Katie and Bliss sat in a booth near the windows, ordered soft drinks, and after they were both sipping from their sodas, Katie, green eyes sparkling, said, "Go ahead. Ask me about Mason." As if she saw the protest forming in her half-sister's eyes, she added, "And don't give me any backtalk about not being interested. I'm a journalist, you know, write part-time for the *Rogue River Review* and you just happen to be one lousy liar, Bliss Cawthorne."

That much was true, and since Katie had already guessed that she was, at some slight level, emotionally involved with Mason, there was no reason to argue the point. "All right. So I'm interested. A little."

"A lot, I'd think."

"A little."

"Okay, okay. The way the story goes is that Mason had

an affair with Terri Fremont years ago. She got pregnant and he, after losing his job at John's, er, your—well, my dad's place, too, I guess. Gosh, this is complicated. Anyway, Mason married her and moved to Montana or somewhere. His sister—you remember Patty, don't you?" When Bliss shook her head, Katie waved her hand as if to dismiss the girl. "She was a wild one and Mason felt like he had to take care of her after his mother died. Anyway, she moved in with Mason and Terri, and I suspect there was hell to pay. Then Terri miscarried and the marriage was in trouble. The baby was all they had in common, the only reason they had walked down the aisle."

"Miscarried?" Bliss repeated, jolted. "But Dee Dee . . ."

"Deanna. I know. She came along right after the miscarriage, I guess." Katie's face twisted thoughtfully. "I don't exactly know all the details, probably no one does, but I'm sure . . . Well, I think I've got the story pretty much straight." She took a long sip through her straw. "As I said, I really don't know Terri that well and Mason's pretty tight-lipped about everything concerning his private life. All I'm sure about is that the split wasn't amicable at all. They were separated for a couple of years and ended up getting a divorce. Terri, who hired some hotshot attorney from Portland, came out smelling like a rose."

"How's that?" Bliss asked, knowing she shouldn't be listening to such blatant gossip, but she couldn't help herself. When it came to Mason, she couldn't seem to learn enough. The thought rankled her. She detested women who were forever trying to find out more about certain men, but here she was, pumping her half-sister for information on the one guy she should forget about.

Katie swirled her drink with her straw, and shaved ice danced in the glass. "Because by that time Mason had done well for himself. He'd saved for years, bought a ranch in

Montana, discovered oil on the property and then started buying other places. He threw himself into his business as if he had something to prove. Worked twenty-hour days if you can believe the local gossip. Terri left the marriage a wealthy woman—well, wealthy by Bittersweet standards. I doubt if she'd cause much of a stir in New York or L.A." Katie tossed down her straw and gulped down the remainder of her drink.

"What about his sister?"

"Patty?" A dark cloud passed behind Katie's eyes. "Don't know," she admitted. "She has a place over near the river, but she's gone a lot. Very private person—kind of weird, I think. Never got over her mother's suicide." Frowning slightly, Katie glanced at her watch and found a way to change the subject. "I think we should talk to Tiffany."

"Now?" Bliss was stunned.

"No time like the present." Katie dropped a few dollars onto the table and pretended that she didn't hear Bliss's protests that she would pick up the tab. "Come on." Katie was already on her way to the door.

With trepidation as her companion, Bliss slung the strap of her purse over her shoulder. "Don't you think we should call her first? Give her some time to get used to the idea?"

"Probably." But Katie shouldered open the door and walked briskly toward her convertible. "Trust me, she won't be that shocked. I already introduced myself a couple of weeks ago."

"But—"

"Come on. You're not a coward."

"No, just cautious."

"Oh, I don't believe that one for a minute. No daughter of John Cawthorne's is cautious."

"Okay, okay." There seemed to be no talking Katie out of her half-baked plan, and Bliss reluctantly climbed into her half-sister's disreputable car. "You know, she might not be all that interested in meeting me."

"Never know until you try." Katie jammed the car into gear.

Bliss settled back in the seat and sighed. The truth of the matter was that she wanted to know more about her older half-sister, and if the truth were known, the fact that Tiffany was Mason's landlord only added to her interest.

"This could be the best thing that ever happened to you!" Katie took a corner a little too fast and Bliss slid in her seat.

Or, Bliss thought, *it might just be the worst.*

The air-conditioning was on the fritz and Mason's office was an oven. Even with the windows partially open, the room was stuffy and warm. Sweat collected around his collar and hairline, and he thought of dozens of reasons to take the rest of the day off. But he couldn't leave quite yet. Edie was in the outer office and, as the door between their rooms was ajar, he heard her humming to herself as her fingers flew over the keyboard of her computer.

"So I'm not sure where I'll be," Terri said over the phone. "Bob has a place up on Orcas Island and it's absolutely beautiful in the summer."

"Dee Dee needs a permanent home."

"So you've said."

"Terri, for once, think of her."

"Like I don't?" she replied, her voice elevating an octave. "Do I have to remind you that I've raised her almost single-handedly these past eight years?"

Here we go again. "No, Terri, but I've told you I'd like her to live with me."

She snorted. "Forget it, Mason, I'll let you know what I

decide. Remember, you've got her for a couple of hours tonight. I'll drop her off later."

"Wait a minute—"

Click.

"Terri? *Terri?*" But she'd hung up. "Damn it all to hell." He kicked at the wastebasket and sent it flying against the far wall.

"Are you all right?" Edie asked.

"Just fine," Mason growled as he slammed down the receiver and fought the urge to swear a blue streak. His head pounded and if he thought it would do any good, he'd drive over to Terri's place and— And what? Scream and yell? Beg and plead? Threaten? No way. The only thing Terri understood was money. Lots of it. He had to calm down and work this out with a cool head and an open checkbook.

Slowly counting to fifty, he stood and stretched his spine, balled and straightened his fists. His desk was cluttered and now, where the wastebasket had spilled, papers had spewed onto the floor. He picked up the can and retrieved the trash and vowed never to let that woman get to him again.

He'd spent the better part of the day going over profit-and-loss statements, dealing with attorneys and accountants, and wrestling with decisions about his business, his daughter, and, of course, Bliss. He'd foolishly thought he could forget her. Wrong. It seemed that with each passing day he was more obsessed with John Cawthorne's daughter.

Cawthorne. He was another headache in and of himself. A real head-case, that guy.

Resting a hip on the corner of his desk, Mason spied the deed to Cawthorne's ranch on top of one stack of papers. Brynnie had signed it, the thing was legal, all he had to do was record the transaction with the county.

Or sell it back to her.

Hell, what a mess.

He rounded the desk, found a bottle of Scotch in the cupboard by the window, unscrewed the cap and took one long, fiery swallow. As the liquor burned a welcome trail down his throat, he discovered that all of his anger with the old man had evaporated, and the vengeance he'd nurtured over the years—the need to prove himself to Bliss and her father—had faded with time. He didn't need Cawthorne Acres. Unfortunately what he did need, he realized with a sinking feeling, was Bliss.

"Get a grip, Lafferty," he chastised. She was still off-limits. Always would be. And he had other problems to deal with. If he wasn't going to settle down at the Cawthorne ranch, he needed a place big enough for himself, Dee Dee, and a housekeeper-nanny. *Or a wife.*

He took one more tug off the bottle, screwed on the cap and shoved it back where it belonged. A wife? No way. He'd tried that once before and look what a mess he'd gotten himself into. *Yeah, but you married the wrong woman. You knew it at the time.*

He folded the deed and slipped it into the inner pocket of his jacket just as the phone rang.

"Jarrod Smith, on line one," Edie called through the open door.

"Got it." Mason picked up the receiver. "Hey," he said, "what's up?"

"It's Patty." Jarrod's voice was grim, without any trace of humor whatsoever. "I think I've found her."

Chapter Ten

"I've got a bad feeling about this," Bliss thought aloud, but Katie, determined that the sisters should meet, was threading the car into the slow stream of traffic that ran through Bittersweet. "You know I already met Tiffany once."

"I heard. Mom said Octavia told her about it."

"Tiffany never said a word about who she was or that we were sisters or anything."

"She was probably shocked."

"Beyond shocked. Way beyond," Bliss said, remembering the horrified look in her half-sister's eyes when she'd mentioned who she was.

"Well, she should have said something, but didn't. We'll give her a second chance." Katie gunned through a yellow light, then eased up on the throttle as they passed hundred-year-old churches with spires and bell towers and wound down tree-lined streets flanked by stately old manors.

"She's Mason's landlady," Bliss ventured.

"Mmm." Katie sent her a sidelong glance. "Thought you didn't care about him."

"I don't, much."

Katie didn't say a word, but looked as if she were swallowing an I-knew-it-all-along smile.

Bliss's stomach tightened as Katie turned the corner to

the street where both Tiffany and Mason lived. She told herself that her paranoia was ridiculous as Katie parked at the curb in front of the ornate Victorian house.

Bliss steeled herself for her meeting with her other half-sister. A sprinkler sprayed jets of water over the parched lawn and a black cat sunned itself on the pavement of the driveway near a basketball hoop. Bliss didn't know what to expect. It had been over a week since she'd stopped by looking for Mason and had inadvertently introduced herself to Tiffany, and in that time she hadn't heard a word from her. At Katie's swift pace she walked up the brick path to the porch. Once at the front door, there wasn't any time for second guesses. Katie pressed the button for the bell.

The door opened and Bliss stood face-to-face with her older sister again. Tiffany Nesbitt Santini looked no more like her than Katie did.

Chin-length black hair framed a heart-shaped face. Eyes, a soft brown, were surrounded by thick lashes and tanned skin stretched tautly over high, sculpted cheekbones. Her mouth was wide, full-lipped and set in a tentative smile.

"Katie," she said, shifting her curious gaze to the petite redhead. The smile faded a little.

"Hi." Katie seemed suddenly nervous.

"And Bliss." Tiffany's grin disappeared. "I wondered when you'd figure it out and be back."

Bliss's heart did a nosedive. Any warmth in Tiffany's eyes had disappeared and there was a slight stiffening of her backbone. "I thought we should meet."

"We did," Tiffany replied.

"No. You met me. You didn't give me your name."

"You didn't bother to ask."

"I know, I didn't think of it."

"Because you were anxious to find your 'friend' Mason."

Boy, this woman had a wicked tongue. Bliss gave herself a swift mental kick for agreeing to Katie's screwball plan. The least they could have done was given Tiffany the courtesy of a telephone call.

"Can we come in?" Katie acted as if she didn't sense any of the nuances of the conversation, as if she didn't feel the tension simmering between her half-sisters. But it was there, evident in Tiffany's cool stare and frosty demeanor.

"If it's not too much trouble," Bliss added, half hoping she'd refuse them and this ordeal would be over. So Tiffany didn't like her. Big deal.

"Sure. Why not?" Tiffany's voice had all the warmth of the inside of an igloo.

A million reasons why not, Bliss thought, but pressed on.

Guardedly, the eldest of John Cawthorne's three daughters stepped out of the doorway and allowed them both to pass. Katie, as if she knew the place, took a right into an old parlor with gleaming hardwood floors covered partially by a floral-print carpet and wing chairs. A small camelback sofa was set in front of a marble fireplace and cushions covered the bench seats of two bay windows.

"I didn't expect company," Tiffany explained.

"Mommy? Who is it?" a small voice called from the second floor.

"Ms. Kinkaid—you don't know her, honey. She's here with a . . . a friend."

A flurry of footsteps heralded the entrance of Christina. Her eyes were wide like her mother's and her black hair shone nearly blue as she careened into the room. Tiffany's harsh countenance softened a bit. "I think you've both met my daughter."

The smiling cherub flung herself into her mother's waiting arms, but she eyed Bliss with unveiled suspicion, much as her mother did.

"Well, uh, wow, this is awkward, isn't it? Where are my manners? Please"—Tiffany waved toward the chairs—"have a seat. Can I . . . offer you something to drink?"

"Naw. We just had a soda downtown," Katie said as Tiffany set Christina onto the floor and the little girl barreled out of the room. The sound of small footsteps scurrying up the stairs reached Bliss's ears. Katie made an idle gesture with one hand. "I thought it was time we all got together."

"I've been thinking about it, too," Tiffany admitted, her cheeks flushing slightly. She fiddled with the chain on her watch. "I know I should have said something the other day when you, Bliss, came looking for Mason, but . . . well, you took me by surprise and I didn't know what to say. Then, as the days passed, I decided I didn't have to do anything until I was ready."

"Or someone forced your hand," Katie said with a shrug.

Tiffany nodded and splayed her fingers in front of her. "Look, I believe in telling it like it is, so to speak, and I've got to tell you straight-out that I don't like what's happening."

"You're not the only one." Bliss was so uncomfortable, she wanted to climb out of her skin and disappear. Instead, she sat on one of the cushions in the window seat overlooking a side yard filled with heavy-blossomed roses and a rusting swing set.

Katie plopped onto the couch. "Have you made any decisions yet?" she asked Tiffany as she ran a finger around the stitching on one arm. "About the wedding? You know that Dad—or John, or whatever it is I'm supposed to call him—really wants you to come to the ceremony."

"I got the invitation. And he called. But I don't think so. You know, just because he's had a change of heart, or some kind of personal epiphany or whatever it is, I can't just forget all the years that I didn't know of him." She wasn't smiling and looked as if her mind was cast in concrete. Bliss suspected that no one pushed Tiffany Santini around.

Katie was just as stubborn. "I can't make up your mind for you, but—"

"No buts about it. I'm not going. And you're right—you can't make up my mind for me."

Amen, Bliss thought, but Katie, forever the steamroller, plunged forward. "Don't you think it would be a good idea if we all tried, if possible, to bury the hatchet, so to speak?"

Tiffany lifted an already-arched brow. "Why?"

"Family unity. Solidarity. All that stuff."

Bliss's stomach clenched.

"Solidarity," Tiffany repeated with a little cough. "*Family* unity. That's rich." With determination flashing in her dark eyes, she settled onto the ottoman of one of the overstuffed chairs. "Let's understand each other. You want to go, Katie, because, after all, your mother and father are finally getting married. And Bliss"—she turned those wary eyes in her middle sister's direction—"it makes sense for you."

"But not you?" Bliss asked, trying not to appear as nervous as she felt.

"No, not me, and I don't think I really have to explain myself."

"Why don't you try," Katie suggested.

A flash of anger flitted through the eldest's eyes. "Okay, if that's what you want. It's been hard for me, okay? And all this nearly killed Mom. She lied at first, told me my dad was dead. I guess that way she thought I wouldn't feel so abnormal, but the truth of the matter was that I was born illegitimate, unwanted by a father who preferred another woman over my mother."

"No!" Bliss gasped. "Dad didn't know Mom until after—"

"Doesn't matter." Tiffany held out her hands to cut off Bliss's protest. "Katie asked and I just answered truthfully. I think there've been enough lies as it is."

Bliss gulped. It was time to leave. Past time. Obviously, Tiffany didn't have any of Katie's need for family unity.

But Tiffany wasn't finished. "I know what the local story is. My grandmother filled me in. It goes something like my mother didn't love John Cawthorne, didn't want to marry him. Nor did he want her. I was the result of a fling." She rolled her eyes and shook her head. "Anyway, for all my mom's tough words, I learned later from my grandmother that it about killed her when he married a rich woman from San Francisco, a woman of breeding, so to speak, and then you came along and were treated like a princess."

Heat soared up Bliss's cheeks and for a second, hot tears touched the back of her eyelids.

"I wasn't going to say anything," Tiffany added, as if she could see the pain ripping through her half-sister. "But you two asked. The way I see it is that my mother struggled to raise me, and she taught me never to depend upon a man—any man. She never married, refused to even date much, and was of the opinion that most men were rats or even worse. When things got tight, there was Grandma to depend upon."

"Aunt Octavia," Katie clarified. "She's not everyone's aunt but everyone calls her that, and she is Tiffany's grandmother."

"Yep, and she somehow helped keep my mother sane, I swear, during those . . . well, the rough years."

Bliss rubbed her sweating palms on her pants. "You mean when Dad married Mother?"

"Yeah. But I thought it was because my dad had died." Tiffany nodded and plucked at the fringe on the cushion of the ottoman. "Anyway, she got over it—at least I thought she did. Then, when I married Philip, she nearly didn't come to the wedding. He was older, and Mom was certain he was a father figure to me, the only father I'd ever known. She read all sorts of self-help books and told me that I was mixing up love and security and— Oh, well, it doesn't matter. I'm sure you didn't come here to hear my life story, so put away the violins and handkerchiefs. I'm not really bitter, just not interested in the prospect of dealing with a dad I've never known."

"But you live in the same town as him. It seems silly to ignore your own father." Katie was nothing if not dogged.

"Let's get one thing straight," Tiffany retorted. "He never was my father. It takes more than getting someone pregnant to earn that title." She glanced out the window, then added, "Maybe that's a selfish way to look at it, but too bad. As for John Cawthorne's wedding—what's that all about? Brynnie's said those supposedly sacred words more times than anyone should. I think they should run off and elope. Have some kind of reception when they get back." Hearing herself, she rolled her eyes. "Like I care."

"You might more than you want to admit," Katie ventured.

Before Tiffany could answer, the front door flew open. Thud! The doorknob banged hard against the wall.

"Stephen?" Tiffany was on her feet in an instant.

"Yeah?" a voice cracked, and in the foyer a boy in his early teens appeared. His hair was black and shaggy, his brown eyes filled with distrust. Every visible muscle appeared tense, as if he expected to make a run for it at any moment. He would be handsome in a few years, Bliss supposed, when his jaw had become more defined and his face had caught up with his nose.

"I think you'd better meet someone," Tiffany said, taking his tense arm and propelling him into the parlor. "This is Bliss Cawthorne. John's daughter."

His eyes narrowed. "Another one? Cawthorne? You mean 'the princess'—"

"Actually, she's my half-sister," Tiffany said quickly, as if to cut off whatever derogatory comment he was about to make. "She's lived in Seattle with John and his wife."

The princess. The second time she'd heard it in a few minutes. So that was what they'd called her behind her back, what they really thought. Why had she so stupidly agreed to come here? Because Katie had practically shanghaied her, that was why.

Stephen's gaze was positively condemning. "Oh." He didn't say anything for a few long seconds, but Bliss was instantly embarrassed that she was the legitimate daughter, the one who bore her father's name, the odd woman out, so to speak. "Well, aren't you the lucky one?" he finally whispered, sarcasm lacing his words. "What do you want from—"

"Don't, okay? Just don't say it," Tiffany warned.

Tossing a hank of black hair out of his eyes, Stephen shifted from one dirty sneaker to the other. "So, can I go now?"

"*May* I, but sure."

Bliss could almost feel the boy's relief.

Tiffany let go of his arm. As he bounded up the stairs two at a time, he didn't give his mother or her guests so much as a backward glance.

"I think it's time I got back," Bliss said, standing. She saw a movement through the window and spied Dee Dee, Mason's daughter, sitting in a patio chair. Wearing cutoff jeans and a sleeveless T-shirt, she lazed, one foot resting on the opposite bare knee as she flipped through a magazine and petted a black cat that was curled up in her lap.

The girl seemed pensive and slightly sad, Bliss thought.

Glancing at her watch, Katie scowled, tiny lines forming across her forehead. "Oops. You're right. I've got to scoot and pick up Josh from his friend's house so that I can get him to baseball practice. Well, uh, gee, I really don't know what to say, except maybe thanks for letting us come by and bend your ear," she said to Tiffany.

"No problem." Tiffany walked to the door, but didn't ask them to return as they stepped onto the porch. "And just for the record, tell *your* father that if he wants to talk to me, he can call himself, or stop by—not that I have any interest in dealing with him. But I think it was underhanded to send you two."

"It wasn't his idea," Katie assured her. "It was mine."

Tiffany didn't reply, just arched a disbelieving brow as she closed the door.

"Boy, that was a good idea," Bliss mocked.

"What do you mean? I think it went well, all things considered." Together, Katie and Bliss walked beneath the shade trees and around the corner of the main house, where Bliss caught another glimpse of Mason's daughter.

"Are you kidding?" Bliss couldn't believe her ears and decided right then and there that Katie Kinkaid was an eternal and somewhat-myopic optimist.

"I suspect that deep down she likes you," Katie added.

"Oh, right."

"I mean it."

"Then I'd hate to see how she treats an enemy."

"Don't worry about it." Katie slid a pair of sunglasses onto her short nose. "If there is a problem, and, for the record I don't think there is, you'll win her over. It'll just take time." She opened the car door, but Bliss hesitated.

"Just give me a second, okay?"

"What for?" Katie glanced at her watch.

"I'll only take a minute." Bliss was already heading along a path winding through a rose garden and arbor. Butterflies and bees flitted in the air as she turned from the side of the house to the backyard where Dee Dee was still perusing a slick teen magazine.

"Hi," Bliss ventured, not sure why she wanted to connect with this kid, but knowing deep down that it was important.

Dee Dee looked up, but didn't smile. "Oh. Hi."

"Saw you out here reading and thought I'd see what you were up to."

"Waitin' for my dad."

"He's not here?"

"Naw." She shrugged as if she didn't have a care in the world, but a shadow of worry slid through her eyes and

Bliss suspected Deanna Lafferty was used to hiding her feelings. "Mom just dropped me off."

"Is he expecting you?"

Again a lift of one shoulder. "Who knows?"

"Can you get into the house?"

"Tiffany will let me in." She chewed on her lower lip and looked at the main house. "It's okay."

"You're sure?"

Her expression changed and Bliss read "Yeah, and what's it to you?" in the set of her jaw. Great, she was making friends left and right today. "I'm fine, okay?"

"Sure. See ya around." With a wave, Bliss was off and she caught a glimpse of Tiffany at the kitchen window. The pane was open and Tiffany seemed to be washing dishes or something, but Bliss guessed she'd heard the entire exchange. Good. At least Dee Dee had an adult to keep an eye on her.

"What was that all about?" Katie asked, once Bliss had settled into the passenger seat of her car.

"Just checking."

"On Mason or his daughter?"

"Dee Dee seemed unhappy."

"Don't blame her. Terri's talking about pulling up stakes again, this time to Chicago, and Dee Dee doesn't want to be so far from her dad."

"But Mason just moved here."

"I know." Katie edged into traffic. "That might be the reason. Terri might not want to be so close to her ex."

"But it would be best for their daughter to be close to both parents."

"I'm not judging. Just telling you what could be happening." Once outside the town limits, Katie lead-footed it, leaving Bittersweet in a trail of dust. She fiddled with the dial on the radio, came up with an oldies station that was playing "Ruby Tuesday" by the Rolling Stones, and while

Mick Jagger sang through the speakers, she drove like a maniac past the fields and hills that led back to the ranch. Exhaust spewed from the tailpipe and the wind streamed through Bliss's hair, but she barely noticed.

Her mind was on Mason's doe-eyed daughter, and she felt a twinge of remorse that she'd ever been jealous of the sad girl.

"You know," Katie said, oblivious to the turn of Bliss's thoughts. "Tiffany's got her own set of problems, what with J.D. Santini and all."

"Her . . . brother-in-law, right?"

"One and the same. Kind of a cross between James Dean and the Marquis de Sade, if you ask me."

"That bad?"

"Well, not really, I suppose. Good-looking, sexy, with an attitude that won't quit. He's not cruel, I don't think, but he's certainly a thorn in Tiffany's side. Ever since her husband, who was quite a bit older, died, he's been calling giving Tiffany advice on how to raise the two kids."

"I'll bet she likes that," Bliss replied with only a trace of derision.

"Not a whole lot, no."

"I don't think she'll be coming to the wedding," Bliss said.

"Uh-oh." Katie eased up on the throttle when she spied a sheriff's cruiser speeding in the opposite direction. She checked the rearview mirror to make sure the deputy hadn't decided to make a quick U-turn and tail her. "Oh, she'll come, all right. I know she appears kind of stuffy and reserved when you first meet her, but trust me, she'll warm up to you, and if nothing else, curiosity will entice her to the ceremony."

"I don't know." Bliss wasn't convinced. She wasn't even sure about Katie's feelings. "Tiffany seemed to resent me."

"Of course she does, but she'll get over it. I already told you I think she's gonna like you, but give it a little time, will ya? Remember, Bliss, you're the one kid our father claimed. You grew up privileged, while Tiffany and I had to scrape by. Now, it never really bothered me because I didn't know that John was my father until a little while ago and we had a big happy, if poor, family, but Tiff, she's lived with a real downer of a mother who lied to her, and it sounds like now that she knows the truth, her mom's made no big deal that she's still bitter about it. Never married. Wouldn't take a dime of support from John."

"How do you know this?" Bliss asked, as Katie cranked on the wheel and the convertible rolled into the driveway of the ranch.

"Mom."

"Brynnie knew?"

"She and John have always been close and I know that probably bothers you, but . . . well, there it is. . . ." Her voice faded as she stared through the bug-spattered windshield. "Uh-oh. What's going on?"

Bliss had been looking at her half-sister but as she turned she spied an ambulance, its lights still flashing starkly. Parked at an odd angle near the front door of the house, the white-and-orange emergency vehicle loomed before Bliss like a specter. Her heart nearly stopped. "Oh, God. It's . . . it's Dad!" she cried, her throat closing and fear congealing her insides. "He's had another heart attack!"

"You don't know anything of the sort—" But Katie stepped on the brakes. The convertible skidded to a stop only feet from the ambulance.

Bliss's heart turned to stone.

Paramedics were wheeling a gurney out of the house. Wheels rattled and creaked, and an ashen-faced John Cawthorne lay on the thin white mattress.

"Dad!" Bliss was out of the car in an instant.

Brynnie, sobbing hysterically, was following close behind the gurney and Oscar was yapping and bounding, confused by all the activity. Horses and cattle grazed lazily, unaffected by all the human drama, and a few of the ranch hands were standing around, grim-faced, their hands in their pockets, their cheeks bulging with chewing tobacco. From somewhere—probably the dash of the ambulance—a radio crackled and the entire scene seemed surreal. Bliss's legs felt like lead as she ran toward her father. Her heart was beating a dread-filled cadence and her eyes burned with tears she didn't dare shed.

"What happened? Is he all right? Where are you taking him?" she asked, surprised she wasn't shrieking.

"Slow down and stay out of the way." The shorter paramedic sliced her a look that brooked no argument. "We're taking him in to town, the medical center. If the doctors there think he needs more specific care, he'll be transported to the hospital in Medford."

The hospital. Mom had died in Seattle General. Dad had nearly lost his life, as well. "Oh, my God."

"He's gonna be all right," Katie predicted, but beneath her freckles her skin had turned the color of the sheets draping her father's thin body.

Let him be all right, Bliss silently prayed as she grabbed one of John's hands.

"Please, miss, stand aside," the round paramedic with thinning blond hair ordered. Bliss stepped back and let her father's fingers slide through her own.

"I'm his daughter," Bliss said.

"So am I," Katie added.

"Just stand back and let the men do their jobs." Mason was striding from the front porch. Bliss's gaze touched his and she saw fear in his eyes; fear and something else—something deeper and more personal. He looked so big, his shoulders so wide. His jaw was tense, his expression hard and determined.

"Oh, John, I'm so sorry, so damned sorry," Brynnie

wailed as she, still trying to pull on her sandals, followed the attendants. “Not now, dear God, not now!”

“Everyone give us some room!” The paramedics were loading the gurney into the back of the ambulance.

“It’s his heart, I just know it. He can’t breathe,” Brynnie said, her eyes and nose red.

No! This couldn’t be happening. Not after he’d survived the first attack. Bliss swallowed back tears. “I’m coming, too.”

Brynnie climbed inside and Bliss was about to do the same when Mason grabbed her arm. “You can ride with me.” She wanted to fight him, but didn’t. Right now she needed his strength. She didn’t kid herself that he cared about her, but it didn’t matter; not until this crisis had passed.

“What—what are you doing here?” she asked, but deep in her heart, she knew the answer. He’d come to see her father; there had been an argument. John Cawthorne had lost his cool and his already-weakened heart had quit working.

Sirens wailing, the ambulance took off.

“I can drive,” Katie offered, her face ashen as she glanced at her watch. “I just have time to pick up Josh and then we can—”

“Don’t worry about it, I’ll take her,” Mason interrupted.

Bliss was already on her way to his pickup. She couldn’t think, couldn’t believe that this was happening. First her mother’s painful death, then her father’s heart attack. Had he survived only to die a few months later? *Please, God, no. Not now!*

As she reached the door of Mason’s truck, she stopped, and the damning truth hit her as hard as a belly punch. She sagged against his rig and turned on him. “Don’t tell me, Lafferty. You’re the reason my dad’s had another attack.”

“I don’t know,” Mason admitted, his face grim as he hurried to his pickup. Mason opened the door for her, then slid behind the wheel. “I told you this place was too much for your father." He slammed his door shut and switched on the ignition.

"So you had to come by and badger him again." Fear and anger took hold of her tongue. "I don't know what it is with you, Mason, but you should leave him alone."

"Believe me, I am," he said, jamming the truck into gear.

"Oh, sure, and that's why you came out here to pick a fight with him."

"I didn't pick a fight, Bliss." He popped the clutch and the truck took off. "In fact, if you want to know the truth, I came out here to sell the place back to Brynnie for what she paid for it."

"What?"

"That's right," he said, slipping his aviator sunglasses onto his nose. "I'm out of this mess with your father. As far as I'm concerned he can do whatever he wants with his ranch. I don't want it."

Chapter Eleven

"Wait a minute. You don't want the ranch? After all this legal maneuvering and arguing and angst?" Bliss couldn't believe her ears. "Come on, Mason, what happened? You came out here to sell back Brynnie's share to her and what—my dad collapsed? Give me a break."

"Believe what you want to believe." His lips barely moved as he spoke.

The interior of the pickup was hot. Stuffy. Too close. Bliss cranked down the window and looked away from Mason's sharp-honed profile. She couldn't think about him and the last time they'd been together; not now, not when her father's life was in question. In the distance, the horrifying shriek of the ambulance's siren sliced across the arid fields.

Mason slid her a glance. His mouth was tight, his jaw hard, his knuckles white as he gripped the steering wheel.

She took a deep, calming breath. "Okay, okay, no more accusations," she said. Nervously Bliss stared through the dusty windshield. Her throat clogged and she couldn't help but wonder if at this very moment her father was fighting for his life or if, like her mother, he'd slipped away. She bit her lip and crossed her fingers. Surely she wouldn't lose him. Not now, she thought, echoing Brynnie's words. "Just tell me what happened."

"I thought we—you and I—needed to talk, so I stopped by, looking for you," he said. "I wanted to speak to you first before I offered John and Brynnie the place back. But you weren't around and Brynnie invited me in for a glass of iced tea. So I decided to wait.

"I was in the kitchen talking to her when John came in from working outside." He slid a glance in Bliss's direction. "I don't mean to scare you, but he didn't look all that great. He was red in the face and sweating like nobody's business. He took two steps into the house, saw me and stumbled. I caught hold of his arm and we both ended up on the floor." The corners of Mason's mouth turned down. "Your father lost consciousness. Brynnie dialed 911 and I tried and failed to revive him."

"Oh, God," she said, feeling tears burn behind her eyelids. As angry as she'd been with her dad, she loved him, didn't want to lose him. "I—I should have been there."

"There wasn't anything you could have done. John won't slow down—you know that as well as I do. He's not happy unless he's going twice the speed of sound."

"You don't think he's going to make it," she said, stunned.

"Don't give up." Mason placed a hand on her shoulder. "You know your dad. He's a fighter. He was still breathing, his heartbeat still strong when the paramedics arrived." He offered her the hint of a smile. "If anyone can beat this, it's your old man."

"I hope you're right," she whispered, wrapping her arms around herself. She stared out the open window and fought tears. It wasn't like her to cry, yet right now, knowing she might lose her only surviving parent, she wanted to break down completely and shake her fist and scream and tell the whole world that it wasn't fair.

Mason's hand was comforting and she wished there was time for him to fold her into his arms and tell her everything would be all right, that her father would live a robust life, that somehow she'd learn to accept John's bride as well as the half-sisters she hadn't known existed. And that, crazy though it seemed, they would all be one big happy family. Of course, it was a pipe dream.

"I, uh, saw Dee Dee today," she said, as much to break the silence as to keep her mind off her father.

"Today?"

"At Tiffany's."

He checked his watch. "Terri said she'd drop her off for a couple of hours, but it was supposed to be later this evening. Are you sure?" Concentration furrowed his brow as they reached the outskirts of town.

"Yes, I spoke with her."

"For the love of Mike, that woman!" His mouth flattened over his teeth. "Look, I'll drop you at the clinic, then check on Dee Dee, but I'll be back."

"Fine," she said, knowing that he had to look in on his child, but feeling disappointed nonetheless. All too quickly she was becoming dependent upon his strength.

At the clinic, Mason gunned the truck into a parking space near the ER entrance. Bliss was out of his pickup before it had completely stopped moving. "I'll be back," Mason promised, then drove off. Bliss nodded and straightened her shoulders. She'd get through this. Somehow. No matter what happened.

She strode through the automatic doors and found Brynnie, ashen-faced, wringing a shredded tissue in her hands. She was seated on the edge of one of the well-used plastic couches in the waiting area.

"How's Dad?" Bliss asked.

"I don't know anything," Brynnie responded as she dabbed at the corners of her eyes. Mascara ran down her cheeks despite her best efforts. "The paramedics seem to think it was just heatstroke, but the doctors are running tests anyway. Oh, Lordy, Bliss, I don't know what I'll do if I lose that man. I've loved him so long, and now . . . now that we finally have the chance to be together, he might . . ." She dissolved into tears, and Bliss, unable to resist, wrapped her arms around the older woman as Brynnie sobbed in earnest.

For all her faults, Brynnie did seem to love John Cawthorne, and Bliss had trouble disliking a woman who cared so deeply.

"I should never have sold part of the ranch to Mason. I thought it would help, but it backfired on me. John will never forgive me."

"Sure, he will. Mason says he'll sell it back to you."

"I know, I know, but I'm afraid it's too late. John will never trust me again."

"Shh. You don't know that."

"Where is Mason?"

"He had to check on Dee Dee, but he said he'll be back soon."

"He's a good man, Bliss. No matter what your father says."

"I know."

People came and went as the minutes ticked by. After nearly half an hour, Mason returned with his daughter in tow. She looked small and frail beside him; her eyes were wide, wary, and stared at Bliss as if she were some kind of oddity.

Mason guided his daughter to a chair by the windows where potted plants were growing in profusion and a rack of well-used magazines was propped against a post. After one last suspicious glance cast in Bliss's direction she dug into her oversize bag and drug out a thin paperback novel. Mason nodded at Bliss, but stayed near his young charge.

"What's taking so long?" Brynnie asked, gnawing on her lower lip.

"Don't worry. It always takes a while. Dad will be fine," Bliss assured the older woman, all the while wishing she could believe her own words and aware of Mason's gaze boring into her. "He wouldn't miss your wedding for the world."

Brynnie laughed despite her tears and blew her nose so loudly she woke a baby who was sleeping in his mother's arms in a nearby chair. The mother smoothed the baby's curls and softly hummed a lullaby to quiet the child who nestled even closer and sighed as his eyelids drooped again. Bliss looked away from the tender scene. Ever since returning to Bittersweet it seemed that everywhere she went she was faced with shining examples of motherhood and was constantly being reminded of her own childless state.

"I . . . I need a cigarette," Brynnie admitted and eyed the No Smoking sign with distaste. "You know, nowadays, they make you feel like a criminal just because you need a little hit of nicotine. Big deal."

"Well, this *is* a health-care facility."

"Yeah, I know. And I've tried to quit, but old habits die hard. Even the ones that will kill you." She laughed again, coughed a bit and patted the edge of a tissue against the corners of her eyes.

"Go ahead. I'll wait in here," Bliss said, relieved that Brynnie seemed to be calming a bit. "If there's any news I'll come find you."

"Promise?"

"Absolutely."

As Brynnie walked outside, Mason said a few words to Dee Dee, then crossed the room. He hitched his chin toward the windows and beyond, where Brynnie was rifling through her purse. "She's not so bad, now, is she?" he asked.

"Brynnie?" Bliss sighed as she watched Brynnie shake out a cigarette and light it with trembling hands. "No. I guess not. She loves Dad." Bliss bit her lower lip. "That much is obvious. And Mom is gone, but . . . I had this belief that marriage should last forever, that two people could be faithful for a lifetime, that . . . Oh, I don't know." She shook her head. Right now, nothing mattered except her father's health.

Mason rubbed his jaw. "I would never have guessed you for a romantic."

"I'm not a— Look, I just believe in commitment."

"Hard to come by these days."

She cringed inside because she knew he was telling the truth. "People just don't try hard enough."

He eyed her speculatively, but didn't say a word, and she suspected he thought her incredibly naive. So let him. She had her convictions.

The woman with the sleeping baby was called into one of the rooms. She disappeared for a few minutes, then returned not only with the infant, but also with a girl of about twelve with a cast that ran from her fingers to her shoulder on her right arm.

"Ms. Cawthorne?" a nurse paged.

"Just a minute."

"I'll wait out here with Dee Dee," Mason said.

Bliss waved to Brynnie, who took one last drag and stuffed her cigarette into the sand of an ash can filled with other used cigarettes. She hurried inside. "Come on, I think they're going to let us see Dad now," Bliss said, shepherding the older woman down a short hallway to a bed surrounded by hanging sheets.

Her father, pale and gaunt, eyes slightly sunken, lay staring at the ceiling. His thin hair was mussed, his expression grim and angry. "What the hell am I doin' here?" he demanded.

"You—you collapsed," Brynnie said, choking back tears. "Oh, baby, are you all right?" She nearly stumbled against the metal railing of the bed to reach for his hand.

Her fingers laced with his despite the IV dripping into the back of his wrist.

"I'll live," he grumbled, apparently not too happy about the prospect. "Seems that every time I wake up I'm in some damned hospital."

"A habit you'd better break," Bliss said.

Brynnie patted his arm tenderly. "I talked to Mason and he's made me an offer to buy back the ranch and, oh, John, if that's what will make you happy, I'll do it. I—I had no business trying to tell you what to do or make you do what I wanted even if it was for your own good. It was stupid of me to sell out. Stupid, stupid, stupid!"

"We'll see," John said with a sigh. He looked as if he'd given up on life, and a little part of Bliss died. Too many times in the past her father's anger had taken hold of his tongue and he'd been rash, unreasonable and sometimes nearly cruel, but she'd love to see some of the old fight in him today. Instead, he looked old and beaten down.

"The paramedics were right," a doctor said as he pushed aside the curtain. "Heatstroke." The name tag on his white coat identified him as Dr. James Ferris. He eyed John's chart. "Has anyone suggested to this guy that he should slow down?"

"Bah!"

"Only his cardiologist," Bliss interjected and was rewarded with a warning glare from her father. "And a few other doctors."

"So this is a hearing problem, eh?" the doctor joked as he picked up his patient's chart and made a note.

"Listening problem," Bliss corrected.

"I hope you're having fun at my expense," John retorted grumpily. "Now, when can I get out of here?"

"Tomorrow, if you're lucky." The doctor clicked his

pen and jammed it into his pocket. "I still want to run a few tests and talk to your doctors in Seattle."

"What do they know?" John complained.

"You listen to them." Brynnie's lips were compressed with new determination. "I'm not about to become your widow before I get to be your bride."

"Hogwash. I'm not dying."

"Not yet," the doctor said. "And probably not for a while. But I want you to stay overnight for observation."

"Doesn't seem like I have much choice in the matter."

"You don't," Bliss said, straightening one of the crisp sheets covering her father's thin body. He'd always been such a robust, strapping man, but now he seemed frail.

"I'll stay with you," Brynnie promised.

"He's going to be moved to a private room. We've only got a couple here, but one's empty and I can't see sending him to the hospital in Medford. The room's on the other side of the admitting desk and down a short hallway. Room three. You can wait for him there if you want to."

"Oh, go on. Go home." John grimaced as he shifted on the bed and Bliss was reminded that he was a terrible patient, hated being sick or laid up, had no tolerance for anyone who tried to wait on him. But at least she caught a glimpse of the man he used to be, the man who'd spent his life giving orders rather than receiving them. Good luck to the nurses who had the night shift.

"I will in a minute," Bliss said, patting her father on the shoulder.

Brynnie didn't budge. "I'm sticking around. You couldn't get rid of me if you tried, John Cawthorne." A heavy-set nurse had to walk around her to check Bliss's father's blood pressure, temperature and IV drip. Brynnie glanced up at Bliss. "You run along, now. I'll take care of your dad."

"I don't need anyone taking care of me."

"See, he's getting better already." Brynnie winked at Bliss. "I think someone's waiting for you."

"Who?" John demanded. "Oh, for the love of Mike, don't tell me that Lafferty's here!" Color boiled up his neck and cheeks.

"Oh, calm down, or I'll call that doctor and have him admit you for the rest of the week," Brynnie warned.

"I'll see you later, Dad." Bliss brushed a kiss against her father's temple and he patted her hand.

"You're a good kid."

"Remember that when I insist you follow doctor's orders." Feeling as if an incredible weight had been taken off her shoulders, she hurried to the waiting area where Mason had taken a seat and was involved in an argument with a preteen boy who sat stubbornly next to Katie. Dee Dee was still in her chair, legs crossed, pretending to be absorbed in her book, though her eyes peered over the tops of the pages as she watched her father.

"You have to show some respect, Josh. Not only for your mom, here, but other people as well."

Josh—Katie's son, Bliss assumed—was pouting and at Mason's crisp words his lower lip protruded another half inch.

Katie saw Bliss and was on her feet in an instant. "How's John?" she asked, her face a mask of worry.

"He'll be fine. Heatstroke." Bliss filled them in on the details and Josh dug at the carpet with the toe of his worn sneaker. Katie introduced her reticent son, then pummeled Bliss with questions while Mason, arms crossed in front of his chest, expression dark and serious, listened intently to every word she said. There was a part of him she didn't know, couldn't understand, a mystery that she hadn't unraveled. Would she ever? she wondered and found herself staring at the hard slant of his jaw and the thin seam of his mouth. Did he care for her as she had begun to care for him? Or was his interest solely because of the ranch and this need she sensed in him—a need to outdo the man who had fired him years before? How much of John Cawthorne's speculation—that Mason was only using her as a way to get to her father—was true?

He was offering to sell his portion of the ranch back, wasn't he? How bad could he really be?

"Well, I'm going to see him as soon as he's in his own room," Katie said, ignoring any advice to the contrary.

"Ah, Mom," the boy whined.

"You, too, kid. He's your grandfather."

"Yeah, right. Since when? A few weeks ago? Big deal." Josh tossed a wayward lock of hair from his eyes and scowled as if the world had wronged him.

"It is," Katie insisted.

"Yeah, so where was he before? Huh? He knew you were his kid and he just looked the other way." Josh rolled his eyes expressively. "Real great guy."

"All that's changed."

"Come on, there's nothing more we can do. Let's get out of here," Mason said. "Dee Dee, are you ready?"

She looked up and her lips pursed for just a second. "Sure." Then, as if sensing her father's disapproval, she tossed her book into her bag and was on her feet.

"I'll take you both to dinner," Mason announced.

"You don't have to," Bliss protested.

"I *want* to."

"I'm not hungry." Dee Dee fidgeted with the strap of her bag. She glanced at Josh and rolled her eyes. "Besides, Mom said she'd be back by now."

Mason's jaw clenched. "I know, but she was supposed to—"

"Wait a second," Katie, ever vigilant, interrupted. "Why

doesn't Dee Dee come over to our place for a while? Josh and his friend Laddy just finished building a tree house and the neighbors have a litter of eight puppies. I'll call Terri and square it with her."

Dee Dee's eyes lit up. "Puppies? Oh, Dad, could I?"

"I don't know—"

"Please, Daddy," Dee Dee begged, and Bliss watched as Mason's heart melted.

"Don't you have plans later with your mom?" Mason asked.

"Mom and Bob." Dee Dee's nose wrinkled at the thought.

"Don't worry. As I said, I'll give Terri a call on my cell," Katie said, zipping open her purse and scrounging for her phone. "She can either pick her up at my place or I'll run her home. It's no big deal."

Mason, it seemed, couldn't deny his daughter anything, and in a matter of minutes the change of plans was arranged and Dee Dee remained with Katie and Josh.

Nonetheless, Mason wasn't pleased as they left the hospital. "Damn that woman, why can't she make a plan and stick to it?" he muttered, then shot Bliss an apologetic glance. "Not your problem."

"I don't mind."

He ran stiff, frustrated fingers through his hair. "Terri's talking about moving again," he admitted, once they were walking across the parking lot. Heat shimmered in waves from the hot asphalt and the air was still even though it was late afternoon.

"Where?"

"The San Juan Islands, I think, or Chicago. It depends on Bob." He slid his aviator glasses onto the bridge of his nose and she couldn't see his eyes, but his entire demeanor had stiffened.

"Bob is—"

"Her fiancé or live-in or whatever you want to call it. He's older, has kids my age and . . . Oh, hell, I don't like the situation. I moved down here to be close to Dee Dee, have a little more influence in her life, and wouldn't you know, Terri's decided to take off again." He opened the door of the truck and helped Bliss inside. The vinyl seat was hot to the touch even though he'd left the windows cracked, and an angry yellow jacket was buzzing loudly, pounding its striped body against the windshield. Mason slid behind the steering wheel, swatted the bee out the open window, then twisted on the ignition.

Bliss glanced at the clinic and sighed.

Mason slid a glance her way as he eased through the parked vehicles. "Your dad will be okay, you know."

"How would I?" she asked.

Mason snorted. "John Cawthorne's too stubborn to give up the ghost that easily."

"You didn't see him after the heart attack in Seattle."

He couldn't argue. Didn't.

"It scared me."

"I didn't think anything scared you."

She let out a hard laugh. "If you only knew."

They drove back to the ranch in silence as the sun lowered over the western mountains. A tiny breeze kicked up and crickets began their twilight songs. Mason parked by the garage and walked her into the house. It was odd being alone with him here, in her father's home, and she suddenly felt tongue-tied and awkward.

The house was too close, too reminiscent of another time and place. She helped herself to two sodas and carried them outside to the back porch. Shadows lengthened across the lawn.

"What will you do if Terri does move again?" she

asked, unscrewing the top from a bottle of cola and handing it to him.

"Fight her, I suppose." He took the drink and rolled the bottle between his hands. "I can't follow her across the country, but I need to be close to Dee Dee. I made a mistake letting Terri take her away from me in the first place. I should have demanded that she stay in state. We lived in Montana then. . . ." He frowned and took a long swallow. "Doesn't matter. It's all water under the bridge. It wasn't my first mistake." His eyes found Bliss's. The back of her throat tightened, just as it always did when he looked at her so long and hard. "I've made a lot of them."

She fumbled with her bottle, but finally twisted off the cap. "We all have."

He leaned a shoulder against the post supporting the overhang of the porch. "My worst was losing you."

"Wh-what?" Her head snapped up and she nearly dropped her soda.

"You heard me." He smiled ruefully. "What do you think buying this place was all about?"

"I thought you wanted it to prove a point. With my dad. He fired you a long time ago, humiliated you, and you thought that by buying this place you could get back at him."

"That's part of it, I guess. But it wasn't really his land I was after. It was his daughter."

She froze, not certain she understood everything he was saying. "Look, what happened between us was a long time ago."

"Was it?" He took a long swallow from his drink and she watched his throat work.

"Yes."

"What about now?"

Oh, God. "Now?"

He set his drink on the porch rail, removed hers from her grip and placed her untouched bottle next to his. Then, standing only inches from her, he didn't touch her, didn't inch even the slightest bit closer, but said, "I want you, Bliss. As much as I ever have."

There it was. Hanging in the air between them. A statement so direct and frightening that Bliss didn't know what to say. She wanted to step away, to put some distance between herself and this man who knew just what to do to upset her world, but she didn't, and she held her ground, staring up at him and wishing he would take her into his arms and kiss her as she'd never been kissed before.

"You didn't," she finally said. "You . . . you had your chance and you left me."

"Wrong." His gaze centered on her lips. "I always wanted you, Bliss," he said, his voice so low it was barely a whisper. "I just didn't know how to go about it."

"You're lying," she accused, but saw the naked truth etched in his features, the pain of baring his soul.

"I wish it was different with us, but it isn't."

"That's how it has to be."

"No way."

She looked up at him, saw the passion stirring in his eyes and felt a trembling deep within her. The world seemed to shrink. Mingled fragrances of dry earth, bleached grass and blossoming Queen Anne's lace didn't diffuse the scents of leather, soap and aftershave that clung to him, nor did the coming twilight dim his blatant sexuality.

What was wrong with her? Why would she fall for his lines all over again? What kind of fool was she?

She only hoped that he would leave soon and she would be away from him and would no longer notice the hard angle of his jaw, the dark secrets in his eyes or the way his jeans hung so low on his hips.

He was, after all, just a man.

But the only man who had ever been able to turn her head around and get under her skin.

Well, that had happened years before; a lifetime ago, it seemed. This time around, she was older and hopefully wiser.

He reached forward and she thought—hoped—that he would pull her into his embrace. Instead, he brushed a lock of hair from her cheek. At the feel of his fingertip, she trembled. Quicksilver images of his body, naked and hard, glimmering with sweat as he'd made love to her, flitted through her mind.

"Take a ride with me," he suggested.

"A ride?"

"To Cougar Creek. Come on, Bliss. What have you got to lose?"

Just my heart. She swallowed hard. "Nothing."

Didn't he know how dangerous being alone together would be? Didn't he care?

"Good." He stuffed his hands into the back pockets of his jeans. "We can take us a thermos of coffee, or a bottle of wine."

"Could we?" she teased, warming to the idea.

His grin was infectious. "You know," he added, "I thought I recognized Lucifer in the south pasture. I suppose he's still a mean son of a gun."

"The meanest. Dad says Lucifer's still a handful but not as young or as full of the devil as he once was."

"None of us are."

She noticed a shadow chase through his eyes, as if he, too, was remembering the fleeting past they'd shared so many years before. Suddenly she was leery. Being alone with him was tantalizing, but oh, so perilous.

"I—I don't know. It's been a long day and—"

"Coward."

"I'm not—"

"So you still remember how to ride, city girl?" His voice was teasing, but deeper-sounding than usual.

The air between them grew thick. "I think I can manage."

"Good." His smile was positively evil. "Then what are we waiting for?"

Chapter Twelve

By the time she'd called the hospital to check on her father, perked a pot of coffee, poured it into a thermos and wrapped a few cookies in aluminum foil, the sun had settled behind the mountains and twilight had descended. The first few stars were winking in a lavender sky, and a half-moon hung lazily over the horizon.

Mason was waiting for her in the paddock near the stables. Two horses, Lucifer and Fire Cracker, who was snorting and pulling at her tether, were saddled and tied to the fence.

"It's, uh, getting late," Bliss said, and Mason slid her a knowing smile.

"Don't tell me you've become so much of a city slicker that you're afraid to be out past ten? No one's going to mug you out here, you know."

"I was thinking of the horses. In the dark, they could step in a rabbit hole or stumble or—"

"They're both more surefooted than either you or I," Mason said, opening the gate. He untied the animals, took the thermos, cup and foil package to tuck into one of the saddlebags. "Come on." Climbing astride Lucifer, Mason quickly pulled on the reins before the stallion tried to turn his head and take a nip out of Mason's leg. "No, you don't."

Mason chuckled and shook his head. "Still full of it, aren't you, boy?"

Bliss laughed as Lucifer rolled his blue eyes and tossed his head in frustration. "I don't know who I feel more sorry for. You or the horse."

"The horse, definitely. I'm going to show him who's boss."

"This I gotta see." Bliss's worries evaporated as they rode through a series of connecting paddocks and corrals, then took off through a huge field of yellow stubble. The horses loped easily over the rolling ground while grasshoppers and a covey of quail fluttered out of their path.

Bliss, despite her worries, felt suddenly lighthearted and free. All her concerns about her father's health, his upcoming marriage, her newfound sisters and mostly her volatile relationship with Mason, vanished in the clean air that tore at her hair and stole the breath from her lungs. Life was good, if complicated.

They rode through the pine trees and along a deer trail that wound upward to a craggy ridge overlooking the creek. A hawk soared high in the violet sky as stars winked and the moon cast the ground in shades of silver. Somewhere in the distance an owl hooted, only to be answered by a coyote whose cry was nearly drowned by the rush of water slicing through the canyon.

Mason climbed off Lucifer and the horse shook his great head, rattling the bit of his bridle. "This place hasn't changed much."

"No," Bliss admitted, as she slid to the ground. While the rest of the world had careened into the future in a mad rush of fax machines, telecommunications, computers, and cellular phones, out here the land was the same as it had been for centuries. Fewer wild creatures roamed the hills, and Native Americans no longer claimed this part of the world, but the geography itself seemed unmarred by civilization.

He poured coffee into the cup, handed it to her, then took his from the lid of the thermos. They sat in silence, steam rising from their drinks as they let the dark mantle of the night surround them.

"So tell me about Dee Dee," she said when the silence became uncomfortable and she found herself sliding glances at his profile. Damn, he was sexy. Crooked nose, high cheekbones, hard jaw, dark beard-shadow and heavy eyebrows over intense eyes gave his face character while his body was lean and muscular, rawhide-tough and strong.

"A great kid. Despite her parents."

"You must've done something right."

"I don't know what."

She sipped from her cup and the hot brew burned a path down her throat. Dear Lord, what was she doing here, alone with Mason beneath the stars, as a summer breeze played over the land?

He turned to face her and her heart kicked into a faster, more potent cadence. "So—so what happened between you and Terri?"

"Not much. That was the problem."

"Oh."

"Your old man convinced me that I should leave and marry her, that she was pregnant with my kid."

"Wasn't she?"

"Apparently not." His words were bitter and harsh.

"But Dee Dee—"

"Wasn't *the* baby. That one, I suspect, never existed."

"What?" Bliss was stunned.

"Oh, Terri claims she miscarried, and before I knew what hit me, she was pregnant again. I think she lied about the first pregnancy because she and I . . . Well, we weren't together much and then you came along. All of a sudden she turned up pregnant and then you nearly were killed in the accident. Your dad offered me money—more money than I'd ever had before—to disappear and do the 'right thing' by Terri, so I did. Then she 'loses' the baby. Before I can figure out if I should divorce her, she's pregnant again."

"With Dee Dee."

"Yep." He took a long swallow from the thermos lid. "And that pregnancy was one of the best things that ever happened to me." He lifted a shoulder. "But no matter how much you love your kid, if there're no feelings between you and the mother, then the marriage is doomed."

Bliss felt empty inside. All the years of envy and jealousy and misunderstanding were such a waste, such a horrid, painful waste. "If only I'd known," she said with a sigh. "No wonder there's so much bad blood between you and Dad."

"He never thought I was good enough for you," Mason said. "I was a poor kid who had to look out for his younger sister, a screwup who had no business being involved with his daughter, 'the princess.' The accident only proved him right."

"It didn't."

"In his mind, Bliss." He took another gulp of his coffee and tossed the dregs into the grass.

"Well, not in mine."

"Is that so?"

"Mmm." She caught the gleam in his eyes and her pulse jumped.

"Don't tell me you didn't regret getting involved with me."

"Okay," she teased, smiling. "I won't."

One side of his mouth lifted, revealing an off-center slash of white. "You're a maddening woman, Bliss Cawthorne."

"So I've been told."

He was suddenly serious. "You know, I never meant to hurt you."

"You didn't," she lied.

"I wish I could believe you." He leaned back on his elbows and stared at her. "If I could change things—"

"You wouldn't. You have a beautiful daughter, a successful business . . . What more could you want?"

"I already told you earlier."

"I want you, Bliss," he'd said. Not *I love you*. Not *I want to marry you*. It was more than she should have expected.

"I don't know," she said as the breeze ruffled her hair. She reached forward, spanning the small distance between them, and touched the back of his hand with her fingers. That one gesture was her undoing. The heat of his skin, the cords running along the back of his hand, caused her blood to ignite. She felt her pulse begin to throb, saw his gaze shift to the hollow of her throat.

With a groan, he moved closer. His fingers linked through hers and an intimate heat, like none other she'd ever felt, passed from his skin to hers.

Stop this, Bliss, while you still can. But it was too late. She was mesmerized by the depths of his eyes, the curve of his lips, the flare of his nostrils. He pulled her next to him and his mouth, wet and hard, found the pulse point in her neck.

No! No! No! a part of her screamed.

Yes, oh, yes! a deeper, more feminine part responded as Mason's fingers twined in her hair. His lips tasted and touched, pressing soft kisses along the column of her throat. "I've wanted you for so long," he whispered in a voice that was rough with need. "So damned long." His lips found hers again, and desire, new and hot, danced wantonly through her blood.

She couldn't think, could scarcely breathe as his hands lowered and he cupped both breasts in his rough hands. Bliss's heart nearly stopped as he buried his face in the cleft, and through the thin cotton of her blouse his breath fanned her skin.

Somewhere deep within her a wanting, warm and moist, began to awaken. A night bird sang a soft song and a breeze stirred the long grass and madrona leaves. Her head lolled back and passion, so long denied, awakened in a rush that stole the breath from her lungs.

"Bliss," he whispered against her throat before lifting his head and staring into her eyes again. Even in the darkness she saw streaks of brown in his golden gaze, witnessed his own apprehension before he lowered his head and kissed her full on the mouth.

She couldn't resist. Her blood pounded in her head and the touch and smell of him invaded her senses. His tongue flicked against her teeth, then delved farther. And yearning, like a silken cord, unwound deep in her core and spread throughout her body. She knew she should stop, that touching him, allowing his hands upon her body would only lead to disaster; but being with him was too seductive, and when he lifted her blouse from her jeans, she didn't stop him. Nor did she protest as one by one, the buttons were undone and her skin was exposed to the breath of the breeze. She felt the lapels part as the soft cotton slid over her shoulders and his fingertips traced the path of the fallen fabric.

"So beautiful," he murmured as he tugged on her bra strap and bared her breast to the pale light of the moon.

She could barely breathe and rational thought escaped into the night. The air was warm and silky, his touch forbidden and so, so wanted. He kissed the tip of her breast, watching as her nipple puckered willingly. Her spine curved as if pulled like a bowstring, and silently she offered herself to him.

His hand was rough and hard against her nipple, his fingers callused as he lifted her breast and brought it to his lips again. Slowly he laved the little bud, teasing and tasting, breathing fire over her wet skin.

A needy moan escaped her lips. Heat roiled deep between her legs. Desire swept through her blood and she was certain her heart, pounding so loudly it echoed against her ribs, would surely break. She couldn't give in to him, but had no will to stop his lovemaking. "Bliss—" he whispered across her nipple, and some final wall of resistance inside her crumbled. "Tell me to stop."

"I—I can't," she admitted.

For a second, he lifted his head. His jaw tightened and he stared straight into her eyes. She reached forward and unbuttoned the top fastening of his shirt. His teeth gritted and he grabbed hold of her wrist with fingers that felt like steel. "You're asking for trouble."

"I know." Her voice was low and husky. She slid another button through its hole.

"Listen to me—oh, for the love of—" He drew her into his arms and locked his mouth over hers as she pulled his shirt from his waistband and in one swift movement he discarded the unwanted clothing. Bliss's hands explored his body, the corded muscles of his shoulders, the mat of curling hair on his chest and the taut planes of his abdomen.

He let out a low, primeval sound when she touched his nipples with her fingers and his lips became more demanding. He reached for the waistband of her jeans, yanked hard enough that her button fly gave way in a series of pops and the denim slid easily over her hips and thighs.

"Bliss. Sweet, sweet Bliss," he whispered, lowering himself, kissing each of her breasts and the hollow between them, then moving lower to the flat of her abdomen where he circled his tongue slowly around her navel.

A spiral of heat and need wound through her insides as his tongue slid along her skin. "Mason, oh," she cried as his hot breath invaded the thin lace of her panties. She wriggled against him and he kissed the lace and the downy curls beneath it. "Please," she begged in a voice that was not her own. "Please, oh, oh, ooh!"

His tongue worked magic through the fragile barrier of lace and she closed her eyes, her entire body centered where he touched her. Desire throbbed between her legs. She moved against him, silently begging for more until at last he stripped her of that last shred of clothing and kissed her intimately.

The world seemed to collide with the stars. She gasped for breath and convulsed. She was on fire, needing more. Wanting only this one man. Her body, slick with sweat, convulsed again and again before he kicked off his jeans and parted her legs with his knees.

"We should stop—"

"No!" *Oh, God, please, no!*

"But I can't. Bliss . . . I can't—" He lifted her buttocks and thrust into her, hard and deep, breaking that fragile barrier she'd held on to for twenty-seven years.

She let out a cry of ecstasy and pain.

He quit moving, his eyes wide. "Lord, Bliss, you're a virgin!"

"Was," she said. "Was. Oh, Mason, please don't stop, don't ever stop." Her fingers pressed deep into his shoulders.

"But—"

"I want you," she said, opening her eyes and staring into his. "I've always wanted you."

"And I want you. Oh, darlin'—" He let out a groan of surrender and then began to move, slowly at first, then faster and harder as Bliss's pain vanished and she matched his tempo. Her heart thundered, her breathing came in short anxious gasps, her body arching up to his. His hands held tight to her buttocks, drawing her closer as the world swirled in a vision of light and color.

"Bliss . . . I . . ." His voice trailed off and she watched sweat run from his temples. Somewhere deep inside a dam broke and she jerked in a contraction of joy. With an ecstatic cry, he went still atop her just as her spirit soared to the heavens and the kaleidoscope of colors behind her eyes became a warm blaze of light.

I love you, she thought desperately, but bit her tongue before the hasty words could reach her lips. This was sex, nothing more. The loss of her virginity, yes, but still just a coupling of two people who were not in love.

Stupidly, tears burned behind her eyes because she'd always thought that when she gave herself to a man, it would be for the time-honored and glorious emotion called "love."

He cradled her face in his big hands and looked deep into her eyes. "Bliss . . . ?" He kissed her forehead and cheeks and must have tasted the salt of her tears. "Are you all right?"

"Perfect."

"Yes," he said with a reverence that touched her heart. "You are."

Oh, God, was he serious? "If you only knew."

"I do." Twirling a strand of her hair around his finger, he slid to the side of her and with one leg possessively pinning her against him, added, "What I didn't know was that you were still a virgin."

A stain of embarrassment washed up her neck in hot, humiliating waves.

"You should have told me."

"Oh, sure. At this age." She managed a thin smile, but didn't tease an answering grin from his lips. "It's probably some kind of world record or something."

He levered up on one elbow and stared down at her. "I doubt that we should call Guinness."

"Good. Then it doesn't matter."

"No?" Still he was skeptical and with one hand he reached forward and touched her nipple with one long finger.

"I think it was long past time to give it up," she said, clearing her throat.

"So why not earlier? And don't give me that line about not meeting the right man, 'cause I won't buy it."

"All right, maybe I just didn't trust anyone, okay?"

"But you do trust me." He didn't mask any of the skepticism in his words.

"As I said, it was time, don't you think?"

"That's your call, Bliss." With a wicked grin he pulled her into the crook of his shoulder. His breath stirred her hair as he spoke. "What I think is that we—well, make that I—should have been more careful. I didn't have . . . protection."

She stiffened and stared upward where leaves of low-hanging branches shifted in the moonlight. The smooth beauty of the moment was shattered. "Believe me, you don't have to worry about any disease from me."

"Nor me," he admitted. "I was tested last year. Twice. Since then I've been careful. Until now."

"Don't worry about it." She tried to pull away from him, but he held her fast.

"It's you I worry about," he said, as if he hated the words. "I didn't mean for this to happen."

"Neither did I, but there it is." She was near tears again. This should have been the happiest, most definitive moment of her life. Instead, she wanted to melt away. Already he regretted making love to her. "We're both adults. You didn't force me into doing anything I wasn't ready for." With renewed energy, she pulled away from him. "Let me go, Mason."

"I can't." He held her fast. "Why me, Bliss?"

"I told you it was time."

"It's more than that."

"Meaning what?" she demanded. "That I was waiting for you? Is that what you think?"

"I don't know what to think." he admitted, staring at her as if for the first time. "But you're over twenty-five and—"

"Don't remind me, okay?" she said jerkily. Yes, she'd been a virgin, and no, she didn't have a husband, or children, or any reason to think she would anytime soon, and though those things bothered her, she wasn't going to let them get her down. She was young, had a career, a life in Seattle. She didn't need Mason's pity.

No, only his love.

"Bliss, I didn't mean to imply—"

"Look, you don't have to say anything, okay?" She wrenched away from him and this time he let her go. Quickly, before she broke down altogether, she snatched up her clothes and dressed, sliding her legs into her panties and jeans, still feeling new and achingly feminine. As she buttoned her blouse, she whistled to her horse and Mason, still naked as the day he was born, grabbed hold of her hand.

"What the hell's going on?"

"Nothing," she lied.

"Bliss, I think we should talk."

"Maybe we should have talked more before we . . . we—"

"Made love?"

Oh, God. Her throat tightened and she blinked against a wash of tears. She couldn't face him, didn't want to cry like some fragile female, some spoiled *princess*, for heaven's sake! She had to get away, had to avoid saying something she would regret. "I—I have to go."

"You're running away," he accused.

"Like you did?" The minute the words were out, she regretted them. She saw the tensing of each of his muscles, the dark fury in his eyes. "Forget I said that. But don't accuse me, okay? Maybe I am running away. I don't know. But I need time, Mason, to think all this through."

"Ten years wasn't enough?"

She glanced up and stared into eyes as clear and amber as priceless Scotch. "I guess not." She pulled her hand away and though her heart was breaking, managed a sad smile. "Goodbye, Mason," she said, hating the finality of the words.

"It was good, but now it's over?" he asked, taunting her.

"It was good, but it never really began." She swung into the saddle and didn't look back. She couldn't. Because if she saw him again, all hard sinew, muscle and bone, his face chiseled and strong, she'd never be able to look away again. She loved him, that much was certain, and it was a cross she would bear for the rest of her life.

Chapter Thirteen

"You had to do it, didn't you?" Mason glared at his reflection in the steamy mirror, scraped away a swath of shaving cream and whiskers and mentally kicked himself for having made love to Bliss.

Though he'd had no conscious plan to seduce her, he hadn't been able to stop himself from spending more time with her, from seeing her, from suggesting the evening horseback ride to the ridge. Pursing his lips, he tried to avoid cutting himself as he finished shaving, then washed his face. He was standing naked in front of the mirror and had the fleeting thought that if Bliss were in the room, he probably should wear a towel wrapped around his waist, or his boxer shorts.

He stiffened just at the thought of her and ground out several oaths. What was he thinking? Why the devil would Bliss ever be in his bathroom in the morning? Just because they'd made love didn't mean that they ever would again, that they were having an affair, for the love of Pete, or that they might consider tying the knot.

As he threw on his clothes, his mind was running in wild, perilous circles. Just as it had all night. Throughout the long, dark hours, he'd been haunted by the image of Bliss's perfect face, the fragrance of her skin, the sound of her laughter. There had also been worries about Dee Dee and thoughts of another sort—memories of the years he'd struggled to prove to himself and the rest of the world that he was as good as anyone else, that the poor boy from the wrong side of the tracks could make good.

Except that he'd screwed up a few times. Seriously screwed up. There was the marriage that hadn't worked, a sister he'd promised to protect but who was constantly in trouble, a few bad deals and his daughter. His heart twisted at the thought of Dee Dee. So beautiful. So bright. So neglected. But no more. Dee Dee deserved security and a home. Here, with him. She couldn't be forever uprooted as Terri chased after this man or that dream. Nope. That part of his life he intended to settle today.

As for Patty, he hadn't yet spoken to her but Jarrod had assured him that she'd been located in Mexico and was flying home. If she knew anything about Isaac Wells's disappearance, she hadn't admitted to it. Mason would find out. One way or another. He'd promised his mother he'd take care of Patty and he'd do just that, though Patty would probably have none of it.

But Bliss Cawthorne was another matter altogether. What in the world was he going to do with her?

Bliss. The image of her face teased him again as he pocketed his keys and wallet. He should never have made love to her, never have taken that darkly seductive step, but he had, and in doing so he had expected that he might regret his desire but he didn't anticipate that he wouldn't get enough of her.

She was a virgin. Had never given herself to a man before.

Who would have guessed?

So what're you going to do about it?

There was, as he'd learned so often before, no going back. But he did have the ability to change a few things in his life.

He slipped into his shoes and flew down the stairs with more purpose than he'd felt ever since returning to Bittersweet. He had a few matters to take care of at the office, then he planned to have it out with Terri. Dee Dee wasn't going to the San Juan Islands or anywhere away from him. If he had to go back to court, he would. But Terri would probably be just as happy with a little cash instead. She'd always had a mercenary streak, even when it came to her daughter.

"I don't know," Terri said, rubbing her forehead as she sat at the kitchen table, which was covered with scraps of cloth as she pieced together a quilt. From her position at the table she could watch the television in the living room where a soap opera was in progress. Dee Dee was outside, lying on a chaise longue near the small pool of the apartment complex.

Leaning against the sink, Mason stared out the window and watched his daughter, sunglasses covering her eyes, reading another book.

Terri said, "I think I'd miss her too much."

"You'd see her at Christmas, in the summer and whenever else you wanted to. The way I see it, Dee Dee needs a home and some security," he said.

"Oh, like she'd get that from you?" Terri laughed and rolled her eyes. "Don't forget you're a workaholic, Mason, and you're always zipping from one place to another. If there's a problem with the ranch, you're back in Montana, or the spread in Wyoming. Now you think you'll settle down here."

"I will."

"Why?"

"Because it's time."

She skewered him with her wide eyes and shook her

head. She still looked young; that pixie quality had never left her despite the lines fanning from her eyes and creasing her forehead. "It's because of Bliss, isn't it?" she said, sadness heavy in her voice.

He didn't answer.

"I knew it. You never forgave me for lying to you about the baby, and you never got over her." She shook her head and sighed. "Oh, Mason, we were such fools." Opening a cupboard drawer, she withdrew a pack of cigarettes.

"I thought you quit."

"I did. Again. But every time I'm around you, I need a cigarette to relax." She lit up and blew a stream of smoke toward the ceiling. "I did love you, you know. A long time ago."

"You had a funny way of showing it."

"Yeah, well . . ." Sniffing loudly, she glanced into the living room. "We both made mistakes. I suppose you're getting married, right?"

"Don't know yet."

"Then how can you talk about security? For God's sake, who's gonna take care of Dee Dee when you're off on business?"

"She'll go with me or I'll have a live-in nanny."

"Or you'll marry Bliss Cawthorne."

"We haven't discussed it yet."

"You'd better talk it over with her old man, you know," Terri said. "And then you'd better come clean with Bliss. There are things she still doesn't know about that whole mess ten years ago. Oh, hell"—she jabbed out her cigarette—"what do I care? Bob wants to get married and move up north, you know that, and, well, he's not crazy about kids."

"Sounds like a great guy."

"At least he loves me, Mason. That's more than you

ever did. If you want to keep Dee Dee, okay, we'll try it out and—"

"No. We're not going to try it out. We're going to do it. No one changes his or her mind. I've already talked to my attorney and we'll make it legal. As I said, you'll see her whenever you like, but I'll have custody. And instead of the child support I've been paying you, you'll get a sizable lump sum."

She lifted a curious eyebrow. "How sizable?"

He had her and he knew it. Good. He reached for his checkbook. "Name your price, Terri. What's it worth to you?"

Bliss scooted back the chair at her desk. So she and Mason had finally made love. She chewed on the edge of her lip and thought, as she had since returning from the ridge, about the only man she'd ever cared for—ever loved. "Oh, you're the worst kind of fool," she told herself as she tossed down her pencil and ignored the plans for a remodel of a warehouse on the Seattle waterfront that had been sent to her and lay open on the desk in her father's den. Work, which usually interested her, held no appeal—not this morning when the sunlight was streaming off the mountains and sparkling in the dewy grass.

Last night she'd watched as Mason had returned, unsaddled and unbridled Lucifer. He hadn't so much as glanced at the house where she'd stood at a window. Instead he'd climbed into his truck and driven away, leaving her alone with her thoughts.

She didn't believe that he'd used her, wouldn't even consider her father's protests that Mason was only getting close to her to get back at him. No, the attraction that she and Mason felt for each other was deep enough to cross time barriers, strong enough to dim the past with all its pain.

So here she was, contemplating loving a man she'd sworn to avoid.

Every time the phone had rung she'd nearly jumped out of her skin, hoping that Mason had decided to call. Each time, she'd been disappointed. She hadn't heard a word from him all day, but then, she supposed, it was her turn to make a move in his direction. If that was what she wanted.

She heard a car in the drive and her heart did a quick little leap. Pulling the old curtains aside, she saw Katie's convertible approaching the house. Her hair was wild and free, her smile wide as she parked, and though Bliss was still thinking about Mason, she was glad for the distraction that her half-sister was sure to bring.

A few seconds later, Katie was ringing the bell on the front porch and Bliss threw open the door. A wave of heat rolled inside. "Come in," she said, before the younger woman had a chance to say a word.

"I just stopped by to let you know that John's being released, but Mom's insisting he stay with her in town. She wants him where she can keep her eye on him, and, really, I don't blame her."

"Neither do I," Bliss replied, still unsure exactly how she felt about this dynamo of a half-sister but willing to give her the benefit of the doubt. "Would you like something to drink or eat?"

"Yeah, a glass of water would be good, then I've got to look under the hood. My car acts like it's about to give up the ghost and it hasn't even reached two hundred thousand miles yet."

"Imagine that," Bliss said dryly.

She poured them each cups of water with ice, handed one to Katie, then followed the redhead outside where her bug-splattered car was resting in the shade of a spruce tree. Above their heads fragrant needles rustled in the hot breeze, and from the safety of a high branch a squirrel scolded

Oscar, who whined and barked and ran in circles at the base of the tree.

Katie popped the hood and while she bent over the engine, she talked. "Hold this a sec, would you?" She took a long swallow of water, then handed the cup back to Bliss. "You know, those brothers of mine would know exactly what's wrong, but where are they when you need them, huh? Around? No way. Probably somewhere raising hell. Oh." She lifted her head and offered Bliss a knowing glance. "They're really not as much trouble as all that. Even the twins with their reputations aren't bad guys—just, well, *irreverent* would be a good word to describe them." She turned back to the cooling engine, touched it delicately as the radiator gave out a warning hiss. "Too hot to do anything with right now," she said, blowing her bangs out of her eyes and accepting her glass of water again.

"I decided to drop by and fill you in because I have a few minutes while Mom and Josh pick up John." She scratched her head and frowned, her forehead puckering thoughtfully. "You know, I'd like to pretend that all this is okay and we could be one big happy family, that I was big enough to make nice-nice for Mom's sake, but the truth of the matter is, I'm not cool with everything that went on between them and though I want them both to be happy, I don't think I'll ever be able to call John 'Dad.'"

"I don't blame you." Bliss lifted a shoulder, as if she didn't care, but she was glad that Katie was having the same kind of mental dilemma that she did. The situation was beyond complicated.

"Mom wanted me to tell you that while John's recuperating at her house, you can come over any time."

Bliss wasn't sure about that. She still had more than her share of reservations where her father and Brynnie were concerned. "How long will he be there?"

"Well, that's the problem, isn't it?" Katie said nervously,

and Bliss suspected they were finally getting down to brass tacks—the real reason for her half-sister's visit. "You know that Mom sold her portion of this place to Mason, though no money changed hands—the deal hasn't closed yet. Now Mason's willing to sell it back to her or John or whoever, which is good, I guess. But the thing is that she did it in the first place behind John's back. Mom should have talked it over with your dad first, I think. I mean, they're getting married and all, so why the secrets? If you ask me, when two people decide to tie the knot they should be able to trust each other implicitly, be able to talk over everything. I mean *every* thing." She picked at a sliver in the fence rail while Bliss felt sweat collect between her shoulder blades. "Call me a dreamer, but that's what marriage means to me."

"I guess it means something different to everyone," Bliss said, remembering her parents' union and knowing now that it was based on lies and deception. She took a long swallow from her glass. "Sometimes I wonder if this wedding is ever going to come off." Her father and Brynnie's relationship seemed more tenuous as the days passed. *Oh, yeah? And what about your relationship, if that's what you'd call it, with Mason?*

Katie took a final swallow of water, tossed the melting cubes onto the grass and handed her glass to Bliss. "Look, I've got to run soon. Josh'll be home in half an hour." Her eyes darkened with a personal pain Bliss could only attribute to her son.

"You're worried about him."

"Him and a lot of things. But, yeah, he's at the top of the list. Raising a kid—especially a boy his age—alone isn't exactly a piece of cake."

"What about his father?"

Katie frowned. "Took off when I got pregnant. Haven't heard from him since. I decided I could raise my baby alone and I haven't really had to. Mom's always helped out." She studied the horizon, but Bliss suspected she wasn't observing the mountains or lowering sun, instead she was looking inward, to a private place only she could see. "I don't talk much about Josh's father. It's easier that way, although my curious son has been asking a lot of questions lately." She lifted a shoulder. "What about you? No kids, I know, but why haven't you ever married? And don't tell me you never met the right kind of guy, 'cause I won't believe it. With your looks, money and connections, my guess is that men—most of them potential 'right guys'—were flocking all over you."

"Maybe the right guy turned out to be the wrong one." Bliss eyed the cattle lumbering in the fields of the lower hills and tried not to let her thoughts turn toward Mason again. "Mom and Dad's marriage wasn't exactly picture perfect, but then you know that. Mom always wanted me to date—and I quote—'a strong, moral man with social standing, not some riffraff or rough-and-tumble cowboy like I did.'"

"Oh."

Bliss plucked a piece of dry grass from a clump near the fence post. "According to my mother, no one was good enough for me and I really wasn't interested."

"Because of Mason," Katie guessed shrewdly.

"What?"

"Hey, I've lived here all my life, heard the gossip, and it doesn't take a genius to put two and two together. You got involved with Mason and John gave him the old heave-ho about the time of your riding accident up on the ridge. Your dad blamed Mason for what happened." She glanced at Bliss, then continued. "Terri was pregnant, Mason married her, and you've never given your heart to another man, right?" Her green eyes were dark with unasked questions and Bliss found it increasingly impossible not to like Katie Kinkaid.

Pride inched Bliss's chin up a notch or two. She wanted to argue, but thought better of it. Wasn't Katie reaching out, talking to her, being the sister she'd never had? "Something like that," she admitted. There was more, a lot more, but some things were private and couldn't be shared, especially with a stranger who just happened to have turned out to be a half-sister.

"Well, good."

"Good?" Bliss couldn't believe her ears. For years, Margaret had paraded eligible suitors in front of her face, begging her to find someone to share her life with and get over whatever it was that had been eating at her—especially if it had to do with a certain cowboy John had told her about.

"Yeah. Good." Katie tossed her hair away from her face. "Now you and Mason can get together. He's divorced, you've never married and the rest can become, as they say, history."

"I think that's a little premature."

"Ten years is a long time."

Bliss bristled. "Listen, if anyone needs a man, it's you."

Katie's small jaw became granite. "Believe me, Bliss, no one ever *needs* a man, but sometimes it's nice to have one around. I'm doing just fine on my own."

"So am I."

"Well, I wouldn't pass Mason up, if I were you. He loves his kid and is a good man. Last night we had Dee Dee over, you know." She thought for a minute. "She's a good kid—a little on the quiet side—but then I'm used to Josh, who's more than outgoing. But I'd only been around Dee Dee a couple of times before, but I liked her. She made sense. It's too bad her folks don't see eye-to-eye."

"Mason's crazy about her."

Katie's smile was wistful. "I know, and Terri doesn't realize what a godsend that is. There are so many fathers who are deadbeats or more interested in themselves than their kids." She sighed, then shook off the wistfulness that had come over her. "Anyway, as I said, Mason's a catch, Bliss, and now that you're my sister I guess I have the right to give you some advice. Don't make the same mistake twice."

"I'll try not to," Bliss replied, a little unnerved at Katie's boldness. Sure, they were related by blood, but that didn't give her half-sister the right to try and run her life.

Katie dusted her palms together. "Time to tackle the car again." She walked back to the worn-out convertible and stuck her head under the still-open hood. Perplexed, she wiggled a few wires, then unscrewed the caps on the battery. "What I wouldn't give to have taken auto mechanics in high school. Damn." She replaced the caps and wiped her fingers on her jeans. With a sidelong glance at her half-sister, she said, "So you're out here all alone for the next few nights."

"I've got Oscar." At the sound of his name, the dog gave out a yip and wagged his tail, but his head was still craned upward as he focused on the squirrel.

"And Mason, if you want him."

Bliss stiffened. "Give me a break."

"Don't tell me he's not interested." Katie closed the hood with a loud clunk. "I may not have ever been married, but Mom's walked down the aisle enough for the two of us. I've seen love and maybe even been there once myself. You, Bliss, have got it bad, and so does Mason."

"You don't know—"

"Sure, I do. I've known Mason a long time. So have my brothers. He's in love with you, Bliss, whether you want to know it or not. Well, speak of the devil." A satisfied smile stole over her face.

Oscar gave a quick little bark as Mason's truck rolled into the drive.

Katie laughed as she walked toward the driver's side of her car and Bliss's pulse, though she was loath to admit it, skyrocketed. "Someone just proved my point."

Mason waved to Katie as she climbed into her rattletrap of a convertible and twisted on the ignition. The engine coughed twice before catching. Then Katie gunned it, and in a plume of blue smoke, the old car lumbered down the drive.

Bliss stood her ground and wished she knew what to say to this man who could turn her world upside down with one long, slow, life-altering kiss.

Mason felt a tightening in his gut at the sight of her. Dear Lord, Bliss Cawthorne was beautiful and seductive and sexy without even trying to be. As he braked, she smiled slightly, the wind catching in her sun-streaked hair. His heart stopped for a second that was destined to change his life forever. He didn't have a reason to be here, but all day long he'd thought of last evening and making love to her. The image of her blue eyes, dusky with desire, her lush lips and rosy-tipped white breasts had filtered through his mind time and time again.

"Well, Mr. Lafferty. I didn't expect to see you so soon."

"No?" Was she kidding? "I thought we needed to talk."

"I suppose," she agreed, though her eyes were bright with suspicions. She rolled one palm toward the heavens. "What do you want?"

"What do I want?" he repeated as he stared at her. *You. I want you, Bliss Cawthorne, and I always have. I wish things were different between us, and God, I wish I never had hurt you.* He crossed the span of the driveway and stood so close to her he saw the slight trembling of her lip and caught the light scent of her perfume. "There are lots of things, Bliss."

"Such as?"

"I wanted to see you again." He searched her eyes.

She swallowed hard and some of her false bravado slipped away. "Look, just because we made love doesn't mean you have some kind of responsibility, a duty to—"

"Is that what you think?"

"To tell you the truth, Mason, I don't know what to think."

He believed her. She'd never looked more confused in her life. Well, he intended to set one thing straight. Before she could back up a step, he gathered her into his arms and lowered his lips to meet hers. Her mouth was soft and supple and yielding, her body warm and inviting. With a groan, he held her fast, hands splaying over her back, his blood pumping through his veins.

Lifting his head he stared into eyes that reflected his own passion. "Now that we've settled my sense of 'duty,'" he said, running a thumb over her lower lip, "let's talk about us."

He felt her stiffen. "I thought I told you goodbye last night."

"You didn't mean it."

She lifted a teasing eyebrow. "Didn't I?"

It was all he could take. "No way, lady," he said and heard her gasp as he lifted her deftly off her feet and carried her into the house.

"Mason, stop! Let me down!" she cried as he marched determinedly down the short hallway to the bedroom where he'd first carried her bags years ago.

He dropped her onto the old double bed and as she landed, fell onto the sagging mattress with her.

"What do you think you're doing?" she demanded.

"Making love to you."

"What? No—" He cut off her protests with a kiss that started in his lips but touched him so deeply that his groin tightened and his erection, already at half-mast, stiffened in anticipation.

Her arms wound around his neck and she sighed contentedly into his mouth. "Why is it I can never say no to you?" she asked as she opened the buttons of his shirt.

"Because I'm so damned irresistible."

She laughed. "Oh, that's it," she said.

"Why else?" His breath fanned her ear and she couldn't think. His hand caressed her breast and she moaned. From that moment onward, she was lost.

He spent the night and it seemed natural to wake with his arms around her, his face buried in the crook of her neck. How many years had she dreamed of opening her eyes to see the sunlight caress the contours of his face? His beard had grown overnight and his eyelashes brushed the tops of his cheeks. In slumber there were no lines of worry disturbing the skin of his forehead, no creases of suspicion pulling at the corners of his mouth.

I love you, she thought, but didn't dare utter the words. This was an affair, nothing more; the culmination of years of old dreams. They weren't kids any longer, but adults with their own sets of problems; their own lives. He ran several ranches and a corporation or two, she was working on becoming a partner in the firm where she worked in Seattle. He had an ex-wife and a daughter; she had Oscar, who, by the sounds of the whining at the bedroom door, needed to go outside.

She threw on a robe, padded down the hallway and let Oscar out the front door. Delores, the cook and housemaid, had the week off, but a few of the ranch hands had already parked their trucks near the barn.

Out of habit she started the coffee and was unloading the dishwasher when she heard the shuffle of bare feet on the floor. She turned and found Mason, dressed only in his worn jeans, rubbing his jaw and glancing out the window. His hair, mussed and falling over his forehead, made him seem younger than his years and his broad shoulders were tanned. But she couldn't ignore the scar that ran around his upper arm, a reminder that his arm had nearly been torn from its socket as he'd tried to save her all those years ago.

"Good morning," she said as the coffeepot gurgled to life.

"It is, isn't it?" One side of his mouth lifted in a playful smile that she found absolutely endearing. She'd miss that smile as well as his lips upon her skin when she returned to Seattle.

"The best. Coffee'll be done in a second."

"Good."

"How about breakfast?"

"You get dressed and I'll buy."

"No reason," she countered. "I can cook."

"What d'ya know? Three languages, ballet, a B.A. in architecture *and* she can cook."

"That's a Masters in architecture," she reminded him as he walked up behind her, wrapped his arms around her waist and kissed the back of her neck.

"My kind of woman."

She laughed and felt him fiddle with the belt of her robe. "Hey, wait a minute—"

"Breakfast can wait," he growled against her ear as the robe parted and he lifted her from her feet.

As it was, breakfast was forgotten.

The fax machine whirred to life and Bliss waited, pushing aside the drawing she'd been working on. It had been four days since her father had been released from the hospital, and each night she'd spent with Mason. They'd talked of everything and nothing, but never once broached the subject that seemed forbidden to them. The future was off-limits. He was worried about his sister and his daughter; she was concerned about her father and the marriage that was once again "on." By the end of next week, Brynnie would officially be her stepmother.

And then what? Pack up Oscar and return to her life in Seattle?

Twiddling her pencil, she walked to the fax machine and read the memo from the office—another bid and a friendly note from one of the partners asking her when she planned to return.

"Never," she thought aloud, then caught herself. Because she wanted to stay here in this tiny town to be near her father? Or Mason? Or both?

Disgusted by the turn of her thoughts, she decided to drive over to Brynnie's to see John, but she'd barely made it out the front door when a brown station wagon pulled into the drive and parked between two of the pickups used by the hired hands.

Tiffany Santini climbed out of the car, glanced at a couple of the workers who were unloading hay into the barn and hurried to the front porch.

"Oh—did I come at a bad time?" she asked, seeing the car keys swinging from Bliss's fingers.

"No, come on in. I was going to visit Dad, but it can wait."

"He's not here? I thought he was released from the hospital."

"He was, but he's staying at Brynnie's for a little while. Come in." Bliss was glad for the distraction and the truth of the matter was that she was intrigued by her slightly uptight older half-sister. She didn't expect they'd become friends overnight, but at least they could get to know each other.

On the front porch, Tiffany said, "Look, I want to be honest with you. I heard that he was rushed to the hospital, that they thought it was his heart but it turned out that he'd gotten too much sun or something—and I didn't know what to do."

"It's hard."

"I thought the decent thing to do was to stop and see him and yet I didn't think he'd ever really done the decent thing by me or Mom, so . . . I waited. Anyway, here I am and I'm wondering what in the world I should say to you or to him." She rolled her large eyes.

"Well, come on in." Bliss held open the screen door. "I've got coffee or iced tea or—"

"This really isn't a social call," Tiffany snapped, then caught herself. A small line formed between her eyebrows. "I—I don't know what it is."

"Neither do I, but if we don't talk, we'll never find out, will we?" Bliss was wary of this woman and yet she was curious. There was, after all, the same Cawthorne blood running through their veins.

Tiffany hesitated for a second, then must have decided that leaving would look cowardly because she nodded stiffly and followed Bliss inside. Her dark brows rose as she entered the ranch house for the first time, Bliss guessed. "It's not as if he was—or is—a big part of my life."

Bliss let that little jab slide by as they walked into the living room and, for the first time, Tiffany's eyes took in the watercolors of Indians and cowboys, the river-rock fireplace, the scatter rugs and marred wooden floor.

"So, now that you've been in town a few weeks and met your stepmother-to-be, how do you feel about John's marriage to Brynnie Perez?" Tiffany asked suddenly.

Dropping her keys into her purse, Bliss stopped at the fireplace and decided to tell the truth. No reason to pussyfoot. She and these newfound sisters had a lot of ground to cover if they were to ever get along. That, she decided, staring into Tiffany's eyes, was a mighty big if. "Of course, I resented Brynnie when I first found out about her. How could my father—my *father*—have carried on an affair for so many years? I knew he was no knight in shining armor—"

Tiffany snorted her agreement.

"But I thought he had more morals than a tomcat." She shoved a shank of hair around her ear. "I was all set to hate Brynnie on sight. This was the woman who had defiled my mother's reputation, had been the 'love of my father's life,' who had been married a zillion times and had let another man claim Katie as his when she was really Dad's. It was crazy. Like I'd just walked *Through the Looking-Glass* or entered *The Twilight Zone.*"

"But you accept it?"

"I don't have much of a choice, do I? I mean, I can't tell my father what to do and anyway, as far as I was concerned, the damage was already done."

"To your mother."

"Yes, and to my idea of what my family was." Bliss sighed. "So I fought it for a while, decided I couldn't do anything and then, of course, I met Brynnie."

Tiffany walked to the window and stared through the panes to the front porch. "And let me guess how this little fairy tale ends—you fell in love with her, too, and now we're supposed to all be one big happy family."

"Wrong. I thought I'd hate my father's mistress on sight. And I decided I could live with that. You know, be outwardly civil while inwardly cold. But—and I wouldn't want my mother, if she were alive, to hear this—Brynnie's a hard person to hate."

Tiffany didn't respond, just ran a finger along the windowpane as she stared outside.

"So-o-o, I'm trying to put all my prejudices away if I can. I'm trying to convince myself that it's time to look forward, not backward. But if you want to know the truth, I'm having a rough time with all of it, okay? It's not easy, but there it is." She lifted a palm.

"There are always choices," Tiffany argued, though she didn't elaborate and Bliss guessed that she was talking about her own private problems.

"Dad didn't give you many."

Tiffany paled. then said, "No, he didn't. And you probably want to know how I felt about it. Well, I felt rotten. Once Mom came clean and told me the truth, I was sick to think that he didn't love me enough to claim me."

Bliss was horrified. "That's not what it was like. Tiffany, you've got to understand that—"

"What?" Tiffany said hotly, then appeared to bite back another sarcastic remark and sighed audibly. "Look, it's not your fault, but I blamed you. When I finally wanted to know more about my 'dad'—if that's what you could call him—I asked around about John. It turns out my grandmother had a wealth of information and was more than happy to let me know every intimate detail of my father's life. That's when I found out about you and discovered that you had this privileged life up in Seattle—that you had Dad—so I made the mistake of calling you 'the princess' in front of my son."

Her cheeks colored as she explained. "You seemed to have everything—anything a daughter could ever want. You and your mom had my father's name and his money and everything while my mother struggled, never married, and worked two jobs just to raise me. Even though my grandmother was and still is supportive, it was hard. Real hard." Tiffany turned back from the window and offered an unhappy smile. "Obviously, coming here was a mistake. I'm not going to your dad's wedding and I'm not going to act like the past didn't happen, okay? I can't."

She turned and Bliss caught hold of her arm. "I understand your frustration."

"I doubt it."

"Okay, so maybe I can't. But I think we should try to get to know each other."

Tiffany silently appraised her. "I was wrong. I shouldn't have called you 'princess.' Pollyanna would have been more appropriate."

"Maybe so, but no matter what happens," Bliss said, unable to hold her tongue, "I'm not going to be bitter about it or carry a huge chip on my shoulder."

Tiffany shook her head. "Good for you, Bliss."

"Would it be so terrible to get to know each other?" Bliss asked, and wondered why it was suddenly so important. So what if Tiffany didn't want to have anything to do with her? She'd lived all her life not knowing she had a half-sister, so why push it?

Tiffany's eyes were cold as ice. "I just don't know if there's any reason to pursue this. I'm not going to make any bones about not liking your father. And trust me, I'll never think of him as mine, so, as for you, all that I feel toward you right now is idle curiosity."

"But you came over here."

She shook her head. "I guess I was feeling guilty, but I

can't for the life of me figure out why. The thing is that even though I don't care about John Cawthorne, I wouldn't want him to suffer, so I'm glad to hear that he's recovering. Other than that, I don't have much to say."

Bliss dropped her hand and Tiffany left.

Why Bliss felt a sense of loss, she didn't understand. As far as she was concerned, Tiffany Santini had never been her sister and never would be. Tiffany had decided.

Brynnie's house was situated two blocks from the park and painted a faded shade of salmon. It had once been a small cottage but had been expanded over the years to accommodate various husbands and additional children. A wing from the kitchen shot into the backyard, the attic had been turned into a bedroom/loft and the garage had been converted into an apartment attached to the house by an open breezeway. A few petunias splashed color from barrels placed by the front door, where the torn mesh of the screen needed replacing. Three cats lazed on a cracked driveway.

As Bliss knocked on the door, she heard her father's voice through the screen. "I told you, this isn't happening—"

"Come in, the door's open," Brynnie yelled over John's deeper, angry voice.

"I don't care what any damned doctor says, I'm not lyin' around here twiddlin' my fingers and toes." John Cawthorne was seated on a plaid couch and pulling on a boot. His face was red, his jaw set and Bliss knew from experience that he wasn't going to change his mind. "Hi, kiddo," he said as Bliss entered, then went right on ranting at Brynnie.

"I have to check with the accountant about my insurance payments and the foreman of the ranch about how much feed we'll need this winter. Bill Crosswhite's got a bull I might want to buy or use, and I'd like to see the animal myself. Then there's the properties up in Seattle—the house is up for sale and the boat. I've got two empty warehouses that someone wants to convert to apartments and . . ." His voice trailed off as he realized both women were staring at him as if he'd lost his mind.

"And what about the wedding?" Brynnie asked. "Are you gonna be able to squeeze that in?"

"Of course, but—"

"We're supposed to talk to the preacher this afternoon."

"The preacher. Right." John rubbed the side of his face and scratched at the silver stubble on his jaw. Rather than address the subject, he asked Bliss, "How're you doing out at the ranch all alone?"

"I'm not really alone, Dad. You've got workers."

He snorted. "Such as they are."

"Well, they're keeping things in line and Mason has been by a couple of times."

"Great," her father grumbled. "He's probably gonna change his mind again and find a way to finagle me and keep the damned place." He shot Brynnie a damning glance. "Or has he been hanging around because of you?" He eyed his daughter and reached for his other boot.

"I don't think all of Mason's motives are evil." she said with a smile.

"Is that so? Listen, Blissie, don't defend that bastard to me. He's even gone so far as to work a deal with Brynnie behind my back. Helluva guy, that Lafferty."

Brynnie, who had been reading her horoscope in the newspaper, said, "That was my fault, John Cawthorne, and you know it. Now Mason's trying to make amends and the least you could do is be big enough to see it." Obviously irritated, she snapped the paper, then dropped it onto a coffee table already laden with empty glasses, ashtrays, magazines and books of matches.

John was having none of it. "That bastard hurt my baby."

And so have you, Dad, she thought silently. *With all of your lies.*

"Come on, let's not fight," Brynnie said to John. "I don't know why you're so darned ornery today. You know you're not supposed to be getting all riled up. Just lie back down, switch on the television and wait for Reverend Jones."

"I just can't stand lyin' around doin' nothin'."

"The doctor said that if you take it easy, you can move back to the ranch soon—"

"The doctor can shove it, for all I care. Blast it all, anyway." He yanked on his boot, rolled to his feet and stood without so much as swaying. If nothing else, John Cawthorne was blessed with more than his share of grit and willpower.

Bliss cleared her throat. "I thought you should know that Tiffany stopped by. She was looking for you, but when I told her you were here, she decided she didn't want to come looking for you."

John's face softened. "Well, I'll be."

"Don't get your hopes up, Dad. She wasn't all that friendly."

"But she tried."

"Yeah." Bliss nodded and didn't bring up the fact that she and her elder half-sister had nearly had a shouting match. She'd said enough. Whatever happened next was between Tiffany and John.

"See there?" Brynnie sniffed. "I've always told you there is a God and He's watching over you."

So who was watching over Mom? Bliss wondered, when Margaret Cawthorne lay dying and her husband, though seemingly concerned, was involved with another woman. She gave herself a quick mental shake. She had to quit thinking in those terms. Her mother, rest her soul, was gone.

Yes, her father had been unfaithful, less than true, and a liar, but that was all in the past. Now he was marrying a woman whom Bliss couldn't find it in her heart to hate. As she'd told Tiffany, she couldn't dwell on the sins of years gone by but had to focus ahead, on the future. With her father.

And with Mason.

She pushed that wayward thought aside. Mason and she were having an affair—that much was true. And she knew that she loved him, but never had he said he loved her; never had she felt that he cared for her as she did for him.

Once again, she'd let him play her for a fool. But not for long.

As soon as John and Brynnie were married, she was moving back to Seattle.

What was the old saying, something like it was better to have loved and lost than never to have loved at all?

Bliss wasn't convinced.

Chapter Fourteen

"This time, Mason, you've really flipped!" Patty Lafferty hoisted one of her bags into the back of his truck. Overhead, a jet taking off from the airport roared upward into the cloudy heavens. "Do you really think I was somehow involved with Uncle—if that's what you'd call him—Isaac's disappearance?"

"You took off around the same time."

"Give me a break." Eyes as gold as his own sparked angrily. "So what?" She glared at her brother as they stood toe-to-toe in the airport parking lot. "You don't believe me."

"You've lied before."

"Not about something like this! Oh, Mason, come *on*!"

He frowned at her and wished he could believe her, but she'd been in more scrapes than he cared to count.

"Swear to God!" She licked two fingers and held them up beside her head as proof of her integrity and innocence. "Scout's honor."

He snorted.

"Oh, for the love of God, Mason, think about it. Why would I help Isaac disappear?"

"You tell me."

Another jet screamed down the runway.

"I can't!" She threw her hands up in the air. The wind

caught the long red-blond strands of her hair, tossing them in front of her face. "Why won't you trust me?"

"Past history."

"I just went to Mexico for a while." She climbed into the cab of the truck and played with the frayed hole in the knee of a disreputable pair of jeans.

"Maybe you'd like to tell me why?"

"Maybe not. It's none of your business." Her jaw was set and she slid a pair of sunglasses onto the bridge of her nose.

"Why won't you tell me?"

"I didn't do anything illegal, okay? I just needed to get away for a while. Fun and sun, that's all."

"And you couldn't call?"

"I didn't want to. Whether you know it or not, Mason, you're not my keeper." She fished into her purse, pulled out a tube of pale pink lipstick and applied it without benefit of a mirror. "And don't give me any guff about a promise to Mom, okay? It doesn't wash anymore. I'm way too grown-up to have an older brother breathing down my neck." She slipped the cap onto her lipstick tube and tossed it back into the messy interior of her bag.

Mason, starting the engine, was still suspicious.

"You know, Mason, you should lighten up." She found a decorative elastic band, scraped back her hair and snapped the band into place. "You're starting to imagine things."

He jammed the truck into gear and drove through the parked cars. Sunlight glinted off windshields and fenders, while people with bags of every sort and size clustered in knots at stations for the shuttle. Was he imagining things? He didn't think so. He cared about his sister even though she'd given him nothing but grief ever since he could remember.

"You know, Patty," he said as he slowed to pay for his short stay in the parking lot. He handed the attendant in the booth a ten-dollar bill and waited for change. "It wouldn't hurt you to settle down."

She laughed as the gate opened and he drove through. "Oh, yeah, what's this? You know the old saying, the pot calling the kettle black or some such hogwash. You could take some of that advice yourself."

He slid his sister a knowing glance. "How did Jarrod find you?"

At the mention of Jarrod Smith's name, Patty's expression changed. She avoided Mason's eyes. "You know your old friend. He could find a black cat in a dark room on a moonless night."

"I'm surprised he didn't come back with you."

Patty lifted a shoulder. "I didn't invite him," she said and reached into her bag for a pack of gum. She made a big show of unwrapping a stick before plopping it into her mouth. "I think he said he'd be back in a few days, in time for his mother's wedding. I didn't really pay a lot of attention. He made sure I got on the flight and I took off."

She seemed to take sudden interest in the other cars on the freeway as Mason melded his truck into the flow of traffic, then slid lower in the seat, as if she intended to get a little shut-eye. "Jarrod did tell me that you were seeing Bliss Cawthorne again," she said.

"She's back in town."

"Is that good news or bad?"

Definitely good, he thought, but kept his feelings to himself. He knew Patty was just trying to distract him and, damn it, her ploy worked. Now that his sister was safe and, for the moment, out of trouble, he could concentrate on other things. Terri was coming around about Dee Dee, and that left Bliss.

Bliss.

What in the world was he going to do with her?

Ask her to marry you, that's what. You can't take a chance on losing her again.

His jaw slid to one side and he adjusted the air conditioner to lower the temperature in the cab. He'd struggled with his feelings for over a week. She was the one woman he'd sworn to avoid and now he couldn't get enough of her. Making love to her was pure heaven. Holding her close at night was something he wanted to do for the rest of his life. And she'd be leaving soon. John and Brynnie's wedding was scheduled for the end of next week. Then Bliss was planning to return to Seattle.

That thought settled on him like lead. It was time to come clean. As soon as he'd deposited Patty at her apartment, he'd have it out with old man Cawthorne.

Bliss gave Fire Cracker her head and felt the hot summer air stream through her hair as the game little mare raced over the dry stubble of the field. The sky was on fire, deep shades of magenta and gold blazing over the western hills, as the sun set in a splash of brilliance.

It was a glorious evening and Bliss felt a rush of adrenaline as Fire Cracker's hooves thundered over the dry acres. Cattle and horses dotted the hillsides, and shadows grew long at the base of trees. How could she ever leave? In the past few weeks she'd grown to love this ranch, just as her father did. And despite all her talk to the contrary, she'd fallen in love with Mason.

Not that he loved her.

She kneed Fire Cracker and the mare leaped over a dry streambed, sailing through the air and landing with a bone-jarring thud on the other side. A field mouse scurried for cover. Birds flew and scattered.

Bliss would be returning to Seattle in a few days, as soon

as her father was married and off on his honeymoon. At that thought her heart twisted. She would miss this place; miss the freedom, the quiet nights, the smell of leather and horses, her father's grumblings and the prospect of getting to know her half-sisters. But most of all, she'd miss Mason.

"Idiot," she muttered as the barn, stables and outbuildings came into sight.

She pulled up on the reins and caught her breath as the mare slowed to a walk at the paddock near the stables. Dirty but exhilarated, Bliss climbed down from the saddle and walked Fire Cracker into the darkened interior.

She spent the next forty-five minutes cooling the horse down, then brushing her sleek hide before offering a measure of oats and bucket of water. "You know," she admitted, scratching the mare between her ears and avoiding being swatted by the sorrel's tail, "I'm going to miss you, too."

She'd considered moving down here. Lord knew, her father was doing his best to promote it. Now that he'd moved back to the ranch and was feeling better, he'd thought of every bribe imaginable to keep her in Bittersweet. Not only had he given her the horse, he'd promised her land, offered her a job, suggested her sisters needed her; but she'd been undeterred. Her job, her friends, her entire life was in Seattle.

But Mason was here. Her soul darkened a bit. She loved him. More than she ever had. And that was a problem. Once before, she'd been involved with him and the love affair had been one-sided; now, since they were older, the only difference was that they were physically intimate. Just because they'd made love was no reason to think that they had a future together.

He had his corporations, his ranches, his own life and a daughter.

"Oh, stop it," she told herself as she finally let Fire

Cracker out of her stall. Bucking and snorting, the horse romped to the middle of the corral and immediately dropped to the ground where she rolled back and forth, her legs kicking wildly in the air, a cloud of dust billowing from beneath her. "Great. All that brushing for nothing." Bliss chuckled as she walked toward the back door of the house.

Lights were already glowing from the windows as the sky darkened and night crept over the landscape. Oscar, lying on the front porch, let out a quiet "Woof" and thumped his tail, but Bliss barely heard him. Through the screen door she heard the sound of voices. Loud voices.

"Look, Lafferty, I don't like the game you're playin' with Bliss." John Cawthorne's voice brooked no argument.

Bliss stopped dead in her tracks. Mason was here?

"I'm not playing any games." Mason's voice, clear, calm and cold.

"She's falling for you again. Just like before."

"This time it's different, Cawthorne."

Different? What was he talking about? Bliss's heart was like a drum, pounding out a wild, erratic cadence.

"Trust me." Mason's voice was stern. Determined. Oh, God, how she loved him. She was about to walk inside, but held back. The air was charged and she knew, deep in her heart, that she should just walk back to the stables and forget every word that was being said. Or she should announce herself and barge into the kitchen. But still she hung back, her throat as dry as a desert wind, her heart pumping madly.

"The day I trust you is the day I give up the ghost, Lafferty. I wanted you as far away from my daughter as possible. I thought I made that clear a few years ago. Seems to me we had an agreement."

"It's off."

"I paid you good money."

Bliss bit her lip. She knew about the cash. So what was the big deal? She reached for the handle of the door.

"Just like the money you paid Terri to pretend she was pregnant?" Mason demanded.

What? Bliss's heart stopped. Surely she'd heard wrong.

"Don't know what you're talkin' about, son."

"Sure you do, Cawthorne. Paying me to stay out of Bliss's life wasn't enough, was it? You bought yourself some insurance by sweetening the deal with Terri. Fortunately for you, she was only too willing to go along with the scam."

No!

"You're just blowin' smoke, Lafferty."

"Am I?" Mason snorted. "I only wish I'd been smart enough to demand the results of a pregnancy test before I married her."

Oh, God, please, no! Bliss's knees nearly gave out. With one hand she balanced herself against the post supporting the roof. Was she hearing correctly? Had her father actually talked Terri into lying? Paid her off? *What?*

"If I live to be a hundred," Mason said, "I'll never believe another woman."

"Even Bliss?"

"I think we should leave her out of this."

"She's the reason you and I are at odds, boy."

A few passing seconds seemed like an eternity. "Bliss wouldn't set me up and try to trap me into marriage with a baby—even a nonexistent one like Terri did."

Bliss's insides were shaking.

"And besides, Terri was coached, wasn't she? By you."

No!

John clucked his tongue, then sighed audibly. "So Terri blamed me? Always knew she couldn't be trusted."

"I saw the records, Cawthorne. When I got suspicious I paid a kid who worked in the lab for a copy of all of

Terri's reports. When I confronted her, she told me the whole sick story.

"Of course by the time I got the news, it was too late." Bliss heard the scrape of boots. "I was already married and guess what? By that time Terri really was pregnant."

"And you ended up with a daughter."

"The only bright spot in this whole sordid deal. In fact, Dee Dee was worth all of this. But now, it's time to come clean."

"You want me to tell Bliss."

"I think it would be a good idea."

"It'll never happen, Lafferty," her father said, but his tone was less firm than before. "Because, unless I miss my guess, Bliss will never believe you."

Dear God. Was her father really so controlling that he would interfere in her life to the point of all this lying and deceit? Fury pumped through her blood and her fingers curled into fists of rage. To think that—

"It was Margaret's idea."

"What?" Bliss couldn't stop the word and suddenly there was silence—hollow, soul-numbing silence. Steeling herself, she yanked hard on the door handle and marched, ready to do bodily harm if necessary, into the house. Oscar gave out an excited yip and followed her inside, but she ignored the dog and glared at her father. "Why are you lying?" Bliss asked her father.

"So that's the way it was. I wondered," Mason said. His face was set and hard, his eyes slits as he stood, his hips balanced against the kitchen counter, his arms folded over his broad chest.

The odors of day-old coffee and floor wax drifted to her nostrils. The only noise for a few long seconds was the hum of the refrigerator and the ticking of the clock.

"I didn't know you were listening," her father said.

"I didn't mean to, but I think you'd better explain."

Sighing loudly, John reached into his breast pocket for a nonexistent pack of cigarettes and avoided the accusation in Bliss's gaze. He found a plug of tobacco in his back pocket.

"It's the truth," he admitted with a lift of one thin shoulder. "Margaret was undone when I let it slip that you were getting involved with one of the ranch hands. She was certain you were going to make the same mistake she did, and since she knew all about Brynnie . . . Well, she threatened to expose Brynnie as my mistress, divorce me and take me to the cleaners. In addition to all that, she was determined to make sure that you never spoke to me again."

Trembling with rage, Bliss leaned over the table and stared at her father—so old, so tired, so forlorn. "I don't believe a word of this."

He blinked before looking at her again. "It's true, Blissie, and you meant so much to me that I caved in and bribed Terri to claim she was pregnant. Then, after the accident, when you were so hurt. I worked a deal with Mason." He wiped a hand over his brow and closed his eyes for a second.

"Oh, Dad, how could you?" Bliss suddenly felt cold to the marrow of her bones. She didn't want to believe that either of her parents would be so manipulative.

"It was for your best interests," her father said.

"*My* best interests? Didn't I have a say in them?" Stunned and reeling, she nearly fell into one of the chairs at the table and fixed her gaze on the man who had sired her.

"You were seventeen. Didn't know up from sideways."

"But it was my life. Mine!" She thumped her fingers against her chest. "You had no right—"

"I saw you with Lafferty and knew it would only be a matter of time before you got yourself into big trouble, so I went along with your mother."

"I can't believe it." Bliss cradled her head in her hands. All these years. All the lies. "You . . . you could have ruined so many lives. Mine. Mason's. Terri's."

"No one was really hurt," John argued.

"Untrue. We were all hurt." She felt the sting of tears behind her eyes at the thought of her parents' betrayal. Whatever were their reasons, there was no excuse, no explanation good enough to justify their actions. "Just because I wasn't 'of age' or whatever you want to call it, didn't mean I didn't have feelings, that I shouldn't have some say in my life!"

Her father's jaw was rock hard. "I did what I thought best."

"Because you were coerced into it by Mother."

"She loved you more than life itself, Blissie. You know that." He blinked, as if the thought of his wife and how he'd treated her brought tears to his eyes. "We were the best parents we knew how to be."

"I can't believe this," she whispered.

"Believe it." Mason's voice was hard and the wrath in his gold eyes reflected his years of pain. "We were both deceived, Bliss."

"And what about you?" she demanded, hurting and raw, as she stared at Mason. "Taking money from Dad, staying away from me and never looking back." Mason, too, had used her.

"I'm sorry," Mason said. "I should have come to you in the hospital and explained—"

"Explain what? That twenty-five thousand dollars meant more to you than I did? That . . . that you were willing to marry another woman rather than face me again? I never thought I'd say this," she whispered, anger burning through her, "but you're a coward, Mason Lafferty, and I thought I loved you. For years I believed . . ." Hot tears stung against her eyelids. "I—I mean— Oh, just forget it." She couldn't stand to remain another second in the house, turned and hurried out the door.

"Bliss, wait!" Mason yelled. "Oh, before I forget why I came here, Cawthorne, this is yours." There was a slap of paper on a hard surface. "The deed to this place, signed back to Brynnie. Now it's official. I don't want your spread anymore, Cawthorne. I don't want anything of yours."

"Includin' my daughter?"

Bliss didn't wait for Mason's answer. She ran down the steps, across the yard to the paddock where Fire Cracker was grazing. *Run. Get away now. You've already lost your heart to Mason, but you can't let him know.* Tears streamed from her eyes. Dear God, she'd fallen in love with him all over again. The one man she didn't dare trust with her heart seemed to have it in a crushing grip that she couldn't pry open. How many nights had she dreamed of lying naked in his arms, oblivious to anything but the feel of his breath against her bare skin? How many hours had she spent thinking of him, wondering if there was any way they could have a future together?

"Wait a second!" Mason's voice and the sound of his boots crunching on gravel caught up with her.

She headed straight for the mare. Hearing the commotion, the horse snorted and pricked her ears forward. Overhead, swallows disturbed from their nests, dipped and fluttered near the eaves of the stables.

"I said, 'Wait,'" Mason nearly yelled as he caught up with her.

She whirled and almost ran into him in the darkness. "Why?"

"Because we should talk this out."

"We could have. When you found out the truth—which, it sounds like, was years ago. But no, you kept it a secret. Were you ever going to tell me?" she demanded, angling her furious face upward and feeling heat pulsing in her cheeks. Curse the man! He was just too damned sexy with his thin lips, thick-lashed eyes and taut, tanned skin over high, angry cheekbones. Just staring into his lying eyes caused a rolling, needy sensation deep inside her. A sensation she suddenly hated.

"If and when I thought it was necessary."

"If *you* thought it was necessary. What about me? This was my life, too, you know." Brushing the condemning tears from her cheeks, she added. "I don't need any man—not my father and certainly not you—trying to protect me or keep secrets from me, or do whatever it is you thought you were doing. Okay?"

"I did what I thought was best."

"Yeah. Just like Dad. Next time, ask me. Better yet, don't. There won't be a next time."

She strode into the stables and grabbed a bridle. Mason followed and took hold of her arm. "Slow down, Bliss. We need to talk."

She whistled to the mare—the way she'd learned from Mason so many years before.

"You should have thought of that before," she said as the mare clomped up to her. Deftly, she snapped the bridle over Fire Cracker's lowered head. "Goodbye, Mason," she said, untying Fire Cracker's reins.

"Maybe you should listen to my side of the story."

"And maybe you should go straight to hell," She swung onto the mare's dusty back.

His eyes were dark with old, hidden demons. "I've already been there and back." He stepped forward as she jerked on the reins and dug her heels into the mare's sides. "Bliss—"

"Hi-ya!"

Fire Cracker took off in a thunder of hooves and over the

noise Bliss thought she heard Mason call after her. *"Damn it, woman, I love you."* The words toyed with her mind, but she shoved them aside and told herself she hadn't heard anything but the voice of the wind.

Mason experienced a sense of déjà vu as he watched her race away. The mare galloped through the twilight-dark fields and he felt every muscle in his body grow tense. Though it was a hot, sticky night, with only a few clouds drifting over the glittering stars, he was reminded of another time, in this very spot, when heavy raindrops had veiled his vision and Bliss had ridden, hell-bent for leather, into the heart of a lightning storm.

This time was different.

Or was it?

A deep, frightening dread inched up his spine and though he told himself he was every kind of fool, that he didn't believe in fate, or premonitions, or anything remotely touching predestination, he couldn't shake the feeling.

He'd come here to give the old man his deed back, and that accomplished, he should just have left, but instead of his footsteps taking him to his truck, he half ran to the tack room, snagged a saddle, blanket and bridle and found Lucifer grazing in a nearby field. With a sharp whistle, he gained the stallion's attention and within minutes he was astride the blue-eyed pinto, chasing after Bliss and feeling his fear mount with each of the animal's swift strides.

"Come on, come on," he urged Lucifer as he silently cursed himself for not watching which of the old cattle trails that webbed over the base of the hills she'd taken. He rode by instinct, sweating beneath his shirt, his eyes narrowed on the terrain ahead.

At the base of the hills, he guided Lucifer upward, heading along one of the dusty paths, hoping to catch a glimpse of Bliss or her dogged little horse. He stopped twice, listening for the sound of hoofbeats and hearing nothing but a train rumbling on distant tracks.

"She'll be all right," he told himself. "She's got to be. Come on, you miserable piece of horseflesh. Run!"

Beneath branches, through swarms of insects, around stumps and boulders the game horse ran. Across patches of moonlight and past a creek with a tumbling waterfall that sprayed a soft mist, he rode until at last the trees gave way to the ridge.

His heart stopped. He saw her silhouette, darker than the surrounding hills, astride Fire Cracker and riding wildly past the very tree struck by lightning ten years before. The old trunk was leafless and dead, the core burned black by the decade-old bolt from the sky.

"Slow down!" Mason yelled. "Bliss!"

She twisted in the saddle, her hair fanning around her.

"I love you!"

She froze, but the horse kept moving.

"Bliss—"

She gathered the reins back, slowing the mare while rocking.

"Move," he yelled at his mount. "Come on!" He remembered the last time, how she'd nearly died. Because of him. Again! "Oh, sweet Jesus!" He kicked his horse forward. Bliss toppled. She screamed. Thud! She hit the ground with bone-cracking certainty.

Mason vaulted off his horse. "No, oh, God, no!" He reached her in an instant, dragged her crumpled body to his. "Bliss, Bliss, oh, love," he whispered, holding her and praying to a God he'd had no words with in years that she was all right. He couldn't have hurt her again, couldn't have been the cause of any more pain. But a bruise and scrape marred the perfect skin near her temple and she sagged limply, as if there were no life left in her.

"I love you," he said and felt tears clog his throat. "Please, sweetheart, don't . . ." He couldn't lose her. Wouldn't! She was breathing shallowly, but her eyes fluttered open for an instant and a faint smile touched her lips.

"Mason," she mouthed.

"Hang in there, baby, I'll take care of you."

"I . . . I know . . ." Then she drifted off again and he felt the cold mind-numbing fear that she might be lost to him forever. He whistled to his horse, rose to his feet and carried her gently. She wasn't going to die on him, nor was she going to leave him.

It had been ten years and he wasn't going to wait any longer. This woman was the only woman he'd ever loved, the only one who could touch his heart. Somehow, some way, he was going to save her.

Bliss felt as if she were drowning. The water was warm and calm, a blackness dragging her under.

"Can you hear me? Bliss?"

A voice. Mason's voice. Oh, Lord, how she loved him. "Blissie. Wake up now."

Her father. And he sounded worried. So worried. About her.

"Don't leave me." Mason again. She would never leave him. Why would he think . . . ? She struggled to open her eyes only to allow a blinding flash of light to pierce her brain. Pain exploded at her temples.

"Did you see that?"

"She's comin' around."

"Mason?" she said, but no sound escaped her and her throat felt as dry as sandpaper.

"I'm here, darlin'," he replied and she felt his hand, big and callused, rubbing the back of hers. Again she tried to force her eyes open and this time, despite the painful brilliance, she managed to blink and stay awake.

"Where—where am I?"

"At the hospital in Medford," Mason said. His face, all harsh planes and angles, was hovering over hers, and she watched as relief washed over his features.

A doctor appeared, nudged Mason aside and shone yet another light into her eyes as she lay on the starched white sheets. "You're going to be all right," he assured her, though she hadn't been worried "You'll be able to go to your father's wedding."

"Good."

"Just as long as she goes to hers," Mason said.

She blinked again. "Wh-what?"

The doctor moved aside and Mason took her hand, linking his fingers through hers. "Marry me, Bliss."

"Now, wait a minute—" her father protested from somewhere behind Mason.

"Forgive me and marry me." Mason swallowed hard. "I love you. I want you to be my wife, to be Dee Dee's stepmother. To be the mother of my children, our children."

Tears filled her eyes. Her heart melted. *Children. Mason's children.*

Mason kissed her on the temple. "I've always loved you, Bliss Cawthorne, and I swear, I'll love you for the rest of my life."

"And I'll love you for the rest of mine." Her voice was weak and cracked, but her conviction was strong. Managing a smile through her tears of joy, she stared into the golden gaze of the man she'd loved for as long as she could remember. "There s nothing to forgive, Mason, nothing. And of course, I'll marry you."

"Oh, hell," her father said.

"No, Dad, it's heaven," she assured him.

"Whatever makes you happy, Blissie," her father said, his voice filled with emotion.

"Maybe we should plan a double ceremony," Mason teased.

"I don't think so," she said. "I don't want to share our wedding day with anyone but you."

Her father cleared his throat. "Whatever you want. Brynnie will be thrilled and your sisters— Hell, I forgot. Katie's been worried sick about you."

"And Tiffany?"

There was a pause. "She's still not talkin' to me, but she called Katie once and this hospital twice. She's concerned about you, kiddo. Looks like you might have finally won her over."

Bliss wasn't sure but she smiled inwardly. Sisters . . . and children . . . and, of course, a husband. Mason.

"I'll go give Brynnie a call. She'll tell your sisters. Love ya, kid," her father said, touching her lightly on the shoulder. "Try and forgive a foolish old man for trying to protect his daughter, would you?"

"Sure, Dad," she said, just thankful to be alive. She wasn't happy with what he'd done and there were still some issues they had to resolve, but she'd give him another chance because she truly believed that both of her parents had thought they had her best interests at heart. She heard her father leave the room and vowed to work things out. With him. With her half-sisters. With Mason's daughter. Somehow, she would make things work.

"So as soon as I get the doctor to spring you from here," Mason said, interrupting her thoughts and staring down at her with his incredible gold eyes, "I'll expect you to start making wedding plans."

"Will you?"

"Unless you want to elope." His smile was positively and deliciously wicked.

"It doesn't matter," she said. "Just as long as you promise to be with me forever."

"No longer?"

She laughed, and he winked at her.

"It's a deal, Bliss Cawthorne. You and me. But only until forever."

"Should we shake on it?" she asked, grinning, her heart so filled with happiness she thought it might burst.

"Shake on it? Hmm." His eyes twinkled. "We could, but you know, I had something else in mind. Something more . . . intimate."

She sighed and rolled her eyes. "You're trouble, Lafferty. Big trouble."

"I am," he agreed. "But only with you, love. Only with you."

A FAMILY KIND OF GAL

To Mom and Dad
You are the best

Chapter One

So this was the place.

With a jaundiced eye, J.D. Santini studied the immense house with its apron of drying lawn and Apartment for Rent sign posted near the street where he'd parked. Gray clapboard accented with bay windows, black trim and a smattering of white gingerbread, this was where Tiffany had run.

Wonderful. Just damned great.

His gut clenched and he told himself that he wasn't throwing her out of her home. Not really. And certainly not right away. What he was doing was for her own good. In her kids' best interests.

Then why did he feel like Benedict Arnold?

"Hell."

Pocketing his keys, he climbed out of his Jeep. The dry heat of southern Oregon in mid-July hit him square in the face.

Bittersweet. A fitting name for the town, he thought; as good a destination as any if a person wanted to turn tail and run. Which is what she'd done.

His jaw clenched when he thought of her. Tiffany Nesbitt Santini. Sister-in-law. Gold digger. *Lover.*

Damn, he hated this.

Get over it, Santini. What did you expect when you took the job with the old man? You dived headfirst into this mess and your eyes were wide-open.

He reached into the back seat of his Jeep Cherokee for his beat-up duffel bag and briefcase.

It was now or never.

Damn, but "never" sounded appealing.

His leg still pained him when he walked, but he hitched the strap of his bag over his shoulder and made his way up a brick walk that needed more than its share of new mortar.

He tried not to notice the crumbling caulking around the windows and the trickle of rust that colored the downspouts as he climbed the two steps to the front door.

This house and its sad need of repair are not your problem.

Right, and the Pope wasn't Catholic.

Everything Tiffany did affected him. Whether he wanted it to or not. She was the widow of his brother, mother of his niece and nephew, and the only woman whom he'd never been able to forget.

And trouble. Don't forget the kind of trouble she is.

He jabbed on the bell, heard the chimes peel softly from the interior and waited impatiently. What could he say to her? That, unbeknown to her, he owned part of this old house, because her dead husband, his older brother, had been an inveterate gambler? That he thought it would be better if she sold the place, bought something newer and more modern, that it would be best if the kids were . . . what? Moved again? Uprooted to live close to the Santini enclave? He snorted at that thought. For years he'd avoided being roped into the tight-knit-to-the-point-of-strangulation clan, but then he was a man. It was different for him, wasn't it? He didn't have kids.

A black cat darted through the shadows of overgrown rhododendrons and azaleas. Footsteps dragged through the house and the door was opened just a crack.

"Yeah?" Suspicious thirteen-year-old eyes peered out at him through the slit.

"Stephen?"

The eyes narrowed. "Who're you?"

J.D. felt a shaft of guilt. The kid didn't even recognize him. That wasn't Stephen's fault so much as it was his. "I'm your uncle."

"Uncle? You mean—?"

"J.D."

"Oh." Stephen's voice cracked and his skin, olive in tone, was instantly suffused with color. A flicker of recognition flashed in his eyes. He opened the door farther, standing aside as J.D. hitched his way into the foyer.

"What happened to your leg?"

"An accident. Motorcycle. The bike won."

"Yeah?" Stephen's eyes gleamed and the hint of a smile slid over his lips. He would be a good-looking kid in a few years, but right now he was a little rough around the edges. Soon his jaw would become more defined and his face would catch up with his nose. The boy reminded J.D. of himself and his own misdirected youth. "You've got a motorcycle?" Stephen asked, obviously awed.

"I did. It's in the shop."

"What kind?"

"A Harley."

"Cool."

He couldn't have impressed the kid more if he'd claimed to be a millionaire. "It doesn't look so cool now. Funny what plowing into a tree does to a bike."

Stephen managed the ghost of a smile. J.D. noted that Stephen's black hair was shaggy, his brown eyes filled with distrust, and his muscles so tense that J.D. half expected him to make a run for it at any moment.

"Is your mother here?"

The kid's gaze fell to the floor and he seemed to be

studying the intricate floral patterns of a throw rug at the foot of the stairs. "She's . . . she's not around right now."

"She's in jail!" a little voice chirped from the landing. A pixieish face, pink-cheeked and surrounded with black curls, was stuck through two balusters.

"What?"

Stephen shot his sister a killing look. "Hush, Chrissie."

Jail? J.D. eyed the boy. "What's she talking about?"

"Nothin', Chrissie doesn't know what she's talkin' about."

"Do too!" the imp retorted indignantly.

Stephen worried his lip for a second, then shrugged, as if he didn't care one way or the other. "Okay. Mom's down at the police station."

"Why?"

"Dunno," he mumbled, obviously lying. "I just got stuck baby-sitting."

"I'm *not* a baby!" Christina dashed down the stairs on her chubby legs. The blue-black curls bounced and her eyes were wide with wonder.

"You're here alone?" he asked.

"Ellie's downstairs." Christina dashed across the hall and through a swinging door leading into the kitchen.

"Who's Ellie?"

"Mrs. Ellingsworth." Stephen shifted uncomfortably from one foot to the other. "She lives in one of the apartments downstairs and when Mom has to work, Ellie looks after Chrissie."

"And you?"

Stephen's spine stiffened. "I don't need a baby-sitter."

This was getting him nowhere fast. J.D. set his bag and briefcase onto the floor. "So . . . when will your mom be back?" Something was up—something the kid didn't want him to know about.

"Dunno. Soon, I guess." Stephen was prickly, but must have heard the rudeness in his voice because he added, "You can, uh, wait for her here or in the parlor, if ya want . . . or—"

Christina barreled out of the kitchen and ran to one of the narrow, beveled-glass windows flanking the front door. "Mommy!" she cried with delight. She threw open the door and raced down the steps.

J.D. turned and saw Tiffany climbing out of a sedan she'd parked in the shaded driveway.

Tall and slim, with shoulder-length black hair that framed an oval face, she was more than attractive; she was downright gorgeous, the kind of woman who expected and received more than her share of male attention.

"A male magnet," his mother used to say.

Folding some papers into an oversize bag, she looked up, saw Christina flying across the yard and offered her daughter a smile that froze as her gaze landed directly on J.D. Her eyes, a gold color J.D. had always found disturbing, hardened and the skin stretched taut over her high cheekbones was suddenly suffused with color. "Hi, honey!" she said to her daughter as she scooped the three-year-old up from the ground.

"Lookie who's here."

"I see." She seemed to steel herself in her sleeveless white blouse, still crisply pressed and stark against her tanned skin. She walked toward the front door and the slit in her khaki-colored skirt moved enough to show off her long, well-muscled legs.

Yep. There was a reason his divorced brother had fallen so hard and fast for Tiffany Nesbitt. The same reason that had nearly done J.D. in. Nearly.

From the foyer, Stephen cleared his throat. His voice cracked again. "Mom . . . Er, Mom. Uncle J.D. is here."

"So I see." She lifted a finely arched brow. White lines of irritation bracketed her lips. "Jay."

"Tiff." His damned pulse elevated a fraction.

"Looks like your timing is impeccable as always," she said with more than a trace of sarcasm.

"What's going on here?" J.D. asked.

Still carrying her daughter, she walked into the house and shut the door. "A misunderstanding."

"With the police?"

"The juvenile authorities," she corrected, her gaze skating to her son for an instant before returning to J.D. She flashed him a look that warned him not to dive too deeply into these murky waters. Whatever was going on, it was serious. Christina wriggled and Tiffany set her daughter on the floor. "You know, J.D., of all the people I expected to run into today, you're the last."

"I should have called."

She lifted a shoulder as if she didn't give a damn, but barely restrained fury snapped in her eyes. "Not your style."

His jaw tightened, but he supposed he deserved the blow. "No."

Stephen glanced up through the shaggy bangs. "I'm takin' off. Me and Sam are goin' fishin' and swimmin'."

"Sam and I," Tiffany corrected as if on automatic pilot. "You're supposed to be grounded."

"I thought we had a deal." Stephen rubbed his nose with the back of his hand. "I did all the chores and my homework."

"Isn't school out for the year?" J.D. asked.

Tiffany shot him another harsh glance. "Summer school."

"Yeah, and it's dumb," Stephen grumbled. "Look, I just want to go swimmin'."

Tiffany glanced at her watch. She looked about to argue

with the boy, then thought better of it. Probably because J.D. had shown up. “Okay. But be back by five.”

“Ah, Mom. Come on, it’s summer—”

“Five or don’t go at all,” she said firmly.

Stephen obviously wanted to take her on but thought better of it and chewed on the corner of his lip instead.

In J.D.’s opinion, the odds were better than ten to one that the kid wouldn’t make curfew. He knew what the boy was thinking; he’d been there.

“And your room is clean?”

“Clean enough.”

“Stephen,” she reproached gently.

“Clean enough for me and it’s my room, okay?” He was already through the front door and grabbing a beat-up skateboard that was propped against the side of the house. The board sported peeling decals of what J.D. assumed were the names of alternative rock bands. “I’ll see ya later.”

“Five. Remember.”

“Yeah, yeah.”

Watching him leave, Tiffany worried her lower lip between her teeth. “Teenagers,” she said in a tone so low he almost didn’t hear the concern in her voice.

J.D. didn’t blame her for being apprehensive. Stephen needed to be sat down on, and hard. The kid had an attitude and it wasn’t going to get any better over the next couple of years.

Sighing softly, Tiffany shook her head as if she were having a private conversation with herself and losing. Badly.

“Since you’re here, I assume you wanted to see me.”

He tensed at her choice of words.

“Come into the kitchen,” she said curtly. “Christina, you, too.” Sandals clicking in agitation, she marched down the hallway, throwing herself through the pair of swinging doors.

J.D. hauled his bags with him and followed, catching one

of the doors as it swung back at him. The kitchen was at the back of the house and looked like something out of *Better Homes and Gardens*. Sunlight spilled through the windows, giving the room a warm, golden glow. Shining pots and pans hung from the ceiling over a center island while bundles of fragrant herbs, suspended from hooks, scented the air. The refrigerator was adorned with a three-year-old's artwork, notes about repairs that needed to be done to the house, and emergency phone numbers.

Homey.

Charming.

And as phony as a three-dollar bill.

Tiffany reached into the windowsill for a bottle of aspirin and shook two white tablets into her hand.

"Headache?"

"At least." She turned on the tap, grabbed a glass from a nearby cabinet, filled it and tossed the pills and a huge gulp of water down her throat. "Now, what is it you want, Jay?"

J.D. set his bags on the floor and leaned a hip against one of the cupboards. A needle of guilt pricked his conscience as he thought about the deed to this house tucked into a pocket of his duffel bag. As much as he disliked Tiffany Nesbitt Santini, he didn't relish adding to her problems.

"There must be something. You didn't drive all the way down here from Portland just to say hello."

"No, but I did come to see you."

He noticed the slight catch of her breath, the widening of her eyes, but the look of anticipation was quickly masked. "Why do I have a feeling this isn't going to be something I want to hear?"

An older woman wearing oversize coveralls, a straw hat and gardening gloves appeared at the back door. Sunglasses covered her eyes and in one hand she held clippers and a bouquet of roses.

"I thought I heard voices," she said as she shouldered open the screen door. She stopped short at the sight of J.D. "Oh, I didn't know you had company."

"Roberta Ellingsworth, this is my brother-in-law, J.D. Santini."

"Pleased to meet you." J.D. offered his hand.

The woman chuckled as she, still holding the roses, extended her gloved fingers.

"You, too. Call me Ellie. Everyone does."

"Ellie, then," J.D. replied.

"I brought these in for you," she said to Tiffany as she released J.D.'s hand.

Tiffany was already reaching for a vase. "Thanks. They're lovely."

"I helped pick them!" Christina announced.

"That you did, honey," Ellie acknowledged, handing Tiffany the roses and winking at the little girl. "You were a big help."

"So were you," Tiffany said, sniffing the fragrant blooms. "Thanks for pinch-hitting with the kids."

"Any time, honey, any time."

"Would you like something to drink? I've got iced tea or coffee—"

"Oh, not right now, but I'll take a rain check," the older woman said, wiping her brow and lifting her sunglasses as if to peer at the strange man in Tiffany's kitchen more closely. "It's about time for my program." Her eyebrows rose a fraction as she looked at J.D. "I try not to miss my soap."

Tiffany grinned and her eyes sparkled with sudden merriment. "Don't tell me—Derek's evil twin has kidnapped him and is going to marry Samantha in his place."

Ellie laughed. "Close enough, honey, close enough. On *This Life Is Mine* you never know what can happen. I'll see you later." She was peeling off her gardening gloves. "Nice meeting you," she said to J.D. before leaving.

"My pleasure." J.D. watched her slowly descend the steps, then round the corner to disappear from sight.

"Ellie watches the kids for me when I'm at work, and believe me, she's an absolute godsend," Tiffany said, her smile fading a bit, and then, as if she'd belatedly realized that she'd been a little blunt earlier, she added, "So how about you? I've got coffee or iced tea"

He shook his head.

"Something stronger?"

"Later, maybe."

"Later?" she asked, her gaze moving to his duffel bag and her eyes narrowing enough that he noticed the curl of her eyelashes. "Don't tell me you're planning on staying?"

"For a while."

She tensed. "How long a while?"

"Till I accomplish what I set out to do."

"Don't talk to me in riddles, okay?" She arranged the roses in the vase, added water and set the bouquet in the center of the old table. Christina hovered near the back door. "Can I do drawing?" she asked.

"Great idea," her mother replied, wiping her hands on a kitchen towel. She reached for a pack of crayons on the counter, only to have her daughter turn up her little pug nose.

"I want to draw outside!"

"Outside?"

"With the chalk."

"Why not?" Tiffany scrounged in a drawer filled with cards, pencils, keys, batteries—anything a person could imagine—until she came up with a box of colored chalk.

Beaming, Christina snagged the prize from her mother's outstretched hand and scurried out the back door. The screen slammed behind her as she rushed to plant herself on the cracked concrete patio, upon which she began to doodle in pink, yellow, green and blue.

Tiffany watched her daughter until she was engrossed in her task, then turned to face J.D. "So, *brother-in-law*, to what or to whom do we owe the honor of your presence?" she demanded, then shook her head at the question. "No"—she held out her hand as if to ward off his words—"let me guess. You're here on a mission. Just checking up on your brother's widow. Trying to figure out if she really is the right kind of mother to raise Philip's kids."

She'd always been smart. Calculating. He leaned a hip against the center island. "I'm here on business." That wasn't a lie. Well, not much of one.

"Sure. That's why you're standing in my kitchen. With your bag. Come on, Jay, you can do better than that." She closed the short distance between them and a hint of her perfume teased his nostrils. It was the same fragrance she'd worn the last time he'd seen her. Touched her. He gritted his teeth and decided it was time to take the offensive.

"Before we get into all that, why don't you explain what you were doing with the juvenile authorities?"

"I don't really think it's any of your business."

"Isn't it?"

"I can handle my children," she said with a cold smile. "No matter what the rest of the Santini family thinks." With a quick glance through the screen door to assure herself that her daughter was safely out of earshot, she lowered her voice. "I *know* what your father thought of me when I met Philip. I *know* he tried to convince Philip that I was a no-good, gold-digging woman who was barely an adult, one who looked at Philip as a . . . a father figure," she said, pain sweeping through her eyes.

You don't know the half of it, he thought with another stab of guilt.

"And I heard that you tried to talk Philip out of marrying me."

The muscles in J.D.'s shoulders tensed. "Careful, Tiff," he said. "I had my reasons."

She flushed and her eyes sparked with anger. For a second he thought she might slap him. "None of them good, Jay," she said through lips that barely moved. "None of them good."

"Good, no. Valid, yes."

"Philip and I had a . . . a strong marriage." Her chin inched up a notch as if she dared him to challenge her.

"If it worked for you."

"It did."

He bit back a sharp retort and stared down at her. His gaze lingered on her lips for a second before lowering to the neckline of her blouse, where her skin was flushed with anger, her pulse leaping at the base of her throat. His bad knee throbbed, his stupid crotch was suddenly tight and he realized that he still wanted her. As he always had. Hell, what a mess.

"Mind if I sit down?" he asked, then didn't wait for an answer, but slid into one of the tall ladder-back chairs that flanked an old claw-footed table.

"Suit yourself." She ran stiff fingers through her hair, then seemed to realize she was being too defensive. Waving with one hand, as if to disperse the cloud of fury surrounding her, she said, "Come on, Jay. Why don't you tell me what you're doing down here? If it isn't to spy on me, there must be a reason. The last I heard, you hated all things that had to do with me or this town."

"Hate's a pretty strong word." But she was right. He didn't trust her and as far as Bittersweet, Oregon, went, he had plenty of reasons to despise this small town filled with small-minded citizens.

Folding her arms over her chest she lifted one delicately arched eyebrow, silently urging him on.

"As I said, I'm here on business."

"In Bittersweet?" She shoved a lock of blue-black hair

from her eyes. "Don't tell me you chased an ambulance all the way from Portland down here."

That stung. "I left the firm."

"No way." She cocked her head as if she hadn't heard him correctly. "But I thought you were a partner."

"I was. Sold out."

"So," she encouraged, suddenly wary, "why?"

"Dad offered me a job with his company."

She laughed without a drop of mirth. "Come on. Don't give me that worn-out line about an offer you 'couldn't refuse,' Jay." She rolled her eyes. "Oh, this is rich. You with Santini Brothers. I never thought I'd see the day."

"Neither did I." He stretched his bad leg and rubbed at the pain in his knee through his jeans. "Since I was down here on business anyway, I thought I'd check up on you and the kids."

"Ah. As I suspected." Her shoulders slumped a bit and she looked at her nails. "Since when do you care?" she asked in a voice barely above a whisper.

She always had been forthright. Nearly to the point of being rude. Well, two could play that game. "I've always cared."

Her eyes darkened for a second. A shadow flickered in their whiskey-colored depths and the pulse in the hollow of her throat, above the deep V of her blouse, beat a fraction more rapidly. Hell, she was beautiful. No wonder his brother hadn't been able to resist her. Neither had he.

"So how have you and the kids been doing?"

"I already told you. We're fine."

"No problems?"

Her jaw tensed a bit. "None that we can't deal with, Jay," she said and wished he'd just disappear. She glanced out the window and spied Christina drawing stick figures on the walk. "You can tell your dad that we're doing fine. No, change that." She waved expansively. "Tell him we're great.

Not a care in the world." She'd never gotten along with Philip's father, Carlo, nor with his mother, for that matter. As his second wife, so many years younger than her husband, Tiffany had been looked upon as a bimbo, a fraud, a little girl who didn't know her own mind and worst of all, as someone who was after all the Santini family's wealth. Considering the circumstances, all those thoughts were nothing but a cruel, ironic joke.

And what did J.D. care? When had he ever? Her heart pumped a little at the sight of him and she silently called herself an idiot. He was just as ruggedly male as she remembered him, with his long, jeans-clad legs, black hair in need of a trim and penetrating silver-gray eyes.

"What about the juvenile authorities?"

Her fingers tightened into fists. "Don't worry about it."

His smile was cynical and downright sexy. If a woman noticed. Tiffany told herself she didn't. She'd known J.D.—James Dean Santini—too many years to trust him. She'd let down her guard a couple of times and in both instances she'd gotten herself into trouble—the worst kind of jeopardy. It wouldn't happen again. Too much was at stake.

"You know, Tiff, you're still a member of the family."

"Since when?" she retorted, skewering him with a look that, she was certain, could kill. She pointed a long finger at him. "I've *never* been considered a part of the family. Over fourteen years of marriage and neither one of your parents accepted me." *Nor did you*, she silently seethed, but held her tongue. There had been enough pain borne on both sides. She had always longed to be part of a real family, one with a father and mother and siblings, unlike her own small group of relatives. Shivering inwardly, she pushed those thoughts aside and stubbornly refused to think of them even though, at the end of this very week, her father—her biological father, for that was all he really was, a man who had donated his share of genes to her DNA—was marrying his longtime mistress.

Wrapping her arms around her middle, she walked to the window that overlooked the backyard. A smile teased her lips as she watched her daughter.

Right now, the little girl was chasing after the cat, Charcoal, as he darted between the shrubs.

"What kind of trouble is Stephen getting himself into?" J.D. persisted. She'd forgotten how determined and maddeningly single-minded her brother-in-law could be.

"Nothing that serious."

"Just serious enough that you had to talk with the authorities."

Silently counting to ten, she rotated her neck and worked out the kinks. "You know, J.D., the last thing I need right now is to be grilled or given some kind of lecture by you. I don't know why you've decided to come to visit right now, but I'm sure it wasn't just to harass me."

He snorted. "Just a simple question."

"Don't give me that. Nothing you've ever done is simple or without a purpose."

"And you're dodging the issue."

"Because it's none of your business, *counselor*."

"The kid's my nephew."

She whirled on him. "And you've never given a damn."

"I'm giving one now." His expression was hard and demanding, just as she remembered, his eyes relentless and piercing. He hadn't changed much except for the fact that she'd never before seen him seated in one position for so long. He'd been too restless, too filled with nervous energy. But now he was waiting.

"He got caught with alcohol about a month ago," she admitted as if it wasn't the big deal she knew it was.

"At thirteen?"

"Yes, at thirteen. He was with an older boy, the brother

of one of his friends, who was throwing a party. Anyway, the neighbors complained, the police showed up, everyone ran, but Stephen and a couple of other kids were caught. Even though Stephen hadn't been drinking, he got himself into some hot water. A juvenile counselor was assigned to his case and just a few minutes ago I was speaking with her."

J.D.'s eyebrows slammed together. "And you don't think this is serious."

"Serious enough," she admitted, though she wasn't going to let her bachelor brother-in-law, a man who'd never had any kids, know just how worried she was. It was too easy for him to criticize. "Stephen will be all right."

"If you say so."

"He's a teenager—"

"Barely."

Tiffany bristled. She stepped closer to him and tried vainly to keep her temper in check. "Don't start passing judgment, J.D. You remember how much trouble you can get into during those years, don't you? According to Philip, your adolescent exploits were practically legendary."

His jaw hardened and he climbed to his feet. He winced, then hitched himself across the room to stare out the window over the sink.

"What happened?" she asked, angry with herself for being concerned. J.D. Santini was the last man she should care about. "Did you hurt yourself?"

"Tore a couple of tendons. It's not a big deal."

"When?"

"A few months ago. Motorcycle accident."

"Oh." So there was still a bit of the rebel in him. Good. For some reason she didn't want to examine too closely, she found that bit of information comforting, but she couldn't dwell on it. Wouldn't. "No one told me."

"Why would they?"

"Because, dammit, I am still part of the family."

"I was laid up for a few days. No big deal. Believe me, if it had been life-threatening, you would have been notified."

"Before or after the funeral?"

His jaw tightened. "You act as if you're ostracized. The way I remember it, you came down here and cut the ties, so to speak, because you wanted to."

That much was true. She'd run fast and hard to get away from the suffocating grip of the Santini family.

"Let's not get into all that," she suggested. "It's water under the bridge, anyway. Why don't you tell me why, if you're working for the company, you're in Bittersweet?"

"Dad's interested in buying some land around here someplace. Potential winery."

"And you're the expert?" This wasn't making a lot of sense.

"Looks like."

She didn't remember him being so evasive. In fact, the J.D. she'd known had been blunt and direct, a man who could make you squirm with his intense, no-nonsense gaze, thin-lipped mouth that rarely smiled and somewhat harsh demeanor. With raven-black hair, thick eyebrows and sculpted features, he never gave an inch and was known to call them as he saw them. And never had he worked for his father. The way Philip had told it, J.D. the renegade, eleven years his junior, was forever at odds with his old man. But then who could get along with Carlo Santini, patriarch with the iron fist and closed mind?

Something wasn't right. She sensed it and began to perspire. She cracked open the windows in the kitchen nook. "You know, Jay, you're the last person, the very last, I expected to cave in and join the family business."

"Life has a way of not turning out the way you expect it, Tiffany. Haven't you learned that by now?" His lips barely moved, his eyes caught hers in a breathtaking hold that she hated, and she felt the first trickle of sweat slide between her shoulder blades. Her stomach did a slow, sensual roll, reminding her of just how easy it was to fall prey to his charm.

But not now. Not again. Never.

She swallowed hard and avoided his eyes. Suddenly the kitchen was much too small. Too close. She needed a reason to break up this unexpected atmosphere of intimacy with J.D.

"Oh, gosh, it's almost three," she said, staring pointedly at her watch. "Christina," she called, looking through the window and spying her daughter drawing on the side of the garage with a piece of yellow chalk. "Time for your nap."

"No nap!" The little girl dropped the chalk.

"Excuse me," Tiffany said, hurrying out the back door and feeling the much-needed breath of a breeze touch her face and bare arms. It had been a long, strained week capped by a hellish day speaking with Stephen's counselor. On top of it all, she'd learned that her father—John Cawthorne—actually expected her to show up at his wedding after thirty-three years of pretending she didn't exist. Fat chance!

Charcoal, who had been rolling over in a spot of sunlight, scrambled to his feet and dashed under the porch. "Come on, sweetheart," Tiffany cajoled her daughter as she picked up broken bits of chalk and stuffed them into the tattered pack.

"I not tired."

"Sure you are."

"No, I not!" Christina's lower lip protruded and she folded her chubby arms across her chest.

"Well, Bub and Louie are tired and they're waiting upstairs in bed for you. It'll just be for a little while." She hoisted her daughter into her arms and Christina, still pouting, didn't protest.

Unfortunately J.D. had watched the entire display from the kitchen window. Tiffany wished he'd just go away. She didn't need any member of the Santini family, especially not J.D., intruding into her life right now—or ever, for that matter. She knew they all thought she hadn't been good enough for Philip while he was alive, so they could all just go and take the proverbial leap.

She carried Christina into the back of the house, mouthed, "I'll be back in a few minutes" to her erstwhile guest, then lugged the tired three-year-old through the hallway and up the stairs to her room.

This part of the house, aside from the addition of the bathroom, was as it had been for nearly a hundred years and Christina's room was a small alcove that overlooked the fruit trees in the backyard. The bedroom next door belonged to Stephen, and Tiffany's was across the hall. There were two occupied apartments in the basement and a third one—an empty studio—on the top floor. The ground floor of the carriage house that flanked the backyard was rented, while the upper level was, at the moment, standing empty.

"There you go," she said, as she tucked Christina under a hand-pieced quilt her grandmother had made. She arranged Bub, a floppy-eared stuffed rabbit missing one eye, and Louie, a black-masked toy raccoon, beside her daughter.

"Just a little while," Christina insisted.

"That's right." Tiffany leaned over and planted a soft kiss on the little girl's forehead. Christina, whom Tiffany had dubbed the "miracle" baby, had been an unexpected blessing three years ago, long after she and Philip had decided that one child—Stephen—was enough. Philip had two nearly-grown children from his previous marriage and he hadn't thought it was necessary to "overpopulate the world," especially when he'd already been "paying a fortune" in child support.

Gazing down at her daughter now, Tiffany was thankful that God had seen otherwise, and that despite the use of birth control and Philip's lack of interest, Christina had been conceived. "Destiny," she'd told her husband upon learning the news.

"Or a curse," Philip had replied with a scowl. "How many kids do you think I can afford?"

"It's just one more."

"That you planned," he stated flatly, insisting that she'd intentionally tricked him by not using her diaphragm. The fight had simmered for days, with Philip brooding and spending more time at the office. Philip had slept in the den for nearly two weeks, acting as if she wasn't even in the same house with him until she'd confronted him and flown into a rage.

"I want this baby!" she'd told him. "Stephen needs a sister or brother."

"He's got one of each."

"Half-siblings who don't live with him." She'd advanced upon him as he'd sat in his chair, holding the newspaper firmly in white-knuckled fists, his jaw set, his nostrils flared in a seething, silent rage. "I didn't plan to have this baby, but now that it's coming, I consider it a gift and you should, too."

"I'm too old to be a father again."

"But I'm not too old to be a mother. It'll be all right," she'd said, aching inside. She wanted this baby so badly. "I'll make it right."

His snort of derision and snap of the sports page had been the end of the argument.

Tiffany had been crushed by Philip's attitude but determined to bear this child and bring it into a loving world.

Eventually, after brooding and pouting for a week or two, Philip had come to terms with the prospect of diapers, formula and interrupted sleep. He'd come home with a bouquet of spring flowers and told her that another baby, though not in his plan for the future, might be the best thing that had ever happened to him—to them and their marriage. "It'll either keep me young or make me old real fast," he'd said.

Tiffany felt a pang of remorse for a man she'd thought she loved, then stepped out of the room as Christina yawned and sighed softly, her eyelids slowly lowering.

J.D. was waiting for her, his hips resting against the balustrade, arms folded across his chest, jaw set with determination. As she closed the door gently behind her, he cocked a thumb at the open door to the third floor. "You've got an empty room upstairs."

Obviously, he'd already checked it out.

"That's right. I'm hoping to rent it soon."

His grin was slow-spreading and positively wicked. "Well, Ms. Santini, I guess this is your lucky day."

No! She steeled herself. Surely he wasn't suggesting . . .

"That's right, Tiff," he said, as if reading her expression. "It just so happens I need a place to stay while I'm in town."

No way. She couldn't have him this close. He was too intrusive, too damned sexy. But then, he always had been.

"Sorry, Jay, but I don't rent week to week, or, uh, month to month for that matter. I, uh, always insist upon a six-month lease, first and last month's rent, and both a cleaning deposit and a security deposit."

"Do you?" One dark eyebrow lifted in mocking disbelief.

"Always."

"Fine," he said, his eyes gleaming as if he loved calling her bluff. "Just show me where to sign."

Chapter Two

"This is crazy," Tiffany muttered under her breath as she climbed the curved stairs to the top floor. J.D. followed after her, his steps uneven as he hauled his damned duffel bag and briefcase with him. As if he really intended to rent the place.

There was no way! He was the last man on earth, the *last* person to whom she would hand over a key to her house.

"A little crazy," he conceded as he reached the top and tossed his bag onto the stripped mattress of the antique brass bed. She saw the white lines around the corners of his mouth and watched as he limped slightly to the French doors that opened onto a small balcony overlooking the backyard then set his battered briefcase on the floor.

"You should try to find something on the ground level."

"Should I?" he mocked, then tossed his hair out of his eyes. "Don't worry about it, Tiff."

"Why do you need a place in Bittersweet, anyway?"

"I told you, the winery—"

"I know, but why here? Why not in California? Sonoma or Napa."

"Dad likes to do business in Oregon."

"There are lots of vineyards in the Willamette Valley, closer to Portland." Her mind was spinning. What would it mean to have the Santinis here, in her hometown, her place of refuge? She'd thought when she'd moved here, to this house that Philip had bought as an investment, that she would have the time and distance she needed to start over, to keep from thinking about the pain, about the guilt.

"He thinks the climate is better here for what he wants to do. He's already got a couple of wineries up north."

"I know," she interjected, remembering all too well the rolling hills of Santini Brothers' vineyards, the place she'd met her future brother-in-law.

J.D. lifted a shoulder as if it made no difference to him. "As I said, I'm just checking out some possibilities."

"And in the meantime you thought you might stop by and look in on me, see if I'm being the model mother I'm supposed to be," she snapped angrily. For as long as she could remember, Carlo Santini hadn't trusted her. He had thought she wanted his son in order to get a chunk of the Santini money. What the Santini family hadn't understood was that when she'd met Philip, it wasn't his family's wealth that had attracted her, but his aura of sophistication, his charm, his way of making her feel loved for the first time in her life. She'd been young, naive and impetuous. Well . . . no longer.

And as for Philip's money, that had become a moot point: there wasn't much.

"No one's ever accused you of being a poor mother," J.D. said, turning the crank to open one of the windows. A breeze, fresh with the scents of cut grass and roses, whispered into the slope-ceilinged room.

"Just a lousy wife."

He didn't respond.

"I know what they thought, J.D.," she said, unable to leave the subject alone. "I heard them say that I was looking for a father figure, that I needed an older man because I didn't grow up knowing my dad."

"And what do you think?"

"I think I loved your brother. End of story. Not that it's anyone's business."

His jaw tightened.

"Just because I was raised by a single mother didn't mean I was insecure or needed an older man to take care of me." She swiped a speck of dust from the coffee table and hoped she didn't show her true emotions. Inwardly she cringed at the accusation. Especially this week, the subject of her own parentage was difficult enough to consider when she was alone with her thoughts. When anyone else brought up the taboo topic, she saw red.

"No reason to get so defensive."

"No?" she challenged. crossing the short space separating them. "Then what's the real reason you're in Bittersweet, Jay? And don't give me any garbage about the winery, okay? There are dozens of little towns down here around the border. Some in Oregon and more in California. It's more than just bad luck that you're here."

His eyes, gray as the dawn, held hers and she braced herself. What was it about J.D. that seemed to bring out the worst in her? Whenever she was around him, her usually smoothed feathers ruffled easily. One disbelieving look from his suspicious eyes and she was itching for a fight, more than ready to defend herself and her children.

"Look, do you really want to rent this place?" She waved widely, taking in all four-hundred square feet of living space. It was sparse, with only room for a bed, bureau, table, love seat and television. The kitchen consisted of a small stove, refrigerator and sink tucked into an alcove. The bathroom was confining and bare bones with its narrow stall shower, toilet and sink.

"It'll do," he allowed in that drawl she found so irritating.

"But you won't be down here long, so why bother?"

He studied his fingers for a second, then looked at her again. "Maybe you're right, Tiff. Maybe I just want to be close to you." He eyed her carefully and her breath caught in her throat.

"For all the wrong reasons," she said, then regretted the words.

"Are there any right ones?"

"No!" she said so quickly that she blushed. "Of . . . of course there aren't." Clearing her throat, she added, "Well, if that's the way you want it—"

"I do."

He was too close. Perspiration broke out along her spine. This wasn't going to work. "Then I guess there's nothing more to say but make yourself at home."

"I will."

Why she found those last words so damning, she didn't know, but as she hurried down the stairs she was struck by the feeling that her tightly woven little world was unraveling by the minute. First, as a widow and single mother, she had to deal with an adolescent boy who was on the verge of trouble. Possibly big trouble. Next, she'd suddenly been faced with her biological father—a man she'd been told throughout most of her growing-up years was dead. Now that man, John Cawthorne, was trying to become part of her life. And he didn't walk alone. No, the man carried baggage and lots of it in the form of two other daughters—Tiffany's half-sisters, whom she didn't know and wasn't sure she cared to. And lastly, J.D. and the Santini family. Too much. It was all too much.

"Wonderful," she muttered in the second-floor hallway, where she peeked in on a napping Christina before continuing downstairs. "Just great."

Why right now, when everything in her life was spinning out of control, did she have to face J.D. again? The mercurial and volatile nature of her emotions concerning her brother-in-law had been the bane of her existence ever since she'd married into the Santini family. Nothing would change now that J.D. had moved in. In fact, she was certain that things would only get worse.

"I just don't get it," Stephen said as he tucked his skateboard into a corner of the back porch. The board was battered and scratched, the decals for Nirvana and Metallica nearly worn off, the wheels not quite as round as they'd once been. He yanked open the screen door and walked into the kitchen where Tiffany was trying and failing to balance her checkbook while cooking dinner. "Why's *he* here?" Stephen didn't bother hiding the sneer in his voice or his dislike of his uncle, a man he thought was intruding into his life.

"Business."

"Yeah, monkey business if ya ask me." Stephen wiped his hands down the front of his jeans and tossed his too-long hair from his eyes. "I don't like this."

Neither do I, Tiffany was tempted to say, but held her tongue. Her feelings for J.D. were far more complicated than simple like or dislike. Too complicated to examine very closely. "He won't be around that much," she said as daylight was beginning to give way to dusk. She snapped her checkbook closed and put the statement back into its envelope until she had more time to go through it. It wasn't that she couldn't make the figures add up, it was that it seemed impossible to stretch her salary and the rent she collected far enough to cover all her expenses.

"Good," Stephen grunted, eyeing the barbecue sauce that was simmering on the stove.

The temperature still hovered near eighty and a hummingbird was flitting near the open blossoms of the clematis that draped over the eaves of the back porch. Bees droned while a woodpecker drilled loudly in a nearby oak tree and the muted sound of traffic reached her ears.

"Is he eatin' with us?" Stephen asked.

"I don't think so."

"Good."

"He *is* your uncle," she reminded him gently. *And he's your brother-in-law, whether you like it or not*, she told herself. J.D. had signed his six-month lease, given her a check and started carting his few belongings up the stairs. His limp was noticeable, but just barely, and she wondered if his brush with death had been the cause for his reconciliation with his father. Or had it been because Carlo had lost his eldest son?

Her heart squeezed at the thought of the accident that had taken Philip's life. Guilt, ever her companion, encroached upon her, wrapping its fingers around her heart. She had loved Philip once, but it had been such a long time ago.

"So why did you have to see the counselor today?" Stephen asked for the first time. He rubbed one elbow with the fingers of the opposite hand, a nervous trait he'd developed from the time he was four years old.

"She just wanted to talk to me."

The cat cried at the back door.

"Come on in, you," Tiffany said with a smile, then noticed as she held open the screen door that the small tear in the mesh was getting larger. Sooner or later it would have to be fixed. Charcoal streaked inside.

"I *know* she wanted to talk to you. But why?" Deftly plucking a bunch of grapes from a bowl on the table, Stephen leaned insolently against the doorframe and began plopping the juicy bits of fruit into his mouth.

This was the opportunity she'd been waiting for, because deep down, though she would never admit it, she was scared. Scared to death.

"Well, she started out by asking about you—you know, just checking on how things were going."

"She just saw me the other day."

"I know, but she had a few more questions. She's worried about you, Stephen, and frankly, so am I."

"I'm fine, Mom."

If only she could believe it. Oh, Lord, how she wanted to trust her boy. "She had a few questions about your relationship with Mr. Wells."

He froze for a second, then spat the seed from his grape into the sink. "I worked for him. Big deal."

"What do you know about him? They think you know something about why he disappeared," she said, finally admitting what the juvenile officer had implied. It was ridiculous, of course. It had to be. Isaac Wells had disappeared over a month ago, vanished without a trace. Whether it was foul play or by his own intention, no one knew what had happened to the elderly man. It was the biggest mystery Bittersweet had seen in years. Though Tiffany believed without a doubt that her son was innocent of any wrongdoing, she wanted to hear it from Stephen himself.

"I don't know nothin'."

"That's what I said, but now someone, and I don't know who, has come forward and said that he . . . well, or she, for that matter, saw you out at the Wells place on the day that Isaac disappeared."

Stephen blanched and Tiffany's heart seemed to fall through the floor. "Someone saw me?"

"That's what she said."

"Then they're lyin'. I wasn't near the place."

"You're sure?"

"Don't you believe me?" he cried, licking his lips nervously, his eyes round with an unnamed fear.

She ached to trust him. "Of course I do, but—"

"But what?" Stephen interrupted.

"But it's your word against this other person's."

"Whose?"

She turned her palms to the ceiling and wished her love was as blind as it had been a few seconds before. "I don't know, really," she said. "But you've had a fascination with that ranch for a long time."

"Yeah. I liked old Isaac's cars. That's all. Come on, Mom, you don't really think I had something to do with him up and leaving—or maybe even being killed?" Stephen asked, clearly astounded by her apparent lack of trust.

"Of course not. But I know you were there before."

"For cryin' out loud, Mom, I drove his old Chevy once. Yeah, I admit it, I did. But that's all. It wasn't like I was going to steal it or anything. I would never do anything like *that*." His face was as pale as death. He swallowed so hard, his Adam's apple bobbed. "I . . . mean, I didn't— Oh, gosh, what're you saying?"

"I know you didn't hurt Mr. Wells, Stephen," she said, instantly filled with remorse. "Oh, honey, I know you didn't have anything to do with him disappearing, believe me." She took hold of his arm only to have it ripped from her overly protective fingers. "But . . ." He was staring at her with the eyes she'd loved from the minute he was born and her heart hurt that she would have to broach such an awful topic. "Look, Stephen, I trust you and I love you, but I do want to know what you were doing there that day—the time you were caught by Mr. Wells. Then I want to know why you lied about it."

There. It was finally in the open.

Stormy eyes glowered from beneath dark brows. "I didn't—"

"Uh-uh-uh," she warned. "Come on, honey."

His jaw worked and he looked out the window, pretending interest in the white trail of a jet that was slicing across the sky. His broadening shoulders slumped as if from an invisible weight. "The day that I took the Chevy—it was just because I was bored. Well, and because I was dared, I guess."

"Dared?"

"By Miles Dean, don't you remember?"

How could she forget? Miles Dean, a couple of years older than Stephen, was a bad influence on her son. "I didn't lie about it. Wells caught me, made me do some extra chores that he didn't pay me for and that was it. You know all this."

"Go on." Nerves strung tight, she walked to the stove and stirred the tangy sauce with a wooden spoon. Though it was warm in the kitchen, her fingers felt like ice. "What about the day that Isaac was last seen?" she asked and watched her son swallow hard, as if the lump in his throat was as big as a cantaloupe.

"Okay, okay. The next time, the *last* time I was there," he said, nudging the edge of the carpet with his toe, "it was another dare, okay?"

"Oh, Stephen, no."

"It's true." He shoved both fists into the front pockets of his baggy jeans. "Some of the kids knew I'd worked for the old guy and that I knew where he kept his keys to his vintage cars, since I'd spent a few days working for him, so . . . I . . ." He hesitated, as if he was afraid to say what was on his mind.

"So you what?" she prodded, surprised at his candor. This was a secret he'd managed to keep.

"Miles Dean, he dared me to swipe the keys." Stephen bit his lower lip.

"Again? Why?"

"I—I don't know." He looked genuinely filled with regret. "Maybe he was gonna drive one of 'em. He liked that old Buick, but anyway it was the day the old man split."

Her throat was as dry as a desert wind, her pulse pounding out, No, no, no, in her ears. *Don't ask it, Tiffany. You don't want to know.* But she couldn't stop the question from forming on her lips. "And did you?"

"Take the keys?" He shook his head vigorously. "Heck, no! I climbed the fence and was going to sneak into the barn but I just had this . . . this weird feeling. I can't really explain it. I looked over my shoulder at the house and there was Mr. Wells, sittin' in his rocker, a rifle on his lap, starin' at me." Stephen took in a deep breath. "It was weird, Mom. *Really* weird. So, so I—I took off." He looked at the floor and blushed. "I was scared and I ran and Miles was really mad and . . . he threatened to beat the—er, tar out of me."

"And that's why you couldn't admit that you were there?" she asked.

He nodded mutely, tears of mortification causing his eyes to glisten.

"Oh, honey—" She wanted to enfold him in her arms, but didn't dare. The look he shot her warned her to keep her maternal instincts under wraps.

"And you never saw him again?"

Stephen shrugged. "I don't think anybody did," he whispered in a voice that was barely audible over the hum of the refrigerator, the bubble of the simmering sauce and the stutter of the woodpecker tapping at the oak tree outside the window.

"Why didn't you tell the police?"

"I said, I was scared."

"So am I," she admitted, tapping the wooden spoon on the edge of the saucepan. She believed her son, but wished he'd come clean earlier; that he'd trusted her enough to confide in her. The timer chimed, reminding her to check the coals she'd lighted in the barbecue.

"Mommy?" Christina's voice filtered through the doorway just as the little girl, dragging her blanket behind her, toddled into the kitchen.

"Well, look who woke up." With a smile, Tiffany picked up her daughter and placed a kiss on her crown. "Are you still a sleepyhead?"

"No!" Christina snorted out the word and rested her head on her mother's shoulder.

"Yeah, right," Stephen muttered under his breath as he plucked another grape from the cluster in the bowl and tossed it into the air before catching it in his mouth. "Grumpy Gus."

"I'm not a Grumpy Gus!" Christina grouched.

"Shh! Of course you're not, sweetheart." Tiffany sent her son a look that would cut through steel. "Your brother was only teasing you."

"He's a big . . . big . . . dumbhead."

"Oh, wow, like that's a problem," Stephen mocked. "A dumbhead, Chrissie? Is that what I am?"

"Enough!" Tiffany said. "Come on, sweetie, you can have some grapes while I put the chicken on the grill."

"I *hate* grapes."

Tiffany set Christina into a chair at the table and Stephen, on the other side, had the audacity to cross his eyes.

"Lookie what he's doing. I *hate* you, too, dumbhead."

"Christina, don't call your brother any bad names and you, Stephen, should know better than to bother her when she's still sleepy. You weren't all that sunny-side up when you used to wake up from your nap."

"Make him take one now!" Christina said in the bossy tone she'd adopted since turning three.

"I'm too old for naps."

"But not to set the table," Tiffany said as Stephen, grumbling under his breath about "women's work," got to his feet and searched in a drawer for place mats.

"So how come we're not going to the wedding?" he asked as he slid three woven mats onto the top of the table, then reached into a cupboard for glasses. She heard the sound of footsteps on the back porch and turned to see J.D. through the screen door. Instantly she tensed. Living in the same house with him was sure to be torture.

"The wedding?" she repeated.

"You know. Grandpa's." He scowled as he said the word, as if it tasted foul.

She opened the door and J.D. strode in. "Wedding? What're you talking about? Your grandparents have been married for over fifty years."

"He's not talking about the Santinis," Tiffany said, wishing she could drop the subject, but J.D. was going to find out sooner or later. In a town the size of Bittersweet, gossip spread like a windswept wildfire. "My father's getting married on Sunday."

"*Your* father?" He scowled slightly, his eyes narrowing. "But I thought— Well, I always had the impression that he was either dead or out of the picture."

"He seems to be back in. Big time." She pulled a pan of chicken from the refrigerator and carried it outside, then forked the meat onto the grill. The chicken sizzled on the hot rack. "Stephen, bring out the pan of sauce on the stove—and the wooden spoon."

J.D. came through the door with the items in question. "Tell me about your father."

She hesitated, took the pan from his outstretched hand and began drizzling barbecue sauce over the chicken. She didn't really want to discuss the wedding with her brother-in-law, but she had no choice. "It's a long story, but it seems my biological father is really John Cawthorne. I found out years ago, but it was easier to keep up the lie my mother had started when I was a little kid—that my dad was dead."

"Easier?"

"Then thinking he just didn't give a damn," she said in a

voice barely audible because her kids were still arguing at the table on the other side of the screen door.

"Cawthorne?" he repeated as if the name was vaguely familiar.

"Yeah, a cowboy-turned-developer-and-businessman. Married. One daughter. Well, one legiti—" She held her tongue as both her children had turned their heads in her direction. "Uh, would you, uh, like to eat with us?" she asked as much to change the subject as anything else. She set the lid onto the barbecue. J.D. Santini was the last person she wanted to spend time with and in the corner of her peripheral vision she caught a glimpse of her son rolling his eyes theatrically.

J.D. hesitated, then shook his head. "Thanks, but another time. I just wanted to work a deal with you."

"A deal?" She was instantly wary.

"I'll need a phone until mine's connected."

"No problem." She let out the breath she hadn't realized she'd been holding. The man made her so damned nervous. She picked up the empty saucepan and spoon and told herself not to let down her guard for a minute. J.D., she reminded herself for the fiftieth time, was a man to avoid. If possible. "There's the wall phone in the kitchen."

"Seen it."

"And an extension in my bedroom on the second floor."

"The kitchen will do."

He started up the two steps leading to the back porch and Tiffany felt a wash of color flood her cheeks. "Fine."

"When the bill comes, I'll take care of the extra charges." He hesitated. "Thanks."

"No problem." But it was. Everything about him seemed to be a complication in her life. "I was serious about dinner," she added, knowing she was making a big mistake, but unable to stop herself. She was going to live in the house with him for the next few months. If life was going to be tolerable, they had to get along. "Look, it's not a big deal, but I thought we should try and . . . and . . ."

"And what, Tiffany?" he asked, his eyes as dark as slate.

What was it about one of his looks that could make her feel like a fool? "Never mind. I was just being polite."

He looked over his shoulder to the well-used barbecue and the smoke escaping from a hole in the lid. Furrows etched his brow and suspicion tightened the muscles of his shoulders. "I think we're past being polite."

"Then we should go back a step or two, don't you think?"

He shoved his hands into the back pockets of his jeans. "What is it they say? Something about never going back."

"Then they're wrong." She stepped closer to him, close enough to notice the few flecks of gray at his temples. "You barged in here. Asked all sorts of questions about me and the kids. Demanded to live here. So I think—no, I *insist* that we be civil and, yes, at times even polite to each other. If we don't, I can guarantee our new living arrangements aren't gonna be worth a single red cent."

He glanced toward the house and the kitchen, where her kids were lurking near the open door. He nodded. "Thanks for the offer," he said. "Another time, maybe. Thanks." Then he went through the screen door and Tiffany didn't know whether to be relieved that he was gone or insulted that he hadn't accepted her invitation. It had been her way of offering an olive branch, a way to bridge the gap that had been forever between them.

Not forever, she reminded herself. There had been a time when she'd been close to her brother-in-law. Too close. She swallowed hard and let out her breath as she watched him walk through the kitchen and press a shoulder against the swinging door to the hallway. She wondered if his limp was permanent but decided it didn't matter. Any way you looked at it, J.D. Santini was a very sexy man. Just the kind of man she didn't need around here.

"J.D.'s a jerk," Stephen said as she returned to the house and set the empty saucepan in the sink.

"Let's not tell him, okay?" Tiffany flipped on the faucet and rinsed the small pot.

"Why not?"

"'Cause it's not nice," Christina said with a knowing nod that caused her curls to bounce precociously.

"Big deal. I thought we were always supposed to tell the truth."

Tiffany placed a bowl of pasta salad on the table, zapped some leftover garlic bread in the microwave and decided to ignore her son's need to vent some of his anger. How could she defend J.D.? The man was an enigma and someone she was certain would only cause her trouble.

She poured the kids each a glass of milk and hesitated, thinking she might have a small glass of wine, then discarded the idea. As long as J.D. was living here, she would need a clear head.

Who knew really why he was in Bittersweet? Judging from past experience, she realized she couldn't trust him.

J.D. was and always had been dangerous. If she were smart, she'd stay as far away from him as possible.

Even if he was living in her house.

The kid was already in trouble with the law.

"Hell." J.D. sat on the edge of his new bed and ignored the mental image that leveled a guilty finger in his direction. It wasn't his fault that Stephen had decided to rebel. What thirteen-year-old wouldn't? Stephen had lost his father, been uprooted and moved to a new town, and become the man of the family all in one fell swoop.

It was too much for any boy. No wonder the kid was full of piss and vinegar.

What a mess. And J.D. wasn't going to make it any better.

He rifled through his duffel bag until he found a crisp manila envelope. Inside the packet was the deed, bill of sale and proof that this house—Tiffany's home since the accident that had taken Philip's life—belonged to the Santini family. Well, at least most of it. A portion—one fourth, to be exact—was still hers; the rest had been signed away to pay off Philip's gambling debts.

"Great," J.D. said, tossing the envelope onto the foot of the bed and wishing he hadn't agreed to step into Philip's shoes in the first place. He'd never wanted to work for his father, had avoided anything to do with Santini Brothers Enterprises for years, but then, after Philip's death, he'd felt obligated. His parents had been devastated by the loss of their eldest, and his father had hoped to "step down," or so he'd claimed. At the same time J.D. had become jaded with the law, tired of the constant courtroom battles and legal arguments he'd once thrived upon, sickened that settlements and awards were always more important than justice.

His motorcycle accident had been his own personal epiphany. When a colleague had suggested he sue the manufacturer of the bike, or the highway department, or the parents of the kid he'd swerved to avoid, he'd decided to chuck it. J.D. had been pushing the speed limit, the accident had been his fault; he'd nearly lost his life and he wasn't going to blame anyone or anything but himself.

But the accident had made him take a good long look at himself and what he did for a living.

When his father had offered him the job, he'd accepted, as long as they both understood it was temporary. He wasn't going to be sucked permanently into the fold.

For the time being he took the job that Philip, in dying, had vacated. Carlo kept talking about retiring and had tried to lure J.D. into becoming more involved—about someday running the multifaceted company—but deep in his heart, J.D. didn't believe his old man would ever voluntarily give up the reins of an operation he'd started nearly fifty years earlier with his own brother, who had retired five years ago. Not so Carlo; the day Carlo Santini quit work was the day he gave up on life.

One of the first duties of J.D.'s employment was to deal with Tiffany. The family wanted to be certain that she and the children were dealt with fairly, but Carlo had never liked his second daughter-in-law, nor had he forgiven his son for divorcing his first wife. Whether he admitted it or not, Carlo blamed Tiffany for the marriage breakup, though she hadn't even met Philip until after his divorce was final.

Or had she?

J.D. really didn't give a damn. He only had to do his job down here, find the right piece of land for the new winery, then make tracks. He'd check on the kids, make sure the widow Santini was handling things okay, inform her about the ownership of the house, then return to Portland.

He couldn't wait.

He tucked the legal papers inside his bag again and stuffed the duffel into a drawer. Walking stiffly across the room he sat on the edge of the windowsill and looked into the backyard where Tiffany, in the gathering dusk, was watering some of the planters near the carriage house. She was humming to herself, seemingly at peace with the world, but J.D. sensed it was all an act. The woman was restless; disturbed about something. Ten to one it had to do with her little foray down to the police department today. She set down her watering can and glanced up toward the window.

He didn't move.

Through the glass their gazes met. J.D.'s stomach tightened. His pulse raced. As he stared into those amber eyes, something inside him broke free. Memories he'd locked away emerged and turned his throat to dust. He remembered touching her, kissing her, feeling her sweet, forbidden surrender. God, she was beautiful.

She licked her lips and his knees went weak at the silent, innocent provocation.

Or was it innocent?

Damn it all to hell. Sweat tickled the back of his neck. Desire crept through his blood.

She looked away at first, as if her thoughts, too, had traveled a sensual and taboo course. She turned her attention back to the planter boxes and J.D. snapped the blinds closed. This couldn't be happening. Not again. Not ever.

His fascination for his deceased brother's wife was his personal curse, one he'd borne from the moment he'd first laid eyes on her.

Chapter Three

"Did you hear that we're getting a new neighbor?" Doris, the owner of the small insurance agency where Tiffany worked, asked the next day. Tiffany was just settling into her chair, balancing her coffee cup in one hand while reaching for the stack of mail sitting on the corner of her desk.

"Who is it this time?" Tiffany took a swallow of coffee and snagged her letter opener from the top drawer. In the small cottage converted into offices there had been everything from acupuncturists to a toy store, a bead shop and a phone-card business. All had failed.

"An architect," Doris said with a wry smile.

Tiffany froze. "You don't mean—?"

"Yep. Bliss Cawthorne's going to be right next door."

"Great." Tiffany sliced open the top envelope as if her life depended upon it. She didn't need to be reminded of her half-sister, her *legitimate* half-sister. Not this week.

"Thought you'd be pleased." Doris's eyes gleamed from behind thick, fashionable frames. Near sixty and divorced, she had the energy and stamina of a woman half her age. "She already stopped by this morning, asking about tenant's insurance, spied your nameplate, and after half a beat, said she'd be back later."

"To see me."

"I guess." Doris lifted a shoulder and rolled her chair back as the fax machine whirred to life. "Uh-oh, looks like someone found us. Probably from the main office." Adjusting her reading glasses, she walked to the fax machine and waited for the paper it spewed forth. " Another memo about Isaac Wells, wouldn't you know," she said, clucking her tongue and shaking her short blond curls. "Aren't we lucky to have policies out on him. I wonder what happened to that old guy."

"You and everyone else in town," Tiffany said uneasily. Any talk of Isaac's disappearance reminded her that the police thought Stephen knew more than he was telling. She shivered. Impossible. Not her boy. He was only thirteen.

Doris snapped up the page of information.

"When is Bliss moving in?" Tiffany asked in an effort to change the course of the conversation. How would she deal with seeing her half-sister every working day? Bliss Cawthorne, "the princess." John's indulged and adored daughter. The only one of his three offspring allowed to bear his name. *Get over it*, she told herself as she settled into her morning routine, opening letters and invoices and scanning each with a practiced eye. It wasn't Bliss's fault that their father was an A number-one jerk, a man who'd ignored both of his other daughters for years. Until it was convenient for him.

Now, after his brush with death, he wanted to make everything nice-nice. As if the past thirty-odd painful years could be swept away. Just because he'd had himself a heart attack, he wanted to start over. Well, in Tiffany's estimation, facing one's mortality didn't do a whole lot toward changing the past.

Give it a rest, she told herself and, taking her own advice, buried herself in her work. Several policyholders came into the office to pay their bills or fill out claim reports.

Tiffany worked through lunch, balanced the previous day's invoices, made her daily trip to the bank, and had found time to chat with Doris about the kids and Doris's planned trip to Mexico while eating a container of strawberry yogurt at her desk.

It was nearly quitting time when the bell over the door tinkled and Tiffany glanced up. Her insides tightened a bit as she recognized Bliss, her face flushed, striding to the front counter.

Wonderful. Tiffany's good mood disappeared.

With cheekbones a model would kill for and eyes as bright as a June morning, Bliss Cawthorne looked like a woman who had everything going for her. Slim and blond, she exuded the confidence of a person who knew her own mind and had never wanted for anything. She wore a white skirt, denim shirt, wide belt and sandals. Upon the ring finger of her left hand she sported a single pear-shaped diamond, compliments of her fiancé, Mason Lafferty, a local boy who, despite his poor roots, had returned to Bittersweet a wealthy, successful man.

Bliss practically glowed, she seemed so happy, and Tiffany had to stanch the ugly stream of resentment that flowed whenever she was face-to-face with her half-sister. Fortunately, their meetings had been few and far between. Until now.

"Hi," Bliss said with a smile.

Tiffany forced a grin. "Hello."

"Did you sign the lease?" Doris asked and Bliss, her steady gaze never leaving Tiffany, nodded.

"Looks like for the next year at least, I'll be your neighbor."

"Welcome aboard," Doris said, walking around her desk to shake Bliss's hand. Her bracelets jangled in the process and she grinned widely enough to show off the gold caps on her back teeth. "It'll be nice to have another woman around here, won't it?" she asked, cocking her head in Tiffany's direction.

"Absolutely."

"It's just us and Randy around back. He organizes guided tours into the wilderness—canoeing, backpacking, trail riding, whatever." She fluttered her fingers by the side of her head, as if dismissing Randy's occupation. "Seth was in the office you're renting. Semiretired accountant, but he had a cancer scare last winter and decided to sell his business."

There was nothing that Doris liked more than gossip and she didn't get as many opportunities as she wanted, so she was anxious to bend any ear she could.

"I hear you're marrying that Lafferty boy."

Bliss's grin widened. "Next month."

"Pretty soon after your father's big to-do," Doris observed.

"I guess it is." Bliss was a little noncommittal, and Tiffany realized that her half-sister had her own reservations about their father's impending nuptials. Not that Tiffany blamed her. It seemed that the old man had kept Brynnie, his bride-to-be, as his mistress off and on during most of the duration of his first marriage to Bliss's mother, Margaret. The guy was a creep. A slime. *And you've got his blood running through your veins whether you like it or not.*

"I've decided to take out the renter's policy," Bliss said, as if the subject of her father's wedding was a little touchy. "I've listed all the assets—computers, fax machine, copier and furniture." She and Doris began discussing the policy as Tiffany printed invoices. She heard Doris giving Bliss her best sales pitch for life, auto and liability insurance while slipping her a business card.

"We could take care of all your insurance needs and we'd

be right down the hall," Doris was saying as Tiffany pulled the billings off the printer.

"I'll think about it."

"And talk to your dad. We could help him out, too." Doris nodded toward Tiffany. "I've asked Tiffany to call him and show him how we could help out, but she—"

"Doris!" Tiffany reproached, shaking her head. That was the trouble with her boss. Doris didn't understand the word *soft* when it was applied to sell. " You don't have to talk to John," she said to Bliss. "Doris can call him herself."

"I suppose," Doris said with a theatrical sigh. "But I should wait until after the wedding."

"Good idea."

"You can't blame a girl for trying, now, can you?" Doris slipped a thick bundle of papers into an envelope and handed the packet to Bliss.

"Wouldn't dream of it," Bliss replied, tucking the envelope into her leather bag. "I, uh, was hoping that you and I," she said to Tiffany, "could have lunch or coffee or something. You know, get to know each other."

"As long as it's what you want and not John's idea."

"Tiffany!" It was Doris's turn to appear aghast.

"Bliss understands," Tiffany said. "Ever since John came back to Bittersweet, he's been trying to steamroller me into doing things I'm not comfortable with."

"That's between you and Dad," Bliss said.

"So you're not going to try and pressure me into attending his wedding?"

"Wouldn't dream of it." Bliss sounded sincere. "But it's up to you. This whole concept of a new family—stepmother, half-sisters and the like—hasn't been easy for me to swallow, either. But I'm trying. And I'd like to start by having coffee or . . . a glass of wine . . . or whatever with you. But it's your choice." She glanced back at Doris, who was assessing the situation between the two half-siblings with surprised eyes. "Thanks." To Tiffany, she added, "I'll give you a call."

"Any time."

Bliss left and Doris stared after her. "You could have been more friendly, you know."

"Just because she bought a policy—"

"That has nothing to do with it. You should be friendly because she's your damned sister, Tiffany."

"Half-sister."

"Whatever." Doris straightened the papers on her desk. Her lips were pursed into a perturbed pout, little lines appearing between her plucked eyebrows. "You're lucky, you know. A sister—even a half-sister—is a special person. More than a friend." She cleared her throat. "There isn't a day goes by that I don't think of mine."

Tiffany cringed and felt like an insensitive oaf. Doris's sister had died less than a year ago from heart disease. "I suppose you're right."

"There's no 'supposing' about it. I am right. It's not Bliss's fault that her father's a jerk who never claimed his other kids. The way I look at it, Tiffany, you have a chance to have a family now. Your father, well, you can take him or leave him. Your choice. But your sisters, they're gifts. Now, let's go over these casualty reports, then you can tell me about your love life."

"There isn't much to tell," Tiffany said.

" A situation that needs to be remedied and I just happen to know a divorced father of four, forty years old, six-foot-three with gorgeous blue eyes and a smile to die for."

"I'm not in the market."

"He has a great job, nifty sense of humor and—"

"And I'm still not in the market."

"You can't mourn forever, honey," Doris said, her eyebrows lifting over the tops of her glasses.

"I'm not mourning—not really."

"Then why not go out, kick up your heels a little?"

"When the time is right."

Doris walked to the coffeepot and poured its last dregs into her mug that seemed permanently stained with her favorite shade of coral lipstick. "You've got to make it right, Tiffany."

"I will."

"When?"

"Soon," she promised but knew she was lying. She wasn't interested in men right now. There was a chance she never would be. *So what about J.D.?* that horrid voice in her head nagged, and Tiffany did what she did best: she ignored it.

"You've come to the right place," the Realtor, an egg-shaped man with freckles sprinkled over every square inch of his exposed skin insisted as he drove J.D. along the winding, hilly roads outside Bittersweet. The grass was bleached dry and wildflowers bloomed in profusion along the fencerows while Max Crenshaw blabbered on and on about the merits of one farm over another.

"I don't know much about growing grapes down here and I'll admit it right up front. But there're several wineries around Ashland and Medford, up the road a bit. They seem to do a bumper business, and the soil here grows about anything."

J.D. was barely listening. He gazed through the dusty windshield at the small herds of cattle and the occasional thicket of oak trees that dotted the fields flashing by. Nondescript music wafted from the speakers of the older Cadillac and was barely audible over the rush of cool air from the air conditioner and the drone of Crenshaw's voice.

"Been here all my life, let me tell you, and I've seen

cattle farms turned into llama and ostrich ranches. . . . You know times change, so I'm sure we'll find the right place. . . ."

J.D. tried to pay attention, but his mind strayed. To Tiffany and her kids. There was more trouble in that house than she was willing to admit. Stephen was well on the path to becoming a juvenile delinquent. J.D. could read the signs—the same signs that he'd displayed as a youth. As for Christina, the imp had woken up in the middle of the night wailing and sobbing. Through the floorboards J.D. had heard Tiffany's hurried footsteps and soft voice as she'd run to her daughter's room and whispered words of comfort.

Yep, she had her problems at the old apartment house. There were four tenants besides himself. Mrs. Ellingsworth, whom he'd already met, occupied one basement unit, an art student lived in the other, and a recently married couple resided on the main floor of the carriage house. The upper story was empty, recently vacated by a man named Lafferty.

He'd learned all this from Max Crenshaw as they'd driven from one place to the next. The Realtor seemed to know everything that happened in Bittersweet.

"Now, I'm gonna show you something that I don't have listed yet—well, no one does, but it's part of our latest local mystery and since we're driving by anyway . . ." Crenshaw braked at a run-down old ranch with a small cabin near the front of the property, a couple of sheds and an imposing barn at the back. Vast, untended acres stretched behind the house.

"Weird deal, this," Max said as he nosed the Cadillac into the drive, shoved the gearshift into Park and let the car idle. "You mind?" he asked as he rummaged in his breast pocket and came up with a crumpled pack of cigarettes.

"No."

"Good. I'm tryin' to cut back, but, hell, you know how

it is." He shook out a cigarette, offered one to J.D. and punched in the lighter.

"No, thanks."

"Ever smoke?"

"Years ago."

"Wish I could quit. Anyway, this place belongs—or belonged, depending upon what you want to believe—to a guy by the name of Isaac Wells."

"Did it?" J.D. was suddenly more interested in the dilapidated cabin and desolate acres.

"Yep. Old Isaac lived here all by himself. Never married. Had a sister who died a long while ago and some brothers who have scattered to the winds, but, oh, a month or two ago, Isaac just up and disappeared." The lighter popped and Max, after rolling down his window, lit up. "Weird as hell, if ya ask me. No one's heard anything from him. You'd think if he died or was killed, someone would've found his body by now. If he was kidnapped, he would have been ransomed, though what for I can't imagine. Some of the people in town think he had money locked in a deposit box in one of the banks or buried in tin cans around the ranch, but that's all just hearsay as much as I can tell." He smoked in silence for a few minutes. "You know, if he just took off on his own, someone he knew would have heard from him, wouldn't they?" He shook his head and jabbed his cigarette out in the ashtray. "Anyway, this place could be on the market—I'm sure as hell looking into it. Then again, it might stay just as it is forever."

J.D. studied the abandoned acres through the windshield. The house was small, in need of paint, with a couple of windows that were cracked. The barn, built of cedar planks that had weathered gray, was huge and sprawling; the other outbuildings looked worn and neglected. The entire spread seemed lonely. Desolate.

"He was an odd one, old Isaac, but didn't have any enemies that I knew of. Like I say, it's a mystery."

"Without any clues?"

"If they've got 'em, the cops aren't saying." He shifted the car into Reverse. "Let's mosey on down the road a piece. I've got a couple more ideas. The first place—the Stowell spread is listed with a Realtor in Medford. It's about a hundred acres, well-kept and the owners are anxious to sell, would even agree to terms—not that your company would need them—but let's take a look-see just in case."

He backed the Cadillac out of the drive and J.D. watched Isaac Wells's place disappear from sight in the sideview mirror.

Max prattled on. The boring music continued to play. The miles rolled beneath the wheels of the old car and J.D. itched to be anywhere else on earth. With each passing minute, he felt that he'd made the biggest mistake of his life by showing up in Bittersweet.

Juggling two sacks of groceries, Tiffany managed to unlock the front door. "I'm home," she called out, but knew before no one answered that she was alone. On a chair in the parlor, Charcoal lifted his head, then arched his back and stretched lazily. "Anybody here?" she said to the house in general, then sighed. "I guess it's just you and me, eh?" The cat yawned and padded after her to the kitchen.

A note in Mrs. Ellingsworth's chicken scratch told her that she had taken Christina to the park. Stephen was still at his grandmother's house doing yardwork. She set the sacks on the kitchen counter and started unpacking the groceries only to notice that the wedding invitation she'd tucked away was on the counter, lying open, seeming to mock her.

"Great," she muttered, fingering the smooth paper.

While she was growing up John Cawthorne had never

been around. She'd never even met him until a few months ago, and for years—*years*—she'd believed him dead. So it seemed unbelievable to her that now, when she was thirty-three years old, a widowed mother of two, she, should be expected to forgive and forget. Just like that. Well, guess again.

For the dozenth time in as many days she read the embossed invitation.

Mr. John Andrew Cawthorne and Ms. Brynnie Perez
Request the Honor of Your Presence
at the Celebration of Their Marriage
on Sunday, August 7th
at 7:00 p.m.
at the Chapel of the Rogue
Reception Following
at Cawthorne Acres
R.S.V.P.

"Fat chance," she whispered to herself.

As far as Tiffany was concerned, John Cawthorne's upcoming marriage was a sham. She wanted no part of it and had refused to attend the nuptials. Even though John had called over, even though she'd felt a ridiculous needle of guilt pierce her brain for not accepting the olive branch he'd held out to her, she'd held firm.

Scowling against a potential headache, she retrieved a handwritten note that was still tucked inside the envelope. In a bold scrawl, good old John had tried to breach a gap he'd created when he'd turned his back on her mother thirty-three years ago.

Dear Tiffany,

I know I don't deserve your support, but I'm asking for it anyway. Believe me when I say I've turned over a new leaf and more than anything I want you and your sisters to be part of my family.

God knows, I've made more than my share of mistakes. No doubt I'll make more before I see the pearly gates, but, please find it in your heart to forgive an old man who just wants to make his peace before it's time to face his Maker. In my own way, Tiffany, I love you. Always have. Always will. You're my firstborn. I hope you will join me and your sisters at the wedding.

Your father,
John Cawthorne

Father. There was that painful word again. Where had he been when her mother was working two jobs trying to raise an illegitimate daughter? Where had this wonderful "father" been during her growing-up years when she'd needed someone—anyone—to explain the complexities of the male of the species? Where had he been when she'd gotten married and had no one to give her away at the small wedding? What had he thought when she'd had children—his grandchildren?

John Cawthorne didn't know the meaning of the word *father*. She doubted that he ever would. She curled the letter in her fist, felt the edge of one sheet cut into her finger and tossed the crumpled pages into a wastebasket near the back door. Why was she even thinking of the man?

Because in a few days it will be his wedding day.

So what? So he was finally marrying the woman he'd professed to love after all these years—a woman who had collected more husbands than most women had pairs of earrings.

As for her "sisters," she wasn't sure she had anything in common with either of them. Bliss was a few years younger than she. Just as she'd appeared today in the agency, Bliss seemed always to be a cool, sophisticated woman who had been born with the proverbial silver spoon firmly lodged between her teeth. She had always had John Cawthorne's name; had never experienced the feelings of loneliness and despair at being poor or different from other kids who, even if their parents had divorced, knew who their father was. Tiffany was fairly certain she wouldn't get along with Bliss Cawthorne.

As for her other half-sibling, Katie Kinkaid—well, Katie was a dynamo, a woman who was naive enough to think she could change the world by sheer willpower.

Tiffany had nothing in common with either of them. Not that she cared. She went upstairs, changed into jeans and a sleeveless blouse, scraped her hair back into a functional ponytail, then returned to the kitchen where she started unpacking the groceries. She was just about finished when she heard the sound of voices in the backyard. Folding the grocery sacks and placing them under the sink, she glanced through the window and spied Mrs. Ellingsworth carrying Christina toward the porch.

"Mommy!" the three-year-old cried as Tiffany opened the screen door. Christina scrambled out of the older woman's arms and ran up the back steps.

"She's plumb tuckered out," Ellie said.

"Am not." Christina yawned nonetheless and the corners of her mouth turned down.

"Well, I am. I wish I had half that kid's energy." Ellie mopped her brow as Tiffany held the door open and leaned down. Christina flew into her arms.

"We swinged and got on the merry-go-round," she announced, her cheeks flushed.

"Did you?"

Ellie laughed as she stepped into the kitchen. "A few times."

"Bunches and bunches of times," Christina said, then

struggled out of her mother's arms and chased Charcoal outside.

"She's a goer, that one," Ellie said, chuckling and watching through the mesh as Christina found an old tin pie plate on the back porch and toddled down the yard. "She'll be tired tonight."

"Good." Maybe then she would sleep through till morning without the nightmares that had plagued her since Philip's death. "Taking her to the park was above and beyond the call of duty."

"Any time. She's a joy, that one." Then, as if realizing they were alone for the first time, Ellie asked, "Isn't Stephen back yet?" Before Tiffany could answer, she added, "That's odd. Octavia called and asked him to come over to mow the lawn. Said it would only take an hour. That was, when?" She checked her watch again. "Nearly three hours ago."

"Figures," Tiffany said. "I didn't find any note from him, but this was lying open." She pointed to the invitation on the counter.

"Was it?" Ellie's face puckered thoughtfully. "I didn't see it."

"Stephen must have found it and left it here." Tiffany checked for another note, found none, and told herself not to worry, that Stephen was probably just with his friends fishing or swimming or hanging out. . . . But where? "Well, I suppose I'll hear from him before too long," she said. "Now, how about a glass of iced tea or lemonade?"

Ellie reached for a tissue from the box on the counter and dabbed at her forehead. "I could use a drink, believe me. A vodka collins sounds nice, but it's a little early. Besides I've got a date."

"A date?" Tiffany repeated, surprised. "Who's the lucky guy?"

The older woman positively beamed. "Stan Brinkman.

Retired. Once owned a roofing company that he sold to his sons. He's widowed, too, and spends his summers up here and drives a fifth wheeler down to Arizona each winter."

This was news to Tiffany. "How long have you known him?"

"Long enough." Ellie gave an exaggerated wink and walked to the door. "I'll tell you all about it later." With a wave she was out the door, pausing long enough to say a few words to Christina who was feverishly plucking blades of grass and dropping them into the pie tin.

The phone rang. Tiffany grabbed the receiver on the second ring and still watching her daughter through the screen, said, "Hello?"

"Mom?" Stephen's voice cracked.

"Oh, hi, kid." She rested her hip against the counter. "All done with Grandma's lawn?"

"Uh . . . a long time ago."

There was an edginess in his voice and she realized something was wrong. Very wrong. She froze. "So where are you?" she asked.

He hesitated.

"Stephen?"

"I'm at the police station, Mom, and . . . and someone wants to talk to you."

Chapter Four

"You're where?" Tiffany sagged against the kitchen wall for support. Dear God, this couldn't be happening.

"I said I'm down at the—"

"I know what you said, but how did you get there? Are you all right? What happened?" A jillion thoughts raced through her mind, none of them good. when she considered her thirteen-year-old son and his recent knack for getting into trouble.

"Yeah. I'm okay."

"You're sure?" She wasn't convinced.

"Yeah. The officer wants to talk to you."

"Wait, Stephen, should I come get you—"

"Mrs. Santini?" an older male voice inquired. "I'm Sergeant Pearson."

Tiffany's throat was dry, her heart a beating drum. "What's going on? Is my son okay?"

"Aside from a shiner and a sore jaw, I think he'll be fine." The sergeant's voice was kind but did little to soothe her jangled nerves.

"What happened?"

"He and another kid, Miles Dean, got into a scuffle down at the Mini Mart."

"A scuffle?" she repeated, anxious sweat causing the

back of her blouse to cling to her skin. The older boy's father, Ray Dean, had been in and out of jail and it looked like Miles was following in his old man's footsteps. What in the world was Stephen doing with him this time?

"The boys got into a quarrel. One thing led to another and a couple of punches were thrown. The clerk gave us a call and we picked 'em up. All in all, your boy's fine."

Relief caused her shoulders to droop but she rubbed at the headache pounding in her forehead. "And Miles?"

The officer hesitated and Tiffany felt a niggle of dread. "Miles always manages to get himself out of trouble."

Nervously she twisted the telephone cord in her fingers. "Are there any charges filed against Stephen?" she asked. Despite a breeze gently lifting the curtains as it slipped in through the open window over the sink, the temperature in the kitchen seemed to have elevated to over a hundred degrees.

Tiffany stretched the cord and looked outside to see that her daughter was still busily making mud pies in the dirt.

"None against your son."

"And Miles?"

"That remains to be seen."

"Can I come and get him now?"

"Actually, an officer will bring him home. They should be there in about ten minutes."

"I don't have to sign anything?"

"No—but just a minute." Pearson's voice was muffled as he spoke to someone else. "Yeah, she's waiting for him. Now listen, Stephen, no more horsing around, right?"

"I won't," her son mumbled as if from a great distance.

"I mean it. The next time it could be real trouble. And I'm gonna have to report this to your juvenile counselor."

There was another muffled response that Tiffany couldn't discern. A second later Sergeant Pearson was on the phone again. "Okay, he's on his way."

"Good." Or was it?

"Look, Mrs. Santini, this incident at the Mini Mart, well, it doesn't amount to much more than a couple of kids getting into a difference of opinion and taking a swing or two on a hot afternoon. However, the way things are today, we tend to worry. If either of the boys had pulled a weapon—a gun or a knife—this could have turned out bad."

Her thoughts exactly. A chill slid through her despite the heat. Guns. Knives. Weapons. She had moved to the small town of Bittersweet to get away from the gangs and violence of the city, but it seemed that no community was immune. Not even a little burg in southern Oregon. In this part of rural America, boys were given hunting knives and rifles routinely about the time they hit the age of ten or twelve, as if the owning of a weapon was a rite of passage from childhood to becoming a man. "I'll talk to Stephen."

"Do that," Pearson advised. "I think a ride in the squad car and having to come down to the station probably gave him a scare."

"Let's hope so."

She was ready to hang up, to wait for Stephen and see that he was okay, then read him the riot act if necessary, but Sergeant Pearson wasn't finished.

"There is something more, Mrs. Santini," he said, and there was a solemnity in his voice she hadn't heard before. She was instantly wary, her fingers tightening around the receiver.

"Yes?"

"As I said, the boys were fighting about something—who knows what, maybe even a girl. At least that's what the clerk at the Mini Mart thought she heard, but there was some discussion about Isaac Wells."

Tiffany froze. "Pardon me?"

"The man who disappeared. Owned a place on the county road just out of town."

"I know who he is," she said, trying to keep the irritation

and, well, the fear, from her voice. Deep inside she began to tremble. "I just don't see what he has to do with Stephen."

"Probably nothing. But when we emptied your son's pockets—just part of procedure, you know—he had a set of keys on him."

"Keys?" she repeated, having trouble finding her voice. "To my house," she said, but knew she was only hoping against hope. Stephen had one key. Only one. No set.

The sergeant hesitated. "Maybe. But the chain is unique and engraved." She closed her eyes because she knew what was coming. "Initials I.X.W. I'm thinkin' it could be for Isaac Xavier Wells."

"I see."

"Talk to your boy."

"I will," she promised as she hung up and felt as if the weight of the world had just been dumped upon her shoulders. None of this was making any sense. Why was Stephen still hanging out with Miles Dean? What was he doing with that set of keys? What was the fight about? And, what could Stephen have to do with the old man whom he'd worked for, the man who'd disappeared?

She walked to the back door and noticed John Cawthorne's wedding invitation on the counter. By the end of the week her father—well, if that's what you could call the snake-in-the-grass John Cawthorne—would be getting married. But Tiffany couldn't think of that now. Suddenly she had more important things to consider.

"Mommy!" Christina shouted from the backyard.

Tiffany managed a tight smile as she opened the window over the sink. "What's up kiddo?"

All smudges and bright eyes, Christina, standing beneath a shade tree, proudly showed off her latest creation of mud and grass piled high in the tinfoil plate that had once held a chicken pot pie. A clump of pansies had been thrown onto the top for color. "Lookie!"

"It's beautiful," Tiffany said as Charcoal mewed loudly at the back door.

"You want a bite?"

"You bet," she lied, trying to push her worries about her son far to the back of her mind. She'd deal with Stephen when he arrived home. "A big bite." She pushed open the screen door. Charcoal slunk into the kitchen.

Christina, holding out her prize, started to run up the back steps.

"Watch out!"

Too late. With a shriek Christina stumbled over one of Stephen's in-line skates and pitched headlong onto the porch. Tin pie plate, grass and clumps of mud flew into the air.

Tiffany was through the door in a second, picking up her daughter just as Christina took in a huge breath and let out another wail guaranteed to wake the dead in the entire Rogue River Valley. Tears streamed and blood began to trickle from a raspberry-like scratch on Christina's knee.

"Mom-meeee!" Christina sobbed as Tiffany held her.

"Shh, baby, you'll be fine." Tiffany hauled her daughter into the house to the small bathroom off the kitchen.

"It hurts!"

"I know, I know, but Mommy will fix it."

In the medicine cabinet she found antiseptic and a clean washcloth. As Christina, seated on the edge of the counter, wriggled and sucked in her breath, Tiffany washed each scratch and cut on her knee and chin.

The doorbell rang.

Probably the officer with Stephen in tow. "I'll be right there!" she called out over Christina's whispers. Balancing her daughter, she reached into the medicine cabinet for a package of bandages.

The bell chimed sharply again.

"Just hold your horses," Tiffany muttered, placing a bandage over the biggest area of Christina's wounds. "Come on, sweetie, we'd better answer the door." She tossed the washcloth into the sink, picked up her sniffling daughter and carried her to the front door. Expecting to have to apologize to a police officer and Stephen, she yanked on the knob and found herself face-to-face with J.D.

"You were going to get me a key," he reminded her.

"Right." His key had been the last thing on her mind. He shot a look at Christina and his brows drew into a single, condemning line. "I didn't think about it. The back door was unlocked." She shuffled her daughter from one hip to the other while Christina blinked back tears.

"What happened here?" J.D. asked.

"I falled down!" Christina said with more than a little pride. All of a sudden she was like a soldier home from battle, showing off her war wounds.

"That you did." Tiffany pressed her lips to Christina's curly crown. "Well, come on in—" She waved to the back of the house and then stopped short as she looked over his shoulder toward the street. "Oh, no."

J.D. turned in time to see a police cruiser easing up to the curb. His gut clenched, an automatic reaction from too many conflicts with the law when he was a kid. In the house, Tiffany paled and J.D. realized that for a beautiful woman, she looked like hell. Her normally cool facade had slipped, her hair was falling out of a makeshift ponytail, and her clothes—faded jeans and a sleeveless blouse—wrinkled and smudged with dirt were a far cry from her usually neat and tidy, no-nonsense appearance.

"Excuse me." Like a brushfire devouring dry grass, she was past him in an instant. Holding her daughter to her, she dashed down the two steps of the porch to the edge of the lawn, where shade trees lined the narrow street.

J.D. followed, his eyes narrowing as the rear door of the police car opened and Stephen sheepishly crawled out. All of J.D.'s worst fears congealed right then and there, and he wondered if Tiffany was at the end of her rope as far as the kids were concerned.

Christina was dirty and bleeding, like a refugee from a war zone. Stephen didn't look much better. Most of his usual bravado had evaporated and his face was bruised, one eye nearly swollen shut. Scarcely a teenager and yet, it seemed, on the brink of big trouble with the law.

Not good. Not good at all.

But then J.D. had suspected as much.

"Mrs. Santini?" The officer who had driven the car, a short man with thick, wavy brown hair and wire-rimmed glasses, approached.

"Yes."

"Officer Talbot, Bittersweet Police."

"Hi."

He glanced at J.D. "Mr. Santini?"

"Yes, but I'm not the boy's father."

Brown eyebrows sprang upward, over the tops of the policeman's glasses. J.D. thrust out his hand. "J.D.," he said. "I'm Stephen's uncle."

Stephen shot J.D. a suspicious glance that spoke volumes, then reached into the back seat of the patrol car for his battered skateboard.

"You might want to have his eye looked at," the officer said to Tiffany. "Helluva shiner, if you ask me."

"I will," Tiffany promised as Christina buried her face into the crook of her mother's neck, smearing blood and dirt on the long column of Tiffany's throat.

"I'm okay," Stephen mumbled, a hank of black hair tumbling over his forehead and partially hiding the eye in question.

"I still think it should be checked," Tiffany said, her nervous gaze skating over Stephen's injuries. Then she asked, "How's the other boy?"

"Looks about like this one here." The officer touched Stephen on the shoulder. "Let's hope this is the last of it."

Sullenly Stephen studied the ground.

"It will be," Tiffany promised as Talbot offered a patient smile, then turned back to his car just as the interior radio crackled to life. Talbot's pace increased and he climbed behind the wheel of the cruiser. He snapped up the handset of the radio.

"What happened?" J.D. asked Stephen. The cruiser took off.

"Nothin'."

"Black eyes like that don't appear by themselves."

With a disinterested lift of his shoulder, Stephen carried his skateboard and sauntered toward the house.

"Wait," Tiffany commanded. "I think we should have your eye checked at the clinic or the emergency room."

"I already told you it's okay."

Christina, as if sensing all of the attention was focused on her brother, sniffed loudly. "My chin hurts."

"I know it does, honey." Tenderly Tiffany placed a kiss upon her daughter's temple. "We'll fix it while we take care of your brother," she assured her daughter.

Stephen snorted. "I don't need you to take care of me."

"Sure you do," she quipped back and followed him inside. J.D. didn't hesitate but walked past a fading Apartment for Rent sign and up the two steps to the front porch.

"Gosh, Mom, just get off my case, okay?" He rolled his one good eye and with as much attitude as he could manage, he dashed up the stairs. An instant later a door on the second floor slammed and within seconds the sound of angry guitar chords filtered down the stairway.

Tiffany hesitated as if she wanted to chase after him, but finally shook her head. "I'll just be a minute," she said to J.D. and he noticed the worry in her amber eyes, as if some of the fight had left her.

His heart twisted stupidly. "You need some help?"

She looked at him straight on, those intense gold eyes holding his for a second. He saw the beat of her pulse at the base of her throat and some of his suspicion melted. Maybe she was just an overworked single parent. "Thanks, but I can manage," she said coolly as she carried Christina to the little bathroom tucked beneath the stairs. "I have the extra key, if you just give me a minute I'll get it for you. It's in my purse, in the kitchen. Why don't you wait for me there—have some iced tea or . . . whatever is in the refrigerator."

"Fair enough." The scent of her perfume teased his nostrils as she closed the door behind her and his groin tightened at a sharp, poignant and oh-so-sensual memory. *Don't go there, Santini.* Silently he called himself a blind fool, then strode to the kitchen. He nearly banged his head on one of the pots suspended over the cooking island and resisted temptation upon spying a plate of home-baked cookies that rested on the edge of the counter.

Christina let out a yelp. "Stop it, Mommy!" she cried, then he heard Tiffany's voice, hushed and soothing, though he couldn't make out the words.

Gritting his teeth, he opened the refrigerator, found a couple of bottles of beer tucked inside the door and pulled one of them out. What the hell was going on here? One kid was banged up and the other beaten to a pulp before being escorted home by the police. Despite all her intentions, good or not, Tiffany seemed to be sliding in the motherhood department.

He twisted off the cap and tossed it into the wastebasket under the sink.

"Owww, Mommy, that hurts!" Christina was admonishing, her voice trembling.

"Shh, honey, it'll just sting for a minute." Tiffany's voice faded again. Disturbed, J.D. walked out the back door into the hot afternoon. The covered porch opened onto a wide backyard. A swing and two rocking chairs were pushed against the worn siding and planters filled with blossoming petunias, marigolds and some other flower he didn't recognize, splashed color against the porch rail. A small foil pie plate had landed upside down on the top step and a spray of mud, flower petals and grass littered the walk.

J.D. eased past the mess and stepped onto the sun-dried lawn. Philip had bought this place—an investment of sorts, as their father was interested in expanding to this part of the state—just a year before his death. All the buildings—house, garage and carriage house—were painted a soothing dove gray and trimmed with black shutters and doors. The white gingerbread trim and steeply pitched roofs added a touch of Victorian élan that, he supposed, appealed to nostalgic types who felt more comfortable in a rambling old manor than in a modern, utilitarian apartment house. Those renters would gladly forgo the convenience of a dishwasher for the gloss of original handcrafted woodwork.

He took a long sip from his bottle and felt the cold beer slide down his throat. Philip had never intended that his small, second family would move down here, but then Philip hadn't planned on dying suddenly at forty-eight. Scowling, J.D. took another cool swallow. A hornet buzzed past his head while a neighbor's dog began to bark incessantly, only to be scolded by a woman's sharp voice.

"Cody, you hush!"

The dog ignored her and kept yapping.

A wail from a discordant guitar screamed down from the open window on the second floor of the main house. Squinting, J.D. looked up and saw his nephew standing in the middle of his bedroom. Biting his lower lip, Stephen bobbed his head, a hank of dark hair falling over his eyes while he banged on the strings. As if he sensed he was being watched, Stephen glanced through the window and the guitar immediately fell silent. He disappeared from view.

J.D. wondered about the kid. Would he make it? Stephen seemed about to embrace the wild side of being a teenager. Just as he himself had done. J.D. had had a broken nose, stitches running up one leg from an automobile wreck and a juvenile record that fortunately had been cleared before he reached adulthood. Stephen seemed about to embark on the same dangerous path away from the straight and narrow—a path that included drinking underage joyriding in "borrowed" cars, shooting BB guns at mailboxes and generally raising Cain.

"Hell," J.D. muttered under his breath as Tiffany, with Christina in her arms, stepped outside.

The little girl had a bandage on her chin as well as her knee, but she was clean again, face scrubbed, with no trace of the tears or dirt that had tracked over her round cheeks.

Tiffany, too, had taken the time to release her ponytail and apply lipstick. Her glossy black hair framed her face which, aside from the touch of lipstick, was devoid of makeup. Nonetheless she was a striking woman. No doubt about it. With high cheekbones, pointed chin, straight nose and those golden eyes accentuated with thick, curling lashes, she had a way of making a man notice her. Add to the already fine-featured eyebrows that arched so perfectly they appeared arrogant and the image was complete.

"Are you Daddy's brother?" Christina asked. Her eyes rounded as if she'd just made the connection.

"That's right."

"Daddy's in heaven," the imp said so matter-of-factly it was almost chilling.

"I know." J.D.'s jaw tightened.

"He's not coming back."

He exchanged glances with Tiffany and her eyes warned him to be careful. "I know that, too."

"Are you staying in a 'partment?"

"For a while," he said and felt more than a trace of guilt.

"How come?"

Good question. He noticed Tiffany stiffen, the tremulous smile on her lips freezing. "Uncle Jay is here on business—for his work—and . . . he decided to visit us."

"That's right," J.D. said, mentally noting that it really wasn't a lie. "But I'll be in town awhile."

Tiffany's mouth tightened a little.

Bored with the conversation, Christina wriggled and Tiffany set her on the ground. "You know, Jay, I still can't picture you working for your dad. You were always . . . well . . . you know."

"The black sheep, the son who swore he'd never work for his old man, the guy who did everything he could to keep his distance from anything remotely associated with Santini Brothers Enterprises."

His off-center smile was a little self-deprecating and his eyes, gray as evening clouds, darkened as if a summer storm were gathering in his soul. Tiffany tried not to notice. She'd been caught in the web of those eyes before and wouldn't make that mistake again. She couldn't. He tipped his bottle back and drained it. "As I said before, the prodigal had a change of heart because his older brother died." The grin fell from his face.

She folded her arms over her chest and sighed. "Life has changed for us all."

"Hasn't it, though?" His gaze touched hers so intimately she shivered, then looked away.

"So what's going on with Stephen?"

If only I knew. "He's nearly fourteen."

"And already in trouble with the law."

"Nothing serious," she countered, ready to defend her son against anyone and anything, including his uncle if need be. Rather than meet the questions in his gaze, she went to the back porch, grabbed a broom and swept up the remnants of Christina's mud pie.

"Looks serious to me." J.D. followed her and rolled his bottle between his palms.

"You should know about being a rebellious youth."

He hesitated, then set his empty bottle on the rail. "That was a long time ago, Tiffany." The way he said her name sent a stupid little thrill down her spine and an unwanted memory started to rise to the surface of her consciousness, a memory that she'd sworn to bury so deep it would never appear again. But there it was, in her mind's eye. Clear as the day it had happened: J.D. stripped to the waist, drips of sweat sliding down the finely honed muscles of his chest and abdomen.

"You can't just forget the past, pretend it didn't happen." Her throat constricted and she wanted to call back the words, but it was too late.

"It would be better if we could sometimes," he said, and she knew in a heartbeat that he, too, was fighting unwanted memories; forbidden, painful recollections of something that, if acknowledged, would only cause more damage.

This conversation with its intimate overtones was getting her nowhere in a big hurry. She swept the last of the drying pansy petals into the shrubs and noticed that Christina was busy plucking blades of grass and tossing them into the air. "Don't worry about Stephen," she said a little too sharply. "I can handle him."

"It's a tough load. Teenage boy, little girl, part-time job, and running this place."

"Not a problem, J.D. Well, at least not yours." She forced a confident smile and wiped her hands on her jeans. No reason for him or any of the Santini family, for that matter, to know any of her troubles.

"It looks like you could use a man around here."

"Excuse me?" she said, nearly stammering at his gall. "A man? Is that what you said, that I could use a man?" She let out a puff of disbelief. "Let's get one thing straight, Jay. I *don't* need a man. Not now. Not ever. I—we're just fine."

"Are you?" He hooked his thumbs in the belt loops of his jeans and she was suddenly aware of his bronzed forearms, all muscle and sinew, where his sleeves had been rolled up. His fingers framed his fly and she looked up sharply to see an amused smile slash across his face. Set defiantly, his jaw showed the first shadow of a dark beard and his teeth flashed white as he spoke. "Let me tell you the way I see it," he said, moving closer. Too close.

Tiffany's heartbeat quickened.

"Your daughter is only three, probably doesn't really understand what happened to her daddy, your son is on his way to becoming a major delinquent, this house is falling down around you, and you're dead on your feet."

"Is that what you see?"

"On top of all that, you're trying to deal with being a widow and single parent."

"Not that it's any of your business."

"These kids are my brother's."

She rolled her eyes and fought a surge of anger. "Come on, J.D., you haven't shown much interest in them until now. Why all of a sudden? Don't tell me that just because you had a motorcycle accident you've had some kind of epiphany, because I won't believe it. It's not your style."

"And you know what my 'style,' as you call it, is?" His voice was low. Way too sexy. It brought back all those old, ridiculous emotions that she'd fought for much too long a time.

"Unfortunately, yes. I think I already mentioned that you're too independent, irreverent and self-serving to work for your father."

His eyes glinted with male challenge. "No doubt he'd agree with you, but he didn't have much choice because he seems to think blood is thicker than water."

"Is it?" There was no use continuing this conversation. "Time will tell." She turned toward her little girl. "Chrissie, I'm going into the house and check on Stephen. Stay in the backyard."

The imp, squatting and watching a butterfly flit from one dandelion head to another, didn't reply.

"I'll watch her," J.D. offered.

"The gate's locked, she'll be all right," Tiffany retorted. "You don't have to—"

"I said I'll watch her."

Fine. What did she care? "I'll just be inside," Tiffany said rather than argue with the man. She stalked through the house and up the stairs, telling herself that she only had a few weeks with J.D. so close at hand, several months at the most. She could handle it.

She had no choice.

A DO NOT ENTER sign was posted on the doorknob of Stephen's room. Tiffany ignored it, tapped lightly on the door and opened it herself.

Stephen was half lying on his unmade bed, staring up at pictures of models and rock bands and fast cars that he'd taped to the ceiling. His guitar lay across his abdomen and his injured eye was nearly swollen shut. He rolled it toward her as she approached. "I want you to come with me to the emergency clinic and I don't want to hear anything else about it," Tiffany said.

"Forget it."

"We're going, and right now. I can't take a chance with

your eye. So come on and get into the car. On the way there you can tell me why you and Miles got into it."

"It wasn't a big deal."

"Of course it was, Stephen. Otherwise you wouldn't have landed at the police station sporting the biggest shiner I've ever seen." She stepped over CDs and video games to stop at the window. Christina had climbed into the old tire swing and had conned J.D. into pushing her. Tossing her black curls over her shoulder, the three-year-old clung to the ropes suspending the swing from a branch of the old apple tree and laughed delightedly. Tiffany sighed. When was the last time Christina had laughed—really laughed? When had Philip pushed her in a swing, or helped her onto a slide, or sat on the other end of a teeter-totter? Never. He'd never had the time, and here was J.D.—with most of his weight resting on his good leg as he shoved on the worn black rubber—sending Christina into a slowly spinning circle in the shade of the leafy tree.

Muttering under his breath, Stephen set his guitar aside and climbed to his feet.

"The officer said there was talk about a girl."

Stephen snorted. "It wasn't about a girl."

"Then what? Isaac Wells?"

Stephen's muscles tensed. Suspicion slitted his good eye. "I already told you that I don't know nothin' about him taking off."

"I know, but the officer on the phone said you were found with keys that might belong to Mr. Wells."

Stephen paled to the color of chalk.

"No way."

"They have the keys down at the station. With Mr. Wells's initials on them." She paused at the door and her son, chewing nervously on the corner of his lip, nearly ran into her. "You want to explain?"

"They weren't mine."

"Then whose?"

His jaw worked in agitation. "I—I don't know."

"Stephen—"

"I mean it, Mom. I found 'em. In, in, the park when I was in-line skating."

"And you didn't tell me or turn them in to the police?" Oh, how she wanted to believe him, but this was way too much of a coincidence.

"No."

"You know that the police are going to take those keys out to Mr. Wells's place. If any of them fit in the locks of his house or his cars, they'll have a lot more questions for you. A lot."

Stephen's lips clamped together and Tiffany realized it was useless to argue with him at this moment. She'd give him a little time to think things over, but then she intended to get to the bottom of whatever it was that was bothering him.

"Wait for me in the car," she told her son, and stopped at the back porch where Christina, her small hand fitted snugly in J.D.'s large one, was skipping toward the house.

"Unca Jay says we can get ice cream," she announced.

"Does he?"

"After dinner."

"That'll be a while, honey. I've got to run Stephen to the clinic. Come along."

She reached for Christina's hand, but her strong-willed daughter thrust out her little bandaged chin. "Ice cream," she ordered.

"In a while."

"Now."

"Come on, Christina," Tiffany said, exasperated. Who was J.D. to try and interfere? *Give it a rest*, she reminded herself. He was just trying to help.

Or was he? She didn't trust her brother-in-law's motives. This sudden change of heart about his brother's family had to be phony or, at the very least, exaggerated. Nervous sweat broke out between her shoulders.

"I'll come with you," J.D. offered.

"You don't have to—"

"Come! Come!" Christina cried merrily as she tugged at J.D.'s arm.

"I want to," he said. his eyes serious as his gaze caught her. "I'll watch Christina while you get Stephen stitched up."

"You don't have to take care of us, you know," she retorted, feeling cornered. "This . . . We . . . aren't your duty. Don't you have work or something better to do?"

"Than look after my brother's kids?"

"They don't need looking after. They have a mother."

"But not a father."

"Oh." She laughed without a hint of mirth as a horn began to blast impatiently. Stephen. She started for the car. "So now you're applying for the job. Substitute dad? Give me a break."

With lightning speed, he grabbed her arm with his free hand and spun her around to face him. "Give *me* one, Tiffany," he said, his face suddenly stern. "From the moment I set foot here you've been baiting me and fighting me."

"Maybe it's because I don't trust you."

His jaw slid to the side and he dropped her wrist.

"Come *on*," Christina insisted, pulling on his other hand. He waited. The car horn blared again.

"Fine, fine! Come with us!" Tiffany said as she marched across the dry grass and fished inside her purse for her keys. Christina sprinted ahead and crawled into the back seat.

J.D.'s voice, calm and so in command that it irritated her, chased after her. "You know, Tiffany, we don't have to fight."

She stopped short and her temper flared. "Of course we do, Jay. It's what we've always done."

"Not always," he reminded her and she, remembering too vividly how intimate they'd been, how she'd let down her guard before, felt fire climb up her cheeks.

"There are some things better left forgotten," she warned before opening the door of her car and motioning Stephen to climb into the back seat. Grumbling, he did as he was bid and J.D. slid into his recently vacated spot. He winced a little as he dragged his bad leg into the warm interior. Sweat dripped down the side of Tiffany's face as she inserted the ignition key.

Just get me through this, she silently prayed and flicked her wrist. The engine caught on the first try. If only the rest of the evening would go so well. But what were the chances, now that she was trapped with J.D. for the next hour or so? Slim and none leaped readily to mind, along with several wanton, and unwanted, illicit memories.

J.D. slipped a pair of sunglasses onto the bridge of his nose and Tiffany slid a glance in his direction. Wearing the aviator glasses he reminded her of the first time she'd seen him, and she willed that memory to fade.

She didn't have time to dwell on the past. Not now, not ever. They drove to the clinic in silence.

Only much later, after Stephen had been stitched up and they had returned home to a late dinner, had she, after spending hours with J.D. and her children, finally unwound.

Alone in the bathtub, with cool water surrounding her and the lights dimmed, she remembered, in vibrant Technicolor, the first time she'd come face-to-face with J.D. Santini.

She closed her eyes, sighed, and finally let all her old emotions come to the surface. It had been nearly fifteen years ago, she'd been eighteen at the time and more naive than any girl should have been.

She could almost hear the sound of champagne bottles popping over the strains of "The Anniversary Waltz" played by a pianist seated at a baby grand so many years ago. She'd been much too young, had thought what she'd felt was love for an older man and had never expected to run into the likes of James Dean Santini.

But she had, and she remembered the first time she'd seen him as clearly as if it had been only this afternoon. . . .

Chapter Five

Tiffany rested in the bathtub and remembered that evening so long ago. . . .

"Look at that rock!" Mary Beth Owens, a friend who had graduated with Tiffany this past spring, reached for Tiffany's hand and eyed the diamond sparkling on her ring finger. "Wow," she breathed, her eyes as bright as the stone.

Blushing, Tiffany pulled her hand away and concentrated on lighting the candles that would warm the serving trays for the wedding reception she and Mary Beth were catering at the Santini winery in McMinnville.

"I would *die* for a ring like that. Philip must be loaded," Mary Beth gushed as she placed napkins with the name of the bride and groom onto a long cloth-covered table already laden with hors d'oeuvres and empty champagne glasses. A silver fountain was flowing with sparkling wine, the pianist was warming up and the guests, arriving from the church, filtered among the folding chairs in the huge tent that was the center of the reception. Under its own separate awning stood a round table crowned with the tiered wedding cake; to the right was another table laden with gifts. Near the entrance to the main tent an ice sculpture of two entwined hearts was starting to drip. "So what's he worth? Do you know?" Mary Beth asked.

Tiffany only smiled. The truth of the matter was that she didn't know and really didn't care. Money wasn't her reason for planning to marry Philip.

Mary Beth, ever the gossip, pushed a little further. "The way I hear it, Philip's in line to inherit all of this." She gestured widely, her fluttering fingers encompassing the acres of vineyards, stately old brick manor, the winery buildings and the natural amphitheater tucked into the hills where the reception was being held. Vast and well-kept, the Santini winery was one of the most well-known in the region, but Tiffany wasn't interested in the profit-and-loss statements of the company. Philip's potential inheritance wasn't on the list of reasons she'd fallen in love with him.

"You know," Mary Beth confided in a hushed whisper, "there are two brothers, but Philip's the good one. The other—" She rolled her eyes. "Big, big trouble. Always has his father in knots or court or worse."

"Is that right?" Tiffany wasn't interested.

Mary Beth nodded, her head bobbing rapidly. "Good-looking as all get-out and just plain bad news. Always in trouble with the cops. My mom says that J.D. Santini is all piss, vinegar and bad attitude."

"Sounds like a real winner." Tiffany hadn't heard much about him, didn't really care. All she knew was that Philip's brother was quite a bit younger than he and had no interest in the family business. Whenever she'd asked about him, Philip had just shaken his head and sighed. "James is just James. I can't explain him. Wouldn't want to try." Truth to tell, Tiffany wasn't all that interested in the guy.

She lighted the final candle beneath a silver chafing dish and nearly burned her fingers on the match.

"Are you and Philip gonna have a spread like this?" Mary Beth asked, clearly awed.

"No." Tiffany shook her head. "He was married before, so we agreed that we'd just have a private ceremony."

"Bummer. You should at least have a gown and bridesmaids and— Oh, look, here's the limo."

Sure enough, a white stretch limousine rounded a bend in the winery's private drive to park near the manor. The bride, a willowy blonde in a beaded gown, emerged still holding hands with her groom, a short, balding, wealthy dentist who had been married four times previously.

"Being married before didn't stop Dr. Ingles from having a big to-do."

That much was true, but the good dentist's fifth wife, the pampered daughter of a local television celebrity, had wanted a lavish wedding since this was her first and, as she'd been quoted as saying, her groom's "last." Tiffany didn't care about the ceremony; the less pomp and circumstance, the better, as far as she was concerned. She couldn't imagine a huge church wedding without the support of a father to give her away. Besides, as the bride she insisted upon paying for the event herself and her budget was limited. "Where's the punch bowl for the kids?" she asked, turning the subject away from her own situation.

"All set up. Over there. André handled it." Mary Beth motioned toward yet another table, then turned her attention to her job and Tiffany was relieved that she didn't have to make any more small talk. She smiled to herself as she spied Philip, tall, dark-haired and in command. She'd met him three months earlier at another event where she'd worked. He'd stayed late and offered to drive her home. She'd declined, refused to give him her number, but he'd persisted and within two weeks they were dating. Sure, he was older than she—fifteen years older—but it didn't matter, she kept telling herself.

Before meeting Philip, she had planned to start college

in the fall, intending to take business courses at Portland State University while working two part-time jobs.

But then Philip had asked her to marry him and she'd said yes. He was everything she wanted in a husband. Stable. Smart. Educated. Successful.

The age factor didn't bother her. His ex-wife and he were cordial if not friendly, and his kids—a boy and a girl—were twelve and ten and weren't a worry. She, as an only child with a single mother, wanted to embrace a large family. She would love Philip's children as if they were her own as well as have her own children someday.

But things weren't perfect. Philip's parents, devout Catholics, had never approved of his divorce and didn't want him to remarry. And her own mother, who had struggled in raising Tiffany alone, had warned her to wait.

"You're only eighteen," Rose Nesbitt had said, shaking her head as she'd dusted the piano bench where countless youngsters had sat as Rose had spent hours trying to teach them what had come so naturally to her. "Give yourself some time, Tiffany."

"Philip doesn't want to wait. He's thirty-three, Mom."

"And too old for you."

"We love each other."

"He thought he loved someone else once."

"I know, but—"

"But it didn't last." Her mother had tossed her dusting rag into a plastic bucket that held cleaning supplies. "Just give it time." She had sighed and rubbed the kinks from the back of her neck. "Real love isn't impatient."

"Why wait?"

"Why rush in?"

"Because Philip wants to," she'd argued.

"This shouldn't be all his decision, honey. You're talking about marriage. Two people. Give and take. I know I'm not one to talk because I've never walked down the aisle, but I just think you should slow down a little. Date boys your own age."

That was the trouble. They were boys. Tiffany had never felt comfortable with them. They were too young, too immature, too stupid. Philip was none of those things and as she watched him now, walking briskly between the rows of beribboned chairs, his hair starting to gray at the temples, his smile fixed and professional, she felt an inward satisfaction that this man loved her.

Unlike the father who had abandoned her and her mother before she'd been born.

"Hi," she said as Philip stopped at the table on his way to the bar where Santini wines were being served.

"Hi."

"Everything set?"

"Looks like." She smiled up at him and Philip winked at her.

"Good job, kiddo. I'll see you later." He disappeared into the throng of guests that were arriving as if in a fleet. Valets parked cars, the pianist played, she and Mary Beth served and the best Chardonnay, Chablis, and claret the Santini Brothers Winery offered flowed like water. Guests in designer gowns and expensive suits talked, drank and nibbled at the appetizers.

The bride and groom cut the cake, sipped from crystal glasses, smiled and glowed, then started the dancing on a platform set near a waterfall and fishpond.

The scene was romantic and Tiffany told herself to be practical; she didn't need this kind of expensive wedding and reception. She wasn't interested in limos and a designer wedding dress and all the show. She just wanted to marry Philip.

She was standing at her post, nearly forgotten as the guests had gathered around the bar and dance floor, when she caught her first glimpse of the stranger.

Tall, lean, hard as nails, this was a man who obviously didn't belong with the others.

In faded jeans and a matching jacket tossed over a white T-shirt, he stalked toward her tent. Tinted glasses covered his eyes and yet she could feel him staring at her with such intensity she wanted to run away. She didn't. Instead she managed a frosty smile. "May I help you?"

"You tell me."

"You're with the Ingles party?"

"If this is the Ingles party."

Should she call security? No. Just because he wasn't wearing a suit and tie didn't mean he wasn't invited. Every family had its rebel. "We have lobster thermidor or beef Wellington or—"

"You're Tiffany Nesbitt?"

Who was this guy? "Yes."

He reached across the table, grabbed her left hand and held it up to the light. Her ring caught one of the last rays of the setting sun, glittering brightly on her finger.

The man's jaw tightened, his already harsh features grew more taut. She yanked back her hand somehow and suddenly felt the ring she loved was ostentatious and obscene. "And you're . . . ?"

"J.D."

Her stomach dropped. Her throat turned to sand. She was staring into the hard expression of the hellion.

"Philip's brother."

"I . . . I recognize the name."

"Good." His smile was as cold as death. "Looks like we're going to be related."

She couldn't hide her dismay. While Philip was refined and polished, this guy was as rough and edgy as a cowboy fresh from a two-week cattle drive. She tried to retrieve her rapidly escaping manners. "Pleased to meet you, James."

"No one calls me that."

"But Philip—"

"Is a snob. The name's J.D. or Jay." He reached into the breast pocket of his T-shirt for a pack of cigarettes. "Let's keep it simple."

"Fine," she said, feeling a general sense of irritation. What was James—oh, excuse me, *J.D.*—doing crashing the party in disreputable jeans and tattered jacket? He lit up, surveyed the crowd from behind his tinted lenses and rested a hip against the table. Tiffany tried to ignore him as she helped another couple of guests. But he never left her side. Standing in the shade of the tent, arms folded across his chest, lips razor thin and compressed, he smoked, then crushed the cigarette beneath the worn heel of his boot.

Tiffany hoped that Philip would return, that he would rescue her from having to make small talk with this guy; but her fiancé was busy, moving from one cluster of guests to the next, doing what he did best as vice president in charge of local sales for the winery.

She sensed rather than saw J.D. observing her, knew that he was watching her every move. She felt like a horse at an auction and was nervous, wary, her muscles tense.

"So what is it you do?" she finally asked, tired of the uncomfortable silence that stretched between them.

He slid his sunglasses from his nose and eyed her with a gaze that was as gray and cold as the barrel of a gun. "What do I do?" he repeated. "Depends upon who you ask, I guess."

"Pardon me?"

"My father thinks I'm a borderline criminal, my mother thinks I can walk on water and my brother sees me as a big pain in the ass. Take your pick."

"What do you think?"

One side of his mouth lifted in a smile that couldn't decide whether to be boyishly charming or wickedly sexy. "I'm definitely not an angel."

Goodness, was he flirting with her? Her silly heart raced at the thought. "I believe that."

"Smart girl."

Night was falling, shadows deepening across the grass. Candles and torches were lit, adding warm illumination to the luster of a new moon and the light from a sprinkling of stars. The piano player was into waltzes and love songs and Tiffany longed to be with Philip and away from his brother. Whereas Philip was strong and silent, a man whose patience and understanding added to his allure, this man was all pent-up steam and energy, a man who would have trouble finding satisfaction in life.

"So when's the big day?" J.D. asked. He fished into his breast pocket for his cigarettes again. Shaking the last one out, he crumpled the empty pack in one hand.

"Excuse me?" She began to pick up empty plates and cups since it was time to shut down the tent.

"Your wedding day. When is it?"

"We haven't decided."

He clicked a lighter to the end of his filter tip. "Doesn't sound like Philip. He has his life planned down to the last minute. He's probably already picked out his cemetery plot."

She cringed inside. That much was true. Philip balanced his checkbook to the penny, filled his gas tank when the needle hit the one-quarter mark, wore his suits by the days of the week and, as far as she could tell, his only vice was that he liked to gamble a little. But just a little.

"Philip would like to get married before Christmas," she said, then instantly regretted the words as J.D. surveyed her with eyes that called her a dozen kinds of fool.

"For tax purposes?" He sucked in a lungful of smoke.

Because we're in love, she wanted to cry out. The tent was too dark, too close, and Philip's younger brother too . . .

male—the kind of male a smart girl avoided like the plague. "It makes sense."

"Does it?" He gave her a last once-over and tipped his head. "Good luck. I think you're gonna need it."

"I doubt it."

"You haven't lived with my brother yet. I grew up with him." He sauntered away and spent some time talking to the bartender while, disdaining his family, he got himself a bottle of beer rather than the traditional Santini glass of wine.

She watched as he found a tree to lean his shoulders against, then smoked and slowly sipped his drink as night fell.

What did J.D. know about Philip? They were eleven years apart in age and light-years apart in maturity. *Don't let him rattle you*, Tiffany, she told herself as she blew out the candles under the warming trays and chafing dishes. She knew the entire Santini clan was against her marriage to Philip. J.D. was just up-front about it.

She saw J.D. off and on that summer. Their conversations were brief, cordial and detached. He didn't bother hiding his disapproval of her engagement, and she bit her tongue whenever she was around him, which, thankfully, wasn't often. He dated several women, all sophisticated, rich and brittle, none of whom he spent enough time with to justify introductions to the family.

J.D. made Tiffany nervous and fidgety, too aware of herself and his all-too-virile presence. She'd found out through snippets of conversation that he'd finished college and was thinking of applying to law school, though Philip found it ironic that his brother, who had come as close to becoming a criminal as anyone in the family, would want to practice law.

"But there are all kind of attorneys, I suppose," Philip had confided to Tiffany. "Some who believe in the system.

others who try to use it to their advantage. I'm afraid James is going to be one who bends the law to fit his own skewed perception."

Tiffany wasn't so sure, because for all his faults—and there were more than she wanted to count—J.D. possessed an underlying strength. He had his own code of ethics, it seemed. Still, the less she was around him, the better she felt.

She made it through that summer and into fall, dealing with J.D. from a distance, talking with him as little as possible when they were forced together, and generally avoiding not only him, but the entire Santini family. Carlo had made it abundantly clear he thought his eldest son should, for the sake of the family and his children, wait to get married. J.D. thought his brother should forget about walking down the aisle altogether and Frances, Philip's mother, didn't like the fact that Tiffany was fifteen years her son's junior. "She'll get used to the idea," Philip assured Tiffany, but his mother barely tolerated her.

"You can still back out," her own mother said only two weeks before the wedding. It was early October and Indian summer was in full force. The days clear and warm, the nights crisp and bright.

Tiffany was feeling the first twinges of cold feet. She knew she wanted to marry Philip, to be his wife and the mother of his children, but everyone else seemed to be pulling them apart.

The occasion was a dinner at his house, ostensibly to celebrate the upcoming nuptials, but Carlo had drunk too much of his own wine and become surly, Frances had repeatedly touched Philip's arm and brought up his ex-wife and children, and J.D., seated across from Tiffany, had caught her eye time and time again. His gaze wasn't openly hostile, nor was it friendly; just intense. He managed a smile or two during the meal but clearly felt as uncomfortable with his own overbearing family as she was.

Philip, Carlo and Mario, Carlo's brother, were leaving for a convention that night in Las Vegas. Upon Philip's return, he and Tiffany were to be married. She only had to get through this dinner and the next week, then she'd become Mrs. Philip Santini. Sweat broke out on her forehead as she tried to concentrate on the conversation while picking at her rack of lamb and seasoned potatoes. To make the meal even more uncomfortable, every once in a while Mario and his wife would lapse into Italian and everyone at the table, aside from Tiffany, understood the conversation. She sensed that she was being spoken about, but never heard her name and silently prayed that the ordeal would be over soon.

God, it seemed, had other plans.

The family lingered over coffee and sherry as the clock in the front hallway of the old brick house chimed eight.

"Don't you have a nine-thirty flight?" Frances asked, startled as she counted the chimes. They were over an hour away from the airport.

Philip glanced at his watch. "It is getting late. We'd better get a move on, Dad." He looked across the table. "You wouldn't mind giving Tiffany a lift home, would you, James?"

Tiffany froze. The thought of being alone with J.D. truly alone—was terrifying. "I thought you were going to drop me off," she said, trying to pretend that she didn't really care one way or the other.

"Change of plan. We're running late, so you'll need a ride." Philip winked at her and for the first time, Tiffany wondered if he was being a bit condescending.

"But—" She looked across the table at J.D. and caught the amusement in his gaze.

"Don't worry. I'll be good," he said. "Trust me."

Her words caught in her throat and she swallowed hard. She wanted to argue, but couldn't risk making a scene in front of Philip's parents. They already had reservations about her and she couldn't let them think she was a spoiled, insecure little girl. "Fine," she agreed with a smile that felt as phony as it probably looked. She'd foreseen something like this happening with Philip's schedule so tight, and she'd offered to drive herself to his father's house, but Philip had been adamant about their arriving together.

Now, it seemed, she was stuck with J.D.

She had no option but to make the best of a very bad situation. Philip and his father left, Tiffany offered to help with the dishes, but her prospective mother-in-law waved off her attempts and told her the servants would take care of the mess. Within half an hour she was riding on the bench seat of J.D.'s pickup, clutching the strap of her purse as if her life depended on it and trying to make small talk. He was, after all, going to be her brother-in-law. It was ridiculous for her to be on edge every time she was near him.

"Tell me," he said as they drove along the narrow country road cutting through the hills surrounding Portland, "what is it you see in Philip?"

"Excuse me?" What did he care? Storm clouds brewed in the night sky, obliterating the moon and hiding the stars. Fat drops of rain began to splatter onto the windshield.

"I mean, let's face it. He's nearly twice your age."

She bristled. "So I've heard."

"I'll bet." Shifting down, he took a corner a little too fast. The storm began in earnest. Rain peppered the windshield, drizzling down the dusty glass.

"Are you going to try and talk me out of it?"

"Could I?" He slid a glance in her direction and her pulse jumped.

"No."

"Didn't think so."

Headlights from an oncoming car illuminated the inside of the pickup with harsh, white light, instantly casting J.D.'s face in relief. Tiffany looked away from his strong profile. His hard, thin lips, tense jaw, eyes squinting as he drove, were far too sensual, far too male. The oncoming car passed them and the interior was dark again.

He poked the lighter. "Well, I guess it's your funeral."

"Wedding. You mean it's my wedding."

"Whatever." The lights of Portland came into view and Tiffany felt a sense of relief as J.D. lit a cigarette from the pack on the dash. She just needed to get out of the truck and away from Philip's disdainful brother. What did it matter what he thought or what anyone thought? All that was important was the one simple fact that she and Philip loved each other.

"You know, you could just try and accept the situation," she said finally as he cracked a window. The smell of fresh rain mingled with smoke. "You don't have to be antagonistic."

"Is that what I am?"

"At least."

"You'd rather I be what? Friendlier?" He snorted, smoke shooting from his nostrils.

"That would be a start."

"Would it?" He let out a huff of derision as he cranked the wheel around a corner. "How much friendlier would you like?"

Bristling, she quietly counted to ten. "Look, J.D., you don't have to try and bait me, okay? I just think we should be civil."

"Why?"

"Because we're going to be family."

The look he sent her could have cut through granite. "I've got more than my share of family." He eased into the lane for the Sellwood Bridge and as they crossed the inky

Willamette River, he tossed his cigarette out the window. The ember died in flight.

"Just tell me what it is that you don't like about me," she said as he angled the car through the city streets. It was time to deal with all this pent-up and ill-directed hostility.

"It's not you," J.D. said.

Liar.

"Turn here," she prompted when he nearly missed her street "If it's not me, then what's the problem?"

"You really want to know?" Tires skidded on the wet pavement.

"Yep. That one, third house on the right."

He parked at the curb directly under a streetlight and cut the engine. Rain pounded on the car roof. "Philip already made one mistake when he got married the first time."

"And now you think he's making another."

He gazed at her with eyes as dark as coal. "Definitely."

"Well, excuse me if I seem offended," she said as his gaze shifted to her throat and the smoky air in the cab was suddenly stifling. She cranked down her window. "But I am. Philip and I are in love and we want to— Oh!"

He reached for her so suddenly, she didn't have a chance to react. His arms were around her, his mouth claiming hers with a wild abandon that stole her breath. She tried to push away, but he only tightened his embrace, his arms like steel bands surrounding her as his lips moved sensually over hers.

Her heart thudded, her pulse hit a fever pitch and the small soft moan that escaped her throat sounded like a plea.

He shifted, drawing her closer, his tongue sliding easily between her lips.

Closing her eyes she sagged against him, wanting more— only to realize what she was doing. *This was wrong. So very wrong.* She stiffened and pushed him away, half expecting a fight. Instead he let her go and his smile in the darkness was silently mocking.

"That's why you shouldn't marry Philip," he said, and she wiped her lips with the back of her hand.

"Go to hell."

He laughed as she scrabbled for the door and shot out of the truck as if she'd been propelled from a cannon. Her skin tingled with a wash of hot, deep color and she stumbled up the steps of the walk to her house. What kind of a fool was she? Why had she let him kiss her, touch her, create a whirlpool of want deep inside? She fumbled with her keys, unlocked the door and slid into the dark interior.

Oh, God, oh, God. Despair flooded her. What had she done? Slamming the door, she threw the dead bolt, as if the twist of an old metal lock could keep her safe from the horror of her own actions.

It was only a kiss, she told herself. A kiss. Big deal. Philip probably wouldn't even care.

Then why was her heart still pounding, her lips tingling, her insides quivering? There were names for women who did what she'd done.

Tease.

Flirt.

Two-timer.

Those were the good ones. The harsher, cruel names that she wouldn't even think about nibbled at the edge of her conscience and made her shake with shame.

She covered her face with her hands. It was only a kiss. One he forced upon her. She hadn't expected it. But she'd reacted, dammit.

Sagging against the inside of the door, she heard the tires of J.D.'s truck squeal and its engine roar, as he drove away.

Thank God.

"Don't come back," she whispered, clutching her throat

and trying to still her heart. " You damned bastard, don't ever come back!"

But come back he had. Years later. And now, like it or not, he was living in the same house with her. Worse yet, that same ridiculous sexual hunger that she hadn't felt for years had resurfaced.

And this time she was free.

Chapter Six

Thank God it's Saturday, Tiffany thought as she wrote out a list of weekend jobs. She was already on her second load of laundry, waffles were warming in the oven and she'd pulled out her basket of cleaning supplies. Stephen could mow the lawn and wash the car while she tackled the floors and windows. As for her nemesis and newest tenant, he'd left early this morning. Before she'd gotten up, she'd heard J.D.'s Jeep fire up and roll down the drive. She was grateful that, for the next few hours, she didn't have to face him.

Ever since he'd rented the room upstairs, she hadn't been able to quit thinking about him. "Stupid woman," she grumbled, as she heard Christina stirring in her room.

"Mommy?" her daughter called from the upper hallway.

"Down here, sweetheart." She smiled as she heard footsteps running toward the stairs.

"Someone's here."

"What?" she asked just as the doorbell chimed.

Thinking she had a prospective new tenant, Tiffany smoothed her hair and headed for the foyer. Christina was standing on the bottom step and holding on to a corner of her tattered blanket. She was staring unabashedly out one of the narrow windows flanking the door. A tall, thin man with blue eyes and a nervous smile peered through.

All Tiffany's muscles tightened as she recognized the bold features of John Cawthorne, the lying, cheating jerk who had the audacity to call himself her father. He literally held his hat in his hands, his big-jointed fingers worrying the brim of a dusty Stetson.

"I don't believe this," she muttered under her breath.

"Believe what?" her daughter asked guilelessly.

"Oh, nothing. Come here, honey," she said to Christina.

"Who's he?" The little girl stared straight at the stranger who had spawned her mother.

Tiffany's throat tightened. "My . . . Your . . . Uh, Mr. Cawthorne." Lifting Christina and balancing her on one hip, she braced herself, then opened the door.

"I thought we should talk," he said without so much as a "Hello." His eyes brightened when his gaze landed on Christina and for a fleeting instant Tiffany wondered if he could care for his granddaughter at all. Was blood really thicker than water? If so, why had it taken him over thirty years to figure it out?

"Now?"

"Before the wedding."

Her voice nearly failed her. "Well, then, I guess it better be now, because we're running out of time, aren't we?" Telling herself she was every kind of idiot on the planet, she added, "There's really not a whole lot to discuss, but come on in."

You're asking for trouble, she silently thought as she led him into the kitchen and tried to come up with an excuse to get rid of him. So what if he was the man who had sired her? Where had he been when she'd needed a father, when her mother had needed a husband, or at the very least, a lover she could depend upon?

Tiffany let Christina slide to the floor while John, damn

him, eyed the refrigerator with its artwork, grades and personal notes to the family.

"I've got waffles in the oven," she said to her daughter and wished Cawthorne would disappear. She had nothing to say to him. Nothing.

"Not hungry," Christina said, winding a ringlet of her dark hair and eyeing the stranger suspiciously.

John turned and smiled, his eyes actually warming as he met his granddaughter's curious gaze for the first time. "So you're little Christina." Tiffany's heartstrings tugged ludicrously. This was *not* the way a family was supposed to be. Despite her own upbringing, she foolishly believed in the traditional family—of parents, grandparents, aunts, uncles, cousins. Holidays spent together. Vacations. Memories.

Fool.

"Christina, say hello to Mr. Cawthorne," she said.

"She can call me—"

"Mr. Cawthorne." Tiffany sliced her father a glare that dared him to argue.

His jaw worked for a second. "You can call me John," he replied and Tiffany nodded as she found a pot holder and pulled the plate of warm waffles from the oven.

Christina climbed into her chair and as Tiffany forked a waffle onto her plate, she lost interest in the stranger and her mother's reaction to him. "I want syrup," she ordered.

"I'd like some syrup, *please,*" Tiffany corrected as she opened a bottle of maple syrup and doused the waffles to Christina's satisfaction.

"Where's Stephen?" John asked.

"Still sleeping." Automatically she cut her daughter's breakfast into bite-size pieces, then poured a small glass of cranberry juice.

"I'd like to see him."

She couldn't believe her ears. After thirteen years, suddenly it was important that her estranged father connected with them. "Let's go into the parlor and talk." Without asking, she poured them each a cup of coffee from the glass pot warming in the coffeemaker, then handed him a mug. "If you want sugar or cream—"

"Black is fine," he assured her.

"Good. Chrissie, we'll be in the parlor."

"'Kay."

Why she was even being civil to the man, Tiffany didn't understand. Gritting her teeth, she led him through an arched doorway and into the small, formal room at the foot of the stairs. For a man with as much wealth as John Cawthorne, the room with its re-covered camelback couch and secondhand floral rug tossed over floors that needed refinishing probably seemed simple and unrefined, she thought, then changed her mind. Wasn't he marrying Brynnie Anderson Smith McBaine Kinkaid Perez? There was a simple woman with far-from-refined tastes. Perhaps this room done in peach and forest green with its hardwood floors and lace curtains wasn't as quaint as she'd first thought. And so what if it didn't suit John Cawthorne's tastes, whatever they were? She loved it. The parlor was light, airy and filled with pictures of Tiffany's family. Her mother, Rose, and grandmother, Octavia, smiled from portraits hung on the walls. Stephen's baby pictures and school photos were displayed on several shelves of a built-in bookcase. Christina's toddler shots were mounted on one wall and a framed portrait of Philip and Tiffany on their wedding day stood on the mantel, but nowhere was there even a snapshot of John Cawthorne or anyone remotely connected with him.

And that wasn't going to change.

"Have a seat." Tiffany offered and John shook his head.

"I'd rather stand."

"Suit yourself." She settled into an antique wing chair and

tried to relax. Impossible. This man, frail though he appeared, had humiliated her mother and abandoned her. She couldn't forget that fact. Ever. She could be civil, but that was all.

He set his hat on the rounded arm of the couch and sipped from his cup. "This is good."

"You didn't come all the way over here to check out whether or not I could brew coffee."

He winced. "Nope."

"Didn't think so." She waited and he studied the dark liquid in his cup as if he couldn't find the right words to say what was on his mind. As if she didn't know.

"You know I'm getting married Sunday."

"I'd have to be a hermit not to know."

"You got the invitation?"

"Yes."

He shifted from one foot to the other and she noticed how old he looked. Tired and worn. Like a scuffed, sagging cowboy boot whose heel had worn to nothing. *Don't do this, Tiffany. Don't feel sorry for him. He left you for thirty-three years. All of your life. Until now. When he wants something.*

"I was hoping you and the kids would attend," he said in a voice that was barely audible.

"I, uh, I don't think I can do that."

He swallowed hard and closed his eyes for a second. "I don't blame you. I know I've been a pitiful excuse for a father to you, but—"

"No father, John," she said as her throat began to close and tears threatened. "You've been no father to me." This was ridiculous; she couldn't be crying for this man who had done nothing in all his life for her or her children.

"All that's gonna change."

"It is?" She couldn't believe her ears. "Just like that?" She snapped her fingers.

"If you'd just give me a chance."

"Oh, please—"

His lips compressed. "Look, Tiffany, this isn't easy for me," he said, his voice firmer. "I'm not the kind of man who likes to admit to his mistakes. Hell, I know I fouled up with your ma. With you. I don't blame you for hating me, but I'm here because deep down, whether you want to admit it or not, we're family."

"Family isn't about blood ties," she retorted, standing as she blinked against the hot tears filling her eyes. "It's about love, sharing, commitment. It's about being around when you're needed, about sharing the good and the bad, helping bear the pain. Family isn't just about being together at weddings and births and funerals, it's about supporting each other every day of your life."

She stared at him and he managed to look ashamed for a second. "What can I say?" he asked, staring into his cup again and shaking his head. "I've changed. I nearly died after that last heart attack and I realized, then, what's important in life." Clearing his throat he looked at her and she bit her lip to keep from crying. "You are, Tiffany. You and your children. I won't lie to you and say that I loved your ma. Lord knows, we were never meant to be together. But you and the grandkids, that's a different story."

There was a snort from the vicinity of the stairs and Tiffany glanced over her shoulder to find Stephen, his black hair rumpled and sticking out at odd angles, his good eye still a slit, his injured one swollen shut, standing on the landing.

"Oh. Stephen. Uh, you know John Cawthorne."

"Yeah." Stephen straightened a bit and walked down the remaining steps. "Grandpa." He spat the word as if it tasted bitter.

"Yes. He's your grandfather."

John managed a tight smile and extended his hand.

"How're ya, boy? What happened there?" He nodded to Stephen's black eye as the boy crossed the foyer, shook his hand for a mere instant and shrugged.

"A fight."

"Did ya win?" One of John's gray eyebrows rose expectantly.

"No one wins in a fistfight," Tiffany interjected.

"Sure they do."

Sullenly Stephen lifted a shoulder again. "I did okay."

The room was tense, suddenly devoid of air. "There's breakfast in the oven. Waffles." At that moment Christina barreled into the room. Syrup was smeared over her lips and across the scrapes on her chin. A few strands of her hair were stuck to her cheek.

"I see you're busy," John said as he set his cup on a table. "Just remember I'd love to see all of you at the wedding tomorrow."

"You mean that?" Stephen asked.

"Absolutely."

The boy looked at his mother. "We goin'?"

"No." She wasn't going to change her mind.

"Give it some thought," John countered and for a ridiculous second, Tiffany felt sorry for him.

"I can't imagine I'd change my mind."

If possible, Stephen's eyes narrowed more suspiciously. Christina asked, "What wedding? You mean with brides?"

John grabbed his beat-up hat and bent down on one knee. "That's right, but only one bride. Her name's Brynnie and she would think it was just great if you were there," he said to Chrissie, then straightened. "If all of you were there."

Stephen's head tipped to one side as he eyed the stranger who was his grandfather.

"Don't count on it," Tiffany said, but the ice in her voice

had melted and she felt a ridiculous stab of guilt for being so cold. "We're busy."

"Sure." He smiled sadly but didn't accuse her of the lie. "I'll be seein' ya."

With that he squared his hat on his head and was out the door in a minute.

"Weird guy," Stephen said as he walked to the window and stared outside. Through the glass Tiffany saw the man who had sired and abandoned her climb into a shiny silver truck—so new it still sported temporary plates. "He's rich, right?"

"Rumored to be."

"Maybe you should be nice to him, you know. Go to that wedding."

"So that I'm in the will?" she said and rolled her eyes. "I don't think so, Stephen. Money isn't everything."

"But he is your dad."

"That depends on what you think a father is," she said. "Now, let me get Christina dressed and you go in and have breakfast. Then you and I had better talk."

"About what?"

She picked up her daughter and started for the stairs. "We'll start with Miles Dean and end up with Isaac Wells."

"I told you everything I know."

"So I forgot. You can tell me again. Come on, Chrissie, time for a bath."

"I don't want a bath."

"Too bad." Tiffany chuckled as she climbed the stairs and touched the tip of her daughter's nose. "You need one. Big time."

"J.D. Santini." J.D. extended his hand to the lanky man on the other side of the desk in the small office. The building was quiet; the other businesses on the second floor had shut down for the weekend. "I appreciate you coming in to meet me. I hear this is a busy weekend for your family."

Jarrod Smith lifted a shoulder. "I come from a big family. There's always something going on." A sardonic smile sliced his square jaw. "Mom's getting married and yeah, it's a big deal, but it's not the first time or the second. Have a seat." Jarrod waved toward one of the two empty chairs facing his old metal desk. J.D. settled into a plastic cushion that protested against his weight.

"I'll get straight to the point. I heard that you're running your own personal investigation into Isaac Wells's disappearance."

Jarrod nodded. His eyes bored into J.D.'s. This man was intense.

"Well, the police are sniffing around my nephew, I think, and I want to find out why." J.D. sketched out his relationship to Tiffany and her children and his concerns for Stephen.

"Rumor has it the kid mixed it up with Miles Dean yesterday," Jarrod said.

"Ended up with a shiner that won't quit."

"And the police found a set of keys on him. Keys they think belong to Isaac Wells."

"The boy didn't do anything to the old man."

"No one's proved anything was done to him. Isaac might have just up and taken off on his own," Jarrod reminded J.D. as he picked up a pencil and turned it thoughtfully between his fingers. "But I agree with you. Ever since Tiffany Santini moved down here, her boy's had more than his share of scrapes with the law. Until now they've been minor. Nothing like the Wells mess."

J.D. relaxed a little. Smith seemed to be on his wavelength. "So what happened to Isaac?"

"That's the million-dollar question," Jarrod admitted. "People usually don't just disappear without a trace. Sooner or later he'll turn up."

"Alive?"

"We can only hope."

J.D.'s stomach clenched. What had Stephen gotten himself into? He reached into his back pocket and slid out his checkbook. The pain in his leg twinged a bit. "What kind of a retainer do you want to prove that the kid's innocent?"

Jarrod snorted. "I'm already working on the case."

"I know, but everyone needs incentive." He snagged a pen from a cup on the desk.

With a smile that bordered on evil, the investigator shook his head. "Believe me, I've got plenty." He stood and thrust out his hand again. "I'll keep you posted."

J.D. had no choice but to take the man's hand. "I'd feel better if we had some kind of agreement."

"You've got my word. That's good enough," Smith insisted. "Trust me, I'm going to find out what happened to Isaac, come hell or high water."

"Okay, kiddo, I want the entire story. Beginning to end," Tiffany insisted as she nosed her car into traffic. Mrs. Ellingsworth was watching Christina and she and Stephen were alone, on their way to do some errands. He hadn't wanted to accompany her, not with so many questions hanging in the air, but she had forced the issue and won.

"'Bout what?"

"Let's start with yesterday," she said as they drove along the tree-lined street. Joggers and dogs ran on the sidewalks, dodging mothers with strollers near the park. "Do the keys the police found on you belong to Isaac Wells?"

Staring out the passenger window, Stephen lifted a shoulder.

"Do they? And don't give me any song and dance about you finding them in the park. That's not what happened and we both know it."

"Okay," he said, rebellion flaring in his eyes. "They were his."

Her heart plummeted. "Oh, Stephen."

"You wanted to know."

"I need to know the truth." Her hands began to sweat "Let's hear it."

He sighed as if pained. "It's not a big deal."

"Wrong. It's a very big deal. The man is missing. No one knows where he is or even if he's dead or alive. And you lied to me."

"It was nothing, okay?" Frowning, he flipped his hair out of his eyes. He rubbed his elbow with the hand of his other arm. "I told you that Miles Dean had dared me to take 'em."

"Right, but you said that you didn't. That you saw Mr. Wells on the porch and changed your mind."

Stephen worried his lower lip with his teeth. "I did see Mr. Wells. On the porch, just like I said. But that was after I'd swiped the keys. He didn't say nothin' to me, just stared me down, and I took off."

Her insides twisted. "You have to tell the police the truth."

"I know." He stared out the passenger window and his shoulders slumped in resignation.

"Why didn't you before?"

His Adam's apple bobbed nervously. "Because . . . because Miles told me if I so much as breathed a word of it, he'd kill us."

"You gave him the keys?"

"No." He was emphatic as he shook his head. "I don't know why, but I didn't feel right about it, so I hid 'em in a box in my room. Then I thought I'd sneak 'em out to the ranch and put 'em back, but . . . I never got around to it. There was all that yellow tape around the house, sayin' it was a crime scene and . . ." He shrugged. "I thought I'd wipe 'em clean of any fingerprints and toss 'em into the creek. I was gonna do it when I ran into Miles at the Mini Mart."

Calm down, Tiffany, she told herself as her fingers held on to the steering wheel in a death grip and she felt sweat dampen her spine. Don't judge, don't yell just listen. "Okay. What did Miles want with the keys?"

"Don't know." Stephen was as pale as death, but he appeared to be telling the truth.

"Is he planning on stealing one of Mr. Wells's cars?"

"Who knows? It doesn't matter. I never gave him the keys."

"Thank God." She braked at the hardware store where she had planned to pick up some supplies, but thought better of it. "Let's go down to the police station. You can tell Sergeant Pearson what you just told me."

"No way."

"Yes, way." She wasn't going to take no for an answer. Slowing at the intersection, she waited for the red light to change, then took a right. The police station was in the older part of town, not far from the park.

Stephen squirmed uncomfortably in his seat. "Mom, please, don't make me do this."

"You don't have a choice, Stephen."

"But Miles will kill me."

"I doubt it," she said, though she knew the older boy's reputation for violence. Miles was a tough kid who was angry at the world. "I'll handle Miles."

Stephen snorted as the courthouse came into view. Old brown brick, the building was three stories and housed the circuit court, the parks-and-recreation department, the mayor's office, library and, of course, the police station. "I hate this place," Stephen grumbled as she glided into a parking spot beneath the spreading branches of a maple tree.

"Good. Then let's avoid it. All you have to do is stay out of trouble." She cut the engine, pulled her cell phone from her purse and called Ellie so that the older woman wouldn't worry if they were gone longer than expected. "We'll come home as soon as we're done here," Tiffany promised her.

"Oh, good gracious." Ellie, who believed Stephen was an angel, was worried. "Don't let them bully him into saying anything he doesn't want to."

"I won't."

"Well, I'll be here with Christina. Now, don't you worry about us."

"I won't." She hung up, flipped the telephone closed and stuffed it into her purse. "Okay, kid, you're on," she said to her son as she opened the car door. Mumbling under his breath, Stephen reluctantly climbed out of the car. She started for the building, then stopped dead in her tracks as she spied Katie Kinkaid. her younger half-sister, striding across the hot asphalt.

"Oh, great."

"What?" Stephen asked. his attention drawn to the red-headed woman fast approaching. "Uh-oh."

"Tiffany!" Katie waved one hand frantically in the air. Wearing a pair of khaki slacks, a white scoop-neck T-shirt and tan jacket, she headed toward them, the heels of her sandals slapping against the pavement. In her right hand she hauled an oversize leather briefcase.

"This is the one who's your half-sister, right?" Stephen whispered.

"One of them."

"The other one's 'the princess.'"

"We shouldn't call Bliss that."

"*You* named her."

"I know, I know. Shh." She pasted a plastic smile on her lips. "Hi, Katie."

"Hi." Katie's wide smile was bright and infectious. Her green eyes sparkled, reflecting the afternoon sunlight. "Oh, gee, what happened to you?" she asked, cocking her head for a better view of Stephen's injuries.

"Nothin'."

"Doesn't look like 'nothin" to me," Katie said, her face suddenly a mask of worry.

"A disagreement down at the Mini Mart," Tiffany clarified and Katie's eyes rounded.

"That was *you*? Gosh, I get to write about it, you know. Along with the obits and gardening news, I type up the police reports and while I was getting the info, I heard there was a scuffle down at the Mini Mart yesterday, but I didn't know who was involved." She touched Stephen's temple and he jerked away. "Of course, if I'd really wanted to know, all I would have had to do was have coffee down at Millie's, I guess."

"It'll be in the paper?" Stephen was horrified.

"Nope. Because you weren't cited. Looks like you lucked out this time. . . . Well, maybe not, judging from the size of that shiner. I'll bet it hurts."

"A little." Stephen was noncommittal.

"Well, be careful, would you? You've got a dynamite face and I'd hate to see it all banged up before you were twenty." Adjusting the strap of her briefcase, she faced Tiffany. "I heard John came to see you this morning."

Tiffany nodded and steeled herself for the onslaught she felt was coming. "He showed up around nine, I think."

"I told him it was a mistake."

"Did you?"

"Hey, we all have to handle this the way we think is best. I'm going to the wedding, of course, even though I'm not sure I totally approve. But it is both my mother and father, and if they can find some happiness together . . . Well"—she turned her free palm skyward—"so be it."

"If that's the way you feel." Tiffany wished her own

emotions were so easily defined. Ever since seeing her father this morning, she'd been in knots, second-guessing herself.

"It is. I'd like to see Mom happy."

"Will this do it?" Tiffany asked, trying not to sound as skeptical as she felt.

"Time will tell, but I can't see any reason to rain on their parade. Sure, John was a jerk—" She slid a glance at Stephen, but Tiffany waved her concern aside.

"Stephen knows the story."

"Then he realizes that his grandfather made some mistakes in his life. Major mistakes. But now he's trying to rectify them. I figure why not give the guy a chance."

"I can think of a few reasons."

"Yeah, I suppose, but I figure it's time to let bygones be bygones."

"I don't think I can," Tiffany admitted, though she felt a tiny twinge of guilt.

"Hey, whatever you want to do is your business. But the wedding could be fun. At least the reception out at Cawthorne Acres will be. If you don't have anything better to do, why don't you and the kids show up? Josh, my son—you probably know him from school, Stephen. He's some kind of cousin to you and he'd love it if another boy around his age came."

Tiffany couldn't find a way to say no without getting into another argument. "I—I'll think about it."

"Do." Katie checked her watch and sucked some air between her teeth. "Oops. I'm late already. See ya." Half jogging to an ancient convertible, she climbed inside. With a clank, pop and cloud of black smoke, the car started. Waving, Katie wheeled out of the lot.

"Wow," Stephen said, watching Katie, her red hair flying, disappear around a corner.

"She's a real go-getter." Squinting against the midday sun, Tiffany added, "I didn't know we were related until we moved down here."

"You always said you wished you had a sister or a brother," Stephen reminded her. "Every time Chrissie bugs me and I tell her to get lost, you tell me how bad it was for you growing up without any other kids."

"I do, don't I?" Tiffany said, touched by the irony of her predicament. Throughout her childhood and awkward teenage years, she'd felt so alone growing up with only her mother and a grandmother as family—three women who depended solely upon each other. Every night on her knees by her twin bed, she'd prayed for a sister or a brother.

Or a father.

Old, forgotten loneliness crawled into her heart—the same painful feeling of being alone in the world she'd hoped would disappear when she married. She'd bound herself to an older man, from an established family, with two kids of his own, and had hoped to raise three or four children of her own and become part of a huge, chaotic and happy family. Philip had come up with his own plans. More children hadn't been a part of them.

Clearing her throat, she turned toward the police station. "Come on, kiddo. We'd better get this over with."

Stephen looked as if he'd just as soon drop dead, but they walked past parked cars and spindly trees until they came to the wide double doors of the century-old building.

"This is a waste of time," Stephen grumbled.

"I don't think so." She pushed the door open. "Come on."

Inside the police station there was no air-conditioning and the few windows that were open were barred or screened, reminding Tiffany of where they were. The offices were now smoke free, but the walls and ceilings were stained by years of cigarette smoke that had hung cloudlike in the corridors and rooms. Stephen's feet seemed to drag on the industrial carpet, but they made their way through a maze of hallways to Sergeant Pearson's battle-scarred desk. Papers, memos, photographs and books were piled high. Three near-empty coffee cups were placed strategically around a computer screen.

A thick-set man with a crew cut that didn't much hide the fact that he was going bald, Pearson sat at his desk. He cradled the earpiece of his phone between a meaty shoulder and his squat neck, and managed to scribble notes on a legal pad covered with doodles.

"Uh-huh . . . And what time was that . . . ? About eight last night? That's when the dog started barking?" He held up one finger, indicating that he was about through with his call, then waved them into the two molded-plastic chairs tucked between his desk and a partition separating his space from the next cubicle. "Don't worry. We'll look into it," he promised the person on the phone, then hung up and shuffled his papers to one side of the desk. "Stephen. Ms. Santini. What can I do for you?" he asked. He leaned back in his chair.

"Stephen has something he wants to tell you."

"Is that right?" Ted Pearson's smile wasn't the least bit friendly. "Good. Since the keys we found on Stephen yesterday fit into the ignitions of several of Isaac Wells's cars, I think it's time we had a chat." He raised his voice. "Jack, you want to come hear this?" he asked and a tall rangy man appeared from behind the partition. "This is Detective Ramsey. He's been working on the Wells case."

"Call me Jack." He shook hands with Tiffany and Stephen.

"Mrs. Santini, and her son, Stephen."

"Tiffany." She shook hands with the tall man and wished her palms hadn't begun to sweat.

His smile seemed sincere. He swung a leg over the corner of Pearson's mess of a desk and said, "Okay, Stephen, let's hear it. Shoot."

"Wait a minute."

J.D.'s voice rang through the offices.

Tiffany froze. Now what? Glancing over her shoulder, she watched as J.D., his limp hardly noticeable, made his way along the short hallway until he was standing beside her. "I'm the boy's uncle. What's going on here?"

"Who invited you?" the detective asked.

J.D.'s smile was cold and there was a spark of challenge in his gray eyes. "I invited myself. J.D. Santini." He thrust out his hand. "And I guess I should mention, I'm an attorney."

Jack eyed him warily. "A criminal attorney? The boy doesn't need representation."

"Good." J.D. stood right behind Stephen as if to shield him from an attack to his backside. "As I said, I'm Stephen's uncle and his attorney if he needs one. So." He rubbed his hands together and pinned both officers with his harsh gaze. "Now, what's this all about?"

Chapter Seven

"You are *not* a criminal attorney," Tiffany said under her breath as J.D., in his new role of concerned uncle, escorted them outside the courthouse. A hot summer breeze blew through the streets, causing dust to swirl and rustling in the leaves of the maple trees.

"They don't know that."

"The police aren't the enemy, J.D." They crossed the parking lot and she wanted to throttle him. Who was he to play the role of concerned father? "Besides, you have no right"—she stopped at her car and whirled, thrusting a finger into his chest—"*no right*, to come barging in there."

"I thought you might need a little help and all I did was to encourage him to tell the truth without falling into any traps. Stephen did fine." His eyes when they found hers stopped her cold. An awareness of something dangerous and primal slid through her and she had trouble finding her tongue.

"I think I already told you that I . . . we . . . are doing fine on our own."

"Are you?" He gestured to Stephen as the boy slid into the passenger seat of her car. "He looks like he just came out of a war zone and he's getting into more than his share of trouble."

"I'm working on it, Jay."

"Then what about Christina? I've heard her scream in the middle of the night."

"I don't think this is the time or place," she said. The conversation was twisting in directions that she couldn't control.

"When?"

"What?"

"When would be the time and place?" he asked. "Whether you know it or not, we need to talk."

She shot a glance at Stephen and saw him staring at her with wary eyes. "Later."

"How much later?"

"I don't know—"

"Tonight," he said.

"No, the kids—"

"They can stay alone for a couple of hours."

He waved to Stephen as he made his way across the parking lot to his rig. Stephen lifted his hand halfheartedly and J.D. nodded. Without a backward glance he climbed into his Jeep and drove away, leaving Tiffany to simmer and stew. Angry and confused, she slid into the sun-baked interior of her car and quickly started it.

"What was that all about?" Stephen demanded. He fiddled with the buttons of the radio, changing from station to station.

"Who knows?" Checking her rearview mirror, she backed out of the parking lot.

"I don't remember him hanging out with Dad a lot."

"He didn't."

"So why's he here now?" Stephen settled on a station that Tiffany didn't recognize, then slumped in his seat and stared glumly through the window.

"I don't know. He's just concerned, I guess."

"Is he really a lawyer?" Stephen asked, chewing on his lower lip and rubbing his elbow nervously.

"Yes." She felt a needle of fear prick her scalp. "Why?"

"Just wonderin'," Stephen said, but Tiffany read more into the question and her heart sank. "Stephen," she said softly. "Do you need an attorney?"

"No," he answered quickly. Too quickly.

Careful, Tiffany, she cautioned herself. *Tread lightly.* "You're sure?"

"I was just curious, okay? It's not a crime." He stopped short at his own words, blushed and punched another button on the dash. Settling back in his seat, he chewed on a fingernail and closed his eyes as a song Tiffany recognized from one of his Nine Inch Nails CDs thrummed through the speakers.

Leave it alone, she told herself. *This isn't the time.* She drove through town and tried not to worry. Everything was going to be all right. Stephen had his share of troubles, but he wasn't a criminal, for goodness' sake. He was just a thirteen-year-old boy who was confused by his father's death and his recent move. For the first time she wondered if uprooting him had been a good idea. There was a chance he would have felt more secure in Portland with his old friends.

Now he was scared.

And so was she.

J.D. couldn't concentrate. Seated at the small table in his apartment, he shuffled the papers he'd received from the real-estate agent—information about the half-dozen properties that would work for his father's latest idea for expansion into a new winery and vineyards, but the words blurred.

He unscrewed the cap of his thermos and poured hours-old coffee into his cup. Frowning at the bitter taste, he added a splash of bourbon he'd bought for just that purpose.

For all of his life, he'd never had a problem keeping his thoughts on track. In high school, despite the fact that he'd spent more time rebelling than studying, he'd breezed through his classes. College hadn't been tough and he'd managed to work full-time and attend law school.

When he'd finally started working for a large firm in Seattle, he'd been able to spend hour after hour in the law library, or at his desk, poring over old cases, reviewing and researching, and generally working eighteen-hour days. He could get by on four hours' sleep and kept in shape by running the hills of the city while honing his thoughts on whatever case he was working on at the time.

He had chased ambulances—or, as he preferred to call it, he'd been a "personal injury" lawyer. That was where the money had been; that was where he could help individuals fight corporations, insurance companies, hospitals or whoever had wronged them.

He'd never been one to lose sight of his goals. Never been unprepared. Never been distracted. Well, almost never. The women he'd dated, slept with, or nearly loved, hadn't been interesting enough to deter him.

Except for his brother's wife.

Tiffany Nesbitt Santini had been the exception—and, he was afraid, his undoing.

Swearing under his breath, he took a long swallow from his cup and felt the coffee and alcohol hit his stomach in a warm, welcome flood.

Tiffany had gotten to him from the start.

Maybe it was because J.D. had always been competitive to the point of being considered cutthroat. Maybe it was because he'd always vied with his brother for his family's attention. Maybe he just hadn't liked being second-born. The fact that Philip had been a screw-up made it worse.

When Philip had dumped his first wife and kids, J.D. had been furious. He'd nearly beaten the living tar out of Philip, for all the good it had done. In J.D.'s opinion, Philip had failed his wife and kids by getting involved with another woman, and then he'd started to gamble more than he should. It was as if he'd given up all sense of responsibility and jumped feetfirst into a raging mid-life crisis. As soon as his divorce was final, Philip had moved on from that woman and zeroed in on Tiffany, who, in J.D.'s opinion, was far too young and naive for his older brother.

His family considered her a gold digger, and maybe she had been, but she'd stuck by Philip, given him another couple of kids, and, to J.D.'s knowledge, had never run around on his brother.

And J.D. had wanted her.

From the get-go.

Badly.

"Forget it," he snorted, as he heard Stephen tuning up his guitar. Discordant music rose from the room below. Tapping the edges of his real-estate reports on the table, J.D. stuffed them into his briefcase where he spied the deed to the house. Now, there was a problem. One he couldn't solve. His father owned most of the place. It was J.D.'s unenviable job to determine if the apartment house Tiffany ran and called home was worth the time and effort of keeping it. The old man didn't necessarily want to cut the mother of his grandchildren out of what was rightfully hers, he just wanted to know if the property was a viable investment. It was Carlo's contention that Tiffany and the kids could live closer to the family in a more comfortable home. As Carlo was estranged from the grandchildren from Philip's first marriage and it didn't seem that J.D. would ever have children, the old man was deeply interested in Stephen and Christina.

But he didn't give a damn about Tiffany. He'd made that clear on more than one occasion.

Rubbing the area of his thigh that still bothered him, J.D. decided to call it a night. It was after ten and he was beat.

He gulped the last of his coffee and wiped his mouth with the back of his hand. The thrum of guitar chords had stopped and the house was quiet. He went to the window and stared through the clear panes.

Past the leafy branches of the trees in the backyard, he spied a few stars that were bright enough to defy the lights of the town. Low in the sky was the moon, or half of it. He stretched and glanced down to the lawn where Tiffany was watering a few potted plants.

Her gauzy white dress caught in a breeze that teased at the hem, giving him a few glimpses of her bare legs. Unaware that she was being observed, she bent over each terra-cotta container and sprinkled the showy petunias, pansies and geraniums placed strategically around the drying grass. Her slinky cat wound about her bare feet, rubbing against her calves.

God, she was beautiful. Her black hair was wound into a knot pinned to the back of her head, but strands of hair had escaped to frame her face and nape. Thoughtfully she bit her lower lip, showing off a hint of pearly teeth as she plucked dead blossoms from the plants.

He couldn't resist. Knowing he was about to step over an invisible but very definite line that he might not ever be able to recross, he set his papers and coffee cup aside and grabbed the neck of a bottle of wine he'd bought earlier in the day. The Cabernet was local and J.D. had decided to check out the competition. Quickly he headed downstairs.

The steps creaked a little but the second level was quiet with only a nightlight in the bathroom offering partial illumination. He hurried down the final staircase to the first floor. A radio was playing softly in the kitchen but the only light was a glass-encased candle flickering on the table.

Quietly he opened several cupboards before finding the glassware, then plucked two wineglasses from a shelf and didn't bother to question his motives. The corkscrew was in a drawer with odds and ends of kitchen utensils.

He slipped noiselessly through the screen door and stood on the porch for a second. Tiffany was near the carriage house, refilling her plastic sprinkler at a faucet and he watched as she watered the planter boxes of impatiens.

Only when she'd turned and faced him, did he step out of the shadows of the porch.

"Oh." She froze, then recognized him. "For the love of Pete, Jay, you scared me." Wiping drips of water from her hands, she approached and he tried not to notice the way her dress hugged her breasts or the slight bit of cleavage that was visible at the neckline. Nor did he concentrate on the way her hips moved beneath the thin fabric.

He lifted up the bottle. "I brought this as a peace offering."

She stopped only inches from him and lifted a dark, suspicious brow. "Because—"

"Of our disagreement."

She shook her head and laughed. The sound was musical and vital. "If you buy a bottle of wine every time we disagree, you're going to go broke fast."

"You think?"

"No, I know."

"Then," he said, placing the glasses on the rail of the porch and beginning to slice the foil surrounding the cork with the tip of the corkscrew, "maybe we should just call a truce."

"You think that's possible?"

He skewered her with a look that made her swallow hard. "Anything's possible, Tiffany. You know that."

She looked quickly away as he placed the bottle between his knees and pulled the cork.

"It's late."

"Yeah, but where're you going?"

"Upstairs. To bed."

He left that line alone and poured them each a glass. "You can spare a few minutes."

She looked like she wanted to bolt, but took the glass and together they sat on a bench beneath a willow tree in the backyard.

"How about a toast?" he asked.

"To what?"

"Better days?"

She smiled sadly and he was undone. For an unreasonable second be wanted to enfold her in his arms and tell her everything would be all right. Instead he studied the ruby-dark depths of his glass. She squared her shoulders and nodded. "Better days," she agreed, touching the rim of her glass to his. "Lots of them."

"Amen."

They both took a sip and the night seemed to hold them closer. Faint light fell from the windows of the nook where the candle burned and somewhere down the street a dog gave a soft "Woof." Crickets chirped from hidden crevices and the rumble of traffic, slow-moving and sparse, was barely audible.

"So," she finally said as if the silence between them was unbearable. "How did you just happen to show up at the police station today?"

"When I got back here, I heard what was going on from Mrs. Ellingsworth."

"Ah," she said, taking a swallow. He tried not to watch the motion of her throat, but it was impossible. "Discretion isn't one of Ellie's strong points."

"No?"

She frowned at her glass. "No. But she's honest, kind, loving, fun, and she adores my children." With a half smile, she added, "I guess I can live with her need to gossip."

"She's just lonely. Wants someone to talk to."

Tiffany nodded and twisted the stem of her glass between her fingers. "So how's the search coming?" she asked. "Have you found a place for the winery?"

"I'm narrowing it down."

"To—?"

"A couple of places. One of which is the Wells ranch."

Tiffany sighed. "It seems we never can get away from that place, can we?"

"I told you I'd help," he said.

"And I told you I don't need any." She took another long swallow from her glass and he drained his.

"You're a lousy liar, Tiffany."

"What?"

"You heard me. You need a lot of help. You've got a house that's falling down around you and a job that takes a lot of your time. On top of that you're worried about your son and I don't blame you. Right now Stephen's rebelling all over the place. Maybe it has to do with Philip's death, but maybe it runs deeper. No one knows, but the simple fact is that he looks like he's been in a prison fight and he's probably still in some trouble with the police. Whether you admit it or not, you're afraid that he's somehow connected with Isaac Wells's disappearance."

"He's just a boy!" she protested.

"A boy who might know too much. He's running with a rough crowd, getting into fights and you don't know how much else, but the fact of the matter is he ended up with Isaac Wells's keys."

"It was a dare."

"One he shouldn't have taken," J.D. said, seeing her face whiten in the night.

"Then there's your daughter."

She gasped. "Christina's fine."

"Is she? Why the nightmares every night?"

Tiffany bristled and set her drink on the ground. What was J.D.'s game? What did he want? "What do you expect, Jay? She was barely three when she watched her father die, for God's sake. Of course that's going to cause some trauma But it's normal. She's been to a child psychologist." Tiffany crossed her arms under her breasts and glared at him. What did he know about raising kids? About becoming a single parent? About dealing with a truckload of guilt because your husband died in an automobile accident while you survived? About facing yourself every morning knowing that you were at the wheel of the car when it slid out of control? Her stomach twisted into painful knots and she cleared her throat.

"I'm just concerned," he said so quietly that for a split second, she believed him.

"Why all of a sudden? Most of Stephen's life you haven't been around."

"I had my reasons," he said.

"Which were?"

He leveled her with a gaze that caused her heart to knock. "You don't want to know."

"Of course I do."

He lowered his glass to the ground and grabbed her bare shoulders in his big, callused hands. She started to shrink from him, but held her ground and inched her chin up a notch. "If you want to know the truth—"

"I do." Or did she?

"Most of my reasons for staying away had to do with you, Tiffany."

"With me?" she whispered, then stared into his eyes. Dark with the night they made promises of slow seduction, of a forbidden desire that no amount of time could erase. Memories cascaded through her mind, erotic images that tumbled, one after another, of the one night, just after Philip's death, when she'd given in to him, of the few desperate hours when she'd clung to him in her tormented and anguished grief. "You're right," she said, swallowing hard and trying with all her heart to forget those painful-yet-bittersweet memories. "I don't want to know."

"Too late." His fingers tightened, he lowered his head and his mouth slanted over hers as familiarly as if they'd been lovers just last night.

A small sound filled her throat—not the note of protest she'd intended, but a soft plea. His arms surrounded her and she knew she should pull back from him, slap him across his cocky jaw, but she couldn't find the strength. Instead she closed her eyes and for one glorious, taboo moment she kissed him back, opening her mouth, feeling the slick penetration of his tongue.

Her skin tingled. Her pulse clamored. Her blood heated.

He wound his fingers through her hair and the rubber band holding it in place broke, allowing the thick tresses to tumble free.

Stop this madness, Tiffany, stop it now. While you still can. But her protests were forgotten as his lips moved to her cheeks and eyes. His body pressed against hers and her nipples tightened expectantly.

Deep inside she began to palpitate, with a quivering need that chased away all her doubts.

"Tiffany," he said on a sigh, and his breath was hot against her skin. He kissed the length of her neck and rimmed the circle of her throat with his tongue.

Her head lolled backward and silently she offered him more. A dozen reasons to push him away entered her mind only to be thrust aside by the greater urge to love and be loved, to feel a man's hands, his lips, his tongue.

His fingers scaled her ribs and his thumbs reached forward, each warm pad pressing against breasts, seeking and finding that taut button beneath her dress, then moving in gentle circles, stirring her blood, stoking the already heated fires of desire that made her skin so hot that perspiration dotted her skin.

He found the front buttons of her dress, easing each pearl fastener through its hole, parting the fabric so that the warm night air caressed her suddenly bare skin. An ache formed deep between her legs and she knew in an instant that she wouldn't stop him; that no matter how far he wanted their lovemaking to progress, she would gladly receive him.

His tongue licked her collarbone and she whispered his name.

"Jay, oh, please—oooh!"

He kissed her through the lace of her bra and she cradled his head against her as his lips found her nipple. Through the fabric he suckled and she could barely keep her balance on the bench. One of his hands reached around her, rubbing her buttock as he teased and kissed her breast.

"Aaaahhh!" A terrified scream pierced the night.

"Christina!" Tiffany sat bolt upright. J.D. released her.

Buttoning her dress and calling herself a moron, she raced to the house, up the back steps and through the door.

"Mommy!" the little girl cried. "Mommeee!"

"I'm coming, sweetheart!" Tiffany flew up the stairs.

J.D. was on her heels.

"Daddy! Daddy!"

"I'm here, baby," Tiffany said, running down the hallway and tearing into her daughter's room. "Right here."

Christina was in the middle of her bed, rocking back and forth, tears streaming down her little face. Tiffany scooped her daughter up and held her tightly, kissing her cheeks, holding her buttocks with one arm and her head with the other. "It's all right, Chrissie, Mommy's here. I'll always be here."

Sobbing, Christina clung to her. "I scared."

"I know, honey, I know. But there's nothing to be scared

about. I'm here." She dabbed at her daughter's eyes and taking up Chrissie's favorite blanket sat in the rocker near the bookcase, the rocker she'd used when the children were infants. J.D. stood in the doorway, looking as if he wanted to say something, but he held his tongue and a second later Stephen, his hair at odd angles, half staggered into the room.

"Nightmare?" he asked and Tiffany nodded.

"Bad dream!" Christina whispered.

"You gotta do somethin' about it," Stephen said, rubbing his eyes and yawning.

"I'm trying. Shhh."

"Yeah, yeah." Stephen rolled his eyes at his uncle, then returned to his own room.

"Can I do anything?" J.D. asked, his face tense.

She shook her head, but held his gaze as Christina, giving up a tiny sigh, snuggled against her. "We're fine," Tiffany said and ignored the doubts in his eyes. "Just fine." She picked up the well-loved floppy-eared stuffed rabbit and tucked it into her daughter's arms. "Here's Bub." Then she pressed a kiss to her daughter's curly head and kept rocking.

Thankfully J.D. took the hint. "If you need anything—"

"I won't."

"I'll be upstairs." She held her breath as she heard him climb the steps to the third floor. Christina calmed as she always did and her eyelids slowly lowered as the tempo of her breathing steadied. Humming softly, Tiffany continued to rock until she felt her daughter's bones turn to butter.

Gently Tiffany tucked Christina into the bed and tiptoed into the hallway. She left the door ajar and walked toward her own room, pausing for a second at the open door to the third floor.

It was an invitation from her brother-in-law. She let her

fingers run alongside the edge of the door and thought long and hard about his silent offer. A part of her longed to dash up the stairs and throw herself into his arms. Another part restrained her. J.D.'s invitation was one she couldn't accept. She'd been a fool to kiss him tonight. Letting him touch her and feeling all those long-buried sensations was tantamount to emotional suicide. With renewed determination and more than a trace of regret, she closed the door and walked to her room.

She could never, never let J.D. get close to her again. It was just too dangerous.

Slowly she unbuttoned her dress and caught a glimpse of herself in the freestanding mirror. Her hair was mussed, her dress wrinkled, her face still flushed. "Oh, Tiffany," she said. "Be smart. For your kids' sake."

She tossed her dress into the hamper and slipped on a cotton T-shirt, then slid between the sheets of her bed and turned off the lamp. Why couldn't she just tell J.D. to take a hike? To leave her and her small family alone?

Because you want him, Tiffany. It's just that simple.

And oh, so complicated.

Once before, she'd given in to temptation and she'd lived to regret it. She shuddered and closed her eyes. It had all started with the accident, the damned accident that had altered the course of her life forever. She'd been driving down from the mountain after a day of skiing. Philip had dozed off in the passenger seat. The kids had been in the back of the sedan, Christina strapped in her toddler seat while Stephen, exhausted and half asleep, was listening to his headphones. It had been nearly nine months ago, but she remembered it as vividly as if the horrible night had just been this past week.

* * *

The snow had been blinding as she'd eased down the steep hillside, not realizing that within minutes her entire life would change. . . .

The snow just wouldn't let up. Fat flakes fell onto the windshield before the wipers could scrape them off. Ice had collected on the wiper blades and the steady glare from the headlights of the cars driving up the mountain were giving her a headache.

She'd never liked driving in the snow in western Oregon where it usually began to melt only to freeze over again, leaving a layer of ice on the pavement.

Road crews were working around the clock and she comforted herself with the fact that the road past Government Camp on Mount Hood had been sanded and plowed and resanded. Yet her studded tires slid a little as she rounded a corner and she looked forward to finding dry, or wet pavement, at the lower elevations.

She was wearing gloves and her ski clothes and the heater was blasting hot air, yet she felt chilly inside. She punched a button on the radio, hoping to catch the weather forecast, but the signal was weak at this altitude, with the craggy peaks of the Cascade Mountains causing interference, so she settled for an old Otis Redding song that crackled and sputtered through the speakers.

Another set of headlights approached. She tried not to stare at the intense beams but she experienced a strange sensation, one that reminded her of a doe transfixed by the glare. *Relax.* The sound of a truck's engine rumbled and its tire chains buzzed over the muffled music.

It's just a truck. Big deal. There are dozens of them on this stretch of road, no matter what the conditions.

She tapped the brakes. They slid just a bit, then grabbed. Good.

To be safe, she eased as far to the right as she dared, but

the guard rail was low in spots and the black canyon that gaped beyond her viewpoint worried her.

Honk!

She jumped, her foot slipping on the brake.

The truck's horn blasted again.

Her fingers tightened on the wheel. She pumped the brakes lightly.

Nothing.

Don't panic! But the truck was roaring toward them on the left and to the right was the gaping darkness of the edge of the cliff.

Honk!

"Philip," she said as the truck's horn blared again. "Philip!"

"Wh-what?" he said around a yawn.

"The truck, oh, God!" At that moment the semi seemed to swerve and come right at them.

"Jesus!" Philip was instantly awake. He grabbed for the wheel.

"Wait!"

She hit the brakes. They locked. The car shimmied.

"Holy Mother Mary!" Philip was wide-awake and swearing, yanking at the steering wheel.

"Don't! Philip!"

The car slid sideways as the truck, only feet away, loomed like the very specter of death. "Tiffany! Crank the wheel! Pump the damned brakes! Get us out of here!"

"I'm trying!"

"Mom?" Stephen's voice cracked with fear.

She managed to turn just enough, but the truck, rolling past and out of control, clipped the rear end of the sedan. It spun wildly. She tried to stop, but hit a patch of ice and suddenly the car slammed through the guardrail and into the abyss.

"Oh my God!" Philip cried.

Tiffany screamed, and Christina let out a wail.

"Oh, no, oh, no, oh, no," Stephen muttered as the car, with a bone-jarring thud, scraped down the side of the mountain and skidded downward. Faster, faster, the wheels spinning, the brakes useless.

"Stop! For God's sake—"

Bam! They smashed into something. Hard. The windshield shattered. Glass sprayed. The car spun around.

"Mommy!"

"I'm here, sweetie."

"For the love of Christ!"

Again they were rolling rapidly forward. Faster and faster.

"Damn it, stop the car!"

"I can't!"

She saw the creek. Silver water slicing through the canyon, "Oh, my God—"

The wheels hit water. Bam! Every bone in Tiffany's body jarred. Ice-cold water ripped through the shattered windshield.

"Get out!" Tiffany yelled.

She scrambled for her seat-belt buckle.

"Mom! Dad!" Stephen's voice was strangled by terror. He was flailing in the back seat. Christina cried. Philip was cursing. Wild, raging water flooded the interior.

"Get out. Everyone get out!" Philip yelled.

Christina was crying and Stephen, too, was screaming.

"Tiffany, for God's sake, get to the shore." Philip was opening his door as she fumbled with her seat belt. The latch refused to give. "I'll get the kids."

"I can't get out!" Stephen's voice was filled with panic. It was black and dark and so damned cold. Water gurgled and swirled, splashing and rushing around them in an icy current.

Tiffany's fingers fumbled with the safety-belt latch.

"Get out! Get out!" Philip was outside the car, attempting

to open the back door. "Christina, hang in there! Stephen, try to get out of the car!"

Tiffany was shaking, her fingers numb, but the latch finally gave way and she shouldered open the door only to fall into waist-deep water. Her feet slipped on the rocks, but she clung to the car, fighting the current, praying that they would all get out of this alive. So cold she could barely move, she found the back door and tried to pull it open. It wouldn't budge.

"I can't get out!" Stephen yelled.

"The safety locks!" Philip shouted. Tiffany couldn't see him but heard him splashing in the icy water. Christina was crying weakly.

"Get out the front!" she yelled to her son as the car filled with water. "Hurry!" She felt, rather than saw, Stephen crawl over the front seat to hurtle through the open door. Miraculously she caught his arm.

Sputtering and shivering, he clung to her.

"Christina!" she cried.

"Got her." Philip's voice sounded so far away.

"Okay, hang on to me. Let's try to get to shore," she yelled into Stephen's ear, though she had no idea how wide or deep the creek was. It could be a river, for all she knew.

"This way." Stephen stepped around the car only to be half-dragged underwater.

"Philip!" she cried, but there wasn't an answer. "Philip!" Oh, God, had he drowned? Did he have the baby? "Philip!" Where was he? She strained to listen but heard only the wild rush of the river. "Philip!"

"Dad!"

Her heart stopped. "He's got Christina, don't worry," she said to her son though she was dying inside. Her husband. Her baby. Where were they? Dear God, keep them safe! Oh, please!

"Mom?" Stephen's voice was faint, his teeth chattering and she realized that she was numb all over. Not a good sign.

"Try to get to the shore," she managed.

"Where?"

If she only knew. Frantically she looked around. Blackness everywhere. Only inky, cold, terrifying blackness. They could be in the middle of the creek or close to one bank. Who knew? But they couldn't stay in the freezing water. They'd both die from hypothermia.

Which way?

"M-m-mom, I'm so cold."

"Hang on, Stephen." How long had they been in the water? "Philip!" she cried and strained to hear. Far away there were voices. "Listen!"

She looked up and saw a bobbing light. The freezing water whirled and danced madly around her.

"Hey!" a male voice boomed. "Anyone there?"

"Help! Oh, God, help us!"

"Hang on, we're comin'," the voice assured her and she clung to Stephen and the car, trying to stay conscious, praying that her husband and daughter were safe.

She didn't remember the rescue. It had taken over an hour and both she and Stephen, suffering from hypothermia, had passed out. She awoke in a hospital in Portland to the news that she and both children had survived, but Philip, as a result of his efforts to save Christina, had died on the way to the hospital. No attempts at reviving him had been effective.

Tiffany was barely out of the hospital, hardly able to function from grief and despair, when she had to arrange a funeral. All of Philip's family was at the long, mind-numbing service. She was a widow. Alone with her children.

J.D. sat between his parents and sister-in-law, not so much as touching her or offering any sign of condolence during the funeral. White-faced, drawn and tense, he'd partially shielded Tiffany from the rest of the family.

But it hadn't worked. Philip's father, Carlo, had been grim and forbidding, his black eyes boring into Tiffany throughout the eulogy. Frances, seated at her husband's side, wouldn't even look in Tiffany's direction, but shunned her and pretended that her daughter-in-law didn't exist.

Philip's ex-wife, Karen, a short blond woman with huge blue eyes, clung to her ex-mother-in-law and sobbed loudly, blowing her nose and sliding furtive glances at the woman who had, eventually, replaced her in her ex-husband's heart. She wailed loudly, while her children, Robert and Thea, were stoic and grim. Philip's older children were both in college, both acting as if they'd rather be anywhere in the world but at the funeral home, both seeming more bored than grief-stricken.

Throughout the service Tiffany held on to both of her children. Christina sat on her lap, and Stephen, pale and wan, was beside her in the pew.

Even without the harsh glares cast in her direction or the cold shoulders meant to shut her away from the rest of the family, Tiffany didn't have to be told that the entire Santini clan blamed her for Philip's death. She'd been the one who'd insisted upon going skiing that day. Philip had only indulged her. And she'd been behind the wheel at the time of the accident.

There had been a gathering of family and friends at the Santini winery in McMinnville after the funeral and gravesite service. Tiffany had never felt so alone in her life. Everyone was coldly polite and the hours went by at an excruciatingly slow pace. She just wanted to be alone, to hide and lick her wounds, to mourn her husband and plan her future; her children's futures.

The words of sympathy echoed in her heart.

"Sorry about your loss."

"A tragedy. Such a tragedy."

"I don't know what Carlo will do without him. And Frances . . . My, how this has aged her."

"Good luck to you and the children."

But after a few kind words—a courtesy to the Santini family—the mourners let her be, each finding his or her small group at the gathering, each whispering and talking about the accident, sending her looks that bordered on pity but oftentimes were tinged with hate.

She'd put on a brave face for nearly two hours, sipping too much wine and fighting back tears of desperation, when a voice behind her said, "Let's get out of here. I think you've done your time for today."

She whirled to find J.D. with her coat and the kids' jackets. Somehow she managed a thin smile and shook her head. "Thanks, but I have my own car."

"I know." Carefully, he removed an empty wineglass from her hand. "I think I should drive." For once he seemed sincere. Almost kind. "This has been a rough day."

"Amen," she agreed, and didn't bother to argue. She gathered up Christina and Stephen and handed J.D. the car keys. On the ride home, she closed her eyes, grateful for someone's thoughtfulness—even her irreverent brother-in-law's.

At the home she'd shared with Philip in northwest Portland, she managed to get the kids into bed before she felt herself coming undone. "I don't know how to thank you," she said as J.D. lingered in the kitchen.

"Brotherly duty."

"Above and beyond the call, if you ask me." She poured herself another glass of wine, though she was already light-headed. She was a widow. A widow, for goodness' sake. The future, once so certain, seemed suddenly bleak as it stretched endlessly before her. "Join me?"

"I think I've had enough."

"Me, too." But she took a long swallow of last year's Santini Brothers premium Pinot Noir. Feeling dead tired, she kicked off her high heels and leaned over to rub her arch.

"I'll help you to bed."

"You don't have to."

"I know. But don't fight it." He eyed the wine bottle and scowled. "Didn't the doctor prescribe some tranquillizers for you?"

"Haven't taken any."

"Don't. Not until you're sober."

"I am sober," she argued, and defiantly drained her glass.

"Come on, I'll help you upstairs."

"I don't need any help," she lied, determined to appear independent. She'd fall apart when she was alone.

"Fine."

She started for the staircase and nearly stumbled. J.D. caught her and sighed. "Come on, Tiff. I know it's been hard."

His gentle words, so unexpected and sincere, caught her off guard. With a tender smile, he managed to pierce the emotional armor she'd worn since the accident. Tears gathered in her eyes for the first time since the funeral service. "I'm . . . I'm okay."

"So you've been trying to convince everyone."

"But I am."

"Sure."

She swayed again and he picked her up, swinging her off her feet as deftly as if she weighed nothing. "Come on, Tiff, let's put it to rest." He carried her upstairs and down a long hallway to the bedroom she'd shared with Philip. Once there, he placed her carefully on top of the bed and brushed a strand of hair from her eyes. "It's all right to break down, you know."

Her chin wobbled and tears drizzled from her eyes.

"You were married to the guy."

"I'll miss him."

His jaw hardened. "It's only natural."

She dabbed at her eyes and sighed. "Oh, God," she admitted, "I'm so scared."

He stared down at her for a long moment, then shrugged out of his jacket, tossed it over the back of a chair and lowered himself onto the bed beside her. The old mattress squeaked as if in disapproval. "You'll be all right," he said, wrapping his arms around her and holding her close. His breath whispered across her hair and she let go of the storm of tears that had been building for days. Sobs racked her body as he held her, keeping her safe, whispering soft words of encouragement. She didn't fight him but let him hold her and by the time she fell asleep, emotionally and physically exhausted, the front of his shirt was wet with her tears and smudged by her makeup.

During the night, he'd pulled the covers around them and when she awoke sometime before dawn, her head aching, she turned and found him staring at her with eyes a deep, smoky gray. She didn't say a word. Didn't have to. He kissed her gently. Once. Twice. A third time.

Something inside her stirred. They kissed again—longer this time—and his lips were warm and gentle; his hands, when they touched her, were loving.

He didn't ask.

And she didn't say no.

Yet they took comfort in each other. Loving, kissing, stroking and finding solace in their shared grief.

In the morning, it was over. All the quiet comfort of the

night was gone and guilt, her companion ever since, lodged deep into a very private place in her soul. . . .

J.D. had left and never once called her. Nor had he written or stopped by. She'd moved to Bittersweet, and, until that day just last week when he'd shown up and rented the upstairs room, she hadn't seen him again.

She'd thought what they'd shared was long over. A mistake. A one-night stand.

Now she knew differently.

And it scared the heck out of her.

Chapter Eight

"I'm just telling you she's doing the best she can," J.D. said into the mouthpiece of his telephone. It had been installed on Friday and he'd finally decided to report to his father.

"She's no mother," Carlo insisted, then his voice was softer as he turned away from the phone. "No prune juice . . . I don't care, Frankie, I won't drink it. Just coffee and toast. We'll have brunch after Mass."

"I think you're wrong." J.D. wasn't afraid to stand up to the old man.

"About Tiffany?" Carlo snorted. "What would you know?"

"She loves her kids."

"Love, shmove. Stephen's already in trouble with the law, isn't he?"

"A little," J.D. lied. There was no reason to bring up the Isaac Wells mess; not until there was concrete evidence as to Stephen's involvement. J.D. intended to take care of the situation—without his father's interference. "She's got problems, but she seems to be handling them."

"Sure." Carlo didn't bother hiding his sarcasm. "What happened, J.D.? Have you fallen under her spell like your brother—may he rest in peace—did?"

If you only knew. "I'm just telling you what I've observed."

"Yeah, and remember, if it wasn't for her, he'd be alive today."

"You don't know that, but let's not get into it again."

J.D. wasn't foolish enough to point the finger at Tiffany for Philip's death, but his parents needed someone to blame, someone to punish for the loss of their firstborn.

"You're already standing up for her and you've hardly been there a week yet." Carlo sighed in disgust. "Sending you down there was probably a mistake."

"Probably," J.D. countered, refusing to be baited by the irascible old man. "You know I go by gut instincts."

"Humph. And what does your gut tell you about a new winery?"

"Still working on it, but I'll fax you copies of the most promising," J.D. said, thankful that his father had dropped the subject of Tiffany, if only for the moment. Frances was chattering in the background. "Your mother wants to know if you're keeping up with your physical therapy, if your leg is any better."

"Stronger each day."

"Good. I'll pass the word along. You'll call again?"

"Soon," J.D. promised as he hung up. He was surprised that he'd stood up for Tiffany, that he was changing his mind about her. He rubbed the tension from his shoulders with his right hand.

Tiffany wasn't quite what he'd expected when he'd driven to Bittersweet. Stronger than he'd suspected, a better mother than he ever would have thought, she gave the outward appearance of being a responsible woman trying to make it in the world. Even if, as his parents were convinced, she'd been a gold-digging girl looking for a father figure a long time ago, she'd grown up, blossomed and done her best with the kids.

"Dammit all, anyway," he growled.

No matter what, she was a problem.

For him.

He wanted her. More than he'd ever wanted a woman. He'd given in once, when she was grieving and alone. She'd reached out and he'd reached back, going too far. He'd felt like a heel ever since, and yet he couldn't stop thinking about her, wanting her, needing her. Taking a room in this house with her just one flight down the stairs had been a mistake he'd probably regret for the rest of his life.

Tiffany Nesbitt Santini was the one woman on this earth whom he should avoid. Being with her was a betrayal of his dead brother. It didn't matter that he and Philip had never been close. Blood was supposed to be thicker than water. Honor and loyalty to a person's family were more important than lust. And yet, where Tiffany was concerned, J.D. was able to toss away his deepest convictions.

Well, he couldn't just turn tail and run. No, he had to face her. Until he'd finished his business down here and could return to Portland.

To what?

An empty apartment.

A domineering father.

A worrywart of a mother.

A job he detested.

"Hell," he ground out, then decided he had to do something—anything to keep his mind off her and his hands occupied. He'd start with the fence. One section of the old boards sagged and that was just the beginning. There were more projects around here to keep him busy. The porch was rotting, the windows losing their seals, and the roof and gutters needed attention. He could keep himself busy for a couple of weeks and maybe do some good for his sister-in-law and her kids. *Just stay away from her, Santini.* He found his shoes and hitched his way down the stairs.

His leg still bothered him, but it was healing without the physical therapy that his mother seemed so focused upon.

On the second floor he hesitated outside Christina's room, then poked his head inside the partially open door and saw that the little girl was still sleeping. The bed was rumpled, the one-eyed rabbit on the floor again, but the imp was tucked into a fetal position, her thumb near her lips, as if ready to be sucked at any moment. He smiled to himself and walked the few paces to Stephen's room where he rapped gently on the door, despite the DO NOT ENTER sign hanging from its knob.

No response.

He knocked a little more loudly.

"What?" was the groggy response.

J.D. took that as a sign to enter. He twisted the knob and shoved the door open to gaze upon a mother's nightmare. The kid' s room was a mess. Clothes, towels, magazines, CDs and guitar picks were strewn all over the floor. A sleeping bag, unrolled, was kicked into the corner and the wastebasket overflowed with candy wrappers and empty fast-food drink cups. Stephen's guitar, with one string broken and curled, was propped against the end of the bed and a set of weights was rolled against a wall housing a low bookcase. "What d' ya want?" Stephen asked, then opened his good eye a crack and spied J.D. His demeanor changed instantly from surly to wary.

"You could lend me a hand." J.D. stepped inside, crunching a corn chip beneath his shoe.

"Doin' what?" Stephen rubbed his face groggily and with an exaggerated groan sat up in the bed.

"Some things to help your mom. A couple of downspouts need to be replaced, the gutters cleaned, the rail of the porch should be shored up, there's a broken step on the back porch, the windows need recaulking—"

"I get the idea." Stephen flopped back on the bed. "Maybe later."

"In half an hour."

"How about three hours?"

"Be ready." J.D. didn't give the kid a chance to worm out of the chores. He found Tiffany in the kitchen, wearing a soft yellow bathrobe and slippers as she poured pancake batter onto a griddle already sizzling with oil. At the sound of his footsteps, she glanced over her shoulder. Hot color washed up her neck and cheeks, and her eyes, gold in the morning light, slid away from him.

"Morning, Jay," she said as if he'd come down her stairs at eight in the morning every day of her life. She plucked a few fresh blueberries from a colander and dropped them onto the heating griddle cakes.

"Hi. I stopped by Stephen's room and tried to nudge him out of bed."

She smiled and cleared her throat as if neither of them were thinking about last night and the kisses they'd shared on the bench outside. Just at a whiff of the memory, his damn crotch tightened.

"How'd that go over?"

"Oh, you know, like the proverbial lead balloon."

"I'll bet. He usually sleeps in on Sunday. No summer school." She smiled and showed the hint of a dimple. "Stephen's not known for being overly enthusiastic in the morning."

"Is any teenager?"

She shook her head, the dark strands gleaming in the morning light that streamed through the windows of the nook. "There's coffee in the pot if you're interested."

"Thanks." He poured himself a cup from the glass carafe and tried not to notice how her hips shifted invitingly beneath the terry cloth. "I've been thinking, Tiffany."

"Always a dangerous sign."

"About Stephen."

All her muscles tensed and her spine stiffened slightly. "What about him?"

"We both know he's not involved in Isaac Wells's disappearance."

"Of course he isn't," she snapped testily. "He's only thirteen, for crying out loud! How could he be involved?"

"He's not. You're right. But my guess is that he knows more than he's saying."

"Knows what?" She kept her back to him as she worked, but he knew he had her undivided attention. "Oh, this is ridiculous. He's just a boy."

"Then why didn't he come clean weeks ago?"

"What are you saying, Jay?"

"It could be he's protecting someone."

"Who?" she asked, looking over her shoulder, her eyes darkening to the shade of amber he found so mesmerizing. In the terry-cloth bathrobe with her hair piled haphazardly on her head and the barest touch of makeup, she was damned near irresistible.

"I thought you might have the answer to that one."

Sighing, she blew her bangs from her eyes. "Stephen doesn't confide in me all the time." She flipped the pancakes deftly. "You know I think this is all a wild-goose chase on your part and the police's, but I'll ask him."

"Good." He wondered what the kid knew. What was eating at him. Sipping from his cup, J.D. opened one of the windows near the kitchen table and tried to ignore the scent of Tiffany's skin. Ringlets, still wet from her shower, framed her face and straggled invitingly at her nape. Again his groin tightened. His blood stirred as it always did when he thought about Tiffany and what sweet pleasure it was to make love to her. There were so many barriers between them—most of his own making, but barriers that needed to be scaled. "About last night—"

"Last night?" She froze, one hand holding the spatula.

"In the backyard."

"Oh." The back of her neck turned a vibrant shade of red. "I, uh, I don't think we should talk about it." She waved her spatula in the air as if she could physically block the train of conversation.

"Why not?"

"Because . . . Because . . . Oh, I don't know." *Because you confuse me. Everything about you makes me challenge my own convictions.* "Let's just chalk it up to bad timing, okay?"

"It was more than that."

Was it? Oh, Jay, part of me wants to believe you, but I just can't. "I don't want to hear this." She scraped the pancakes from her griddle and tossed them expertly onto a platter.

"We can't run away from it."

"Sure we can." She poured more batter onto the griddle and as the pancakes started to cook, turned to face him. "I've got a lot to deal with, Jay. A helluva lot. I don't need or want any man—even you, believe it or not—complicating things."

He smiled and she rolled her eyes, grabbed another handful of berries and tossed them onto the cakes.

"I'm not trying to complicate anything."

"Oh, right." She shook her head and sighed theatrically. "Maybe you can't help it," she said. "Maybe it's a part of your makeup, in your genes." She smiled a little. Goodness, he was handsome, even in the early morning. Unshaven, his black hair a little too long and shaggy to be fashionable, he looked rugged and hard and unbending. A man to avoid at all costs.

"I just thought we should discuss what happened."

"What happened was a mistake. Period. You're my brother-in-law. Nothing more. Even though Philip's dead and your family already despises me. My kids are dealing with the loss of their father in their own ways and I don't think that I have any right, or . . . or . . . desire—" He lifted one eyebrow, silently calling her a liar, and she sighed. "Okay, bad choice of words, but you know what I mean. I'm not ready to, well, you know, make things more difficult for anyone. Including myself."

Smothering a smile, he took a sip from his cup, then set it on the counter. "You're kidding yourself, Tiff."

"No way." She turned the pancakes and he came up behind her and slipped his arms around her waist. She wanted to push him away but she couldn't find the strength, or the desire. He dragged her closer, nestling her buttocks between his legs, allowing her to feel that he was already aroused. Deep inside she sensed a dangerous warmth spreading through her bloodstream. "Jay, don't—" she started to protest, then stopped. Because she wanted him. That was the simple and horrid truth.

He nuzzled the back of her neck and she let out a soft moan. "I'm warning you—"

"Good." His arms tightened around her slim waist. "Warn all you want."

"This isn't a good idea."

"The worst," he agreed.

"I mean it, Jay."

"You're gorgeous in the morning. Well, really, you're gorgeous at night, too."

"And you're incorrigible."

"I can only hope." Turning her in his arms, he rested his forehead against hers. Morning sunlight glistened through the windows and the odors of drying herbs and sizzling griddle-cakes mixed with her feminine scents of soap and lavender. His lips found hers and she opened her mouth as easily as a flower to the sun. The bathrobe slid open and his hands slipped around her waist, feeling her bare skin, the weight of her firm breasts unencumbered by a bra.

"Jay," she whispered as he lowered himself to his knees. She closed her eyes and he kissed first the top, then the underside of one breast before leaving a wet kiss on the nipple. "Oooh," she whispered and he took the anxious bud into his mouth. He teased its tip with his tongue and teeth and she leaned against the counter for support. With his hands, he parted the skirt of her robe and his fingers skimmed the insides of her legs. She sagged a bit and he reached higher just as she started.

"The breakfast," she gasped, and looked down at him in horror. " Oh, no, no, no." What had she been thinking, letting him kiss and touch and pet her so thoroughly right in the middle of the kitchen on a bright sunny day? The kids could have come downstairs or Mrs. Ellingsworth could have shown up on the back porch and caught them acting like a couple of hot-blooded teenagers. "For the love of Saint Jude," she whispered, scraping the burning pancakes off the griddle and tossing them into the sink to be devoured by the disposal. "I don't know what got into me," she said, pouring the last of the batter onto the griddle.

"Don't you?" He laughed wickedly and she blushed to the roots of her hair.

"Look, Santini, instead of bothering me—"

"Bothering you? Oh, lady, you don't know how much more I could bother you if I set my mind to it"

Maddening. That was what he was. "Why don't you make yourself useful? Pour orange juice or set the table or something."

"I've got a better idea." He kissed her cheek and she shot him a glare she hoped could cut through steel. "Call me when it's time to eat." Taking his cup of coffee with him, he walked to the back porch, then sauntered to the garage.

Pretty high-handed of him, she thought, until she saw him return with a carpenter's belt slung around his waist and a ladder over his shoulder. Within minutes he'd propped the ladder against the side of the house and had climbed to the second story where he started pounding, presumably to secure one of the shutters surrounding one of her bedroom windows—a shutter that had hung at an angle ever since she'd moved in.

She shouldn't trust him, she told herself, as she started frying bacon and added the last of the berries to her pancakes. She always suspected him of having his own agenda and yet the memory of his touch caused her insides to melt.

With a clang of ancient pipes, water from an upstairs faucet began running. Obviously Stephen was up and showering.

Soon both of her children had padded downstairs. Christina was still in her pajamas and dragged her blanket with her. Stephen was wearing distressed jeans and a faded T-shirt. His hair was wet and his expression was sour, which wasn't unusual and often didn't disappear until his second helping of eggs or bowl of cereal.

"Mommy!" Christina ran across the kitchen and flung herself into her mother's waiting arms.

"Good morning, kiddo."

"I'm hungry."

"Well, breakfast is ready." Tiffany helped her daughter into a booster chair. "How about you?" she asked Stephen.

He slumped into one of the wooden chairs that surrounded the table and slid a glance toward the window where the ladder and the toes of J.D.'s boots were visible. "What is it?"

"Blueberry pancakes and bacon. Eggs if you want them."

"No eggs!" Christina cried, shaking her head as Tiffany snagged an oven mitt from the counter and pulled out the platter of pancakes. She slid one onto a plate, drizzled it with blueberry syrup, then pronged a slice of bacon from the frying pan.

"Careful, it's hot," Tiffany said, placing the plate and a small fork onto the place mat in front of Christina. "What about you?" she asked Stephen. "Eggs?"

"Naw. Just pancakes."

As she was fixing a plate for her son, she opened the window over the sink and invited J.D. to join them. Christina grinned as she saw her uncle climb down the ladder, but Stephen's mouth tightened at the corners.

"Are we goin' to the wedding?" he asked when the eggs were cooked and they were all seated around the table. He stared at Tiffany through a fringe of too-long hair.

"No." She didn't bother to elaborate. "I think you'd better go down to the barbershop this week."

"I want to go to the wedding," Christina insisted. "I want to see brides."

Stephen snorted contemptuously. "There's only one."

"So?"

"You don't even know who's getting married."

"Who is it?" the little girl demanded.

"Our grandfather, that's who," Stephen said.

It was on the tip of Tiffany's tongue to argue with her son and tell him that John Cawthorne would never be his grandfather, but she held the hateful words back. Why lie? Who knew what the future would bring? Though she saw no reason to celebrate his marriage to his longtime mistress, she hoped she wasn't so bitter about her lonely childhood that she couldn't someday be civil to the man and his wife.

"Have you considered going?" J.D., seated across the table from her, cut into his stack of pancakes with the edge of his fork.

"Fleetingly."

"But—"

"I'm not ready. Not yet." Using her fork, she shifted her

scrambled eggs around on her plate and realized the turn of the conversation was affecting her appetite. "I'm not sure I ever will be."

"I think we should," Stephen said, settling low on his chair.

"Why?"

"Why not? He wants you to."

"I know, but—"

"Are you chicken?"

The light banter fell away. Tiffany's heart squeezed hard. "No," she replied. "It has nothing to do with fear. I just don't think I should . . . honor—if that's the right word, or maybe validate would be better—this man's decision."

"Why not?"

"It's a long story. Goes back to when I was a little girl and he wasn't around."

"But he wants to be around *now*. Doesn't that count?" Stephen asked, eyeing her with such scrutiny she wanted to squirm out of his line of vision.

"It counts. A little."

Stephen reached for the syrup and poured a rich purple river over his stack of pancakes. "I thought you always said it's important to forgive." Tiffany's throat constricted. Her son had a point and there was more going on here than the typical teenager-parent argument. Stephen might be trying to tell her that she was lucky to have a father—even a latent, unconventional one like John Cawthorne. After all, Stephen had lost his own dad and was a little like a ship without an anchor, drifting emotionally. He probably needed a positive male role model in his life. Somehow John Cawthorne, who had kept a mistress for years while married to another woman and who had fathered two children out of wedlock, didn't seem the best candidate.

"I'll probably forgive John someday."

"But you won't call him your father?" Stephen prompted.

"Being a father is more than a question of biology and genetics."

"Yeah, sure." Stephen shot her a look that called her a liar and a hypocrite as he pronged a forkful of pancakes. "You're always telling me to give people a chance."

"Is that what you want?" she asked and her son looked away.

"Dunno," he admitted, then nodded. "I think we should go to the wedding."

"Too late." She felt a sheen of perspiration coat her body.

"I want to go!" Christina said, her face smeared with syrup, her hands a sticky mess.

"Not this time."

"He's our grandfather!" Stephen challenged.

"I know, but—"

"This is something your mom has to deal with in her own way," J.D. interjected and Tiffany felt as torn as she had when she'd first learned of John Cawthorne's wedding.

"Maybe later we can all get to know each other," she said, realizing that her son was somewhat isolated down here. He'd left friends in Portland when they'd moved. The few he'd made here were trouble. She took a long swallow of her coffee and thought about the cousins that he had. Her half-sister Katie had a boy, Josh, a few years younger than Stephen and Bliss was going to marry Mason Lafferty, who had a daughter, Dee Dee, from his first marriage. Surely there would be a baby on the horizon. And Katie had three brothers, none of whom were married, but who might link up with women who already had children.

With bone-chilling certainty Tiffany realized that Stephen was reaching out for a family, longing for more than he had, searching for a father figure. *Just as she had when she'd been his age.*

Tears stung her eyes and her hands shook as she set her cup on the table. "We can't go to the wedding today, but—"

"You mean *you* won't go," Stephen interrupted.

"But I'll see that we get together with your . . . grandfather and his new wife soon."

"Goody!" Christina said, throwing up her hands and losing a piece of bacon from her fist. It fell to the floor only to be sniffed at disdainfully by a curious Charcoal who had been sunning himself near the window.

J.D. looked like he had more to say, but one glance at Tiffany seemed to tell him that she was having trouble with the discussion, so he quickly changed the subject to fixing up the house with Stephen's help.

"What do you mean?" Stephen asked when J.D. suggested they start with the fence.

"We'll shore it up, replace a few boards and then work on the porch or the windows."

"I don't know how to do anything like that."

J.D.'s eyes glinted. "Then it's time you learned."

Though Stephen acted as if he'd do just about anything to escape from his uncle's proposed list of duties, he finished his breakfast, dropped his plate into the sink and followed J.D. outside. Tiffany, still recovering from her son's interrogation, cleaned the kitchen, then helped Christina take a shower while J.D. and Stephen tackled everything from the gutters to the back porch.

It was almost as if they were a small family.

Be careful, Tiffany, she cautioned herself. *That kind of thinking might land you in trouble. Big trouble. J.D. is your brother-in-law. Not your husband!*

But Christina didn't know it. She seemed to be in heaven hanging around outside, a satellite who orbited around her uncle. Stephen, on the other hand, made no bones about the fact that he felt used and overworked. He grumbled continuously as he and J.D. cleaned the gutters and straightened the fence. He complained that he was supposed to meet friends, that his back hurt, that he was tired, but his uncle would have none of it and ran the boy ragged.

They stopped around one for sandwiches and lemonade, then went back to fixing the back porch where it sagged. Meanwhile, with the sound of hammers pounding nails ringing through the house, Tiffany changed the beds, did the laundry and caught up on some neglected paperwork.

Christina had protested vehemently against a nap and was starting to get cranky around three-thirty. By that time, Stephen looked exhausted and J.D. finally released him from his duties.

Stephen was on the phone in a second and had made plans before Tiffany could say anything. "We're going swimming," he announced.

"Who?"

"Me and Sam."

"Sam and I," she automatically corrected.

Stephen rolled his eyes while Christina chased a grasshopper through the dry lawn.

"Be back by six for dinner," Tiffany told her son as he grabbed his scarred skateboard and sailed down the sidewalk.

"I'm not hungry."

"You will be," she called after him.

"Yeah, yeah," he said before adjusting his balance and coasting agilely around the corner.

"He's not such a bad kid." J.D. said, watching Stephen vanish past a stand of pine trees and draping an arm familiarly over Tiffany's shoulders. They stood at the edge of her rose garden near one side of the house. Honey bees buzzed around the blooms and their fragrance filled the hot air. Why did it feel so natural for his hand to rest on her shoulder? Why did the scent of his after-shave tickle her nostrils and make her think of tumbling into bed with him?

"Never said he was." She shrugged and slid away from his touch.

"I was kidding, Tiff. You've always stood up for your kids and your family. Even Philip."

"Why wouldn't I?"

His eyes narrowed on the distant horizon, but Tiffany suspected he wasn't watching the jogger and the black Lab running along the sidewalk, or that he noticed a van full of kids and a harried mother drive by. No, his mind was turned inward and he was focused on his own vision, his private viewpoint. "Philip wasn't a saint, you know."

"And you are?" She plucked a dying rose from its thorny stem and an angry bumblebee, buzzing indignantly flew out of the petals as they dropped to the ground.

J.D.'s laugh was without a drop of mirth. "A saint? Far from it."

"What is it they say about casting stones?" She twisted another dying bloom from the nearest rosebush, then decided to wait until she'd located her gardening shears to finish the task. "I know Philip gambled, Jay." She squinted up at him as the late-afternoon sun was still bright, the day hazy and hot. Perspiration began to collect on her scalp. "And I realize that he cheated on his first wife." Her brother-in-law's eyes registered surprise. "He told me about sneaking around on Karen when Robert and Thea were still toddlers," she admitted. "Granted, he didn't confess until after we were married, but still, he told me."

"Maybe he thought it would be better coming from him rather than hearing it from a stranger."

"Well, he was right. As far as I know, he never betrayed me, and even if he did, what good would it do now to know about it?" she asked, searching his face for any kind of clue as to what he was trying to say. She'd known Philip's flaws as well as anyone. "The fact of the matter is that he died saving Christina's life."

"So he *is* a saint."

"Just a good man. With his share of faults."

J.D., if he was going to argue, didn't get the chance because at that moment Christina finally caught the bug she'd been chasing and let out a horrified squeal. Brown stain covered her fingers. "He's bleeding on me." She dropped the grasshopper as if it had bitten her.

"It's just his spit," J.D. said with a laugh.

"Spit?" Christina was horrified.

"We used to call it tobacco juice," Tiffany said, hauling her daughter into her arms.

"It's icky!" Tears rolled down her eyes.

"Come on, let's clean you up, then get something to eat."

For once her daughter didn't protest and after a bath, a peanut-butter-and-jelly sandwich and glass of milk, she settled down to watch television. Tiffany started dinner by cooking pasta for a salad and mixing the dressing in the blender. J.D. stopped his work for a bottle of cold beer, then continued to work outside, fixing a leaning handrail and several window latches. Exhausted from a long day, Christina dropped off in her chair and rather than rouse her for dinner, Tiffany carried her upstairs and tucked her into bed.

After she'd picked up a few scattered toys in Christina's room, Tiffany finished making the salad and checked the time. Stephen was already half an hour late and she was a little nervous. The kid always pushed her and was forever ten or fifteen minutes late, but a half hour was longer than usual.

"Don't borrow trouble," she told herself as she tossed shrimp, green onions and artichokes into the pasta salad, then turned on the oven to preheat. Stephen would be home soon. After all, he'd mislaid his watch a few weeks back. He'd probably just lost track of time.

Chiding herself for being a worrywart, she glanced up

the drive as she walked outside to the corner of the house where J.D., wrench in hand, was fixing a broken outdoor faucet. The handle had fallen apart and he was replacing the worn piece with a new one.

"You don't have to do all this, you know," she said. "It's not part of the rental agreement."

"Just wait till you get my bill."

"Oh, right. And how much will that be?"

His eyes glinted wickedly. "Well, Ms. Santini, we're not talking dollars and cents, you know."

"No?"

"Uh-uh. I was thinking more along the lines of a trade. Tit for tat. I scratch your back, you scratch mine. . . ."

She laughed. "I don't even want to know what you're thinking."

"It's twisted," he teased.

"Mmm. Sounds interesting."

"If you only knew." He winked at her, then turned his attention back to the task at hand. Setting his jaw, he gave a final tug on the wrench and twisted on the faucet. For the first time in months water spewed out of the tap and didn't spray at odd angles from the spigot.

"You're a natural," she said with a laugh.

"If you think this is good, just wait until you see me sink my teeth into a double valve, if there is such a thing."

At the sound of tires crunching on gravel, they both looked toward the street. Tiffany thought Stephen might have found a ride home, but her son wasn't anywhere in sight. She began to worry a little more.

A Dodge pickup that had seen better days rolled into the drive and the man behind the wheel, a lanky stranger, climbed down from the cab. Tall and slow-moving, he crossed the expanse of grass and approached them. "You in charge?" he asked J.D.

"Not usually."

The man, his hair a dark shade of blond, nodded toward the Apartment for Rent sign in the front yard. "I'm lookin' for a place to stay for a few months."

"I'm Tiffany Santini, and this is my brother-in-law, J.D." She offered her hand. "This is my place," she said and noticed J.D.'s mouth tighten a bit.

"Luke Gates."

He shook her hand, then offered his to J.D., who hadn't smiled since the pickup had stopped in the drive. Obviously Jay had reservations about the stranger who looked like he was more comfortable in a saddle than in the bucket seat of a truck.

Tiffany sized him up. His clothes were clean but worn, pride kept his spine straight and his eyes, she thought, had seen more than their share of pain. Crow's-feet fanned from his eyes and calluses on his hands suggested that he wasn't afraid of hard work. "I've got two units available, one in the basement of the main house, the other over the old carriage house. I ask for first and last month's rent, a security deposit, cleaning deposit and references."

"I imagine you do." His smile was slow, and his west Texas drawl nearly imperceptible. "Got both. Let's see the one over the carriage house."

"This way."

J.D.'s limp had nearly disappeared as he followed them around the house, then went back to work cleaning a patch of asphalt on the far side of the garage. He'd already told Tiffany he thought it would be a good place to hang a basketball hoop for Stephen. "A boy needs something to do when he's got time on his hands. He can shoot baskets, hit a tennis ball against a wall, or work out with a punching bag, but you need to give him something to do here, preferably something that he can do alone or with his friends, so that they'll hang out at the house. Assuming that's what you want."

"I'd rather have them where I can see them than at someone else's place."

"Good point."

They'd settled on the hoop.

Luke Gates nodded as he walked into the upper unit of the carriage house, though, Tiffany suspected, he'd decided to rent it before seeing the patina on the hardwood floors, the red brick of the fireplace or the single bedroom. She guessed he'd made up his mind before he'd even parked his truck.

Luke signed the papers in her kitchen, offered her a list of references and paid the rent and deposits with cash. Crisp one-hundred-dollar bills.

This wasn't the first time she'd been given currency up front, since renters who hadn't yet opened local bank accounts sometimes had enough cash on them, but it always made her a little wary. Never would she carry that amount of money in her purse, but Luke acted as if it was natural and he intended to move in that very night.

"So where're you from?" J.D. asked as they walked outside to the spot where Luke's truck was parked.

"All over."

"You must've started out somewhere."

"Yep."

"But not from around here," J.D. prodded.

"Nope. Texas. A little town east of El Paso." With an enigmatic smile, he climbed into his truck, ground the gears and backed out of the shady drive.

"I don't trust him," J.D. said once the truck had rounded the corner, leaving a trail of smelly blue exhaust in its wake. They stood on the porch together as the shadows of evening began to stretch across the parched grass.

"You don't trust anyone," she observed, but understood

what J.D. was saying; Luke was the kind of man who made people edgy, not so much by what he said as by what he didn't say—a man who didn't give out much information but took in a whole lot.

"Not true." One side of J.D.'s mouth lifted and Tiffany's heart skipped a silly little beat. As easily as if he'd done it a thousand times before, he wrapped his arms around her waist. "But people have to earn my trust and it takes time."

"Does it?"

His face was so close to hers that she noticed the webbing of colors—blue and green—beneath the gray of his eyes. "Yep. A long time." He kissed her then, and her insides melted. His lips were firm and warm. So damned inviting. She and he were becoming familiar—way too familiar—and the feel of him, of his hands locked behind the small of her back, was a sensation she didn't want to give up. Ever.

When he lifted his head, she smiled, sighed, then rested her head against his shoulder. "James Dean Santini, what in the world am I going to do with you?" she asked as the moon began to rise.

"Good question. I was just thinking the same thing about you."

"They say that great minds think alike."

"Do they?" he asked, his voice deep, his gaze so intense that she had to look away, at anything. She chose her watch and felt a frisson of dread. "Stephen's so much later than usual."

"He's a thirteen-year-old boy."

"I know, I know, and he's chronically pushing his curfew back, but not by more than fifteen, maybe twenty minutes."

"He'll show up." J.D. was confident. Always.

"I hope so."

He folded her into his arms again and kissed her temple. "Worrying isn't going to help."

She knew it, but couldn't help the edge of concern that

nagged at her. Lately Stephen had been getting into more and more trouble. It wasn't the pack of cigarettes she'd found in his room that bothered her, but this business with Isaac Wells and the fight with Miles Dean the other day. Not to mention his general bad attitude.

"It'll be all right," J.D. promised, as if reading her mind.

"I hope you're right."

Somewhere not too far away church bells tolled, the chimes ringing through the town and echoing off the surrounding hills. Tiffany lifted her head and sighed.

"Something else is bothering you," J.D. said, touching her chin with one finger.

"Hear that?" The melodic bells continued to peal and Tiffany's heart squeezed painfully.

"Late service?"

"Nope." She rubbed her arms as if to ward off a chill. "I think my father just got married."

Chapter Nine

"I've called everywhere," Tiffany said, hanging up the kitchen telephone and leaning heavily against the wall. "He's gone."

"We'll find him," J.D. insisted. "Ask Mrs. Ellingsworth to watch Christina and we'll start looking for him."

"Where?"

"You tell me."

Don't panic. He's fine. He's got to be. With trembling fingers she dialed Ellie's number and tried to remain calm as the telephone rang. When the older woman answered, Tiffany explained what was going on.

"I'll be up in a second," Ellie said without hesitation. "Now don't you worry."

If only that was possible. These days, worry seemed to be Tiffany's middle name.

True to her word, Ellie was at the back door within minutes and bustling them both outside. "You know how boys are, never can keep track of time. My Charlie, he was the worst. Gave me every gray hair on my head, I swear." But the concern in her eyes betrayed her. She, too, was upset.

"It's so unlike Stephen to be this late," Tiffany said, once they were in J.D.'s Jeep and driving through the narrow streets and alleys of Bittersweet. Dusk had given way to the deeper shades of evening and a few streetlamps had begun to glow.

"Relax." J.D. patted her knee as he shifted down. "Let's start with the obvious. Tell me where his friends live."

"Okay. Let's think. He said he was with Sam—Sam Prescott—but when I called over there, no one answered."

"Where does Sam live?"

"On the outskirts of town, to the north, near the water tower."

J.D. maneuvered his Jeep through town, past the park and shopping mall to a residential district. The Prescotts resided in a log cabin that had been in the family for generations. The house was dark, the porch light burning when Tiffany hurried up the front path to the door. She rapped firmly on the old oak panels, then jabbed at the doorbell, but though the buzzer went off inside, no one answered.

"Something's really wrong," she said, spying Sam's ten-speed chained to a post supporting the roof of the porch and his skateboard left near the steps. "If Sam were with Stephen he'd be on his bike or skateboard."

"You think."

"I know." Though the evening was warm, she felt a chill deep in her soul and rubbed her arms where goose bumps had taken hold. Where was Stephen? Thoughts of injury, kidnapping or worse skated through her mind. She noticed the uneaten bowl of cat food and two rolled newspapers left on the front porch, as if no one had been home for a couple of days. "It's possible the Prescotts are out of town," she admitted.

J.D.'s expression hardened as he, too, noticed the signs of inactivity at the house. "Looks that way, doesn't it?"

"So Stephen lied," she said, disheartened. Ever since Philip's death, her son had become more secretive, and he'd started lying about the time of Isaac Wells's disappearance.

"I think we should go over to the Deans' house. They live in a mobile home about two miles up the road."

J.D. didn't waste any time. He drove unerringly to the Dean property and pulled into a weed-choked drive. Two disabled cars sat rusting by a vegetable garden surrounded by a high chicken-wire fence to keep out the deer. Besides the mobile home, there were a shed and a lean-to barn by which a skinny horse stood. flicking flies with his tail and trying to find any blade of grass in the small paddock.

Tiffany was out of the Jeep before it stopped. She hurried up a couple of weathered steps, nearly banged her head on a hanging pot overflowing with dying geraniums and pounded on the door. Vera Dean, Miles and Laddy's mother, opened it a second later. She was tall and thin, with a fading beauty that matched her worn-off lipstick, short, shaggy blond hair and tanned skin stretched taut over high cheekbones. She looked as tired as a plow horse after a day in the fields, and her smile, friendly at first, fell as she recognized Tiffany.

"Hi, Vera. I'm sorry to stop by unannounced, but I'm looking for Stephen," Tiffany said. "He's missing and I thought he might have come here."

"After the fight he had with Miles?" Vera shook her head and reached into the pocket of her jeans for a leather case that held a pack of cigarettes. "No way."

"You're sure?"

"Absolutely."

Tiffany wasn't convinced the woman was telling the truth. "Could I talk to Miles?"

Vera unclasped the case and stared at J.D., looking him up and down as he stood on the step behind Tiffany. "Miles isn't here."

Warning bells clanged in her mind. Both boys, known to get into trouble together, were missing. "Do you know where he is?"

"Miles?" She let out a throaty laugh. "Nope. That boy's just like his old man. Never around when you need him. But I'll let him know you dropped by." She shook out a long, slim cigarette and held it between two fingers. "Anything else?"

"No. Just please have Miles call me when he gets in."

"Will do." She shut the door and Tiffany walked back to the car, convinced that the boy would never get the message.

"Friendly," J.D. observed sarcastically.

"She doesn't like me. Or Stephen."

"Any particular reason?"

"Not that I know of, but I don't take it personally. She doesn't get along with many people. Her husband, Ray, is a guy who hires on at local ranches and he's been in and out of jail since he was nineteen. Right now he's out, but no one thinks it'll last."

"You know a lot for a newcomer to Bittersweet."

"It's a small town. Everyone has his nose in everyone else's business. I hear it all day long—down at the insurance office or when I'm having coffee down at Millie's or, if all else fails, from my renters."

They drove toward town as the stars winked in the dark sky. Tiffany leaned her arm out the open window and tried to imagine where her son had gone. Was he with Miles, and more importantly, was he safe? Oh, dear God, she prayed, please, let him be all right.

"I have an idea," J.D. ventured as he slid her a glance.

"About Stephen?"

"Mmm." He drove through town, but didn't head toward her house. "Remember this morning at breakfast? Stephen seemed pretty determined to go to the Cawthorne wedding."

She felt her shoulders sag as she remembered the conversation about her father. "It was just talk."

"Was it?" J.D. asked as they passed the post office.

"It's his new thing—try to argue Mom into a corner."

"Or he could have been serious."

"Why?"

J.D. lifted a shoulder. "Curiosity. Or a need to connect with his mother's family. Who knows?"

Tiffany didn't want to believe that Stephen would openly defy her. Not this way. "He . . . he wouldn't have gone to the wedding. No way. Same goes for the reception."

" A few days ago you were certain he knew nothing about Isaac Wells's disappearance. Now you're not so sure."

"He must be somewhere else." She didn't want to believe that her boy would lie so blatantly—especially about this—and yet, she couldn't overlook any possibility. Staring out the bug-spattered windshield, she realized that J.D. wasn't listening to her arguments anyway. He was driving out of town in the direction of Cawthorne Acres, John's ranch. The thought hit her like the proverbial ton of bricks. "You're not really going to take me to the wedding reception, are you?"

He lifted a dark brow. "Seems as if you were invited."

"I know, but—"

"We'll just see if anyone's seen Stephen."

"No!" She was emphatic.

"Got any better ideas?"

She wanted to come up with something—anything other than her estranged father's wedding—but she couldn't. Her stomach twisted into tight little knots. " All right, we'll check," she finally conceded because she couldn't think of another place Stephen would have gone. "Discreetly," she said, hating the thought. "We'll inquire discreetly. I don't want to cause a stir." Then she looked down at her attire. Jeans and a short-sleeved blouse. Everyone else would be dressed to the nines for the wedding. Not that it mattered. She'd suffer any kind of humility; just as long as Stephen was okay.

"There won't be a stir," J.D. assured her as he slowed at

the lane leading to John Cawthorne's place. The gate was open and the curved sign that spanned the lane read Cawthorne Acres. A black ribbon of asphalt sliced between moon-washed fields of cut hay. In the pasture on one side of the road a few bales had yet to be hauled to the barns. They stood like unmoving, rectangular sentinels in the dry stubble. On the other side of the lane, long-legged foals romped and bucked around a small herd of serene older horses. Silvery moonlight played upon their white markings, making them appear ghostlike.

At the end of the lane, the ranch house and grounds were ablaze with lights.

Tiffany's stomach tightened and her fingers curled into fists of anxiety as she saw dozens of cars parked in the lot between the house and barns. More vehicles had been directed into one of the fields while still others were parked along one side of the lane.

Dear God, what am I doing here? she thought as J.D. eased his Jeep behind a sports car nearly a hundred yards from the house. *You're only here to find your son. Nothing more. Remember that.*

"It's now or never," J.D. said and Tiffany steeled herself. She climbed out of the Cherokee and was hit by the strains of "The Anniversary Waltz" being played by a small dance band. The notes carried on a breeze tinged with the scents of cut grass and honeysuckle. A faint odor of cigarette smoke wafted through the summer air and the hum of conversation grew louder as they approached the single-story house.

Millions of tiny white lights decorated the trees and fence line, as if it were the Christmas holidays instead of the beginning of August.

Guests, dressed in everything from silk and diamonds to denim and rhinestones, wandered the grounds. But no Stephen. "This is insane," Tiffany muttered under her breath as she followed a path that led behind the house. Rounding the corner by the back porch, she nearly slammed into a woman walking in the other direction.

"You decided to come after all!" Bliss, dressed in a shimmery silver-blue dress, smiled widely. Her blond hair was pulled into a French braid and her eyes sparkled as brightly as the thousands of tiny bulbs. Beside her was a tall man with light brown eyes and sun-streaked blond hair. His hand was placed firmly in the middle of Bliss's back.

"I don't know if you've met Mason," Bliss said. "My fiancé, Mason Lafferty. This is Tiffany Santini, my half-sister."

Somehow, despite the worry congealing her insides, Tiffany managed to make the appropriate noises as well as introduce J.D. as her brother-in-law and explain why they'd shown up. "We decided to come here because I'm worried sick about Stephen and he isn't at any of his friends' houses. No one knows where he is but he was interested in coming to the wedding today and I thought . . . I mean, J.D. thought he might have shown up here."

Bliss's smile had slowly given way to a frown of concern. Tiny lines of anxiety etched her forehead. "I wish I could help out, but I don't remember seeing him," she said, looking to Mason for support.

"Don't ask me, I've never met him." Mason glanced around the crowd that had collected around the rim of a temporary dance floor in the backyard. "There are a lot of kids here, though."

"It's true." Bliss's eyes clouded with genuine worry. "There were a few boys about Stephen's age at the ceremony, and more here." Her gaze swept the area. "But it's easy to get lost in this place."

Tiffany's stomach, already tense, tightened another notch. "You don't mind if we look around?"

"Of course not. Dad will be thrilled that you're here," Bliss said.

"Not if he found out I came here because I lost his grandson." Why did her tongue still trip over the word?

Bliss nodded. "But you should let him know. He does care about you and your kids. I know that sounds weird, considering all that's gone on and how he dealt with you in the past, but I've seen firsthand the pain he's been going through, the struggles. He would want to help find Stephen and he'd be mad as a hornet if we didn't let him know Stephen was missing."

Tiffany's heart was drumming, her pride dissipating by the minute. "I'll take all the help I can get," she said fervently. When J.D. had suggested coming to this party, she'd been reticent, but a part of her had hoped that she would locate her rebellious son, stay long enough not to offend anyone, then hightail it back to her house. Now, all she wanted was to find Stephen.

"He's not here," she whispered to J.D.

"We don't know that yet."

Again, Tiffany searched the faces of the people talking in small clusters. She recognized a few of the townspeople, and several of the kids, but she didn't see any sign of her son. Music filtered through the throng. On the dance floor Brynnie, dressed in a lacy creamy-white gown that showed off her ample cleavage, smiled radiantly up at her new husband. Her flame-colored hair was pinned in curls to her crown and decorated with tiny rosebuds and sprigs of baby's breath. Her face was flushed, her eyes bright, merriment fairly oozing from her expression.

For a second Tiffany forgot her worries and watched as John Cawthorne twirled his bride around the makeshift floor, dancing as if he were a man twenty years younger, a man who didn't fear another heart attack or facing the Grim

Reaper. Dressed in a gray tuxedo, he swirled and dipped, causing Brynnie to laugh out loud.

They stared into each other's eyes as if they were high school sweethearts about to embark upon a new adventure instead of two older people who had kept up a clandestine love affair for years; a man and woman who had brought an illegitimate daughter into the world and let another man claim that child as his own. Katie had grown up thinking Hal Kinkaid was her father. Neither her mother nor her biological father had discouraged the lie—until a few months ago.

John was an adulterer, a cheat and a liar. Brynnie was a loose woman who had married a string of men before finally claiming the love of her life as her husband. There had been lies, neglect, dishonor and betrayal; but tonight, under a kind, pearlescent moon, with romantic music filling the air and champagne flowing from a silver fountain Brynnie and John looked for all the world like a couple in love.

Like they belonged together.

Tiffany's heart tore. She would never be a part of her father's life. It had been his choice when she was a child, it was hers as an adult. Her throat was hot, her eyes burned a little as she turned to J.D. "I don't see Stephen."

"Neither do I, but I'm going to start asking some questions. Why don't you walk around, see if there is anyone here he might hang out with?"

"Okay," she said and started working her way through the crowd She smiled at people she met, managed a few words to those she knew, but her eyes were forever moving, hunting, seeking a glimpse of her child. She paused beneath the branches of a large locust tree in the backyard and silently prayed that Stephen was all right.

"The bride has requested a snowball dance," the bandleader said over the microphone before the melody of "The Blue Danube" filled the air. Tiffany was vaguely aware of John and Brynnie dancing as she wended her way through the guests gathered around the dance floor. She saw several boys she recognized but didn't know their names and when she questioned one lanky, pimply-faced kid, he said he hadn't seen Stephen since the end of the regular school year. *This is a wild-goose chase. He isn't here! Dear God, where is he?*

"Switch," the bandleader instructed and Brynnie and John broke up to pull two unsuspecting people onto the floor. Brynnie nabbed her eldest son, Jarrod, who eased his mother around the parquet as if he'd done it all his life, while John took hold of Bliss's hand and led her to the middle of the temporary dance floor. Tiffany, though she fought the urge, couldn't help but watch her father and half-sister, smiling, laughing, gliding easily in front of the crowd. To her absolute horror, she experienced a little nudge of envy.

Don't do this, she warned herself as she edged closer to the dancers.

Bliss looked like she belonged on the dance floor. She was in perfect step, smiling and laughing, tossing back her head, her cheeks tinged a deep pink, her eyes glimmering as she danced with her father.

As if they've done it a hundred times before.

They probably had. Not that it mattered. Tiffany didn't care. The past was long gone and right now, her only purpose was to find Stephen. That was why she was here. Nervously she scanned the crowd. Oh, this was getting her nowhere.

"Switch."

She barely heard the bandleader's command as she started toward the back door of the house. There was a chance, though slim, that Stephen, if he had come here, was inside.

"Dance with me." Strong fingers surrounded her arm.

Oh, no.

Her heart sank as she whirled around and faced the man who had sired her. Reflexively, she jerked her arm away. She was about to tell John Cawthorne to leave her alone, just as he had for most of her life, when she realized that over fifty pairs of curious eyes were trained her way. This was her chance. If ever she wanted to pay him back, to mortify him for all those years of neglect, she could simply stomp away and show her utter disdain for a selfish son of a bitch who'd never so much as sent her a birthday gift or a card at Christmas. She could not only personally belittle him but publicly embarrass him at his own wedding reception. If she had the guts.

"I—I"

"Come on, Tiffany. You're here. Let's get to know each other." His hint of a smile belied the inner torment she saw in his eyes.

"But—" She blushed and bit back all the angry words that wanted to leap to her tongue. What satisfaction would she get out of ruining his day or his bride's party? "Okay," she finally acquiesced. "Why not?"

Brynnie was already dancing with one of her twin sons, Nathan or Trevor McBaine, Tiffany didn't know which. Jarrod had found Patty Lafferty, Mason's willowy sister, and Bliss was molded to her fiancé. Stiffly Tiffany took the floor, feeling self-conscious and out of place. Unlike Bliss, she hadn't been trained in dance, but she'd grown up with music, through all the years her mother had taught piano. Rose Nesbitt would die, would absolutely have a heart attack, if she suspected that Tiffany was turning coat and waltzing with the enemy.

"I'm glad you came," John said as he maneuvered her past Bliss and Mason. "I really didn't expect you to."

"It—it wasn't planned."

"Doesn't matter." He grinned down at her and she felt like

a heel, not that she had any right to her ridiculous emotions. She couldn't forget how he'd ignored her growing up, neglected her for over thirty lonely years.

"I came because I'm looking for Stephen."

"He didn't come with you?"

She shook her head, stepped on his toe and wished the damned song would end. "He's missing. Been gone a couple of hours. J.D. thought he might have come here."

She felt her father tense, his muscles stiffen, his hand tighten around hers. "But I saw him earlier."

"Here?"

"Yes." He looked instantly confused. "I mean, I think I did. It was either here or at the wedding. I know because I recognized him and spoke with him. I asked about you, but he was evasive."

There was no way to avoid the truth, no reason for Tiffany to lie. "He, uh, attended behind my back. Lied about it. Said he was going swimming with a friend."

"I see," her father said and a wounded look crossed his eyes. "Well, I guess I can't blame you for how you feel." He sighed audibly and his shoulders slumped a little. "What is it they say, 'Time heals all wounds'?"

"Or wounds all heels," she said automatically, then wished she could call the words back when she noticed his lips flattening over his teeth.

"Well, for what it's worth, I'm glad you're here, Tiffany, no matter what the reason. Don't worry about Stephen. He's here somewhere, I'm sure of it. Enjoy the reception."

"Switch," the bandleader called out just as the tempo of the music changed. Her father released her. She turned and walked quickly off the dance floor just as she recognized the first strains of "And I Love Her," an old Beatles tune.

She ran smack-dab into J.D. "Found him," he said, cocking his head in the direction of the stables. A few boys had gathered in the shadows, perched on the fence rail like birds on a telephone wire. "Stephen's over there," he said, and when Tiffany started to bolt toward the group, J.D. held her hand. "Let him be, Tiff. I already talked to him and gave him the lecture of his life about scaring you the way he did. He knows you're going to tear into him, so wait a few minutes. Let what I said sink into his brain and allow him to sweat about what you'll do to him. Then you can go for it."

Her knees went weak with relief. "I'm just glad he's okay."

"But he did lie and sneak around."

"I know. I'll deal with it. Believe me."

"Later." J.D. manacled her wrist in his strong fingers and pulled her back to the dance floor. "Right now, let's indulge ourselves."

She shook her head vehemently. "I think I disgraced myself enough for one night."

"Not yet," he said, propelling her to a space on the rapidly shrinking floor. "There are hours and hours yet for you to really make a fool of yourself."

She giggled despite herself. "Flatterer." With a smile, she added, "Hey, don't I get a say in this? Aren't I the one who's supposed to be looking for a new partner?"

"You found him," he replied and his expression was so intense that her breath got lost somewhere in her lungs. For a heartbeat the sounds of the reception faded, the lights and music blurred and she fought against the feeling that they were alone and intimate. He tugged on her hand, pulled her tightly into his embrace and sighed against her hair. "Isn't this better?"

"Much," she admitted, though she didn't want to think about the consequences of pressing her body to his, of swaying to the music in the evening-dark night. Other couples danced around them. John had found his youngest daughter and Katie, in peach silk, was beaming up at him as she danced. Brynnie had, presumably, chosen the second of her twins to dance with, though Tiffany wasn't sure. For all she knew, Brynnie could have been dancing with the same brother. Mason and Bliss had found new partners but their gazes sought each other continuously.

For a few wonderful minutes, Tiffany closed her eyes, rested her head against J.D.'s chest and lost herself in the feel of his body, so long and lean and possessive. The scent of his after-shave filled her nostrils and she heard the beating of his heart, comforting and steady.

Why was it that being in his arms felt so right when she knew deep in her heart it was wrong? Why did his touch thrill her as no one else's had? There had been men who had tried to date her when she'd moved to Bittersweet. A widowed rancher with a hundred-acre spread bordering Cougar Creek and three half-grown daughters had shown interest, and a divorced insurance adjuster who lived in Medford had called a few times. She hadn't responded to either. She'd been grieving, trying to get over the guilt surrounding the accident that had taken Philip's life, while attempting to keep her small family intact. She hadn't had time for a relationship of any kind; but with J.D. her silly heart wanted to make an exception. The touch of his splayed fingers against the small of her back was erotic, even through her blouse; the sensation of his breath fanning her hair made her tingle.

What was wrong with her? This was J.D. Santini, for crying out loud. Her brother-in-law. A man she was no more sure of than sand shifting beneath her feet.

"Okay, let's switch again," the bandleader said, and reluctantly J.D. released her.

"You go ahead and dance," she said, slipping away from him and breaking off the magic that she felt existed between them, "but I'm going to have a talk with my son." She couldn't be swayed by the seduction of the night, nor let her mind wander into the dangerous territory of thinking J.D. was anything but her brother-in-law.

But he wasn't about to be left behind. He caught up with

her as she rounded the house and wended her way through the parked cars toward the barn. Four boys sat on the top rail of the fence and the smell of cigarette smoke burned in the air.

Stephen was at one end of the group and he watched her approach with openly suspicious eyes.

"We need to go home and talk." she said without making any small talk or allowing her son time for introductions.

"Why?"

She motioned toward the other boys. "You want to go into it here? In front of your friends?"

In the paddock a horse snorted loudly, then plodded away. The boy sitting next to Stephen on the rail, a kid Tiffany didn't recognize, slid farther along the fence, putting some distance between his body and Stephen's, as if in so doing he would avoid some of the fallout from her wrath.

Stephen wasn't going to be cowed in front of his friends. His eyebrows drew together and he glared at his mother as if she were the problem. "I came here because I wanted to," he said boldly. "You wouldn't bring me."

"So you lied."

"You're the one who always says family's so important."

Stephen's eyes flashed with challenge and in that slice of a second, Tiffany witnessed the man he would become.

"You're changing the subject."

"John Cawthorne's my grandpa."

"He's a stranger."

"And he'll always be one if we don't get to know him."

Where did all this logic come from? And why did he care about a grandfather who for years had pretended he didn't exist? Fuming, she tried to understand her son, who, until the past year, had tried to please her. Now, it seemed, he drew strength, even enjoyed, defying her.

"It's time to go home, Stephen. Whatever it is you

wanted to accomplish by breaking the rules, it's over. Come on."

He hesitated and Tiffany nearly stepped forward, grabbed him by his rebellious thirteen-year-old arm and yanked him off the fence, but just as she found the inner strength not to give in to the impulse, J.D.'s fingers tightened over her wrist, restraining her from further humiliating her son in front of his newfound friends.

Grudgingly Stephen hopped to the ground and started striding toward the lane where the Jeep was parked.

"Tiffany!" Katie, holding her skirt in one hand was waving frantically as she weaved in and out of the haphazardly parked cars. "You're not leaving already, are you?"

"I think it's time."

"But we never even got to talk— Oh, hi," she said to Stephen. "I'm Josh's mom, but you know that, don't you?" She turned her thousand-watt smile on J.D. "Don't tell me, you're Philip's brother."

"J.D. Santini." He extended his hand and Katie shook it in both of hers.

"Glad to meet you. But please, don't leave yet. The party's just beginning. I'm just thrilled that you decided to show up. I know it means a lot to John and to my mom. They have this wild notion that we can all become one of those big blended-patchwork kind of families."

Tiffany hazarded a glance at her son. Was that what he wanted? A large family, complete with aunts, uncles, cousins and grandparents? How could she blame him? Hadn't she, at his age, longed for the very same thing? "Maybe, in time, it'll all work out," she offered and didn't add, *But I wouldn't hold my breath.*

"Sure." Katie seemed convinced. "It won't be easy, but, hey—" She shrugged. "Why wouldn't it work? We're all adults—well, most of us," she added, winking at Stephen.

"I'm looking for Josh right now. I don't suppose you've seen him?"

"He was, uh, playing in the hayloft with some of the younger kids," Stephen said, obviously uncomfortable, as if he'd broken some code of honor by telling a parent where to find her son.

Katie rolled her eyes. "He's probably ruined his new slacks and jacket. I just bought them for this deal and I was hoping that he wouldn't grow out of the blazer before he wore it again—say, for Bliss's wedding—but now it's probably ruined. Oh, well, such is the life of a single mother."

Tiffany thawed a little. Katie's warmth and enthusiasm were downright infectious. Besides, she and Katie had so much in common. Not only were they John Cawthorne's illegitimate daughters, but they were both struggling as single parents and working women.

"We really do have to go," Tiffany said. It wasn't a lie. Mrs. Ellingsworth had been pressed into duty to watch Christina, and Tiffany wanted to take Stephen home and set down the rules.

"Then call me for lunch someday," Katie replied.

"I will." Tiffany didn't know if she was ready to embrace this ready-made family, but one lunch wouldn't matter. As Katie headed for the barn, Tiffany asked Stephen, "Didn't you bring your skateboard?"

"Oh, yeah. I'll get it." He jogged over to a shiny Dodge pickup, reached into the back and withdrew his wheels. "I, uh, got a ride out here from the wedding," he explained when he rejoined them.

"You went to the ceremony?"

"Uh-huh." He lifted a shoulder.

"Who gave you a lift out here?" She bristled, as she didn't recognize the truck. She hoped he wasn't foolish enough to ride with strangers.

"Trevor McBaine."

One of Katie's twin brothers. Part of the extended family. Perfect, she thought with more than a hint of sarcasm.

"He's got a kickin' truck."

"That he has," Tiffany said tightly. She didn't know whether to throttle her son or hug him close and beg him not to pull any more stunts like this.

They climbed into J.D.'s Jeep and didn't say a word all the way home. J.D. stared through the windshield as he drove and Tiffany, rather than blast her boy, fiddled with the controls for the radio until she found a station that was clear.

The atmosphere inside the Jeep was tense, and the ride, only twenty minutes long, seemed to take forever. Before the truck had stopped completely in the driveway, Stephen had unbuckled his seat belt and was out the door and across the lawn. He slammed up the back steps and Tiffany told herself to give him time to cool off. But she couldn't. She was too angry herself.

J.D. cut the engine. Tiffany unclasped her seat belt and reached for the handle of her door, but J.D. caught hold of her shoulder, restraining her. "Give him time to think things over before you rip into him."

"I think he needs to know what he put me through."

"I know," J.D. said with an exaggerated patience that made Tiffany's blood boil. "I don't have a doubt that you want to tell him exactly how you feel, but wait until you've both had time to think about it."

Irritated, she retorted, "Is this the voice of experience talking?"

"It is."

"Oh, right," she said. "Since when did you become a parent?"

His nostrils flared and his eyes flashed. "I was talking from the kid's point of view—a troubled kid. I've been there."

"Forgive me for thinking like a mother, okay? But I think it's more important to be a parent than a friend." She jerked her arm away from him. "If I remember correctly you were the one who pointed out that I was having trouble with my son."

"You are," he agreed, his face set.

"Well, it's my problem, okay? I'll handle it how I see best." Her eyes held his for a rapidly accelerating heartbeat. "It's not your responsibility to step into Philip's shoes, you know. It's not your fault that he died."

He eyed her for a second and she felt as if the interior of the Jeep had shrunk, become far too intimate. "Funny," he said in a soft voice. "That's exactly what I was going to tell you."

Her chest tightened and she looked away. "Your parents blame me."

He didn't argue. "They're having trouble with all of this."

"Did your father send you down here to spy on me?" she asked—the question that had been on her mind from the moment she'd found him on her front porch springing to her lips.

"He was worried about the kids."

"Was he?" Anger shot through her. "You know, Jay, of all the things I would have expected from you, it wouldn't be that you'd end up as some kind of gopher . . . or . . .or what do they call spies these days? Moles? I can't believe you'd come down here to be a mole, or whatever you want to call it, for your father."

"I'm not."

"Then why are you down here?" she demanded, poking a finger at his chest. " Why are you in a room in my house? Why didn't your father send someone else—someone with more experience—down here to check out possible vineyard sites? You know, this whole thing has been bogus from the start!"

"Have you ever thought that I might be here because I couldn't stay away?"

"From what? Me?" She shook her head and reached for the handle of the door again. "Oh, come on, Jay, it's been months since Philip died. *Months.* If you really cared, you would have— Ooh!" He pulled her close and kissed her so hard she couldn't breathe for a second, couldn't think. Strong arms wrapped around her, preventing her escape.

Fire screamed through her blood. Desire shot through her insides, turning her liquid. Oh, why was it always like this with him? He groaned as his kiss deepened and erotic images flashed through her mind.

"Tiffany," he said and his voice cracked a bit. He lifted his head and she saw in his eyes a raw pain she didn't understand. "I do care, Tiffany," he admitted, though he seemed to hate the words. His arms, strong and warm, were still wrapped around her. "I care too much. Way too much."

Her heart pounded for a small second. Oh, God, how she wanted to believe him, to drown in his words, to trust in the concern in his eyes; but she couldn't. This was J.D. Santini, her brother-in-law, a man who felt some kind of obligation, a duty to his dead brother's memory and widow. "Then don't, Jay," she said, tamping down that stupid little romantic part of her heart that cried out to give him a chance. "Just don't care. I . . . we . . . The kids and I are doing fine." She kept her voice devoid of emotion. "We don't need you."

The lie hovered between them for a second. He stared deep into her eyes as if in so doing he could search her soul. She wanted to kiss him, to hold him, to tell him that she loved him— Dear God, she loved him?

That thought scared her to the bone, turning her blood to ice. Of all the men in the world, she couldn't fall in love with J.D. Santini.

Never.

Before he could guess the turn of her thoughts, she fumbled for the door latch, scrambled out of her seat and raced across the lawn as fast as if Lucifer himself were on her heels. She only hoped that she could run away from the awful truth. She couldn't love J.D. Santini. *Wouldn't!*

Behind her she heard the Jeep's engine fire again. With a screech of tires, J.D. backed out of the drive. Tiffany didn't turn around, just dashed up the two steps of the porch and propelled herself through the front door. He was leaving. Good. The more distance between his body and hers, the better. But it was only temporary. He'd signed a lease for six months.

Six months!

Inside, she slammed the door shut and sagged against the wall. She was perspiring and gasping for breath, her mind spinning in restless, unending circles. She'd never make it. Never. She couldn't face living in the same house with him for the next two days, let alone half a year.

She couldn't see J.D. again. Not now. Not ever. Unfortunately; she didn't have a choice.

Chapter Ten

"Write up an offer. Five-percent less than the owners are asking. Make it contingent on the soil analysis and water report." J.D. eyed the surrounding acres of the Zalinski farm and told himself that he wasn't making a hasty decision, that these three hundred acres were the right piece of property, that he wasn't grasping at straws just to leave Bittersweet and Tiffany in his dust.

It had been days since the wedding and he'd barely seen her since. The tension between them was stretched to the breaking point; it was time to leave.

Max Crenshaw tugged at his tie and grinned widely. Beads of sweat slid down from his bald pate, over his fleshy cheeks and along his neck to disappear beneath his collar. "This is a good choice," he said with a wink. "And the sellers are motivated. The offer shouldn't be a problem."

"Good." J.D. liked what he saw. The farm consisted of a stone house, barn and outbuildings set in rolling hills with a creek that zigzagged through the fields. Pine and oak trees offered shade around the buildings as well as fringed the neat acres now planted in grass. A few head of cattle grazed on dry stubble while sheep and goats occupied pens closer to the barn, and a tractor with a trailer hitched behind was parked on the knoll of one grassy field. The exposure and drainage looked right, the soil was known to produce high-quality grapes for Santini Brothers' Sémillon, a white Bordeaux wine. The Cabernet Sauvignon and Merlots would be perfect for a new blend of red wine his father wanted to try. As far as J.D. could see, this place would be perfect.

And he could leave.

Before he got too entangled in Tiffany's life.

Before his heart was involved.

"I'll stop by your office later today and sign the offer, then fax a copy to my father in Portland," J.D. told the Realtor. "He'll want to see all the information you've got on this place. If there is any problem with water rights or the property being sublet or rented, he'll need to know about it."

"Shouldn't be a concern. The Zalinskis have already moved and the acres are being used by a cousin who lives near Ashland, but he knows that they're trying to sell. He'll move his animals and equipment on the spot. Not a problem," Max said with a congenial nod. J.D. could almost see the wheels turning in the real-estate agent's mind as he mentally calculated his commission on this place. "I've done some digging with the title company and I think we're all right. Aside from a small mortgage with a local bank, the property is free and clear. But I'll get a title report and see that all the paperwork is done."

"Fair enough." J.D. slid into Max's car and told himself that this was the first step. Soon he'd be able to extricate himself from this little town and return to Portland where he could start working for his father in earnest.

The thought made his jaw clench. He'd never been one who pursued his own happiness, or worried much about it. He considered life a challenge, one with rewards as well as disappointments, and he'd prided himself on being his own man, not his father's flunky as Philip had been.

But he'd changed. Absently J.D. rubbed his thigh, the old pain from his accident returning with a twinge of conscience.

Max turned the car around in the dry grass by the garage and headed down the long, winding lane to the main road. He was still going on and on about the location of the property, resale value and such, but J.D. wasn't paying much attention because as they drove toward town, the dry acres of Isaac Wells's ranch came into view. "Let's stop here," he said suddenly and Max shot him a glance.

"But you're already making an offer on the Zalinski place."

"I know, I know. I just want to check something out."

Always one to please, Max turned into the drive and cut the engine.

"I'll be right back," J.D. assured him and ignored the No Trespassing sign posted on the gate. He climbed over the graying slats and hopped to the ground on the other side. His leg pained him a little, but he jogged around the side of the small house with grimy windows, overgrown garden and weed-choked lawn. Behind the house was a woodshed and farther back, a huge barn. A padlock kept the door in place, but one window was open a crack and J.D. looked into the gloomy interior to see four automobiles parked inside. The concrete floor was swept clean and the smell of oil filled his nostrils. Tarps had been thrown over the vehicles and from the accumulation of dust, he concluded that none of the cars had been moved in months.

The barn was surprisingly neat and tidy, as if Isaac had prided himself on the old car collection. Tools, all neatly placed on racks, covered one wall; shelves filled with books, wax, cleaning supplies and small replacement parts filled another. Hubcaps and old license plates were hung higher on the empty wall space, as if Isaac had spent a lot of time out here.

Odd.

Why would a man just up and leave?

Had he been forced? Had there been foul play? Or had he just left voluntarily for reasons known only to himself?

It just didn't make any sense.

But Stephen had some idea of what was going on. J.D. was willing to bet on it. He just had to find out what the boy knew. J.D. owed it to the kid. To Philip. To Tiffany. His jaw clenched as he started back towards Max's car.

Tiffany. How the devil was he going to erase her from his mind? He could leave Bittersweet; that part was easy. But he had a deep worry that he'd be taking her with him—in his head, and, dammit, in his heart.

He kicked at a dirt clod, sent it reeling against the barn and told himself it didn't matter. He just had to get the hell out.

"That Dean boy was over here again," Mrs. Ellingsworth said as Tiffany tossed her jacket over the back of one of the kitchen chairs. The scents of cinnamon, vanilla and nuts filled the room.

"Mommy!" Christina, standing on a chair near the sink, raised her flour-smudged hands.

"Hi, sweetie." Tiffany dropped a kiss onto Christina's crown and touched the tip of her daughter's tiny nose with her finger. "What're you up to?"

"Ellie and me is making cookies."

"I see that," Tiffany said, and held her tongue rather than correct her daughter's grammar. "What kind?"

"Peanut butter and jelly."

"Just peanut butter," Ellie said. "When this batch is done,

we were planning to go out and get a hamburger, then go to the library for storytime, then stop at the park on the way home and play in the fountain."

"And feed the ducks!" Christina said.

"And feed the ducks." Ellie chuckled deep in her throat and winked at the little girl she'd affectionately dubbed, "the granddaughter I'll never have."

"Can you come, too?" Christina asked her mother.

"I hope so. I'll try to meet you there," Tiffany promised, and gave her daughter a hug.

"You bring Unca Jay."

"Him, too?"

"Yep." Christina nodded her head sharply as if she called all the shots. "I like him."

Ellie lifted a knowing brow. "So do I," she said.

Me, too, Tiffany thought, but kept her feelings to herself. J.D. Santini was a pain. A sexy, intelligent, stubborn, pain in the backside. And she was falling in love with him.

As Christina turned back to the ball of dough on a flour-dusted cutting board, Tiffany dragged her thoughts away from her brother-in-law. "You said that one of the Dean boys was here. I assume it was Miles."

"Whichever one is the older." Ellie wiped her hands on the oversize apron that covered her clothes. "I never could keep those two straight."

"Miles is a few years older than Laddy."

"Then he's the one. He came around here right after Stephen got through with summer school, I think. You know, I usually get along with kids—all kids, no matter how old they are. But that one, he makes me uncomfortable, let me tell you. Shifty-eyed, like he couldn't tell the truth if his life depended on it." Ellie picked up a spatula and wagged it under Tiffany's nose. "That father of his is a no-account,

I'm afraid. He's been in and out of prison for as long as I can remember."

"I know," Tiffany said, fighting a headache that was pounding behind her eyes. "It's not Miles's fault that he's got Ray Dean for a dad."

"No, but it's not your fault, either, and now he seems to be your problem all of a sudden."

Tiffany couldn't argue that point.

"Anyway, the two of them, Stephen and Miles, left a little while ago, but they're supposed to be back by six."

"Good." She told herself not to be nervous. So Stephen was hanging out with Miles again. It wasn't the end of the world. Or was it? When Stephen and Miles were together there was always trouble brewing.

The timer dinged and Ellie put on an oven mitt before removing a batch of cookies. "Okay, pumpkin, you and I, we've got ourselves a date." She untied her apron and helped Christina from her chair. Aside from the one cookie sheet and Christina's messy cutting board, the kitchen was clean.

"I finally managed to say a few words to the new tenant," Ellie commented as she reached for her purse. "Handsome devil."

"Is he?" Tiffany wasn't going to rise to that bait. From the minute Ellie had moved in, she'd been playing matchmaker.

"Almost as good-looking as that brother-in-law of yours."

Tiffany cocked an eyebrow at the friendly older woman. "Almost?"

"That J.D.'s got something, honey, and don't tell me you haven't noticed. On top of that, he's lots more outgoing than Luke." She looked through the window to the carriage house and wiggled a finger at the upper story. "Luke's been in the place for what—several days now? Gee, almost a week, I guess—I can't keep track—but I haven't hardly seen him."

"Maybe he's avoiding you," Tiffany suggested with a smile.

"Don't be teasing, now. I think you might be on to something there. He's not avoiding me, per se, but everyone in general. A real recluse. Probably has some deep, dark secret from his past."

"Probably," Tiffany said, swallowing a smile. Sometimes the older woman's imagination ran away with her. In Tiffany's opinion it was because of all the spy and mystery novels Ellie devoured.

"Ah, well." The older woman sighed and turned her attention away from the window. She took Christina's small hand in her wrinkled one. "We'll be back in a few hours. Right, Chrissie?"

"Right!" Another strong nod of affirmation. "Bye, Mommy." Christina held up her arms to be hugged and Tiffany swung her off her feet.

"Be a good girl for Ellie, won't you?"

"I will."

"She always is," Ellie insisted, but Tiffany rolled her eyes.

As they left, Tiffany finished washing and drying the last of the cookie sheets, then went upstairs to change. Pausing at the open door leading to the third floor, she ran a hand down the woodwork and wondered about her brother-in-law. Since their last argument on the night of John Cawthorne's wedding, she and J.D. had avoided each other and kept to themselves.

Grudgingly she had taken his advice and tried to reason with Stephen, but her son seemed to be slipping away from her. She knew that it was only natural. As the years progressed Stephen would start withdrawing from her, but she wasn't ready for it, nor could she turn a blind eye to his rebellion. The strain in the house had been nearly palpable and everyone was feeling the pressure.

Even Christina had sensed the stress and been grouchy from the tension in the air. The little girl was finally getting over a summer cold that had caused her to sniffle and cough for three days. But she hadn't woken up screaming. During the past week Christina had slept through the night.

That was the good news.

J.D. was the bad.

James Dean Santini. The enigma. She'd tried to avoid him, but it had proved impossible with him living upstairs. Every night she'd thought about him, only one floor away, as she'd lain in her bed.

There weren't enough cold showers in the world to keep her mind from replaying in sensual detail the few kisses they had shared, the intimate caresses. *You're just lonely*, she'd told herself over and over again. *And it's been a long time since you've been touched or held by a man. What you're feeling is normal. It's just too damned bad you're feeling it about J.D. Santini.*

She walked into her bedroom and kicked her shoes into the closet. Aside from the tense atmosphere at home, she'd suffered an incredibly long day at the office. The fax machine had refused to work, the new insurance rates from the company had caused a dozen customers to call in with complaints or ideas about how to lower their premiums, she'd helped two clients fill out accident reports and, to top it all, the computers had decided to take the day off.

She pulled on a pair of shorts and a V-necked T-shirt, then snapped her hair into a ponytail.

Barefoot, she padded to Stephen's room and eyed his clutter. Empty pop cans and dishes littered the room. His bed was unmade and there were magazines, comic books and video-game cartridges scattered across the floor.

Whether he liked it or not, the kid would have to clean up the mess. She only hoped it wouldn't take a fire hose and an exterminator to get the room clean again. The phrase " A man's home is his castle" flitted through her mind, and she thought a more apt description would be "A boy's room is a garbage dump."

At the sound of an engine, she crossed to the window, her naive heart soaring at the thought that she would see J.D. again. Instead she spied Luke Gates's pickup pulling into the drive. Ellie was right. He was an interesting but mysterious man. He was quiet, kept to himself and hadn't caused any problems so far. Crossing her fingers, she hoped against hope that he'd turn out to be a perfect tenant, because she needed the money to stay in the black.

Now, if she could just lease the other unit in the basement, she could probably make ends meet. Probably.

Rubbing the kinks from her neck, she walked downstairs and hit the landing just as the front door burst open. Stephen, his face red with exertion, his eyebrows drawn into a single harsh line, his young jaw set, strode into the house.

"Hi."

He nearly jumped out of his skin. "Mom. Gosh, I didn't see you."

She hurried down the last few steps and started for the kitchen. "Didn't mean to scare you," she said. "Christina and Ellie made cookies. You want some?"

He hesitated, then shrugged. "Sure."

"Ellie said you were with Miles."

Every muscle in his body tensed. "So?" He snagged a couple of cookies from the cooling rack.

"Where'd you go?"

Tossing his hair out of his eyes, he shrugged. "We just hung out at the river."

"But you didn't swim." His hair and clothes were bone-dry and there was a hint of smoke tinging the air surrounding him.

"Nope."

She knew prodding him any further would get her nowhere, so she changed tactics. "How's summer school?"

"Bo-ring." He opened the refrigerator and pulled out a jug of milk.

"You doing all right?"

"Yeah. Why?" Grabbing a glass from the cupboard, he averted his eyes and paid attention to pouring the milk.

"Just checking," she said. She reached for a cookie and took a bite. "It's a mother's job, you know."

"Crummy job, if ya ask me."

"Oh, I don't know. I kind of like it." She smiled and tousled his hair.

Rolling his eyes, he said, "It sucks."

"Let's not talk like that."

"Fine. I'm going to a movie tonight." There was only one theater in Bittersweet and the movies it showed could sometimes be rented at the video store.

"Are you?" she asked. "You were grounded, remember?"

"Until today."

She couldn't argue the point. He'd done his time for his disappearing act. "Okay, but first clean your room."

He seemed about to argue, but wisely held his tongue and washed down whatever words he was about to utter with a big gulp of milk.

"Who're you going with?" she asked, hoping he hadn't made plans with Miles Dean.

"Sam."

She didn't bother hiding her relief. "Okay. So who's driving?"

"Sam's older brother, Seth. Is that okay?"

She decided to trust him. Seth was almost twenty and

worked at one of the mills around town. He seemed to be a straight arrow. "Just come home right after the movie, okay?"

"Yeah. No problem."

She only hoped so. It hadn't been that long ago that the police had been questioning him about Isaac Wells's disappearance, though she hadn't heard a word since the interrogation at the police station. She had tried to convince herself that the police had found other leads, other suspects, but she still shuddered every time the phone rang, fearing that the long arm of the law was about to reach out and grab her son.

But that was crazy. She believed Stephen. Surely if he knew more about the old man's disappearance, he would confide in her. Or would he?

Trust him, Tiffany. He's your son.

Jarrod Smith looked as frustrated as a barking dog who'd treed a raccoon and couldn't get anyone's attention. He paced back and forth in his office and gave J.D. a quick update on the Isaac Wells case. "The police have had several leads, none of which amounted to anything. Originally, they thought some of Isaac's relatives or friends were involved. They were convinced the old man had been the victim of foul play—murder, kidnapping, you name it. But nothing seems to fit." He offered J.D. a sheepish look. "I hate to say it, but it beats me what happened to Isaac. It almost looks as if he just got up and walked away."

"Why would he do that?" J.D. asked.

"That's the question that keeps everyone coming back to square one—that he must've been forced to leave or lost his marbles. Every day in this business, you hear about old men and women snapping and just wandering off." He rubbed the bridge of his nose as if to clear his head. "But I've talked to a lot of people who knew Isaac better than I did. A lot.

None of them think he was suffering from some kind of dementia or paranoia or schizophrenia, or anything else. Supposedly the old guy was sharp as a tack. Spent his time running that ranch and babying the classic cars in his barn. Other than that, he kept to himself." Jarrod settled on the corner of his desk, one leg swinging in agitation. "I even thought that he might have staged the whole thing in hopes of somehow getting the life-insurance money. I thought whoever was the beneficiary of his policies might be in on the con, but nope. All he had in life insurance was enough to bury him. So if he left, he walked away from a ranch worth about a hundred and fifty, maybe two hundred thousand dollars—though it was mortgaged for quite a bit—and his old cars, which he supposedly loved more than his half-breed bloodhound that died a month or so before he disappeared."

Jarrod picked up his coffee mug, saw that it was empty and scowled. With a thump, he set the mug onto the desk. "How about a beer?" he asked. "I'll buy."

J.D. nodded. "Sounds good." He liked Smith, who seemed to be a straight shooter. Everyone he'd met in this small town was starting to appeal to him—which was odd. He'd never thought he would like anything to do with a tiny burg and the small minds he always assumed would occupy it. He'd been wrong. Not that he would ever live here. No way. He was making tracks as soon as possible. Once they were outside the office building, Jarrod showed him a shortcut through a couple of back alleys that he'd used for years. "An escape route when I was a kid," he explained. "Believe me, I had my own share of trouble back then, but not half as much as my brothers. Trevor and Nathan gave my mother more gray hairs than she'd ever like to admit." The late-afternoon sun was still warm but a cool breeze shot between the buildings.

They walked through a back door to the Wooden Nickel

Saloon and slid into a booth. The interior of the restaurant/bar was decorated with Western memorabilia—everything from two-handled saws, wagon wheels and saddles, to lanterns, mining picks and the heads of stuffed animals; their glassy eyes surveying the premises from high above the bar. Embedded in the thick, clear plastic of each tabletop were genuine plug nickels surrounded by glitter that, J.D. assumed, was supposed to represent fool's gold.

They ordered a pitcher of beer distributed by a Portland microbrewery that J.D., as a VP of Santini Brothers Vineyards and Winery, had personally inspected.

The bar was nearly empty, with only a few stools occupied and one pool table in use. Above the barkeep, mounted on its own angled platform, was a television tuned in to an all-sports network where the scores of the previous day's baseball games were being flashed. Over the click of billiard balls, the clink of glasses and the whisper of conversation, country-and-western music drifted from hidden speakers. J.D. didn't recognize the song or the singer and really didn't give a damn. The music just added to the backwoods, rural America atmosphere that was beginning to appeal to him.

A buxom blond waitress clad in tight jeans, boots, checkered shirt and cowboy hat deposited a frosty pitcher of beer and a bowl of some kind of party mix, then poured two glasses. "Anything else?" Her smile was genuine; her green eyes actually held a spark of interest.

"Naw, Nora. This is fine. Thanks."

"Just let me know if you want something." She winked at Jarrod, then sauntered back to the bar.

Jarrod took a long swallow, let out a deep breath and set his glass on the table as Nora swung over to another table, deftly scooping up her tip as she swiped away rings made by the half-full glasses. "Went to school with her older sister, April," he explained, glancing at Nora's backside as she leaned over the table. "I dated April for a few months, took her to my senior prom. Nora was just a little kid at the time."

"All grown up now," J.D. observed as Nora, smiling at several customers, hurried back to the bar.

"Yep." Jarrod glanced over his shoulder and watched as she wiped the bar with a thick white towel, then cleared his throat and turned back to J.D. "If you're asking what Stephen knows about Wells's disappearance, I really can't tell you. You'd be better off getting the facts from him, but I doubt that he's involved. He might have some ideas—kids are always telling tales—and he probably swiped the old man's keys as a prank that nearly blew up in his face, but no one—not me or the police—really suspects that he did anything. They're just interested in what he's heard. The strong-arm tactics down at the station were just to scare him into telling them what he knows."

J.D. should have felt relieved, but he didn't. He still suspected that Stephen was holding back, hiding something important, though what, he couldn't imagine.

As he and Jarrod finished the beer they talked about the baseball season, the past NBA draft and everything and nothing. J.D. learned that Smith had been with the police before breaking out on his own and becoming a private investigator.

When Jarrod asked about him, J.D. mentioned that he was a lawyer, who, until recently, had been involved in personal-injury cases.

"So when Philip died, the old man pressed me into service," he continued. "I didn't jump on it at first, but after an accident on my motorcycle, when I had a few weeks to think about things, I decided to join the family business, at least temporarily." He drained his glass. "Philip's death made it clear that life's too short not to try some new experiences."

Jarrod studied the two inches of beer in his glass. "I heard you were making an offer on the Zalinski place."

J.D. tensed. "Just this morning."

"You know what they say about gossip traveling faster than the speed of light in a small town."

"One of the reasons I like the city."

Jarrod shrugged. "It's not so bad here. Sure, there're a lot of people sticking their noses in everyone else's business, but it works both ways. If you're ever in trouble, everyone in town's willing to pitch in and help you."

"Except in Isaac Wells's case."

Jarrod sighed. "Have to admit," he agreed, "that one's got me stumped." He leaned back in the booth. "So how're you and your sister-in-law getting along?"

The muscles of J.D.'s shoulders immediately tightened. His jaw clenched and he braced himself as if he were expecting a physical blow. "Well enough." Where had this come from and where was it going? J.D. wondered. Smith didn't seem the kind to pry into another man's personal life.

"She's a beautiful woman."

J.D. nodded.

"Had a few tough breaks, what with her old man skipping out on her mother and then losing a husband at her age."

"She's holding up." J.D.'s fingers gripped his glass as if his life depended upon it.

"She's strong. Well, all of John Cawthorne's daughters are. Must be in their genes. Take my sister, Katie. Tough as nails. Growing up with three brothers, she had to be." His gaze clouded for a minute. "She's had her share of troubles, too, and managed to get by. Nothing that happened broke her." He said it almost in wonder. "She's an amazing woman. In fact, Katie's one of the most upbeat people you'll ever want to meet. But she's pushy as all get-out. When she wants something, watch out, she'll just steamroll her way through." Jarrod chuckled, then sobered as he poured a half glass of beer from the pitcher.

"As for Tiffany, she's different from Katie. Quieter. More thoughtful." He rubbed the edge of his jaw. "It can't be easy trying to raise two kids so far apart in age, especially when the older one seems hell-bent on rebelling. Yep, Tiffany Santini is a helluva woman."

J.D. narrowed his gaze on Jarrod. "Is there a reason you're telling me this?"

"Just reminding you what a lucky guy you are to be related to her."

"Seems as if you're related, as well."

Smith grinned. "I know. When John married my mother, I ended up with two stepsisters. I guess I'm lucky, too."

"So it would seem," J.D. said, finishing his drink.

Jarrod reached into his wallet and dropped some bills onto the table. "This one's mine," be added when J.D. pulled out his money clip.

Rather than argue. J.D. tucked the clip back into his pocket. "Fair enough, Smith. but the next time it's on me."

Jarrod didn't argue.

"So I thought. if you're not too busy. we—you and Bliss and I—could meet for lunch tomorrow." Katie suggested from the other end of the telephone line.

A cold sweat had collected between Tiffany's shoulder blades. "I guess that would be all right," she heard herself saying. Katie was trying so hard to get the three of them together. Too hard. But it was inevitable they would meet at some point in time, and Stephen had already let her know that he wanted to belong to a larger family. "How about one-thirty? Doris will be back by then."

"Great! I'll set it up with Bliss and we'll meet you at the Blue Moon Cafe. They've got outdoor tables."

"I'll see you then," Tiffany promised and hung up. Great. She was going to have to deal with her sisters whether she wanted to or not.

She heard the front door open.

"Tiffany?" J.D.'s voice rang through the house. Tiffany braced herself. The tension between them had been so thick she was certain it could have been sliced with a butcher knife.

"In here." She was in the hallway when he met her.

"Where are the kids?"

"Out for a couple of hours or so. Christina's with Mrs. Ellingsworth and Stephen's with some friends at the movies—"

"Great."

Great? Why didn't she think so?

"It's time we took a little time off and celebrated."

Something in his voice gave it away. She felt a cold. dark emptiness as she said, "A celebration. Why? No, don't tell me. Let me guess. It's because you're leaving."

He paused, his gray eyes holding hers for an intimate second. "It's what you've wanted since the moment I walked in your front door."

Oh, dear God. No. The thought of the house without him caused a new dread to fill her heart. "But—but your lease is for six months."

"I know." He rubbed the back of his neck in an attempt to ease the knots of tension in his muscles. "But I'll keep the apartment because I'll be back."

Her stupid heart soared at the thought. "When?"

"Off and on, probably a couple of days a month."

"That's all?"

A smile slid from one side of his mouth to the other. "Don't tell me you'll miss me."

She managed a cold smile. "In your dreams, Santini."

"Always."

She froze and something in his eyes beckoned her, touched that part of her soul she'd tried to keep hidden. "Come on, Tiff," he said, his voice low. " There's something I'd like to show you."

"What?"

His flinty eyes sparked as if with a very private secret. "The reason I can leave sooner than expected."

"Oh," she whispered and felt as if she'd been kicked in the gut. "Sure."

"Isn't that what you wanted?"

"Yes. No." Confusion tore at her. She'd told herself a million times over that if only J.D. would go back to Portland, or L.A. or Timbuktu, for that matter, her life would be better, but now, faced with the fact that he would be gone, she felt none of the elation she'd hoped for. "I, uh, don't know."

His eyes searched her face, as if hunting for a hidden message, a silent clue to her feelings. For a second she thought he would kiss her. Instead he pulled on her hand. "Come on, Tiff."

She couldn't resist.

Before she could come up with one bit of argument she was inside his Jeep, sitting close to him and staring out the windshield as the main streets of town faded behind and they were on a winding country road, slowing for a tractor pulling a mower, whipping around a truck towing a horse trailer, and avoiding squirrels that dashed frantically across the strip of asphalt that carved through the hills.

"Ever heard of the Zalinski place?" J.D. asked. The windows of the Jeep were open and the hot breeze that filtered in ruffled his hair and tugged at her ponytail.

"I've met Myra Zalinski at the agency. They moved."

"But they hadn't sold their farm. Until today."

"*You* bought it?"

"Actually, Santini Brothers did." He drove past Isaac Wells's property and Tiffany felt a chill as cold as death when she wondered what had happened to the old man. Where was he? And what, if anything, did Stephen know about his disappearance? *Nothing. He knows nothing! Remember that, Tiffany. Trust your son.*

A little farther up the road J.D. turned into a winding drive that was little more than two graveled ruts. Tall weeds grew along the sides of the lane and between the tire tracks, scraping the bottom of the Jeep. A few cattle stood in the surrounding fields and a creek, little more than a trickling stream in the late summer, wound its way into a tiny valley where the house sat, its windows shut tight, the curtains drawn.

"What made you choose this place?"

"Size, price, proximity to the freeway, the general appearance of the land, and a gut feeling." He slid her a knowing glance as he parked the Jeep near an ancient oak tree with spreading branches. "It's not a done deal yet," he said, "but it looks like it should fly." His mouth drew tight at the corners and he drummed his fingers on the steering wheel. "Just what Dad was looking for."

She didn't know what to say. Part of her wanted to tell him adios so that she could get back to living her life the way she wanted, without Santini eyes watching her every move and judging her. Another part had decided that she liked having him around, that he wasn't cut from the same cloth as his father, that he really did care about his niece and nephew. Yet another part—one she didn't scrutinize too closely—wanted him to stay because she was fool enough to love him. An ache had already begun to settle around her heart and she tried desperately to ignore it.

"So you think you can grow grapes down here," she

said, trying to sound lighthearted, while a part of her was withering inside.

"Not just grapes. The *best* grapes."

"Oh, right." She couldn't even summon a laugh. He was leaving. *Leaving.* A cold wind swept through her soul and she suddenly felt empty and desolate inside.

"Well, Santini Brothers won't be the first winery. There are quite a few vineyards between Bittersweet, Ashland and Jacksonville. We'll just have to see if we can make our mark."

"And grab your share of the market."

"If Carlo has his way."

"He always does, doesn't he?" she said, and for a second he hesitated, as if he wanted to tell her something that hovered on the tip of his tongue. Clearing his throat, he looked away and lifted a shoulder. "Most of the time. Come on. I'll show you around."

He reached into the back seat and pulled out a backpack that he slung over one shoulder before getting out of his Jeep. "For the celebration," he explained as they walked to the house, a stone cottage that was nestled in a grove of trees. A swing set that had seen better days was rusting by the side of the house and an herb garden, now going to seed, had encroached upon a flagstone patio that overlooked the creek.

"It's beautiful—well, it will be." Forcing her thoughts away from the heart-wrenching fact that she'd have to patch her life back together without him, Tiffany tried to show some interest in her father-in-law's next project. She looked past the obvious need for repairs to the house and grounds. On the far side of the cottage, away from the shade, a vegetable garden with an arbor flanked an orchard of fruit trees and a small raspberry patch. A breezeway separating the garage from the house was trimmed with lattice that stretched into a grape arbor.

"The first season's harvest," J.D. joked, lifting one of the hundreds of clusters of tiny green grapes. He grabbed her hand, linking their fingers and causing a silly little thrill to climb up her arm.

Don't think about it, she told herself. *For once, enjoy the moment. He'll be gone soon and then where will you be? Alone. Again. Hasn't every man who ever was a part of your life left? First your father, then your husband, now J.D.* Her throat turned to cotton and a pain, needle sharp and hot, ripped through her heart.

She told herself that she was being a ninny, that he didn't care for her, had never cared for her, and any feelings she was harboring for him were just silly, romantic whimsies.

Remember, Tiffany, you can't love this man. You just can't!

But she did. The simple, unalterable and painful fact was that she loved him. Wrong or right. For better or worse. Cringing inside at the turn of her thoughts, she was just a step behind him as he showed her around the grounds, pointing out reasons this farm was better than the others he'd seen.

The sun dipped below the horizon and the few clouds hanging low over the western hills blazed brilliant orange and magenta as J.D. followed a path from the house to the barn. Swallows were nesting in the rafters and screeched their disapproval of anyone in the vicinity. A few frogs began to croak and in the distance a coyote sent up a lonely howl.

"It's peaceful out here," she said. "Different from the city."

"Just a tad." The barn door was on rollers and he shoved it open. It creaked and groaned, as if protesting their entrance before finally giving way.

"Needs a little oil," she observed.

"A lot of oil. The whole place needs work. Obviously, but

not more than I expected. Both the house and this barn are over a hundred years old and even though they've been updated, the wiring's shot, plumbing needs to be redone and the house reroofed. But with some time, money and effort I think the cottage could be restored and turned into a gift shop and this place could be converted into a winetasting room." He motioned to the musty interior with its time-darkened beams, wide stalls and hayloft. High overhead a round window let in the last shafts of daylight and an owl, disturbed, fluttered in the rafters.

J.D.'s eyes narrowed thoughtfully, as if he were already imagining what the converted farm would look like. He led her through a back door where the pasture dropped off steeply into a natural bowl. "This could be tiered and landscaped into a natural amphitheater that could be rented for parties, or summer concerts or weddings."

"Just like the vineyard where you and I met," she said automatically, then felt like a fool for mentioning something so personal.

"The same idea." He shoved his hands into his pockets. "Didn't think you remembered."

"How could I forget?"

He eyed her for a second, as if trying to read her mind. A small smile toyed at his lips. "You were catering the wedding and trying your best to look grown-up."

"And you were doing your best I-don't-give-a-damn-about-anything impression."

"Did it work?"

"Oh, yeah. Big time. Everyone who saw you thought you were the reason we'd hired security guards."

He lifted one eyebrow. "That was a long time ago."

"A lifetime," she admitted, a trifle breathlessly. It was happening again, this feeling of closeness and intimacy that she wished didn't exist.

"You weren't married yet."

"Neither were you," she retorted.

"Never have been."

"Why not?" she asked, but before he could answer, she added, "And don't give me the line about not finding the right woman, Santini, because I wouldn't believe it."

He hesitated for a second and when his gaze returned to hers it was dark, intense. The wind seemed to have died and it was so quiet she heard the sound of her heartbeat in her ears. "Maybe I found her, but she was promised to someone else."

Her breath caught in her throat.

"In fact, she was engaged to my brother."

Oh, God. There it was. So many times since Philip's death she'd wondered. Had the one night she'd spent with J.D. been, as she'd told herself, just two people trying to console each other in their grief? Or had it been more? This was dangerous territory, very dangerous, and yet she couldn't resist stepping over the imaginary line she'd drawn in her mind. "For me," she said, swallowing against a lump in her throat, "commitments aren't to be broken."

"I know."

"I . . . I loved your brother."

His jaw tightened almost imperceptibly.

"I know your family thought I married him for his part of the Santini estate, or for the fact that I never knew my own father and was searching for a replacement, but the truth is I fell in love with Philip. It might not have been the wild passion people expect to find, and it certainly changed and became . . . more difficult as the years went by, but I loved him nonetheless."

J.D. snorted. "So did I." His lips flattened into a thin, self-deprecating line. "Why do you think I stayed away for so long?"

"I . . .I didn't know."

"Why do you think I'm leaving now?"

"Oh, God, don't say it—"

"Because I can't stand the thought that I want my brother's wife." His expression was grave. "I saw your marriage falling apart," he admitted. "I know that Philip became . . . less enchanted and I beat myself up because a part of me wanted it to fail."

"No. Please, Jay." Somewhere deep in her being there was a rendering, painful and filled with remorse. Her heart was pounding so loudly he could surely hear its erratic cadence. "I . . . I don't think we should be talking like this," she said in a voice she barely recognized as her own.

"You asked."

"But . . ." Somehow it seemed wrong, such a betrayal of Philip's memory. "It's just that what happened between you and me was . . . was . . ."

"Not supposed to," he finished for her, his jaw tight, his nostrils flaring slightly. A muscle worked in the corner of his jaw and his hands balled into fists of frustration as he gazed upon the still waters of the pond and saw past its clear depths to the bottom of his own soul, his private hell. "I know. Believe me, I know."

"I had no intention—"

"Neither did I," he said crisply, as if to dismiss the subject. They walked down the natural bowl in the hill to the pond and a thicket of cottonwood, pine and oak that guarded one bank. The sky was turning a deep shade of lavender and a soft breeze raced across the pond.

Guilt, never far away, nudged even closer. She'd been faithful to Philip, never so much as touched another man. Her heart had been with her husband. Always. Except for a few lonely moments when she'd thought of J.D., of his kiss, or what might have been. But she'd never said a word, never lifted the phone to call him, never uttered his name in the middle of the night when Philip, off on business or a gambling junket, hadn't been around. She rubbed her arms to ward off a chill before she realized how warm the evening was.

A hawk flew overhead, lazily circling in the dusky sky, but Tiffany hardly noticed because of the man beside her. *Rebel. Black sheep. Hellion.* Names she'd heard Philip call his younger brother. Foolish names that weren't true.

"On to better things," he said, as if he'd chased the ghosts of his past away. From the backpack he withdrew a bottle of wine. "I thought we should christen this place."

"And how did you want to do that?" she asked, her stupid heart racing at the prospect.

"I'll show you." He pulled a jackknife from the pocket of his jeans and flipped out the corkscrew. "Santini Brothers' award-winning private reserve." With an exaggerated flourish, he uncorked the bottle. "Want to sniff the cork?"

"I'll trust you," she said, then saw the stiffening of his spine. "I mean—"

"I know what you meant." He set the bottle on a flat rock near the edge of the pond to let it breathe, but he was tense, his muscles flexed. "And the fact of the matter is you don't trust me." He looked at her with eyes that flashed a silver gray. "You never have."

"I think that goes both ways, Jay. From the moment you laid eyes on me you went out of your way to let me know that I wasn't good enough to marry your brother."

"It wasn't a matter of being good enough."

"No?" She didn't believe him. "Then what?"

"I thought you were too young for Philip."

"It really wasn't any of your business, was it?" she

demanded, stepping closer to him, elevating her chin and skewering him with a stare meant to melt steel.

He didn't so much as flinch. "I guess I made it my business."

"But you had no right," she said, all the years of pentup frustration surfacing. "Just like you have no right to come down here and force yourself into my life."

"Is that what I'm doing?"

"Yes! You seem to think that you . . . you can do anything you please and damn the consequences."

"Not true, Tiffany. If it were, then things would be different between us."

"Would they? How? Oooh!"

He grabbed her. Strong arms surrounded her and his mouth, hard and unyielding, pressed firmly over hers. Her breasts were crushed against his chest and she couldn't breathe, could barely think as he pushed the tip of his tongue to the seam of her lips.

A thrill swept through her and she opened her mouth willingly. A thousand reasons to push him away slid into her mind. A thousand-and-one reasons to hold him close chased them away. His tongue explored her mouth, touching, tasting, tickling, and her knees turned liquid.

Large, callused hands massaged her back, moving sensuously over the light cotton of her T-shirt. Fingers dipped beneath the waistband of her shorts and heat invaded her blood.

Her resistance fled. Common sense failed her.

His weight pulled them to the ground and he trembled as he kissed the patch of skin exposed by the neckline of her shirt. Her fingers tangled in his hair and she refused to pay attention to any lingering doubts still clouding her mind. She didn't protest when he lifted her T-shirt over her head, didn't offer any objections as he kissed the top of each breast so sensually that she ached for more.

She pulled his shirt over his head, mussing his hair, then touched the thick mat of hair covering his chest. She traced the indentations of his muscles and she felt his abdomen contract when she toyed with the rim of his navel.

"You're asking for trouble," he whispered.

"I know. I just hope I'm going to get it."

"Oh, yeah, lady." He unhooked her bra and stripped it away. "Oh, yeah." His breath was hot and seductive, his fingers pure magic as they skimmed over her.

She arched upward as he kissed and licked her breast, teasing and toying as she writhed beneath him. Like a slumbering animal, desire awoke, stretching and yawning deep inside her, aching to be filled.

"Jay," she whispered, his name floating on the evening breeze.

"Right here, love," he assured her as his fingers found her zipper and it opened with a hiss. She sucked in her abdomen as her shorts were pulled over her hips and she was suddenly naked, aside from the scrap of lace between her legs.

"You are beautiful," he said, kissing her belly button, his breath and tongue tantalizingly close to the apex of her thighs. "So beautiful." Lowering himself, he pulled on her panties with his teeth, deftly removing them before inching back up her legs with his mouth.

Her throat was as dry as a desert, her blood on fire. She arched as he discovered her most intimate recesses and caught her buttocks in his hands.

"Jay, oh, Jay," she moaned, her eyes closed, her body glistening with perspiration.

Somehow he kicked off his jeans and parted her legs with his knees. "Stop me now," he said through gritted teeth and she shook her head.

"Don't ever stop."

"You don't know what you're asking," he said, but lost control. Arms surrounding her, he thrust deep, fusing his body with hers only to retract and push forward again. Tiffany moved with him, her body catching his rhythm, her mind closed to all thoughts but the powerful pulsing need that he alone could fill.

She dug her fingers into the muscles of his upper arms, pressed her heels into his calves. Hot desire swirled through her. Her breath was suddenly far too shallow, her lungs too tight. The world tilted on its axis and somewhere in the heavens a star burst into a billion sparks of light.

He cried out with a sound as primitive as the night, and Tiffany lost herself, body and soul, in J.D. Santini—the one man who had no right to her heart.

Chapter Eleven

"So who's the new renter?" Katie asked as she dunked a french fry in her tiny cup of catsup and bit off the end. The three half-sisters were seated at an outside table in the garden of the restaurant, a large umbrella offering shade from the summer heat, flower boxes spilling blooms in profusion.

"You don't miss much, do you?" Tiffany asked, not entirely comfortable with Bliss and Katie, who seemed to have hit it off already.

"I'm a reporter, remember?" Katie grinned and dabbed at her lips. Perspiration dotted her smooth forehead.

"His name is Luke Gates. He's from a small town in west Texas. Other than that, I don't know much about him. He pretty much keeps to himself."

Katie wrinkled her nose as if she smelled a story. "I wonder what he's doing here."

"You're always looking for a mystery," Bliss said.

"Not a mystery. A scoop. There's a difference." She took a sip of iced tea and settled back in her chair. The umbrella wasn't big enough to shade the entire table and Katie had to squint a bit, even though she was wearing wire-rimmed sunglasses. "I'd really like to crack the Isaac Wells case, let me tell you. Now, *there's* a mystery and a scoop."

Tiffany froze. The topic was too sensitive.

Bliss cleared her throat. "I wish it were over, too."

Katie thought aloud. "The old man, for no apparent reason, just up and vanishes. Some people, including the police, think he might have met with foul play. They have suspects, but they're reaching for straws. I've been trying to come up with a reason why anyone would do the old guy in. He wasn't very friendly and made his share of enemies, but none who would want to kill or kidnap him. And if he was kidnapped, why no contract or ransom demands? Gosh, I don't get it."

"No one does," Tiffany said and picked up her glass of cola. Beads of sweat slid down the outside of the glass and she swirled the melting ice cubes. She thought of her son and knew in her heart that he wasn't involved. He was only thirteen, for crying out loud, and yet she was worried. Worried sick.

"So, Tiffany," Katie said, holding one hand over her glasses to shade her eyes, "what's the deal with you and J.D.?"

Tiffany was taking a sip from her drink and nearly choked. "What deal?"

"You tell me. I saw you at the wedding reception, dancing with him. The man's in love with you."

"Love?" Tiffany shook her head despite the soaring of her heart. If only she could believe that J.D. really cared. "He's just here on business."

Bliss and Katie shared a knowing look. "Right."

"It's true. He's buying a farm for his father's new vineyard and winery."

"I know all about the Zalinski farm being sold," Katie said. "And I've heard the rumors about the Santini Brothers Winery expanding to southern Oregon, but that doesn't explain why the guy couldn't keep his hands off you last Sunday."

Tiffany felt heat steal up the back of her neck. She remembered all too vividly J.D.'s lovemaking, but she didn't want to attach any emotions to it. Not yet. "J.D. and I are—"

"Don't say it." Katie shook her head. "If you tell me you're just good friends, I think I'll scream."

"That might be overreacting a tad," Bliss said.

"I know what I saw."

"It's Tiffany's business." Bliss sighed and smiled at her older sister. "When Katie gets an idea in her head—"

"This isn't an idea. This is gut instinct."

"Fine. Whatever you want to call it," Bliss said with infinite patience. "But I've learned you've kind of got a one-track mind."

"A reporter is nothing if not dogged."

"Some people might think of it as stubborn or mule-headed." Bliss winked at Tiffany and Katie rolled her eyes as she fanned herself with one hand.

"For the first time I get why sisters complain about each other." Katie swept her bangs out of her eyes. "And I thought brothers were bad."

"I just think you should give Tiffany some breathing space."

"It's all right," Tiffany said, even though she felt decidedly uncomfortable. "My feelings for J.D. . . . Well, they're complicated."

"That's always what people say when they don't want to admit they're in love."

Love? In *love?* Was it so obvious? "Is that the voice of experience talking?" Tiffany asked and Katie nodded.

"Maybe."

"I've got kids," Tiffany said, opening up more than she expected. "It's not so easy getting . . . involved again."

"Tell me about it." Katie laughed.

"How do they feel about their uncle?" Bliss asked.

"Christina adores J.D. Since he's moved in she's always chattering on and on about him. She's experienced some bad dreams since Philip's death, but they've just about stopped." Tiffany ignored the rest of her lunch—a chicken salad—and leaned back in her chair. "I'm taking Christina to the park this evening. The local theater is putting on a kids' play, and she wants J.D. to go with us."

"Is he?"

Tiffany shook her head. She hadn't even asked him.

"This is a mother-daughter bonding thing," she said.

"It sounds wonderful," Bliss said and for the first time Tiffany realized that the woman she'd always thought of as "the princess" wanted children.

"And Stephen?" Katie ventured. "How does he feel about J.D.?"

"Good question." Tiffany didn't understand why she felt she could confide in these two women who, though her half-sisters, were still strangers to her. But, for the first time in her life, she didn't overanalyze the situation. It felt good to talk things over. "He's . . . he's more difficult. He did see J.D. as a threat at first. You know, he thought, after the accident and Philip's death, that he had to be the man of the house, but then he's still a kid." She lifted her shoulders. "As I said, it's complicated."

"Look, there's something I want to ask each of you," Bliss said and nervously took a gulp of her iced tea. "I know this is odd, considering all that's happened, but I want you to think about it anyway. You both know that Mason and I are getting married. It's going to be a small wedding down here and I thought it would be nice if the two of you would stand up for me."

Oh, God. Tiffany didn't know what to say. Yes, she felt closer to these two women than she'd expected, but she wasn't convinced that it would last. One confidence shared over lunch wasn't a commitment of friendship or sisterhood. Or was it?

"Well, sure." Katie's eyes sparkled at the thought. "Why not?"

A thousand reasons why not! Tiffany looked away.

"I . . . I don't know."

"I don't need an answer immediately," Bliss said. "And I understand why you might have reservations. As I said before, you need your own space, but I would love it if you would do this for me."

"Don't you have friends who would want to be in your wedding?"

"I suppose. But now I've got two sisters. Well, half-sisters. And even though I'm not crazy about what Dad did and I hate to think of how my mother must have felt, I think it's time to move on, not dwell on the past, and look to the future. I always wanted sisters . . .or brothers, for that matter . . . and now that I know about you two, well, it only seemed right."

"John didn't put you up to this?" Tiffany asked, still not trusting the man who had sired her.

"He doesn't even know about it. Neither does Mason. This is all my decision."

"Well, count me in." Katie finished her drink in one long swallow.

Tiffany felt cornered. If she didn't agree, she'd appear headstrong and one-sided, when the truth was she didn't know how she felt about her half-sisters. Some of her anger had dissipated over the past few weeks. But, on the other hand, if she jumped on this bandwagon she might not be able to jump off, and she didn't want to appear weak. "I'll think about it," she said, but then remembered her own wedding day—how she would have loved to have sisters in attendance, or even a father to give her away.

"Do. Just let me know in a couple of weeks."

"I will," Tiffany promised. Could she do it? Accept this olive branch that Bliss was offering?

"Good."

"It'll be a blast!" Katie predicted.

The waitress came with the check and before the others picked it up, Bliss snagged the bill. "This one's on Dad."

"What?" Tiffany's head snapped up.

"He insisted."

"No way. I can pay my share," Tiffany said. She wasn't about to take any charity from John Cawthorne. No way. No how.

"Fine with me." Katie tossed her napkin onto the table. "I've got to run anyway."

"But—"

"Let him pick up the damned tab," Katie said as she slung the strap of her purse over her shoulder. "The way I figure it, it's the least he can do."

Bliss nodded. "You don't have to love him, Tiffany. You don't even have to like him. But let him buy you lunch."

"Fine." Tiffany wasn't sure she liked the idea, but she had more important things to worry about. J.D. and Stephen were at the top of the list.

At the small table in his room, J.D. reread for the thousandth time the deed and the note his brother had signed.

The contract was ironclad. Aside from a few thousand dollars' equity, Santini Brothers owned this apartment house lock, stock and barrel. And unless Carlo could be convinced to sell the place, Tiffany couldn't do anything about it.

So much for her independence.

So what are you going to do about it? he asked himself and felt remorse tear at his soul. He'd made love to her. His brother's wife. True, Philip was dead, Tiffany was a free woman, and yet J.D. didn't feel right about what had happened.

Yeah, but you planned her seduction. You took her and the bottle of wine to the Zalinski place for the express purpose of making love to her.

His jaw tightened and he saw his reflection in the window. Alone in the house, his bags packed, he had time to think, time for recriminations, time to realize that, like it or not, he was in love with his brother's widow. "Hell," he ground out and reached for the telephone. The room was hot. Stuffy. The heat of late afternoon setting in after a long day. He punched out a number he knew by heart, waited until his father had answered and said, "Hi. It's me, Dad."

"Jay. How's it going?"

"I want out." No reason to beat around the bush.

His father's silence was condemning. "You're kidding."

"No joke."

"You've hardly been in the job six months."

"I know, but it's not working."

"Why?"

"A dozen reasons. I should never have taken the job in the first place." He waited a second and softened his voice. "I'm not Philip, Dad."

"You're telling me." Was there a hint of disgust in the old man's voice? J.D. really didn't care. He couldn't be a part of Santini Brothers as long as his father insisted on pulling everyone's strings.

"Listen, Dad, I'm driving to Portland tomorrow. I'm selling my stock, my boat, my bike and my condo and I'm paying off Philip's debts to the company."

"But why—"

"Tiffany needs this place. Her kids need it. I want her to own it free and clear."

"I'm not trying to push my grandkids out of a home," Carlo said. "I just want them closer."

"Forget it. This is their home. Now, I'm paying off the debt and you're accepting it, or we're going to court."

"Always the lawyer."

"Always." J.D. wasn't taking no for an answer.

"You don't have to do this."

"Of course I do, Dad."

"She's got her claws into you."

"Big time."

Carlo sighed. "I don't know what's going on down there, son, but if that woman's turned your head around—"

"What? You'll what?" J.D. demanded. "Find a way to tie her up financially even more than she is? Strap her so that she'll be forced to move closer to you and Mom?"

"Would it be so bad?"

"Yeah, Dad, I think it would. She's her own woman. Independent and tough. She's dealing with her own problems and seeming to get by without any of our interference. The least you could do—*we* could do—is have a little faith."

"But—"

"Draw up the necessary papers. I'll see you tomorrow. Goodbye." J.D. clicked off and half expected his father to call back and the phone to jangle insistently. Thankfully it didn't. J.D. opened the window a crack to let in the evening breeze that was turning the leaves of the tree next to the house. Along with a breath of cool air came the sound of voices, young voices, drifting up from somewhere near the carriage house.

"I mean it, Santini, if you breathe a word of this to anyone, you're dead meat."

J.D. looked into the yard and saw Stephen and another

boy, one who looked a little older than he, standing on the asphalt beneath the new basketball hoop.

"I'm not sayin' nothing to no one."

"You'd better not. We had a deal."

"I know, Miles."

So the scruffy-looking kid with the two-toned blond hair and bad complexion was the infamous Miles Dean. He didn't look all that intimidating; in fact, truth to tell, he seemed more frightened than tough.

"Yeah, well, you already screwed up once."

"It . . . it was an accident."

"You were hiding the keys from me, you little freak. If you woulda given 'em to me like you said you would, then the cops wouldn't have found 'em."

"If you wouldn't have started hitting me, the cops never would have come."

Miles's eyes slitted and he took a step toward Stephen. "Just don't do it again. Stick to the story. You know what'll happen if you mess up again."

J.D. had heard enough. He was on his feet, hopped over his duffel bag that was packed near the door, and was down the two flights of stairs in an instant. He flung himself out the back door and across the lawn before the two boys knew what was happening. At the sight of him, Miles started walking away.

"Not so fast," J.D. said, reaching the older boy and taking hold of his arm.

"Let go of me."

"Not yet." J.D. wasn't going to be intimidated.

"Leave him alone," Stephen ordered, his eyes wide.

"Not just yet." But J.D. abandoned his grip and placed both hands on his hips. "I overheard part of your conversation."

There was stunned silence. Mosquitoes whined around them as the heat of the day began to recede.

"You shouldn't threaten people," J.D. said.

"Crap!" Miles muttered.

"Now why don't you tell me what's going on. What do you know about Isaac Wells's disappearance?"

"I don't know nothin'," Miles spat out.

"No? Then why all the scare tactics while you tried to intimidate Stephen here?" He hooked a thumb at his nephew, who was as pale as death and sweating like he'd just run a marathon.

"I don't know what you're talkin' about!" Miles sneered.

"No? Then let's find out. We'll go down to the police station together. Call your mother, see what she has to say."

"You can't."

"Just watch me."

"No, don't!" Stephen insisted.

"Why not?"

"Because—because—" Stephen looked to Miles for support, and in that instant, Miles jerked his arm free and ran. Like a fox being chased by hounds, he vaulted the fence and took off through the neighboring yards. J.D. had half a notion to run after him, but decided the kid wouldn't get far on foot.

"You shouldn't have done that," Stephen said. "This has nothing to do with you."

"Of course it does," J.D. countered, turning to face his nephew. "Because you're involved."

"So?"

J.D. eyed the boy. "I care."

Stephen snorted. "You're not my dad." Needle-sharp pain seared J.D.'s brain.

"Just because Chrissie thinks you're hot stuff, doesn't mean I have to." Stephen was on a roll and all his fears came tumbling out. "I've seen you and Mom, you know. Seen you together, and Christina's just a little kid. What does she know, huh? She was messed up when Dad died, started having all those nightmares and now . . . now, just 'cause you're here, that seems to be over, but they'll come back. Just as soon as you leave." His eyes flashed a blue challenge and J.D. inwardly cringed. The kid might be right. Christina had seemed to attach to him and if he left—no, *when* he left, which was going to be tomorrow morning—the little girl would be disappointed.

Or devastated. Maybe worse than she was when you arrived down here, Santini. Boy, have you made a mess of things. The worst part of it was that, he, too, would feel the pain of separation, he'd started to think not only of Christina as his little girl, but of Stephen as his son.

"I'm your uncle, Stephen. I care."

"Yeah, right."

"It's true."

Stephen's jaw worked. He stood his ground, his fists clenched, his nostrils flared, more bravado than conviction straightening his spine.

"Now, why don't you tell me about Isaac Wells."

"Nothin' to tell."

J.D. caught his arm. "Just start at the beginning. And this time, no lies."

"Let go of me!" Stephen said, immediately defensive.

J.D. released his grip. "I just don't want you to run off like your friend."

"Miles Dean isn't my friend."

That was one for the good guys.

"That's a start. Tell me about Isaac Wells and his car keys."

"I can't." Stephen shook his head and his skin turned the color of chalk.

"Sure you can."

"Oh, gosh," Stephen said, chewing on his lower lip anxiously. "You—you don't understand."

"Try me."

Stephen blinked rapidly. "Miles will kill me."

"He's not going to kill anyone."

"You don't know him. Or . . . or his dad."

"Ray Dean?" J.D.'s ears pricked up. "What about him?"

"He's back in town and he's . . . mean."

"Either talk to me or to the police." J.D. felt sorry for the kid. Obviously he was in big trouble, wedged between the proverbial rock and a hard place, but J.D. couldn't help him if he didn't know the truth.

"I *can't.*"

"Why not?"

Stephen hesitated. He rubbed one elbow with his other hand and nearly jumped out of his skin when Charcoal galloped out from under the porch. "Oh, God."

"Whatever it is, it can't be that bad."

Stephen looked over his shoulder and his eyes were wide with fear. "You don't understand. If I say anything to you, or to the police . . . they'll hurt Mom and Chrissie."

J.D. saw red. "Who?" he demanded. "Who'll hurt them?"

"No one." The poor kid's voice cracked on the lie as he tried to backtrack, but J.D. grabbed his shoulders and shook him.

"Listen to me, Stephen. No matter what you're involved in, no matter what happened, I'm going to help you. You got that?" When the boy didn't answer, but just looked at the ground, J.D. shook him again. *"You got that?"*

"Yeah." Stephen nodded.

"Okay. So what's going on? Who's threatening to hurt your mother and sister?"

Stephen swallowed hard. His lips were chalk white. "It's Miles," he said. "Miles and his dad."

"So Ray's involved."

"No . . . yes . . . Oh, man . . ." Stephen shoved his hair from his eyes. "He's . . . he's been in jail before and he . . . he's the one who wanted Mr. Wells's keys."

"Why?" he asked, turning the information over in his head.

Stephen shook his head. "I dunno. He heard I stole the keys once and drove one of the cars. Miles told him and then Miles dared me to do it again and bring him the car and keys, but I didn't. I messed up, stole the keys but didn't get the car and . . . and . . . Well . . . I decided I couldn't be a part of whatever it was, so I didn't turn over the keys. I thought I'd get rid of 'em, but then Mr. Wells disappeared and . . ."

"And what?" J.D. demanded. The kid couldn't clam up on him now.

"I . . . I just hid 'em. Miles got real mad. Beat me up. Told me he and his dad were going to hurt Mom and Chrissie if I didn't give 'em the keys, and then the police came and . . . and I got in big trouble."

J.D. held Stephen at arm's length and looked him straight in the eye. He felt a connection with this boy, his brother's son, who was so much like him. "Well, Stephen," he said, his jaw rock-hard, "I think it's time to get you out."

Carrying a sleeping Christina, Tiffany tried to open the back door, but it was locked.

"What in the world?" she wondered, balancing her daughter as she fumbled in her purse, fishing for her keys. Stephen should have been home hours ago and J.D. was normally around at this time in the evening. She glanced around the driveway and noticed that his Jeep wasn't in its usual spot.

Good.

Then she wouldn't have to deal with him.

A part of her ached to be with him, to relive the lovemaking they'd shared, and yet she still needed time to think, to sort things out.

Christina yawned and opened her eyes.

"We're home, sweetie," Tiffany said as she found the key and managed to unlock the door. "Stephen?" she called, but no one answered. "Great." She glanced at the table and saw no note, but didn't panic. Not yet.

"Let's get you upstairs and into bed," she told her daughter, and for once the little girl didn't protest. Within twenty minutes Christina was washed and tucked into her bed, snoring softly and sucking her thumb as Tiffany turned out the lights.

The house seemed empty without her son.

And without J.D.

She walked outside where evening had settled and down the flight of steps to Mrs. Ellingsworth's apartment. The door opened after the first rap of her knuckles against the panels. Curlers were wound through the older woman's gray hair and her face, devoid of any makeup, appeared older than usual. "Sorry to bother you, but I was looking for Stephen."

"Isn't he here?" Ellie frowned thoughtfully.

"Not that I can tell."

"Well, he was. He and that other boy—you know the one I mean, the hooligan—well, he looks like one—"

"Miles Dean." Tiffany's heart nearly stopped. There was more trouble simmering in the summer night. She could feel it.

"The older Dean boy, if that's the one," Ellie said, nodding. "Never can keep those two straight. Anyway, he and Stephen were here earlier. I saw them through the kitchen window." She pointed to the window in question. Though her unit was on the lowest level of the house, it still got natural light as the lot sloped sharply on the north side.

Tiffany tried to forestall an inevitable feeling of dread. "Thanks."

"Don't mention it. Oh—" She snapped her fingers. "Did you ask J.D. where Stephen went?"

"He's not here, either."

"Isn't he? Funny, I thought I heard his Jeep earlier. Oh, well." They chatted for a few minutes more, then said good-night. Tiffany, lost in thought and worry, walked up the steps and was rounding the corner to the backyard when she caught sight of Luke Gates locking the door to his upper-story unit of the carriage house.

He offered her a slight smile. "Evenin'."

"Hi, Luke," she said and then asked, "Have you seen Stephen anywhere?"

Luke gave a curt nod. "Earlier. With J.D. and that scruffy-lookin' friend of his."

"Miles?" What did J.D. have to do with it? Worry set her teeth on edge.

"Don't know his name." Luke flashed her a crooked smile. "I just caught a glimpse of them earlier, then heard a truck or some kind of rig pull out. Thought it was probably J.D.'s Jeep."

"Thanks."

"Anytime."

As Luke climbed into his old truck, Tiffany headed back to the house. What was going on? She felt a dread, as cold as a north wind, cut through her soul as she walked up the stairs, checked on a sleeping Christina, then made her way to Stephen's room.

It was cleaner than usual, thanks to his efforts during the period when he'd been grounded, but she found no hint in the scattered CDs and magazines as to where he'd gone. *He's probably with J.D. He'll be all right*, Tiffany tried to convince herself as she ran her finger over the top shelf of his bookcase and noticed the little car he'd fashioned from wood and entered a race with years ago when Philip had been alive. *But Miles Dean is involved and that spells trouble. Trouble with a capital T.*

Having found no clues to Stephen's whereabouts, she

left his room and hesitated in the hallway. The door to the third floor had been left open, was slightly ajar. Beckoning. Though she felt a sense of guilt for invading J.D.'s privacy, she mounted the stairs to the loft tucked under the eaves. She took one step into his room, turned on the lights and tensed when she saw his duffel bag, fully packed, standing ready near the door. He was leaving. Just like that. After they'd made love.

Though she'd known it would happen, had tried to prepare herself, a part of her withered in pain. Why had she expected anything different? He was just a man, and like most of the men in her life, he was leaving her.

Don't dwell on it. Buck up.

But the dull ache around her heart only increased. She walked to the window to look through the branches of the night-darkened tree when she noticed his briefcase, open, and a document spread upon the table.

Don't look at it.

But she saw her name—and Philip's—on the contract.

The contract?

With trembling fingers she picked up the pages and read each of the pages. Slowly, as she sifted through the legalese, she understood the reason why J.D. Santini had come to Bittersweet. It wasn't just to buy a winery. It wasn't to see his niece and nephew. It wasn't to check on her. No, the reason he'd shown his face down here and rented an apartment from her was because he was checking out his father's investment in this house, this Victorian manor she'd called home. Her heaven.

Only it wasn't hers.

Santini Brothers owned the lion's share of it. Philip had signed away most of what she had assumed was her equity. Nothing much was left.

And it had been J.D.'s job to come and give her the news. Only he'd chickened out.

Tears burned behind her eyes. Betrayal raged through her soul. How had she trusted him? Believed in him? Made love to him?

Because you're a fool for that man. You always have been and you always will be.

Her knees turned to jelly and she sagged against the table. The first tears began to rain from her eyes and she heard the sound of an engine. Swallowing hard, she looked out the window and braced herself as J.D.'s Jeep came into view. Her fingers curled over the damning papers and she forced her leaden legs to move. It was time to have it out, once and for all.

Chapter Twelve

"Who do you think you are?" Tiffany flew across the dry grass like an avenging angel. Her eyes were as bright as twenty-four-karat gold. her face flushed, her beautiful lips compressed into a furious pout, her black hair streaming behind her. In one hand she had papers, legal papers, clutched into a wad.

J.D.'s stomach tightened. Every muscle in his body tensed as he climbed out of the Jeep. He knew why she was furious. Stephen didn't.

"Mom—"

"Go into the house, Stephen," she ordered.

"But—"

"You heard me!" So angry she was shaking, she stopped at the Jeep's fender. Her eyes, luminous and burning with wrath, focused on J.D. "Your uncle and I have something important to discuss."

"We took care of it," Stephen said.

"You what?" Her perfectly arched eyebrows drew together.

"At the police station—"

"She's not talking about the Isaac Wells case," J.D. clarified.

Tiffany stumbled backward a step. "Isaac Wells? Police?"

She looked at her son for the first time. "What are you talking about?"

"What are *you* talking about?" Stephen asked.

"I think we'd all better sit down." J.D. reached for Tiffany's arm because she looked as if she might fall over, but she recoiled as if the mere thought of his touch sickened her.

"Just tell me what's going on."

"Stephen had a long talk with Sergeant Pearson down at the police station."

"Oh, God—" Her voice failed her. She blinked and clasped a hand to her chest. The papers—the damning deed and note—fluttered to the ground, suddenly forgotten.

"It's all right, Mom," Stephen said.

"All right?"

"Stephen explained what's happening. Why he's been acting the way he has, what the deal was with old Isaac's keys," J.D. told her as he reached down for the note and deed. Folding them together, he added, "I'd venture to guess that right about now, Ray Dean and his son Miles are being questioned."

"Ray Dean?" she repeated. "What's he got to do with anything?" She licked her lips. "I knew he had been released but . . . is he involved in this?"

"It looks that way."

"Oh, Lord." Her legs seemed to wobble again.

J.D. reached for her arm and this time she didn't back away. He helped her into the kitchen and noticed how homey the room appeared with its hanging pots, fragrant herbs, and children's artwork on display. He'd miss this place, he realized, feeling a pang of regret. He'd miss the house, the kids and Tiffany. God, how he'd miss her.

"Tell your mother everything you told the police and me," J.D. said, once Tiffany and Stephen were seated at the table. He poured her a glass of water, which she ignored, and he wished there was something, anything he could do to erase her pain. Though she was relieved that her son was only a minor player in the drama unfolding around Isaac Wells's disappearance, he was involved nonetheless.

"So . . . so Miles told me if I didn't do what he said and get him the keys and the car, his old man would hurt you, Mom. You and Chrissie." Tears filled Stephen's eyes and he looked more boy than man at the moment. Tiffany couldn't bear to see his pain. "I thought I should try to protect you."

"Oh, honey, you didn't have to—"

"Yeah, Mom, I did. Dad wasn't around, so who was going to take care of you?"

Her heart swelled and she got up from her chair, pulled her son to his feet and embraced him. Tears ran down her face and she felt his frightened sobs against her shoulder. "You don't ever have to worry about taking care of me, Stephen. I'm the one who does the taking-care-of around here. It's my job. It's what I want to do." She stared at J.D. over her son's shoulder. "I'm in charge, honey," she whispered, kissing Stephen's temple and feeling the scratch of new whiskers against her chin.

"I don't think you'll have to worry," J.D. said. Leaning against the counter, his long legs stretched in front of him, his hands at his sides supporting his weight against the counter's edge, he looked damnably sexy, but Tiffany told herself she was immune. Never again would he get to her. "The police have zeroed in on the Deans. No one knows for sure what's happening with Isaac Wells yet, but it's only a matter of time. I called Jarrod Smith and he's working on the case independently. My guess is that the old man will turn up in a few days."

"You think Ray Dean's held him hostage?"

"Possibly."

"But you're not sure?"

"Not yet" He pushed himself upright. "The important

thing is Stephen is out of it. His testimony will lead the police in the right direction. Pearson called his juvenile counselor and in light of the situation—that he was coerced, but then came clean—the local authorities will talk to a judge and expunge any charges, no matter how minor, against Stephen."

Tiffany's heart lightened. "That's the best news I've heard in weeks."

"J.D. did it," Stephen said with something akin to awe for his uncle in his voice. "He's the one that insisted I get a break because of all this."

"Is that right?" She looked at the man before her with new eyes.

"I have taken my share of criminal law," he admitted, "though it was a long time ago."

"I guess I owe you a debt of thanks."

"Do you?" He pulled the wrinkled documents from his pocket and she stiffened. The note.

"Listen, honey, why don't you go up to your room?" Tiffany said to her son. "Uncle Jay and I have something to discuss."

"What?" Stephen demanded, looking from one to the other. "What?"

"It's personal," Tiffany said. "I'll explain later."

Stephen hesitated, but J.D. nodded. "Go on up. This'll only take a minute or two."

Not certain, Stephen started for the swinging doors. He paused just as he reached them, then studied the floor for a few seconds. "Does this have anything to do with me?"

"No!" they said in unison.

Stephen managed a thin smile. "Good I thought maybe I was in trouble again." He disappeared through the doors and Tiffany heard his footsteps on the stairs. A few seconds later he'd tuned up his guitar and notes were wafting through the floorboards.

"I should tell him not to wake Christina," she said, but decided it wasn't the time. Instead, she turned and faced the man she loved, the man who had taught her that it was all right to be done with grieving, the man who had used her so callously.

"What's going on?" she demanded.

"It's simple. I came to Bittersweet to tell you that you don't own the house, that Santini Brothers do. They bought Philip out to cover his gambling debts."

Pain burned through her soul.

"So I'm tossed out? Me and the children?"

"Nope." He tore the deed and note in half, then half again. "It's forgiven."

"What?"

"The debt. It's been taken care of."

"How?"

"My father's had a change of heart," he said, still shredding the documents and letting the small confetti-like pieces fall to the floor.

"You paid him."

He didn't answer.

"You didn't have to, you know. I would have taken care of it" She should have been offended but found the gesture somehow comforting. Maybe their relationship wasn't for naught "I'll pay you back."

"Don't worry about it."

"I said I'll pay you."

"Drop it, Tiffany. You and the kids, you're part of the family."

"Don't lie to me, Jay. It belittles us both. I never have nor will I ever be part of the Santini clan. That was your father's choice. Not mine."

His jaw worked. "I said, things have changed."

She didn't believe him, but changed the subject to the worry that had been gnawing at her for the past hour. "You're leaving, aren't you?" Her voice was barely a whisper.

"In the morning."

"Nice, Jay." She couldn't hide her disappointment. How would she live without him? These past few weeks had been glorious torments, a kind of bittersweet pleasure that she would miss. As she would miss him. She looked at him and wondered if she'd ever be blessed with his smile again, ever feel his lips on hers, ever quiver at his touch. *Oh. foolish, foolish woman. Pull yourself together. He doesn't care about you. Never has. Never will. Your love for him is a joke.*

"And when were you going to tell me about the deed?" she demanded, chasing away her painful thought of love or the lack of it. "Or were you going to wait until Carlo decided to evict me?"

"That's not happening." He was firm.

"Isn't it? Then why all the secrecy? Why didn't you tell me the truth?" she demanded, walking closer to him, stopping only when the toes of her sandals brushed the tips of his boots.

His jaw slid to the side and he stared at her with an intensity that stole the breath from her lungs. "Why?" he countered. "You want the truth?"

"Absolutely."

His mouth tightened at the corners and his eyes took on the color of midnight "Because, lady, from the moment I set my eyes on you again, I knew that I was lost."

"'Lost'?" What was he saying? The room was suddenly hot. Way too hot.

"That's right, Tiffany." He pushed his head forward, bending so that his nose was a hair's breadth from hers, so close that his clean male scent enveloped her. "The second you climbed out of your car the first day I was here, it was all over for me."

"I—I don't understand."

"I'm trying to tell you that I fell in love with you, dammit."

"In love with me?" Could she believe it? No way. Her insipid heart took flight.

"That's right."

For a heartbeat there was silence. Hot, condemning silence. She swallowed hard. *Love? J.D. loved her?*

"I don't know what to say."

He straightened and a look of weary defeat gathered in his eyes. "You don't have to say anything, Tiff." Shaking his head he started past her, but she reached out and grabbed the crook of his elbow.

"Wait."

Beneath her fingers, his muscles tensed. He looked at her over one muscular shoulder with eyes that reflected a pain that tore at his very soul. "For what?"

"Me," she whispered, swallowing the lump forming in her throat. "Wait for me."

He closed his eyes.

"I love you, too, Jay." Tears spilled over at the admission. "I . . . I have for a long, long time."

For a second he didn't move and then his eyes flew open, he grabbed her and kissed her hard on the lips. Her arms wound around his neck and his circled her waist. They clung to each other as if they'd been separated for years, star-crossed lovers who had at last rediscovered each other.

When finally his head lifted from hers, he cracked a smile. "So?"

"So marry me, Santini," she said with a low chuckle. "Make an honest woman of me."

"I don't know if that's possible."

Tossing her head back, she giggled. "Try me."

"All right. You're on. We'll drive to Portland tomorrow, find a justice of the peace and be married in the afternoon."

"No way. I did the quickie marriage before. This time we're going all out. My son's going to give me away. My daughter's going to be the flower girl and my sisters . . ." She surprised herself. "My sisters will be there."

"What about your father?"

A cloud crossed Tiffany's mind and her heart squeezed in the same painful manner it had for all of her lonely life, but she decided it was time for a new beginning. Time to bury all her pain. "He'll be invited. To be a guest, nothing more. If he shows up, fine ."

"And if he doesn't?"

"His loss."

J.D. placed a kiss on her forehead. "Are you sure about this?" he asked.

"As sure as of anything I've ever done."

"We still could lose the house. Dad might not approve."

"Then we'll move, won't we?" She felt lightheaded, freed of the blackness that had shrouded her for so long. "But what about your job?"

"Already quit." He regarded her with twinkling eyes. "You know, I think there're some ambulances down here just dying to be chased."

"No doubt."

"Besides which, I'm not destitute, you know."

"No?"

"No. But we do have one more obstacle to overcome."

"What's that?"

"I want to adopt the kids."

"But you're already their uncle."

"I know." A dimple showed in his cheek. "But when they're ready, I want them to think of me as their father."

"Do you think that'll happen?" she asked skeptically.

He twirled her off her feet. "Haven't I been telling you all along that anything's possible?"

"That you have, J.D.," she admitted.

"Then, for once, Tiff, trust me."

"I do," she promised, and he kissed her as if he would never stop.

Epilogue

Two weeks later Tiffany twirled in front of the mirror. The blue silk dress swirled around her like a cloud. "It's beautiful," she said, turning to face her half-sisters.

"Yep. Looks great." Katie, dressed in an identical gown, agreed.

"Good." Bliss flopped into a chair at the dressmaker's shop where she had ordered not only her wedding dress but the two bridesmaid's gowns, as well.

Tiffany felt a sense of family. She and J.D. were going to marry, her half-sisters and she were discovering each other, and her kids, finally, had settled down. Under J.D.'s influence, Stephen seemed to be trying to walk the straight and narrow and Christina was on cloud nine.

"Okay," Bliss said, "let's get out of here. I'll buy you both a soda."

"I think we deserve gin and tonics after this ordeal," Katie teased as she peeled off her dress and handed it, along with the marked hem to Betty, the shop owner.

"Well, how about a glass of Chablis instead?"

"You're on!"

They changed and walked outside where the afternoon sun was glistening overhead. The streets of Bittersweet were shaded on this edge of town, the traffic slow.

"I can't believe that both of you are getting married," Katie said with a sigh as they walked to Bliss's Mustang convertible which was parked in the shade of a giant oak tree. The top was down and Bliss's dog, Oscar, a golden mutt of about twenty pounds, gave out an excited yip and, at Bliss's command, hopped into the back seat.

"You'll be next," Bliss predicted as she slid behind the wheel. Katie climbed into the back and petted the dog while Tiffany took her place in the passenger seat.

"No way. I've got too much to do before I get married."

"Such as?" With a flick of her wrist Bliss turned on the ignition. The sporty car roared to life.

"Such as finding out the story behind Ray Dean and Isaac Wells."

"Can't you leave it to the police?" Tiffany asked as Bliss pulled out of the parking lot.

"And miss the scoop of a lifetime? No way."

Wind breezed through their hair as they drove. Tiffany leaned back and smiled. Life was definitely improving.

"So, what've you learned about your newest tenant?" Katie asked.

"Luke? Not much. He keeps to himself."

"I wonder why?"

"Why don't you ask him?" Tiffany asked.

"I just might." Katie laughed, the sound tinkling and light over the growl of the engine, and Tiffany smiled as her house came into view. In a grand gesture, as an early wedding gift, her father-in-law had given her the title to the house. He had refused payment from J.D. and was desperately trying to wheedle his son back into the Santini Brothers fold. But J.D. was determined to hang his shingle in Bittersweet.

"Mommy!" Christina flew out the front door as Bliss pulled into the drive. J.D. was on her heels. His limp had all but disappeared, and his eyes glittered mischievously.

Oscar hopped out of the car and washed the little girl's face with his long tongue. Christina giggled with delight.

As Tiffany climbed from her seat, J.D. held the door open for her. "Glad you're home."

"Are you? Gee, and I thought you loved baby-sitting," she teased.

"I do."

At that moment Luke Gates's dilapidated pickup pulled into the drive. He parked and slowly stretched his way out of the cab. "Here's your chance," Bliss said to Katie in a stage whisper, and the younger woman grinned widely.

"You're right." She climbed out of the car. "You know me," Katie said, straightening. "I'm not one to pass up an opportunity."

"What's this all about?" J.D. asked.

"It's a long story." Tiffany smiled as J.D. wrapped his arms around her and Katie crossed the lawn toward the tall Texan. "But don't be surprised if you read about it in the *Review.*"

"Uh-oh. Katie's on to a hot story," J.D. guessed.

"She only hopes," Bliss said and Tiffany sighed contentedly, glad to be a part of this scattered, but loving, family.

Someday she might even forgive her father.

Someday.

For now, her focus was on loving J.D.

A FAMILY KIND OF WEDDING

Chapter One

"I'm countin' on you, boy. Now that Dave's gone, all his mother and me got left is the thought that he might have left himself a son or daughter. Don't know if it's true, you know, but he mentioned something about it the last time we spoke to him." The old man's voice cracked. "You let me know, hear?"

"Will do," Luke Gates promised, cursing himself as he slammed the phone down. How had he gotten himself roped into this mess? Sweat ran down his back, and the sweltering heat of the September day seemed worse in the confines of this tiny top-floor apartment of an old carriage house in southern Oregon.

In Luke's estimation, Ralph Sorenson should do his own damned dirty work. What the hell was Luke doing, getting caught up in an old man's hopes and dreams that were bound to cause nothing but heartache and pain? So the old man thought he had a grandson. So he hoped that Luke would find the kid. So he was going to pay him to do it. Big deal.

But it was. When it came to money, Luke had been born with a weakness, a hunger for it. Having grown up dirt-poor, tossed around from one aunt to another, constantly reminded that he was "another mouth to feed" and that he must "earn his own keep" had only fostered his drive and need to chase after the almighty greenback.

But this job might be too much.

Ralph was pushing. Too hard. But then, the old man was desperate.

Luke's stomach curdled as he thought of the heavy-bodied man who had helped turn him from a hellion into a decent-enough businessman. Luke had never known his own father, and Ralph was the closest thing he now had to family. He supposed, under the circumstances, the reverse was true, as well.

But still, the thought of dragging forgotten skeletons out of closets and digging up innocent people's lives didn't appeal to him.

Not so innocent, he reminded himself.

Ralph Sorenson deserved to know his own flesh and blood. Who cared if it fouled up some woman's life? And besides, there was a pile of money involved.

Telling himself it didn't matter what he thought, Luke yanked on his favorite pair of boots and headed outside. Pausing on the upper landing of the staircase, he felt the impact of the late afternoon. The air was as dry as a west Texas wind and the September sun merciless. Just the way he liked it.

Sliding his key ring from his pocket, he hurried down the flight of stairs and strode across the patchy dry lawn to a spot of concrete by the garage where his pickup leaked a little oil. He'd lived here for a couple of weeks and planned to stay until he could make the old ranch house livable. It would take a little doing, even by his spartan standards.

A crow cawed angrily from an eave of the main house, a massive Victorian complete with gables, shutters and gingerbread trim. The turn-of-the-century home had been divided up some years back and now had several apartment units ensconced within its century-old walls.

He heard the sound of tires on gravel. A convertible, belching blue exhaust, the engine knocking out of synch, careened into the drive. The driver, a red-haired woman he'd caught glimpses of before, stepped on the brakes. She was out of the car before it stopped rolling.

"Hi!" She waved.

What was her name? Katie Something-or-other, he thought—a relative, maybe a sister, of Tiffany Santini, the widow who was his landlady.

Katie strode toward him with an air of confidence he found refreshing. A mite of a thing with fiery red hair, a sprinkling of freckles over a pert little nose and a pixie-ish jaw, she didn't dally. Sunglasses covered her eyes. "You're Luke Gates, aren't you? I've seen you around here and I always wanted to introduce myself." She flashed him a smile that wouldn't quit, the kind of thousand-watt grin that beautiful women used to get what they wanted. Her hand was already outstretched as she marched up to him. "I'm Katie Kinkaid, Tiffany's sister—well, half-sister really." Her teeth were a set of pearls that were straight enough except for a small, sexy overlap in the front two and her face was flushed, as if she'd been running. He could do nothing but accept the small hand that was jabbed his way.

"Glad to meet you," he drawled, though he wasn't really sure. Katie struck him as the kind of woman who could steamroll right over a man even though she was only a couple of inches over five feet.

"Me, too." She shook his hand crisply, then let it drop. "Don't suppose you've seen my son around here, have ya? He's ten going on sixteen, got reddish-brown hair and is about yea tall." She gestured with the flat of one hand to the height of her opposite shoulder. "He's usually moving about a billion miles a minute and he's been spending a lot of time hanging out here with Stephen in the last day or two."

Luke knew the kid she meant. A gangly kid always on the go. "I think I've seen him," Luke allowed with a flick of his gaze toward the back porch. "But not today."

"Hmm." She shoved her bangs from her eyes and the scent of some flowery perfume teased at his nostrils. "Tiffany said something about taking the kids out to the farm—you know, the old Zalinski place that Santini Brothers Enterprises bought for their latest vineyard and winery. They probably just haven't gotten back yet." She slid her sunglasses off her nose and chewed on one bow as she squinted down the length of the driveway. "I guess I'll just have to wait." Pausing for a second, she turned her attention back to Luke. "So, I've been meaning to ask ever since I first saw you, what brings you to Bittersweet?"

"Business."

She was a pushy little thing. She gave him the once-over, a swift glance up and down his body, and her expression said it all. In faded jeans, a T-shirt and his scruffy boots, he didn't look like the typical three-piece-suit-and-tie businessman. But then this was Bittersweet, Oregon, not New York City or L.A.

"What kind of business?"

He had to get the word out sooner or later. Though he was going to do a little bit of detective work for Ralph, that was only part of his reason for hanging around. The ranch was his real purpose and now that the sale of the property was a done deal, he saw no reason to keep it to himself anymore. "I bought a spread a few miles outside of town and I'm hoping to convert it into a working dude ranch."

Her eyebrows arched up as she slid her shades onto the bridge of her nose again. "You mean for tourists to come down here and round up wild horses, and brand cattle, and, well, do all that macho outdoorsy cowboy thing—kind of like the movie *City Slickers*?"

He couldn't help but smile. "Not that elaborate, but, yeah, that's the general idea." There was a whole lot more to it than that, but he didn't see any reason to fill her in—or anyone else, for that matter—with the details. Not just yet. Until he was sure of them himself. Besides, she had a way of distracting him. In white shorts and a sleeveless denim blouse, she showed off a tanned, compact body with more curves than a logging road in the Cascade Mountains. The V of her blouse's neckline gave him a quick glimpse of cleavage between breasts that were more than ample to fit into a man's palm.

He caught himself at the thought and shifted his gaze back to the truck. Katie Kinkaid's all-American-girl-next-door good looks were heightened by a bit of raw sensuality that gripped him hard and caused a ridiculous tightening in his groin.

Obviously it had been way too long since he'd been with a woman.

He even noticed the dimple that creased her cheek when she smiled. She was sexy and earthy, yet exuded an innocence and charm that, if he let it, might get under his skin.

"When do you plan to open the doors?" she asked, and he cleared his throat for fear his voice would betray him.

"By early next summer. Soon as the winter snowpack melts." He wasn't used to being grilled, wasn't sure he liked it.

"Where is your ranch, exactly?"

"Outside of town about three miles or so." He decided to end the conversation before she dug too deep. She was a nosy one, this Katie Kinkaid. If he let her, she'd talk to him all afternoon. "I gotta run."

"Wait a minute. I'm a reporter with the *Rogue River*

Review—that's our local paper—and I'd like to do a story about the ranch when you open."

So that was it. He should have known.

When he hesitated, she barreled right on. "You could think of it as free advertising." She angled her face upward for a better look at him and he thought he noticed a hint of defiance in the tilt of that impish chin.

"Thanks. I'll let you know."

"Here—let me give you my card." Whipping open a small purse, she scrounged around for a second, extracted her wallet and edged a clean white business card out of a slit behind a picture of her son obviously taken a few years back. "Here. Just give me a call, or I'll contact you." She looked up at him expectantly as he flipped the card over and over between his fingers.

"I don't have anything like this yet," he admitted. "The deal just went through, but I'll call you later."

"Or I'll call you," she repeated quickly, as if she thought he was giving her the brush-off. Apparently she was used to being in charge.

"Fine. Nice meetin' ya." He slid her card into the back pocket of his jeans and walked to his truck. A black cat that had been sunning himself on the hood, perked up his head; then, as Luke opened the driver's door, the animal shot to his feet and hopped lithely to the ground.

"Oh, come here, Charcoal," Katie said, bending down and picking up the slinking feline. "That's a boy."

As Luke rammed the truck into gear, cranking on the steering wheel, he caught a glimpse of Katie in the rearview mirror. One hip thrust out as she cradled the cat against her chest, dark glasses hiding her eyes, lips tinged a soft peach color, she exuded a natural sensuality that caught a man off guard and squeezed tightly. Too tightly.

His gut feeling about her was simple: Katie Kinkaid was a woman to avoid.

Katie was still petting the cat, staring down the driveway and asking herself a dozen questions about the enigmatic cowboy who had taken up residence in Tiffany's carriage house when J.D. Santini's Jeep roared into the drive. J.D., Tiffany's brother-in-law and soon-to-be husband, was behind the wheel.

Katie stepped aside as the rig rolled to a stop.

"I'm sorry we're late," Tiffany apologized. Her face was flushed, her gold eyes bright as she climbed out of the Cherokee. "We went to the farm and the kids swam in the lake and . . . Well, we just lost track of time."

J.D. stretched out of the rig. His grin was wide, a slash of perfect white teeth against a dark complexion.

"Don't let her kid you," he said, winking at Katie. "Stephen, Josh and Christina amused themselves and this one"—he slung his arm familiarly over Tiffany's shoulders—"couldn't keep her hands off me."

Tiffany burst out laughing and nudged him in the ribs with her elbow. "Dream on, Santini," she teased, but she wasn't able to hide the sparkle in her gaze. She was, without a doubt, totally and gloriously in love.

Katie didn't feel the least little bit of envy. She believed in love—for other people. It just wasn't in her cards. "I haven't been here long and besides, I got to meet your new tenant."

"Luke? Hmm." Tiffany frowned slightly. "He keeps to himself most of the time."

The boys climbed out of the back of the Jeep and Christina, Tiffany's three-year-old daughter, hopped to the ground. The minute her sandals hit dry grass she ran, black curls bouncing at her shoulders, plump little arms stretched upward to J.D., the man who was her uncle and was about to become her stepfather. "Piggyback ride!"

"Sure, dumpling." J.D. lifted her to his shoulders. Christina giggled and clung to J.D.'s head and for the first time in a long while, Katie felt a touch of sadness that her son hadn't yet met his father. In time. All in good time, she, told herself.

"Hey, Mom, what're you doin' here?" At ten, Josh had teeth that were still too big for his face, freckles that stood out and huge, deep coffee-brown eyes.

"Picking you up."

"Already?"

"You've got soccer practice."

"Not until five."

"He can stay—" Tiffany started to offer but caught the quick shake of Katie's head.

"Another time."

"Okay, but at least come into the house for a quick glass of iced tea or lemonade. There's something I need to talk about."

"It sounds mysterious," Katie said.

"Everything sounds mysterious to you. Believe me, this isn't anything you'll want to write in the paper."

"You never know," she teased. After having grown up in a houseful of older half-brothers Katie was overjoyed to discover she had not one, but two half-sisters. For most of her life she hadn't known that Tiffany was her sister; it was only after her husband died that Tiffany had decided to move to Bittersweet where her grandmother, Octavia Nesbitt, had spent most of her life.

The boys took off for the house at a dead run and by the time Katie, Tiffany and J.D. had crossed the shaded backyard and climbed the few steps to the back porch, the wail of an electric guitar screamed through the open window of

Stephen's room. "My son, the rock star," Tiffany said with a laugh.

"I wanna see!" Christina wriggled unsteadily on J.D.'s shoulders until he helped her down to the floor. She scurried ahead of them through the open door of the house and clambered up the stairs. The airy kitchen smelled of dried herbs and wildflowers that were bunched and hung from the exposed beams overhead. Artwork, schedules and old report cards decorated the refrigerator while a rack of copper pans was suspended over a center cooking island.

"I'll bet the boys are gonna love her wanting to get in on the action." Tiffany opened the refrigerator and hauled out a pitcher of iced tea.

"If they're like my brothers," Katie said, "they'll lock the door and tell her that because she's a girl she's not allowed inside. It's a plot by all older brothers to mess up their younger sisters' self-esteem."

"Didn't seem to take in your case," J.D. observed as Tiffany poured them each a glass.

"Careful, Santini, you're outnumbered here," Tiffany warned him as she sliced a lemon and dropped wedges into the drinks. She handed Katie her glass and waved her into a chair at the table. Leaning thoughtfully against the counter she asked, "So, are you ready for the wedding this weekend?"

"Can't wait." Katie took a long sip of tea. "How about you?" She pressed the cool glass to her forehead as Tiffany settled into a chair.

"I'll be okay, I guess. I'm thrilled for Bliss and Mason, but . . ." She let her voice trail off as she took a swallow of cold tea.

"Don't tell me," Katie guessed. "You're still having trouble dealing with dear old Dad."

Small lines of concern appeared between Tiffany's eyebrows. "Let's just call him John."

"Okay, so the fact that John Cawthorne is going to be there is bothering you."

"Not only that he's there, but that he's giving the bride away." Tiffany sighed and, resting her chin on her open palm, stared through the window. "It . . . it brings it all out in the open again."

Katie knew what her half-sister was talking about. The situation had been painful for everyone involved. John Cawthorne had sired one daughter out of wedlock and hadn't bothered to marry the girl—Tiffany's mother. According to Tiffany, there was no love lost between Rose Nesbitt and John Cawthorne. But he hadn't finished fathering daughters. He'd married a woman named Margaret from San Francisco and she'd borne him a second daughter—the legitimate one—Bliss.

Not one to ever be satisfied, John had started living a dual life—part of the year in Seattle with Margaret and Bliss, the other down here in Bittersweet where he met and fell in love with Brynnie Anderson, who, in between several husbands, carried on an affair with Cawthorne. As luck would have it, Brynnie, who already had three sons, got pregnant with John's third daughter. However, Katie had always assumed her father was Hal Kinkaid, her mother's third husband, whose name she was given. No doubt about it, the family situation was one tangled mess of relationships and emotions. "So, what're you going to do when you and J.D. get married?" Katie asked.

"I want to go before a justice of the peace."

"No way." J.D. set his glass on the table and skewered his bride-to-be with determined eyes. "This is my first and last marriage and I want it done right."

"I know, I know. Then . . . then I suppose that Stephen will give me away."

"Fine." J.D. seemed satisfied. "Now that I've exerted my

testosterone-filled rights, I think I'd better make a quick exit." He walked to Tiffany and brushed a kiss across her ebony crown. "Besides, I've got some paperwork to finish, then I've got to call Dad. I'll be down in a couple of hours." He hoisted his glass in Katie's direction. "Ms. Kinkaid," he said with a lift of one corner of his mouth. "It's been a pleasure. As always."

"You, too, J.D."

Carrying his glass, he walked briskly out of the room and Tiffany's gaze followed longingly after him.

"Boy, have you got it bad," Katie observed.

"That obvious, huh?"

"You could hang a flashing neon sign that reads 'I Love J.D. Santini' around your neck and it would be more subtle."

"Oh, well, I guess I should be more discreet."

"Not at all! Love's great." Katie believed it with all her heart; it just didn't seem to work for her. "Which brings us back to Bliss's wedding this weekend. How're you gonna handle the John situation?"

"I don't know," Tiffany admitted. Rubbing one temple, she leaned back in her chair. "What do you want me to do? Make up with the man? Let bygones be bygones and pretend that he didn't ignore me for over thirty years?" She shook her head and swirled her glass. Ice cubes and slices of lemon danced in the amber liquid. "I'm sorry. I didn't mean to sound bitter, and in all fairness, John . . . he's been good to the kids and to me lately, ever since his damned heart attack. But I can't just erase the past."

"No one's asking you to."

"Just to sweep it under the carpet for a while?"

"No way, but maybe . . . Well, if you want to, just give him a chance. That's what I've decided to do."

"You don't have a mother who uses his picture for a dartboard." Tiffany's lips pulled into a tight little knot.

"Nope. My mom married him. Imagine that." Katie let out a low, disbelieving whistle. The conversation had turned too heavy. Way too heavy. "So what about you and J.D.? When're you going to tie the knot?"

"Later in the fall, we think, though . . . Well, I don't think I'm ready for all the fuss of a big wedding."

"But you have to!"

"I've been married before."

"So were Brynnie and John."

"I know. My point exactly." Tiffany studied her glass and frowned. "We'll see. I think we should give it a couple of months."

"Why wait?" Katie knew she was impetuous to a fault but when two people were so obviously in love with each other it seemed silly to put off the inevitable. Though she tried to ignore it, she was a romantic at heart.

"Actually," Tiffany admitted, "there's something I was going to discuss with you, something that has to do with me getting married."

"What?" Katie asked, unable to contain her enthusiasm.

"Well, J.D.'s dad has finally convinced him that he and I and the kids should move out to the new farm that Santini Brothers is converting into a vineyard and winery."

"The old Zalinski place." Katie had already heard the news.

"Right. Even though J.D. argued with him and told him there was no way he was going to be involved with the company business again, Carlo can be *very* persuasive when he wants to be, so . . . as the old saying goes, he made J.D. an offer he couldn't refuse. Not only did Carlo give me the deed to this house free and clear, but he is offering us the farmhouse if we'll agree to live on the grounds. J.D. will still practice law for other people but he'll be a consultant of sorts for Santini Brothers." Glancing around the kitchen, Tiffany added, "It's probably time I started fresh anyway. I moved here when Philip died and both of the kids hated it. Stephen openly rebelled and Christina suffered from nightmares. All that seems to have gone away, but J.D. and I and the kids need a new start. A place of our own."

"Sounds great. Too good to be true."

"Almost. But the problem is I'll need someone to run this place—you know, manage the apartments and live on the premises. I thought it would be perfect for you and Josh. You could stay here rent free, collect a salary and still work for the *Review*."

"You're kidding!" Katie's head snapped up.

"Dead serious. You could sell your place or rent it out," Tiffany said, before draining her glass.

Katie didn't know what to say. She gazed at the kitchen filled with all of Tiffany's things—her baskets and shiny pots and hanging bundles of dried herbs. "I . . . I don't know. I'd have to think about it. Talk it over with Josh."

"Do. You've seen the place, of course, but let me give you the grand tour, show you what you'd be in for. Let's start at the top." They climbed two flights of stairs to a studio apartment set under the eaves. J.D. sat at a small table with his laptop computer glowing in front of him.

"Missed me?" he asked, as Tiffany approached him.

"Terribly," she replied dryly. "I just couldn't stand it."

His smile stretched wide and he leaned back in his chair to stare at his fiancée. The silent message he sent her fairly sizzled and Tiffany's cheeks burned red. "Well . . . uh, this is the smallest unit." She pointed out the tiny kitchen and bath, then, with a sidelong look at her husband-to-be, led Katie down to the second floor.

"He's incorrigible," she muttered.

"Along with a whole list of other things," Katie teased. When Tiffany eyed her skeptically, she added, "All good. All very good."

They toured the second story with its three bedrooms and bath. The rooms were compact, with high ceilings and tall windows. The master bedroom, Katie noticed, had a view of the carriage house where Luke Gates had taken up residence. She thought of the rangy Texan—a sexy, raw-boned cowboy with a slow-growing smile and a quiet manner. But beneath his easygoing exterior she sensed there was a deeper person, a man who had more than his share of secrets. Or maybe her reporter instincts were working overtime. Everyone accused her of searching out mysteries, stories and scoops where there were none. Nonetheless, she stared through the glass at the carriage house and said, "Tell me about Luke Gates."

"Not much to tell," Tiffany admitted. "But he's the perfect tenant. Quiet. Clean. Keeps to himself. Pays on time."

"He's from Texas, right?" Katie asked, spying the bridesmaid's dress for Bliss's wedding hanging from a hook on the back of Tiffany's closet door. Draped in plastic, it was a blue gown identical to the one Katie was to wear.

"Somewhere around El Paso, I think, although it seems to me he mentioned something about spending some time working at a ranch near Dallas. But I really can't remember. As I said, he doesn't say much." She slid an interested glance in Katie's direction. "Why?"

"Just curious." The truth of the matter was that Luke was the most interesting man to show up in Bittersweet in years. Not that it mattered.

Tiffany raised one dark brow. "Good-looking, isn't he?"

Katie lifted a shoulder. "Only if you like the cocksure, I-don't-give-a-damn cowboy type."

Tiffany laughed. "Don't we all?" she said in a whisper, as if she expected J.D. to hear her.

Katie didn't answer, only grinned as they left Tiffany's room, walked down the short, carpeted hallway and stopped at a six-paneled door with a large DO NOT ENTER sign swinging from the knob.

"Yeah, right." With a wink at Katie, Tiffany gave the door

a sharp rap with her knuckles, then twisted the knob and walked into what could only be described as a "healthy mess"—just the kind Katie's own boy loved. Cards, marbles, shoes and clothing were strewn over the floor, a bookcase was crammed with video games, books, baseball cards, tennis racquets and empty soda cans. Posters of rock stars and baseball greats decorated the walls, and the bed was a disaster, the edges of the mattress visible beneath rumpled sheets and a cover that was draped half on the floor. In the middle of it all, Josh and Stephen were thumbing through a sports magazine while Christina rummaged through the closet. In Katie's estimation this was a ten-year-old boy's idea of heaven. "We have a deal," Tiffany explained. "Every Saturday morning—which is coming up in a few days, Stephen—he cleans this up, changes his sheets and puts everything away to my satisfaction. Then he can go out with his friends and I don't bug him until the next Saturday."

"Awesome," Josh said, showing off his preteen vocabulary as if he knew the meaning of straightening up.

"If you guys need any snacks, I bought some chips and cookies this morning."

"Cool," Josh said and the boys, with Christina hurrying after them, scrambled out of the room.

"I quit fighting this mess because I had bigger problems with Stephen," Tiffany admitted and Katie remembered the boy's run-in with the police. Stephen had been questioned about Isaac Wells's disappearance because he'd been hired by the reclusive farmer to do odd jobs and had, at one time, stolen the keys to Isaac's classic car collection.

"How's Stephen doing?"

"Better." Tiffany sighed. "I hate to admit it, but J.D. has been a big help. Everyone told me that a boy needs a positive role model, a man to look up to, but I didn't want to believe it. After Philip died I wasn't going to ever get married again." She picked up a couple of empty cans and brought them with her. "Then J.D. came along—well, actually kind of pushed his way into my life. I had to let him because he was Philip's brother and the kids were his niece and nephew, but I never expected . . . Oh, listen to me. I'm rambling. Come on, let me show you Christina's room."

They walked through a half-open door to a charming room filled with a canopied bed, stuffed animals and a box of toys. A lacy dust ruffle matched the curtains that framed a view of the side yard. Katie's heartstrings tugged a bit. She'd always wanted a little girl, a sister for Josh, but, of course it wasn't going to happen. Having a daughter was part of a pipe dream—one she'd given up long ago. Now, she had to concentrate on her son and her career. Period.

In the next twenty minutes, Tiffany showed her through the living quarters on the first floor of the house, then pointed out two apartments in the basement, and an upper and lower unit in the old carriage house.

The boys were shooting baskets near the garage and Christina was chasing Charcoal across the lawn by the time the tour was over.

"So, what do you think?" Tiffany asked as Katie slung the strap of her purse over her shoulder.

"It's definitely a possibility." The truth of the matter was that she wanted to say yes right then and there. "I'll think about it," Katie promised, but she'd already half made up her mind. She could rent out her house and save money, spend more time with Josh and concentrate on her career without constantly worrying about making the mortgage payment. She might even be able to trade in her car for a slightly newer model.

"Right now all the units are occupied except for the third floor that J.D.'s using as his office. I'll start advertising the space as soon as we move. Uh-oh. Chrissie! Watch out!" Tiffany raced across the backyard. Her daughter had tripped and tumbled over an exposed root. For a second there was no noise as Christina's tiny face screwed up and turned a deep shade of purple. The scream was next, a pained wail loud enough to cause the boys to give up their game.

Tiffany scooped Christina up off the ground. "It's okay," she said, brushing bark dust from the little girl's tangled black curls.

Tears streamed down Christina's cheeks and she cried, "Mommy, Mommy, Mommy!" over and over again.

"I think it's time for us to leave," Katie said. "Josh! Let's go."

"Oh, Mom, can't I stay a little longer?"

Christina was sobbing and gulping air now.

"Nope. It's time."

"But—"

"Hop in the car, bud. Now!" Josh cast her a I-can't-believe-you're-so-unfair look, but she ignored it and turned back to Tiffany who was brushing aside Christina's tears with a finger. "Thanks for the offer. I'll talk to Josh and give you a call."

"Good."

The back door of the house burst open, then slammed against the side of the house. J.D. hurtled down the steps. His face was a mask of concern and his eyes focused hard on Christina. "What happened?" he demanded, sprinting across the backyard with long, athletic strides. At the sight of J.D., the child brightened visibly.

"A minor catastrophe." Tiffany was holding her daughter close and Christina, who had been quieting down, started crying hysterically again.

"Is that right? Looks pretty major to me. Come here, dumpling," he said, prying Christina from her mother's arms. "Let's make sure you're gonna live."

Christina's tears stopped and she offered J.D. an impish

smile that made Katie think her injuries weren't quite as painful as she'd let on. But then, she was only three.

"I'll see you later," Katie said as Josh climbed into the passenger seat. She waved to the small family as she climbed behind the steering wheel. She tried to start her car. The ignition ground and she pumped the gas before the convertible coughed twice, then sputtered. She swore under her breath and said a quick little prayer. Again she twisted the ignition. With a sound like the crack of a rifle, a spurt of blue smoke shot out of the tailpipe and the engine caught. "Good girl." Katie patted the dash. At least the darned thing was running. She only hoped that the temperamental car wouldn't die as she backed out of the drive.

"Can we stop and get a hamburger?" Josh asked. He adjusted his seat belt and leaned his seat into a half-reclining position.

"I suppose. I was planning pasta salad for dinner but"—she glanced his way and saw the expression of distaste on his oversize features—"I guess a bacon cheeseburger and a basket of curly fries sounds better."

"And a milk shake."

"Chocolate."

"Good deal, Mom." Josh gave her a thumbs-up. "I *hate* pasta salad."

"I know," she said and swallowed a smile as she reached over to rumple his stick-straight hair. Right now, staring out the bug-spattered window, he reminded her of his father; a man she hadn't seen in eleven years, a man who probably still didn't know he had a child. Her hands started to sweat against the wheel. For years she'd told herself that Dave didn't need to know he had a son, that he'd run out on her and left her pregnant without a backward glance, that he didn't deserve Josh's attention.

Lately, however, seeing all the mistrust and damage that had occurred because of her own father's lies, she doubted the wisdom of a hasty, emotional decision made when she was a scared, pregnant teenager. Wouldn't it be better for Josh to know his dad? To understand where he'd come from?

Wouldn't she, as a teenager growing up, have given her right arm for the truth? She owed that much to her son.

Chapter Two

"I hate to say it, Katie, but what you need is a man." Jarrod Smith, Katie Kinkaid's oldest half-brother, slammed down the hood of her old convertible and swiped at a mosquito that had hovered near his head. The minute she'd arrived home after dropping Josh at soccer practice, she'd called her brother to check under the hood. But she hadn't wanted or needed his advice on the sad state of her love life.

"I think what I need might be a new car." Katie frowned at her ancient two-door—a gem in its day—and wondered how she could possibly afford the payments on a newer model. Her gaze traveled from the single-car garage to her little bungalow, the place she and her son had called home for nearly a decade. Two windowpanes were cracked, the dryer was temperamental and the carpet should have been replaced years before. No, she couldn't swing buying a new car right now.

"This"—Jarrod thumped a greasy finger on the faded finish of her convertible—"is the least of your worries." Wiping the oil from his hands onto a soiled rag, he shook his head. Sweat dampened his brown hair and slid down the side of his face. "You've got Josh and—"

"And I don't need a lecture. Least of all from you," she said, irritated that the subject of her being a single parent was a matter for discussion. Just because their mother had married for the fifth time this summer and her two half-sisters were planning to "do the aisle-walk thing," as the media now called it, didn't mean that she needed to hook up with a man. Independent to a fault, she supposed people thought her, but she couldn't imagine being tied down to one man. Not that she didn't have a fantasy now and again. Raising a boy alone was no picnic, but she wasn't sure a husband and stepfather would help the situation. In fact, she was certain it would do more damage than good. "No one ever *needs* a man, Jarrod," she said, leveling a gaze at him that she hoped would burn into his hard-edged heart. "Least of all, me."

"I'm just telling you that it wouldn't hurt." He glanced around the backyard where a rusted basketball hoop hung at an odd angle from the garage and the dandelions battled it out with the crabgrass for control of the lawn. Weeds choked the flower beds and the patio furniture needed to be treated for a severe case of rust. Yep, the whole place needed a makeover—and badly. Even her old hound dog, Blue, who was lying in the shade of the porch, one silvering ear cocked though his eyes were closed, could probably use a flea bath, a teeth cleaning and a "buff and puff" from Elsie, the local dog groomer.

It didn't make Jarrod's suggestion any more palatable. She was a woman with a mission, imagined herself launched into a career in high-profile journalism. It was coming her way, and soon. She might already have been sent her one-way ticket to fame and fortune—if the anonymous letter she'd received in this morning's post was to be believed.

"A man, Katie," her brother repeated.

"You're like a broken record or CD, these days." Planting both fists firmly on her hips, she asked, "So what do you suggest? That I take in a roommate so that I don't con my lazy, no-good self-serving half-brothers into doing odd jobs like fixing the dryer or the dishwasher or the car for me?"

A crooked smile tugged at the corner of Jarrod's mouth. "Now, that's an idea." He swiped the beads of perspiration from his forehead and left a grease stain on his brow.

"Or should I just take out an ad in the personals, hmm? 'Wanted: Handyman and part-time father. Must do light housework. References required.'"

"Maybe you should just get married," he said, and Katie bristled at the thought.

She wasn't interested in marriage with anyone. Wasn't even dating. For a second her thoughts skipped to Luke Gates; then, horrified, she cleared her throat as well as her mind. "Our family has enough of that going around," she grumbled as they walked toward the back porch where several wasps were busily constructing a muddy nest in the corner of the ceiling. Blue struggled to his arthritic legs and his tail whipped back and forth. Katie couldn't let the subject drop. "If you haven't noticed, Jarrod, I don't have time for another man in my life. Believe me, Josh is enough."

"He's one boy."

"And a great kid," she said automatically as she tugged open the screen door. A jagged tear in the mesh was getting bigger by the day, but she ignored it as she always did. She had bigger worries, but she wasn't about to tell her older brother that she was concerned as all get-out about her son, that it was hard as hell to raise a boy alone, that sometimes it scared her to death. Nope, she'd somehow deal with Josh and whatever challenge he came with. He was worth it.

The interior of the kitchen was sweltering—nearly ninety degrees according to her indoor-outdoor thermometer. Though the window over the sink was ajar, no summer breeze slipped through to dissipate the smells of maple syrup and bacon that hung in the air from the breakfast she'd made hours before. Whining, Blue lifted his nose toward the sink where the frying pan was soaking in greasy water.

"Trust me, boy, you don't want it," Katie advised.

Swinging his gaze around what he called "a thousand square feet of chaos," Jarrod asked, "Where's Josh?"

"At soccer practice. Earlier he was at Tiffany's. He and Stephen have kind of bonded, I guess you'd say."

"Better than you and Tiffany?"

"Actually, Tiff and I are getting along just great," Katie said. "She wants me to rent out this place and take over hers." She explained quickly about Tiffany's offer earlier in the day. "So Tiffany and I don't have a problem."

"Real sisters, eh?"

"Half-sisters."

"Close enough." He winked at her and she grinned. "Like you are to me."

"Right."

"So John's getting his wish."

"Not completely, but this ragtag family is finally coming together a little, I think. Tiffany has agreed to be in Bliss's wedding and I *never* would have thought that was possible." There was still some envy on Tiffany's part because Bliss was John Cawthorne's only legitimate daughter, but things were working out.

Katie snagged a peanut from a bowl on the table and plopped it into her mouth. "I would never have thought that Tiffany would agree to be in Bliss's wedding."

"See? Finding a man didn't hurt Tiffany's disposition, did it?"

"Oh, get over yourself. So now men help women's personalities? Come on, Jarrod, that kind of thinking went out with hula hoops."

"I'm just pointing out a simple fact."

"I'm *not* getting married, okay?" Biting her tongue

before she said anything she might really regret, Katie took up her scratchy sponge and scrubbed the frying pan so fiercely, she wondered if she'd scrape the Teflon right off the metal. Though she relied on her brothers from time to time, they—especially Jarrod in his current older-brother mood—could be worse than irritating. "My marital status is, as they say, none of your business."

He had the audacity to laugh. "But your car is."

"Touché, brother dear," she said with a sigh. "Want something to drink?"

"Got a beer?"

"Nope. Bottled water, tomato juice and grapefruit juice."

"Thanks anyway. Too healthy for me. I think I'll pass." He grabbed a handful of peanuts and tossed them one by one into the air, catching them in his mouth—a trick he'd perfected before Katie had even entered grade school.

"Thanks for helping out," she said over her shoulder.

"Any time." He was out the door and it slapped shut behind him. Katie rinsed her hands and dried them quickly. Since Josh was at soccer practice, there was just enough time for her to do some research for a story she was investigating—the biggest news story in Bittersweet in years. She found her purse and slung the strap over her shoulder as she breezed out the back door. Someone had to solve the mystery surrounding Isaac Wells's disappearance and she was determined to get the ball rolling. One way or another, her byline was going to be on the story when it broke.

Astride a tired sorrel mare, Luke squinted against an ever-lowering sun. His bones ached from over six hours in the saddle, and sweat had collected on his back. Dust covered his hands and face and all he wanted was a cool shower and a cold bottle of beer. As the horse eased down a steep cattle trail, Luke eyed the rough terrain of rocky cliffs, narrow ridges and scraggly stands of oak and madrona. The place wasn't exactly Eden. Not by a long shot.

He'd spent the afternoon following deer and cattle trails that fanned across the hilly, sun-dried terrain. Thickets of scrawny trees offered some shade, but for the most part the earth was covered with brittle, bleached grass, rocks and a sprinkling of weeds. There wasn't more than five acres of level land, and not much more of rolling hills. Most of the spread was mountain-goat country, with craggy hillsides, narrow ravines and a slash of a creek that zigzagged its way through the canyon floor.

But it was perfect for trail rides and the small cattle drives he planned to organize as part of the working dude ranch he envisioned. Better yet, the eastern flank of the spread abutted a huge parcel of national forest service land that was open for the type of backpacking, hunting or camping he was going to offer to his clients.

He frowned and wondered if, for the first time in his thirty-six years, he would finally find some peace of mind. "Not a prayer," he said to the mare, a game little quarter horse who, he'd been told by Max Renfro, the onetime foreman of the place, was named Lizzy.

Especially not until he found Ralph's grandson or granddaughter. If there was one. Just because Dave had mentioned ten years after the fact that he thought he might have fathered a kid, didn't necessarily mean it was true. Luke could be chasing after the gossamer fabric of an old man's dreams—nothing more.

He clucked to the horse and nudged her sides. They started down the south slope.

A glint of metal flashed in the distance.

"Whoa."

From his vantage spot on the hill, he had a full view of the Isaac Wells place. It had been unoccupied since the old guy had disappeared but it had attracted its share of curiosity seekers despite the lengths of yellow police tape that had been strung across the main gate. According to Max Renfro, the sheriff's department was always having to run someone off the place.

Sure enough, there was a car in the drive—a convertible, he realized—and Luke felt an uneasy sensation stir in his gut. He reached into his saddlebag and pulled out a pair of binoculars.

Lifting the glasses to his eyes, he spied Katie Kinkaid, as big as life, climbing over the fence and ignoring not only the police tape but the No Trespassing sign posted on the gate.

Luke's jaw grew hard as he watched her shade her eyes and peer into the windows of the dilapidated old house. Luke had never met Isaac Wells, but his mysterious disappearance a while back was well-known. So what was Katie Kinkaid doing, nosing around the neglected spread?

"She's a snoopy thing," he remarked to the horse, then remembered that she was a reporter of some kind or other. She leaned over to look through one window as if she were trying to see beneath a half-lowered shade, and Luke's gaze settled on her rear end, round and firm beneath her shorts. His mouth turned to sand and he suddenly felt like a schoolboy for staring at her. Who cared if she was wandering around the abandoned farm? It wasn't any of his business.

But the rumors he'd been hearing in the taverns and coffee shops—talk of possible kidnapping, burglary and murder—cut through his mind. What if Isaac Wells had been the victim of foul play? What if he'd been killed and the murderer was still on the loose?

It's not your problem, he told himself and decided he was only borrowing trouble. If there was a culprit involved in the Isaac Wells mystery, he was long gone. There probably wasn't much danger anyway. The whole Isaac Wells mess was probably blown out of proportion, grist for the slow-turning gossip mill in this part of the country. He took one final look at the fiery redhead. She was standing now, one hip thrown out the way it had been earlier and as she turned toward him, he noticed the now familiar pucker of her full lips, the arched eyebrows pulled together in concentration.

He swallowed hard as his gaze skated down the column of her throat to the gap between the lapels of her blouse, to the hint of cleavage he'd seen earlier. He gritted his teeth and looked away in disgust. He wasn't used to the earthy pull of this woman, the desire that singed his mind every time he looked at her. "Come on," he ground out, clucking to the horse and urging her back down the steep grade.

He couldn't worry about Ms. Kinkaid or anyone else, for that matter. He'd learned long ago that he could only take care of himself.

At that particular thought, he scowled. Reaching flatter ground, he pressed his knees into Lizzy's sweaty sides. Though she was tired, the mare responded, her strides stretching as they reached the lower hills where the grade was much gentler and the stables were in sight. Her ears pricked forward and she let out a little nicker at the small herd that had gathered by the weathered fence.

"Yeah, and they miss you, too, Lizzy," Luke said, already feeling at home on this dusty scrap of land. All of the outbuildings needed new roofs, the siding of each was crying out for gallons of paint, and there were few windows that didn't require replacement of at least one new pane.

But he was getting ahead of himself. First he had to find out if Ralph's son had fathered a child around here. It shouldn't be too hard. He'd already started checking birth notices for ten and eleven years back. Tomorrow he'd drive to the county courthouse to check records there and, of course, there was always local gossip—as good a place to start as any.

He cooled Lizzy down and stripped her of bridle and saddle, then set her free in the closest field. With an eager nicker, she joined the small herd gathered near a solitary pine tree. A few half-grown foals frolicked around their more sedate dams while a roan gelding rolled on the ground. His legs pawed the air madly and he grunted in pleasure as brown clouds of dust enveloped his body. Luke smiled. All in all, the horses looked healthy and alert. Good stock. Ten head if you counted the two fillies and one colt.

The cattle were another story. They roamed the hillsides freely and were rangy and lean—not exactly prime beef. But they would do for what he had in mind.

His plan was to start renovations on the main house as soon as the building permits were approved by the county, work through the winter, then start advertising in January. In order to be in full operation this coming spring, he'd have to hire at least basic help—a cook and housekeeper, along with a few ranch hands and a part-time guide or two. Hopefully he'd have his first group of clients in by mid-May. He figured he'd run the first two years in the red but after that, he hoped to turn a profit.

He had to. All his hopes and dreams were tied up in this old place, he thought with a humorless smile.

Years ago, he'd had other visions for his life. He'd thought he'd settle down and raise a family, save enough to buy his own place and live out the American Dream. But things hadn't worked out the way he'd thought they would. His stomach clenched when he thought of his marriage. Hell, what a mess. Seven years of bad luck. Then the divorce. As bad as the marriage had been, the divorce had been even worse.

Well, it was over. A long time ago. Since then, he'd worked his butt off to save enough money to buy a place of his own and this, it seemed, was it. So he'd better make good.

He locked up, then climbed into his old truck. With a flick of his wrist, he turned the key. Tomorrow he'd start by cleaning out each of the buildings and checking on the permits again—just as soon as he'd done a little digging into the past. He figured it wouldn't take long to discover the truth. If Dave Sorenson had fathered a kid eleven years ago, someone around a town as small as Bittersweet would know. It was just a matter of time before he found out.

"Don't do this to me!" Katie cried.

She tromped on the accelerator of the convertible, pushing the pedal to the floor, but the car continued to slow. The engine had died and she had no choice but to roll onto the shoulder of the road.

"Perfect," she grumbled sarcastically. She was nearly three miles outside of town, the sun was about to set and she was wearing sandals that would cut her feet to ribbons before she could catch sight of the town limits of Bittersweet. "Just damned perfect."

The car eased to a stop, tires crunching on the gravel.

Valiantly she twisted the ignition again.

Nothing.

"Come on, come on." She tried over and over but the convertible was as dead as a proverbial doornail and wasn't about to budge. "Great. Just bloody terrific!" She thought of her half-brother and his efforts under the hood a short while ago. "Nice try, Jarrod," she grumbled, but couldn't really blame him. He was a private investigator, an ex-cop, and never had been a mechanic. Just because he was male didn't mean he knew anything about alternators or batteries or spark plugs or whatever it was that made a car run.

With a pained sigh she dropped her head onto the steering wheel and whispered, "A cell phone, a cell phone. My kingdom for a cell phone." Sweat ran down the back of her neck and within seconds a lazy bee buzzed and hovered near her head.

Katie drew in a long, deep breath, then gave herself a quick mental shake.

"Okay, okay, you're a smart woman, Kinkaid. When Jarrod worked on this he might have messed up and didn't reconnect a wire or hose properly. It's probably no big deal." She buoyed herself up as she slid from behind the steering wheel and looked under the hood. The same engine she'd stared at earlier in the day sat where it always had, ticking as it cooled in front of her. Everything appeared in order, but then she didn't know up from sideways when it came to cars. Gingerly, hoping not to burn herself or smear oil all over, she jiggled a few wires, poked at the hoses, checked the battery cables and saw nothing out of the ordinary. Not that she would recognize it if it was.

In the distance, beyond the last hill, the sound of an engine reached her ears. "Hallelujah!"

Ignoring all the warnings she'd been given as a schoolgirl, she stepped around the car and raised her hands. On this road she was most likely to come across a farmer or ranch hand, or a mother toting her kids into town.

A battered pickup crested the hill and her heart nosedived. She recognized Luke Gates's truck before it ground to a stop.

"Great," she muttered sarcastically. "Just . . . perfect." She told herself she should be relieved rather than disgusted, angry or embarrassed. After all, he was a man she trusted. Well, sort of. At least, as far as she knew, he wasn't a rapist or murderer or any other kind of criminal.

He parked just ahead of her car and opened the truck's door. Long, jeans-clad legs unfolded from behind the wheel and leather boots that had seen better days hit the ground. "Trouble?" he asked as he slammed the door shut.

"A little." Katie's heart drummed a bit faster and she mentally berated herself for letting his innate sex appeal get to her. What did she care if he was tall and lean and irreverently intriguing? She'd met a lot of men in her lifetime—*a lot*—who were just as good-looking, rebelliously charming and sensual as this guy.

Hadn't she?

"Looks like a lot of trouble to me."

"I guess. It just died on me," she said as he bent to look under the hood.

"And it was runnin' fine before?"

"No, not really." Standing next to him, her bare shoulder brushing against his forearm, she explained how the car had been giving her fits and starts over the past six months. "It zips along just fine, then something goes wrong. I have a mechanic or one of my brothers fiddle around with it and it finally begins to run again. Or, worse yet, it stops on me and with enough prayer and sweat I manage to get it going again, only to take it into the service station where it purrs like a kitten." She slid the convertible a spiteful glance. "Then the mechanics can't find anything wrong with it." Frustration burned through her veins. "It's what you might call 'temperamental.'"

"Maybe it's just old and worn-out. How many miles you got on her?"

"Two-hundred-and-twenty-some thousand, I think," she said with a shrug.

He let out a long, low whistle. "As I said, she's just tired. Think how you'd feel if you'd gone that far."

"Sometimes it feels as if I have," she grumbled, and frowned at the engine.

"Get inside and try and start it," he suggested.

"It won't go anywhere."

He cast her a look she couldn't comprehend. "Maybe not, but I'll get a better feel for it if I'm watching the engine attempt to turn over."

"Okay. Okay." She climbed into the car, twisted the ignition and heard the engine grind laboriously.

"Again," he ordered and through the crack where the hood was raised she saw his arms reach deep into the cavern that housed the engine. She pumped the gas and turned the key again. Grinding. Slower and slower, then nothing.

Three more times she tried before he slammed the hood down in frustration. "She's dead."

"I knew that much."

He eyed the sky, judging the daylight. "I think I'd better drive you back to town and we can call a tow truck."

"Wonderful," she muttered sarcastically, but reminded herself that at least she wasn't stranded or alone.

She hoisted herself into the passenger side of his truck, an older model with new seat covers and a thick layer of dust. Both windows were open and as Luke steered the rig onto the empty road, late-summer evening air streamed inside, tangling Katie's hair and cooling her skin.

Glancing at her watch, she frowned. "Oh, this is just perfect," she said, unable to hide her sarcasm.

"Something else wrong?"

Why did she feel like an incompetent around him? She wanted to look and play the part of the clever reporter—sassy and bright. Instead she felt like a frazzled woman who couldn't quite get her act together. "I'm supposed to pick up Josh from soccer practice in five minutes."

She folded her arms across her chest in frustration. "Damned machine." Casting her would-be savior a glance, she swallowed her pride yet again. "I hate to ask, but would you mind swinging by Reed Field to pick Josh up? It's pretty close to the high school."

"Not a problem," he said, and she fell back against the seat.

"Thanks. I owe you one."

"Don't worry about it."

But she did. She didn't like owing anyone; especially a stranger she'd barely met. This time, it seemed, she had no choice. Feeling the wind brush against her cheeks, she stared through the bug-spattered windshield and watched as the sun sank behind the western hills to stripe the sky in vibrant shades of gold and pink. All the while she was aware of the man beside her—a sexy stranger with a Texas drawl, that seemed to bore right to the very center of her. Angry at the turn of her thoughts, she tapped her fingers nervously on the armrest.

"You okay?" Luke slid a glance her way as he braked for a corner.

She stopped fidgeting. "Fine."

"So what were you doing over at the Wells ranch?"

Every muscle in her body tensed. "You saw me?"

With a quick nod, he turned onto the main highway leading into town.

She had no reason to lie, though the question made her edgy. She'd had no idea she was being observed. Well, a private detective she wasn't. "I thought I'd go check things out," she admitted, feeling suddenly foolish, like a kid caught with her hand in a forbidden cookie jar. "I've been by the place quite a few times ever since Isaac disappeared, but I haven't really pried much—well, not as much as I'd like to."

"Nosin' around for a story?"

"Not just a story," she admitted, trying to contain the excitement she always felt at the thought of uncovering a mystery and being the first to report it. "I think this is the scoop of the century around here." She turned her head to stare at his profile as he shifted down. His face, all hard planes and angles, was a study in concentration. "Where were you that you saw me?"

"At my new place."

"Your new . . . ?" Her throat went dry and she licked her lips as she realized where he was going to live. At the Sorenson ranch. Dear Lord, no. Her heart turned to stone and she had trouble breathing for a second. "Don't tell me you bought out Ralph Sorenson." She could barely say the name. A sick sensation curled in her stomach.

"That's it."

Oh, God. Her fingers clenched into tight fists. Slowly she straightened them. This was no time to fall apart. "You know Ralph Sorenson?"

"Sure do." He slowed as they passed the sign indicating they'd entered Bittersweet's city limits. A few streetlights had begun to glow as the first shades of evening slipped through the narrow streets and boulevards of Bittersweet. "Ralph helped me out of a jam a long time ago, gave me a job and treated me like a son ever since."

"Did he?" She felt the color drain from her face and her heartbeat thudded through her brain. "I suppose you met his son," she said, trying to sound lighthearted when deep inside she ached.

"Dave?" His smile faded and something dark and dangerous skated through his gaze as he glanced in her direction.

"Y-yes. Dave."

"I knew him," he admitted, his voice suddenly flat. Was

it her imagination or did he suddenly grip the steering wheel more tightly? "Helluva guy."

"Is he?" she asked, her own question sounding far away when she thought of the one boy she had loved, the one to whom she'd eagerly given her virginity, the father of her only son.

"Was," Luke said, flipping on his turn signal and wheeling into the gravel lot beside the high school.

Her heart turned to ice at the implication. Luke rubbed his chin as he pulled into a parking spot. He cut the engine and looked at her with troubled blue eyes.

"I thought the news would have gotten back here by now." She felt a chill as cold as Alaska in January and braced herself for words she'd never expected to hear.

"Dave Sorenson died six months ago."

Chapter Three

Katie's world tilted, the underpinnings giving way. All that she'd held true for years shattered, bursting through her brain in painful, heart-slicing shards. *No! It couldn't be. Dave Sorenson was alive.*

But the look Luke Gates sent her convinced her that he was telling the truth, that this wasn't some sort of cruel, hateful joke.

Josh's father was dead.

"Dear God," she whispered, her throat raw, the insides of her nose and throat burning with sudden, grief-riddled tears. "I— I . . . I didn't know." She cleared her throat and looked away, blinking rapidly against the wash of tears. Her throat was so thick she couldn't swallow, her eyes ached. For years she'd considered trying to find Dave Sorenson and telling him the painful but glorious truth that they had a son—a wonderful, lighthearted boy she'd named Joshua Lee—but she never had. She'd always thought—*assumed*—that there would be time; that the perfect moment would somehow appear for confiding to Josh the fact that his father was a man whose circumstances had forced him to move to Texas; a man who, at the time of Josh's conception, had been little more than a boy himself; a man, who at that tender age, couldn't have been expected to settle down. Then she'd thought, in this silly fantasy, that she'd eventually track down Dave and give him the news. She'd told herself he would be mature and would understand, and that Josh would somehow connect with his father. But . . . if Luke was telling the truth, it was too late. Josh would never know his father.

"Katie?" Luke's voice startled her.

"It . . . it can't be." She glanced at him and saw a storm of emotions she didn't understand in his expression. "He was so young—not much older than me." She drew in a long, disbelieving breath.

"I know." His face showed genuine concern. "Are you okay?"

"Yes . . . fine . . ." But it was a lie.

"You're sure?" Obviously he wasn't convinced.

"No. I mean, yes." She blinked rapidly, refusing to break down altogether. Inside, she was numb. Shaking. Grieving painfully. But she couldn't let Luke Gates or anyone else know how devastated she felt. This was too deep. Too personal. Dabbing at an escaping tear with the tip of her finger, she stared out the window. "I, uh, knew Dave. . . . He was in the twins'—my half-brothers'—class in high school and he hung around the house sometimes. I liked him and I didn't know that . . . that he'd . . ." She swallowed hard, then let out a sigh that started somewhere deep in her heart. "You shocked me, I guess," she admitted, trying desperately to recover a bit when her entire world seemed shaken, rocked to its very core. Forcing an empty, faltering smile, she asked, "What . . . what happened?" Then, as she looked through the windshield, she said, "Oh, no."

Focusing for the first time on her son's soccer team, a ragtag group of kids in shorts and T-shirts who were coming off the dusty field, she saw trouble. The boys' faces were red, perspiration darkened their hair and grass stains smeared their jerseys. Part of the team was still kicking a ball around, a few others were gathering up their bags and water bottles, but what held her attention was the group huddled around the coach who was helping a sweaty kid who bit his lip as he limped toward the parking lot.

Josh.

Her already-battered heart sank even further.

Luke reached for the door, but Katie was ahead of him, out of the pickup like a shot. "Josh?" she called, waving her arms madly. "Over here!" His face was so red she could barely make out his freckles and every time he started to put some weight on his right foot, he winced, then bit his lower lip. He had one arm slung around his coach's shoulder and he hobbled slowly. Though tears swam in his eyes, his chin was jutted in determination as he made an effort not to cry.

"What happened?" Katie asked when she reached him. Luke had gotten out of the truck and was leaning on a fender.

"Little accident," the coach explained. "Josh and Tom were fighting for the ball and Tom tackled him. Josh went down and twisted his ankle."

"Let me see—" She bent over and eyed the injured foot. His shin guards had been stripped off but the swelling was visible through his sock. She clucked her tongue and when she tried to touch his leg, Josh sucked in a whistling, pained breath.

"Heck of a way to start the season," the coach, a man by the name of Gary Miller, said.

"I can still play," Josh protested.

"Only if the doctor says so." Gary helped Josh to Luke's truck. "I think he should have that ankle X-rayed."

Katie nodded. "We will."

"Where's the car?" Josh asked as he slowly climbed into the bench seat of Luke's truck.

"It's a long story."

"Don't tell me. It broke down again."

Katie's head was beginning to throb. She didn't want to

think about what else might go wrong. First the convertible had broken down, then she'd heard the devastating news that Dave had died and now Josh was hobbling, his ankle twice its normal size. "Yep, the car conked out again."

"I thought Uncle Jarrod was gonna fix it— Ooh!" Josh sucked in his breath as he shifted and tried to slide across the seat.

"He did. Sort of. Come on, let's get you to a doctor." She squeezed onto the seat with her son and slammed the pickup door shut.

"I'll call you later and see how he is," the coach said and reached through the open window to rumple Josh's sweat-soaked hair. "It was a great practice until you and Tom got into it."

Luke took his place behind the wheel. "Where to?"

"Cawthorne Acres, I suppose." Katie was already thinking ahead. "My mom's probably there and we can borrow her car."

Luke twisted the key in the ignition. "That's clear out of town."

"I know, but—"

"Isn't there an emergency-care place around here somewhere where we can get that ankle looked at?"

"About half a mile that way," she said, pointing up the street. "But I hate to bother you—"

"No bother at all," he insisted and rammed the truck into gear. There was no reason to argue with him, so Katie guided him to the small clinic and felt pretty useless as Luke carried Josh into the emergency area. She'd been here before, not long ago, when John Cawthorne had collapsed and her mother had been worried that he'd suffered a second heart attack. Fortunately his condition had been diagnosed as heat stroke and he'd survived.

Josh's injury wasn't life-threatening. The worst that would happen was that he'd be in a cast for a few weeks.

Yet she hated the thought of him being in any kind of pain or laid up. Katie wiped her hands on the front of her shorts.

"Look, you can go now," she said to Luke, once the paperwork was finished and a nurse had come with a wheelchair to whisk Josh to the X-ray lab. "I'll call Bliss or Tiffany or Mom or someone to come get me."

"No reason."

"But it could be a while. He might have to see a specialist."

Luke eyed her. "Why bother someone else," he drawled, "when I'm here already?"

"You probably have better things to do."

He lifted a shoulder as if his own life were of no concern. "If there was something pressing, I'd let you know."

She was too worried to argue, and while Luke sat on one of the plastic couches and thumbed through a sports magazine that was several months old she fidgeted, paced, and tried not to worry. A jillion thoughts rattled through her head, most of them mixed up with Luke, Josh and Dave Sorenson. How could Dave have died and she not have heard about it? It was true that he and his folks had moved away over ten years before and they had little contact with anyone in Bittersweet, but they'd still owned the ranch next to Isaac Wells's place. Usually, bad news had a way of filtering back to a small town. Katie's heart ached and her head pounded with an overwhelming and desperate grief. What could she tell Josh?

For years she'd kept the name of her child's father a secret. Only she and her mother knew the truth. Even her twin half-brothers, Nathan and Trevor, who had known Dave in high school, had been spared the bitter fact that one of their friends had done a love-'em-and-leave-'em number on their half-sister. Her hands felt suddenly clammy, her heart as cold as the bottom of the ocean.

"Josh is gonna be all right," Luke said as she passed by

him for the thirtieth time. He gestured toward her anxious pacing. "You know, if you're not careful you're gonna wear a patch right through the floor."

He smiled, but it seemed guarded somehow and she wondered about him. From the minute he'd blown into town he'd been a mystery, a man without a past—a tall, lanky Texan with a sexy drawl and, seemingly, no ties. She'd fantasized that he'd held some deep, dark secret that she, as the local reporter with her ear to the ground, would uncover. Instead, he'd dropped a bomb that threw her life into unexpected and unwanted turmoil.

Luke studied her over the top of his magazine. "Can I get you something? A cup of coffee?"

"The last thing I need is caffeine."

"Decaf, then."

"Or maybe a tranquillizer." She knew she was overreacting, but she was a jumble of nerves today.

His grin widened a bit and the crow's feet around his eyes deepened. "This is probably the place to get one."

"I was kidding."

"I know." He slapped his magazine closed. "I think we should call a tow company for your car."

"Oh . . . good idea, but I need to be here."

"As soon as Josh is released." He snapped his magazine open again and turned his attention back to the article he'd been perusing. Katie sat down, but couldn't endure the inactivity. Seconds later she was pacing again, her brain pounding with the problem of how she was going to tell Josh that his father was dead. She wanted to ask Luke what had happened to Dave, but thought she had better wait until they were alone, and she felt more in control.

Within twenty minutes Josh was wheeled back into the room. He was wearing a brace on his leg and a woman doctor with short brown hair, wide eyes and round glasses approached. "Are you Josh's mom?"

"Yes. Katie. Katie Kinkaid."

"Dr. Thatcher." The doctor extended her hand and shook Katie's. "I think Josh here is going to live a while longer," she teased; "Nothing appears to be broken, but I'm going to send his X rays to a specialist for a second opinion, just in case. What I see is a pretty severe sprain. He'll need to lie down and elevate his foot for a couple of days. The ankle should be iced, to begin with. I've prescribed some mild painkillers that he can take for the first forty-eight hours or so and I'd like to see him use crutches until the swelling goes down."

Katie listened and nodded but wondered how in the world she was going to keep an active ten-year-old off his feet. Short of strapping him to the bed, she didn't have many options.

With Luke's help, Josh hobbled to the truck and they drove straight to the pharmacy where they picked up Josh's prescription and rented crutches five minutes before the place closed for the night.

By the time they pulled into the driveway of her little bungalow, night had fallen and the streetlights gave off an eerie blue glow. Crickets chirped softly and from a house down the street music wafted—some piece of jazz that seemed to float on the breeze. Blue, lying on the back stoop, growled his disapproval of the newcomer as Katie unlocked the door and Luke helped Josh up the steps.

"Hush!" Katie said sharply and the old dog gave off one last indignant snarl. "Don't mind him, he's getting old and grouchy," she said, but fondly patted Blue's head. She snapped on the porch light and the aging dog tagged after them as they entered the kitchen.

Once Josh was in his room and lying on his bed, Katie

propped his leg on pillows, then rinsed a washcloth with water in the bathroom. "I guess you'll have to use this to clean up," she said as she handed him the wet cloth and eyed his cramped room. "You know, Josh, if you agree to keep up with your homework and don't abuse the privilege, I'll bring in the little TV set that's in the kitchen."

"Really?"

"Mm-hmm. But homework comes first. School's just started, so we don't want to get behind."

"'We' won't," he promised with a grin.

"I can take care of that." Luke went back to the kitchen and returned to Josh's room with the thirteen-inch TV. Balancing the TV on the top of an already crowded bookcase, he adjusted the rabbit ears and found a baseball game in progress.

"Awesome."

Luke tossed Josh the remote control.

"Now, you promise to do everything the doctor says and keep up with your schoolwork?"

"Course." Josh nodded vigorously. For the first time since they'd picked him up, Josh smiled as he leaned back on his twin bed and immediately clicked the remote control to a different channel and one of his favorite sitcoms.

Blue, eyeing Luke suspiciously, slunk into the room and after circling a couple of times settled on the rug beside Josh's bed. Resting his graying muzzle on his paws, he glared up at Luke as if he were the devil incarnate.

"You be good," Katie warned the old dog and he managed one thump of his tail. She turned her attention back to Josh. "Now, kid, is there anything else you need? How about something to eat?"

Josh's dark eyes sparkled. Already he was getting used to being waited on. "Pizza?"

"Tomorrow, maybe. *If* we get the car back."

"Papa Luigi's delivers."

"As I said, tomorrow." She winked at her son. "Right now, I think I'd better scrounge something up from the refrigerator."

He pulled a long face, which she ignored. "How about you?" she asked Luke. "I'm going to whip up some sandwiches if you're interested."

"You don't have to—"

"Of course I don't. But I do feel like I owe you." He hesitated, then lifted a shoulder as they stepped into the hallway where the door to Katie's room was half open, almost inviting. Inside, a Tiffany lamp burned at a low wattage, reflecting on the windows and spreading a warm pool of light over the lacy duvet and the pink and rose-colored pillows that were piled loosely against the headboard of her bed. The decor was outrageously feminine, with antiques, scatter rugs and frills. Oddly, she was embarrassed that he was looking into her private sanctuary where she worked on her columns, worried over Josh, and dreamed about her career; a room where no man had ever dared sleep. She felt her heart pound a little and when Luke's eyes found hers again, she realized she was blushing.

"So, how about ham or turkey on white bread?" she asked blithely, as if men looked into her bedroom every day of the week.

"Sounds great."

"Good." She walked briskly away from her room and, once she and Luke were in the kitchen, she let out her breath again. Why seeing him so close to her most private spot in the world disquieted her, she didn't know; didn't *want* to know. But there was no doubt about it—this easygoing Texan put her on edge.

He looked awkward and big and out of place in her kitchen. "I'll make the ice bag the doctor ordered," he offered, as if he, too, needed something to do. "Just point me in the right direction."

"Good idea." She handed him the tools he needed, then spread mayonnaise on slices of white bread. He found ice in the freezer, cracked the cubes from a tray and smashed them into smaller chunks with the small hammer she'd dug out for him. Once the ice was crushed, he rustled up a couple of plastic bags, put one inside the other and brushed the ice shavings inside.

"You've done this before," she observed, slapping ham, turkey, lettuce and tomatoes on the bread.

"Too many times to count."

"Do you have kids?" she asked automatically and he hesitated long enough to catch her attention. She'd never thought of him as being married or having children, but then she didn't know much about him. Not much at all.

"Nope. No kids of my own. But I've spent enough time with teenagers to get in this kind of practice. I've worked on crews with kids where we bucked hay, strung fence, roped calves—the whole nine yards. Someone was always getting kicked, or falling off a rig, or being bucked from a horse or whatever." He glanced up at her and she felt her breath stop at the intensity in his eyes. So blue. So deep. So . . . observant. She felt compelled to look away to break the silly notion that there was some kind of intimacy in his gaze. What was it about him that made her nervous? She was used to men and boys, had grown up with three brothers, yet this man, this stranger, had a way of making her uncomfortable. She pretended interest in slicing the sandwiches into halves. "So you've done a lot of ranching."

"Yep."

"In Texas?"

"All over. Wyoming and Montana for a spell, but mainly Texas."

"And that's where you met Ralph Sorenson?"

He nodded and his eyes fixed on her with laser-sharp acuity. "Years ago." He handed her the bag of ice, and though there were dozens of questions she wanted to ask him about Ralph and Dave and his life, she carried the ice pack, along with a platter of sandwiches, down to Josh's room.

She couldn't help wondering what Luke thought of her and her cramped little home. Filled to the gills with memorabilia from her youth, antiques, and enough books to make her own library, her house had a tight, packed-in feel that bordered on cramped but felt right to her. A string of Christmas lights was forever burning over an old desk she'd shoved into a corner of the living room and her walls were covered with pictures and doodads she'd collected over the years.

To her it was home and, if she moved to Tiffany's house, she'd take every bit of her life—the mementos from her past—with her.

She didn't know but guessed that Luke Gates lived a more austere existence. She imagined he'd be as content to sleep under the stars with a buffalo robe for warmth and a saddle for a pillow as he would in a feather-soft bed with eider-down pillows and thick blankets.

Josh had inherited his mother's need for keepsakes. Posters covered the walls of his room, and model planes hung from the ceiling. His desk was littered with baseball cards, trophies, books and CDs and his floor space was crowded with toys he'd just about outgrown. "You okay?" she asked, seeing that her son was channel surfing, flipping from a docudrama about the police to the baseball game.

"Fine, Mom. Don't worry."

"I'm your mother. It's my job."

"Oh, right." Josh rolled his eyes.

While Blue lifted his head in the hopes of snatching a

dropped morsel, Katie handed Josh the plate. "Better than Papa Luigi's," she said. "You've got my personal guarantee."

"Sure."

"Ask anyone in town." She tucked the ice bag around his ankle.

He sucked in his breath and stiffened, tipping his plate and nearly losing a sandwich to the floor and the ever-watchful Blue. "Jeez, Mom, that's cold."

"It's supposed to be."

"I know, but, Mom, it's *freezing* cold."

"That's the general idea," she deadpanned. "It's ice."

"I don't want it."

"You have to. Wait a second." She went to the linen closet in the hall, found a thin washcloth, then wedged it between the bag and Josh's bare ankle. "Better?"

"Lots." He nodded, bit into his sandwich and turned his attention to the little black-and-white TV where a batter was sizing up the next pitch.

"Good." She patted him on the head and resisted the urge to overmother him and kiss his cheek.

By the time she'd returned to the kitchen Luke had settled himself into one of the chairs that surrounded the small table she'd bought at a garage sale three years earlier. His long, jeans-clad legs stretched out at an angle to the middle of the kitchen floor and he was sliding his finger down the open Yellow Pages of the phone book. "Tow company," he said to the question she hadn't yet voiced.

"Oh, right. Good idea." She hated to think of her disabled car and the hassle of getting it fixed. She couldn't imagine being without wheels for even a few days and shuddered to think that it might stretch into weeks if the mechanics couldn't find the problem or get the part. On top of the inconvenience, there was the money to consider—extra money she didn't have right now. Again she thought of Tiffany's offer and she realized it was just a matter of convincing Josh. But whether he liked it or not, they would have to move; it only made sense. She set a platter of sandwiches on the table and then poured Josh a glass of milk. Holding the glass in one hand, she paused to pick up a scrap of turkey left on the cutting board, then headed back to Josh's room.

By the time she'd handed Josh his milk, thrown Blue the morsel and returned to the kitchen, Luke was on the phone and instructing the towing company as to the location of her car. "We'll be there in forty-five minutes," he promised and hung up. "All set," he said, winking at her.

Stupidly, her heart turned over.

"All-Star Towing to the rescue," he elaborated.

"Great. Thanks." She scrounged in a drawer and found a couple of napkins that hadn't been used for her Independence Day picnic. Emblazoned with red and blue stars, they gave a festive, if slightly out-of-date, splash of color. "I, uh, appreciate all you've done for me."

"All in a day's work."

"Only if you're into the Good Samaritan business." He smiled and she felt herself blushing for God only knew what reason. Motioning to the stack of sandwiches on the platter, she added, "Please . . . help yourself. We believe in self-service in this house."

"Good."

"Is there anything else you'd like—something to drink? I've got juice, milk and water. Or coffee."

"Decaf?" he asked, lifting a blond eyebrow. "Isn't that what you said you needed earlier?"

"Yeah, yeah, but I lied." She measured grounds into a basket, then poured water into the back of the coffee maker. With a flick of a switch, the coffee was perking. "I think I need to be turbocharged right now."

"Aren't you always?"

The question caught her off guard. "How would you know?"

"Seen you around," he said.

"Where?" She was surprised he'd noticed. She knew she didn't exactly meld into the wallpaper, but she didn't think Luke Gates was the type of man who paid attention to most women. He seemed too aloof; too distant.

She took a seat at the table as the smell of French roast filled the air.

"I've seen you over at the apartment house with your sister and a couple of times in town. That convertible of yours is hard to miss."

"It's been a good friend," she admitted. "I hope it isn't dead for good."

"I'm sure it can be resurrected, but it might cost you a bit."

"Doesn't everything?" she thought aloud and reached for half a sandwich.

"I suppose."

The phone rang as the coffee brewed and Katie spent a few minutes explaining to the soccer coach about Josh's ankle. Gary Miller was concerned and they decided that Josh should forgo practice and games until he'd received a clean bill of health from the doctor. "Here, I'll let you speak with him yourself," Katie offered, and carried the portable phone into the bedroom. Josh talked for a few minutes, handed her the phone again and turned back to his program. By the time she'd returned to the kitchen, the coffee had brewed. She was pouring two cups when the phone jangled again.

"Could you?" she asked as dark liquid splashed into her favorite mug.

"Sure." Luke snagged the receiver. "Hello?" He waited, then said, "Kinkaid residence . . . Hello . . . ? Hello?" He paused and his eyebrows drew together. "Is someone there?" He paused again. "Hello? Oh, for the love of Mike." He hung up and stared at the phone.

"No one?"

"Oh, there was someone on the line," Luke said, glaring at the instrument as if he could see through the phone to the face of the person on the other end. "But he was put off when he heard my voice."

"Or she."

"Or she," he agreed, rubbing the side of his face thoughtfully.

Katie lifted a shoulder. "They'll call back if they really want me. Probably thought they got the wrong number when you answered."

"Maybe." He didn't seem convinced and his demeanor made her edgy. "You get many hang-ups?"

"My share: Along with solicitations and wrong numbers. Come on, eat. We don't have a lot of time if we're gonna pick up my car." She handed him a cup of coffee, then settled back into her chair.

"I guess you're right." He reached for half a sandwich and they ate in relative silence. It was odd, she thought, to have a man other than one of her brothers sitting across the table in her tiny kitchen. She'd grown up with three half-brothers and more than a handful of stepfathers, but she'd never settled down with a man, never felt comfortable with one in her house. There had been other boys and men in her life, of course, before and after Dave. She'd dated on and off over the past ten years but she'd never allowed herself to fall in love; had always found an excuse to break off a relationship before it deepened into something emotionally dangerous.

She'd been accused of being "too picky" by her oft-married mother, or "too flighty" by the twins, and "too bull-headed about that damned job," by Jarrod, but the real reason she hadn't settled down was that she hadn't wanted to. She believed a woman should stand on her own two feet before she started leaning on a man. Any man.

Besides, she had Josh to consider and a career to promote. Just because Luke Gates was interesting didn't mean anything.

He checked his watch and finished a gulp of coffee. "I think we'd better get rollin' if we want to meet the tow truck."

"You don't have to do this," she said, giving him another out. "I have dozens of relatives who would help me."

Luke nodded as he carried his plate to the sink. "I know, but let's just say I like to finish what I start."

She thought about arguing with him, but changed her mind. For whatever reason, he was willing to help her, and she decided to accept his aid. She dumped the dishes into the sink, told Josh what was going on, then locked the door behind her on the way to Luke's pickup.

As they drove away from town, the night seemed to close in around them. Stars twinkled seductively in the blackened heavens and a slice of moon cast a shimmering silver glow over the countryside. The dark shapes of cattle and horses moved against the bleached grass of the surrounding fields and hillsides and only a few headlights from oncoming cars illuminated the truck's cab as they passed.

Katie hugged the passenger door. Even with the window rolled down, the pickup seemed too small; too intimate. She told herself she was overreacting, but she noticed the position of Luke's hand on the gearshift lever, the way his fingers clutched the knob and how his sleeve was pushed up to his elbow, allowing her a glimpse of tanned skin dusted with gold hair.

So male.

So close.

Don't be ridiculous. He's just doing you a favor, for

goodness' sake. There's nothing more to it than that. All her life her silly imagination had run away with her and she'd been forever reining it in. Tonight; it seemed, her fantasy was that Luke Gates, sexy and mysterious, was trying to think of ways to be alone with her. What a joke. Yet she felt her heart pounding in the pulse at her neck, and couldn't ignore the sensual, all-male scents of hay, dust and leather that clung to him.

Get over it, Kinkaid. The last complication you, need in your life right now is a man—especially a quiet, mysterious stranger you don't have one scrap of solid information about. Think about Josh. Think about the Isaac Wells story. Think about your career. And for God's sake, forget any silly romantic fantasies you have about this man!

She bit her lip and, drumming her fingers on the edge of the window, she stared into the night until they crested a small rise. Her car, looking abandoned and lonely, was parked just where she'd left it.

Luke pulled onto the shoulder on the opposite side of the road. "Let's try it one more time," he suggested as he helped her out of the cab. His fingers as he grabbed her hand were warm.

"And what if it starts?" She hopped lithely to the ground.

"We pay the tow-truck driver and send him on his way."

"Just my luck—having to pay for service I don't need." She let go of his hand.

"It hasn't happened yet."

"It's not going to." Crossing her fingers, she unlocked the car and climbed into the dark interior. "Here goes nothing," she said under her breath and discovered as she turned the ignition that she was right. The engine didn't so much as spark. "Satisfied?" she asked Luke.

"I guess I have to be." He leaned one hip against the fender and tried not to notice the shape of her leg as she climbed out of her beater. She slammed the door shut with a quick movement of her hip and his crotch tightened. A million questions about her pricked at his mind, but he ignored most of them. He wasn't interested in her. Just as he wasn't interested in any woman.

He caught the scent of her perfume on the breeze and wondered what it would be like to kiss her. She was different from the kind of woman who usually attracted him—small and compact rather than tall and slim. He'd convinced himself that he liked a woman who was as quiet as he, thoughtful and soft-spoken, but this redheaded dynamo had changed his mind.

Not that he'd do anything about it.

"You're sure the towing company knows where we are?" she asked, her eyebrows puckering together in concern.

"Yep."

She checked her watch, glanced up the road and frowned. He imagined a dozen thoughts streaking through her mind all at once. "Your last name's Kinkaid," he finally said.

"Uh-huh."

"But your father's John Cawthorne, right?"

"Don't you know the story?" She turned eyes that were as dark as emeralds in his direction. "I thought everyone did."

"I'm new in town."

"But you know that Tiffany is my sister—er, half-sister."

"That much I gathered."

"I guess I should be embarrassed about all of this," she confided, as if glad for something to talk about. "The truth is, my family is what you might call 'different'—well, way beyond conventional. I didn't even know I had half-sisters until this year." She explained how her father had sired three different daughters with three different women, Bliss being the only legitimate one.

"No way around it, the whole thing was a scandal," Katie

admitted, "because rather than break up John's marriage, which would have been horrible, Mom married Hal Kinkaid and told him I was his. The only other person who knew the truth was John."

"And he allowed it?" Luke asked, disgusted with the man.

"At least he didn't put up a fight," she allowed, obviously trying not to show the little bit of pain she still felt over the fact that her biological father hadn't claimed her for most of her life. "John didn't want a divorce or to lose Bliss. So . . ."

"You grew up living a lie."

She lifted a shoulder and sighed sadly. The breeze caught in her hair, lifting it from her face, and Luke felt a possessive need to place an arm around her shoulders and pull her close, to hold her and comfort her.

"It's not that big a deal now. I never much liked Hal, anyway. He was a jerk, so I didn't cry many tears when he and Mom split up. You have to remember, it was kind of a tradition with my mother to marry a guy for a few years, then divorce him and marry someone else."

Katie shook her head as if to dismiss the negative sound of her last statement. "Mom isn't a bad person, just kind of flighty. Impulsive, I guess you'd say, especially when it comes to men. To her credit, though, she always loved John."

"Even though he was married to someone else."

"Yeah. Weird, huh?"

"To each his own," he said, though he didn't believe it. Marriage was marriage. You didn't step over the line. You didn't cheat. He'd felt the sting of that whip himself and had vowed at the time that he'd never be flogged again. "So . . . what about you?" he asked. "I thought Kinkaid was your married name."

"My what?" she demanded. "I've never gotten married, but I see what you thought—because my name is different from anyone else's in my family." She laughed nervously. The subject was touchy.

"Yep."

"I guess you'd say I never met the right guy."

She glanced away as if embarrassed and he mentally kicked himself from one side of hell to the other for the look of pain he'd brought to her pixie-like features. Still, he couldn't give up. There were just too many unanswered questions. "So . . . what happened between you and Josh's father?"

"Josh's father," she repeated, then cleared her throat and looked away. "He and I . . . We were just kids." Nervously she rubbed her arms and the sound of a truck's engine cut through the night.

Headlights appeared over the rise and Katie let out a sigh of relief—whether it was because help was on the way or because she'd managed to avoid a painful topic, he couldn't guess. "Thank God," she said, then forced a smile. "The cavalry did make it, after all."

With a squeal of brakes, the big tow truck slowed, then idled in the road while Katie looked up to the driver in the raised cab and explained how her car had died. He was a kid—barely out of high school, it looked like—but he wheeled his big rig around like a pro. Within a few minutes he'd winched the disabled car onto the bed of his truck. Once the convertible was secure, he filled out the paperwork to ensure that Katie's wheels would end up at Len's Service Station.

"I hope this doesn't cost me an arm and a leg," she thought aloud as the tow truck eased onto the road and was off in a cloud of dust and exhaust.

"Shouldn't."

"I've got my fingers crossed." The worry etching tiny lines across her smooth forehead gave him pause. He noticed the pulse beating at the base of her throat and the way the wind snatched at her hair.

For a second the urge to take her into his arms was so strong he nearly gave in. Standing alone at the side of the road with the sound of the truck's engine fading in the distance and the stars flickering in the sky, he was tempted to pull her against his chest and rest his chin on her crown. She was small and warm, smelling of lilacs and honey, and he knew she'd feel like heaven against him.

She glanced up at him with those luminous eyes and he had to set his jaw against the overpowering urge to kiss her until they both couldn't breathe.

The thought struck him hard and he shoved it quickly aside. He cleared his throat. "We'd better get a move on."

"Oh, right." She, as if having read his mind, couldn't get to the pickup fast enough. The entire way back to her house she sat pressed against the passenger door, as if she, too, was touched by the growing intimacy between them, and it scared her to death. She looked like she hoped to bolt the minute he pulled into her driveway.

He switched on the radio, played with the buttons and finally settled for a rock station that was usually more heavy-metal than he liked. They didn't talk much and he tried to ignore her, but his mind was racing down a path that was as dark as midnight; a path he didn't like.

Who was Josh's father?

The kid was ten or eleven. Just the right age.

But it would be too much of a coincidence for Josh to be Dave Sorenson's son. Too much. There were dozens of kids Josh's age who didn't live with their dads. Besides, Ralph wasn't sure if Dave had fathered a boy or girl or any kid at all, for that matter. Ralph Sorenson's grandchild might be just a figment of the old man's imagination, a pipe dream that he couldn't yet give up.

Still, the thought that Josh Kinkaid might be Ralph

Sorenson's grandson burned deep in Luke's brain. Like it or not, he'd have to check out the kid's birth records. He slid a glance at Katie as the lights of Bittersweet glowed ever closer. She leaned against the window of the passenger door and chewed nervously on a fingernail.

As if sensing him watching her, she dropped her hand and Luke turned all his attention to winding through the tree-lined streets of the small town. From what he understood, she'd lived here all her life. It shouldn't be too hard to check out the truth. The knot in his gut bothered him; she'd reacted strongly to the news of Dave's death, with the emotion of someone who was more than just a casual acquaintance.

Was it possible?

Could she and Dave have been high-school sweethearts? Lovers? His fingers tightened over the steering wheel in a death grip as he cruised around the final corner to her house. Hell, what a mess.

He wheeled into the driveway and parked inches from the sagging door of her dilapidated garage. From the open window of Josh's bedroom, Blue gave out a sharp, no-nonsense bark.

"Guard dog," Luke observed, switching off the ignition and trying to ignore the tension that seemed to invade the pickup's dark interior.

"He thinks he is, I guess." Katie managed a smile that was feeble at best. Nonetheless, that slight twitching of her lips touched Luke in a place he'd long forgotten. "My guess is that if Joe Burglar ever did show up, Blue would turn tail and run. Deep inside he's a chicken." She leaned her head against the back of the seat. "But he's loyal and good-hearted. Always glad to see me." She nodded slightly, to herself. "I've had him longer than I've had Josh. Mom gave Blue to me on my sixteenth birthday." She shoved her hair from her eyes. "Most of the kids were hoping for a car and all I wanted was a puppy to love and . . ." Her voice trailed off as if she'd said too much, as if she'd let a little of her soul slip past her outgoing, breezy, take-the-world-by-storm facade.

"Anyway, Mom gave me this gray bundle of energy with the brightest eyes you've ever seen. He wiggled like mad, peed on the floor and washed my face with his tongue and I . . . I just fell in love with him. He's been with me ever since." She cleared her throat and slapped her hands on her thighs as if to change the subject. "Well, so much for soppy, maudlin puppy stories. I, uh, guess I should thank you." Turning to face him, her eyes shining with a bit of unwanted moisture, her lips full over a forced smile, she started to speak again. "You've been—"

He lost all control. The resistance he'd so painstakingly constructed disintegrated as quickly as a match striking and bursting into flame.

"Wonderful— Oh!" Without thinking he placed his hands on either side of her face and kissed her with an intensity that he hadn't felt in years.

Her lips were warm and pliant, her skin soft beneath the calluses of his fingers. Her breath caught in a swift, sharp intake and Luke felt a rush of desire, warm and seductive, flow through his bloodstream.

She moaned, then pulled back to lean against the passenger door. He dropped his hands and inwardly called himself a dozen kinds of fool. What had he been thinking? Kissing her, for God's sake! He couldn't, wouldn't be distracted by a woman—any woman. Especially not one who might just be the mother of Dave Sorenson's kid.

"I . . . I . . . I don't know what to say. . . . And that—being tongue-tied, that is—doesn't happen to me very often." She bit her lip and stared at him with wide, forest-green eyes.

"Don't say anything." He grabbed the steering wheel. "I was out of line."

She reached for the door handle of the pickup. "Maybe

we both were. I"—she hooked her thumb toward the house—"I've got to go. Thanks. Thanks again." She was out of the truck and up the path to the back of the house as quick as lightning.

He watched her hurry up the steps, her shorts white in the moonlight, her hair bouncing as she ran. At the porch she cast one final, fleeting glance in his direction, then, with a quick wave, opened the door and disappeared into the cozy, cluttered little bungalow.

"Idiot," he growled under his breath as he flicked on the ignition. "Damned fool moron." Throwing his rig into reverse, he rolled back to the street, flipped on his lights and headed toward his rented rooms in the old carriage house.

He thought of her mouth rubbing so sensually against his, and his damned crotch tightened again. What was it about her that got to him?

"Damn." He'd been a fool for a woman before, a long time ago, and he'd sworn then that it would never happen again.

Until now, it hadn't been a problem.

But then, he'd never met a woman like Katie Kinkaid.

Chapter Four

"Ninny!" Katie glared at her reflection in the steamy bathroom mirror as she brushed her teeth. What had she been thinking, kissing Luke Gates?

The answer was that she had never let rational thought enter the equation. She'd sensed he was about to kiss her in the pickup, had felt the darkened cab seem to shrink, but she hadn't had the guts, the nerve or whatever-you-wanted-to-call-it to open the damned door and slide out of the truck before his lips had touched hers and the world had changed forever.

Worse yet, she'd spent all night thinking about her reaction, remembering the feel of his hands as he'd taken her face between his palms and gazed into her eyes while his lips had pressed so passionately against hers. Oh, Lord, here she was, thinking about it all over again, feeling tingly inside and stupidly wondering if he'd ever kiss her again. She grasped the sides of the sink for support and mentally counted to ten before letting out her breath.

"Get a grip, Kinkaid," she said to the woman staring back at her in the mirror. "You don't know a thing about this guy." She leaned under the faucet and rinsed her mouth.

Steadfastly she told herself that she wasn't going to be

swayed by one intimate gesture. She had too much to think about today, the first being her son.

Josh was still sleeping—the result of watching television until the wee hours of the morning. She'd checked on him, seen that his leg was still elevated, and changed the bag of ice that had long since melted. Blue whined to go outside and Katie obliged, filling his water dish and pouring dog food into his bowl on the back porch. Butterflies and bees flitted through the flowers that grew along the edge of the garage and two wrens flitted to a stop on a sagging bit of her gutter. She smiled to herself and told herself it was only sane that she should move.

Buying this little house had been difficult, a real stretch for her. She'd borrowed the down payment from her mother and convinced the previous owner, an old man who had been moving to California to be with his eldest daughter, to accept a contract with her. No sane banker would have loaned her a dime at the time.

But she'd proved herself by paying promptly each month and this little cottage had been her home ever since. She sighed. Now she and Josh were going to move. She supposed it was long overdue and the repairs that she'd put off—painting the interior, replacing windowpanes, cleaning the gutters and shoring up the sagging garage—would have to be done for the next tenant.

Leaning against a post that supported the overhang of the porch, she smiled as her old dog nosed around the backyard and she thought of Luke Gates—elusive cowboy with the killer kiss. Her whole body tingled at the thought and she pushed herself upright, slapping the post and telling herself that it was time to forget about one stupid act of intimacy. Inside the house, she phoned Len's Service Station and was told that her car was in the process of being checked out by the mechanic. Len would call her back as soon as he figured out what the problem was. "Wonderful," she said with more than a trace of sarcasm as she hung up and imagined she heard the sound of a cash register dinging each time one of the mechanics fiddled with the wires and hoses attached to the engine. For the fiftieth time she promised herself that she would sign up for an auto mechanic's class offered by the local community college.

But not right now. She picked up the receiver again and quickly punched out the number of her office. Winding the cord around her finger, she stared out the window and waited as the phone rang.

"*Rogue River Review*," Becky, the gum-chewing receptionist answered in her typically bored voice.

"Hi, it's Katie. I'll be a little late because Josh had an accident. Nothing serious, but it's gonna keep me home this morning." After explaining to Becky what had happened, she was connected with the editor and repeated herself, telling him about her car and Josh's injury. "I'll work here until I get the word on the car, then I'll be in," she promised.

She'd had a second phone line installed months ago so that she could, over the summer months, work from the house while Josh was home for vacation and was grateful that the powers-that-be at the newspaper understood.

She hung up, feeling a little better, grabbed a soda from the refrigerator and settled in at her desk. Hidden in the top drawer was the letter. Was it a fake or the real thing? She reread the typed words she'd memorized since receiving it in yesterday's post.

Dear Ms. Kinkaid,

I've read your accounts of my disappearance with some degree of fascination. Though others have written similar stories, your columns have been the most insightful.

Therefore I decided that you were the person to trust.

I would have come forward earlier, but circumstances have prevented me from doing so.

I will contact you again soon.

Sincerely,
Isaac Wells

Katie's heart beat a little faster each time she read the short note. When she'd opened the hand-scrawled envelope yesterday, she'd been stunned. Was it a prank or had Isaac Wells really reached out to her? And why? Why not go to the police or just come home? What "circumstances" had prevented him from returning? If he'd been kidnapped, he surely wouldn't have been allowed to write the missive. Was he running from the law? Or an old enemy? She pulled out a thick file and skimmed its contents—copies of police reports, the columns she'd dedicated to the Isaac Wells mystery, notes from interviews with what little there was of his family and friends.

What had happened to the old guy? Had there been foul play involved? Leaning back in her chair she tapped the eraser end of a pencil to her front teeth as she scanned her own articles for the millionth time.

Wells, who owned the ranch so close to Luke Gates's property, had been a loner. Mason Lafferty and his sister, Patty, were his only relatives living in the vicinity.

He had resided in the area for over sixty years, but had kept to himself, wasn't very friendly. Some people in town thought he was a miser, even a cheat. There was talk of him being involved in some kind of crime, but, as far as Katie could learn, it was all just gossip.

He'd never married, never fathered any children and had lived alone for most of his life. He'd gotten by meagerly, and had struggled for years to keep his scrap of a ranch afloat. But he'd had a passion for old cars and had owned a collection of classic and antique cars that he'd restored himself. He'd hunted once in a while, usually deer or elk. He hadn't been a churchgoer, and had been a solitary man who didn't talk much—a man whom no one, including the few members of his family, really knew. Despite local conjecture, he'd never been in serious trouble with the law.

Why would he take off?

Had he been coerced?

Had he been getting senile and just wandered away?

Or had he left on purpose?

No one, including the police, insurance-company investigators or his family, seemed to have much to go on.

Until now. Katie stared at the note with a jaundiced eye.

The letter certainly could be a hoax. The postmark was from Eureka, California, which was barely a hundred miles south. Anyone could have driven down the coast and sent it. His signature—the only part of the missive aside from the address on the envelope that was handwritten in ink—looked authentic, but it wouldn't be too difficult to forge.

So, now, what to do?

Katie took a long pull from her bottle of soda. A lot of people had been questioned about Isaac's disappearance. Ray Dean, a local thug who had been in and out of prison several times, was the most current "person of interest" in the case. Ray had recently been paroled, but most of the people in Bittersweet believed it was only a matter of time before he was arrested again for some kind of crime. So how could he be involved? She decided it was time for her to find out.

After letting Blue back into the house, she spent the next couple of hours at her desk writing the story about receiving the letter. She polished the text, then reworked an article about the new school-district administrator and another on the making of applesauce using other fruits and berries to change the color and flavor of an old favorite.

"Not exactly Pulitzer material," she muttered under her breath, because though the community was interested in the warm folksy articles that the *Review* was known for, she preferred something meatier, something with a little flash. When she'd completed her work, she e-mailed the columns to the office, then reviewed her notes on Isaac Wells again.

"Who knows?" she said, snapping off her computer as she heard Josh stirring. Rubbing a crick from her neck, she made her way back to her son's room and found him dozing again. She folded her arms under her breasts, leaned against the doorjamb and watched him sleeping so peacefully. *The sleep of the innocent.*

In repose Josh looked a little more like Dave than was usual. Or maybe it was her imagination working overtime. Ever since learning of Dave's death, she saw flashes of him in their boy. Which was ridiculous. Everyone who met Josh thought he was the spitting image of his mother.

Still, Katie saw the resemblance to his father in the shape of his eyes, the slight bump in his nose, even the way he walked.

And now Dave was gone. Her throat grew thick with memories she'd repressed for over ten years. She'd been young and foolish, anxious to grow up. Dave, just a little older than she was, had had the same wide brown eyes and thick eyebrows he'd given his son. He'd been a quiet boy who had moved from Texas with his mother and father. The first friends he'd made in town had been her half-brothers, Nathan and Trevor, two hellions if ever there were any.

Katie sighed as she stared at her son. How could she tell him about his father? That there had been a poignancy, a deep sadness in Dave that had touched her heart? Whereas

David Sorenson had been drawn to her wild brothers and their outgoing, tomboy of a sister, she'd been attracted to his shy smile and clever, dry wit. *Oh, Dave*, she thought, *why did you have to die?* And how? She'd never even asked. So stunned by the news, she hadn't voiced the question as there hadn't been much opportunity and she hadn't been sure she wanted to know.

Guilt, an emotion she tried to ignore, pricked at her mind. Dave, while he was alive, had the right to know that he'd fathered a son and, dammit, Josh should have met his father. When Dave and his family had left Bittersweet, she'd told him that her period was late, that there was a chance she was pregnant, but that her monthly cycle was irregular. He'd never called and asked what had happened, and by the time she was certain she was carrying his child, her pride was wounded, her heart broken, and she refused to try and track him down like some pathetic, unwanted woman. Looking back now, she realized she had probably made a mistake.

Her throat grew tight and she told herself that no good came from self-recriminations, that she could mentally beat herself up, but what was done was done. She just had to tell Josh the truth, and, of course, inform Ralph and Loretta Sorenson that they were grandparents.

Easier said than done.

A dozen worries skated through her mind. What if they decided they wanted partial custody of Josh, that this boy was all they had left of their only son? Conversely, what if, upon learning that Dave had fathered a child, they didn't want to deal with Josh, and felt that seeing him was too painful a reminder of their late son? What if they didn't believe her, thought she was lying, or worse yet, was trying to scam them because they were a wealthy family that, after Dave's death, had no heir?

Just as she chided herself for borrowing trouble, Josh

stirred and blinked. "Mom?" he asked around a yawn. He stretched one arm over his head.

"How ya feelin', bud?"

He wrinkled his nose. "Not great."

"How about breakfast—or lunch? It's nearly noon."

"Whatever."

He started to climb to his feet and winced. "Ouch."

"Hey. Use the crutches."

"I just gotta go to the bathroom," he complained and hopped on one foot down the hallway.

Don't nag him, she reminded herself as he managed to shut the bathroom door behind him. *He's gonna be grumpy for a while. He's in pain, but he's got to do for himself.* Rather than overmother him, she went to the kitchen and finished her cola. She'd just tossed the empty bottle into a sack on the back porch when she heard the bathroom door open, then the sound of Josh hopping to his room. He muttered something under his breath that she probably didn't want to hear.

Blue whined at the back door and while she held it open, she heard the uneven cadence of crutches hitting the floor as Josh hitched his way down the hall. She was wiping the counter when he paused at the archway leading to the dining room. "Is the car okay?" he asked, leaning forward on his crutches in order to scratch the old hound behind his ears.

"We can only hope. The mechanics at Len's seem to be baffled." She held up both her hands, showing him that her fingers were crossed.

Blue grunted in pleasure.

"I think we should get a new one."

"Do you?" Josh had been pushing for a new car for the past couple of years. "And give up the cool convertible?"

Rolling his eyes theatrically, he nodded. "It would be cool if it wasn't a billion years old. I think we need something like a Corvette or a Porsche or . . . or a Ferrari."

"Oh, sure. Or maybe a Jaguar or—"

"A BMW."

"In your dreams," she said, flashing him a smile.

"Mo-om!"

"Back to the real world, bud. What can I get you for breakfast?"

"We *need* a new car."

"You get no argument from me on that one. I just have to figure out how to pay for it." She tossed her sponge into the sink. "If you want me to make you something to eat, speak now or forever hold your peace."

He bumbled his way across the kitchen and half fell into the chair Luke had occupied the night before. "How about a double-cheese bagel?"

"You're in luck. There's one left." She reached into the cupboard and while opening the plastic bag with one hand, she pointed a knife at his bad ankle. "Keep that raised, okay?"

"Okay," he grumbled and hoisted his foot onto the seat of a second chair. His hair was rumpled and he was still wearing his soccer uniform from practice the day before.

"We'll have to figure out a way for you to take a shower," she said as she sliced the bagel and slipped both halves into the toaster.

"*I'll* figure it out."

"Okay, okay. Whatever." She bit her tongue to keep from saying anything more and scrounged in the refrigerator until she found a tub of cream cheese.

"So why was that guy with you last night?" Josh asked and she looked up sharply to find him staring at her with curious eyes.

"You mean Luke."

"Yeah. Why was he here?"

"He rescued me when the car broke down." The toaster popped. Quickly, as she slathered the bagel halves with cream cheese, she ran down the details of the night before and only left out the fact that Luke Gates had kissed her. That was one little fact that no one would ever know. It had been a mistake. A big one. She wouldn't be surprised if Luke was as embarrassed about it as she was—if he even remembered.

She placed the bagel halves and a glass of orange juice on the table in front of Josh.

"So why did he hang out? Why didn't you call Uncle Jarrod or Uncle Trevor or—"

"I offered," she interrupted. "But I guess Luke just wanted to see it through and make sure I was okay."

"Humph." Josh bit into his bagel and she let the subject drop.

The telephone rang sharply. Katie snagged the receiver before it had a chance to jangle again.

"Ms. Kinkaid?" a gravelly voice asked.

"Yes."

"This is Len down at the service station. I took a look at your car and I've got some bad news."

"What?" she asked, feeling a headache starting to pound at the base of her skull.

"You really need a new engine, or at least to have this one rebuilt."

"No." She felt a sudden weight on her shoulders. Even though she'd told herself she was prepared to hear the worst about her car, she'd held out a slim hope that the old convertible could somehow be resuscitated.

"'Fraid so. The rings are shot, the distributor cap needs to be replaced, the cylinders are only working at about thirty percent of capacity. . . ." Len rattled off a list of repairs that made her tired. In her mind's eye she envisioned hundreds of dollars flying out of her wallet just the way they did on cartoon shows. "So," he said, and she imagined him scratching the silver stubble that forever decorated his chin, "looks to me like you might want to scrap her out and start over.

For the same amount of money you could get a car a few years newer and probably a helluva lot more dependable."

"I—I'll think about it," she said and hung up slowly.

Josh's eyebrows lifted with an unspoken question.

"That was Len at the service station," she said, deciding not to let this one last piece of bad news bring her down. "Looks like we're going to have a funeral."

"What?"

"The car's officially dead."

Josh's face split into a wide grin. "So we're gonna get a new one?"

"Maybe," she said. "Yeah, probably." How, she wasn't quite sure.

"All-l-l-l ri-i-i-ight!"

"But the most important thing is, we're going to move."

"Move?" he repeated, suddenly serious. "Where to?"

"Tiffany's house."

"No way." Josh looked at her as if she'd just said they were going to be living on Jupiter.

"Yes, way. They're moving to a farm J.D.'s family bought—the old Zalinski place, so Tiffany wants me to be the manager of the apartments in exchange for living there free. We'll be closer to the main part of town and the school. We'll rent this place out and yes, I think we'll be able to afford a new car—just not a BMW."

Josh's smile fell away and his eyes thinned suspiciously. "Wait a minute. Doesn't the guy who was here last night live over there?"

"Yep." She'd thought about Luke residing right next door and she didn't like the rush of anticipation she felt when she considered how close they'd be. "But he won't be renting there for long. He's got a ranch outside of town."

"Good," Josh said as he kicked open the screen door with his good foot so that Blue could saunter outside and lie in his favorite spot in the shade of a rhododendron bush near the back steps. "'Cause I don't like him. I don't like him at all."

Katie bristled a little. "Why not?"

"I don't know. It feels weird when he's around."

That wasn't surprising, she supposed. Josh probably sensed that she was interested in Luke. At that thought she froze inside. She was *not* interested in him. Not really. It just had been so long since a man had shown her any attention, since she'd let a man flirt with her. Remembering Luke's kiss, she touched the tips of her fingers to her lips, then realized that her son was staring at her.

Quickly, fearing he might read her mind, she reached for the phone again. Cradling the receiver between her shoulder and ear, she dialed the number of John Cawthorne's ranch. "I'm going to see if I can borrow Grandma's car 'cause I've got some errands to run this afternoon. Will you be okay here alone for a couple of hours?"

Josh lifted a shoulder. "I'm not a baby anymore."

"I know, I know, but you're only ten—"

"Almost eleven." He stuffed the end of one of the bagel halves into his mouth and Katie heard the sound of someone picking up the phone on the other end of the line.

Her mother answered with a quick, "Hullo."

"Hi, Mom," she said, feeling warm inside at the sound of Brynnie's voice. "It's Katie. I've got kind of a crisis." Then, hearing her own words, she said, "Don't have a stroke, it's not serious—not really, but the car is in the shop again."

"I thought Jarrod fixed it yesterday."

"He tried, but as a car mechanic he makes a great private investigator."

"Oh."

"Anyway, it looks like I'm going to have to go car shopping soon because Len thinks it would cost more to fix the convertible than it's worth. Josh is laid up—a sprained ankle—and I need to run out and do a couple of things, so I was wondering if I could borrow your car."

"Of course you can!" Brynnie didn't hesitate for a moment. She might have had lousy taste in men and had more husbands than a cat had fleas, but she was a good mother and had always put her children first in her heart. Katie had never doubted how much she was loved. "I'll bring it down and sit with Josh for a while."

"But aren't you going crazy, what with Bliss's wedding plans and all?"

"Bliss has it all handled, believe me." Brynnie chuckled and coughed a bit. "Never been married and she's carrying this off like a pro. As many times as I walked down the aisle, I was rattled each time, let me tell you. Now, is Josh all right?"

Katie slid her son a glance. "I think so. His pride might be more bruised than his ankle." Josh, who was reaching for his crutches, didn't seem to hear her comment.

"Tell him Grandma's coming over and I'll take him on in Hearts or Pitch or whatever card game he wants."

"I will," Katie promised.

"Good. Now— What?" she asked, obviously turning away from the phone as her voice faded for a few seconds. "Oh, Katie, wait a minute, your father wants to talk to you."

Katie was still uncomfortable hearing John Cawthorne referred to so casually as her father. As much as she loved her mother, she couldn't forget that Brynnie had kept the truth from her until this past year; that Brynnie let her live a lie, even given her another man's surname.

"Katie?" John Cawthorne's voice blasted over the phone. "What's this I hear about your car givin' up the ghost?"

She went through the whole story again while Josh finished his breakfast, then hobbled into the living room. As she was ending her tale, John interrupted, "We've got lots of rigs out here. If you can drive a clutch, you can have the Jeep. It's just sitting in the garage collecting dust."

She didn't want John Cawthorne's or anyone else's charity. "I just need to borrow something for a couple of days."

"Fine, fine, but there's no sense putting yourself out much. Brynnie'll drive the Jeep into town, visit with Josh and I'll come pick her up later. Now, what's this about Josh hurtin' himself playin' soccer? You know, I told you that game was more dangerous than football. No pads. No protection."

She talked with him for a few minutes, heard for the dozenth time about the pros of football, which was played at the same time of the year as soccer, and how a fine, "strappin'" boy like Josh should get into a decent sport. She hung up, wondering if borrowing the car was worth hearing all the advice. As much as she disliked Hal Kinkaid—a surly, quiet man who seemed to forever carry a chip on his shoulder—at least he didn't butt into her life. In fact, he'd never shown much interest in her at all.

Growing up, Katie had felt neglected and had knocked herself out trying to get Hal's attention. She'd been flamboyant in high school, part of the "wild crowd" who drank and smoked, though she'd drawn the line at drugs. She'd flirted outrageously, gained an ill-gotten reputation and, of course, lost her virginity to Dave. At the thought of her one and only lover, she felt a pang of grief. In retrospect, getting pregnant was the best thing that had happened to her. She'd settled down, suffered the indignities and slurs about being an unwed mother when it wasn't quite as fashionable as it was today, but given birth to the greatest kid in the world. She glanced into the living room where Josh was flopped on the couch with his ankle, propped on the overstuffed arm. Nope, she wouldn't have changed anything about her life. It was just too darned good. Even if she did have to put up with John Cawthorne's opinions on every subject in the world.

When her mother came over to drop off the car, Katie hoped to speak to her in private, tell her about Dave. All in all, Brynnie was the only person in whom Katie could confide.

And what about Luke? Are you going to tell your mother that for the first time since Dave Sorenson, you enjoyed kissing a man, even fleetingly wondered what it would be like to make love to him?

She swallowed hard at the thought. Making love to any man was out of the question right now. She had too much to do to get involved with anyone. Even if she had the time, Luke Gates was the last man in the world she could dare trust.

And yet . . . she couldn't help fantasizing about him a little. After all, what would it hurt? It wasn't as if she would ever get the chance to make love to him.

"Thank God," she whispered and realized that a sheen of perspiration had broken out all over her body.

"Oh, honey, I hope you're not getting yourself into the kind of trouble you can't get out of." Worry pinched the corners of Brynnie Cawthorne's mouth as they walked through the overgrown vegetable garden at the side of Katie's house.

"I'll be fine."

"But a letter from Isaac Wells?" Brynnie bent over and picked a plump cherry tomato from a scraggly vine.

"Or someone who wants me to think he's Isaac." Katie lifted her hair off her neck as the sun warmed her crown. "I just wanted you to know what was going on before the story was printed in the paper. I took a copy of the note for me and one for Jarrod, then I'll drop off the original at the police station."

"I don't like the sound of this."

"I know, Mom, but this could be my big chance."

"Just be careful, okay? You're a mother." Brynnie slid the sunglasses that held her hair away from her face onto her nose.

"I know, I know, and there's something else I wanted to talk to you about." Katie's enthusiasm drained.

Brynnie took a bite from the tiny tomato. "Shoot."

"Luke Gates knows the Sorensons. He said . . ." Her throat tightened and she looked away. "He said that Dave is dead."

Brynnie froze. "But he's only about thirty."

"I know, I know." Katie shook her head and blinked back tears. "I didn't get a chance to ask what happened, but I will." She sniffed and looked away from her mother. "I can't believe it. I always thought there would be time to talk to Josh, to tell him about his dad, have them meet." Her voice cracked. "Oh, Mom, I really blew this one."

"Are you sure? This could be a mistake." Brynnie threw an arm around her daughter. "Maybe Luke got his facts wrong."

Katie sighed and fought tears. "I doubt it, Mom. Luke Gates doesn't strike me as the kind of man to spread idle gossip. I think . . . Oh, God, I think Dave's gone." She took in a long, deep breath. "And someway I've got to tell my son."

"Hold on a second, will ya? Don't rush into anything. This could all be a mistake."

"I doubt it," Katie said. "But I thought I'd ask Jarrod to look into it for me, find out what happened and then . . ." She shuddered inwardly. "And then I'll talk to Josh."

"This won't be cheap," Bliss Cawthorne said as she rolled out the blueprints she'd drawn for Luke on a long low table in her small office. "But I think it incorporates everything you wanted in the most cost-efficient manner."

Luke stared down at the drawings and nodded, but he had trouble concentrating. Ever since being with Katie the night before, he'd thought of little else than the fact that he'd impulsively kissed a woman for the first time in years. He prided himself in always being in control, in taking charge of the situation, in avoiding the pitfalls of getting involved with any woman.

Worse yet, Katie just might be the mother of Dave Sorenson's kid. If, indeed there was a child at all.

"So . . . I enclosed the area between the two existing buildings for the dining hall and added an exterior as well as an interior stairway." From the old blueprints and a quick look at the ranch house, Bliss had drawn a new set of plans according to his specifications and the latest building codes. And the blueprints looked good.

Bliss Cawthorne, Katie's other half-sister, was an interesting woman. Sophisticated and bright, with blond hair and blue eyes, she spoke and held herself well. Yet there was an earthiness to her, a down-home charm that was appealing.

Manicured nails slid across the pages as she explained how she'd created a large kitchen within a small amount of space, enclosed an area between the two buildings that would become an oversize dining room and dance hall when the tables were pushed aside, then incorporated three more bedrooms and accompanying baths on a second level. It would cost him every dime he owned. A big gamble. But then he'd been a gambler all his life.

"Looks good," he admitted. Finally, a place of his own.

"I think it'll work."

"I appreciate you doing this so fast." He'd only made the request ten days ago and even though Bliss was planning her wedding, she'd found the time, energy and imagination to draw up exactly what he had in mind.

"Had to get it done before the big day." She smiled, showing off perfect white teeth that he suspected had once been braced. "It's this weekend."

"So I've heard," he replied. "The talk of the town."

"Bittersweet doesn't have much to gossip about." She rolled the plans into tubes and snapped them closed with rubber bands. "Well, except for my family. I guess we keep the rumor mill in business." She blushed a little as she slapped the plans into his open palm. "If you'd like to come, it's this Sunday at the church in the square and we're having a reception afterward at the Reed Hotel just out of town." She grinned up at him and seemed to sense his unease. "I know that this is sudden, but you are my client and Mason and I would love it if you'd attend."

No way, José. "Thanks, but I don't think I'll make it." He knew the invitation was just because she felt obligated to hand it out. Besides, he wasn't interested.

"If you change your mind, the wedding's at seven and the reception will probably last all night."

A bell over the door to the office tinkled and Luke looked up to see Katie, dressed in a white-and-blue sundress, dash inside. "Bliss, I wondered— Oh." For a moment the red-haired locomotive stopped dead in her tracks. "Hi," she managed, recovering herself as she spied Luke and a rosy color invaded her cheeks as it had her half-sister's a heartbeat earlier. Her eyes held his and in a second he remembered the kiss—the damned touching of lips that had kept him awake all last night. He'd thought of her, fantasized about her, then dreamed of making love to her. He'd woken up on fire and had taken the longest cold shower of his life.

"Get the car fixed?" he asked and she shook her head, fiery red curls brushing her nape in a movement he found ludicrously sensual.

"Nope. You were right, it's dead." She hooked her thumb

to the window overlooking the parking lot. "I'm borrowing one of John's rigs."

"So you two know each other?" Bliss asked thoughtfully.

"Luke helped me out yesterday," Katie explained, giving her half-sister the blow-by-blow of her evening.

Bliss's forehead had wrinkled as Katie finished. "But Josh is okay—the ankle is all right?"

"He'll be fine. For the moment he's enjoying being king of the roost."

"Good, good." Folding her arms across her chest, Bliss asked, "Okay, so now that I know Josh will survive and the car won't, why don't you tell me what you think you were doing poking around Isaac Wells's place? I thought it was off-limits to everybody but the police."

Katie lifted a shoulder. "I know, but I was hoping to find something—some sort of clue, I guess, to what happened to him."

"I thought that was the sheriff's department's job."

"Yeah, but I was . . . well, hoping to look at it with different eyes—a woman's eyes, a reporter's eyes—that I might see something everyone else had missed." She was excited now, talking rapidly, and it gave Luke some insight into how much she loved her job. Katie Kinkaid, ace reporter.

"Isaac's been gone for months," Bliss reminded.

"I know, I know, but—" Katie hesitated, then looked as if she'd decided that confiding in her sister and Luke would be all right. Her cheeks flushed and a smile pulled at the corners of her full mouth. "I want the story. Period. I'm tired of writing about bridge-club meetings and covering the school-board agenda."

"You want something with some mystery to it. Some adventure." Bliss nodded, as if she'd heard it all before.

"At least." Katie looked away and Luke noticed the column of her throat, the way it disappeared into the tangle of bones between her shoulders. She was sexy as hell and didn't seem to know it.

He wondered about the men in her life, then quickly shoved that wayward thought aside. What did it matter whom she dated, whom she kissed, who had experienced the rush of making love to her? His jaw tightened and he fought a ridiculous envy of those unnamed men. All that he cared about was whether or not Dave Sorenson had fathered her child over a decade ago.

"Well, I'd better be shovin' off," he said. "You'll bill me, right?"

"You can count on it."

"Bliss did some work for you?" Katie asked, as if eager to know what he was doing in her half-sister's office. Luke noticed her eyelids crinkle at the corners as if she was trying to put two-and-two together.

No way out of it now. "Bliss drew up some plans for me for the ranch house. I'm going to expand it."

"Oh."

"So you already know that he owns the Sorenson place," Bliss added and Katie again felt that dull ache in her heart, the one that reminded her Dave was dead.

"I heard."

"And I heard that you might be moving into Tiffany's place," Bliss said.

Luke froze. Katie was going to live next door to him?

"I'm thinking about it."

"That's what Tiffany said when I bumped into her this morning."

"I've already talked to Josh and he's game, so I guess I'll rent my place and move in whenever Tiffany and J.D. settle into the farm that they're turning into a winery. I was on my way next door to the insurance office to give Tiffany the news but I wanted to stop by here and see how the wedding plans are going."

"Hectic," Bliss replied. "This is my last day of work"—she pointed a long finger at Luke's blueprints and skewered him with her blue gaze—"so if you want any changes, they'll have to wait for a couple of weeks until I get back."

"They're fine," he assured her and reached for the handle of the door. "Thanks."

"You're welcome." Before he could yank the door open, Bliss added, "I was just trying to talk Luke into attending the wedding and reception."

"Oh, you should come." Katie turned and gave him her thousand-watt smile. "It's going to be the event of the summer."

"I'm not usually one for 'events.'"

"Well, think about it. Just drop by the reception, if you'd like," Bliss invited and he inclined his head.

"I just might." He left feeling that he'd somehow been manipulated by the two sisters, but he didn't much care. He wouldn't attend the wedding, but, hell, he might as well check out the reception.

But it had nothing to do with the fact that Katie Kinkaid would be there, he told himself. Absolutely nothing.

Chapter Five

"You think this is authentic?" Jarrod asked as he eyed a copy of the note Katie had received from Isaac Wells.

Dressed only in frayed cutoff jeans, he toweled his hair and stood dripping on the rocky shore of the Rogue River. His house, a small single-story cabin of shake and shingles, overlooked this wild stretch of water and had been his home for nearly ten years. Jarrod, solitary by nature, lived alone here with his dog and seemed to like it just that way. No women to bother him. No children to care for.

"I wish I knew," Katie admitted. "It would make things a whole lot easier."

"What did the police say?"

"Just that they'd look into it."

A half-grown black Lab bounded up and Jarrod bent down to pick up a stick. "Here ya go, Watson," he said, hurling the stick into the water. The dog jetted into the swift current and caught up with the bobbing piece of wood.

"Do you think it's a hoax?"

"Could be." Jarrod scowled and squinted as the sun lowered over a ridge of hills to the west. Overhead a hawk slowly circled in the hazy blue sky. "But why?" He shoved his hair out of his eyes and chewed on his lower lip. "I don't like it. Something's not right."

"What do you mean?"

"Why would Isaac Wells—or even an imposter, for that matter—want attention from you?"

"Publicity?"

"A man who spent most of his life as a recluse?" Jarrod's eyes followed the dog as he galloped out of the river and, with the prized stick in his mouth, shook the water from his coat. "Tell me you're not going to print it."

"Too late."

"Not smart, sis." His eyebrows slammed into a single, intense line. "You might be playing right into his hands."

"Whose? Into whose hands? Ray Dean's?"

"I wish I knew," Jarrod said.

"Well, maybe we'll finally find out."

"Be careful, Katie. One guy's already missing and don't even think about messing with the likes of Ray Dean if he's involved—and even if he isn't. The guy is a criminal, remember that." Jarrod's eyes held hers for a second. "I wouldn't want anything to happen to you."

"It won't. I'm always careful," she said flippantly. "I just stopped by because I thought you'd want to know."

Jarrod flung the wet piece of wood back into the river.

"I do." His scowl was so dark she nearly laughed.

"Better crack this case quick," she teased, "or I might just beat you to it." She checked her watch and sighed. "Look, I've got to get a move on. I've got another errand to run before I go home. Mom's hanging out with Josh and I said I'd be back by five." With a wave she was off and she refused to let Jarrod's warnings give her pause. He was just in a bad mood because this was one case he hadn't been able to solve. The deputy she'd spoken with at the sheriff's department hadn't been any happier with her. He'd taken the note and asked her if she'd touched it, which, of course, she had, though she'd been cautious as she'd figured someone would check it for fingerprints.

"Curiouser and curiouser," she whispered to herself as she drove away from Jarrod's hermit's abode in John Cawthorne's Jeep. At a fork in the road, she turned toward the hills and angled away from town. As she passed Isaac Wells's ranch she thought fleetingly of the mystery surrounding him, but didn't turn off until she reached the Sorenson place. Her heart thudded with painful memories as she wheeled through an open gate where wildflowers and brambles grew in profusion. The smell of dust, dry grass and Queen Anne's lace hung in the late-summer air as the Jeep bounced over the ruts and potholes of a lane that was once familiar to her.

How had she let the years roll by without once trying to contact Dave, to tell him about Josh? Why had she let pride—always her enemy—come between her and the truth? She swallowed back a lump in her throat as she angled the Jeep around a bend in the lane and the Sorenson cabin came into view. A rambling single-story with a loft, it sprawled between thickets of pine and oak.

Wearing only worn jeans that looked as if they might fall off his hips at any second and a pair of weathered rawhide gloves, Luke was straining against a wayward post in the fence near the barn, trying to push it into an upright position. His booted feet were planted solidly in the dry earth, one muscular shoulder braced against the graying post. Jaw set, lips pulled back with effort, he glanced in her direction, then gave one final shove. The post slowly inched upward and Luke, muscles straining, sweat rolling down his face and back, moved one leg and kicked a pile of stones into the widening hole at the post's base.

Katie felt a jab of disappointment that he wasn't glad to see her, then swept that wayward emotion aside. Feigning disinterest in his sun-bronzed chest with its mat of gold hair, she pretended not to notice how those curly, sun-kissed sworls arrowed down to his navel to disappear in a gilded ribbon past the worn waistband of his jeans.

Her heart fluttered and her stomach did a slow, sensuous roll as he straightened, crossed his arms over his chest and she noticed the striated ridges of his flexed shoulder muscles. Perspiration glistened on his chest, face and arms; dust clung to his skin.

She climbed out of the Jeep and managed a smile that felt as frail and phony as it probably appeared. Just being on Sorenson ground gave her pause. "Hi."

"The convertible's still not workin'?" He kicked the remainder of the stones into the hole, then tested the post by trying to move it with his hands. It held and he grunted in satisfaction.

"No . . . And Len seems to think it's a goner." Lifting a shoulder, she tried to sound cheerier than she felt. "I guess I'm in the market for new wheels."

"Humph." He yanked off his gloves and stuffed them into a back pocket. "Somethin' I can do for you?"

Her heart pounded and her throat went dry. She remembered his hands on either side of her face as he'd kissed her, the desire that had burned through her body. Clearing her throat, she looked away. "Thank you again for helping with the car . . . it's been acting up a lot. I don't know what I would have done if you hadn't come along."

"It was nothing. Really. Don't think anything of it."

She managed a smile and glanced around the outbuildings. "So this ranch was the Sorensons'."

"That's right."

"And you said you knew Dave."

Luke nodded slowly, his eyes narrowing. "Since I was about twenty when I went to work for his old man. I was hell on wheels, in trouble all the time, and Ralph took a chance on me. Gave me a job. That's how I met Dave."

"You became friends?"

"For the most part, when he was around," Luke said as he walked toward the ranch house. Katie fell into step with him. "He joined the army a little while after high school, became career military."

"What happened to him?" Katie asked as they reached the shade of the wide front porch.

Luke frowned. "I'm not sure anyone knows all the details, but he was killed this past year in a freak accident. Helicopter crash during routine maneuvers."

Katie's blood turned to ice. She closed her eyes and held on to the rail by the steps to steady herself.

"Ralph and Loretta took it pretty hard," Luke said.

"I don't blame them." She ran a trembling hand over her forehead. "Lord, what a blow."

"I'm sorry."

She swallowed hard and sagged against the rail. Dozens of memories, yellowed with age, their edges softened as the years had passed, swam through her mind. "So am I," she said roughly, then cleared her throat.

"You knew him well?"

Better than anyone, she thought, then realized that wasn't the truth, either. Dave had kept to himself, for the most part. As naive as she'd been all those years ago, she'd sensed that he was holding back, that even during their lovemaking there had been a part of him he'd kept hidden and remote; a part she would never understand. "I'm not sure anyone really knew Dave," she admitted. "As I said, he didn't live here all that long."

"A year or two, the way Ralph talks about it."

"Yeah, about eighteen months, I think."

"He involved with any girls back then?" Luke asked, and she stiffened.

"I, uh, I don't think he dated much. Why?" She couldn't help but ask. There were questions in his eyes she didn't understand, didn't want to trust.

"Ralph seemed to think he might've had a girlfriend."

"He could have," she hedged. Though tempted, she wasn't about to tell this sexy stranger that she'd been involved with Dave Sorenson. Not until she'd spoken with her son. Josh deserved the truth. All of it. "So . . . tell me about your plans."

She needed to change the subject. She'd dwelled enough on the subject of Dave Sorenson. She'd mourn her first and only lover in private and then confide in her son. Josh might hate her for keeping the truth from him, might never forgive her for not allowing him the privilege of knowing his father, but she couldn't keep Dave's death from him.

Luke hesitated for a second, as if he had more questions, but he eyed her, tugged on his lip and lifted a shoulder. "Let me show you around."

He opened the door and led her into the main house, a building she'd been inside only twice before, long ago, and both times in the middle of the night, with Dave holding her hand and leading her through the darkened rooms.

It hadn't changed much. From the looks of the curtains, she imagined that they were at least twenty years old; the furniture, too, felt as if it had been in the house for two decades. A couch with wooden arms and feet, tables nicked and scarred, a leather recliner that was worn in the arms and where a man's head had rested.

"The entire place will be remodeled," he said as they walked through a small eating area and into the kitchen. He showed her how he planned to push out walls and connect the main house with what had once been the detached garage and bunkhouse. That area would be more rustic, with bunk beds and shared baths, while in the existing house the attic would be expanded into bedrooms with private baths and a back stairs that led to the main hall that could be used for dining or dancing or general recreation.

"If things work out, I'll expand the stables in the next

year or two," he said, leading her down a short hallway and past the door to Dave's room. She felt a sliver of pain pierce her heart again but ignored it as he opened the door to the master bedroom, an expansive room big enough for a king-size bed and an armchair or two. A stone fireplace, dusty and missing a few rocks, filled one corner and a mouse scurried quickly into a hole in the mortar. Long horns were still displayed above a thick mantel, and from one of the exposed beams of the ceiling a wagon-wheel chandelier hung from a wrought-iron chain.

"In time this'll be my living quarters," he said with a crooked smile. "I was going to make it the only guest suite in the place, but decided I didn't want to bunk with the hands." He walked to a window and cranked it open. A soft summer breeze slipped into the room, carrying with it the scent of roses and honeysuckle.

"It'll be nice." She was already envisioning the room as it would be. With a few dollars and a lot of elbow grease, the hardwood floors would gleam, clearpaned windows would give a view of the garden and beyond, to the fenced fields where the hills rose sharply and trees dotted the fence line. In her mind's eye she saw volumes filling the now empty bookcase near the fireplace and warm coals glowing in the grate on a cold winter's night.

"Why did you decide to settle in Oregon?" she asked as Luke opened a door that led from the bedroom to the backyard.

"Ralph and I had a deal. I worked for him for ten years and he kept half of my salary—invested it in some of his real estate. I was supposed to end up with a small spread of his outside Dallas, but he really wanted to get rid of this place, which is quite a bit larger." Luke eyed the craggy hillsides. "I needed an excuse to get out of Texas. This was it." He turned his attention back to her and she felt the weight of his gaze, hot and steady, against her skin.

"Why did you want to leave Texas?"

His lips tightened just a fraction, as if he didn't like the intrusion into his personal life. "It was time. I lived there most of my life."

She sensed there was more to his story, but that no amount of prying would get it out of him. Luke Gates was a private man with a past he preferred to keep to himself. A secretive man. The kind to avoid.

They walked to the front of the house, past the overgrown rose garden and a sagging clothesline. Luke frowned as he eyed the grounds. "It's gonna take a lot of work."

"But it will be worth it, don't you think?" Katie asked, some of her enthusiasm returning.

"I hope so."

"Oh, sure. The area is primed for this kind of thing. Are you going to let your guests brand and rope and whatever else it is a cowboy does?"

"That's just the routine stuff. I'm planning to have trail rides that last from eight hours to four days. Some will be the real thing—roughing it up in the mountains complete with pack horses and a mess wagon. But I'll have the more deluxe groups as well, where caterers will be set up along the trail. Food, drink, and entertainment provided. The only thing the guests will have to do is ride. Their tents, cots and sleeping bags will be set up for them while they're out riding. When they return, they can relax around a gourmet meal and I'll even include portable showers to wash the dust off."

She was impressed. This had obviously been his dream for a large part of his life.

"For the people who want to stay down here on the ranch, we'll not only do the regular work, but we'll have horse races during the day and hayrides at night. They can swim in the river, or raft or canoe if they want to and in the winter—well, not this year, but hopefully next winter—I'll organize ski trips to Mount Ashland or hunting expeditions up in the hills."

"So you'll be open year-round."

"Mmm." He nodded and eyed her speculatively. "This isn't an 'official' visit is it?"

"'Official'?"

"You're not up here scoutin' up a story for your paper?"

"Not today." She offered him a smile. "Believe me, when I interview you for the *Review* you'll know it."

"Good."

She glanced away. "I just wanted to thank you again." *And to find out what happened to Dave Sorenson.* And now she knew—the sad truth. Her heart began to ache again and she knew she should leave this ranch. There were too many ghosts from her past still wandering through the old house. And of course, there was the other problem that came in the form of a rangy Texan who played havoc with her mind—whether she wanted him to or not. "I'd better be off. Josh has probably driven his grandma crazy by now."

"How is he—your boy?"

"Better, I think," she said with a grin. "He's getting a little cranky and my mom always said that a bad mood is a sure sign that the patient is getting better."

"Your mother sounds like a wise woman."

She thought of Brynnie and all her husbands. "Some people might disagree on that one. She seems to get married at the drop of a hat."

"But you don't."

"Me?" she said, startled. "Well, no. I, uh, tend to think marriage is more of a commitment than Mom does."

"Is that why you didn't marry Josh's dad?"

She felt a needle of warning, the way she always did when the subject of Josh's paternity came up. "I told you we were just kids."

"Even so, most men want to do what's right."

"Most boys don't," she replied automatically, then felt a twinge of guilt. "It was complicated."

"Does he see Josh often?" Luke asked, and Katie's heart hitched painfully.

"No." She considered telling Luke the truth; after all, he'd known Dave, but what good would come of it? First she had to talk to Josh, then the Sorensons. And then, her family.

Luke, as if sensing the subject was too tender to discuss, asked, "Can't you stick around a few more minutes? Since you're already here, I thought you might want to see the rest of the place."

"I would. Very much," she admitted boldly as the offer, softly seductive, hung in the air between them. It was true. Katie was tempted; she'd enjoy nothing better than to get to know Luke Gates with his slow, sexy drawl, bedroom eyes and past that had yet to be unraveled. She thought of their one shared moment of passion, that unguarded instant in time when she'd felt his lips on hers, tasted the salt on his skin, experienced his flesh pressing hot against her own. "But I'd better take a rain check." Her gaze held his and she saw in his blue eyes a flicker of something darkly dangerous and ultimately erotic.

"I'll hold ya to it," he said, and her insides turned to jelly. He was too close, too unclothed, and too damned male. But she couldn't just let sleeping dogs lie.

"I really do have to go pick up Josh right now, but maybe I'll see ya around. At Tiffany's. Or Bliss's wedding reception."

"I don't think so." But he hesitated.

"Well, I'll look for you anyway," she said, surprised that she was intentionally flirting with him. Hadn't she told herself a thousand times over to avoid him, that he was all wrong for her, that there was something about him no sane woman would trust?

"I don't think I'll show."

"Your loss." Somehow she managed to turn on her heel and walk to the Jeep without feeling like she was fleeing. But her fingers were shaking and her palms sweating as she jabbed her key into the ignition. "You're an idiot," she told herself not for the first time, as the engine fired and she twisted the steering wheel. With what she hoped looked like a carefree wave out the window, she was off in a cloud of dust and exhaust. "Stay away from him, Katie! For once in your life, be smart!" She glanced in the rearview mirror and along with a vision of her worried eyes she saw him standing watching her, his feet apart, his long, jeans-clad legs stiff as they met at his slim hips. His arms were folded over his bare chest and his jeans hung low enough to show off the bend at his waist.

Katie's throat went dry and she knew right then and there that she was in trouble. Deep, deep trouble.

Chapter Six

Every muscle in Luke's body ached. He'd spent ten hours setting fence posts and cleaning out the stables. He smelled bad and probably looked worse, though the woman behind the convenience-store counter hadn't appeared to notice as she'd counted out his change when he'd stopped to buy a six-pack of beer, a bag of chips and a copy of the local paper.

He pulled into the driveway of the carriage house and parked near the garage. As he grabbed his copy of the *Review* and his sack from the store, the Santini family, dressed to the nines, emerged from the back door of the main house.

Tiffany had her purse in one hand and her other was wrapped around Christina's wrist. Wearing a long, shimmering blue dress she was giving orders to her family, commands Luke heard through the open windows of his pickup. "Now, listen, I don't want any more fights," Tiffany said, leveling her gaze at her son as her small family gathered on the back porch. "You're a lot older than Christina and fighting with her is ridiculous."

The little girl, pleased with the turn of the conversation, smiled broadly, then, behind her mother's back, stuck out her tongue at her brother.

Stephen yanked at his tie, looked about to say something but just rolled his eyes instead.

If Tiffany noticed any part of the exchange she ignored it as J.D. locked the back door. "Now, come on, I just talked to Aunt Katie. She and Josh need a ride."

"Still no car?" J.D. asked. He seemed every bit the lawyer in what looked to be an expensive suit and neat tie.

"Not for a few more days. If I were her, I'd go out of my mind. The good news is that Josh is off crutches and that the phone calls he was getting have stopped."

"What phone calls?"

"Oh, some kind of prank, I think. He'd answer and no one was there."

"Probably kids." J.D. shook his head but every over-worked muscle in Luke's body tightened. He hadn't seen Katie in a couple of days, not since she'd been out to the ranch.

Tiffany had shepherded the family down the back steps and onto the dry grass of the lawn when she spied Luke climbing out of his truck. "Oh, hi!" The worried knot between her eyebrows disappeared as both kids dashed for J.D.'s Jeep. "It's a madhouse as usual around here. If we make it to the wedding on time it'll be a miracle," she said with a laugh. Her eyes skated down his dusty, sweat-stained T-shirt and worn jeans. "I thought—I mean, didn't Katie say that you were going to Bliss's . . ." She blushed and he figured out the rest for himself.

"I think she expects me to show up at the reception."

"You should!" Tiffany enthused.

"I told Bliss I'd think about it."

A horn blared and Luke spied Stephen behind the steering wheel of J.D.'s rig. A broad smile creased his face.

"Stephen, stop!" Tiffany said, shaking her head at her son. She turned back to Luke. "We really do have to run," Tiffany said as J.D. managed to get his soon-to-be stepson to move to the back seat as he was still a few years too young to drive.

Luke waved and headed up the stairs. He tried not to think about Katie dressed up and looking for him at the reception, nor did he want to dwell too long on the thought of a couple making vows. He'd been down that road himself and had ended up being burned. Big time. Good luck to Mason and Bliss. He wanted no part of it.

The carriage house was stuffy and hot, so he cracked the windows, opened a beer and settled into his recliner with the paper. The headline on page one caught his attention: Wells Mystery Deepens. Katie Kinkaid's name was on the story. "Great," Luke growled, taking a long swallow from his bottle. His eyes skimmed the article and his jaw hardened. "Damned fool woman."

There was no doubt about it; she was trying her best to get herself killed.

It's none of your business, Gates. None.

"Hell." He attempted to read the rest of the paper, but his mind kept straying back to Katie and her stubborn fixation on becoming some kind of hotshot ace reporter. In Bitter-sweet, Oregon. Fat chance. No wonder she wanted to jump feet first into this Isaac Wells mystery.

He drained his bottle, then slammed it down on a nearby table. Try as he might, Luke couldn't forget the fact that she was getting crank calls and weird letters.

Dog-tired and irritated as all get-out, Luke slapped the copy of the *Rogue River Review* onto the table and shoved himself to his feet. Knowing he was about to make a huge mistake, he kicked off his boots and stormed into the bath-room.

He yanked off his T-shirt and dropped it onto the floor. What the devil was Katie thinking? Why did she insist upon stirring up trouble? Muttering under his breath about hard-headed career women who had more guts than brains, he twisted on the shower faucet and stripped out of his jeans.

In the past two days he'd half expected her to show up at

his ranch again, half wanted it. Anytime he'd heard a rig slow at the end of the lane, he'd felt an unlikely rush of adrenaline, experienced a clenching in his gut, only to end up disappointed when she didn't appear.

Whether he wanted to admit it or not, there was something about that little spitfire of a woman that got under a man's skin—well, at least his skin.

"Man, you've got it bad, Gates." Disgusted with that particular thought, he stepped under the shower spray and sucked in his breath. Hot water splashed against his chest and ran down his torso. As he scrubbed the dirt, sweat and smell of horse dung from his body, he told himself that Katie Kinkaid was off-limits. Way off-limits. She was the kind of woman who could turn a man's head around, and he needed no part of that. None. And yet . . .

Annoyed, he scrubbed until the dirt under his fingernails had washed away and all the lather that swirled down the drain was white. Why did he care what Ms. Kinkaid did? It wasn't as if she was someone special in his life. As a matter of fact, she wasn't in his life at all. Heretofore he'd helped her out of a jam with her car and her kid, and had made the mistake of kissing her. She'd shown up on his doorstep asking about Dave. That was it. So what if she wrote articles about hermits who disappeared? Who cared that the man had decided to contact her? It wasn't any of his business.

Oh, yeah? What if she's the mother of Dave Sorenson's kid? What then? It sure as hell is your business.

And he was bothered by Katie's involvement in this Isaac Wells mess. The situation bordered on the bizarre. What if the old man was involved in something criminal or sinister? The police had been questioning Ray Dean, a local hoodlum who'd been in and out of prison for years. Though no connection had been made, there was speculation in town that the two men had known each other.

A lot of people had thought Isaac Wells was dead. Maybe even murdered.

Yeah, then who wrote Katie the letter?

That was what bothered him. Was the letter the real thing or some kind of grand hoax? Either way, he was worried.

Angrily he dried his hair with a towel, stepped in front of the foggy mirror and swiped at the glassy surface until he could see his reflection well enough to scrape off his five-o'clock shadow and run a comb through his hair. He'd suspected from the moment Katie had invited him that he would attend the wedding reception, but it galled him to think that he had no will where that woman was concerned. One curve of her lips, a tiny sparkle in her eye, a mocking lift of her eyebrow and he found himself doing things he'd sworn to avoid.

"Damn." He dressed in a white shirt and black slacks, then fingered a bolo tie only to discard it and slide into his best pair of boots. By the time he walked outside it was dusk and the filmy clouds gathering over the moon were beginning to thicken. The air was hot and sultry without the slightest hint of a breeze, and yet he sensed a storm was brewing.

As he walked to his truck, he eyed the old Victorian house. It seemed strangely empty. No lights glowed in the windows, no kids ran in the yard, no angry guitar chords wailed from one of the upstairs rooms. Boxes were stacked on the porch—evidence that the Santini clan was moving out.

And Katie Kinkaid would be moving in. That thought made him edgy and restless. Living less than a hundred feet away from her was much too close. Though she probably needed a man to look out for her, he wasn't a candidate. As he climbed into his truck he tried to take solace in the fact that he wouldn't be here long. As soon as the electricity and phones were connected, he'd set up housekeeping at the ranch.

Oh, yeah? And then what? Are you just going to forget her and the fact that she's wading into dangerous waters? Are you going to ignore the fact that you'd like nothing more than to kiss her until her knees went weak, peel off her clothes and make love to her until dawn? And what about the fact that Josh just might be Ralph Sorenson's grandson? What the hell are you going to do about that?

His fingers tight on the wheel, he drove through town, past the church where Bliss Cawthorne had become Mrs. Mason Lafferty, and on to the old Reed Hotel. A tall three-story building with a Western facade, narrow windows and the original weathered siding, the Reed Hotel had once been a stagecoach stop. Now, after some remodeling and additions, it was the most elegant and historic inn anywhere near Bittersweet.

He handed his keys to a kid who didn't look old enough to drive, but was eager to park the truck, then headed inside. As if it were Christmas instead of early September, thousands of tiny lights winked in the branches of the trees and shrubbery that flanked the front porch. Again, he told himself, he had no business being here—none whatsoever—and yet he climbed the few steps to the open double doors.

Music filtered from within and he didn't have to pause at the front desk; he just followed the tinkle of laughter and buzz of excited conversation to a ballroom that was filled to the brim with the citizens of Bittersweet. A small band was playing a lively tune and couples were already swirling around the floor.

He spotted Katie instantly. In a long blue dress with her red hair piled onto her head, she danced with a guy Luke didn't recognize. Long-legged, with hawkish eyes and a smile that looked as phony as a three-dollar bill, Katie's partner held her close. Too close. As if she were his personal possession. And Katie was eating it up. She talked and laughed, tilting her head back and flirting outrageously with the stranger. Her cheeks were flushed, her green eyes sparkling, her smile positively radiant. Luke's gut twisted with something akin to jealousy and he silently swore.

When offered a glass of champagne by a waiter dressed like an old stagehand, Luke accepted the drink and downed it in one long swallow. The room was crowded, the music a little loud, the room surprisingly stuffy and hot. With two fingers he pulled at his collar and told himself his claustrophobia was way out of line.

Mason and Bliss danced past, she in white silk and lace, he in a black tuxedo. He twirled her off her feet and she laughed gaily, as if she hadn't a care in the world, as if she were completely and truly in love.

The thought sat like lead in Luke's stomach and he snagged another glass of champagne from a tray near a fountain that spouted gallons of the stuff. Hearing Katie's laughter rising above the buzz of conversation, clink of glasses and notes from a dance band, he sauntered outside to a veranda where there was a little respite from the heat.

Several people had gathered on the flagstones, talking and smoking, holding drinks or resting their hips against the stone railing and looking over the creek that splashed behind the hotel.

Two women strolled onto the patio and stood far enough away that he only caught snatches of their conversation.

"Can't imagine what happened to him," one of the women was saying. She was short and round, with hair starting to turn silver and long, well-kept fingernails that rummaged through the contents of her purse.

"So you don't believe the letter is real?" her companion; a wasp-thin woman with harsh features and more makeup than she needed, asked.

"The letter that was printed in the paper? Naw." She

found a pack of cigarettes and shook one out. "If you ask me, Lois, Isaac Wells is gone for good."

At that point Mason strode onto the patio and spying Luke, offered a smile.

"Aren't you supposed to be cuttin' the cake, or toasting the bride or somethin'?" Luke asked as they clasped hands.

"Needed a break." Mason tugged at his collar and Luke noticed the sweat sliding down his neck.

"I hear Bliss has designed a new house for you. That you're going to open up a dude ranch at the old Sorenson place."

"That's the plan." Luke sipped his drink. He wasn't much good at small talk, but felt comfortable with Lafferty; there was something about him that seemed sincere. Beneath the expensive tux was a real, solid man, a fellow rancher who felt a kinship with the earth. The kind of man Luke trusted.

"I'd like you to show me around sometime when work gets under way."

"Come on out, anytime," Luke offered, then asked a question he'd been tossing about all day. "I heard you were related to Isaac Wells."

"Yep."

"What do you think happened to him?"

"Wish I knew." Mason rubbed his chin. "I'm afraid it might become one of those unsolved cases around here, just like the Octavia Nesbitt thing a few years back."

"Nesbitt?" Luke asked. The name was familiar.

"Tiffany's grandmother. Years ago she was robbed—her jewelry taken from her house, even her damned cat stolen. The case was never solved and made everyone nervous. Leastwise, that's what Bliss and her father tell me."

"But no one was hurt?" Luke asked.

"Nope. This is different that way." Mason's eyebrows

drew together. "Can't help but wonder whether old Isaac is dead or alive."

"There you are!" Bliss, breathless, caught up with her new husband. "Hiding?" Her blue eyes sparkled with a teasing light.

"From you?" he asked. "Always."

"Such a charmer." She clucked her tongue and to the delight of the two women on the far end of the patio, Mason swooped her into his arms and kissed her as if he'd never stop. One woman fanned her face, the other turned away, hiding a smile. Luke grinned. He felt the passion between the just-married couple, knew what it was like to want a woman so badly he ached.

When Mason finally lifted his head, Bliss appeared breathless. "Well," she finally said, her cheeks flushed to a rosy hue, "I'd love to steal away to the bushes with you right now, Mr. Lafferty, but we have duties to attend to."

"Too bad," Mason drawled.

Bliss touched him lightly on the nose. "If you're lucky, I'll give you a rain check."

"I'm gonna hold you to it, Mrs. Lafferty."

They linked fingers and she pulled him back into the interior of the old hotel.

Luke finished his drink, then stared through the windows and spied Katie dancing. She was grinning and looking as if she were having the time of her life. He wondered what kind of trouble she was getting herself into. First the letter—be it a hoax or the real thing—then the phone calls to her house where no one answered. They could just have been someone dialing the wrong number, but he couldn't shove them out of his head.

Not that he could forget much about Katie Kinkaid. As the two women drifted back into the ballroom, Luke leaned against the rail and glared down at the darkened ravine. Lights from the hotel reflected on the tumbling water of the creek and he thought he saw a lone man, a black figure, slip behind a thick copse of trees.

The hairs on the back of his neck lifted in warning, even though he told himself that he'd imagined the shadow, or, if there really was someone hiding in the undergrowth, it was probably just some kid sneaking booze from the reception or stealing away from his parents' wary eyes. Luke squinted hard into the darkness and strained to hear a sound—a snapping twig or muttered oath or anything to convince himself that he hadn't imagined it.

Watch it, Gates, you're getting paranoid. Still, he studied the night-darkened banks of the creek. The suspicious part of his mind considered vaulting over the rail and following his instincts, tailing whoever it was and finding out if he was up to no good.

"I thought I saw you sneak in." Katie's voice startled him.

Luke glanced quickly over his shoulder. She was standing only inches from him, her tiny, flushed face angled up to look at him. Her green eyes sparkled and he wondered if she wasn't the most intriguing woman in the universe.

"I suspected that you might decide to put in an appearance after all." Her lips curved into a smile of silent amusement, as if she could read his mind and found his thoughts laughable.

"I think you invited me," he replied, turning and placing his body between hers and the stranger in the shadows—if there was one. A thin sheen of perspiration added an alluring glow to her skin, which was already smooth as silk.

"That I did," she said flirtatiously, and Luke remembered seeing her in another man's arms, how at home she'd seemed, how lighthearted and free. She interrupted his thoughts when she asked, "So . . . how about a dance?"

He hadn't been asked that particular question since high school. "I'm not much of a dancer."

"That makes two of us. Come on." As if she expected

him to come up with some kind of excuse, she grabbed hold of his hand and pulled him into the warm room where couples were gliding around the dance floor. Rather than protest, he went with her into the ballroom. He felt safer inside even though there was probably no danger lurking in the gloomy shadows by the creek. It was just his imagination working overtime.

A song from the big-band era was playing. He'd heard the tune before, didn't know its name, and didn't have time to speculate. Katie fell into his arms as naturally as if she'd been born there. She didn't seem to mind that his dancing was limited. He hadn't lied. He'd had a few dance lessons in physical education when he'd been about twelve and scared to death of the opposite sex; then he'd experimented a little in high school and at rare social events while he'd been married to Celia.

"See?" Katie said, looking up at him with eyes as green as a forest. "This isn't so bad."

"Could be worse," he admitted and wondered why it felt so right to hold her.

"A lot worse."

As if of their own accord, his arms tightened around her. She felt small, warm and pliant as she rested her head against his shoulder. Music and laughter swirled around them. The lights dimmed and Luke's heart pounded. He imagined kissing her again, melding his lips over hers and sliding his tongue between her teeth; imagined slipping his hands beneath her dress and how her skin would feel as he peeled the blue folds of silk from her body.

Tiffany and J.D. glided past. Tiffany's head was thrown back and she was laughing gaily, as if she had the world by its proverbial tail. In a glimmer she spied Katie and winked at her half-sister, as if the two women shared a private joke.

"Mind if I cut in?" John Cawthorne's voice surprised him. "I'm making a point of dancing with each of my daughters."

Luke stepped aside, ended up with Brynnie in his arms and watched as the father of the bride made a big display of dancing with his third daughter. He'd already had a turn with Bliss, who had seemed radiant in her father's arms—as well as with Tiffany, who had danced stiffly, no smile upon her face. Now Katie fell into step with her newfound father as if she'd been a part of his family for years.

"He loves them, you know. Each one," Brynnie said as she and Luke paused for a glass of champagne. "All the hard feelings that existed between the girls and him, well, let me tell you, it's taken its toll. Trying to put this scrappy family together has been hard on him."

"And on his daughters," Luke added.

"Oh, my, yes. Even Katie." Brynnie sipped slowly. Her face was flushed and her fading red hair, precariously curled onto the top of her head, was starting to fall. "Here, would you mind holding this?" She handed him her glass, extracted a bobby pin from her crown and held it between her lips as she expertly tucked the falling loops of hair into place again. "There we go." She pushed the bobby pin to the spot where it belonged, securing her tresses, then took her glass from him. "What I wouldn't do for a smoke," she admitted, "but I'm trying to quit, what with John's condition and all. I suppose you know that he had himself a heart attack."

"I'd heard," Luke admitted, still watching John and Katie move easily around the dance floor.

"That's what started all this—him and me getting together and his obsession with making us all one big happy family." She glanced up at Luke. "I'm not a gambling woman, but I'd bet my life that our family's a little bit like Humpty-Dumpty—darned near impossible to put together. At least, not as fast as he'd like it. Emotions take time to heal. . . . Oh, listen to me. This is a wedding, for goodness' sake, and here I am gettin' maudlin." She blinked rapidly, sniffed, and swept a beringed finger under her eyes. "It's so silly. I guess I just want John to be happy."

"He looks like he is," Luke observed as the music ended. Katie looped her arm through the crook of her father's elbow and they maneuvered through the knots of people clustered around the ballroom floor.

"I hope so," she said fervently as John and Katie approached. John and Brynnie moved off.

"So what did Mom tell you?" Katie asked. "I saw you two with your heads together."

"She was just giving me some background on the family."

"Such as?" she asked as his arms surrounded her again.

"Your mother seems to think there's no hope of bringing your family together." He held her tight and got lost in the scent of her perfume.

"Maybe not, but I think it's time to bury the hatchet and get on with our lives. Bliss is married now, has her own life with Mason and his daughter, Dee Dee—that's her, dancing with her father." She pointed to Mason and a girl of about nine or ten, he guessed, as they danced together. Dee Dee was embarrassed, but Mason swung her off her feet and she couldn't help but laugh. "Anyway, so Bliss is happy and now Tiffany and J.D. are going to tie the knot, so why dwell on the past? Don't get me wrong—John and Mom should never have carried on an affair while he was married. Though, come to think of it, if they hadn't, I wouldn't be here, would I?" She grinned and the reflection of a thousand tiny bulbs in the chandelier overhead shone in her eyes.

"And that would be a shame." Luke brushed a lock of her hair off her cheek and saw her smile slowly fade as she stared at him. The pulse at the base of her throat jumped a little and he was lost in her. He forgot the dozens of people in the room, was alone and intimate with her as the world around them slipped away.

"A . . . a big shame," she said, trying and failing to lighten the mood. She avoided his eyes for a second and he forced himself to think of something, anything other than holding on to her and never letting go.

"So what about you? Both your half-sisters are getting married."

"I have my career," she said automatically and sensed her blood heat. Being this close to Luke, feeling the pressure of his fingers on her back caused her head to swim. Oh, Lord, how had she gotten this close to him?

"And that's the most important thing in your life."

"Second. Josh is first." That was a given, but she didn't want to discuss her son; not with this man who spoke little but asked questions that delved far too deep. Changing the subject was simple. "So, I guess you and I will be neighbors in a couple of weeks."

"More than neighbors," he said, and stupidly her heart took flight as the leader of the dance band announced that the musicians would be taking a break.

"More?"

"You'll be my landlady."

"Oh." She let out her breath and laughed. "Good. It'll give me a little bit of power, won't it?"

His smile was off-center and sexy as all get-out. "A little. But I'll be movin' out myself soon."

"I suspected as much," she said and mentally gave herself a shake when she heard the note of disappointment in her voice. "Come on, it's time you met some people around here." She guided him through the throng where they not only spoke with her half-sisters, and Mason and J.D., but she introduced him to her half-brothers and three quarters of the town. While he seemed to recognize a sprinkling of the guests at the reception, Katie knew them all.

"It's hard to believe there are this many citizens in the town," he whispered to her as she located Josh, who was ignoring his crutches in favor of hanging out with Stephen and a couple of other boys.

"I should go and talk to my son," she said, but hadn't taken a step in Josh's direction before Brynnie caught up with her.

"Come on, come on," she said, tapping Katie's shoulder. "We've got dinner in the dining room and it'll go to waste if we don't eat it."

"In a minute—"

"Now or forever hold your peace."

"I think we'd better not cross my mother," Katie said with a teasing grin.

"Good idea," Brynnie remarked as she beelined toward her twin sons and hustled them in the direction of the buffet.

They dined on salmon, prime rib and venison, though Katie's appetite was nil. She was too keyed up, being with Luke. Touching him and smelling the faint odors of leather and musk that clung to him caused her heart to flutter, her mind to spin, and, apparently, her stomach to shrink. She played with her food, barely eating a bite, sipped a little more champagne, and after the meal, danced to a couple of songs. She then stood beside Luke as Bliss and Mason cut their five-tiered cake and fed each other enormous pieces that left smudges of frosting on their faces. Mason kissed the icing off Bliss's cheeks and she repaid him by swiping a dab of the white confection onto his nose.

The crowd laughed and Katie glanced up at Luke, who managed a smile.

"Silly, huh?"

"But fun," he conceded, staring so deeply into her eyes that she had to swallow hard and her mouth lost all moisture. "I . . . I . . . uh, need to talk to Tiffany," she said to break the spell, the pure madness that seemed to be a part of the night.

Sometime near eleven, Mr. and Mrs. Mason Lafferty ran

out the front door of the hotel and, while being showered with birdseed, ducked into a long white limo that idled near the front steps. As the guests waved and shouted, the newlyweds roared away. Katie felt a faint twinge of envy, then told herself she was being a romantic twit. She was glad that Bliss and Mason were together, thrilled that Tiffany had found J.D. to become her husband as well as a stepfather to Stephen and Christina. What was right for her half-sisters didn't necessarily mean that she wanted the same thing. She couldn't. She didn't dare let her heart be broken again.

They lingered for a while, dancing, talking with friends and sipping coffee as the crowd thinned. She wandered onto the veranda but Luke grabbed hold of her arm.

"Let's stay inside."

"Are you kidding? It must be a hundred degrees in here." She winked at him and tugging on his hand, dragged him outside. "Don't tell me you're afraid to be alone with me, Gates."

"That's not it—"

"Good."

Ignoring the look of unwarranted consternation that twisted his features, she walked across the flagstones and leaned over the rail. From far below, the sound of the creek tumbling over stones and exposed roots reached her ears.

"Tell me about the letter you got," he said, resting a hip against the stone railing and folding his arms over his chest. He stared down into the canyon, his eyes narrowing as if he were searching for something. Or someone. "The one that's supposed to be from Isaac Wells."

"I take it you read the article in the *Review*."

"Every word."

"That's what I like to hear," she teased, then added, "Really, there's not much more to say. I received the note, gave the original to the police and wrote the article. I don't know if it's phony or real." She turned her palms upward. "I guess time will tell."

"Could be dangerous," Luke mused aloud, though his gaze was still searching, his eyes narrowed against the darkness that escaped the wash of light from the hotel's security lamps. "A nutcase."

"You sound like Jarrod."

"Just be careful."

She lifted a skeptical eyebrow. "You think I'm in some kind of danger?"

"I don't know that you're in danger, Katie, but, yeah, it could be trouble."

"Maybe." A needle of fear pierced her heart. How many times had she told herself just the same thing?

"It doesn't worry you? You're a mother and—"

"And what I do shouldn't worry *you*," she interrupted as her anger suddenly flared. Who was he to insinuate that she was messing up her life? She couldn't control her tongue. "If I didn't make it clear before, let me assure you I don't need another brother, okay? Three half-brothers add up to too many—way too many when it comes to giving advice about my life." Turning quickly and seething deep inside, she headed toward the French doors. The last thing she needed—the very last thing—was a man telling her what to do.

Before she'd taken three steps he grabbed her elbow, spun her around and kissed her so hard she didn't know what hit her. She gasped as hot, demanding lips crashed over hers and strong arms surrounded her waist, dragging her close. She started to protest, to push away, but his hands splayed against the exposed skin of her back and a tingle of excitement sped through her blood.

Don't do this, Katie. Don't kiss him. This was what was dangerous—emotionally dangerous. Not the Isaac Wells case.

But she didn't stop and the sound of wanting that

reached her ears came from her own throat. Oh, Lord, what was she thinking?

With all her strength she pushed away. "Is—is that what you do?" she asked, drawing in a shaky breath and hating herself for how weak she was when it came to him. "When a woman gets into an argument with you, do you always grab her and kiss her just to make her shut up?"

"Most women don't get me so riled up," he admitted.

"Don't they? Well, good. That's very good. For you. Because these Neanderthal, 1950s B-movie tactics are . . . are . . ." Damn the man! He was actually smiling, amused by her reaction. Her fists balled in frustration.

"Are what? Effective?"

"I was going to say boorish, or antiquated, or at the very least rude and entirely unacceptable!"

He laughed then. Threw back his head so that his blond hair brushed the collar of his shirt and he laughed.

"This is not funny!" She almost stomped her foot, then decided she'd look even more adolescent than she felt. "Good night, Luke. The evening has been . . . entertaining, but I think I'd better leave now."

"And back off from a fight?" he challenged.

Though she knew she was being goaded, she couldn't stop herself. Like a trout spying a salmon fly on a hook, she rose swiftly to the bait. "I'm not backing off from anything, Gates. If you don't know anything else about me, you should at least figure out that I'm dogged, not afraid of too much, and never, never duck an argument." She was about to say more when Josh, who had somehow rediscovered his crutches, hobbled onto the patio and Katie, wondering if her skin was as inflamed as it felt, told herself to count to ten and cool off.

"Is it okay if I spend the night with Stephen?" he asked.

"But you're still recovering."

"I'll be good. Promise." Josh flashed her his most engaging smile just as Stephen, eating a piece of wedding cake, sauntered outside. His hair was unruly, his tie was dangling from his neck and he licked a spot of icing from the corner of his mouth.

"Why doesn't Stephen come over to our house?" Katie asked, trying not to remember that Luke was standing only inches from her, that he'd kissed her like no other man had ever kissed her, that she didn't know quite how to handle her wayward emotions whenever he was near.

"'Cause we're gonna camp out in the backyard."

Tiffany and J.D. joined the group. J.D. was carrying an exhausted Christina, whose usually springy curls were as droopy as her eyelids. Her head was nestled against J.D.'s shoulder and she yawned broadly. "I take it you've already heard?" Tiffany asked, nodding toward the boys.

"Sounds like they've already cooked up plans," Katie eyed her son and his crutches. "He really should come home and elevate the foot and—"

"Aw, Mom . . . I'm okay." To prove his point, Josh lifted both crutches in the air and walked without so much as a limp. "I'm better. A lot better. Besides, it's almost our house, isn't it?"

"Not quite," Katie said, but shrugged. "It's all right with me if you're sure—" She looked at Tiffany who nodded. "I'll see he takes care of that ankle and in the morning, if he's up to it, he can help Stephen pack his room."

"He doesn't have his pajamas—"

"Don't need 'em," Josh said.

"But I don't want you sleeping in your church clothes. I'll stop by the cottage and pick up anything you need."

"I said I *don't* need anything," Josh insisted.

"He's probably right," Tiffany agreed. "We have double of just about anything he could want. He can have something Stephen's grown out of."

Josh threw Katie a look that begged her to give in.

"If you're sure," she said to Tiffany.

"Positive."

"Okay. I'll call you in the morning." Katie planted a kiss on her son's cheek and he made a hasty retreat on his crutches. Tiffany and J.D. ushered the kids through the ballroom and out a side entrance. As Katie watched them leave, she realized that she'd just lost her ride. "Oh, wait," she called after them. "I need a lift home. . . ."

Luke grabbed her again. "Don't worry about it," he said as she turned and saw the smoky blue of his eyes.

"But—"

"I'll take you home, Katie. It would be my pleasure."

Chapter Seven

In her driveway, Luke braked and cut the engine of his pickup. Katie reached for the door handle. Once before, she'd been in this very truck with the night closing in on them and had felt the sheer intimacy of the moment as he'd kissed her. She didn't want a repeat of that incident. Or at least, she tried to convince herself that she didn't. "Thanks for the ride."

"Maybe I should come in and see that everything's okay."

Her heart nearly stopped. She heard the ticking of the engine as it cooled and the jingle of his keys as he pulled them from the ignition.

"Okay? What wouldn't be okay?" she asked, buying time. Part of her was tempted to invite him in, to take a chance; the other, more sane portion of her mind warned her that she was only asking for trouble. Begging for it. The kind of trouble she didn't need and couldn't deal with. This man was linked to Ralph Sorenson, Josh's grandfather. "For what?" she asked, shoving her shoulder against the door while trying to ignore her elevating pulse and dry mouth. *Come on, Katie, let him in. What would it hurt?*

"I'm not sure. But it's just a feeling I've got that something isn't right."

"Anyone ever tell you you're a worrywart?"

"A few people," he said and climbed out of the cab.

Blue gave a soft bark as Katie inserted her key into the dead bolt and discovered the door unlocked. "That's odd," she said, dropping her keys into her purse. Frowning to herself she walked into the kitchen.

"I'm sure I locked it."

"You remember doing it?"

"No . . ." Flipping on the kitchen lights she tried to think over the rapid beating of her heart. Blue's toenails clicked on the linoleum as he greeted her with a wagging tail and lowered head. "It was real crazy," she said, dropping her purse on the table as she scratched Blue behind his ears. "We were running late. Josh had trouble with the knot of his tie and then had a fit about having to use the crutches and the next thing I knew, Tiffany was knocking on the back door." She shook her head, trying to clear the cobwebs. "I don't remember, but I always lock it. It's habit."

Luke's gaze was thoughtful. Worried. Katie felt suddenly awkward. "Would you like . . . some coffee or soda or . . . anything?" Why did the question sound so lame?

"I'm fine." Jaw set, he strode through the kitchen and into the living room to her desk. Without asking, he pushed the Play button on the answering machine.

"Hey, wait! You can't—"

The machine clicked as someone hung up.

Katie's stomach curled and the hairs on the back of her neck rose. "Who was that?"

"That's what I'd like to know." Luke scanned the desk area. "Just about everyone you know was at Bliss's wedding tonight, right?"

"Of course, but—"

"So who would have expected you to be home?"

"No one," she thought aloud, her skin crawling at the

thought that someone might actually be watching her. "You think it might have something to do with the letter?"

"I don't know. It could be just a mistake, a wrong number, but it might be a crank—either this Wells character or someone looking for him." His gaze fastened on hers. He was stone-cold sober. "But your door was unlocked. Someone could have been in here."

Her knees threatened to give way at the thought.

She laughed a little nervously. "I can't believe—"

"Sure you can. Now take a look around. Does anything seem out of place?"

Walking slowly through her few cluttered rooms, she eyed her belongings, touched a few pieces of furniture and saw nothing out of the ordinary. Everything was just as she and Josh had left it when they had rushed out of the house and into J.D.'s Jeep. She would have sworn that, out of habit more than anything else, she had locked the door behind her.

"Nothing seems to be missing or out of place," she told Luke.

"You're sure?"

"Yeah. Pretty sure."

"Would your dog have allowed anyone inside?"

"Probably, but I don't really think anyone was here," she said, though she had a severe case of the creeps. Thinking that an intruder, a stranger, had been in her house—in Josh's room, for crying out loud—caused a chill in her blood as cold as all November.

"Maybe you should call the police."

"And tell them what? That I left the door unlocked? That I think someone was in here, but nothing is missing or out of place, that someone has been calling and hanging up? What could they possibly do?"

"Stake out the place?"

"On what? Your hunch? Just because I got a letter from Isaac Wells?"

"Yes."

She almost laughed. "Even in a small town like Bittersweet, the police have better things to do."

Scowling, he paced to the front window and stared through the plate glass to the yard. Even with the glow of the streetlamp at the corner, it was dark. "I suppose you're right."

"I know I'm right. There's nothing anyone can do."

"Sure, there is," he said, slowly turning to face her. "I can stay here."

"What?" *Was he out of his mind?* "Here? No way." She couldn't believe her ears. Although a secret little part of her was pleased, the other saner, more rational side of her nature was scared to death.

"On the couch."

"I don't want a bodyguard!" she snapped, throwing up a hand. "I can't believe we're having this conversation. It's . . . it's ridiculous."

"I don't think so." He was firm, his jaw set, his gaze steady. He looked like a man who wouldn't be swayed. But the thought of him in the house alone with her, even on the couch, was unnerving. "I'll be fine. Blue's here with me."

"What if the guy has a key?"

"A key? Wait a minute. I don't think there is a guy, and if there was, why would he have a key to my house?"

"Don't you have one hidden outside for Josh?"

"Yes, but—" She felt the color drain from her face. Was it possible? "You're spooking me, Gates."

"Just trying to get you to see the possibilities."

She went to the back porch, skimmed her fingers over the ledge above the door and found the key. "Still here," she said, holding it up for Luke's inspection. The metal glinted in the glare of the single bulb burning over the door.

"Good. Bring it inside."

"No one was here," she insisted as she tossed the key into a kitchen drawer and met him in the archway to the living room. "You're borrowing trouble."

"Maybe."

"You can't stay here."

"Why not?"

A million reasons. I can't trust myself around you. I don't know you. Having you in my house is more emotionally dangerous than anything. "I hardly know you."

As if he could read her mind, he grinned—a wide, sexy smile that did considerable damage to her self-control. "Maybe this is a way to get to know me better."

"I'm not sure I want to."

His eyes said he didn't believe her. "I'll stay on the couch. Believe me, your virtue is safe with me."

"My 'virtue'?" She couldn't believe what she was hearing. "My *virtue*? Are you crazy, or what? You think I'm worried about my inability to say no to you?" If it wasn't so near the truth, it would have been funny.

"Something like that, yeah."

"Of all the conceited, self-centered, egotistical ideas I've ever heard . . . Hey, what do you think you're doing?" she demanded, following him down the short hallway to her bedroom. He shoved open the door and strode inside as if he'd done it all his life, as if it were his damned right!

Her heart was in her throat as he strode to her sleigh bed in the center of the room. "Luke, you can't—"

He threw back the covers, grabbed a pillow, then reached for the blanket folded over the foot of her bed, an antique quilt her great-great-grandmother had pieced from scraps seventy-five years earlier. "I'll be out there," he said, his smile disappearing as he hitched his chin toward the door, "in the living room. You stay in the bedroom."

"But—"

"Don't argue." To her surprise he reached forward, grabbed hold of her arms, yanked her close and kissed her hard. She opened her mouth to protest and his tongue slid past her lips and beyond the barrier of her teeth. Steely fingers clenched her forearms. She tried to concentrate, to find the words to disagree with his high-handed tactics, to tell him exactly what he could do with all his good intentions, but she was lost.

A small moan escaped his throat and her heart pounded expectantly. His tongue touched hers, explored the roof of her mouth and a thrill, hot and wanton, swept through her blood. She told herself she was being foolish, that she shouldn't let him touch her, but she couldn't stop herself. She heard the zipper of her dress hiss open, felt the cool air touch her back where the silky fabric parted, experienced a rush of desire as the tips of his fingers, callused and blunt, brushed across her skin.

A thousand warning bells rang through her mind as he kissed her cheeks and eyes and throat, but she ignored them all. Her neck arched as her head lolled back and his lips found the shell of her ear.

Don't! Don't! Don't! Her mind screamed as her legs buckled and Luke caught her, sweeping her off her feet. *This is madness! Katie, use your head!* But the alarms ringing through her head couldn't chase away the wonder of the feel of him, the heat of his body, the smell of sweat and musk that lingered on his skin. He placed her on the bed and slipped her dress over her shoulders.

"I—I don't know about this," she whispered, but her words caught in her throat. Kneeling next to the bed, he leaned forward. His lips brushed the tops of her breasts and an ache deep within the most feminine core of her began to pulse.

"Me, neither." His tongue skimmed her breastbone and her skin turned to fire. Nudging the silk bodice of her dress even lower, he kissed her breasts where they bulged above her bra. Inside her, something dark and painful broke. She closed her eyes as the dress slid down, exposing her to the warm lamplight.

Don't do this, Katie! Don't.

Desire, long slumberous, rose and seeped through her veins. His breath was warm, the scent of him arousing. With gentle fingers he edged one breast from its confines. Her nipple puckered in anticipation. As he placed his lips over the hard little nub, she drew in a swift breath. His tongue encircled her nipple until he began to suck slowly, seductively.

Katie's fingers slid through his hair and she fought the urge to cry out as his teeth tugged and pulled and one of his hands pushed her dress past her ribs to her waist. She was breathing fast and hard, her body quivering inside.

"Katie," he whispered, his voice rough as he lifted his head. "I—"

"Shh."

"Oh, hell." The muscles of his face tightened as he battled between good intentions and self-control. "I—I think we should stop. While I still can."

Disappointment welled inside her as he gently pulled the dress back up and over her breasts. His gaze, still bright with passion, touched hers. "I'll be in the living room."

She fought the urge to mew in protest, to beg him to finish what he'd started, to make love to her all night long, and she watched in fascination as he straightened, turned his back to her, and with long, swift strides crossed the room and closed the bedroom door behind him.

Hot tears starred her lashes. Whether the tears were from embarrassment, regret or just plain frustration, she didn't know or care to analyze. She slapped them away with her fingers and told herself she was every kind of fool known to womankind. What had she been thinking, letting this man—this virtual *stranger*—into her home, into her bedroom and darned close to into her bed? "Oh, Kinkaid, you're really losing it," she chided herself, then decided not to dwell on what had happened between them. He was here, on the couch, presumably to help her and that, as they said, was that.

She pulled off her dress, hung it haphazardly on a hanger, then tossed her favorite nightgown over her head. She needed to wash her face, but that would mean walking into the hallway. "So what?" she growled under her breath. Just because Luke was in the house, didn't mean she couldn't do what she had to do. The man wasn't going to intimidate her, for goodness' sake! This was her house. Her life. She snagged her bathrobe from a hook on the closet door, flung her arms into the sleeves and cinched the belt snugly around her waist. She crossed the hall, slipped into the bathroom and went through her nightly ablutions with one ear cocked to the door.

Luke didn't disturb her. A few minutes later she crawled into bed, pulled the covers to her neck and wondered how she'd get one second of sleep knowing that he was just down the hall. Blue, who had padded into the room when she was in the bathroom, circled and dropped into a sleeping position at the foot of her bed. "Good dog," she said around a yawn and he thumped his tail. Sighing, she closed her eyes and the exhaustion of the day took hold. She was asleep within minutes.

A sharp pain in his neck drove Luke to consciousness. He blinked, focusing on the small living room, and realized he was in Katie's house.

The smell of coffee drifted from the kitchen and as he lifted his head, Katie, her hair wound into a knot atop her head, her face scrubbed free of makeup, peeked around the corner.

"Good morning," she said, her eyes sparkling in the dawn light.

"Mornin'."

"Some bodyguard you turned out to be." She giggled and he should have felt irritated by her ribbing, but he managed a thin smile.

"You're safe, aren't you?"

"Yeah, but I don't think it's because of you."

"Well, then, you're wrong. I chased away all sorts of evil types last night."

"Did you?" She laughed and ducked back into the kitchen as some bell rang.

He got up from the couch, rubbed the kinks out of his neck and back, then ambled into the kitchen where she was busy tossing slices of bread into an ancient toaster.

"Breakfast?" Katie asked him.

"You don't have to—"

"No trouble," she insisted with a lift of one shoulder. "Consider it payment for protecting me. Ham and eggs okay?"

She didn't know that he'd stayed awake until dawn, only falling asleep when he'd felt certain that there was no one skulking in the night to threaten her. "Great." He couldn't help noticing the long, graceful arch of her neck, the feminine slope of her shoulders and the nip of her waist where her robe was tied. Beneath the soft velour fabric her hips shifted as she twisted to look at him.

Her eyes caught his for a second and she blushed, a fetching pink hue that climbed her throat and colored her cheeks. In a flash, he was reminded of kissing her breasts. He'd thought of little else all night and had fought the urge to return to her bedroom, press his lips to hers until she couldn't protest and make love to her over and over again. His crotch tightened. "If you don't mind, I'd like to step through the shower."

She hesitated for a second, then said, "Sure. There're extra towels in the hall closet."

"Thanks." In less than two minutes he was under the spray of the showerhead, silently damning himself for his wayward thoughts and the hardness in his crotch. What was wrong with him? Every time he looked at Katie Kinkaid, he wanted to start kissing her and never stop.

It had been just too long since he'd been with a woman. Way too long. He let the hot water work out the kinks in his muscles, washed as best he could, toweled off and dressed. As he opened the bathroom door, he heard Katie's voice.

"I know it's tough, especially for you, but it's something we all have to face, Tiff. Whether you like it or not, John's your father and you have to deal with him. Just like I do." There was a pause, then she added, "Yeah, I know. Okay, I'll start moving stuff over in a few days. I've still got Dad—er, John's Jeep. The convertible is officially dead. Len at the gas station is going to try and sell it or scrap it out and I'll find something else soon. But while I've got John's rig, I may as well start moving." There was a short pause, then she added, "Just let Josh know that I'll pick him up by noon. Thanks again."

She was replacing the receiver when he entered the kitchen. Her face was drawn in concentration until she saw him and grinned. "Well, well, Mr. Gates," she teased, "don't you clean up nice."

"Do I?"

"Here." She handed him a cup of coffee. "Now, sit." At the table were two place settings complete with orange juice, toast, ham, eggs, and hash brown potatoes.

"Yes, ma'am," he drawled in his best Texan accent and

she laughed, the sound as musical as wind chimes in a summer breeze.

They ate and talked as Blue sat on the floor at Katie's side, his brown eyes following each morsel that she forked into her mouth. Every once in a while, she'd toss the dog a tidbit and he'd deftly catch the treat with a snap of his jaws.

It felt comfortable and right in the cozy kitchen. In her fluffy bathrobe and slippers, Katie was innocently seductive, expressive with her hands and eyes as she talked about her job, her son, her ambitions and her family.

"So it's all rather complicated," she admitted as she poured the last cup of coffee. "All those years I'd grown up with and tolerated my half-brothers, never dreaming that I'd end up with not one, but two half-sisters." She grinned, showing off the sexy overlap of her teeth. "Kind of weird, when you think about it. How about you? Any siblings?" She munched on a bite of toast.

"Nope." He shifted uncomfortably in his chair.

"So where are your parents?"

He felt his eyebrows quirk and drained his cup. "My mom took off with some other guy when I was two and my old man was killed in Vietnam when I wasn't much older."

He noticed the color drain from her face. "I was kicked around between a couple of aunts and pretty much raised myself."

"I—I'm sorry."

"Nothin' to be sorry about." He saw the pain in her eyes and refused to let her pity him. "Trust me, it was harder on them than it was on me. I was in and out of juvenile homes for a while until I met my wife."

"Your . . . wife?" she repeated, stunned.

"Ex-wife." He shoved his chair back. "I've been divorced for years."

"Oh." She forced a smile that didn't seem genuine and tiny lines deepened between her eyebrows.

"It's over, Katie. Been over a long time." Why he felt compelled to explain, he didn't understand. "We didn't have any kids together and the last I heard, Celia had divorced her second husband and was on her way to marrying a third—not that I care. I don't even know where she's living now."

She seemed troubled and he felt something tug at his heart. Katie Kinkaid, for all her tough-as-nails-investigative-reporter inclinations, was soft inside, couldn't stand to see anyone hurt.

He went to her chair, reached under her arms and drew her to her feet. "Thanks for breakfast," he said, bending down so that the tip of his nose brushed hers.

"Thanks . . . Thanks for staying here last night." Katie could scarcely breathe. His hands, big and possessive, held her on either side of her rib cage. One corner of his mouth lifted into that smile she found so damnably sexy.

"My pleasure, Ms. Kinkaid."

"Mine, as well." Cocking her head to the side she looked up at him, heard a deep, heartfelt groan develop from somewhere around his lungs, then gasped as he pulled her roughly to him and pressed hard, insistent lips against hers.

In a heartbeat her blood was rushing through her veins, her bones began to melt and she sagged against him, only to be released quickly. She nearly lost her balance and glanced up to find his eyes a smoky blue. "I gotta go," he said.

"Y-yes."

With another quick kiss to her cheek, he turned and walked through the back door. Katie was left with her heart pounding wildly, her thoughts tumbling disconcertingly and a new hunger burning deep in the most womanly part of her. She dropped into her chair and held her head in her hands as she realized that she was starting to fall in love with a man she barely knew.

"Don't," she warned herself, and Blue gave out a bark of agreement.

But she feared it was already too late. Much too late.

A few days later Luke stared at a copy of Josh Kinkaid's birth certificate. Luke smoothed the official paper open on the scarred maple table that had come with his apartment in the carriage house. The name of Josh's father was missing, but the birth date was perfect. With a little math, Luke figured Katie had gotten pregnant about a month to six weeks before Dave Sorenson had left Bittersweet.

It wasn't proof positive, of course; she could have had another lover, but Luke had the painful sensation that he knew for certain that Josh Kinkaid was Ralph Sorenson's only grandchild. His jaw tightened and he wondered where the feeling of satisfaction he'd anticipated in figuring out this mystery was. He was about to earn the money he'd been promised, about to give an elderly man a ray of hope before he died, about to betray a woman he thought he could all too easily fall in love with.

At that thought, he started. He wasn't falling in love! Hell, at best what he felt for Katie Kinkaid was lust. And what did it matter if he let Sorenson know the truth? The man had a right to meet his grandkid, didn't he? Of course he did. Luke kicked out his chair, grabbed his hat from a peg near the door and walked outside to the landing where the sultry evening air was so thick it seemed to weigh against his skin.

Somewhere over the mountains, thunder rumbled and he thought about his livestock at the ranch. He'd better check on the horses and cattle, than return to town.

To Katie.

His gut clenched when he thought of leaving her that morning in her bathrobe. He'd wanted to stay, to carry her back to the bedroom and finish what he'd started on the night of Bliss Cawthorne's marriage. It had been five or six days since then, and the image of her lying on the bed, the shimmering blue gown peeled down to her waist, her gorgeous breasts exposed and crowned with rosy nipples, had haunted him. Day and night. He'd cruised by her house since then, telling himself that he was checking to see that no one was lingering in the shadows of her cottage, that no intruder was hell-bent on breaking in, that he was only checking on her.

And he'd called. Asked her about Josh's ankle and if she'd had any more hang-ups, or if she'd changed the locks. She'd told him in no uncertain terms that it wasn't really any of his business, but he knew that it wasn't his concern that bothered her; it was the unspoken current that existed between them, the passion that they both tried to ignore, that caused her tongue to lash out.

He could break down and knock on her door. Use the same excuse he'd used the other night, about the potential prowler. And they'd end up in bed; they wouldn't be able to stop themselves. But he knew it was a sham, a pretense to see her again.

Trying to convince himself that he'd been overreacting—that no one had been observing them at the hotel the night of the Lafferty wedding, that nothing in her house had been out of place and no one had broken in, that the phone calls she'd received were just a rash of wrong numbers—he climbed down the outside staircase.

The main house was nearly empty; a moving van had carted off most of Tiffany Santini's belongings the day before. Boxes, crates and sacks were piled on the back porch and the windows were dark. Soon, Katie and Josh would be moving in. It calmed him somehow, to think that she'd be near. Sure, there'd be hell to pay because he knew himself well enough to realize that he'd use any reason to get close to her, any excuse to get her into bed with him.

"Damn it all to hell." What was it about that woman that made him want to protect her one minute and make love to her the next?

As he crossed the dry, yellowed lawn he noticed that the sky was dark, thick with swollen-bellied clouds that blocked the sun. He made his way to the truck just as the first fat raindrops began to fall. Inside the cab it was hot, breathless. He opened the windows, shoved the rig into reverse and squinted as rivulets of rain slithered through the film of dust that covered his windshield. He wouldn't think of Katie right now but sooner or later, he'd have to deal with her.

"I don't believe you." Josh, half lying on the rumpled sheets of his bed, stared at his mother with wide-eyed disgust.

Katie cringed. "It's true. Why would I lie?"

"But you did. You lied."

"And now I'm telling you the truth," she said, dying a little inside. "Dave Sorenson is . . . your father." She sat on the edge of the bed and opened the yearbook from her days in high school. "I'd always thought there would be more time. That when you were older . . . Oh, Josh, I made a horrible mistake." Her voice was thick, her throat nearly closed. "Your dad and I . . ." How could she explain a short-term love affair to a boy who wasn't yet eleven? "We were just kids and he moved away. By the time I knew I was pregnant with you, he was already gone and, I think, dating some other girl in his new town." She pointed to Dave's senior-class picture. He looked so young, so boyish, and yet he'd been her first love. "I'm sure he would have loved you a lot, but he never knew about you."

"Because you lied."

"Yes." She bit her lip and fought the urge to break down and sob like a baby. "Yes."

"You should have told me."

She felt as if she'd been stabbed through the heart. Of course she should have. "I know."

He swallowed hard and folded his arms over his chest. Thrusting out his chin, he demanded, "Are you gonna send me to him or is he comin' here, or what?"

"No," she said, summoning every bit of courage she could muster. "He can't. Not anymore. He died . . . a few months ago, I guess . . . and I didn't know it. He was in the military. There was a helicopter accident while they were on maneuvers and . . . and he didn't survive."

Josh gasped and his face, tanned from the summer sun, turned a sickly chalky shade. Tears filled his eyes.

"I don't believe you," he said again.

"It's true."

"How do you know?"

"A friend . . . he told me." For the first time she considered the fact that Luke could have been mistaken or lied, and she mentally kicked herself for not checking it out herself. She was a reporter, for God's sake. She knew better than to take someone's word. She spent days double-checking sources and yet this time, she'd taken Luke's story about Dave as if it were Gospel from the Bible.

But he wouldn't have lied.

"You shoulda told me. Told him about me," Josh said.

"As I said, I'm sorry, Josh." She sniffed as tears drizzled down her cheeks. "So sorry."

"Why didn't you?"

"I—I couldn't. It was wrong. Bad. I wish I could change things, but I can't. I . . ." She sighed and fought the urge to break down altogether. "I just can't. Not now."

He blinked and looked away toward the window that was open just a crack. Outside, thunder rumbled over the hills and rain began to drip down the windowpanes. Blue growled from the living room. With a swipe of one hand Josh wiped the tip of his nose and as Katie touched him he shifted, using his shoulder as a shield, silently shunning her.

They were only inches apart but the distance between them seemed vast. Unbridgeable.

"Josh—"

"Leave me alone."

"Honey, please—"

He hopped to his feet, winced from the pain in his ankle, then skewered her with eyes filled with hatred. With a condemning finger pointed at her nose, he whispered his newfound mantra: "You shoulda told me." His voice cracked and Katie's heart shattered into a million pieces.

"You're right," she admitted, standing and wanting so badly to fold him into her arms. Here in his room where model airplanes, books, CDs and magazines had begun to be packed into boxes for the move. Boxes of memorabilia that his father had never seen. A soccer trophy winked in the harsh light from the overhead fixture—a trophy Josh had never shared with his father. How had she been so selfish? She'd denied her son his right to know his own dad. Just as she'd been denied the knowledge of her biological father. "You're right, Josh. I made a mistake," she admitted, "but I can't change anything now. I can only let you meet your other grandparents—your father's parents. They want to see you."

"Just leave me alone." His chin inched up in rebellious defiance and his cheeks were wet from his silent tears.

"Listen, Josh—"

"I said, leave me alone." He snagged up the yearbook and Katie told herself she had no choice but to let him sort through his feelings, whatever pain she'd inadvertently hurled at him. She swallowed hard. "Think about it."

"I don't want to talk to anybody!"

"Okay, okay, I'll let you be," she said, knowing he needed time to adjust to the bomb she'd just set off in his life. "But Grandma's coming over and—"

"I don't want to see her," Josh insisted, reaching for the remote control and clicking on the small television set to a decibel level guaranteed to shatter glass. "I don't want to talk to anyone."

"You might. Later."

He glared at her with red-rimmed eyes that were filled with silent, deadly accusations. His chin wobbled and his back stiffened in some vain attempt at manhood.

"I'll be in the living room. When Grandma gets here I'll send her in."

"No."

"Josh—"

His lips compressed and she held both hands up as if to fend off an attack. "Okay, okay, bud, I'll give you some time alone, but I think we should talk this out."

"I don't want to talk to you or Grandma or anyone."

"We'll see." She walked out of the room and jumped as the door slammed behind her. Clearing her throat she headed for her desk and told herself it would all work out. Of course, Josh was hurt, disappointed and angry. Of course he wanted to scream and cry and mourn for a father he'd never known.

She sank into her desk chair and sighed, stirring her bangs.

And of course, he was right. She should have told him the truth. Years ago. But she hadn't. Now, it seemed, they would all have to pay the price.

Chapter Eight

"Of course, Josh is upset," Brynnie said, rummaging in her purse for a pack of gum that, it was advertised, would cut down her need for a cigarette. She tossed her keys, eye-glass case, coin purse and wallet onto Katie's table before she found the gum. "Who wouldn't be?" She opened the pack and shook out a stick. With a longing sigh for a smoke she'd sworn to give up, she plopped the gum into her mouth.

Katie swiped at the counter haphazardly with her sponge. "I should have told him about Dave. No. Reverse that." She rinsed the sponge at the sink. "I should have told Dave about Josh." Wiping her hands on a towel hanging over the handle of the oven she glanced down the hallway. "He's been in there over an hour."

"Give him time," her mother advised.

Katie bit her lip. She felt worse than awful. Sometimes she thought that as a mother she'd failed miserably. This was one of those times.

Brynnie eyed the few boxes that were stacked in the corner. "I've got an idea. I'll help you load these into the Jeep and you can take them over to the new place."

"Even though Tiffany and J.D. moved out the other day, I think they still have some things they want to do to the place before I call it home," Katie said, though her half-sister had told her that the house was just about ready and had encouraged her to start moving. "Besides, I can't leave Josh now."

"Of course you can." Her mother wasn't swayed. "Do you really think it makes any difference to him if you're here or a few blocks across town?"

"But if he wants to talk—"

"He can wait. Besides, I'm here. I know the scoop."

"It's my job."

"I'm his grandmother and I've dealt with this kind of thing a lot." Brynnie managed a smile as she popped her gum. "Besides, I kind of owe you one, don't I?"

"Why?"

"For letting you think that Hal Kinkaid was your father." Two spots of color appeared on her cheeks. "I, uh, should apologize to you for that little fib."

"I think it was more than a 'little fib,' but it doesn't matter right now. It's water under the bridge," Katie said, waving off her mother's concerns.

"You didn't think so at the time."

Katie managed a half smile. "Well, come on, Mom, you have to admit that of all your husbands, Hal was the least . . . 'memorable,' for lack of a better word."

"You mean boring."

"That, too." Katie rubbed her arms at the thought of her surly, overbearing namesake. He was a steady worker, but found absolutely no joy in life. "I never knew what you saw in him."

"Neither do I. Not now." Brynnie motioned to the boxes. "Go on, Katie, take these over to the house. Give me a couple of hours alone with my grandson."

Katie hesitated. "If you think it'll work."

With a wink, Brynnie slowly nodded her head. "Guaranteed."

"Okay, okay." Katie walked down the hall to Josh's room

and rapped on the door with her knuckles. Her mother was just a step behind. "Bud?" Katie called through the panels.

"Go 'way!"

So Josh was still in his foul mood. Despite his order, Katie opened the door a crack. "No reason to be rude."

He didn't look her way but she could read the I-don't-want-to-talk-to-you expression on his face. "I'm gonna run some boxes over to the new place, but Grandma's here, okay?"

"I can stay by myself."

"Not while I'm anywhere in the vicinity," Brynnie said. "I never give up a chance to play darts or Hearts or Scrabble with my favorite grandson."

"I'm your only grandson," he grumbled, but a dimple creased one cheek—a dimple Katie hadn't seen since she'd told him about his father.

"Then that makes you extra special, doesn't it?" Brynnie edged into the room and looked over her shoulder. "Go on," she mouthed to Katie as she took a seat on the foot of the bed. "Now, kiddo, what'll the bet be?"

"I dunno."

"I know. If I win, you'll come over and mow my lawn, but if you win, I'll take you and a friend over to the water park next weekend."

"Really?" Josh sent his mother a glance that said he knew he was being conned.

"Of course." Brynnie looked up, caught Katie standing at the crack in the doorway and gave her a curt little wave.

"Okay, okay, I can take a hint," Katie said, relieved that her son seemed to be jollying out of his bad mood. "I'll see you both later."

She packed the Jeep with boxes, coats from the front closet and a few sacks from the kitchen, then drove to the old Victorian house she would soon call home. It felt odd, somehow; she and Josh had lived in the cottage for all of his life. But it was time for a change.

She parked in an open spot by the garage, noticed that Luke's pickup was missing and kicked herself when she felt a pang of disappointment. "Forget him," she whispered under her breath as she started unloading boxes and carrying them into the old house. It seemed empty and cold. Fresh paint, a soft gold color that Tiffany had let Katie pick out, covered the walls and the wood floors gleamed, but the furniture was missing, the hanging pots, the dried herbs and the children's artwork stripped from what had been Tiffany's once-cozy kitchen. No black cat slunk through the shadows and without the wail of Stephen's guitar, the patter of Christina's busy feet or Tiffany's soft laughter, the house was little more than a tomb.

"Cut it out," she reprimanded and busied herself by carrying box after box into the house and leaving it in the appropriate room. She'd finished her last trip and was actually hanging coats in the front hall when she heard the back door open.

Her heart nearly stopped.

"Hello?" Luke's voice filled the empty space.

"In here." Her pulse jumped a bit as he came into view—tall and rangy, in jeans and a faded denim shirt with its sleeves shoved to the elbows, his hair windblown. He brought with him the scents of rainwater and horses.

"Movin' in?" he asked, his blue eyes intense.

"The first load." She shut the closet door and suddenly felt tongue-tied. "I, uh, I'll move the big stuff in a couple of days. My brothers have offered to help with the furniture and appliances."

He glanced around the empty rooms. "Your boy here?"

"At home with Grandma." A pang of regret sliced through her heart at the thought of Josh and his reaction to the news that the father he'd never known was dead.

As if he read the pain in her expression, Luke said, "Wait here, I've got an idea."

"For what—?" she asked but he'd already turned on his heel and was striding toward the kitchen. A second later the screen door banged shut behind him. Curious, she couldn't help but follow the sound and walk into the kitchen where she looked through the window and watched as he dashed through the raindrops to the carriage house, then took the stairs to the upper floor two at a time. A few seconds later he reappeared carrying a bottle of wine and two glasses. She watched as he jogged across the yard and entered the house with the smell of fresh rain clinging to him.

"I think we should christen the place," he said, removing a corkscrew from his pocket and piercing the foil over the cork with the tool's sharp tip. "Come on," he encouraged, as if witnessing skepticism on her face. "Let's do it right. In here." As he started uncorking the bottle he led her into the parlor where bay windows, draped in gauzy curtains overlooked the front yard and a marble fireplace loomed against the opposite wall. The cork popped. "Here, you pour. I'll be right back."

"What now?" she asked, but watched him leave again and didn't argue. There was something enchanting about spending some time alone with him here.

Careful, you'll only get yourself into trouble, her mind warned as she tipped the bottle and the rich, dark Merlot streamed into the two stemmed glasses.

"I wouldn't have thought of you as having anything like these," she observed, holding up one of the goblets and twisting its stem between her fingers as he returned carrying chunks of firewood and kindling. He leaned over the grate and cast a glance in her direction. Over his shoulder he muttered, "Castoffs from the divorce."

"Oh." She didn't want to be reminded that he'd been

married once. Not tonight. "I just meant that you seem more like a guy who drinks beer."

"Sometimes. Whatever suits the mood." He looked over his shoulder again, his eyes a deep, glittering blue. "I think it's good to mix things up, don't you?"

"Of course."

"Good." He turned his attention back to the fire and she noticed the darker streaks of blond where rainwater had run, from the top of his head and the way his neck, at its base, spread into strong shoulder muscles that disappeared beneath the collar of his shirt.

She remembered seeing his bare chest and muscular back and at the thought her pulse elevated and she fought the urge to run. This was too close, too intimate. He was squatting, the worn heels of his boots above the carpet as he leaned forward. His jeans were low on his hips, his waist-band gaping at his spine, but, unfortunately, the tail of his shirt never moved, remained tucked while he struck a match against the sole of one boot and lit the fire. She realized that being alone with him was dammed close to emotional suicide, that her fascination for him was running far too deep, and yet she couldn't resist staying with him.

With a spark and a crackle, flames began to devour the dry kindling and wood. Smoke billowed into the room. "Dammit," he said, reaching quickly above the hungry, snap-ping flames to open the flue. "I forget some people close these things." The chimney began to draw. "You didn't know that my plan was to asphyxiate you, did you?"

She laughed as he straightened, dusted his hands to-gether, then cracked one of the windows. "Better?"

"Much."

"So much for being suave and debonair." He sat on the floor next to her and accepted a glass.

"That's okay. I'm not into the sleek-and-sophisticated type."

"Lucky for me." He offered her a crooked smile that drilled right to the core of her. "How about a toast?"

"A toast? I can't wait to hear this."

"Here's to you, Katie Kinkaid." He touched the rim of his glass to hers and looked deep into her eyes. "May you find your happiness here and may you always be safe."

Her heart nearly crumpled and her throat grew thick, but she managed a frail smile. "And here's to you, Luke Gates," she said, again nudging his glass with hers. "Man of mystery, cowboy and Bittersweet's newest entrepreneur. May the ranch be a raving success."

"It will be." He grinned crookedly, his gaze still holding hers as he took the first sip. Katie's heart thrummed, her throat was as dry as a desert and she sipped from her glass, feeling the red wine slide down her throat more easily than she'd expected. She shouldn't be doing this; the room was much too intimate, the atmosphere seductive.

Firelight played in Luke's hair, reflecting in his eyes and gilding his skin. He stretched out, boots nearly touching the marble hearth, one elbow propping his shoulders upright.

"Tell me about yourself," he suggested.

"Not much more to tell." She took another swallow. "I think you know most of the high points."

"Do I?" One of his eyebrows arched and her stomach rolled over. He was so damned sexy, so raw and male. As he drank from his glass she watched his Adam's apple move and she found the involuntary motion decidedly seductive. What was wrong with her? Why did she always see Luke Gates as a raw, sexual man; not just someone she wanted as a friend. "How about the men in your life?"

"'The men'?" she repeated and smiled. "The dozens of men?" When his smile faded she shook her head. "The truth of the matter is, there just haven't been many."

"There was Josh's father."

Dave. Her heart twisted a bit. "He was a long time ago. I was in high school."

"And since?"

I've dated a little. Nothing serious. I had Josh to think about, to protect, and of course, my job. I . . . I told myself I couldn't get involved with anyone, I had too many responsibilities and maybe it was just a defense mechanism, but the truth of the matter is that no one interested me." *Until you.*

"Most women want a man to be a father to their kids."

"I'm not most women," she said, lifting her chin defiantly.

"I noticed." His eyes locked with hers and in that instant she knew she would make love to him. It was inevitable, like the ebb and flow of the tide. The wine was beginning to warm her blood and the intimacy of the room enfolded her in a soft, seductive cocoon. Raindrops sparkling with firelight trailed down the windowpanes and she felt as if she and Luke were the only two people on earth. She licked a drop of Merlot from her lips and his gaze followed her movement.

Slowly he took her glass from her hand, set it along with his in a corner near the fireplace, then stretched out beside her on the carpet and wrapped his arms around her. She turned her head up expectantly but wasn't prepared for the onslaught on her senses as his lips met hers, his tongue delved between her teeth and a rush of desire as hot as lava sped through her blood.

This time there were no excuses, no interruptions. His tongue and hands were everywhere and without a thought she kissed him back, her arms drawing him closer still, her mind swimming with erotic images as he pressed wet, warm kisses onto her eyes, her neck, her shoulders. He stripped her clothes from her body, leaving her naked, her skin shimmering with perspiration before the fire. And she, too, worked at the buttons of his shirt, tore open the waistband of his jeans, pulled hard and heard a sexy series of pops as his fly gave way.

His body was lean and sinewy, sleek muscles visible through skin that was tanned except for a strip of white over his buttocks. Golden hair covered his chest and his manhood, which was strong, erect and ready.

His fingers caressed her, his lips and tongue exploring each intimate crevice and curve. She tingled inside as she, tentatively at first, and then with more confidence, touched him and heard him moan with deep, hungry pleasure.

She didn't think about the consequences as he rolled atop her, didn't consider recriminations. She arched as he placed his big, callused hands on either side of her rib cage, his fingers splaying around her ribs, his thumbs rubbing her nipples seductively. His hair fell forward, streaked gold and red by the firelight as he bent forward and kissed the tip of each breast. The world began to tilt. He pushed his tongue through the valley of her sternum; then, with his lips, climbed each mound and lingered, laving and sucking at her nipples. Desire, dark and insistent, curled deep inside her, and brought with it a moistness, a wild yearning she hadn't felt in years.

"Katie," he rasped, lifting his head as her fingers dug into the hard, sinewy muscles of his buttocks. "Sweet, sweet Katie."

She opened her mouth to speak but couldn't form a word.

"Is this what you want?"

"Yes." She didn't hesitate. It had been so long. Too long. Winding an arm around his neck, she pulled his head down to hers and kissed him, her mouth open and waiting, her body quivering with a passion she'd feared she'd lost.

His knees parted her legs and he looked one last time into her eyes before he thrust into her as if he'd wanted to make love to her all his life. She gasped as he entered her, holding tightly to the arms planted on either side of her head, and as he withdrew and entered again, rose to meet him. She held his gaze as their bodies joined, moved her hips to his rhythm, felt the sting of anticipation in her bloodstream. All her doubts fled, all her worries disappeared and she was lost in the single purpose of loving this lone, tough man.

Faster and faster he moved and she could scarcely breathe, gasping in short, sharp bursts that matched the crazy beating of her heart.

"Katie," he cried, throwing back his head as he spilled himself into her. "Katie!"

She clung to him, her body convulsing, her universe shattering deep in her soul. He fell against her, breathing hard and holding her close as he rolled to the side.

Tears welled deep in her eyes and he leaned over and kissed each eyelid. "Regrets?" he asked, his expression clouding.

"Relief."

"Good." He held her close, in strong arms that made her feel safe and secure, and she closed her eyes, knowing that the moment would soon end, but making it last for as long as she could. He sighed across her hair and she snuggled close. She wouldn't believe that making love to Luke Gates was anything but wonderful.

A few days later Katie was still thinking about making love to Luke, wondering if it would ever happen again as she carried a box of pots and pans onto the back porch. She stacked the box on top of the growing pile of assorted crates and cartons that waited for Jarrod, Nathan and Trevor on the back porch of her little cottage. Sweat drizzled down her nape and forehead. She mopped her brow, then swiped at a cobweb that dangled from the rafters of the roof.

The rainstorm of a few nights before was long gone and the temperature had soared into the nineties again, proof that summer wasn't ready to give up its searing hold on the Rogue River Valley.

The yard was patchy and yellow, the leaves on the trees just starting to turn gold with the promise of autumn. She'd miss this place, she thought, as she squinted against the sun and watched Blue sniff in the shrubbery for a squirrel or bird hidden deep in the foliage. The old dog moved his head to look at her, wagged his tail, then turned back to smelling the underbrush.

But it was time to move, she decided. Things were changing. Josh on the threshold of adolescence, was dealing with the new changes in his life—about his father's death and accepting a grandfather he hadn't known. Brynnie had gotten through to him. Within a few more years he'd slowly be pulling away from his mother.

Katie had already run an advertisement in the "For Rent" column of the *Review's* Classified section. It was time to move on in many ways.

She went inside her sweltering kitchen, turned on the tap and holding her hair away from her face, drank from the faucet. She swiped the back of her hand over her mouth, then walked to Josh's room. With a rap of her fingers, she called through the door. "Need any help in there?"

There was a pause. Her hand was on the doorknob when he answered. "Nope."

"Jarrod and the twins will be here soon."

"I know."

She wanted to reprimand him, to tell him to try and stop punishing her; but she bit her tongue and decided to give him some space. For the past few days—ever since Katie had told him about his father—Josh had been upset and sullen, offering her the juvenile equivalent to the cold shoulder.

Katie had tried to broach the subject of Dave several

times since she'd first told her son about his father, but Josh had retreated into disgusted silence and had spent his time either at school or with his friends. When he was at home, he kept to his room, watching the small television, playing video games and generally indulging his bad mood. But, the good news was that he was off crutches for good; the doctor had called the Monday after Bliss's wedding with a report that the specialists who had read his X ray had found no indication of fracture in his ankle and physically he was solid again.

And today was different. They were moving and she'd forced Josh into a halfway-decent mood. He'd even offered to help her pack up her desk. A small olive branch, but one that she'd quickly accepted.

Their lives were changing in other ways. As of this day, Katie would live next door to Luke.

Which was another problem.

She'd seen Luke several times since the late afternoon when they'd made love. Each time, he'd been cordial and warm, a sexy, affectionate smile creasing his jaw whenever they'd run into each other. But he hadn't called and hadn't so much as touched her again.

It was almost as if something had come between them, an invisible barrier she didn't understand. She filled another cardboard box with memorabilia from her kitchen, piling in knickknacks and pictures, cookbooks and a few pot holders.

She heard the truck before she saw its rear end back into the drive. As it slowed and parked several feet away from the garage, she heard her half-brothers' shouts.

"Start with the big things—washer and dryer," Jarrod ordered as he climbed out of the cab. "And don't forget the refrigerator."

"As if I'd let them forget anything." Katie stepped onto the back porch as her twin brothers leaped past the two steps and barreled into the kitchen. "But don't worry about the refrigerator. It stays with the place."

"Good. Just point us in the right direction," Nathan told her. His hair was a dark brown, stick straight and flopped over a high forehead beneath which intense hazel eyes bored into her.

She followed her brothers inside and from the archway in the kitchen looked down the hallway to where Trevor was already unhooking the hoses to the washing machine that was wedged into what was euphemistically called a "laundry closet."

Jarrod pushed open the screen door and frowned at the torn, jagged mesh. "I think I made some wild promise about fixing this," he said, sticking a finger through the hole.

"That you did." She winked at him. "And just because I'm moving doesn't let you off the hook, you know. This is still my house and you made a promise."

"Consider it done."

"Oh, sure. Promises, promises," she quipped blithely.

"Hey, are we gonna get some help in here?" Trevor, the more hotheaded of the twins, yelled.

"Duty calls." Jarrod was already halfway there. "Hey, kid. How about giving your uncles a hand?"

Josh, hearing the commotion had poked his head out of his room. Upon spying Katie's half-brothers, he joined in and forgot to cast his mother a disparaging glance before he helped unhook the dryer. Katie mentally crossed her fingers that he'd forgive her.

As the men handled the bigger items, the beds, couches, tables and chairs Katie kept filling boxes from the few cupboards that she hadn't already cleared out.

"I can't believe how much junk you've got," Trevor observed on one trip to the truck. "Can't you get rid of half of it?"

"Didn't have time for a garage sale." She carried a

kitchen chair to the loading area at the rear of the big truck. "Besides, I don't like living as spartan as you."

"Easier that way."

Nathan laughed. He handed an end table to Jarrod who was standing inside the truck. "Yeah. Trevor thinks that a person can get by with a bedroll, a mess kit, and a television."

"Don't need much more," Trevor said, his hawkish features identical to his brother's. The difference in the twins was in their temperament. Nathan was steadier and levelheaded while Trevor was the hothead, always ready for a fight.

They finished loading and the house was nearly empty. Jarrod, Nathan and Josh rode over to the new place in the truck while Katie, with Trevor in the passenger seat and Blue in the back, followed in the Jeep.

"This is gonna be weird," Josh said, once they'd parked and everyone began unloading the furniture. Josh commandeered Stephen's old room while Katie set up her home office in Christina's bedroom.

Josh was right; it felt strange to see her bed and bureau in Tiffany's old room and stranger still to look out the window at the carriage house where Luke Gates lived. As she instructed her brothers on the placement of chairs, tables and lamps in the parlor, she noticed the ashes in the grate, testament to her afternoon of lovemaking with Luke. Their two empty wineglasses stood next to the once-full bottle of Merlot on the hearth.

Images of making love with Luke, of his corded muscles gleaming in the firelight, shot through her mind.

"Looks like someone had themselves a private party," Trevor observed as he and Nathan carried in a bookcase.

"That it does." Quickly Katie reached down, picked up the goblets and bottle, and hoped the back of her neck didn't look as warm as it felt.

Trevor didn't let up. "I wonder who—"

"Hey, pay attention!" Nathan, who was holding one end of the bookcase, wasn't in the mood for conjecture.

"Just put it there, to the side of the window," Katie said, and silently counted her lucky stars that the conversation was dropped. She carried the evidence of her evening with Luke into the kitchen and hoped Trevor's curiosity was sated. She didn't want to think about Luke and what had happened between them. Not now. Nor did she want to explain it to anyone. Especially her half-brothers.

She had too much to do.

An installer from the phone company came and hooked up the telephone and fax line while she was organizing the kitchen. In the midst of the pure chaos of wadded newspapers on the counters and floors, dishes in every available space and cupboards half filled, the easygoing man worked on the outlets, kept up a steady stream of conversation about his grandchildren and managed to install three phones.

Once they were installed, she found her courage along with Ralph Sorenson's phone number and she dialed. One ring, two, three and so on. No answer. No answering machine. She hung up disappointed, but told herself she'd try again.

A few minutes later Tiffany and J.D. came over and they, along with Katie's half-brothers, finished putting things in order. Christina was confused, but contented herself in chasing a nervous Blue through the house and Stephen and Josh holed up in Josh's new room. Though Stephen was three years older and in high school, he didn't seem to mind hanging out with his younger half-cousin when they weren't in school.

"It looks different," Tiffany said as she eyed the parlor and foyer. "And yet the same."

"It'll take some getting used to."

"For all of us." Tiffany showed Katie a file she'd left in the front-hall closet. Inside was information on the house, rental agreements, application forms and extra sets of keys. "I'll get you started and show you how this works," she said, "but it's not all that tough once you get the hang of it, and you can always call me."

"Hey, now that the phones are hooked up, how about ordering pizza?" Trevor called down from the second floor.

Katie grinned. "You think you deserve to be fed?"

"At least. It wouldn't hurt if you stocked the refrigerator with some beer, too."

"Okay, okay. You guys are in charge of the kids. Come on, Tiffany, let's run down to Papa Luigi's and figure out what we need for this crowd."

"Pepperoni!" Josh yelled.

"With double cheese," Jarrod added.

"Naw, get the all-meat special." Trevor was reaching for his wallet. "An extra large and—"

"I'll take care of it," Katie said. "It's on me." She ignored Trevor's offer of money and found her purse wedged between half-filled boxes on the kitchen counter. As she and Tiffany headed outside; Katie glanced up at the upper story of the carriage house, the place Luke temporarily called home. How would it be to live so close to him, to know that he was only a few short footsteps away? She thought again for a second about making love to him on the parlor floor and decided she couldn't dwell on the future or what, if any, kind of relationship she had with him. Only time would tell.

"I was wondering when I'd hear from you again. How's it going out there?" Ralph Sorenson's voice was loud, and filled with anticipation.

Luke had steeled himself for this phone call—a call he hadn't wanted to make. "It's going," he replied, hedging. "Renovations on the ranch house have started and I should be moving out to the spread in a month or two."

"So what about the other? Have you found out if Dave had a kid like he hinted at?"

Luke heard the note of eager enthusiasm in the older man's voice, could almost see Ralph's aging fingers curl, white-knuckled around the receiver. "I'm not certain yet," Luke admitted, "but I've got a couple of leads. Good ones. As soon as I know for sure, I'll let you know."

"It means a lot to me," Ralph said. "It's all I have left of my boy."

"I know. I'm working on it. Trust me." Luke heard the old man sigh and felt like a heel. How had he gotten himself roped into this mess? He turned the conversation to the weather, the price of feed, a new virus that was infecting cattle herds in west Texas—anything but the topic of David Sorenson's child. Stretching the telephone cord so that he could look out the window to where Josh Kinkaid and Stephen Santini were playing one-on-one at a basketball hoop hung on the garage, he leaned his shoulder against the window.

The older kid was winning by a lot, but Josh, even though he still hobbled a little, wasn't a slouch. Luke hated the thought, but he would bet dollars to doughnuts that the kid was Dave's. His age was perfect, and Katie acted so oddly—like she couldn't wait to change the subject—whenever the question of Josh's paternity came up. She'd also been blown away when she'd learned about Dave's death—had turned white as a sheet. Hell, what a mess.

But he couldn't prove it. He suspected only one person knew the truth.

"I'll call in a couple of days," he promised and hung up. It was time for a showdown with Ms. Kinkaid. As soon as her half-brothers and the Santini clan cleared out, Luke would have to confront her.

For a second the image of her lying beneath him, her

eyes wide and verdant green in anticipation, her lips parted in passion as he made love to her, flashed through his mind.

His gut clenched.

He'd never felt so completely satisfied in his life as he had with her; and he'd never felt so guilty for seducing someone. Katie Kinkaid was different from any of the other women he'd had in his lifetime. Very different. And that was a problem. A big problem.

Chapter Nine

That night, after most of the stuff had been packed away, Katie opened the door to Josh's room and smiled as she saw him spread-eagled across the bed, snoring softly, dead to the world. Her heart swelled as she brushed a wayward lock of hair from his forehead, leaned down and kissed his smooth brow. He had been warmer to her today, as if he was getting over the shock of realizing that she had lied to him, as if he were finally forgiving her. *Thank goodness.* She didn't know how much more of the cold shoulder she could take. As she left the room she snapped off the TV and lights, then softly closed the door behind her.

In the next room over, her new office, she rearranged some files on her computer, edited an article on the new Santini winery and vineyards, and went through her notes on Isaac Wells. It had been over a week since she'd received the letter, and she'd never been contacted again. The police had told her nothing and she was starting to believe she'd been the target of some kind of hoax, though she couldn't begin to think why. "Live and learn," she said, frowning and catching a glimpse of her pale reflection, blurred over the words of her article in her computer monitor.

A truck roared into the drive and Katie's heart jumped. The engine died as she opened the blinds and peered through. Luke's truck was parked near the garage, the glow of a security lamp reflecting on its hood. Stretching as he climbed from the cab, he strode across the backyard. His expression was stern, his demeanor that of a man with a mission. Her pulse jumped of its own accord.

He cast a quick look at the house and upstairs to the lighted window. Katie's throat caught. She couldn't look away. He didn't so much as smile, and quickly disappeared from view beneath the roof of the porch. Her porch. Oh, God, he was coming to see her.

Katie was down the stairs in a flash, her bare feet skimming the wooden steps and hallway into the kitchen. She opened the door and found him in the shadows, as taciturn and unfriendly as she'd ever seen him. "Something's wrong," she guessed.

"You could say that."

Her heart went wild. "Come in, come in. What is it?"

Once inside, he grabbed one of the chairs positioned around the table and straddled it. Folding his arms over the back, he stared up at her. Dread did a slow crawl up her spine. In a moment of intuitive divination she knew what this was about.

"I want to talk about Josh's father."

"I figured as much." Her voice sounded strangled, even to her own ears. "Why?"

"It's time."

She wanted to argue, to tell him it was none of his business, but the truth of the matter was out. Now that Josh knew his parentage, there seemed no reason to lie. "I don't see why it could possibly matter to you," she began, rubbing at a spot on the counter with one finger, "but you may as well know that Josh was Dave Sorenson's son. We . . . we knew each other in high school, got involved and then, just before he left, I got pregnant." Her cheeks burned and for a second she thought she might break down altogether, but she managed to keep her voice steady and look Luke in the eye.

"You never told him that he had a son."

"Nope." She shook her head and couldn't hide the regret in her voice. It seemed Luke was determined that she face all her demons. Tonight. "I should have. For Dave. For Josh. I . . . I was young and stupid and naive and hurt. I had explained to Dave before he moved away that there was a chance that I was pregnant, but he didn't seem concerned and then, when I knew for sure, I found out that he'd already hooked up with another girl in Texas. I guess I had too much pride to run after him and give him the news he didn't want to hear—that he was going to be a father." She drew in a long, shaky breath. "So the only ·person I confided in was my mom. No one else knew and she kept my secret. I didn't even tell Jarrod who Josh's dad was and I felt badly about it, because Jarrod saw me through some pretty dark hours. Stood by me and didn't ask any questions or give me any lectures."

Luke raised an eyebrow, silently encouraging her to continue.

"I'm not making excuses. I should have told Dave the truth. I thought I was protecting my son and myself, but really I only ended up hurting Josh." She managed a thin, frail smile. "I made a mistake. A big one."

"Everyone does." Surprisingly, he didn't seem to judge her.

Folding her arms under her breasts, trying to maintain some semblance of poise, she fought tears. "So, cowboy from Texas, what does it matter to you?"

"I already told you that I knew Dave. Worked for years for Dave's father, Ralph."

"Uh-huh." She didn't like the way this was heading.

"And you know I bought my place from him." Luke seemed as tense as she. His shoulders were rigid, his eyes watching her every move.

"Maybe you should tell me what I don't already know." She was careful. Wary. Where was the warm man to whom she'd made love only a few days before?

"As I said, I didn't buy the place with cash, really. I worked for him, he withheld part of my paycheck with the understanding that I'd one day use that money as a down payment on a place outside of Dallas. However, that didn't work out and he offered me full ownership out here instead. It was a deal I couldn't pass up."

He'd told her all this before, but nothing he'd said so far explained the rigid set of his jaw or the lines of silent anger that bracketed his mouth. "So?"

"He asked a favor of me before I headed west."

Here it comes. "What kind of favor?" she asked, not really sure she wanted to know. Her pulse thundered through her brain.

"Ralph asked me to do some checking when I came into town. Before his death Dave had mentioned that he might have fathered a child back here and Ralph wanted to locate that grandchild if he had. That's why I came over here tonight. To get this all out in the open. It's been a secret too long."

Katie's chest was as tight as if it had suddenly been strapped in steel bands. "I had already decided to talk to the Sorensons," she said, though she still felt cornered, as if tracking hounds had been put on her trail and she had no place to run to, her back against the face of a sheer cliff. "But first I had to talk to Josh."

"He didn't know?"

She shook her head and felt beads of sweat collecting at her nape and forehead. "As I said, no one did. Whenever the subject of his father came up, I told him that the man was in my life for a very short period, then gone, that I didn't know much about him anymore. I promised to tell him the whole story some day, but, for the most part, I hedged. I didn't want

Josh to hear things about a father who had left him before he was born, and I thought that if I kept the guy anonymous, and if there was no speculation, no gossip, it would be okay. Of course, that was a mistake. People talk and kids are cruel." She swiped her bangs from her eyes. "You have to understand I was little more than a kid, myself. I'd been teased all my growing-up years because my mom was forever getting married and divorced. It seemed like everyone else's family was stable and mine was this . . . this chaotic mess.

"I know now that it wasn't true. All families have their little secrets." She laughed at the irony. "And of course, I had no idea that the man who was supposed to be my father, wasn't. My mom lied to me, too. I would have *died* if I'd guessed that I was the product of a . . . an illicit affair. That I would be called 'illegitimate.' It was bad enough as it was, and I was determined that I wouldn't put my kid through the same kind of pain."

She leaned a hip against the kitchen island and glanced out to the backyard where moonlight was casting the dry grass in soft shades of silver. "Anyway, of course it was probably worse for Josh to not tell him the truth, but I was young and convinced I was doing the right thing. The trouble with a lie is it feeds on itself and keeps growing. Any time the subject came up, I evaded the issue and told myself he was too young to understand. I thought there would be plenty of time. It wasn't as if Dave had shown any interest in my possible pregnancy, anyway. But then you landed in town with the news that Dave was dead and I . . . I couldn't stand it. I knew I had to level with Josh. I finally talked with him a few days ago."

"How did he take the news?"

"He was stunned. No. *Horrified* would probably be a better word. Then, once the disbelief subsided, he was angry—I mean, really angry with me." She swallowed hard and reached into the cupboard for a glass. "Can't say as I blame him. I was mad that my mom lied about who my father was, but at least I had the chance to meet him and decide for myself how much I wanted John Cawthorne in my life. Josh has no options. I took them away from him." She flipped on the tap, filled her glass and drank to quench the dryness at the back of her throat.

"You did what you thought was best." Luke's voice was low, a balm.

"Yeah, and it blew up in my face." She lifted her glass. "You want some?"

"Naw, I'm fine." Getting to his feet, he went to her and wrapped solid arms around her torso. "You can't beat yourself up for this."

"Oh, no?" Turning to gaze up at him, she saw the sweet seduction in his eyes, heard his sharp intake of breath as her breasts brushed against his shirt.

"Nope." His gaze slid down her face. "Besides, we have other problems."

"Do we?"

"Mmm." His arms tightened, holding her close, and she was pulled snugly to him, her breasts flattening against his chest, her hips pressed intimately to his. Gazing into her eyes, he lowered his head to hers. "This," he said, his breath warm against her face, "is a much bigger issue." His mouth slanted over hers and her blood turned to fire.

So this was the way it would be with him, she realized. Each and every time they touched, passion would ignite. Her arms wound around his neck and he lifted her off her feet. When he started for the stairs, common sense ruled. "We can't," she whispered, struggling to get down. "Not with Josh here."

Luke's eyes were the color of midnight, but instead of releasing her, he carried her outside, across the moon-washed lawn and up the stairs to the carriage house. "If he wakes up, we'll know," he assured her as he kicked open the door and crossed the hardwood floor to the bedroom. He paused long enough to flip the lock behind him, then laid her on the bed and kissed her as if he would never stop.

"So I thought we could have lunch and catch up," Bliss suggested a few days later. Katie, working at the office, balanced the receiver between her shoulder and ear.

Bliss, home from her short honeymoon, was calling from her cell phone and still sounding breathlessly in love. She and Mason had just gotten back to Oregon and were living at Cawthorne Acres, the ranch John Cawthorne had called his own until his marriage to Brynnie. Brynnie had insisted he give up ranching for fear of his having another heart attack and he'd reluctantly sold the ranch to Mason and Bliss. John and his wife would move into town as soon as Brynnie's house was remodeled to suit them. Meanwhile, Bliss and Mason shared the place with them.

"Sounds great." Katie stretched the cord of her phone around the computer monitor glowing on her desk and reached into a drawer for her pen. Her cubicle, or "office," as it was sometimes referred to, was situated in the middle of a huge room that was divided by soundproof barriers that didn't quite do the job. The conversation of other reporters, the clacking of computer keys, even noise from the street filtered through the maze of desks.

"Let's meet at Claudia's at one and I'll call Tiffany to see if she can join us."

"I'll be there," Katie promised, making a note to herself. She had an interview with Octavia Nesbitt, Tiffany's grandmother and president of the local garden club, this morning; then she wanted to talk with the police department and Jarrod about the Isaac Wells case.

Each day, she'd riffled eagerly through her mail, hoping

for another missive from the mystery person, but there had been nothing at work or at home. She'd even checked her mailbox at the cottage, on the off chance that the mail hadn't been forwarded. No such luck.

"Face it, Kinkaid," she grumbled to herself, "you've been led down the garden path." Lately, it seemed, her life had been bedlam. The move had been exhausting, but finally, most of her possessions seemed to have found new places of their own. Josh's ankle was fine and he was back at soccer practice, but the car was still a problem; she'd gone to the local dealer and hadn't been able to locate a used vehicle that suited her. Nor did there seem to be the perfect car in the "Autos for Sale" part of the classified advertisements in the paper. She was still using her father's Jeep, and though John assured her that it was better she be driving the rig than it be gathering dust in the garage, she wasn't comfortable without her own set of wheels. Her convertible, if not all that reliable, had been an old friend. She punched out Jarrod's number with the eraser end of her pencil and prayed that she wouldn't have to leave a message if he was out.

Her oldest half-brother had the decency to answer on the fourth ring.

"Hello?" His voice was curt, all business.

"It's me," she said. "I just wanted to thank you for helping with the move."

"No problem. And I will fix the screen door at the cottage. I promise."

"Good. I'll hold you to it. Now, what's new with the Isaac Wells case?"

"Ah, the real reason you called."

She grinned. "You always could read me like a book."

"Why don't you tell me about Mr. Wells, Katie. You're the one getting the letters."

"Letter. Singular. No more."

"Good. You know I don't like you involved in that mess," he admitted, not for the first time. "Stick with writing about the schools, and recipes and obituaries before your name is in one."

"Very funny."

"I'm serious, Katie. You know the police have been talking to Ray Dean and he's bad news."

Katie knew everything there was to know about Ray Dean, his estranged wife and their two sons.

Ray was a criminal, convicted of theft, burglary and suspected of being involved in other crimes that had never been solved. But he'd never been caught with a weapon or had anything to do with violent crimes. Nothing like kidnapping. Or murder.

"Just tell me you'll keep me posted," Katie nagged and heard her brother swear under his breath.

"I don't know what good will come of it."

"Only give my career the biggest shot in the arm of its life."

"Didn't I stupidly promise that if I find out anything," he said reluctantly, "I'd let you know?"

"I believe the exact words were that you'd give me 'an exclusive.'"

"You got it."

"Great," she said without a lot of enthusiasm, as time was ticking by and she was afraid this case might just end up as an unsolved mystery.

For the next few minutes they talked about the twins, their mother and Josh, then hung up. Grabbing her recorder, notepad, and purse, she flew out the door to where her father's Jeep was parked. The rig was hot, having sat in the sun all day, and Katie made a mental note to find another vehicle. She hated being obligated to anyone, even the man who had sired her.

Katie spent the next two hours interviewing Octavia Nesbitt. With honey-gold-colored hair that was teased to stand away from her small head, oversize glasses, and a big, toothy smile, Octavia was one of Bittersweet's leading citizens. In three-inch heels she was barely over five feet and Katie had never known her not to be dressed as if she were going to the opening of a Broadway play. At eighty, Octavia had the energy of a thirty-year-old, and she wasn't satisfied until she'd walked Katie through her house—the old Reed estate—and had given her a guided tour of her rose garden and greenhouse.

They drank tea during the interview and after the cups were drained, Octavia read the tea leaves that had settled in the bottom of Katie's porcelain cup.

"You're involved in an affair of the heart," she observed, lifting a penciled eyebrow above the top of her thick glasses. "And this man is very special to you."

Katie blushed to the roots of her hair. "Anything else?"

"Mmm." Her brow knitted and her lips puckered. "I can't make it out, but I'd say there was danger in your future."

Katie's heart nearly stopped, then she shook her head as she reminded herself she didn't believe in such nonsense as reading tea leaves, or palms or any other spiritual mumbo jumbo. Still, the odd sensation stuck with her as, after the extended interview, she explained that she was meeting her half-sisters for lunch and Octavia told her to say hello to Tiffany. "Darling girl," she said. "The apple of my eye, and her children . . . so dear. But her mother is such a proud woman—wouldn't take any help from me when she was raising Tiffany. Insisted on doing it on her own. Kind of a martyr, if you ask me. But . . . eventually Tiffany will get her trust fund and Rose will just have to accept it. Well, enough of that . . ." Her eyes twinkled behind her glasses. "I can't tell you how pleased I am that she's marrying J.D."

"She's happy, I think."

"As well she should be." Octavia clapped her beringed hands and looked skyward. "She deserves it. Now—" her owlish eyes fell on Katie again as they walked to the Jeep "you be careful." She touched Katie lightly on the arm. "Whatever it is you're getting yourself into, it's perilous."

"I'll be fine," Katie assured her, but left with an uneasy, nagging sensation that wouldn't let go of her. So what if the older woman saw danger in the bottom of a porcelain cup? "There's nothing to it," she told herself as she drove through the lazy streets of Bittersweet. "Nothing." Reading tea leaves was just the older woman's way of passing time.

But she saw that you were involved with Luke.

"Lucky guess," Katie assured herself as she wheeled into the restaurant parking lot. She locked the car and half jogged to the front door of the little cottage that had been converted into an eatery. Filled with antiques, books and ferns, Claudia's was known for its special soup of the day and cozy, intimate atmosphere.

Tiffany and Bliss were already in a corner booth, chatting as if they'd been friends forever instead of wary siblings who'd only recently discovered that they were related. Over the course of the summer, Tiffany had warmed to Bliss and the animosity that she originally had felt toward John Cawthorne's only "legitimate" daughter had all but disappeared. Slowly, the walls holding them apart were crumbling.

"We had a fabulous time," Bliss was saying as Katie slid into the booth and sat next to Tiffany. "I've been to Hawaii before, but Mason hadn't and—" she sighed dreamily, her honeymoon still fresh in her mind "It was different, being there with someone you love. We want to go back there when we can spend more time. Hi, Katie."

"Sorry I'm late."

"Not a problem. I took a chance and ordered you an iced tea."

"Thanks. So what were you talking about? Your honeymoon, right?"

Tiffany winked at Katie. "I'm trying to get all the details from her."

"Come on, spill 'em," Katie encouraged. "I hear Hawaii is way beyond romantic."

Bliss's cheeks turned a soft rosy hue. "It is. We snorkeled and rented a catamaran, and took long walks along the beach. Maui was breathtaking. You're in a mountain jungle one minute and in a resort on the beach the next."

"I'd love to go there," Tiffany said wistfully.

"Why don't you?" Bliss reached into her purse and came up with a handful of brochures and slapped them onto the table. "Take it from me, it's the perfect place for a honeymoon."

"With Stephen and Christina?" Tiffany thumbed through a brochure with a picture of a couple lying on the sand beneath a palm tree and staring at an aquamarine surf.

"No way. They can stay with me," Katie offered, then turned to Bliss. "You didn't take Dee Dee, did you?"

"Not this time, but we plan to the next."

"See. You can do the same," Katie told Tiffany as a waitress dressed in khaki slacks and a black T-shirt served them the iced tea. "Oh, jeez, I haven't figured out what I want," Katie said, opening her menu while her half-sisters ordered.

She settled on a French-dip sandwich, while Bliss ordered a Caesar salad and Tiffany chose a fruit plate and a bowl of soup. Bliss insisted Tiffany keep the information on Hawaii and Tiffany slipped the pamphlets into her purse. Conversation never lagged. Lunch was served and they ate and caught up, laughed and talked about everything and nothing. Katie felt a warm glow inside; as much as she'd loved her half-brothers growing up, she'd always wanted and needed the intimacy only a sister could inspire.

"Your grandmother says hi," Katie said to Tiffany, explaining about her interview with Octavia. "She's an interesting woman."

"Beyond interesting," Tiffany observed. "Did she give you a cup of tea, then read your fortune?"

"Yep." Katie grinned. "How'd you know?"

"She's done it to me for years. Let me guess She saw romance in your future, right?"

"Yeah."

"What else?"

Katie thought of Octavia's concerns about danger, then decided to dismiss them. It was all nonsense, anyway. "Not much."

Tiffany lifted a disbelieving brow. "That's odd. She usually comes up with two or three predictions. It's her passion."

"Now there's a good topic," Bliss said. "Passion. Why don't you fill us in on this romance you've got going with Luke Gates."

Katie nearly choked on a swallow of iced tea. "I don't think I'd call it a 'romance.'"

"Looked that way to me. At the reception." Bliss nudged her plate aside. "Convenient that he lives in the carriage house."

"'Convenient'?" Katie repeated.

Folding her arms across her chest, Bliss pinned Katie with her incredibly blue eyes. "Isn't it?"

"I don't know if 'convenient' is the right word," Katie hedged, "but, yes, since you're asking, I like him. That's about it. There's really not much more to tell."

Tiffany rolled her large eyes. "Who are you trying to

kid?" Sending Bliss a conspiring glance, she said, "Katie's been interested in him since he first came into town."

"I remember," Bliss agreed, showing off a dimple as she grinned at her youngest half-sister. "You were certain he was involved in some kind of mystery."

"My imagination tends to lean toward the melodramatic."

"Part of your charm," Tiffany said.

"Then, at the reception, Mason and I both noticed that you were very interested in him and that the feeling is mutual," Bliss commented.

"He's an interesting man," Katie admitted, determined not to reveal too much, though it was out of character for her.

"That's it? Just 'interesting'?" Bliss asked with a laugh. "Come on, Katie."

"Okay, okay, a little *more* than 'just interesting.'"

"A lot more," Tiffany guessed. She dabbed at the corners of her mouth with her napkin. "And now you're living right next door. If you ask me it's pretty handy for a romance."

Katie's eyes narrowed. "If I didn't know better I'd guess this was a plot set in motion by two kindhearted, if tunnel-visioned sisters who want me involved with a man." She pointed her finger at the half-sister seated on the bench beside her. "If I remember correctly, you were the one who suggested I move into the main house."

Tiffany giggled. "Guilty as charged."

"Okay, okay," Bliss interjected. "Tiffany might have gotten you to move into the house, but I had nothing to do with it."

"Don't look at me." Tiffany shook her head. "I don't play Cupid. I just needed someone reliable to take care of the renters."

"I would hope so." Katie brushed the crumbs to one corner of her plate. "Because you've got your hands full as it is. When are you and J.D. going to get married?"

Tiffany's gaze slid away. "Soon."

"How soon?" Bliss insisted. "You said something about this fall."

Tiffany bit her lip and leaned over the table. "Our plans have changed a little. I think we might just drive to Reno and elope."

"No!" Bliss's eyes were round with dismay. "You have to have a wedding."

"I agree." Katie had always considered herself practical, but she had enough of a romantic side to think that there should be a little pomp and circumstance, white lace and satin, a wedding cake and flower girls.

"I did the big-wedding bit before. Remember, I was married to J.D.'s older brother. It's like we're already family."

Bliss was having none of her arguments. "But you need a special day, an event, a rite of passage to start your life with J.D."

Tiffany leaned back in the booth as the waitress brought their check. "We'll see."

"Really, Tiffany—"

"Look, Bliss, there are other complications, as well," Tiffany said, then, hearing the edge in her voice, she sighed.

"Oh." Bliss cleared her throat and Katie got the message. "You mean you're not going to have the big church wedding because you don't want to deal with John."

"What would I do, have him give me away?" Tiffany asked, her lips pursing. "That's a joke, isn't it, since he never even claimed me for over thirty years."

Bliss's chin hardened. "Have Stephen give you away. Leave Dad out of it."

"Too late." Tiffany tossed her napkin on the table and reached for the check. "John's already asked to pay for the wedding, just like he's been my father all along." She lifted a shoulder and shook her head. "Maybe if this were my first wedding, maybe if there had been more time since I'd connected with him and accepted him as a father figure of some kind, if not a real dad, then maybe this would work. As it is, I think it's best if J.D. and I scoop up the kids and steal away in the night. When we return a few days later, we'll be married."

"There is an edge of romance to that," Katie allowed.

"Well, it's your decision." Bliss reached across the table and squeezed her half-sister's fingers. "Don't mind me. I just learned at an early age to speak my mind, even when I know that discretion is the better part of valor and I should be shot for being so blunt."

"Forgiven," Tiffany said with a wave of her hand.

"Good, then consider a big wedding."

"I'll think about it," Tiffany promised.

They split the check and Katie headed back to the office. For the next forty-five minutes she worked on her story about Octavia Nesbitt and decided not to mention the tea leaves.

She checked her e-mail and regular correspondence, hoping that someone had answered her "For Rent" advertisement for the house she and Josh had called home for over a decade, or, on the off chance that Isaac Wells had tried to reach her again. No such luck.

By four o'clock, she'd met the following day's deadlines, endured a late staff meeting and left work. Josh was at soccer practice and another mother had offered to drive him home, so Katie had an hour or so alone in the house, an hour she could use to clean and put away odds and ends.

She'd introduced herself to all of her tenants and was particularly fond of Roberta Ellingsworth, known as Ellie, an older woman who lived in a unit downstairs. On the second day Katie had been in the house, Ellie had brought her a home-baked pie and a cluster of asters, then promptly offered to watch Josh whenever Katie needed a hand. All in all, living in the old Victorian manor was beginning to feel like home.

Except for the fact that Luke lived nearby. Being this close to him was unnerving. And exciting. To her disconcertment she found herself looking out the window, watching his comings and goings, waving as he passed by a back window and dreaming of making love to him.

Don't trust him, she told herself when she found herself fantasizing about him again. *You barely know him. He could have a dozen women in a dozen different towns.*

Chapter Ten

"That does it," Ralph Sorenson said, his voice shaking with emotion. "Loretta and I will be on the next flight to Oregon. I've got to hand it to you, Luke. I didn't have much faith in you when you took off, didn't think you'd really put your heart and soul into finding Dave's son, but you did it. And don't think I won't remember that I said I'd pay you."

"I think you should slow down a minute," Luke interjected, trying to tamp down the older man's enthusiasm. "I said that Katie Kinkaid told me that Dave was Josh's father. She told her son as well, but I think you should hold off coming out here until the dust settles."

"Hold off? For the love of Pete, why?"

"To give everyone time to adjust."

"Like hell, boy. I'm seventy years old. It's up to the Man Upstairs how much longer I'll be walkin' on this planet and I don't see any reason to slow down. By next month I could be six feet under."

Luke doubted it. Ralph, though no longer a young man, was as spry and healthy as most men ten years younger.

"Why don't you just give me the boy's phone number and I'll call him up?"

"Wait a second." Luke's head began to pound. "How

about the other way around? I'll have Katie and Josh, if he's up to it—call you."

"Why wouldn't he be up to it?" Ralph demanded.

"He's ten, for God's sake. Give him a break, would ya?"

"I guess you've got a point."

"Good." Luke wasn't convinced that the old man was actually listening to reason, but he had no other options. "I'll let you know how this all turns out."

"Do. Loretta and I . . . Well, we don't get along much. Been separated for years. When Dave died we nearly divorced, but we're hangin' on by a thread right now, Luke, and that thread is Dave's son."

"I'll call." Guilt squeezed through Luke's innards as he replaced the phone. He'd have to talk to Katie again and this time he couldn't be distracted as he seemed to forever be whenever she was near. Just the thought of her brought a tightness to his groin and a longing that he didn't want to scrutinize too closely.

"You're a fool, Gates," he muttered and grabbed his hat from a hook near the front door. The excavating foreman was scheduled to meet him at the ranch to discuss the addition to the house, and he had just enough time to get there.

He'd deal with Katie, Josh, and Ralph later.

"Any more information on the Isaac Wells story?"

Pat Johnson, Katie's editor, asked as he paused at her cubicle and leaned against the edge of her desk. He was all of five feet six inches, but he carried himself as if he were a foot taller. With a shock of white hair, round eyeglasses and small features drawn close together, he was far from Hollywood handsome, but his sharp mind, bright eyes, and quick wit compensated for his lack of pure physical beauty. Everyone loved him. Including Katie.

"I wish," she said, but shook her head. "I've badgered the

police and my brother and a few of Isaac's associates, all to no end. I've even tried contacting whoever sent me the letter through the personal ads in the *Review*, as well as the local paper in California where the last letter was postmarked. So far, nada."

"Too bad." Pat removed his glasses and wiped them clean with a handkerchief from his pocket. "I thought it would be this year's big story."

"Me, too." She offered him a smile. "At least I'd hoped."

"Well, something could still break." He slipped his spectacles back onto his nose and patted the edge of her cubicle's thin walls before moving on.

No one wanted the story more than Katie. Despite the problems and distractions in her life—a new mishmash of a family of half-sisters and brothers-in-law, Josh's attitude toward her, Dave's death, and her fascination with Luke Gates—she was still anxious to solve the Isaac Wells mystery and get the byline.

She forced herself to finish an article on the change in the school district's curriculum, then accessed the Internet and, through cyberspace, found the obituary on David Sorenson of Dallas, Texas. So it was true. Her shoulders sagged a bit. She hadn't doubted Luke's word, but seeing Dave's short life in an even shorter article was strangely sad.

"Great," she muttered under her breath. It was bad enough that she'd been forced to tell Josh about his father's death, but now she was trying to get him to call his newfound grandparents and her negotiations with her son on the subject weren't going well. Josh was interested, but wary. Tonight, if he didn't do the deed himself, Katie would call them. She had to. The Sorensons deserved to know their grandson.

She was grateful for the end of the day. At home, she started dinner and turned on the radio. Josh had a ride home from soccer practice, so she threw together potato salad and baked pieces of chicken in herbs. She wasn't used to the thermostat in the new oven, so she was doubly careful, and as she unpacked what seemed to be an endless number of boxes, she kept an eye on her meal.

The phone jangled just as Bliss, with Mason's daughter, Dee Dee, pulled into the drive. "Hello?" Katie answered, waving Bliss and the girl inside. Holding the phone to her ear with one hand, she kicked open the screen door.

"Ms. Kinkaid?" a gravelly voice asked.

"Speaking."

"This is Ralph Sorenson."

Her heart dropped to the floor and she leaned against the cupboards for support. As much as she'd tried to bolster her own confidence and had told herself that she wanted to talk to Dave's parents, now that she was down to it, she was apprehensive. She felt as if all the blood had drained from her body in that one instant. "Hello," she said, trying to sound calm when she knew that her life was about to shred.

"I don't know how to say this but straight out. So here goes. I know about the boy. That he's David's."

"I see," she replied tonelessly as Bliss and Dee Dee rushed into the room.

"This is very awkward for me."

"Me, too," Katie said and met the worry in Bliss's eyes. "I did try to call you once, but when I didn't get through I'd hoped I could call another time, when Josh was home. . . ."

"Glad to hear it." He sounded appeased and she was relieved. "Difficult as all this is, I have to tell you that I'm pleased to know that I have a grandson, especially now that Dave's gone. It's comforting to know that a piece of him lives on."

"Of course," she replied, her eyes and nose burning.

"But I can't imagine why you chose to hide him from Dave for ten years. It would have done my boy some good to know that he had a son of his own."

"I didn't mean to hide—"

"I guess it don't matter now that Dave's gone—" The old man's voice cracked and Katie crumpled inside.

"I did try to tell him, before he left Oregon," she said, shaking her head at the unspoken, worried questions forming in Bliss's eyes. "He never called or came back to find out."

"So now it's his fault?" The man's voice rose an octave and Katie could almost feel his agitation.

"That's not what I meant."

"I should hope not, missy, because our boy's gone. Gone. It nearly killed Loretta—" His voice cracked again and Katie wanted to drop off the face of the earth.

"Look, I'm sorry about Dave. Really. He was a good person."

"But not good enough for you to contact and tell him about his son."

"That was probably a mistake," she allowed.

"Amen to that one."

"But I was young and scared—"

"Maybe we should be running along," Bliss said as she caught a glimmer of the conversation.

"No, it's fine. Please. Stay," Katie mouthed, placing her hand over the mouthpiece of the receiver.

"Okay. We'll be outside." Without another word, Bliss shepherded Dee Dee outside, found the basketball on the back porch and challenged her stepdaughter to a game of horse.

"I know why you were scared," Ralph Sorenson said. "Can't say as I blame you, but the here and now of it is that Loretta and I have a grandson—the only one we'll ever have—and we want to meet him."

"Of course you do," she said, trying to stay calm. "I think that it would be a good idea." That was stretching the truth a bit, but she couldn't deny Josh the right to see his grandparents, or vice versa.

"Then let's do it. The sooner the better."

She'd forgotten how pushy Ralph Sorenson had been, how Dave had complained of an overbearing father. "Listen, Mr. Sorenson, I said I was sorry and I am. I probably handled this all wrong from the get-go, but the most important person in this situation is Josh. I just want to make sure that he's strong enough to handle this. I think he is. And certainly, very soon, he's gonna want to meet you."

There was another pause, then a sigh. "All right, Ms. Kinkaid. You do what you think is best, but remember, Mrs. Sorenson and I are here waiting, dying to meet Dave's boy."

"I know. I'll let you know when Josh is ready to meet you. Then, of course, I'd love you to visit. You can even stay here at the house, if you want."

"Well . . . that's very kind." The anger in his voice faded away and she thought she heard him sniff, then blow his nose, as if he were overcome with emotion. Her own throat was thick, her hands sweating over the receiver. But she wouldn't break down, wouldn't allow herself the luxury. It seemed that all she ever did anymore was cry, and she hated it.

"Tell Luke that we spoke and assure him that he'll get paid, just as promised."

"I will," she said, wondering at the turn of the conversation.

"I know he told me not to call, that he'd set it up, but . . . Oh, hell, the missus and I, we just couldn't wait for him."

"'Wait for him'?" she repeated uneasily.

"You'll let us know when we can visit?"

"Of course." She hung up, mystified. Why was Ralph Sorenson talking about paying Luke for something now? A hint of an idea pricked her mind, but she didn't want to think about it, couldn't let that little niggle of horrid doubt burrow into her brain.

Bliss, as if sensing the conversation was over, lost her game to Dee Dee, then, while Katie was rummaging in the refrigerator for a pitcher of lemonade, returned to the kitchen. Both mother and stepdaughter were sweating, their faces beet-red, their eyes bright.

"I won!" Dee Dee announced.

"Fair and square," Bliss agreed. "But wait until next time. Then we'll see who's the champ of the court."

"I am, I am!" Dee Dee cried excitedly. She turned big eyes toward Katie. "I'm gonna be a big sister!"

"A what?" Katie nearly dropped the pitcher of lemonade. She turned and saw a blush creep up Bliss's neck.

"That's right," Bliss admitted, her eyes shining with her secret. "I'm pregnant!"

Katie left the pitcher on the counter and hugged her half-sister fiercely. "I'm so happy for you and Mason! When is the baby due?"

"A long time off," Bliss admitted. "I'm really not sure, but in the spring sometime. I'll find out when I go to the doctor."

"A baby!" Tears threatened Katie's eyes all over again. From the edge of her vision she saw Dee Dee gazing up at them both. "Oh, Dee Dee, how lucky you are," Katie said. "I was never a big sister, always the youngest."

"Not me." Dee Dee's smile was back in place immediately.

"Let's have a toast," Katie insisted. She poured them each a healthy glass, sliced lemons and tossed them into the liquid, added a couple of plump strawberries for good measure, then plopped ice cubes into the drinks. "Here." She handed them each a glass and touched the rim of hers to Bliss's. "To the baby and his big sister."

"No way. It's gonna be a girl," Dee Dee insisted.

"Okay. To the baby and *her* big sister," Katie amended.

"What? Nothing for the mother?" Bliss stuck out her lower lip until she couldn't help giggling.

"You get the best part. You get to be a mother," Katie said, "and change diapers, get no sleep, worry yourself silly and . . . I'm only kidding. It's the most wonderful feeling in the world."

"I'm already a mother," Bliss said, cocking her head toward Dee Dee. "Well, kind of."

The girl nodded enthusiastically and Katie was amazed at how quickly Mason's daughter had taken to Bliss. But then, who wouldn't? Bliss Lafferty was special. "Well, listen, I'm going to throw you the biggest, most lavish baby shower Bittersweet has ever seen!" She pointed a finger at Dee Dee's small nose. "You can help me give it—you and Aunt Tiffany."

"Can I really?"

"Really and truly." Katie took a long swallow from her glass. "This is the best news I've had in weeks."

"Speaking of which," Bliss asked as Dee Dee discovered Blue, and dog and girl dashed out the back door. "Who was on the telephone?"

"Oh. That." Katie's good mood instantly shattered. "That was Ralph Sorenson."

"Who?" Bliss's features pulled together as she tried to remember the name and came up blank.

"Dave Sorenson's father. You wouldn't know him, they lived here only a little while."

"Sorenson? Isn't that the guy who owned the place Luke Gates bought? I drew those blueprints for him and it seems like I remember the name."

"Small world, isn't it? Anyway, Dave was Josh's father. I just found out a week or so ago that . . . that Dave's gone. . . . I mean, he's, uh, dead." Her heart squeezed again at the horrid thought. "Died in a helicopter crash a few months back."

"*What?*" Bliss eyed Katie as if she'd just sprouted horns. "Wait a minute. Slow down and start over. From the beginning."

Fighting a losing battle with tears, Katie obliged and as she told her story, she felt as if a great weight, a burden, was slowly being lifted from her shoulders. For the first time in her life she understood the depth of a sister's love, the special bond that exists between sisters in times of joy or sorrow. Who else would listen to her and empathize when she poured out her heart and unburdened her soul?

Bliss listened and chewed on her lip. "Unbelievable," she said when Katie had finished. "What're you going to do?"

"Talk to Josh and try to get him to accept Dave's family. I was afraid that they might want custody or something, but I don't think so. They just want to know their grandson."

"Well, if there's anything Mason or I can do, just call and let us know."

"I will. But I think we're okay, as long as Josh quits blaming me for not telling him the truth. This is my problem. I can handle it." The words sounded much stronger than she felt, but she and Josh had weathered storms before; they'd get through this. "You know the old saying—something about that which doesn't kill us makes us stronger."

"Words to live by," Bliss murmured and Katie changed the subject.

"Let's get back to the baby," she said, sliding into a chair at the table. "I think we should have the shower about a month before the blessed event. . . ." She threw herself into discussing the joyful topic at hand and turned her thoughts away from Ralph Sorenson and his interest in Josh right now. There was a chance that Josh knowing his paternal grandparents would be a blessing, but there was also the risk that it would turn into a disaster; that the Sorensons would become overbearing and insist upon being an integral part of his life. Katie told herself not to borrow trouble and was already mentally organizing the baby shower when the phone rang.

"I'd better get it," she said to Bliss. "It could be Josh. This is his first day back at soccer practice." She snagged the phone on the third ring and silently prayed that the caller wasn't Ralph Sorenson again. "Hello?"

"I'm calling about the ad you ran in the paper."

Her heart nearly leaped from her chest. For a second she'd wondered if the male voice on the other end of the line belonged to Isaac Wells.

"Yeah, I'm looking for a place to rent, so can you tell me more about the house?"

"Oh." Her excitement dropped. But she couldn't be disappointed, because she needed to rent her cottage. She gave the man a quick description of the house and grounds, quoted him the rent and terms, then asked his name.

"Ben Francis. I'm married, but me and the wife don't have any kids yet. No pets, neither. If it's not too much trouble, I'd like to see the place as soon as possible."

"I could meet you there at—" She checked the clock over the stove, mentally calculated when Josh would be home, and said, "Around seven tonight if that works for you."

There was a pause and for a reason she couldn't name, Katie felt a moment of doubt, had the odd sensation that something wasn't quite right.

"That would be good," he finally agreed just as the timer on the oven dinged loudly and Bliss, grabbing a pot holder lying on the counter, took over the duty of removing the steaming pan of savory chicken.

"Let me give you the address," Katie offered, ready to rattle it off.

"No need. Got it this afternoon, from the sign on the front lawn."

She hesitated. "But I thought you got the information

from the paper." Was it her always-overactive imagination or was something wrong here?

There was a beat of silence. "I did. Once I saw the sign, I checked out the ads in the *Review* to find out how much the rent was. Then I called you."

"Oh." Why the devil was she always so suspicious? "All right, Mr. Francis—"

"Ben."

"Ben. I'll see you there."

She hung up slowly and read the questions in her half-sister's eyes. "Someone who wants to rent the old place," she said thoughtfully.

"Someone you know?"

She shook her head.

"Ever heard of him before?"

"No, but before I hand over the keys, I'll check his references."

"Do that," Bliss advised as she drew in a deep breath of fragrant steam escaping from the hot pan. "This—" she pointed at the pieces of chicken "—smells like heaven."

"Does it?" Katie was pleased. "One of Mom's old recipes. I'm really not much of a cook." She winked at Dee Dee, who'd entered the kitchen, followed by Blue. "Don't tell Josh. He hasn't figured it out yet."

Dee Dee giggled and Blue, smelling the food, whined near the counter.

"Ever hopeful," Katie observed.

Bliss drained her glass and scraped her chair back as a station wagon filled with rowdy boys pulled into the driveway. Blue barked excitedly, clamoring to be let outside as Josh climbed out of the fold-down third seat and waved to his teammates. His face was flushed, his hair matted with sweat, but he wasn't limping.

"I think we'd better be taking off," Bliss said. "Mason

will be home soon and, unlike you, Ms. Kinkaid, I don't have dinner ready. I think it'll be take-out Chinese."

Dee Dee wrinkled her nose.

"Oh, come on," Bliss said, giving the girl's slim shoulders a hug as Josh shouldered open the door and dropped his soccer bag in the middle of the floor. "I bet you'll like the fried shrimp."

"You could stay," Katie offered.

"I'll take a rain check. We just wanted to stop by and give you the good news."

"Congratulations." They hugged and Katie's heart swelled. When she'd first learned she had two half-sisters, she'd been wary, not certain of her feelings, especially since Bliss had been pampered and preened—John Cawthorne's "princess." But, being ever pragmatic, Katie had decided to make the best of the situation and from the minute she'd pushed herself into Bliss's life, insisting that both she and Tiffany be accepted, she hadn't regretted it for a minute. Today was proof positive that a loving family—no matter how tattered and shredded and pulled apart—was the greatest gift in life.

Luke eyed the pile of dry earth that had been scraped away from the building site. Kicking at a dirt clod, he examined the dig and was satisfied with the progress. The excavation would be finished in two days; the setting of forms for the concrete foundation that would link the existing buildings was scheduled thereafter, and by the end of next week the framing crew would be at work. He wanted everything done immediately, of course, but knew better.

As he squared his hat on his head and walked to the stables, he reminded himself that patience was a virtue—one that had eluded him for most of his life. He reached through the slats of the fence and twisted on the faucet for the water trough. Clear water gushed through ancient pipes and spilled into the metal drum, splashing noisily. Several mares lifted their heads at the sound. A light bay with black ears nickered in his direction.

"Hello to you, too, Trudy," he said and felt a sense of belonging, of finally having a place in the world he could call home.

It was just a damned shame that he'd be doing it alone. For the first time since his divorce from Celia, he experienced a need to be connected, to be a part of something bigger than just himself. It was an odd sensation, really—one he'd hoped he would avoid for the rest of his life and that, he suspected, had more than a little to do with Katie Kinkaid. That mite of a woman had bored herself under his skin and he found himself thinking about her far too much.

"So stop it," he ordered. She was just a woman. Angry with himself, he twisted off the faucet, and saw that the stock seemed settled down. The foals cavorted, running and bucking and nipping at each other while their more sedate dams, ears flicking at each sound, tails forever switching at flies, grazed and generally ignored the antics of their spindly-legged offspring.

It was a peaceful existence right now, though an influx of guests, ranch hands, and house staff would change that sense of tranquility in the months to come. But then money was money, and somehow this place had to support itself.

"Good night, ladies," he said, but the horses didn't pay any attention. "See y'all tomorrow."

Shoving his rawhide gloves into the back pocket of his jeans, he strode to his pickup and climbed into the cab. Though the windows had been left down, the interior was sweltering. A confused horsefly buzzed angrily between the dash and windshield before finally stumbling upon the open window.

"Good riddance." Luke ground the ignition, jammed the

rig into gear and headed for town. Dust and exhaust billowed in his wake and he thought of Katie. Damn, but he'd love to get her into his bed again. He envisioned her dark red hair, spread around a face that was flushed with desire, imagined kissing the freckles on the bridge of her nose, saw vividly in his mind's eye her swift intake of breath and seductively parted lips as he thrust deep inside her and began making slow, sensuous love.

"Cut it out," he growled. At the end of the lane he noticed that his crotch was suddenly uncomfortable, his arousal stiff, and he wondered if he'd spend the rest of his life fantasizing about that sharp-tongued-but-beautiful woman. He looked into the rearview mirror, saw his own eyes and then barked out a humorless laugh. If he didn't know better, he'd think he was in love.

Yeah, and you sold her and her boy out for money. Some lover you turned out to be!

Maybe it was time to tell her the truth. His fingers tightened over the steering wheel. She might hate him for the rest of her natural life, but, be that as it may, it was a risk he had to take.

Yep, he'd face her, tell her the truth and the devil take the consequences.

"I should be back in about an hour," Katie told Josh, who was grumbling about having to do the dishes. "Maybe sooner. I'm going to the old house to try and rent it." He didn't respond and she touched him lightly on the shoulder. "You can come with me if you want."

"Naw." He shook his head.

"Okay. Ellie-Mrs. Ellingsworth downstairs, is home and she said she'd look in on you if you'd like."

"I'll be okay."

"'Course you will." Katie rumpled his hair, which was

still wet from the shower he'd taken before they'd sat down to dinner. For the first time in a week he'd actually talked to her, told her about soccer practice and a new kid he'd met at school, then even brought up Dave, asking a few questions about him. Eventually she'd offered Josh the opportunity of meeting his paternal grandparents. Josh was interested, but wary. They were strangers to him, but he'd agreed to meet them. Soon. *One step at a time*, she reminded herself, since Josh had been forced to face a truckload of issues this past couple of weeks.

Placing a rental agreement and application into a side pocket of her purse, she headed outside just as Blue, who had been lying docilely on the porch, jumped up and made a racket, startling the blue jays that had collected on the eaves. The birds squawked and fluttered off.

Luke's truck rolled into the drive and Katie's heartbeat began to notch up a bit. She set her jaw and marched over to the pickup as he, in worn jeans and a frayed shirt that he hadn't bothered to button, swung out of the cab.

"Ms. Kinkaid," he drawled, his sexy-as-all-get-out crooked grin growing from one side of his square jaw to the other. "You look like you're about to spit nails."

"That would be a good way to describe it," she agreed, throwing out a hip as Blue, finished with his alarm barking, began sniffing the grill and running boards of Luke's truck.

"At me?" He feigned innocence.

"You'd be a primary target, yes."

"Is there a reason?" But his eyes belied him and she saw in their blue depths a hint of worry.

"Ralph Sorenson called today."

His smile fell away from his face.

"He wanted to come out and meet Josh, and during the course of our conversation—which could only be described as tense, at best—he let it be known that he's grateful to you for finding his grandson and that you'll be paid for your trouble."

Every muscle in his body seemed to tighten and his face, so congenial minutes before, took on the expression of a harsh, unbending cowboy. "You want an explanation."

"Not just an explanation, but a damned good one," she clarified, her fingers curling around the strap of her purse.

Luke glanced at the house. "Maybe we'd better go inside."

"So Josh can hear this? He doesn't much like you, to begin with. I think this would only make things worse."

"Fair enough." He rested his buttocks against the fender of his pickup, folded his arms over his chest and stared so hard at her she nearly looked away. But she didn't. She was too hurt. Too upset. And too damned mad.

"When Ralph and I made the deal on the ranch, he sweetened the pot a tad."

She was shaking inside. She didn't want to hear his confession, but wouldn't have missed it for the world. This was a man she had trusted, believed in, made love with. She'd given him her heart though she'd die before admitting it. And he'd betrayed her. Used her. Played her for a fool. Well, she wasn't having any more of it. "How did he 'sweeten the pot'?"

"A few more dollars if I found out whether or not his son had fathered a child."

She'd suspected it, of course; been darned-near sure that this was the explanation she would eventually hear after her talk with Ralph Sorenson, but the bald facts, the depth of the deception that went into the lie, hit her hard, like a blow to the stomach. "I hope it was worth it," she said through lips that barely moved. Inside she was shaking, quivering with a rage that burned bright in her soul.

"Katie—" He reached for her, but she ducked away, holding up her hands as she backed up a step and shook her head.

"Enough already."

"Just listen."

"I think I've heard enough to last me a lifetime, Gates." She turned on her heel and marched to her father's Jeep.

"If you would let me explain—"

"What?" Again she turned. "How you lied to me? Deceived me? Seduced me? *Used* me and my son for your personal gain? Is that what you want me to listen to? Well, forget it. It's over, Luke." She felt a tiny shaft of sadness. "It really was over before it began." She yanked open the door of her father's rig. "The only thing you need to remember is that the rent's due on the first." She slid into the hot interior and told herself it was better this way. Pumping the gas and turning on the ignition, she was reminded that she'd done just fine without Luke Gates in her life before; she could darned well do it again. She didn't need anyone but Josh.

She reversed into the street, her eyes trained on the rearview mirror, then she threw the Jeep into first and roared away from Luke Gates. This time it would be forever.

Chapter Eleven

Katie pulled into the drive of her old cottage and felt a tug on her heartstrings. She climbed out of the Jeep and walked the familiar path to the back door, smiling as she saw Josh's old basketball hoop still hanging lopsidedly from the garage. The trail Blue had worn from the front of the house to the back was still visible, a crooked ribbon of dirt in the grass, and the vegetable garden, hardly more than a tangle of weeds, displayed a few pumpkins yet to ripen, a couple of oversize zucchini squash and three vines of tomatoes with fruit threatening to rot.

She'd hired a yard crew to clean up the place and repairmen were scheduled to fix the dripping bathroom faucet, sagging gutters and somehow shore up the garage. Jarrod had promised to mend the screen and the twins had volunteered to patch the nail holes in the walls and help her paint next weekend. By then, she hoped, she'd have a tenant to help pay for the upgrades as well as cover the payments on her mortgage.

She heard the crunch of tires on gravel before she saw the nose of a maroon minivan pull in behind the Jeep. A tall, lean man climbed from behind the wheel and she had the vague sensation she'd seen him somewhere before. His hair was a little long and shot with the same gray that silvered his short-cropped beard and mustache. Dark glasses covered his eyes and the bill of a baseball cap shaded his forehead.

"Are you Katie Kinkaid?"

"Yes."

He grinned and showed off white teeth that seemed in contrast to his disheveled appearance. He wore brown coveralls that had a few oil spills on them and a faded red rag, streaked with grease, poked out of his back pocket.

"Hi." His hand shot out and she noticed his fingernails were dirty as she offered her palm and felt the strength of his clasp. "Benjamin Francis." He nodded toward the house. "This is a nice place, looks like it might work for me and my wife. I work at a gas station in Ashland and she teaches preschool."

That explained his work clothes, though she wondered why there wasn't a logo for the station or his name embroidered on his coveralls. There was something about him that didn't ring true, made her ill at ease, though she couldn't explain why.

"Can you give me a look at the inside?"

"Sure." She told herself her case of nerves was unjustified and unlocked the back door. The heat of the day had settled into the house, leaving it sweltering. As she reached for the latch of the window, she said, "I have a few repairs that will be made before anyone moves in. I plan to paint, clean the carpets, wax the floors and—"

She heard him walk in behind her, close the door and turn the lock. "Don't bother with the window." His voice was low, the command sharp.

She froze. "But it's beastly in here and there's a good cross breeze—" Turning, she found him leaning against the door, blocking her way out, and his expression had turned from friendly to hard and calculating.

"I have a confession to make," he said.

But she already understood as she mentally scraped off

his beard and removed his hat. She swallowed back her fear as she recognized him. Her blood turned to ice.

"I'm not Ben Francis."

"I know."

His eyes glinted with a malevolent light. "I don't believe we've met."

"We didn't have to," she said, fighting a feeling damned close to terror climbing up her spine. "I know who you are, Ray Dean. I just don't understand what you want from me."

Luke yanked a clean pair of jeans onto his wet body. His muscles ached and his mind thundered with the accusations that Katie had thrown his way. She was right. Though he hadn't set out to use her, he hadn't been completely honest about his intentions.

"Damn." He snapped his jeans closed and silently cursed himself to as many levels of hell as there were, then added a few more for good measure.

If only Ralph had held his patience in check; if only he'd let Luke talk to Katie himself, explain what he'd been doing, try to let her understand his position. "And what good would that have done?" he wondered aloud. Angry at the world in general and specifically at himself, he jerked a towel from the rack and wiped away the condensation that fogged the mirror.

His reflection glowered back at him through the tiny droplets and he felt as if he were about to explode. He didn't bother combing his hair, just raked his fingers through the wet strands. Muttering under his breath about hardheaded women and the stupid men involved with them, he threw on a pair of old sneakers and a T-shirt that had seen better days, then buckled the worn leather strap of his watch.

He was outside and down the stairs before the door slammed shut behind him. Crossing the yard in swift, ground-eating strides that led him straight to the back door, he ignored the low rumble of a growl old Blue gave him.

Banging loudly with his fist, he waited until Katie's kid, eyeing him with unmasked suspicion, stood on the other side of the screen.

"Yeah?"

"Your mom here?" He knew better. The Jeep was still missing in action, but he thought he'd start at the beginning with Josh.

"Naw."

A wealth of information, this kid. "Do you know when she'll be back?"

Josh's eyes narrowed a fraction. "Yeah."

Luke's patience was wearing thin. "And when is that?"

"Later." He gave a lift of one shoulder. "She said about an hour."

Luke calculated that she'd already been gone twenty minutes or so. He was going to ask Josh where she'd gone even if it wasn't any of his business, but at that moment Tiffany's car pulled into the drive. She was out of the car in a second. Her son, Stephen, who'd been in the passenger seat, was right behind her.

"Is Katie here?" Tiffany asked, climbing the steps.

"At the other house."

Bingo.

Josh opened the door for his aunt and cousin. "Someone's looking at it."

"Good. I need to talk to her, so Stephen and I'll wait if that's okay."

"Great. Where's Christina?"

"She wouldn't get up from her nap, so J.D. stayed with her." Tiffany rolled her palms to the air and winked at her nephew, as if they shared some private joke. "So, I guess it's just you and Stephen."

"Too bad," Stephen said sarcastically. He didn't seem

inclined to hide the fact that he was sick to his back teeth of a sister who was little more than a toddler. "She's a pain."

"She is not. You're lucky to have her."

"Yeah, right."

"Stephen," Tiffany warned, about to say more when her eyes met Luke's. "You'd think that with all the years that separate them, they'd get along."

Josh grinned from ear to ear, eager, Luke supposed, to hang out with his older cousin. He opened the door and Stephen bolted through, followed by his mother, who took over the duties of keeping the screen door from shutting by using her body as a wedge. The boys were already up the stairs. Tiffany smiled at Luke. "Why don't you come in and keep me company while I wait? I'm sure Katie won't mind. That way you can tell me what's happening with the ranch you're fixing up."

"You know about that?"

"Katie happened to mention that you were going to open it up to the public and take in guests sometime next spring."

"That's the plan," Luke allowed as the boys, eating red licorice, ran through the kitchen again, grabbed a couple of skateboards that had been propped on the porch and took off toward the front of the house.

"Hey, wait. Where're you going?" Tiffany asked.

"Just to the store." Josh was already around the corner.

"Be careful and come right back!" Tiffany yelled, then, when Stephen threw her a look that silently told her he wasn't a baby anymore, she turned back to Luke. "Moms are really just pains in the neck for teenage boys."

"Is that right?" He wouldn't know, of course, since he hadn't been raised by his own mother, but there was no reason to confide in her. "He'll grow out of it."

"I hope." She sighed and he saw a glimmer of the worry she'd carried with her as a single mother, a grieving widow. He decided it was a good thing that she'd linked up with

J.D. She glanced around the kitchen. "It's starting to come together, isn't it?" Shaking her head, she admitted, "I never thought I'd move out of here. Never planned to remarry." A tiny smile played at the corners of her mouth. "I guess that just goes to show you that you never know what's around the next corner."

"Nope."

"So—" she motioned to a chair "—just for the record, I think a working dude ranch is a great idea. Why don't you tell me all the details?"

"You sound like your sister."

"I'm not a reporter, but I'm interested. Besides, it looks like we both have a little time to kill before Katie gets back." She offered him a brilliant smile. "I feel kind of strange about sitting in *her* house waiting for her, but knowing Katie, she wouldn't want it any other way."

She heated coffee on the stove as Luke explained his plans. He was hesitant at first, didn't know if he wanted his entire life exposed to a woman he barely knew, but Tiffany, like her dynamo of a half-sister, was easy to talk to. The difference was that this woman was calm and chuckled softly as she cradled her cup in her hands. Katie, on the other hand, was a bundle of energy and would have dominated the conversation while doing a dozen other things.

Tiffany asked questions, made a few jokes, and generally kept the conversation rolling as the minutes ticked by. The boys returned, the wheels of their skateboards grinding on the concrete. Hastily they constructed a jump out of some two-by-fours and plywood, and immediately took to their boards to practice becoming airborne.

"I hope they don't break their necks," Tiffany said looking worried.

"They'll be fine."

"But Josh is still recovering from spraining his ankle."

She started to yell something out the window, thought better of it and held her tongue. "Once a mother, always a mother."

"I hear it's a hard habit to break."

"The hardest." They laughed and watched the boys through the window and Luke checked his watch for the dozenth time. He was starting to feel antsy, though he had no reason. His talk with Katie could wait.

"So, I wonder what's keeping her?" Tiffany finally asked as Luke finished his second cup of coffee. He'd been in the house nearly an hour. "It's odd that she'd leave Josh alone so long." She sighed and lifted a shoulder. "Maybe she had to go to the store." She scraped back her chair, walked to the sink and placed her cup under the faucet. "If Katie doesn't show up soon, I'll have to leave her a note."

"I could take a message," Luke said automatically, but he was starting to get that same damned feeling of anxiety he'd had before when she lived in the other place and she'd been receiving the crank phone calls. *Don't overreact*, he told himself, but found it impossible whenever Katie was concerned. He couldn't do anything but wait.

The phone jangled and they both jumped. "It could be Katie," Tiffany said, glancing to the backyard. "She might be calling Josh to explain why she's late." For some reason he couldn't explain, the muscles in Luke's back tightened and he snagged the receiver before it had time to ring again. "Kinkaid residence."

"Who's this?" a male voice demanded. Luke's fingers tightened over the mouthpiece in a death grip. "Luke Gates. I'm a neighbor. Ms. Kinkaid isn't in right now."

"Where is she?"

Luke's eyes narrowed and he thought of all the hangups Katie had received. "Who're you?"

"This is Jarrod Smith, Gates," the voice said with more than a trace of irritation. "I'm looking for my sister."

He relaxed a bit. The voice fit. He'd only talked to Jarrod

a couple of times, but he was convinced that Katie Kinkaid's oldest half-brother was on the other end of the line. "She's not here right now."

"So where is she?"

Leaning a shoulder against the door and meeting the questions in Tiffany's eyes, he said, "According to Josh, Katie went over to her old place to meet a potential renter."

"When?"

"Over an hour ago."

"Damn!" Jarrod let fly a blue streak and Luke's momentary feeling of calm vanished into thin air. "Let's hope it's legit."

"What do you mean?" Luke demanded.

"It's probably just a coincidence, but Isaac Wells, with his lawyer, walked into the police station not two hours ago. He seems to think he's in some kind of danger from Ray Dean, an ex-con. He also thought maybe because Katie's shown so much interest in the story that Ray might want to talk to her."

Luke didn't like what he was hearing and he'd never put much stock in coincidence; the fact that Katie was late at the same time Isaac Wells had suddenly turned up made him anxious. Still . . . no reason to panic. Not yet. "How do you know all this?"

"I have connections with a friend on the force. We used to be partners. He keeps me informed because I've been working on this from the outside. I'd been checking with lawyers in Eureka, where that letter Katie received was postmarked, widened the circle to include Oregon as I figured Wells would want an in-state attorney. I was on the right track, only hadn't located the guy. Anyway, he and Isaac strolled into the police station this afternoon." Frustration edged Jarrod's voice and Luke decided Katie's oldest half-brother wasn't used to having his quarry elude him. "Katie wanted to know the minute he came into town, so I thought I'd pass on the information."

"I'll let her know," Luke promised.

Jarrod hesitated, as if weighing whether he should confide in Luke, as if there was something more.

"Anything else?" Luke prodded.

"I don't know."

Luke could almost hear the wheels of suspicion turning in Jarrod's mind. Tiffany was standing by this time, her eyes fixed on Luke's face, her expression growing more concerned by the second.

"Maybe I'm just borrowing trouble," Jarrod allowed, "but Wells is starting to claim that Ray Dean has been involved in a lot of crimes the police couldn't pin on him."

"How does Wells know?"

"Wells?" Tiffany repeated, her eyebrows shooting up. "Isaac Wells?"

"Because Wells is claiming that he was his silent partner," Jarrod said. "Says he helped mastermind the crimes and case the places Ray would rob. He left town because Ray was getting out of prison and he was afraid for his life, or something. Anyway, now he's willing to turn state's evidence against Ray Dean in return for immunity from prosecution."

Luke's mind was racing ahead. He didn't give a hoot about Isaac Wells or Ray Dean or how they were involved in crime together. But he sure as hell was concerned about Katie and it looked as if, because of her articles, and the letter Isaac sent her that she published, she might be a link between the two thieves. "Did Isaac Wells write the letter to Katie?"

"That, I don't know. But if he did, he didn't contact her again because his attorney wanted him to deal directly with the police."

Luke's throat felt like sandpaper. He thought about the crank calls she'd received, about the feeling he'd had that someone had been watching her, waiting in the shadows at the hotel and at her home. Even after she'd moved this close to him, he'd spent more hours than he'd like to admit, sitting in the dark, staring out his window, watching the main house, scouring the darkness for any hint of a prowler. But he wasn't convinced. "Do you think Katie's in any danger?"

"I don't know. Hell, I hope not." But there was a note of apprehension in Jarrod's voice that Luke couldn't ignore. "Just let her know what's going on. When she gets in, have her give me a call."

"I will," Luke promised and promptly hung up.

Tiffany motioned toward the phone. "What was that all about?" she demanded. "You said something about danger."

"Isaac Wells is back in town." He gave her a quick rundown as he reached for the handle of the door. "If you want more details, call Jarrod back. There's probably nothing wrong," he said, disturbed and telling himself that he was being a dozen kinds of fool. "I'm going to check on Katie."

"I'll stay here with the kids," Tiffany said, her usually dark skin turning an ashen shade.

"Do that." He ran to his pickup and climbed inside as the two boys stopped their jumps for a second. The way Luke figured it, he could be at the cottage in less than ten minutes. He reminded himself this was probably just a wild-goose chase. Katie was probably safe. She might not even be at the cottage, but he wasn't going to rest until he found her. He backed his truck into the street, flung it into first gear and roared down the street.

He didn't give a damn if he looked like a fool; he wasn't about to take a chance with the life of the woman he loved.

* * *

"I think you and I should go for a ride," Ray said and Katie, rooted to the floor of the cottage, tried to maintain her rapidly escaping wits.

She shook her head.

"Whatever it is you have to tell me, you can say it right here." It would certainly be more dangerous to leave with him. At least she was in an environment she knew, with neighbors just across the fence.

"We could be interrupted."

"So what?" She was thinking fast, trying to get her bearings. If she could get over her fear and if Ray meant her no harm, she might have stumbled on the answer to the Isaac Wells mystery. But what if he did intend to hurt her? What then? Her legs threatened to give out on her and for the first time since her interest in the Isaac Wells disappearance began, she questioned whether or not she wanted to be involved. "You're not in trouble with the police, are you?"

"Always." He lifted a shoulder and she tried to determine if he was carrying a weapon. There were no bulges in the pockets of his coveralls, but a knife would be easy to conceal. Even a small handgun could be hidden somewhere on his body. Not that it made a huge difference—not when there was the size of him to consider. At over six feet and two hundred pounds, he was way too strong for her to try to overpower him. No, she'd have to use her brains.

"Do you know where Isaac Wells is?" she asked Ray.

"No."

"Is he alive?"

"I think so."

"Why?"

He studied her carefully, as if, now that he had her full attention, he wasn't sure how much of his story to divulge. "I have connections."

"Connections? Who? What?"

"Someone trustworthy."

Her mind was racing, her skin prickling with dread. "A snitch? A *trustworthy* snitch?" She tried to keep the disbelief out of her voice.

Ray's lips flattened at the insult. "Has he contacted you since you got the last letter?"

"No." She shook her head. "I thought he would, but I haven't heard a word. No letters or phone calls . . . well, except for some hang-ups."

"That was me."

"You?" She was sweating now, adrenaline rushing through her system.

"But they started coming before the letter was published. . . ." Her voice faded away and she wondered how long this man had been watching her, following her. Her skin crawled at the thought of what he might have seen. "You . . . were watching me?" She thought she might be sick.

"I had to know what was going on."

So Luke had been right. She'd dismissed his concerns as some kind of overprotective paranoia, but his sense of dread had been justified. "Look, if you want me to help you . . ." She let her voice drop off. "Is that it? You want me to do something?"

"I want you to level with me. I think you know where Isaac Wells is."

"I don't." She shook her head. "I swear. The only contact I've had with him is the one letter."

"My source said he was returning to town. Was gonna turn himself in, but first he would contact you."

"Why?"

"Good question. I thought it was so that he could give you some more B.S. and lies that you'd publish in the paper."

"No," Katie insisted and heard the familiar sound of a pickup turning in at the drive.

Ray's nostrils flared, as if he'd encountered a bad smell. "Who's here?" he demanded.

"I don't know."

"Liar."

"Really. No one knows I'm here."

Ray's face clouded. He reached into his pocket and Katie couldn't help but back up a step. There was a horrid click; the sound of metal snapping. A switchblade flashed. "Oh, God," she whispered.

At that moment, the sound of Luke's boots hit the back porch. She looked through the window and shook her head as she spied his rugged face, twisted with concern. "Katie?" He knocked loudly as Ray stepped away from the door. "You in there?"

"Go away!" she yelled.

"Shh." Ray reached forward, grabbing her arm, but she resisted, pulling away, kicking at him with her feet, hearing the sound of Luke swearing and banging on the door.

"Let go of me!" She yanked away, but he grabbed her again, forcing her close, the smell of grease from his uniform filling her nostrils. Hard muscles restrained her and the knife was ever-present in his left hand.

"Katie!" Luke's voice thundered through the house.

"Who's that?" Ray snarled.

"A friend."

"Tell him to get the hell out."

"Luke, go away!" she cried, as worried for him as she was for herself.

There was a split second of silence.

Crash! Glass splintered and sprayed. A body, huddled against the impact, burst into the room and rolled over the broken glass.

"Damn." Ray twirled, lifting Katie off her feet as Luke, recovering, found his footing and, all muscles flexed, eyes glimmering with fire, advanced.

"Stop!" Ray commanded.

"Let her go," Luke ordered through lips that barely moved.

Ray's grip tightened. Katie could scarcely breathe. "Get out!" he shouted at Luke.

"Are you okay?" Luke's gaze touched Katie's for an instant.

"Get out or I'll cut her," Ray threatened. The knife was poised high, glinting in the fading sunlight. "I swear it, man."

"Leave her be." Luke didn't move, just crouched, his gaze trained on the knife.

Fear congealed in Katie's blood. "Let me go," she demanded. "There's no reason for this."

Tense, appearing as if he'd lunge at any second, Luke took a step toward Ray. "Who are you?"

"Stop right there."

The arm around Katie's waist jerked hard and she gasped. Luke froze. Ray pulled her backward, toward the living room, his boots crunching on the bits of glass scattered on the old linoleum.

Katie's heart thudded wildly. There was nothing she could do. "You—you haven't been in this kind of trouble before, Ray," she said.

"Ray?" Luke repeated, his expression wary. "Ray Dean?"

Sweat streamed from Ray's face.

"Just let her go and we'll talk this out," Luke insisted.

"Nothin' to talk about."

"Sure, there is. You told me about Isaac Wells," Katie said. "That you think he's going to frame you or something. Why don't you let me write *your* side of the story?"

She felt him hesitate.

"If you do anything now you'd be thrown back in prison for a long, long time. And Isaac would get away scot-free. Think about your kids," she said, sensing him listening, hearing his breathing slow a bit. "Laddy and Miles need a dad who isn't in prison."

"They're used to it." He glanced at Katie. Luke sprang forward. Startled, Ray stumbled a bit. His hold on Katie loosened a little. She threw herself away from him. "Don't move!" Ray's knife arced downward. Katie, screamed and looked for something—anything—to use as a weapon. Luke caught Ray's wrist, and the knife trembled as the men struggled.

Grunting, swearing, muscles straining, they wrestled each other to the floor. Glass crunched. Katie ran for the door, her feet slipping on the shards. She threw the bolt, shouldered open the door and, screaming for help, grabbed the only thing she could find—Josh's old baseball bat that had been left in the corner.

Sirens wailed in the distance, and a truck roared to a stop behind Ray's van. From the corner of her eye, Katie spied Jarrod bolting out of his pickup. "Get away!" he yelled, running up the steps, two at a time.

But it was already over. Luke, straddling Ray's chest, had him pinned to the floor.

"Hell, Katie what were you thinking?" Jarrod demanded as she followed him into the house. Outside, a police cruiser slammed to a stop.

"I thought I was renting my house."

"What happened here?" a female cop demanded. She and her partner, weapons drawn, ran through the back door. She stopped when she recognized the man sprawled on the floor, pinned by a strong-willed cowboy. "Well, well, well. Ray Dean. Why aren't I surprised that you'd be in the middle of this?"

"Butt out."

"Don't think so." She motioned for Luke to get up. "We'll take over from here, but all of you" her gaze swept the group and brooked no arguments "—will have to come down to the station to give your statements."

Luke didn't look at the cops, but walked straight to Katie and folded her tightly into his arms. "Thank God you're okay," he said, his breath hot as it ruffled her hair. She felt him tremble, heard his heart pounding and wanted to cling to him forever. Tears blocked her throat and her eyes burned. "I was so worried." He kissed her crown and something inside her broke. She let the tears rain from her eyes and drooped against him, all of the fight and fire of her spirit finally collapsing. "Shh. You're okay. I'm here." She felt like a fool, an idiot of a woman, but was grateful that he was here, holding her, coming to her damned rescue.

"It's all a mix-up," Ray insisted as he climbed to his feet and the second cop, Officer Barnes, a thin man of thirty or so with an expression of someone who had already seen far too much, yanked Ray's arms behind his back and snapped handcuffs on his wrists.

"Take it easy! I haven't done anything wrong."

"Right," the policewoman mocked. "Not a damned thing."

"Ray Dean, you have the right to remain silent—" Barnes began reading Ray his rights, but the prisoner would have none of it. He looked at Katie and beneath the anger in his eyes, was a silent plea. "Look, I messed up."

"Big time," Katie said as Luke's arms tightened around her.

"Shut up. You have the right to remain silent . . ." the officer began again.

Ray ignored him. "I want you to write my story. In your paper."

She hesitated.

"Forget it, Dean," Jarrod said. "Just get him out of here," he ordered.

Luke wouldn't let Katie go.

"You said you'd write it!" Dean argued.

"For God's sake, man, you had a knife to her throat!" Luke's face was red, his eyes narrowed in fury.

"I'll think about it," Katie said. Luke tensed.

"Are you nuts?" Jarrod was in her face now, his finger jabbing at her nose. "Do you know what he almost did to you? Katie, use your damned head!"

"This is my life, Jarrod," she replied.

"And you nearly lost it! Get a clue, would you?"

With a prod from Officer Barnes, Ray was led away and slowly Luke released Katie. Jarrod, still fuming, kicked at the broken glass and muttered under his breath about women who didn't have the common sense of fleas.

With Dean in the back seat, the police cruiser pulled away and a few neighbors who had gathered in the yard peeked inside. One, Leona Cartwright, an elderly woman with keen eyes and a hearing aid that helped her miss nothing that was going on in the neighborhood, admitted calling the police when she heard the commotion. "I just thank the Lord that you weren't hurt," she said, basking in the bit of glory that came with being the person to inform the authorities. "I just knew something wasn't right."

"Thanks."

"You'll write about this in the paper, no doubt."

"No doubt," Katie confirmed and Leona, like a preening peacock, beamed, looking from one of her neighbors to the next.

Luke didn't leave Katie's side and by the time the mess was cleaned up, they'd given statements at the police station and had returned home, it was nearly ten o'clock.

Katie, exhausted, was greeted by her entire family. Her father and mother, half-brothers and half-sisters were all milling and pacing around her kitchen, their faces drawn, lines of worry etching their features. At the sight of her sliding out of the Jeep, the family poured onto the back porch.

"Katie, oh, thank God!" Brynnie, smelling of cigarette smoke and perfume, dashed through the door and down the porch steps to fold her only daughter into her arms. "I was so worried."

"We all were," John said as Luke, who had parked behind the Jeep Katie had been driving, walked slowly across the lawn. He hung back, letting the family surround her while

Jarrod's truck screeched to a stop. Rushing over to join the rest of the family, he was still wearing the role of protective older brother.

"I'm okay, Mom," Katie assured Brynnie.

"Thank God." Again, Brynnie's arms tightened around her, then she let them drop. "You're still my baby, you know."

"Yeah, I know."

"Lord, what I wouldn't do for a cigarette."

"Mom!" The screen door opened and banged shut. Josh flew down the steps to hurtle himself into Katie's arms.

Her throat was suddenly swollen, at the gesture of her son. She blinked hard and silently thanked God for her boy. "Hi, bud."

"Are you okay?"

"Fine, fine." She kissed Josh's crown and for once he didn't seem embarrassed that his mother was displaying her heartfelt affection for him.

"What happened? I thought you were just going to try and rent the house." His eyes were wide and now that the worry of her safety was over, he was keyed in on the fact that his mother was some kind of heroine.

"I did. I guess I was duped," she admitted, ruffling his hair. So much for heroics.

"So the guy was a phony."

"Big time."

John Cawthorne stepped forward. "You'd better come into the house and slow down a mite. You look all done in."

"I'm fine," Katie lied.

"Dad's right." Bliss, ever the worrier, held the door open. "Maybe you should rest."

"That's a good idea." Jarrod glared at his half-sister. "And give up the ridiculous notion that you're going to interview Ray Dean for your story."

"Ray Dean? Laddy's dad? He was the guy?" Josh asked,

his eyes round as saucers as his estimation of his mother and her bravery soared into the stratosphere.

"Stay away from the likes of him," John growled.

Tiffany squeezed her hand. "Oh, Katie. Jarrod and . . . and John are right. Ray Dean's a criminal and you're a mother, you can't be taking any chances." For once, Tiffany sided with her estranged father, and Katie saw that this family—ragtag and filled with more than its share of bitter memories, distrust, and skeletons tucked away in every available closet—had come together during this crisis. Unintentionally, she'd drawn them to one another.

"Maybe everyone should hear what Katie has to say." Luke, the outsider, finally put in his two cents worth. He was standing beneath a madrona tree, one shoulder propped against the trunk, his hands shoved into the back pockets of his jeans. "Seems to me that it's her life."

Jarrod was about to argue. He opened his mouth, snapped it shut and then lifted a hand as if in surrender. "He's right."

"Tell us what happened," Bliss insisted.

"Everything," Tiffany added. "Come on, I think we can all fit into the parlor." She held the door open and John urged everyone inside. There wasn't enough of Katie's odds and ends of eclectic furniture to hold everyone, but Stephen and Josh sat on the hearth, Christina was huddled in her mother's arms while Bliss and Mason stood at the windows, Brynnie sagged onto the couch, and the rest were scattered throughout the room, either seated in kitchen chairs they'd dragged into the parlor, or on the floor.

At John's insistence Katie took her place in an overstuffed wing chair and Blue, toenails clicking, entered the room to curl into a ball at her feet. His ears twitched and his eyes moved from one member of the family to the next while Katie launched into her story. Everyone, even her ever-restless twin brothers, listened raptly. Few questions were asked and when she described Luke's dramatic rescue, all eyes turned his way. He stood in the archway between parlor and foyer, his face without much expression. Aloof. And still as sexy as any man she'd ever seen. Her throat caught for a minute as his eyes held hers. In that heartbeat she forgot that he'd betrayed her; remembered only that he'd put his life on the line for her. Before anyone had noticed, she looked away.

"I guess we owe you a debt of gratitude," John commented, eyeing Luke and sizing him up.

"No trouble."

"Nonetheless, you should be rewarded—"

"I don't think so." Luke's back stiffened in stubborn pride, and then Katie remembered that he'd probably already been paid for locating Ralph Sorenson's grandson. Her teeth clamped together; now wasn't the time to bring that up.

"You saved Katie's life," John said adamantly.

"She was doin' okay before I got there."

"Like hell she was," Jarrod retorted, his lips compressed over his teeth, his eyes flashing with frustration at his half-sister's bullheaded streak. "I don't call it 'okay' when you're locked away with a known criminal who has a weapon at your throat!"

"It wasn't like that," Katie protested.

"Damned close."

There was no arguing with him. She glared at Jarrod for a second, then smiled. After all, he was only angry because he cared. "So what happened on this end?" Katie asked, hoping to defuse some of the tension that lingered in the air.

"After Luke left, Tiffany called me. Explained what was goin' on," John clarified.

Tiffany, smoothing Christina's curls, nodded. "I was worried. Luke had already left and I just had this feeling that there might be trouble, so I decided your folks should know what was going on." Her eyes met Katie's and a moment of understanding passed between them, a connection only true sisters share. "So, I phoned the ranch and talked to John."

Katie couldn't believe her ears. For Tiffany to have reached out to her estranged father was a major step. Major. Maybe there was hope for this ragtag family yet.

"Since I was there when John got the call," Jarrod added, "I decided to find out what was going on for myself. Bliss and Mason gathered everyone together here."

"I talked to the police," John said. He stood behind the couch where his wife was ensconced and patted her shoulder. Brynnie reached up and grabbed his fingers in hers. "But they'd already been tipped off. Some neighbor, I think."

"Leona."

"Helluva way to get us all together," Nathan joked.

Katie managed a laugh. "I promise I won't do it again."

"Good." Brynnie pushed herself upright. "I don't think I could live through it again."

"The next time you meet someone interested in looking at that place, give me a call," Jarrod said.

"I don't need—" Katie stopped short. How could she complain about his overbearing, big-brother tactics when he'd risked his life for hers? "Okay, I'll be more careful and take someone with me."

"I'm gonna hold you to it," Jarrod warned, leveling a finger in her direction. But he couldn't hang on to his glower and the smile that twitched at the corners of his mouth let her know that all was forgiven.

The conversation grew lighter and the kids strayed upstairs. Luke, seeing that all was well, tried to leave, but Jarrod stopped him in the foyer near the staircase. “Seems to me you might just be the reason my sister’s alive.”

Luke’s gaze touched Katie, still seated in the chair near the fire. She felt her heartbeat elevate from just that one glance. What was it about him that made her so crazy? It seemed that she was either ready to murder him because he was so bullheaded; or she was melting at his touch, dreaming of making love to him forever. The man was just plain confusing. There were no two ways about it. She climbed out of her chair and went swiftly to the entry hall. A slow smile stretched across Luke’s mouth. “My guess is that your sister here would have done just fine on her own,” he said to Jarrod. Again Luke’s blue eyes found hers. “I just didn’t want to take any chances.”

“I’m glad you didn’t. Stick around,” Jarrod invited.

“Please. Stay. I’m sure this clan is going to be clamoring for food at any second,” Katie agreed.

“I’m already taking care of it.” John joined them in the foyer. “Everyone’s invited out to the ranch. I know it’s late, but we need to celebrate. Brynnie and I’ll pick up ribs and chicken down at Mel’s Barbecue. Meet us at the ranch in an hour.”

Luke started to protest, but John put on his I-won’t-take-no-for-an-answer smile. “It isn’t every day someone saves my daughter’s life, though it has happened in the past.” His gaze slid to Mason for a second, before returning to Luke. “Please, son. It’s the least we all can do.” He stuck out his hand and Luke clasped it firmly. “All right. I’ll be there.”

“Good.” John turned toward the parlor and announced that the entire family was invited.

“It’s so late,” Tiffany said, blushing as Christina yawned and rubbed her eyes. “We need to get her home.”

“She can bunk down on one of the beds in the guest rooms,” Brynnie offered.

"I don't know. . . ." Tiffany looked at Katie, then, moistening her lips, glanced in Bliss's direction. "Okay," she finally said, her shoulders straightening a bit as she seemed, for the first time, to accept her position in John Cawthorne's family. "We'll be there."

Katie could have dropped through the floor. Never would she have believed Tiffany could capitulate.

"Good! Good!" John said, practically beaming. "Come on, Brynnie, we'd better get a move on. We'll see you all in an hour."

Katie was stunned. Every member of the family had agreed to show up at Cawthorne Acres. In a flurry of activity, they left, climbing into individual cars and trucks that roared away from the apartment house, leaving Josh, Katie and Luke standing in the moon-washed backyard.

"Who would've thought?" she said, tousling Josh's hair.

"What d'ya mean?"

"I never thought this family would get together. Never. This is a red-letter day," she said to Luke as everyone dispersed.

"I'm just glad you're okay, Mom," Josh admitted.

"Me, too."

"Why don't you go check on Blue and we'll get ready to go?"

Josh hesitated, as if he were about to argue, then lifted a shoulder. "Sure."

"Good." She turned back to face Luke. "Now," she said as a cloud shifted over the moon, "you and I need to talk."

"Do we?" In the half-light his teeth flashed white and she reminded herself that despite everything she was still angry with him. That he'd deceived her.

"Yep. Just because you probably saved my life today," she continued, "doesn't mean you're off the hook, Gates." She angled her face up to his and said, "There's still that little matter of your deal with Ralph Sorenson. No matter what happened with Ray Dean, I think you used me and my son. For your own purposes."

He stared down at her so intensely she had trouble meeting his gaze. For a brief second she thought he might kiss her, but then she changed her mind when he looked away. His eyes narrowed as he stared into the distance, but, she suspected, he saw only what was deep in his own mind.

"I guess you have the right to think anything you damned well please," he finally muttered. "Can't say as I blame you." He turned on his heel and started toward the carriage house. "Give my regrets to your father and Brynnie."

"But— No. Wait." She caught up with him, touched his arm and he spun again, facing her with an expression of exhaustion and pain.

"Just for the record, Katie," he said slowly, his gaze drilling into hers as if he could somehow find her soul, "I never intended to hurt you." With that, he turned and walked out of her life.

Chapter Twelve

"I don't want the money."

Luke had never thought he'd say those particular words. Since he'd grown up poor, he'd thought, for as long as he could remember, that money could buy him happiness. Not that he needed a lot. Just enough to get by and give himself a little nest egg so he wouldn't have to work until he was ninety. But he'd changed his mind. Katie Kinkaid had seen to that.

Ralph Sorenson, on the other end of the line, and woken from what must have been a deep sleep, wasn't in the mood for Luke's change of heart. "You earned it, boy. It's yours."

"No."

"What the devil happened to you?"

I fell in love. "I just had a change of heart." That wasn't a lie.

"You're just mad 'cause I called my grandson's mother before squarin' it with you," Ralph said. "Well, I admit I was a little impatient, but then you've got to understand there's no reason to wait. That boy is Dave's son. Our grandson. It's time we met."

"I don't think that'll be a problem."

"So you'll get paid."

"Give it to Josh," Luke said. "I'm out of this. Good night Ralph."

"Well, ain't that a fine howdy-do?" The old man hung up and Luke felt only slightly better than he had a while before. He strode to the window and stared into the night. He'd never gotten used to living in town and the blue glare of the streetlights seemed harsh and unforgiving.

Just the way he felt. Staring at the huge apartment house as if it were an enemy, he tilted back his bottle of beer and took a long swallow. He thought of Katie, and deep inside there was an ache—something primal and painful and, in his estimation, way out of line. So she was a beautiful woman. So she had an outlook on life he found fascinating. So what? Disgusted with himself, he drained his long-neck, considered another, then tossed the idea aside.

Alcohol wouldn't help. Not that it ever had.

His conscience was eating him alive. What he'd done to her was unforgivable, and calling and telling Ralph that he was out of the deal was hardly compensation enough. Nope, his refusal of Ralph's bribe was just another incidence of too little, too late.

Which seemed to be the story of his life.

"Where's Luke?" Bliss had asked.

Tiffany, too, hadn't let Luke's absence go unnoticed. "I thought he was coming."

"I specifically invited him," John Cawthorne had grumbled. "Helluva way to act, if ya ask me."

Of course no one had asked John's opinion; John was just forever willing to offer it. While the rest of her family had laughed and talked, eating ribs, chicken, bread and coleslaw, Katie had scarcely been able to take a bite. Everyone had assumed it was from the trauma she'd suffered earlier in the day, but the truth of the matter was that no matter what she did, her thoughts turned back to the rangy cowboy with the Texas drawl and easy smile. Dammit, she'd missed him.

As soon as it was polite, she'd located Josh and said her goodbyes. All of her brothers had warned her to be more careful, whether while renting the house or chasing down stories. Her sisters had told her how great they thought Luke was.

As if they were a couple. What a laugh—a miserable, heart-wrenching laugh. Driving through the darkened streets of Bittersweet, she told herself that she couldn't love a man like Luke Gates. She wouldn't. It was just too painful.

He used you, she reminded herself as she shifted down and turned into the drive of the apartment house. The beams of her headlights washed up against the tailgate of Luke's truck. He was home. Only a few yards away. She told herself it didn't matter if he was living next door or in the middle of the North Pole.

But of course that was a lie. "Lord help me," she whispered under her breath.

"Huh?" Josh, eyes closed, stirred in the passenger seat.

She parked and set the emergency brake. "Come on, bud," she said. "Time for bed."

"I can't make it." He yawned and let his head loll back against the seat again.

"Sure you can. Just try." She managed to help him out of the Jeep, then guided him toward the house and upstairs to his room. He managed to make it as far as his bed, then flopped, facedown, onto the mattress.

She brushed a kiss across the top of his head. "I'll see you in the morning."

As she snapped off the light and closed the door, Josh

lifted his head and tried to stifle a yawn. "I'm really glad you're okay, Mom."

"Thanks, kid." Her heart swelled. "I love you."

"Me, too. And Mom? You know what I said about Luke before, that I didn't like him?"

She nodded, vaguely recalling a conversation when Josh had sprained his ankle. "Yeah."

"I changed my mind. He's okay."

"Good." Why it mattered she didn't know, because Luke had used her. And Josh. "See ya in the morning." She closed the door and went down the hallway to her room. It seemed empty and dark. Even after she turned on the bedside lamp and pulled down the quilt, it felt cold somehow, vacuous and barren.

What had Jarrod said—that she needed a man? She'd never believed him. Until now. Because of Luke Gates. "Oh, Katie, you've got it bad," she said, realizing the aching truth that she loved Luke Gates.

"I never intended to hurt you." His final words had rattled through her brain all night long. But it didn't matter what his intentions had been. He had hurt her. And loving him only made it worse.

"Okay, Katie, I should be shot for this, but I think I made the rash promise to let you know anything I found out about the Isaac Wells case," Jarrod said when she answered the phone the next morning.

"Sounds like you've had a change of heart." She poured herself a cup of coffee and looked through the back window only to discover that Luke's pickup was missing.

"No way. You be careful. But I figure someone down at that rag you work for is going to write the story, so it may as well be you."

"Can't argue with that." Holding the receiver between her shoulder and ear, she scrounged in a top drawer for a pen and a notepad. "Okay, brother. Shoot." She sat at the table and listened.

"Okay, the deal is this. It seems that Isaac isn't quite the loner everyone thought. In fact, he was a crook, or the guy behind the scenes with all the brains. The police don't know for sure, but they suspect Isaac was involved in a string of burglaries that happened around Medford and Ashland a few years back. Ray Dean was his accomplice, the actual thief. Ray took all the risks and got most of the money. Except for one job—the big one."

"Which one was that?"

"When Octavia Nesbitt was robbed."

Katie stopped writing. Her hand froze over the paper. "Wells and Dean were involved in that one?"

"It looks that way. They got away with it and were about to split the loot when Dean was caught for his part in an earlier break-in. He was convicted and, as they say, sent up the river. All that time in prison he kept his mouth shut about the Nesbitt job because it was the biggest one he'd ever pulled off. He had some phony alibi, so the police were thrown off. No one suspected that Isaac Wells might be involved and eventually Dean ended up paroled. The problem was that Isaac had used all the money—either gambled it away, paid off back taxes, used it to keep up that car collection of his, whatever."

"He told them this."

"Not everything, of course, but it's what the police have pieced together. So when Ray was about to be released, Isaac decided to disappear rather than face him. Ray has a track record of being thrown back in jail within months of being paroled, but this time it didn't happen. Isaac began to get worried that Ray would talk, so he turned himself in yesterday and is cooperating with the authorities."

Dumbstruck, Katie leaned back in her chair. "So what about Octavia's jewels?"

"Pawned."

"And her cat?"

"I don't think anyone asked him about her cat. He's probably long gone by now."

"Wow." Katie scribbled as fast as she could. "Why was Stephen a suspect?" she asked, remembering that her nephew had been questioned.

"Never a suspect, but he did have a set of keys that belonged to Isaac Wells—keys that Ray Dean hoped would lead him to the loot. The police didn't know the connection, of course. Not until now."

"So what happens now?"

"Your guess is as good as mine. I think Ray will be sent back to prison and Isaac will get a lesser sentence for turning himself in. I think Octavia's insurance company will probably sue and Isaac will have to give up whatever he has left to pay off the claim. But I'm not sure. That's just conjecture."

Katie chewed on the end of her pencil. "So how did they break into Octavia's home?"

"Isaac knew someone who had once cleaned Octavia's house and knew where she kept the extra keys. The old lady was foolish, I think."

Katie stared out the window toward Luke's apartment. A squirrel was racing along the gutter, then scrambled into the overhanging bows of a pine tree. Blue was barking, running along the edge of the carriage house, his nose tilted into the air, his eyes trained on his quarry. But Katie didn't pay any attention to the squirrel's antics or Blue's frustrated cries. In her mind's eye she saw her story forming, but some of the joy she'd expected to feel the satisfaction of getting her big scoop—was missing. "I owe you, Jarrod."

"Just take care of yourself."

"I will. Thanks."

"No problem."

"You know I'll have to talk to Ray Dean," she ventured, ready for her brother's temper to explode.

"Go ahead. As long as he's behind bars."

The next couple of days were busy. Too busy. Somehow Katie avoided Luke, though she suspected he was the one doing the avoiding. By the time she got up each morning and peeked out the window, his pickup was gone; she didn't hear it return until after midnight. She'd talked to Ralph Sorenson a couple of times and Josh had tentatively gotten on the phone and spoken to his grandfather. Things were still tense, but working out. Eventually they would all meet.

So close and yet so far away, she thought on the second day after Josh had flown out the door, his backpack draped over one shoulder, his hair flopping as he raced up the street to meet the school bus.

She finished cleaning the kitchen, then, against the wishes of everyone in the family, drove to the jail where she planned to interview Ray Dean. She'd already written the story about his arrest and how she was involved. Her editor was impressed, but he wanted more.

Ray, seated on his cot, looked at her through the bars. She sat in a folding chair and listened as he smoked and told his side of the story in painstaking detail. In the end, it seemed, his version only backed up Isaac's rendition. They were both crooks. But Ray, she assumed, because of his record and the fact that he'd actually done the deed, would draw a much longer sentence.

Nonetheless, she got her story.

So where was that overwhelming sense of satisfaction she'd been certain she would feel? Where was her emotional payoff? Instead of a feeling of elation, she experienced a sense of loss. The mystery was over and, though she would probably get to work on more interesting stories in the months to come, she was still the same woman she'd always been just with a different set of problems.

She drove home and found a bouquet of flowers on the front step. She bit her lip as she carried the roses, chrysanthemums, and baby's breath inside. Her fingers trembled and she mentally crossed her fingers that the bouquet was from Luke.

The card was simple: "We're proud of you. Congratulations. Mom and Dad."

"How nice," she said, but couldn't ignore the overwhelming sense of disappointment that dwelled deep in her heart. Though she'd pushed Luke away, now she missed him. "Yeah, well, you're an idiot," she said as she mounted the stairs, started removing her earrings and, once in her bedroom, checked the clock. Josh wouldn't be home for another couple of hours, so she just had time to—

The phone rang shrilly. She snatched up the receiver before it had a chance to ring again. "Hello?"

"Katie Kinkaid?"

The voice was familiar. "Yes?"

"It's Ralph Sorenson again. I've been doing a lot of thinking and even though we've talked a few times, I didn't really tell you what I'm thinking. Mainly that I guess I owe you an apology for the first time I called and I don't want there to be any bad blood between us."

"There isn't—"

"Just hear me out," he insisted, on a roll he didn't want to stop. "When I first called you I was just so damned anxious to get to know Josh, you know, because of Dave's death and all. Anyway, I made that deal with Luke, offered him money to find the boy, because I was so damned lonely."

Her throat ached all over again, as he explained how empty his life was without Dave but that he'd decided that Katie, as Josh's mother, knew what was best when it came to his grandson. He and his estranged wife only wanted what was best for Josh, and to that end they planned to set up a trust fund for him with the money he'd set aside for Luke.

Katie was thunderstruck. Her fingers clamped over the receiver. "But I thought Luke already got the money."

"No way." The old man chuckled sadly. "That boy taught me a little bit about what being a family and putting other people's needs before your own is all about. It's funny, really. Luke never really had a family, didn't know much about his folks, and then his own marriage was a mistake from the get-go, what with his wife running around on him and all."

Katie felt a tear slide down her cheek. What a fool she'd been.

"Listen, Mr. Sorenson—"

"Call me Ralph. We are like family whether we want to be or not."

"I want you to come and visit Josh. I've talked with him and we need to all get together."

There was a moment's hesitation. "You're certain about this?"

"Positive."

"Well . . . sure. I'll let you know. Thank you, Katie."

"And thank you." She hung up, wrote Josh a quick note in case he got home before she returned, then flew out to the car. She needed to talk to Luke and tell him how she felt. She had to swallow her pride and, no matter what happened, admit that she loved him.

Once behind the wheel, she took a deep breath, then jabbed

her key into the ignition and prayed that she hadn't let the one man in the world she needed slip through her fingers.

Luke, pounding nails that had worked their way out of the stable's old siding, raised his hammer again and heard the Jeep before it rounded the corner of the lane. He half hoped it would be Katie driving out to see him, but told himself he was being a fool. Whatever they'd shared was over. Somehow he'd have to get used to living in the same town with her and knowing they'd never be together.

"Tough," he muttered to himself and slammed the hammerhead into the siding so hard as to leave a dent. A whirlpool kicked up dust in the corral, spinning a few dried leaves and blades of grass in a crazy dance. Overhead a hawk circled lazily.

Katie's Jeep appeared and for a moment Luke thought he was seeing things. What could she possibly want? Probably another story now that the Isaac Wells mystery was cleared up she'd need another topic. Maybe she wanted to do a piece on this place. The concrete foundation had been poured; in less than six months he hoped to be open for operation.

He slid his hammer into a loop on his jeans and walked across the gravel lot to the spot where she'd ground to a stop. She hopped out of the cab and marched up to him.

"Do you have anything to say to me?" she demanded.

"Such as?"

"I just got a call from Ralph Sorenson."

"And—?"

"He seems to think he's going to send Josh some money for a trust fund." She threw up one hand and he couldn't tell if she was furious or pleased. "I think this has something to do with you."

"I told Ralph I was out of it."

"Well, you're wrong, Gates," she argued, her eyes crackling like green lightning. "You're in it big time."

"How's that?"

She drew in a long breath and he braced himself. Her cheeks were rosy, the pulse at the base of her throat beating erratically. The fingers of one hand opened and closed as if she was so nervous as to be tongue-tied and the scent of her perfume tickled his nostrils. Damn, but she was beautiful. And she didn't seem to know it. "Because I want you to be," she said, her voice a little softer.

"You do?"

"Yes." She licked her lips and he found the movement ridiculously provocative. "I—I want you in my life, Luke." She seemed embarrassed, but held his gaze. "I love you."

He didn't move, didn't feel the wind play with the tails of his shirt or ruffle his hair. "What?"

"I said, 'I love you.'"

He couldn't believe it and before he could respond, she started to turn. "Wait."

"Why?" She was halfway to the Jeep, when it finally hit him. He caught up with her before she reached for the door handle.

"Katie—"

She shook her head and disappointment darkened her eyes. "Look, just let me go, okay? I've embarrassed myself enough as it is, and—"

"I love you."

"You don't have to say anything. Really."

His fingers tightened over her arms. "I love you, Katie Kinkaid, and I've known it for weeks." All the words that he'd bottled up started tumbling out of his mouth as he tried to convince her of the truth. "It's just that I felt like such a heel because of the Ralph Sorenson thing."

"No—"

"Believe me."

"No, I—"

"Katie, will you marry me?"

The world seemed to stop. The breeze died and the hawk disappeared. It was as if they were entirely alone in the universe with that one simple question hanging precariously between them. "Wh-what?"

"Katie Kinkaid, I want you to be my wife." He reached for her then, and drew her close. "You're not going to make me get down on my knees and beg you, are you?"

She laughed. "No . . . but . . . it would be a nice vision." Swallowing hard, she stared up at him and in her eyes he saw his future. "Of course I will," she said with a grin, "but just tell me one thing."

"What's that?"

"What took you so long to ask?"

Epilogue

The preacher smiled as he looked at Luke and Katie. "You may kiss the bride," he said, then turned to J.D. and Tiffany, "And you, too, may kiss the bride."

The guests filling the hundred-year-old church whispered and chuckled and Katie leaned forward as Luke lifted her veil and kissed her as if she were the only woman on earth.

This double ceremony had been Katie's idea and now, as she felt her heart flutter and broke off the embrace, she grinned broadly.

"Ladies and gentlemen," the preacher announced, "I give to you Mr. and Mrs. Luke Gates and Mr. and Mrs. J.D. Santini."

Katie slid a glance in Tiffany's direction and was rewarded with a smile. *This is the way it should always be*, she thought, with Bliss as their maid of honor, Christina as their flower girl, and their sons as well as John Cawthorne giving them away.

She'd thought Luke would balk at the idea when she'd first suggested it, but he'd agreed, happy to finally be part of a family. Even Tiffany, at first resistant, had gotten caught up in the extravaganza. As the organist began to play, Katie, holding Luke's arm, walked down the aisle. Between the sprays of flowers and the candles, she saw the faces of the townspeople she'd known all her life. Her mother was crying, of course, and John Cawthorne was sniffing loudly. Octavia, Tiffany's grandmother, beamed. She'd been reunited with her cat—the result of a woman who'd bought the Persian years ago—reading Katie's article on the Nesbitt burglary, which was picked up by a paper in Portland. Brynnie and John were considering moving into the apartment house, while Katie, Luke and Josh would take up residence at Luke's ranch.

It seemed fitting, somehow, that Josh would live in the very spot where his father had lived.

Outside, the late-October sun was gilding trees already starting to turn with the coming winter. Katie imagined being snowbound with Luke at the ranch, sleeping in the room with the river-rock fireplace, watching as his dream unfolded and the ranch was up and running. She would still write, of course, but she thrilled at the thought of spending her days and nights with the man she loved.

The two brides and grooms formed a reception line and Katie accepted kisses, hugs and handshakes from friends, neighbors and relatives. Ralph and Loretta Sorenson had met Josh and had stayed for the nuptials. Even Rose Nesbitt had stood proudly and watched Tiffany marry, though, Katie decided, it would be a cold day in Hades before Rose would ever say a kind word to John Cawthorne.

But time could take care of a lot of the pain.

"It was a great wedding," Bliss said as the line dwindled and she stood between her two half-sisters.

"The best," Dee Dee said.

"Oh, I can think of a better one." Mason winked at his wife.

J.D. laughed and kissed Tiffany again. Luke's arm surrounded Katie's waist. "I wouldn't trade this one for the world," he whispered into her ear. "Now, can we go somewhere private."

"Soon," Katie whispered back.

"Not good enough, wife." Not waiting for another second, Luke pulled her behind a thick laurel hedge and, holding her face between his two callused hands, he looked deep into her eyes, then kissed her as if he never intended to stop. Because he didn't.

More from Bestselling Author JANET DAILEY

Calder Storm	0-8217-7543-X	$7.99US/$10.99CAN
Close to You	1-4201-1714-9	$5.99US/$6.99CAN
Crazy in Love	1-4201-0303-2	$4.99US/$5.99CAN
Dance With Me	1-4201-2213-4	$5.99US/$6.99CAN
Everything	1-4201-2214-2	$5.99US/$6.99CAN
Forever	1-4201-2215-0	$5.99US/$6.99CAN
Green Calder Grass	0-8217-7222-8	$7.99US/$10.99CAN
Heiress	1-4201-0002-5	$6.99US/$7.99CAN
Lone Calder Star	0-8217-7542-1	$7.99US/$10.99CAN
Lover Man	1-4201-0666-X	$4.99US/$5.99CAN
Masquerade	1-4201-0005-X	$6.99US/$8.99CAN
Mistletoe and Molly	1-4201-0041-6	$6.99US/$9.99CAN
Rivals	1-4201-0003-3	$6.99US/$7.99CAN
Santa in a Stetson	1-4201-0664-3	$6.99US/$9.99CAN
Santa in Montana	1-4201-1474-3	$7.99US/$9.99CAN
Searching for Santa	1-4201-0306-7	$6.99US/$9.99CAN
Something More	0-8217-7544-8	$7.99US/$9.99CAN
Stealing Kisses	1-4201-0304-0	$4.99US/$5.99CAN
Tangled Vines	1-4201-0004-1	$6.99US/$8.99CAN
Texas Kiss	1-4201-0665-1	$4.99US/$5.99CAN
That Loving Feeling	1-4201-1713-0	$5.99US/$6.99CAN
To Santa With Love	1-4201-2073-5	$6.99US/$7.99CAN
When You Kiss Me	1-4201-0667-8	$4.99US/$5.99CAN
Yes, I Do	1-4201-0305-9	$4.99US/$5.99CAN

Available Wherever Books Are Sold!

Check out our website at **www.kensingtonbooks.com.**